Table of Contents

Chapter 1

McCann was on his way with the others to London for a final press conference. The airship was making its way from Paris, the home of the second astronaut Louis Beaumont. The last four cities on the list were that of the traveller's home nations Seoul, Delhi, Paris and finally London. Louis described it as a 'déplacement du cirque,' going from city to city speaking to the press.

Airships were the preferred mode of air transport now especially since hydrogen was in such common use; they were cheap, clean and quiet. Travelling on the airships was the single part of the media tour McCann enjoyed and he suspected the same of the others. It was a break from the constant exercises in Geneva and the grilling of the media.

McCann was eager to reach London, it was where he was born and raised; a city that had risen from the ashes more than once in the last century. He looked forward to seeing his parents, especially his mother who had flown in from her home in Tel Aviv to see him before he left.

His father had met his mother whilst serving in what was named the oil conflicts, a conflict that ironically made the resource obsolete by the time it was settled. They had separated on good terms after he had joined the Navy, it still wasn't entirely clear why. He suspected they stayed together for him but he didn't really care, they were on amicable terms and never spoke ill of one another so he was content.

The voice of the captain announced over the coms 'You should be able to see London on the left; we'll be landing in about an hour.'

McCann put down his paper and peered out of the window, he could see a few tall buildings, monuments of a bygone era. Most of the tall sky scrapers had been obliterated in the past, what hadn't been destroyed by military strikes had been washed away by tsunami.

Most would have left the city and started a fresh, but like San Francisco in the early 20th century they refused to surrender and built each time from the ashes. Big Ben could be seen in the distant fog, one of the few monuments which had been restored, a testament to man's stubborn resistance to any type of logic. He smiled to see his home slowly advancing.

'Looking forward to the press conference?' jested Ryu.

McCann looked towards her but didn't answer; he smiled before his gaze returned to the city.

'Well I am, the last one and we can finally get down to business,' stated Ryu.

She was itching to get into space and couldn't wait to be the first woman to set foot on the red planet. She wanted to be the first person to set foot on it also and wasn't secretive about her ambitions.

'All good things come to those who wait,' said McCann thoughtfully as he looked out of the port window by his seat.

'So does arthritis and dementia Duncan, I want to lift off before I'm retired by the state!'

By the next day the four Astronauts were in the conference centre, sitting at a desk in front of the press, by now they were a well-oiled machine. Having done this so many times before, alongside all of the other televised interviews that were allowed by the I.S.A they were rarely stuck for words. It started as usual, 'So have you decided who will be the first person to step onto the surface of Mars? Or are you still undecided?'

This was usually directed to McCann as he was the flight commander and the bookies favourite, 'That's for mission control to decide, however we could always draw straws if it came down to it.'

Journalists were taking turns in asking a single question and the next in line stood up 'This is for Louis, since the Paris conference three women have claimed you are the father of their baby and are demanding a DNA before you leave. Do you have anything to say to them or any comment on these claims?'

Louis snarled 'I have nothing to say to those people, I've never met them nor desire to do so.'

'Then you deny you may have fathered those children?'

Louis maintained his snarl as the others smirked 'I've barely had time to sleep and eat in the last year, let alone getting three women pregnant!'

'So you have a problem with being labelled the "Cosmic Casanova" or is it justified?' replied the journalist who just refused to give it up.

'Can we please move on now,' said the man directing the conference to chuckling in the background 'and please no more questions concerning the gutter press, thank you.'

The next to stand up looked at the fourth astronaut 'This is to Hassif, being the only member of the mission without flight experience do you feel awkward or intimidated?'

'I'm not required to pilot anything so no,' replied Hassif 'I'm on the mission to keep the computer systems running. They do most of the flying anyway, we're just cargo until we touch down.'

Hassif, a man selected for his ability with computers. His talents were undeniable, able to analyse and repair any computer failures he was a human back up system. The director then took the mic 'Last question to Major Ryu Yong please,' and pointed to a journalist who took his cue.

'Major how do you feel about having to spend the next seven months with these three men alone? Most women would jump at the chance!'

'Well we've spent the last three years training together so I suppose I'll be able to tolerate another seven months.'

'It seems odd that the I.S.A has selected four bachelors for this mission, why do you think they did that?' asked the press journalist.

'You'll have to ask them, I'd say having a family to think about could cause an individual to be less focused and prone to error.'

The director stood up announcing that was all and the astronauts were shuffled out.

That night while Louis did his Network America interview, Hassif went to see the sights and Yong stayed in the hotel, McCann waited in the lobby of the recently refurbished Savoy hotel for his parents. It was and still is the premier place to stay in London and every room had been booked by the I.S.A for security reasons. The Savoy merged modern elements with the styles of the early twentieth century, quite tastefully. His parents were chauffeured to the hotel and ushered in, his mother hugged him and his father shook his hand.

'How have you been son?' she said in her Middle Eastern accent.

'The same as always mum and how have you been?'

'Good, the family is good too, it's been so long.'

McCann ushered them to the hotel restaurant where they sat and discussed things over a meal. His father sat down and looked around at the restaurant then at his son, 'Well I'd probably have to mortgage my house to eat here again!'

'Oh stop being so vulgar James, always talking about money even now!' snapped Ofra.

'Hey I was just giving the boy a compliment, I wonder if they do doggy bags here?'

McCann laughed with his father but his mother was more concerned with seeing her son before lift-off, she lacked a jovial attitude even at the best of times.

'I have seen that space lift they're going to tie you on, I pray it doesn't snap and you fall back down and crash! Will they test it before you go on it?' his mother whispered to him noticing someone was listening.

'They use the damn thing all the time Ofra!' bellowed James 'It's a lot safer than those rockets, he'll be fine!'

Duncan held his mother's hand across the table and said softly 'The orbital lift is the safest form of transport in existence, you were at more risk on the airship flight here mother.'

'He's got more chance of crashing when landing, now that's the risky part!' stated his father.

Ofra shuddered, 'Could you please shut your mouth about crashing or any disaster?'

James caught a black look from Duncan and decided to remain quiet, he knew better than to antagonise his estranged wife any further in front of his son.

'So how long will you be here Duncan?' asked James in a lighter tone.

'Two more days, I and the others have interviews and other media events to attend then it's back to Geneva.'

James an overweight and balding man in his seventies was beaming with pride 'To think the furthest I ever got was flying transport choppers whilst dodging towel head SAMs, and here I am seeing you a Colonel commanding a mission to Mars.'

Despite his years he, like his son was tall and he still cut an intimidating figure, but at this moment there was nothing intimidating about him merely tearful joy, 'So what about that Korean lady you're going with? Do you think I have a chance, or did that French bastard get there first?'

James and Duncan laughed but Ofra sighed, an Israeli woman of Arab descent she had long curly black hair with a light caramel skin. A great beauty when she caught the eye of a young Navy pilot and even today her looks could be appreciated despite her years.

'She is a nice girl and about your age.'

Duncan cut his mother off 'She's married to her career, or should I say obsessed, she considers men an unnecessary distraction from achieving her goals in life, I don't think she's interested in starting a family.'

'Yes but you need to find a woman you know? You're not so young now. You're successful and good looking, what are you waiting for?'

His mother constantly brought up this subject whenever they spoke, McCann was ill at ease whenever the subject or as he described it "the spectre" arose but it was important to his mother, 'I'll start looking after this mission, all right mother?'

'After the mission!' she shrieked 'I could be dead in a years' time you know? There are many nice girls that would have you right now near us you know?'

McCann rolled his eyes and made promises to come and have a look when the mission was over.

After the meal they moved on to the bar, a 1920's style which seemed to be a prevalent theme throughout the Savoy or at least that's what McCann thought it was. They sat down with their drinks and his father snuck him a cigar which they both lit up. McCann was not allowed to smoke them but he slipped them in here and there, his mother didn't like them but put up with it.

His father questioned him on his crew and what he thought of them and shared some laughs concerning the press. His mother was far too concerned to make small talk that night and most of her conversation was about safety and getting back. McCann spent the evening chatting with his parents as the media buzzed outside as bees around honey. He and his parents could feel the energy of it even whilst hidden from view. After a long meal and discussion it approached 10 pm, McCann informed them it was his scheduled time to sleep and had to go. His parents said their goodbyes and departed, a proud father and a worried mother.

The next day McCann awoke at 8am and had his morning coffee, something he wasn't strictly meant to drink due to caffeine but it was his morning routine and like tobacco he refused to give it up completely. He put on a blue shirt, black trousers and some black trainers which looked similar to shoes; he liked the comfort, and met his comrades for breakfast.

The day was spent going over schedules with I.S.A directors and Louis being told off by the PR department for his out-going interviews. Hassif was sitting at his 3D tablet solving code problems; he said it helped him keep on his toes. The tablet was a device that most people owned, the mobile phone of the 22nd century it had motion detection and the processing power that a hundred years ago a warehouse of super computers would fail to match. For most it was a device that was used for communication, entertainment to even driving your car. For Hassif it was an extra organ, watching 3d projected representations of code and solving the errors using hand gestures and voice commands. It baffled the others in a way that calmed them, providing a sense of security.

Ryu listening intently and digested all the information in her usual disciplined fashion, a stickler for efficiency. Louis joked she probably has a PHD in minimalism. Ryu didn't take chances, if anything was to go wrong it wasn't going to be due to her. In fact Ryu was considered for mission leader and would have got it if it was not for her almost Zen disciplinarianism. It was decided that her personality would negatively impact the other three so they plumbed for McCann.

McCann was a silent type that during a mission only spoke out of protocol when required; he had a rather black sense of humour which probably originated from his parents influence; his father being a jovial optimist and his mother possessing a rather nihilistic streak.

That evening McCann was chauffeured to his Network America interview being held in London. Louis had been there the night before and McCann was expected to raise the tone. Being interviewed by Jerry Habeeb, a respected journalist, "Habeeb's Hour" was the most watched current affairs broadcast on planet Earth. Jerry was dressed in his signature late 21st century style, a collarless shirt with a pocket watch clipped onto the breast pocket. He was in his mid-forties, dark hair receding apart from the peninsula of short hair jutting out in the middle. He was from Boston originally but his Mediterranean features and tan could have put him anywhere from Sicily to Syria, It was only when he spoke you realised where he was born and educated.

McCann sat opposite Jerry; he'd gone over most of the questions earlier that day in the hotel. Dressed in his best charcoal grey Italian suit with a black shirt that sported a small winged collar, he chatted with Jerry before they went on air. Jerry was reassuring him and trying to keep him calm as he did with all his guests; letting him know that nothing too risqué was going to happen.

McCann smiled and nodded, his fine grooming and his bespoke suit definitely exuded that he was relaxed and in control. Though this could be quite deceptive often he gave the impression of a cool exterior only to be the opposite, like a calm pool of water masking a raging torrent below. Tonight however he was calm, he had faced far worse in the past than a TV presenter with some possibly awkward questions.

The music played and the main lights came on along with a green digital on air sign. Jerry looked into camera 1 and spoke in his deep direct voice 'Hello and welcome to Habeeb's hour and tonight we have another one of the intrepid crew of the Athena, Flight commander Colonel Duncan McCann.'

McCann smiled and replied 'Good evening Jerry.'

Jerry continued 'In less than one month Colonel McCann and his three crew mates will lift off for Mars. However it will be two weeks before you even make orbit! Now I've had this explained to me but for the benefit of those that either haven't or still don't understand can you explain this?'

McCann smiled and obliged 'Certainly Jerry, it's actually a very simple principle. There's a ribbon anchored at two ends; one on Earth where we lift off and another in orbit on the station Tsiolkovsky.'

Jerry interrupted 'Right now that's the part I think we all understand, there's a cable between the Earth and the Tsiolkovsky. How do you move up the cable though and why doesn't it snap? I don't understand how it takes the strain.'

'Well first it's a ribbon not a cable and second it's made from nanotubes,' replied McCann.

'So what's the difference between a ribbon and a cable and what the hell is a nanotube!' Jerry asked with a smile.

'Well it's a ribbon because that shape can better withstand or avoid hits from space junk and meteorites, as for nanotubes Jerry you've got me there! That's not my area,' grinned McCann.

Jerry gave a playful puff then continued 'So how do you move up it and why does it take so long?'

'The ship is attached to a crawler that sends cargo to the Tsiolkovsky every month; we're pretty much hitching a ride on it. The crawler itself moves slowly up at first so as not to put too much stress on the ribbon but then gradually gathers pace. It gets its power from a second ribbon, as fuel would weigh it down, and returns via a third ribbon,' replied McCann matter-of-factly.

'Alright, now people have asked if it's possible that the Tsiolkovsky could come crashing into the Earth and push us into another holocaust? A lot of people still aren't comfortable with there being a massive asteroid so close to our planet, let alone the fact it is anchored to us!' inquired Jerry.

This had been the original fear when the orbital lift was being set up, a space station hewn out of and asteroid selected from the asteroid belt so close to us terrified many people. Many believed we were setting ourselves up for a mass extinction and it took a lot of persuading the public before opinion was on the side of the I.S.A.

'The station is very high above us in geostationary orbit, it swings back and forth due to the crawlers but imagine it being like a pendulum. It only swings so far before it has to swing back to its centre. The station is also manned constantly and has state of the art computers with backups and an SI that would correct any deviation with the on board thrusters,' replied McCann.

'Well I hope that helps some of our viewers sleep easier tonight!' quipped Jerry.

McCann had answered these questions before and still people didn't seem to understand that the planet wasn't going to be wiped out. He put it down to the fact that most people often let their hearts rule their heads and fear was a powerful emotion. Some just seemed to get a kick out of doom mongering and spreading panic, thankfully cooler heads had prevailed.

'So what will you be doing once you get to Mars Colonel?' asked Jerry.

'If all goes well we'll be overseeing the final construction of the first Martian base and secure the Martian orbital ribbon,' replied McCann with a slightly excited tone to his voice, but not enough to be detectable unless you knew him.

'So why do we need a manned crew, as far as I've learnt the whole base has been constructed by robots. What are you going to do that they can't?'

'The I.S.A would like some engineers to be there on site to oversee it, make sure the base is habitable, oversee the connecting of the ribbon system and monitor the first crawler. It could be done remotely from orbit but this project has too much invested in it not to send us. We'll be doing several jobs at once, when we're finished Mars should be ready for the first steps in colonizing a new world and I find that very exciting,' replied McCann.

'I see, so that accounts for why this mission has a crew with such a broad scope of expertise. What will each member be doing once there down there, I mean to say what area will their specific responsibilities lay in?' Jerry inquired.

'Well Louis will concentrate on the construction and repair systems, making certain the nanites are all running properly and checking that the architecture is sound. Hassif will be on the computer systems, making sure the central computer is hooked up to the SI and operating properly. Major Ryu will be piloting the drones, doing recon missions of the area such as geo surveys and she will be piloting the drone during the ribbon attachment. I'll be co-ordinating the mission and reporting to Geneva on progress, making certain orders are carried out.'

Jerry gazed at McCann with an expression some might say of envy, which was understandable who wouldn't want to go?

'So how will you return once the mission is complete?'

'We intend to use the orbital lift to haul ourselves to Edwards (The Mars station) and then launch from there back to Earth, if all goes to plan.'

'Now I'd like to talk about how you'll travel between the planets. You're going to use a maser to shoot you there and what's more this has never been done before! Aren't you worried you'll be vapourised or something?' said Jerry with a playful tone.

'No we won't get vapourised; it's actually an old concept just like the orbital lift. Once in space the Athena will open a sail and point it towards the moon, then a large maser on the moon will fire onto the sail pushing the Athena faster and faster towards Mars. One has been constructed on Deimos, the smallest moon of Mars and that will push us back. The Martian one shall be operated remotely from the Edwards.'

'Why are these masers based on moons and is there a chance we on Earth could get hit by them?'

It was something that the doom mongers had been asking since growing tired of predicting another great extinction event thanks to the Tsiolkovsky.

'The masers are placed on the dark side of each moon so we can't shoot ourselves and the moons have no atmosphere so it means there's no resistance. Allowing more efficient power transfer and of course they're closer to the target,' replied McCann.

'What if the Mars maser missed and hit Earth? Isn't that possible and what damage would it cause? Or even worse what if it hit the Tsiolkovsky?'

'Nothing, the chances are miniscule of that happening and if it did there isn't enough power to cause any damage to the Earth. The range of a maser is quite small and you'd need a lot more to budge the Tsiolkovsky from its orbit!' smiled McCann.

'So I'm not going to get cooked in my bed when you're returning?' jested Jerry.

'No Jerry, you'll be fine.'

Jerry looked at McCann 'Now I'd like to chat about your career before the I.S.A. You were a navy pilot I gather; please tell us a little about that.'

'I joined the navy perhaps through a sense of obligation, since it's a family tradition.'

'Is that an obligation to tradition or an obligation to something else?' countered Habeeb.'

'Obligation to the Royal Navy, I was educated and raised there so it seemed a logical choice.'

'So what did you start out as in the navy?' asked Jerry.

McCann smiled as he began reminiscing about a part of his life he hadn't gone over in a long time 'I first entered active service as a flight sub-lieutenant, I was assigned to a missile cruiser for a few years; as part of the crew that flew one of the then newer VTOL transport craft, I was very fortunate to get it as my first job.'

'Then later you went onto serve on a carrier I believe, could you tell me about that?'

On hearing Jerry's request McCann's smile faded as his mind hit upon something else 'Then the world seemed to catch fire again, the Eastern States embargoed South America and in East Asia war was being declared like it was going out of fashion.

I was assigned to HMS Hermes in the mid- Atlantic; as there was a shortage of combat pilots; at first we flew anti-submarine cover for the Americans. After sometime I was selected for the SBS.'

'Could you explain to some of our viewers what the SBS is?' interjected Jerry.

'It's the Special Boat Service the navy's answer to the SAS if you will.'

'How do you get selected and what are the requirements?'

'Anyone in the UK armed forces may apply, if selected there are several fitness and survival tests in different environments culminating in a resistance to interrogation test.'

'So tell us what happened after you joined SBS? Was it as exciting as it sounds?'

'Exciting is very subjective Jerry,' spoke McCann in a serious tone 'it was exciting at times, just not the type of excitement you would welcome. I ended up flying an Atlas VTOL craft, or as we called it the flying crate. It was a fine craft, a massive box with two wings and a jet on each. In flight it looked just like a flying cargo crate, hence its name. I also piloted the smaller Hummingbird.'

'You've not mentioned in past interviews that you were involved with the British assault on Soledad. Could you tell us what part you played in that fateful operation?' asked Jerry.

McCann sat back obviously annoyed at the question but began to explain his part in Soledad, an assault on a coastal citadel in Colombia...

When the United States broke up due to the collapse of the fiat currency system it caused a domino effect, leading most notably to China imploding. However China was by no means the only nation to change drastically, in the turmoil South American nations lost support causing drug lords to take power. The coast of South America from Venezuela to Peru then into Bolivia and Paraguay became autonomous regions run by Cartels and Warlords funded by cocaine (their new currency).

After the Americans had settled on an agreement and the old U.S was broken up into three parts, the Eastern States, which comprised of most of the major north eastern states, and the most conservative, took Japans lead and embargoed the drug producers that endangered the stability of their nation. Eventually they had the Southern Union and Western States on board, then the re-formed EU followed and McCann was assigned to an aircraft carrier. Flying a small craft loaded with torpedoes and depth charges he spent most of his active service hunting submarines that were used to slip past the blockade and deliver the product to the buyer. The HMS Hermes was a King William II class carrier, outfitted with the latest EU made scram drones, air transport and anti-submarine VTOL craft, it was a floating city. Built after the oil conflicts had left the British fleet in tatters and with scram drones in mind; it had been used previously in the subjugation of the African pirate states and only the best were considered to serve on her.

Unlike carriers of the past the scram drones were launched not via a runway but fired from what looked like a rocket artillery launcher. Two giant rectangles split into eight square tubes sat at each end of the ship, loaded with scram drones to fire out when need be.

The scram drone landed by flying into a net at the end of the runway similar to conventional jets but the scram drones had no undercarriage, just as the scram drone approached the net the wings were swept back into the fuselage along with any weaponry and landed on the belly. The material on the belly was very tough and easily replaced, below decks in the hangar, if damaged.

McCann flew a VTOL craft something that required him to actually pilot, rather than sit in a booth safe below decks. Helping the Americans maintain an effective embargo on drugs he spent his days or nights hovering around, dropping sonar buoys and when a target or "drug sub" as they called it was identified he'd fly over and drop a smart torpedo that would hunt it out and hopefully sink it.

It was a routine McCann had got used to and he took pride in his work. One day after his shift he sat in the officer's mess with a hard copy of the Times. In fact he preferred to read papers considered much lower brow. However his superiors would have frowned on it and they wouldn't have lasted long in the officer's mess.

McCann lit up a cigar and sat with a large whisky reading when one of his flight crew sat next to him 'Bloody hell man, are you puffing on one of those cancer sticks again?'

'Why don't you try one Jenkins, no point in being a teetotaller all your life. Look at what happened to Hitler, the man didn't drink or smoke and ended up shooting himself! I'd hate to see you go the same way,' replied the short brown hair of McCann that bobbed over the paper.

'Listen old boy, SBS selection is coming up again this year and you'll never make it by smoking those things.'

Jenkins gestured to the tablet he was holding.

McCann turned down his paper and looked at Jenkins much like a father looking at his naughty son 'Good luck, I hope you make it in this time,' he replied as he turned the paper back up and resumed reading the article on the high court judge arrested for alleged virtual stalking.

Jenkins had been applying for SBS since he first was assigned to active duty; McCann had seen his type before. He had Jenkins classed with the other excitement seekers, he used to call them the "over the mountain squad" as his type were always searching for excitement and glory and it was always just over this mountain. Jenkins mountain was passing SBS selection which he'd failed to do 15 times. 15 times he'd applied and hadn't been asked to try out once. Ever since McCann had known him on the Hermes Jenkins had done little else but twitter on about the SBS.

For the last two years McCann had become pretty tired of listening about it on a regular basis. One of the officers had joked that he'd applied to the SBS selection just to get away from Jenkins. It had soon become a running joke on the ship amongst the officers, although it only seemed to encourage Jenkins.

'Why don't you apply Duncan, the selection quota has gone up to 500 this year more than double the usual!'

This got McCann's attention; he dropped his paper, put his cigar down and took the tablet from Jenkins 'Really? Any reasons given why?'

'No but I think we can all assume that this blockade is going to heat up now,' said Jenkins in his excited tone of voice.

'Perhaps, although maybe they are just low on personnel this year? A lot of retirements?' asked McCann.

He knew that Jenkins had friends who'd made it into SBS and suspected Jenkins finger was close to the pulse of what was happening.

'No, no, no that's not the reason. Manchuria attacked Russia last week and last night Korea broke the siege of Vladivostok!' Jenkins was almost unable to get the words out quick enough.

'Well good for them but what has that to do with the SBS recruiting an extra 300 this winter?'

'Well don't you see old boy? Russia has officially gone to war in China and joined the Japanese embargo. It gives the Americans a free hand to attack the Cartels,' blurted Jenkins.

McCann sat back in his seat and looked at the tablet, by now a small group had gathered around, it did make sense. If Moscow was officially embargoing the drugs, instead of trading weapons to keep it out of their country, then the balance of power was changing. Moscow was about to get embroiled in a war against potentially all the warlords it supplied in China. They wouldn't have the time or resources to be concerned with the South American cartels.

'I'll tell you what Duncan if we both apply and don't make it I'll stop complaining about those awful cigars,' poked Jenkins.

'And if we both make it in?'

'You won't have to listen to me prattle on about being selected for the SBS I suppose!'

The people around them laughed and the officers started egging McCann on. Jenkins brought up the electronic application on the tablet and the laughs became a roar with shouts of 'go on do it!' and 'drinks on me if he applies!'

McCann put his thumb to the tablet and his application was sent to cheers and applause, he looked up at a man in his forties with a moustache standing next to him 'Drinks are on you tonight Peterson!'

Six months, several combat fitness tests and one gruelling RTI (resistance to Interrogation) test later and McCann was flying an A-2 Atlas VTOL craft; transporting squadron Gama and their equipment to the Hermes. He had been selected to apply for SBS and had made it into the final 500 as had Jenkins who was posted with squadron Omega.

McCann was excited to see his old comrades on the Hermes again so soon, he had been as shocked as Jenkins was elated when they both found out their applications had been accepted. There was a great celebration on the Hermes; McCann suspected many were ecstatic to be seeing the back of Jenkins due to suffering years of his god awful yapping concerning the SBS. After a month of fitness, combat and navigation tests they both made it through and got past the RTI test. McCann was put in Gamma squadron, a general purpose squadron that had been running operations in Madagascar. By the time McCann joined most of the pirates had been disbanded and much of it he suspected was a dry run for the Americas.

For the most part he piloted the smaller Hummingbird VTOL, used for small unit insertion and extraction, on the surface it seemed similar to his former job on the Hermes, in reality it was very different. Nearly all the flying was at night and by now he'd developed nerves of steel due to months skimming jungle canopy waiting for the next radar warning or burst of tracer fire attempting to knock him out of the sky.

McCann set the massive transport down on the flight deck, the deck then lowered the transport inside the hangar. The craft was lifted off by an arm and the lift rose up to fit back into the flight deck and make it complete again. The hangar was massive with 5 Atlas transports and a myriad of smaller vehicles and separate bays for drones. McCann opened the rear hatch of the craft and powered everything down, he then marched out and stood in line with his SBS comrades.

All were made present and correct and after a few words from Brigadier General Greetham the men were dismissed and escorted to their quarters. After reaching his quarters and dropping off his gear the bell rang, McCann opened his door.

Standing there was Commander Peterson 'How's the SBS been treating you old chap?' said Peterson as he presented him with a Habanos cigar.

'Thanks Robert,' said McCann as he took the cigar on offer 'I'm still alive so they've done a good job.'

McCann began to put his few possessions away and asked 'So how has it been on the Hermes?'

'Same old, same old, Duncan. So why are you SBS boys here?'

'I can't say anything about that Robert, I'm sorry.'

'Don't worry yourself, Jenkins told me the same thing yesterday.'

McCann looked around rather surprised.

'Didn't you know Jenkins was here old chap?'

'No he was assigned to a different squadron; I don't know where he's been for months. Is he still on the Hermes?' inquired McCann.

'Yes, you've been invited to the officer's mess by Admiral Mansfield at 20:00 hours. Jenkins should be there so bring plenty of good stories for us will you?'

'No problem, I'll be there on the dot.'

'See you later then.'

'Later.'

Peterson left him to finishing tidying up his quarters.

That evening McCann walked into the officer's mess on the Hermes wearing a freshly pressed uniform and sporting his SBS emblem which read "By Strength and Guile". As he stepped in the room erupted to a rendition of "for he's a jolly good fellow".

McCann was rather embarrassed at such attention but he smiled through it.

Jenkins approached him and shook his hand 'Great to see you old boy, how've you been?' he asked showing off his SBS badge with obvious pride.

'Very well thanks, so where have you been hiding out all these months Jenkins?'

'The last three months we were in Guyana, bloody awful place. Six of us were living off bananas and caterpillars for two weeks!' laughed Jenkins which caused McCann to laugh along with him.

'Emails and such weren't permitted not that there was any time for it.'

Next he was approached by his former commanding officer Admiral Mansfield; a man in his fifties and going grey. He was very proud of the fact that two of his officers were selected for SBS and wanted to show them every honour whilst they were back on board. The Admiral approached them and McCann saluted. Mansfield returned the salute then offered his hand which McCann shook. 'So how has my other SBS boy done? It's good to see you on board again McCann,' said the Admiral in a booming voice.

'Well I saved the world once and romanced at least five world leader's wives!' replied McCann with a wink to roars of laughter.

'But most of all I didn't have to listen to Jenkins talking about applying for the SBS!'

Jenkins smiled and the Admiral patted him on the back and led him to the bar where he ordered him a drink. McCann took a non-alcoholic port to go with his cigar. Tomorrow was when the operation began and he couldn't drink anything alcoholic.

The evening went well as he and Jenkins mixed with old comrades and traded war stories, competing in "past acts of gastronomic degradation" as the Admiral described it. Later it got on to speculation as to what was going on with two SBS and one SAS squadron on board the carrier. Everyone knew there was going to be an assault, they just didn't know where and when aside from the Admiral and other top brass from the SBS and SAS. A second British carrier, HMS Prince of Wales, had joined the task force along with the American Carrier USS Constitution.

The Americans had already moved in on the Colombian Pacific coast and it seemed logical the British were going to make a go of the Atlantic coast, whilst the French were fighting their way through Venezuela.

The next day McCann and his flight team were called to the operations room by the Brigadier General. Inside the Admiral and his staff briefed McCann's team on their mission. They were to fly a humming bird into Colombia and insert a team close to Soledad's main military airbase undercover of night. The SAS were to first, take down the radar network and neutralise the missile defence shield; which guarded Soledad and the surrounding area from and air assault. Allowing the SBS to drop larger teams inside to neutralise the port and airbase before the enemy could respond. All this opening the door for the main forces to land and capture the port then surround Soledad and force a surrender before the afternoon.

The SAS had been in the area for weeks already and were prepared to take down the radar net in 20 minutes. With that the Brigadier ordered his SBS to prepare for take-off and wished them good luck.

Twenty minutes later and McCann was skimming the ocean towards the enemy airbase, he could see Jenkins banking off in the direction of Soledad's military port thanks to the electronic display the computer fed onto his helmet visor. He could feel butterflies in his stomach. This was something that comforted McCann and reminded him he was alert, which he kept under control as usual.

Outside it was pitch dark, the display on his visor superimposed the true image of what was outside along with all pertinent information to the mission. McCann could see the beach approaching with Soledad only 3 miles to the west; the port attached to the city and Jenkins moving in close to it.

The Brigadier then came over the comms informing McCann that the radar was down and it was time to insert. McCann increased the speed of the Hummingbird as far as he could and made for the airbase, at that point flares shot into the sky searching for enemy aircraft much like a blind man using a cane to see. McCann landed his craft safely only a few hundred metres from the airbase perimeter opened the rear hatch. His cargo of twenty men and a light armoured vehicle filed out. Once they were clear he lifted off and made back for the carrier reporting the insertion a success.

After having landed on the Hermes McCann was called back to the Brigadier, as he made his way back the flight deck was busy. Scram drones were launching into the sky to intercept the incoming enemies. Crews were waiting on the deck checking and rechecking the Atlas transports that were prepared to drop off cargos of men and tanks. McCann got out of the way and made his way to report in, leaving his flight crew in the hummingbird.

'Flight Commander McCann reporting, Sir,' said McCann saluting the Brigadier.

The Brigadier returned the salute 'Excellent, did you see anything of Jenkins on the way back?'

'No Sir, I witnessed him approaching the port but once the radar was down I didn't see him again. Why is something wrong Sir?'

'He should have made contact with us by now, we'll see. How did your job go McCann, any trouble?' asked the Brigadier getting off the subject of Jenkins.

'No problems Sir, in and out without a hitch nothing to report.'

McCann was still concerned for Jenkins as he turned to look at the tactical display of Soledad and all the objectives. From a quick glance he could see all wasn't going as it should, his concern grew for Jenkins and the squad he had dropped off at the airbase.

Ninety minutes into the operation and the situation had greatly deteriorated, the HMS Prince of Wales had been hit by two fully loaded enemy scram drones and the deck was ablaze. The USS constitution had taken minor damage but was still fully operational, the HMS Hermes had escaped so far, but probably not for long.

The enemy was using the scram drones as guided missiles since the airbase was about to fall into SBS hands. Instead of bringing them back for re-arming the pilots were ramming them into the carriers at Mach 5 and launching a new one. McCann had been ordered to fly into the port and search for Jenkins squadron and extract them if possible. McCann and his team lifted off just as a scram drone flew into the deck and exploded, the damage seemed superficial to the ship but McCann witnessed crewmen being flung around by the impact. Despite his concern for them he concentrated on the job in hand and turned his full attention to Jenkins and Omega squadron.

As McCann approached the port he could see dawn was breaking, now that the glow of the fires on the carriers was behind him. From above he could see the British and Americans had already formed makeshift LZs either side of Soledad but were being pounded by missile fire from within the city. It was obvious that the forces in the city would inevitably surrender but not until they had inflicted as much damage as possible.

Scram drones circled the air like vultures looking for a corpse, when a target within the city was spotted the computer locked on and fired on it with cold mechanical prejudice. McCann found it to be a most distasteful sight so turned his gaze towards the port; where his on board computer managed to identify a damaged Hummingbird smoking on the ground. His heart jumped into his mouth, when he'd got his composure back he hovered around the site for as long as he dared and called it in reporting no sign of the crew. The Brigadier recalled him back to the Hermes, so McCann dutifully turned and made his way to the carrier as an Atlas went the other way to the LZ.

Two days later and the Prince of Wales had withdrawn for repairs. Jenkins and his entire team were still missing and the Americans were preparing to assault Soledad since the citadel commander had refused to surrender and the local cartel was moving an unknown force towards the area.

The enemy had lost their airbase to the SBS who had secured it for the Hermes and Constitution, the port had been secured and all that remained was the burnt out city of Soledad.

'Why don't those bastards surrender?' boomed the Admiral whilst he toured the Hermes early in the morning inspecting the damage with the Brigadier.

'They're afraid of the cartel Sir,' replied McCann who had been spending the morning standing on the deck looking out over the sea at a smoking Soledad in the distance, wondering where Jenkins was.

'Afraid? How do you mean Commander?' asked Admiral Mansfield.

'If you surrender then your family will be executed, however if you're captured whilst in combat that's different, Sir,' replied McCann in a rather philosophical tone.

'So you're saying they're waiting for us to attack so they can give in?'

'No Sir, but I'd bet it's going through their minds right now,' replied McCann staring into the distance 'any word on Jenkins and his crew, Sir?'

'None, we didn't find any bodies just that his Hummingbird was hit by an anti-tank mine. Poor blighter must've landed on the bloody thing. I'm sure he got away Commander.'

'Then why haven't we heard from him Sir? Unless he's either dead or in that city held captive,' said McCann still staring out.

'Don't let it get to you, if we find them I'll let you know, all right?' replied the Brigadier to which McCann nodded in thanks; before returning to looking out over the carrier at Soledad.

Jenkins had been annoying in the past but he was a good reliable man and McCann was worried for his comrade. The citadel was half destroyed by missile fire from scram drones that still circled the city like vultures over a dying animal. They hit it time and again patiently. McCann was fine with a good clean fight but watching Soledad go through the death of a thousand cuts with his friend possibly alive and injured inside was torture.

Later that day the American tanks began to open fire; McCann could hear the boom of the cannons as they smashed a path through the winding, walled city streets of the citadel. By midday the Americans had sliced through the city unopposed, any difficult areas were demolished by tank fire. By that afternoon the General in charge of the city had been found dead. He committed suicide at his HQ rather than be captured and have his family killed.

Jenkins team was discovered in the city, they had split up after the Hummingbird hit a land mine. They'd spent the last couple of days hiding in Soledad, sabotaging enemy communications and defences. Some were captured and tortured, some killed, others somehow made it. McCann was informed that they were being lifted onto the Hermes and ordered to extract them. When the Englishman and his team got to the airbase Soledad was in ruins. British and American soldiers combed the city either suppressing resistance or pulling out corpses which sat in massive rotting piles. The sight of bodies in the hot sun some with bloated tongues thrusting out of the mouths turned McCann's stomach. On landing he saw Jenkins carrying a stretcher with one of his comrades on it, ten of them got on board. McCann kept waiting for the others to turn up until Jenkins walked into the cockpit, in a rather sorry state, and whispered 'That'll be all, you can take off now.'

McCann could smell the stench of rotten flesh on Jenkins as the co-pilot got up to let him sit next to McCann 'It's good to see you old boy, I was worried when I saw your Hummingbird,' said McCann as Jenkins strapped himself in.

'So that was you was it?' replied Jenkins in an understandably tired voice 'I'm sorry but it was too dangerous, couldn't endanger you as well.'

It then went quiet as McCann lifted what was left of Omega squadron back to safety. Within a few minutes the fleet appeared over the horizon. Jenkins looked shocked 'What the bloody hell?' he said breaking the previous silence as they approached the Hermes. He surveyed the damage done by the enemy 'Where's the Prince of Wales?'

'She's had to get repairs, they kamikazied us as we were taking the airbase. All the carriers got hit but the Prince of Wales got the lions share. Five direct hits in all, fully loaded scram drones at Mach 5 into the flight deck The Hermes got hit too but it was a lot less serious.'

'Any casualties?' inquired Jenkins thinking of his crew mates,

'Bates bought the farm along with six hands and Peterson took some nasty burns. It would've been a lot worse if we hadn't got our drones up in the air so quickly. Still it's good to see you alive, how did your boys do?'

'Not so good, we hit a mine on landing and had to abandon the Hummingbird. The port was just a big booby trap full of anti-personnel and anti-tank mines. The vessels in the port had been abandoned and disabled; our only option was to either head for the surrounding countryside or make a dash for the city. We chose the city as the safer option and thought we could still help out. Two days of hell old chap with 20 dead because someone bungled the reconnaissance, bloody awful!' bemoaned Jenkins as he sank back into the seat.

Within two weeks Soledad was secured and being used as a naval base, four years later the last of the cartels was hunted down in the jungles of Bolivia. Those countries conquered were split up between the American nations and those who supported them. The Eastern states taking Ecuador, a location that would place them in good stead in the future.

McCann spent another 7 years in SBS attaining the rank of Colonel in the Royal Marines. Much like the SBS joining the ISA was a similar affair, whilst having a drink at the officers club in London Jenkins brought it to his attention. Jenkins was applying and McCann decided he could do with a change of scene from all the blood and guts, so he went in with him. Jenkins didn't make it but McCann was selected for flight commander based on experience, ability and his psyche profile.

'So that's about the short version of my story Jerry, I hope I didn't send you to sleep?' quipped McCann.

'Well that was a truly fascinating saga and I hope your comrade Jenkins is well and watching this today, but my final question is who's it going to be Colonel? Who has been chosen to set foot on Mars first?' inquired Jerry in a now subdued tone.

'We haven't been told yet Jerry, but I think they're just trying to keep you all in suspense!' smiled McCann.

'Well the bookmakers say it's going to be you, next it's Major Ryu. Are you going to be making any bets before you leave?' jested Jerry in his bombastic manner.

McCann laughed 'No Jerry I'm not a gambling man.'

'Do you have any words prepared in case it's you?' probed Jerry, it was almost a certainty it would be McCann but the I.S.A hadn't released a statement.

'I haven't had time to think about it Jerry, but if it is me I'm sure I'll think of something,' replied McCann.

'Well that's all the time we have, America wishes you a safe journey and we'll see you back here in this studio sometime next year.'

Jerry brought his hand up and McCann shook it 'Thank you very much we'll all do our best to make you proud.'

Chapter 2

Back in Geneva McCann awoke at 7pm sharp, just before the early morning alarm. He got dressed and went to the mess hall to grab breakfast with his comrades. He took a bowl of muesli and a decaffeinated coffee. All food was measured out into exact portions; the I.S.A was leaving nothing to chance. McCann found Major Ryu sitting alone at a table and joined her, she was snacking on some vegetables and rice it didn't look very appetizing but the muesli wasn't exactly bacon and eggs itself.

'Good morning Colonel, please sit down,' chirped Ryu. She was always up bright and early on a morning. She was sharp all the time but McCann couldn't fathom how anyone could be such a bright spark on a morning except for a child on its birthday. Then again today was a special day, lift off was two weeks away, today they would prepare for their final flight to Ecuador to begin their slow ascent to the heavens. Rather anti-climactic compared to the rockets of yesteryear, but far safer!

'Good morning Major, anyone else up yet?' inquired McCann.

'No, just us. I could hear the buzz from mission control in my room I don't know why those two need an alarm to wake them,' stated Ryu.

McCann nodded, mission control had been buzzing all night; checking and re-checking all the systems on the orbital lift, the Athena and their computers at ground zero in Ecuador. So much rode on this that failure was something that the mission director William Faraday had nightmares about; although he let none know of it.

He had been the head of the I.S.A for the last 15 years; the main force behind the push for the orbital lifts, before climbing to his present position. For over 30 years the orbital lift had been a possibility but a massive war of words had raged over it on Earth. The cost, the risk and the fear of a disaster that would eclipse all of mankind's conflicts put together prevented it from being constructed. What had convinced enough leaders wasn't the fact that it would open up the entire solar system; nor the fact that it would slash the costs of launching satellites and allow mankind to perhaps colonize other planets. No it was the fact that Russia had announced they were going to build one. They had selected an asteroid from the asteroid belt. With drones cutting and tunnelling the inside they would construct the station soon. Moscow announced they'd move the Tsiolkovsky into orbit within ten years.

After that an even greater wave of panic and fear struck, having to pay tolls to Moscow for the use of the lift. Mankind as usual showed how petty and pathetic he truly can be. Human life was no longer a concern, now it was the horrifying thought of Moscow having a monopoly on space travel and access to all those resources. Moscow would have been in charge. The European Space Agency quickly broke with N.A.S.A and negotiated before anyone else. Agreeing to pay half the credits for rights and having it anchored on their soil. Moscow waited for everyone else to start making offers, soon the Americans decided it would be cheaper to build their own, rather than win the "Mother of all bidding wars".

Then the Europeans started to back off and consider their own alternatives, smaller satellites but further out, compressed structures and all sorts. Soon the Asians were looking towards getting there, with the resources of India, Japan and Korea they formed their own coalition to build a working orbital lift or space elevator as they preferred to call it. All the time the Russians were speeding towards actually doing it, the others were arguing amongst themselves.

Before long they all realised there was no way to beat the Russians to it but they could get it done shortly afterwards, so the others banded together and the I.S.A was formed. Based in Geneva they decided on building a smaller satellite that was in a much higher orbit. It would require a much longer tether; however a university in India had solved the problem. They could grow nanotubes long enough to do the job without having to weave them together. The Russians were going to weave theirs; a woven tether could take far less stress than one grown in a single piece, allowing the I.S.A to send larger payloads into space. Moscow soon had talks with Geneva; the result was a Russian station using an Indian ribbon anchored in Ecuador with the HQ at Geneva. Moscow entered the I.S.A.

Over the years the old space agencies faded and merged all they had into the I.S.A, this was to be the greatest construction in history. Projections put it as earning more than any other endeavor in mankind's history and offering such advantages militarily that no nation could own it, or at least afford not to have a stake in it.

The I.S.A over the years became its own master. It was now unclear who controlled the organization since no single nation owned enough of it to claim ownership. Yet without Moscow providing a station, India growing the nanotube for the ribbon linking it to Earth, the Eastern States providing the highest point on Earth to Anchor the station; and finally The EU providing a HQ to co-ordinate it all along with the next generation of SI, it would not work.

The I.S.A became autonomous to a certain extent and William Faraday was its director, perhaps the most powerful person in the world? Since he could cut any nation off from space, perhaps, but certainly the most stressed!

Faraday walked into the mess hall and approached McCann and Ryu 'So where are the other two?'

'Haven't seen them yet sir, I'm sure they'll be down presently,' replied Ryu.

A moment later Hassif and Louis walked through the automatic doors into the mess hall, both were smiling. They seemed to have been sharing a joke or some amusing anecdote on their way to breakfast.

'The early bird catches the sky lift boys!' said Faraday turning to the LCD clock on the wall which also displayed a countdown to lift off.

'Don't you worry yourself, we have it all in hand mien Fuhrer!' joked Louis.

Hassif laughed but neither McCann, Ryu nor Faraday were in the slightest bit amused. Louis never took anything as seriously as they thought he should and Hassif was too ready to be his partner in crime.

'Louis, shut your bloody mouth and get your breakfast,' replied Faraday in his stiff upper class English accent, an old Etonian and Cambridge man he didn't have much patience for Louis Beaumont even at the best of times. He tolerated Louis as best he could or perhaps suffered him would have been his choice of words; Louis was unfortunately indispensable unlike his attitude.

'Forgive me mien master!' cracked Louis whilst smiling.

Faraday was on the verge of another explosive rant, McCann had got used to this over the years due to Louis and his antagonistic attitude towards all authority figures.

McCann quickly intervened 'Louis just do it now,' in a stern but calm voice.

Louis went from giggling satyr to having a rather irritated expression; he didn't like being spoken to in that manner. In fact no one had spoken to him that way before he came to Geneva and put on an I.S.A uniform. Many wondered if he'd last one month, but going to Mars was such a powerful lure that he controlled himself as best he could.

He respected McCann and Ryu above anyone else for some unknown reason; perhaps it was their military records. The fact McCann was an ex-SBS pilot and Ryu flew drone scram jets for her country during the Manchurian war. It was the one thing the two had in common other than being the only people Louis ever listened too; whatever the reason, without another word he went over to the counter and ordered his breakfast along with Hassif.

Faraday took a moment to calm himself; the stress of the last few months had been enormous. Faraday felt that the future of humanity itself was on his shoulders and if he made a mistake he would have doomed not just the I.S.A but his fellow man also. Faraday was the San Andreas Fault on legs and no one that knew him envied his position.

'When you're all finished you've got a final physio and psyche test, so report to medical by 08:30 hours. When the doctor releases you meet me in the briefing room, understood?' said Faraday.

'Yes Sir,' replied the four as Faraday walked out through another set of doors.

After breakfast McCann left the mess hall and strolled down one of the many long white corridors to the medical wing. A staff of 50 of the world's best professionals dedicated to ensuring the good health of the four astronauts. The wing was equipped with all the state of the art equipment; the head of the department Doctor Weissmuller could monitor them from his office, even on Mars. Each astronaut had nanites injected into their blood stream; hooked up to a microscopic body monitor, which acted as the nanites central nervous system, injected into the flesh at the rear of the neck. The chip in the neck sent data via the Athena to and from the Doctors main computer in his office, monitoring every aspect of the patient's physical condition.

Nanites had been used in medicine for many years now; they had replaced minor surgical procedures such as removing blood clots or tumors from the body. Weissmuller had developed his nanites to carry out many other emergency procedures if needed and he could do them from Earth. McCann walked into Weissmuller's office, the doctor sat at his computer, a mahogany table with three displays and a silver glove.

Weissmuller a bald man in his 70's sat in his comfortable matching mahogany chair and with one hand in the glove was typing up Major Ryu's report. He tapped different parts of his own hand to give commands and select words, with one hand he could type a report and with his voice he ordered the body monitors to run self-diagnostics and check the hosts for any abnormalities. It was quite a sight to behold, the office gloves were an older technology not used much today, as you could fully interact with speech and had motion detection, but Weissmuller didn't see why he couldn't use both and get his work done twice as fast.

'Good morning doctor, do the nanites give me a clean bill of health?' asked McCann.

'It looks promising Duncan, you shouldn't croak for at least another week!' replied Weissmuller in his thick German accent as he dipped his head and looked over his spectacles at him. For some reason the doctor didn't have his eyes lasered. He said the spectacles helped him think, it seemed a crazy notion but his work spoke for itself.

'You have been a naughty boy whilst you were away Duncan, you know I could have reported you for drinking that caffeine and smoking that cigar, I hope it was a Havana!' said Weissmuller slowly, still looking over his spectacles.

McCann grinned back at the doctor, he had gotten to know the doctor well over the last three years and they had become firm friends 'You know me Frank always living on the edge!'

The doctor gave a slow light laugh 'Don't worry I won't tell the Director, I'm just glad to know that the nanites operated properly. That trip you four had was the furthest distance they've been tested at this year, I just need to have a look at your body to make sure they're doing their job.'

He pointed towards a bed in his office; McCann lay on what was a raised bed which lay on a semi cylinder. Once he lay on it the doctor made a hand gesture with his free hand at a screen on his desk. To McCann's right and left rose two halves of the cylinder until they came together above him. The bed was now completely inside a plastic cylinder. Weissmuller watched one of his monitors intently as it took McCann's readings, loaded them onto his computer, and the information was synced with what the nanites were sending him.

'Excellent,' said Weissmuller after a minute or so, he then made another gesture and the cylindrical casing above McCann broke in two and slowly returned into the other half below the bed.

'You may rise now,' said Weissmuller 'how have you been Duncan, have you had any bad stomachs or headaches? Anything at all please let me know,' Inquired the doctor as he looked at a different monitor now and typed up McCann's report with the glove.

'No I've been fine Frank, no complaints at all.'

'Well you're A+ for the physical Duncan, you can go and have your brains picked now. If I don't see you before lift-off have a safe journey.'

McCann thanked him and made his way down the hall for his psychological assessment; he waited outside the door and touched the pad that served as the doorbell. After a moment the door slid open to reveal a lady in her 50's with red hair sitting on a large comfortable leather chair, she smiled and gestured to the twin of her chair facing her over a coffee table.

'Come in Duncan and please sit down,' said Doctor Valorie Pitt

McCann made his way to the chair. She reminded him of a school mistress or some other strict authority figure, disguising her wrath behind smiles and soft talk, an iron fist in a velvet glove if ever there was one.

'So how was your trip Duncan, did you have fun visiting all those cities?' asked Valorie in her usual soft and calming tone.

'Well I enjoyed seeing my parents, apart from that it was nothing special really.'

'I see, was it good to see your parents together again?' inquired the doctor.

McCann felt very uncomfortable. He was always looking for the ulterior motive behind her questions, especially when it involved relationships and childhood.

'Yes I suppose it was, it was nice to see them together after so many years.'

Then she seemed to quickly change her direction 'So did you get along well with the others? Any problems at all?'

Again it made him uncomfortable he wondered if she had found what she wanted and was digging for something else or was she trying to get him to drop his guard? 'No, it went fine,' replied McCann almost robotically.

The doctor smiled and relaxed in her chair 'You know Duncan it's like having a conversation with my second husband; you're always worrying about what I'm thinking. There really is no need to be so defensive you know.'

'I'm sorry doctor, but this type of thing has always made me feel awkward, it's nothing personal.'

'What type of thing do you think this is Duncan?' asked the doctor calmly.

'It feels like the Spanish inquisition is interrogating me. No offence intended doctor but I am the kind of man that really likes to keep to himself. Long conversations aren't really my forte.'

'Yes we've discussed this before and we still haven't got to the stage of you calling me Valorie yet. Why do you think that is Duncan?'

'Perhaps it's because you make me nervous and I like to keep you at arm's length and not calling you by your name helps me achieve that?' replied McCann in an almost sarcastic tone.

'Very good Colonel, it seems you've read a little in the last few years on psychology ... know thine enemy?' asked the doctor calmly with a wry smile.

'No doctor, it's not you it's just that being analyzed makes me nervous, really I didn't intend to insult you or cause any offence.'

'Really no offence is taken Duncan, after nearly 30 years in this job and 4 husbands it takes far more to get my feathers ruffled!'

McCann gave a smile.

'There is one thing I'd like you to do just for me before you leave Duncan.'

'What's that Doctor?' asked McCann who seemed genuinely intrigued.

In three years the doctor had never made such a request, even her requests in the past were merely orders wrapped up in soft words.

'I'd like you to call me Valorie, not for any reason other than that it would make me feel better, could you do that?'

It seemed a very odd request from a woman who had seemed to be so hard and self sufficient, 'Of course, I'm sorry about not using your name in the past, I didn't mean ...'

The doctor cut him off 'No need Duncan, I'd just like to have you call me by name. After 4 failed marriages this has been one of the most successful relationships I've had with a member of the opposite sex, I just want you to use my name.

Don't worry you've passed the psyche test Duncan, you're one of the most stable people I've ever met.'

The doctor then picked up a tablet and started reading and typing 'Your brainwaves have been fine; I was just confirming that all was good and you hadn't gone nuts since we last spoke.'

'Thank you … Valorie,' replied McCann.

The doctor looked at him and said rather disappointedly 'That was a joke Duncan.'

'Sorry Valorie,' replied McCann.

'Well get going Duncan, you're completely sane and in fine mental condition, good luck … we're all wishing you well,' said the doctor as she gestured to the opening door.

McCann thanked the doctor and promised he'd use her name when he spoke to her in the future, then he briskly walked out as he broke a sweat.

Two weeks later they were at ground zero in Ecuador, inside the hollowed out mountain of Cayambe. Cayambe was actually an extinct volcano and the highest point on the equator. Being the highest point it meant using less nanotubing and less stress as a whole on the orbital ribbon.

The first few hours were spent being prepared by various prep teams, running through emergency drills and breakdowns of the ships systems which they all knew back to front anyway. Faraday was his usual self, with enough pressure running through his veins to crush a submarine. Then the time came to suit up and board the cart that would take them to the Athena. It was an open top cart, mostly for the press of the world. The four got on and were driven through a tunnel and out into what was a titanic cavern filled with loading bays and other tunnels leading off to more bays. The press was allowed in a small area along the carts route and closer to the Athena than the public. The public that were allowed in stood at a distance and watched.

The architecture made the cavern seem like a massive coliseum hewn out of rock. The launch pad or the orbital lift station was surrounded by buildings that made up the coliseum walls and protected the crawlers when they initially started their journey. Also a roof at the top of the volcano could be slid over it all, leaving only the three ribbons coming through in case of very bad conditions. The buildings were occupied by the orbital control centre, dedicated to monitoring the orbital lift, crawlers and the ribbons.

The cart stopped short of the boarding station, the Athena was attached to a crawler. The crawlers were cylinders that encompassed the meter thick ribbon, holding onto the ribbon tightly with rollers. Using powerful magnets powered by a charge from a second ribbon the crawler pulled its way up the ribbon; slowly at first but after some days it would reach quite a high speed, by that time the rollers would have moved off allowing just the force of the electro magnets to pull the crawler and it's payload to orbit in perhaps a couple of weeks.

Usually it took less time but the Athena was a very hefty payload, the sky lift had never been tested with such a heavy load but the engineers were quite certain it was well within safe operating parameters.

The four stepped off the cart and onto the launch station and looked at the Athena for the last time until they reached the Tsiolkovsky. The Athena was a short fat cylinder itself. Forming two distinct sections with a large sphere on the bottom (similar to a gigantic thermometer) which the astronauts couldn't see at this distance due to it residing below the boarding level somewhere in the subterranean floors of the pad where the ribbons were anchored onto reels.

The ribbons were surrounded by a metal cylinder; McCann peered over the edge viewing it. This was where a lot of the work was done by engineers checking that everything was ship shape and removing crawlers on returned; checking them after unloading and placing them on the other ribbon to be loaded in the bay above that McCann, Ryu, Louis and Hassif were in before their skyward journey.

When ready the crawler was hoisted up to the ground level where the payload was attached; so the Athena's rear end was hanging inside the giant metal cylinder below the earth. Also there was a lot of cargo for the Tsiolkovsky, far more than usual. This was due to the fact that the weight had to be equalized around the crawler so that it remained as stable as possible and didn't put any adverse strains upon the ribbon when it moved to the Tsiolkovsky.

The crew in their space suits took McCann's lead and walked along the gangway to the open hatch. They turned and waved to the public while the press jostled for position to snap them, as had been practiced they stepped in one by one. After stepping inside the Athena her hatch closed behind them and the gangway retracted. The Athena shining white with its name in vertical black letters along the cylinder (probably for the press) began to inch its way up the ribbon.

Inside the ship all four were sat in the command room, they had strapped themselves in with their backs to each other as they faced a panel on the wall and monitored the craft. Carrying out checks and answering all mission controls questions they would be spending the next few hours like this. It was one of the most crucial moments of the mission though from the outside, watching a crawler slowly move its way upwards you wouldn't know it. In-fact it was quite the anti-climax, but to those who had been training for three years or more inside and those who'd fought for decades to be at this point it was a very tense few hours. However there was no crisis and the Athena gathered pace as she ascended out of the volcano and into the heavens with her four mortals.

The Athena had been travelling for close to two weeks, attached to the crawler moving faster than a bullet train along the ribbon. The crew however only recognised the speed on checking the computer. The weather had been good with no turbulence so the journey thus far was smooth. The crew took shifts, shuttling between the three sections of the Athena. Sleeping quarters were Spartan with little privacy, bunked down much like a U-boat. However it was still adequate, they would have their meals in the same section and the toilets and showers were separate, located in the mid-section.

McCann awoke and sat up in his bunk, pulled a side panel off the wall and his meal tray slid out, held in place by a taught arm. The inside of the wall panel he'd pulled out was the meal tray and inside the alcove were a series of small panels each with a different meal inside. He had 3 choices for his breakfast meal and chose the mid panel. It was a porridge/muesli concoction put together by the nutritionists at the I.S.A. He also took out his water bottle for the day and a container with orange juice in it.

After eating his first meal of the day he put the remnants in a trash compactor which was also inside the little alcove by his bunk, then replaced his meal tray back in place so that now it became part of the wall again.

The Englishman made his way to the shower; it couldn't be used properly as there was still too much gravity. So he entered the cylinder, closed it then let a little warm water run into a small bowl and sponged his body down. Once finished he then drained the bowl and left. The toilets could still be used however, as they worked better under gravity and wouldn't need the airflow suction system until they were away from the Earth's influence.

McCann didn't shave, he never did it more than once a week normally. He had decided beforehand he'd only shave for the broadcasts that would be released to the media, thankfully Faraday agreed.

Drying his body he returned to the sleeping quarters where Ryu and Hassif were asleep and dressed himself. Pulling out a second panel by his bunk he found his clothes draw, first his underwear, next, he put on his space suit. The first astronauts of the 20th century wouldn't have recognised it as a space suit. It was such a thin and light weight piece of clothing that it was nick named the space glove. It was a space suit of one piece that was no more than 3 cm at its thickest and weighed no more than 10 kilograms. The strength came from a skeleton of flexible fibres woven into the suit; it protected the wearer from the rigors of space whilst allowing them to perform tasks without being impaired by the suit.

The helmet was made out of a tough composite plastic and totally retracted into a neck slot at the back. The only detachable part were the gloves, which were inter changeable with several different designs depending on the work you were doing. The whole thing reminded McCann of some of the more modern fencing clothing he used on the pistes today.

McCann then climbed the small ladder up through the hatch into the command module situated in the top of Athena's thermometer design, Louis was sat in the command chair and on hearing McCann entering he turned in the chair and got up.

'Good morning Duncan, did you sleep well?'

'Very well, how is everything here? Anything to report?'

'No, it's been fine,' replied Louis as he stood aside for McCann to sit 'I've been chatting with Athena most of the time. I can't wait to get to the Tsiolkovsky!' said Louis in a tired voice.

Louis sat down next to McCann at his regular station which primarily monitored engineering.

'How are you today Athena?' asked McCann.

'I'm doing very well Colonel, how are you?' replied the SI of the Athena.

All space faring vessels had some kind of a Synthetic Intelligence but Athena was a massive step forward. She had the closest approximation to a synthetic brain ever put on any type of vessel.

Mankind had possessed the ability for some years now to grow computers. The CPU and many of the parts that made up the central nervous system of a computer could now been breed. It was a costly and difficult process, for now.

Also the SI (Synthetic Intelligence) could be programmed to do what any computer could do, but the higher processes beyond number crunching had to be taught to some degree. Not everyone was happy with the situation, many ethical questioned had been asked, but fortunately so far it hadn't been necessary to confront them.

For instance the question was posed about using them in future droids, could it be justified installing what was perhaps a sentient being that we created into a droid and have it work in slavery? What about weapons? Drone fighters? Or even worse missiles? For now there were few grown SI and only a handful of them could be considered sentient ... maybe, and Athena was one of them.

'I'm good Athena, how was Louis?' asked McCann.

'He is well Colonel, he's improving at Othello,' it was her favourite game 'would you like a game Colonel?'

'Not right now Athena, it's a bit early in the morning for me, maybe later,' replied McCann as he scanned through the logs of the last 14 hours.

'Very well Colonel, if there's anything you need just ask,' said Athena in her soft voice.

'Thank you Athena,' replied McCann.

After checking the logs and doing a systems check on the Athena and crawler McCann relaxed in his chair and started reading the newspapers. Most were running stories of the mission and each day their schedule was reported along with interesting facts concerning the crew, mission and equipment. The gutter press ran far more sensational stories concerning the mission, all ultimately involved sex; usually full of innuendo about who was doing what to who and how.

McCann enjoyed reading the gutter press, much to the distaste of pretty much everyone else. He didn't make a big deal out of it nor did he impose it on others, he just found it entertaining along with what most considered trash TV. McCann enjoyed watching people make idiots of themselves on television. The DNA tests the lie detector tests and finding out the latest innuendo concerning his alleged sex life.

McCann himself saw no shame in enjoying it and was certain most others took the same guilty pleasures. Only that they were too afraid to admit it, fearing the opinion of their piers over their own honesty. Besides someone has to watch it and read it otherwise why would you transmit or print such outrageous material?

McCann had settled on a two page story that started off about how close the crew had become in the last few years, insinuating the obvious. Then ending in describing how in theory an orgy might be conducted in zero G in the Athena's aft section. McCann found the whole thing hilarious, and let out a few sniggers.

'So what does the shit press have to say this morning?' asked Louis with his signature French snarl they'd all grown used to. He knew what McCann was doing since one of the rare times he expressed humour was when sniggering like a schoolboy over trash media.

McCann ignored Louis' disdain and read on continuing to giggle at the ridiculousness of the whole article.

Louis continued 'I don't know why you read that damn trash! You British and Americans have spread it like a plague, trash TV, trash food you damn people do nothing but live on trash! You're like a pig, you know that? Vous vivez que de la merde!'

Louis was working up to one of his outbursts so McCann put down the tablet he'd been reading from 'What's up Louis?' asked McCann in a friendly voice; he detected there was more on Louis mind than a gutter press article. Louis was looking anxious and McCann was curious as to what had set it all off. He knew Louis didn't start cursing in his mother tongue without good reason.

'Those papers, they're full of lies I wish that you wouldn't read that shit.'

'I'm sorry Louis I didn't know I was annoying you, I'll read it later.'

'It's not that, it's just that you read it at all, why do you bother with it?'

'It relaxes me and I enjoy it, if that's a problem I'll stop reading it Louis.'

'No, it's okay, it just makes me angry when I think about what they publish.'

McCann started thinking; Louis was often the focus of the trash media and their innuendos. He noticed that Louis seemed to quite enjoy the attention until about 6 months ago at which point he began to snarl whenever it was brought up. As launch date approached the attention got more intense, private lives were dug into and a lot of claims were made. Around then Louis took on a whole different demeanour, at least at work he did. Louis put on the same smile as always for the cameras but McCann suspected what had caused his abrupt change in attitude, though he never said.

McCann put his tablet back in the holder at the console; he didn't want to aggravate Louis any further. As he did Athena's soft voice spoke from the console, 'Incoming transmission from Director Faraday to Colonel McCann.'

'Acknowledged Athena,' replied McCann.

The image of Faraday came up on the view screen above the console 'Good morning Colonel,' he said in a calm voice. It seemed that the successful lift off and continued smooth voyage had lowered his blood pressure significantly.

McCann replied 'Good morning Sir, nothing more to report everything is ship shape.'

'Excellent Colonel, Athena is working 100% and we confirm that all systems are optimal, how are the four of you doing personally?'

'Everyone has been good, Sir, Louis and Hassif are no more annoying than usual and Major Ryu is running at full efficiency.'

'Excellent, you'll be docking with the Tsiolkovsky in under 36 hours, then after that there will be a press interview the following day with that Habeeb fellow. So make sure all of the crew are clean and shaven.'

'Understood Sir, it's nice to know our biggest worry is an interview, we must be doing well?'

Faraday said in a relaxed tone 'Keep your eyes open Colonel, but yes so far everything has been going to plan. The next time we speak should be on the Tsiolkovsky if all goes well. I just wanted to check in with you personally, good luck with the docking Colonel.'

Faraday's image left the screen, McCann could speak to anyone at the mission control but it was reserved for utilitarian matters. Idle chit chat was forbidden, only Faraday had that privilege, which he had only used to check on their well-being, usually before an important event.

The important event to come was the docking with the space station and then the interview. Jerry Habeeb had been invited to a control room in Geneva at the I.S.A and would pose several questions to the crew. It was a necessity in this day and age, the exploration of space was no longer an endeavour funded by tax payers money. The I.S.A scrounged about for every penny it could, it was policy. Every opportunity to bring in money was used within acceptable parameters.

For instance Faraday wasn't prepared to have a fast food chain slap an advert on the Athena or the space suits. He didn't want to trivialise what they were doing but interviews were a great method of free advertising and a way to bring in extra funds. Network America had paid for the exclusive rights to interview the crew during the mission. At the same time it put the whole endeavour into the media generating interest in the public. That interest brought in many corporations and governments that wanted a piece of the Mars dream. Once there was a foothold on Mars the rest of the system was open, the opportunities for governments and Corporations was massive to anyone that could see ahead.

Mining companies were looking at the asteroid belt, mining an almost infinite supply of minerals in zero G. Right now it wasn't viable economically for them, but once colonies were established the first ones there now, would pull in the biggest profit later. Hydrogen production on Mars was in the more immediate future, the massive polar caps beckoned begging to be exploited. H2O was the most valuable resource in the solar system at the moment, it provided the basics for exploration and exploitation. Hydrogen and Oxygen, the most efficient fuel known, it was required if you were going to send drones to search the belt. Mine it and return the spoils, and once Mars had an orbital lift those corporations would have the rights to a supply of it.

It was expected that there would be an old fashioned land grab in the asteroid belt at some point in the near future. Mining corporations staking claims on the richest asteroids, with court battles following the legal mess. However before that would be Mars. No doubt once a regular human presence was established there would be a lot of prospecting, exploration and research. The Mars base was set up so that all contributors would get a fair shake.

McCann glided into the sleeping quarters to check up on Ryu and Hassif, they were both up and eating their breakfasts. Sitting in opposite bunks they were chatting, McCann said good morning, Ryu was her usual self but Hassif wasn't taking too well to the low gravity breakfast.

'Are you going to be able to keep that down Hassif?' asked McCann.

'Don't get stressed, it's just the gravity, it feels like my meal has a mind of its own. I'll get used to it,' replied Hassif.

'Either that or you'll get used to throwing up in a bag, so that we don't have to dodge your last meal, keep it with you at all times Hassif.'

Ryu nodded towards the plastic bag Hassif had next to him, whatever the gravity if you felt odd you kept it with you. Hassif nodded at Ryu and chewed slowly on the scrambled eggs on toast concoction he was squeezing out of a tubular package, much like a giant tube of tooth paste.

'Everything okay for the docking, McCann?' asked Hassif.

'We're all ship shape; as long as you keep your breakfast down we should dock without a hitch in a few hours. You can both take your time getting ready, meet you in the cockpit,' as he was finishing McCann pushed himself up and into the cockpit.

The Athena was close to the Tsiolkovsky, they had left the atmosphere of the Earth and her gravity hours ago. McCann supposed it wasn't much fun to go to sleep at 1G then wake up at zero G then have to eat your breakfast and go to work. Ryu seemed to cope with it, as she did with most things, without complaint. Hassif wasn't taking it as well but McCann was certain he'd get over it, he always was a slow starter but after he warmed up he quickly adapted. Besides they had three hours, McCann was certain Hassif would be back to his old self before then.

McCann glided into the command module and strapped himself in opposite Louis, who was in a good mood. He couldn't wait to stretch his legs ... so to speak, on the Tsiolkovsky.

'Data stream steady Colonel, Tsiolkovsky has given us the go ahead to begin deceleration,' said Athena in her soft calm voice.

'Very well Athena you may begin deceleration now, how long until we dock with the Tsiolkovsky?' asked McCann.

'T-minus two hours and thirty six minutes Colonel, the Tsiolkovsky reports all systems are optimal, she also hopes to see you soon Colonel.'

'She?' inquired Louis 'you know someone on there McCann?'

'No I don't, who is she, Athena?'

'The SI on the Tsiolkovsky Colonel, she is excited to meet all the crew.'

Louis chuckled 'For a moment there I thought you had a girlfriend McCann, I was about to send an email to your mother!'

'I'm sorry could you clarify that for me Louis?' inquired Athena.

Louis started to laugh but McCann cut in 'Enough, concentrate on the job Louis! He was attempting to be humorous Athena.'

'I'm sorry Colonel, I didn't intend to pry into your personal affairs,' apologized Athena.

'Thank you Athena,' replied McCann as he took a sharp look at Louis who was still smiling.

The Tsiolkovsky was also fitted with an SI of its own, it didn't have one at first, synthetic intelligence was in its infancy.

As the technology developed it was realised that two computer systems running on entirely different software that was normally incompatible could easily communicate with an SI in control of each. An SI could learn any operating language very quickly, with one installed on the Tsiolkovsky and one at Geneva compatibility was no longer an issue.

The Russian SI wasn't as advanced as the Athena when it was installed, but over time it grew in experience, the ability of these computers to grow and adapt made them unique and they quickly became indispensable. Unlike most of the first generation SI it hadn't failed, many shut down due to imperfections when first grown. The imperfections only manifested years later after the SI had developed into sentience; and what by human standards would be called a mental breakdown suddenly took place one day without warning. The Tsiolkovsky had been one of the few that fortunately had no imperfections at "birth". Athena was a next generation SI but the Tsiolkovsky made up for it with experience, in human terms you could say a case of wisdom over intelligence.

Soon Hassif and Ryu joined them in the command module. Ryu sat at the controls ready to take over the deceleration and docking process if the Athena failed. The chances were minimal but nevertheless it was always required to have a human pilot ready to take over.

McCann took a look at Hassif who was busy checking over the software looking for any blips; 'Feeling better Hassif?' inquired McCann.

'Sure,' replied Hassif without looking away from his monitor.

McCann was satisfied, though he noticed he had his vomit bag attached to the velcro patch on his space suit leg. McCann inquired about the crawler with first Louis then Athena, all seemed to be going smoothly.

Right now the crawler was slowly breaking using electro magnets; it would slow down from the speed of a bullet train to that of a cyclist. The powerful engines that allowed the crawler to clasp onto the ribbon with its wheels and manage to push the payload from a slow crawl to that of around 180 MPH were now using those electro-magnets to slow it back down to 10 MPH. The Tsiolkovsky would let the crawler move up inside of her and then bring her to a halt with a magnetic net. The Tsiolkovsky crew were set to over-look the unloading of the crawler. First detaching the crawler then later re-attaching it onto the ribbon going downwards. The Athena would be moved to a separate bay with an atmosphere and prepared for a space launch.

During that time the crew would be guests on the Tsiolkovsky where they could stretch their space legs, take a break and be interviewed by the world press.

The Athena approached the looming hulk of rock that orbited Earth, attached by a few ribbons that had now grown in diameter. Clamped to the crawler she moved towards the gaping hole that the ribbon disappeared into.

The crew watched this mammoth sight through the monitors, there were no portholes on this craft only tiny cameras on strategic points along with heat and radar sensors. The crawler was now moving along the ribbon just on momentum, the engines were turned off. The crawler slipped inside the Tsiolkovsky effortlessly, bringing its payload to a halt just below a collection of metallic discs that were suspended from metal cylinders attached to the cargo bay roof. The ribbon continued upwards into the black hole cut out for it, lined with some light super strong metal. The magnetic discs broke the crawler's approach, as soon as the crawler reached 0MPH it locked the wheels and held itself and the precious payload in place ready for the Russians to unload it.

Now the Tsiolkovsky was in control, the SI monitored as the crew of the station closed the orifice below them. Removing the blue planet from view and leaving a small hole that allowed the ribbon to enter. The robots moved in, their concertinaed arms extended from the walls and clasped onto the Athena. Using the pressure from each arm they held a firm grip on the Athena.

Once four arms had a firm grip the order was sent for the crawler to release her. McCann felt nothing, strapped in inside the command module all four of them watched and waited for at least an hour. Slowly the four arms manipulated the Athena in front of a large entrance that lead to an inter locking bay area. Once in front of the entrance another arm peered through and clasped onto the Athena. Three of the main docking bay arms released, allowing the two arms one in each bay to slowly move the Athena to her new resting place. The bay door they'd come through now slowly came down after the last of the original arms released and retracted back into the first bay, 30 minutes later it was closed, another hour and it was pressurized with an oxygen/nitrogen atmosphere.

McCann had been speaking with the station commander Leon Titov, a well-built man especially for someone who'd spent so much time in space, with a mane of black hair. He was informing McCann that his officers were about to come in and greet them as they left the Athena. McCann concurred, turned off the monitor and told the others to prepare, he went to the sleeping quarters and pulled out an expensive bottle of cognac.

McCann had requested it before the flight, Faraday had permitted it as it was just good etiquette in his opinion. The Tsiolkovsky was almost solely crewed by Russian cosmonauts, Moscow refused to give up its control of the station. Relations between the station and Geneva were often strained with personalities grating on each other; station commanders refusing to take orders from the I.S.A and likewise.

One day a Russian scientist working at the I.S.A was busted for smuggling alcoholic drinks onboard a crawler payload. After an investigation it turned out the reason he had his projects done in a timely manner was due to the illicit cargo he smuggled towards the heavens.

The scientist was reprimanded but the shipments remained, that was the end of any problems with the Tsiolkovsky. Since then all kinds of luxury goods have made their way into orbit. Even today despite the crew containing a larger multi-national I.S.A contingent, the command is still left to the Russians and a bottle of fine old Cognac goes a long way to keeping on the commander's good side.

McCann and his crew could feel the gravity of the Tsiolkovsky as they put on their suits to leave the Athena and visit Titov's crew. The Tsiolkovsky had a small gravity due to tidal forces on the asteroid.

She was held in place by tidal stabilization, the top of the Tsiolkovsky weighing less than the bottom causing the earth to pull on them by different amounts. The larger pull on the bottom part causes it to point towards the Earth; this tidal affect stabilizes the Tsiolkovsky in orbit and creates a small gravity through the tidal forces.

The gravity was enough to get dressed properly in and was no doubt a great aid to the cosmonauts running the station.

Athena spoke softly 'Pressure has equalized and Colonel Titov is awaiting you outside Colonel.'

McCann replied 'Thank you Athena, please open the airlock, we're ready to depart.'

'As you wish Colonel.'

The hatch opened and the four travellers stepped carefully down the steps in the low gravity, holding onto the safety rail. McCann clutched the rail with one hand and a bottle of cognac in the other. Titov and three of his officers stood waiting; Titov was eyeing the bottle and giving a smile of satisfaction.

The bottle had become a symbol of respect, a required tribute; if it weren't there he would have to punish the ISA until reimbursed or suffer the ridicule and scorn of his comrades. Besides Titov wasn't a vengeful man and although he'd have to, he didn't take any pleasure in the prospect of making life difficult for others.

Chapter 3

McCann stepped off the gangway and slowly approached Titov; they shook one another's hand whilst at the same time McCann passed over the Cognac.

'Was your journey troubled at all Colonel?' asked Titov in his best English.

'No it couldn't have gone better and please call me Duncan.'

'Then you must call me Leon,' replied Titov with a friendly smile 'this is Podpolkovnik Cherkesov,' said Titov pointing to the middle aged man next to him.

McCann shook his hand 'Good to see you Cherkesov. I hope you don't mind me using your second name since your first is a bit of a mouthful!'

The crew of the Tsiolkovsky seemed a little taken a back or just embarrassed, Ryu interjected 'Podpolkovnik is Russian for Lieutenant Colonel, Sir!'

McCann suddenly had the desire for something large and heavy to come crashing down, taking the attention away from his attempt at humour. McCann apologised for a faux pas rather than a bad joke since he wasn't sure if anyone recognised his attempt.

Chereksov accepted awkwardly then Titov step forwards whilst offering his hand to Ryu 'It's an honour to meet you Major, the crew have been awaiting your arrival.'

Ryu almost blushed 'Thank you Polkovnik,' she then saluted Titov which made the crew of the Athena even more uncomfortable than they already were.

Titov looked rather embarrassed or flattered or both, it was hard to tell. He returned the salute, shook her hand and said softly 'You must call me Leon, you will join us for a drink before you leave Major? My crew is most anxious to meet you in person.'

Ryu did blush now, McCann stared at Louis and Louis stared back with a quizzical expression, Hassif was no less befuddled. They were all asking each other telepathically "What the hell is happening?"

Ryu seemed to be acquainted with Titov or at least Titov was familiar with her. How did she know him? How did he know her? If she did why hadn't she mentioned it? Why did all the Russians seem to know who she was and want an audience with her as if she were Royalty? All these questions were now burning inside the three male members of the Athena. Ryu was about to get a good interrogation as soon as they could get her alone and wrangle the information out of her.

After the introductions Titov handed the Cognac to one of his junior officers and began to take the crew on a tour, 'Mr. Hassif and Mr. Beaumont, Lieutenant Pankov shall give you a tour of relevant systems.'

Hassif and Louis followed him towards engineering.

'Duncan and Major Ryu please follow me to command.'

McCann and Ryu wearing their silver space suits minus the helmet and gloves followed him along a white corridor constructed of hardened plastic panels. Titov was dressed in his slightly bulkier cosmonaut suit, all white with his RKA and ISA emblems on either side of his chest. The Russian Space Agency still kept their insignia in use; it was all over the station. Whilst others had relinquished control within the ISA many years ago the Russian still refused to make that leap of faith. They still saw themselves as partners rather than subordinates to Geneva.

Titov showed them around the command centre, a large room in the signature Tsiolkovsky dirty white. All the time McCann was making glaring looks at Ryu, she attempted not to notice. McCann had a short chat with the Tsiolkovsky, he considered the SI to be quite amiable for a Russian, though he preferred the Athena. Although both were prompt and pragmatic the Tsiolkovsky left him feeling a little cold whereas the Athena didn't. McCann put it down to being in contact with the Athena for so long. He was certain Titov would find many character flaws in the Athena that put him off.

After a while Titov escorted them to their accommodation on the Tsiolkovsky, each room had two bunks so McCann and Ryu would be bunk mates. Real estate inside the asteroid was at a premium right now. She had to be crewed 24/7 and they were in the process of making new tunnels and constructing new quarters.

Titov invited Ryu to the celebrations at 19:00, allowing her three hours to prepare. The rest of the crew were invited but it was obvious to all who the centre of attention would be. In fact McCann couldn't say that this celebration was for the Athena and the voyage to put down the first roots of humanity on Martian soil. No, it was fairly obvious to him and the others that this was all about Major Ryu and her presence here.

Titov said his farewell after securing Ryu's promise to turn up; next McCann escorted her into their quarters, as if a member of the Gestapo. McCann wasn't the type to beat around the bush. Probably thanks to years of watching the Springer show more than anything else, 'You didn't tell me you were acquainted with Titov or the crew here.'

Ryu smiled 'I didn't tell you because I'm not acquainted with any of them as far as I know, Sir.'

McCann didn't want to play games with her so he just asked 'Alright ... Major ... why does Titov grin like a buffoon when he lays eyes upon you and why are they throwing a party in your favour?' he said rather abruptly.

'Perhaps it's my smile or my stunning personality!' she joked taking pleasure in keeping McCann hanging on.

'Well certainly not your wit!' replied McCann.

'Look who's talking ... Kovnik!' quipped Ryu as she let out a big laugh.

McCann was very taken aback. Ryu was not an emotional person and to see her chuckle was rare however McCann had never witnessed her find anything so amusing as to laugh out loud before.

At that moment Louis and Hassif crashed through the door, 'Is everything alright? We heard a scream!'

To be fair it was far more likely for Ryu to scream than laugh. Yet they were no less curious than McCann and were not passing up the opportunity to interrogate her in private.

'Shut the damn door, Louis,' McCann turned back to Ryu 'my thanks for saving me some embarrassment back there but you haven't answered me. Why is it when you walked into the command centre every single one of them saluted you before me? It was as if I barely existed! And now they're throwing a party in your honour and don't try and tell me it isn't!' inquired McCann as the other two stared intently at Ryu.

Ryu expelled some breath through her nose, the sound she made when she was annoyed or frustrated 'I was decorated by Moscow, I was in the media for a while. It seems some of them remember it, are you satisfied now?'

'To be honest no I'm not!' replied McCann.

'I was awarded the Order of Kutuzov and Suvorov; it was a long time ago.'

McCann knew less about Russian military decorations than Hassif did about getting a date. However judging by the reactions he'd witnessed earlier today he was certain that Moscow wasn't giving them away to the first guy that threw a grenade.

'So what exactly are the medals for?' pushed McCann.

'It was for the assistance we gave in the Russian campaign to repel Qian Jing,' replied Ryu who was growing weary of the grilling. 'Oh and I'm also an honorary Colonel, just in case it comes up,' added Ryu as if it had slipped her mind for a moment.

Louis raised his eyebrows at Hassif and thought to himself 'I wonder how many villages she had to nerve gas to get those?'

Hassif nodded in agreement almost as if he could read his friends thoughts.

'OK you two, get to your quarters there's a party in the lounge at 19:00 we'll see you there,' ordered McCann.

Louis and Hassif left and McCann apologized to Ryu for the interrogation.

That evening the party was going well, most of those attending were gathered around Ryu as she recanted stories of the war. Hassif was mingling with the group around Ryu whilst Louis stood by the makeshift bar chatting.

McCann sat with Titov complementing him on the celebration and the wide array of liquor at hand. Titov plonked an ashtray on the table smiled and produced a brown leather case from his pocket, McCann recognised it as a cigar case.

'What do you have there Leon?' asked McCann.

Titov opened the case to produce 6 cigars lying down alongside each other. Titov had several of his crew stealing quick looks; smoking was prohibited for obvious reasons. Firstly the fire hazard but it also burnt precious oxygen and forced the atmosphere scrubbers to work harder than they should. Some of the looks were disapproving whereas others were of envy. Technically the drink was prohibited also, but in this era things were changing. Earth orbit was no longer some far flung place where total discipline had to be maintained; now it was merely an extension of Earth. The Tsiolkovsky was a Behemoth, a far cry from the likes of Mir. If something went horribly wrong on the Tsiolkovsky it could be dealt with and the SI was meticulous at monitoring and maintaining the rock.

Titov offered the contents of the case to McCann 'I have heard you like to smoke, please be my guest.'

McCann took one of the Robusto cigars, he examined the red and gold band closely and deduced it was a Partagas serie D. McCann wasn't usually a Robusto smoker but he would never turn down a good Cuban, he took one out as did his companion.

Titov then passed him his guillotine cigar cutter 'Relax it's all cleared with the Tsiolkovsky, we can smoke in here when off duty.'

'Thank you,' said McCann as he took the cutter and sliced the cap off his cigar.

He passed the cutter back and he took the silver gas lighter from Titov. Both of them lit up their cigars and began to smoke whilst others gave some odd looks.

'How the hell do you get away with this then?' inquired McCann.

Titov smiled 'We spend a lot of time on this station; the crew is large enough for some of us to have genuine leisure time here. The Tsiolkovsky understands that keeping her crew happy is important, when we can let off stress we work better. She makes certain Moscow or Geneva don't get concerned about our relaxation.'

Suddenly it hit McCann, his crew's information wasn't being relayed through the Tsiolkovsky they were having their details sent via the Athena. For a moment McCann panicked. He hit his communicator and the Athena replied in her usual soft tone 'Yes Colonel? Is there something I can do for you?'

'Athena are you transmitting our bio signs to Geneva?' asked McCann in a slightly shaky voice.

'Yes Colonel, is there a problem Colonel?' asked Athena calmly.

'Shit!'

'I'm sorry Colonel but are you feeling alright, Sir?' asked the Athena softly.

Titov found this all very amusing much to McCann's irritation. However McCann was worried about what would happen when Geneva saw alcohol and nicotine coming through on their readouts. The nanites would inevitably pick up the drinks that were flowing freely and the cigars he and Titov were smoking. McCann asked then began to demand he speak to Doctor Weissmuller. He was causing a stir and many of the Russians peered over at the table he was sitting at with Titov. The heated one way conversation continued as McCann hurriedly paced up and down. He envisaged himself being demoted and blamed for anything that went wrong ... if they weren't recalled before they left the Tsiolkovsky. Ryu, Louis and Hassif were shocked at what they saw, they stood motionless and at a loss.

Finally he got Weissmuller on his communication badge 'Hello? Duncan is that you?'

'Thank god, yes Frank. Listen are you receiving the bio signs?' screeched a desperate voice.

'Not yet Duncan, the next transmission will be in 3 hours, why?' replied the doctor.

The information was sent every 24 hours along with all data recorded by the Athena in a data packet. If the Athena were not in a decompressed launch bay right now he could have headed down and made the arrangements so that he wouldn't be tarred and feathered by Faraday upon his return.

Since the Tsiolkovsky had a direct link to Geneva through the ribbon connecting the two he could get in touch with them and head the data packet off at the pass so to speak. McCann explained his predicament and the Doctor listened. Weissmuller calmed him down and agreed to make sure Faraday didn't see anything he didn't need to. McCann thanked him and the doctor assured him that he'd keep an eye out in the future.

McCann sat back down at the table with Titov, he took a large drag from his cigar and knocked back his Cognac in one go. Titov was grinning; he picked up the bottle 'Another?'

McCann just nodded towards the glass and Titov poured 'I must say the Cognac you brought is very good, Colonel.'

McCann didn't reply he just sat back and tried to relax, the room had gone back to what it was doing before the scene. Titov and McCann began chatting mostly about the Mars expedition. Titov was quite envious, as was to be expected, he was an ex-military pilot who ended up serving in space. For him as with most it was the adventure, now he had grown quite comfortable after having run the Tsiolkovsky for so long and familiarity had overtaken adventure. Meeting McCann reignited that lust and he would have done anything to have joined him. However he was the victim of his own success, he ran the Tsiolkovsky so well that he would never be considered for anything else while he commanded her.

McCann sat and unwound whilst Titov questioned him about details of the mission mostly concerning maintenance of the Martian base at Pavonis Mons. As the evening moved on McCann recovered from his shock and had been having a long interesting conversation with Titov. He had discovered a lot of information about running a large station that he didn't learn in Geneva.

Titov was an encyclopaedia on power conservation and short cuts that weren't covered back on Earth. Titov pointed out that McCann would still have to learn some things the hard way due to a different environment. One point he stressed was converting the water reclamation system as soon as possible. McCann didn't understand it as it was far too technical. Neither did Titov totally, but he promised to have one of his technicians go over it with Louis.

On the Tsiolkovsky the urine had been diverted from water reclamation and into a converted fuel cell. Fuel cells used for the most part refined hydrogen as fuel, although there were many different types in existence that could use an array of fuels, the ISA preferred pure hydrogen as the only by product was pure water; which is fine as long as you can power the 2500C pressure oven to separate water into hydrogen and oxygen, creating the fuel (hydrogen) and the catalyst (oxygen). Which then re-combine in the fuel cell produced power with a by-product of pure drinking water.

The Tsiolkovsky had some problems in its early stages, all of the solar arrays weren't functioning and the station was suffering brown outs. Without the arrays Titov couldn't run the hydrogen oven to cook the water; which in turn powered the fuel cells which in turn powered the water reclamation, atmosphere scrubbers and 99% of the systems on the station. Once the solar arrays broke down and the batteries were out a vicious cycle began. They were using power sent up the ribbon from the base station in Ecuador to stay afloat. That meant a crawler couldn't be powered to simply deliver some liquid hydrogen. With emergency power and brownouts it would take months to get the arrays fixed and everything running again.

Everything was on minimal power and it seemed the new space age had come to a screeching halt thanks to a few solar panels failing. Titov had a meeting with his officers; he needed an idea or something to get those panels back online. They didn't have repair drones for the arrays yet and even if they did he wasn't sure if they had enough power to run them.

A tech made a suggestion at the meeting that sounded quite ridiculous to Titov. He suggested making some alterations to the fuel cells and using urine and oxygen rather than hydrogen and oxygen. There were some uncomfortable looks, some thought he was joking others just thought it was madness, run a fuel cell on urine? It seemed equally preposterous to Titov and under normal conditions he'd dismiss such a suggestion; however under normal conditions the tech wouldn't have suggested it and these were not normal conditions.

The room went silent and the tech took the opportunity to explain the science before someone could speak.

He explained that urine contained hydrogen and it was far more efficient to use urine as you didn't need a hydrogen oven. He went on to point out that in the rural community he grew up in farmers used fuel cells powered by urea; it was easily available and cut their fuel bills since they didn't need to use any hydrogen or any of the other fuels used in the cells.

Titov looked at his chief engineer, the engineer told him that he would consult the Tsiolkovsky and find out if enough of their fuel cells could be converted.

Within a week the station was up and running as normal, the crawlers were sent straight away with repair drones and the arrays were fixed. Titov's position as station commander was cemented the day the arrays were back up and working. Titov told McCann he always had enough converted power cells to keep the station running on urine.

It was a fascinating story and McCann intently listened as he puffed away. When Titov had finished he asked what was wrong with the solar panels. He explained that some of them were faulty due to poor manufacturing, causing a massive failure of entire arrays.

McCann shook his head in disbelief that such a thing could occur while thanking him for the information. The Englishman requested that the same tech speak with Louis and give him the plans whenever he could.

Titov then chuckled and said something in Russian about the future of humanity saved by a pot of piss. McCann understood the jist and laughed as did Titov, both of them enjoying the evening.

As the evening drew on Titov inquired about Ryu, he seemed interested in what she was like when off duty. McCann pointed out she was pretty much the same person. Titov seemed a little disappointed to hear this but nonetheless he didn't appear surprised. McCann asked about her and what she was decorated for.

This time Titov did show some surprise 'You didn't know?' he asked.

'The ISA isn't a military organization, I knew she was a drone pilot during the Manchurian war and a good one, but aside from that she has never expanded on the subject,' replied McCann.

'You know she'd never had any formal training as a pilot before she first flew in combat?'

'No I didn't, so how?'

Titov cut him off and began to explain with a look of satisfaction and mild intoxication.

Titov recalled how during the early part of the war the drug lord Qain Jiang had invaded the now reformed Korea.

Jiang needed a port desperately, to both import his weapons to maintain his position and export his poison to pay for it. Since no one would give him passage to conduct business his choices were either that of fighting with other warlords to the south, attacking the Russians to the east or invading the Korean peninsula.

Korea being the softest target he invaded, with all the armour and air power he could muster, he made a rapid advance. Japan and Taiwan had supported Korea in an alliance to stop the warlords of China but they were under siege themselves and the assault took everyone by surprise. Japan and Taiwan were unable to assist their ally.

China had broken up into a series of kingdoms run by warlords of varying brutality many years ago. Initially they had fought amongst themselves until after several years of fighting they agreed to an armistice. Before this there was little Manchuria was able to do about the blockade. Japan, Taiwan and Korea were the only nations in the region prepared to make a stand against the warlords.

Within the first month most of Koreas drone pilots had been killed in surgical strikes on airbases using nerve gas. The Koreans had years of catching up to do experience wise. Flying drones with computer assistance was standard practice however inexperienced pilots came to rely on it as a crutch more than an asset. Manchurian pilots were successful in every strike they made, always getting their target with small losses. The scram drones they purchased from Russia were tried and tested and the most reliable money could buy.

The Koreans and Japanese had developed their own drones, but they had rarely been used in combat against other drones. As a ground attack drone the AI assistance had worked well, keeping up a total sea blockade. Sinking ships and hitting the odd undefended port, but against another drone in a dog fight the computer assisted crutch was kicked out from under them.

Soon Korea was on the verge of being over-run, without air superiority they couldn't field any ground forces. They had the drones but there were not enough pilots trained in flying them. They were desperate and had no more than a week or two to find enough pilots who could fly them in combat; otherwise Jiang was about to roll into Seoul unopposed. The military sent out dozens of recruiters and locked down the net with adverts for pilots. Within a few days a Lieutenant, one of the many recruiters sent out, came back with a fairly sorry looking group of teenagers which included Ryu.

When asked what they were doing there he explained his younger brother used to compete online. His clan had won the national gaming league in the simulator division, which included the current scram drone simulator used by the military to train their own drone pilots. Apparently they were set to compete at a world tournament before the war broke out.

His superior made no secret that he felt this was a preposterous idea and even questioned the Lieutenants sanity. It sounded like an April fool's joke made in very bad taste, suggesting he allow these scruffy children charge of a scram drone.

However he was under orders to consider everyone and to give every single applicant a competency evaluation versus an AI, no matter what the circumstances. He signed the Lieutenants' tablet with his thumb. Still shaking his head he sent him and his brother's ragtag clan on to the simulation centre.

At the simulators the gazes were no different, mostly of disbelief. The Lieutenant informed the obviously intimidated teenagers to wait in line for their test. He made his way to the Colonel that was coordinating a warehouse filled with every simulator in the country that they could get their hands on. It gave them the ability to evaluate hundreds of applicants at a time. The Lieutenant handed his tablet over, the Colonel looked at him then gestured towards the kids, 'Who on earth are they?'

'They have come to do their duty, Sir,' replied the Lieutenant.

The Colonel didn't like his answer 'Do any of them have a pilot's license? Most of them seem too young to drive!'

'No Sir, however I've seen them fly drones in simulators before. They are better than any qualified pilot I've witnessed. I felt obligated to bring them here.'

'We shall see,' he sighed 'send them to area C. We have some free simulators there, let them fly against the AI Lieutenant,' the Colonel pointed all the way down the warehouse to where block C was.

'Thank you, Sir.'

The Lieutenant took back his tablet after it had been approved with the Colonel's thumbprint.

What they didn't know is that these kids had competed on this very same simulator many times in tournaments. They had all thrashed the most advanced AI along-time ago and in one tournament they had gone up against an SI built in Germany; developed by the military to train the most advanced pilots.

The German scientists had jokingly christened it "The Red Baron". They were proposing the use of Advanced SI flying a wing of scram drones for the Luftwaffe. The scientist showcased it first in Germany and after it had beaten nearly all their best pilots, getting another such demonstration set up was difficult. The Red Baron was resigned to being shown off at gaming tournaments and net programs until the military had gotten over it. Although most air forces were interested in developing the idea behind closed doors, they were frightened by the concept just as much. Of the hundreds of contestants one had beaten it, Ryu, and according to the hosts she had the largest recorded margin against it.

After reaching block C then defeating the AI effortlessly and shocking everyone by doing so they were sent to block D. On arrival they saw there were only 6 simulators divided into two teams of 3. A General and several other officers watched the combat on screen intently as the hopefuls that beat the AI faced off against each other. They all stood making notes and running back the footage; pointing out sparks of talent that could be used and perhaps developed in the short time available.

The busy discussion stopped and the General looked at the ragtag clan that had been lead in by the Lieutenant, 'What's this lieutenant? A joke?' stated General Pak as he approached them.

'No Sir, they've passed the AI and are here to be tested again,' replied the young Lieutenant quickly.

The General looked at them and then starring at Ryu asked sharply 'Where did you learn to fly girl?'

'I learned to fly at home ... Sir,' she replied timidly.

There were some chuckles in the background but the General was not amused, his country was staring into the abyss and his sense of humour was on leave.

'So you're not a qualified pilot then?' he said again in his stern and intimidating manner.

'No, Sir,' she replied.

'What makes you think that you and your sorry group would be any use against Jiang's pilots when our best are in their graves girl?' he barked.

The last question angered Ryu; the General was unaware that her family in the north had been gassed by the Manchurians. Her father died from the nerve gas attack. The village was evacuated with her mother surviving the initial attack, only to die later in a mobile triage centre before any treatment could be given. Her brother was away at university thankfully. Her sister was being looked after by an aunt though she suffered from severe lung problems thanks to the gas and wasn't expected to survive.

Jiang was merciless with the use of nerve agents; it was a quick and easy way to dispose of the enemy. He had no qualms about it being used on civilians for the purpose of terrorizing a population into submission and clearing his path to his goal, which was Seoul and an unconditional surrender.

Ryu gave a hard stare and said calmly but sternly 'Why don't you just give us a chance instead of wasting our time?'

The room fell quiet; the staff were expecting Ryu to be thrown out on her backside. However the General had worse things to worry about than his pride right now and didn't respond to her outburst.

'Very well girl you and two of your friends can get in over there.'

He pointed towards the three booths nearest to her and gestured towards three men waiting to be tested. The three opponents strapped themselves in but the three kids looked at each other and Ryu asked that their chairs be deactivated. General Pak nodded and the seats were deactivated, they had never flown and found the motion to be a distraction.

The test commenced, 6 scram drones in 2 teams of 3 facing off. Flying into a combat zone that they were not permitted to leave during the test. The test was short but the observers were very excited by what they had seen. The next 3 were tested against a fresh threesome, as the last were sent home.

Sure enough they won quickly and easily. Afterwards General Pak approached Ryu 'Very good girl and my congratulations to your friends, give me that Lieutenant.'

He took the tablet and put his thumb to it 'I'll accompany you and your team to block E.'

'Thank you, Sir,' replied the Lieutenant as he smiled quickly at his brother.

The General was smiling with excitement; he had forgotten Ryu's earlier comments as he led them towards the final testing area.

Block E was where the people that made it had a final test against experienced combat drone pilots in one on one situations. General Pak ushered them in, it was much the same as the previous block only there were two booths. Yet one was manned by a proven scram drone pilot.

General Pak approached his opposite and quickly stated 'General I have some applicants that show great promise.'

Then he said under his breath 'Do not judge them by appearance.'

General Kim looked hard at them over Pak's shoulder. It was difficult for him to believe these children who were in need of a haircut and some decent clothes were capable of making the grade, 'Very well, perhaps the young girl in the shorts would like to try her luck first?'

It was hard to tell if he was being sarcastic or not but Ryu got in the booth and General Pak requested her booth seat be deactivated. The techs complied and everyone watched the screen as the combat began. General Pak was transfixed but Kim seemed to be rather uninterested. If it weren't such dark times he'd have thrown the kids out and let the drill Sergeant in-still some discipline into them for an hour or two.

The combat started to get Kim's attention since Ryu hadn't been shot down in the first 10 seconds. His pilot who was one of their best seemed to be struggling to get a fix on her. It was a game of cat and mouse that he just couldn't finish. His pilot was becoming rather frustrated whilst Ryu remained relaxed and focused.

The clan knew what was happening and had seen it time and time again. Her opponent thought he was chasing and just half a second away from ending his enemy; when in fact he was no more than the puppet. The room fell very quiet as the team of techs watched with bated breath, observing the two combatants ascend further into the simulated atmosphere. Twisting and turning around each other in what seemed a dance of death, a dance that Ryu was leading unknown to her opponent. Her clan mates had all been caught out by this strategy at least once.

She manipulated her pursuer into a steep climb, luring him very close before she slammed on the air brakes and cut power to her engine. She also hit the landing parachute, the virtual parachute tore and the cord ripped away from her drone bringing her drone to a relative standstill. Her opponent flew past and before he realised that he was now the hunted; he was shot to pieces by Ryu's cannons, with a Joseon air to air missile fixed onto him turning his drone into a ball of fire just for good measure.

Her opponent in a fit of anger slapped his controls as hard as he could. Kim ordered the techs to continue the simulation, he ordered Ryu to land the drone. She let her drone go into a steep dive, kick starting the scram engines back into life. Without the parachute she landed it softly in the designated area, causing superficial damage if any.

She stepped out of the booth with a beaming smile to cheers from her clan mates, her opponent was not amused. He just had some misfit girl in shorts that had never flown before wipe the floor with him. She made him look like a rookie and he felt extremely embarrassed. The team that had watched the display was quiet and didn't know what to say. General Kim approached her and with a smile 'Welcome to the air force young lady! If your friends can fly half as well as yourself you'll all be having a go with the real thing before the day is over!'

She smiled and gave a little bow; however Ryu felt the animosity coming from the other pilots.

'Tell me where did you learn to fly that well?' asked Kim.

Ryu who was quite bubbly after her victory started rambling 'I learnt from this flight programme at home. Then I used to play it on the net for fun. I was pretty good and joined a clan that competed. We won the nationals and were set to go to Lanageddon again this year in Leipzig. That was until we were attacked, we were favourites to win in the combat simulator section.'

The clan leader and brother of the young Lieutenant stepped forward and stated 'She is the best at the drone simulators. We wouldn't have won the nationals without her and she holds the record against the Red Baron.'

Kim nodded (not that he knew anything about these gaming tournaments) and looked at the young Lieutenant 'Well done Lieutenant it's good to see an officer that will show initiative and take a risk, especially now. We'll test the others first then I want you to get them all into some appropriate clothing. We will see how they do on the real thing.'

'Thank you Sir,' replied the Lieutenant.

Kim put his hand firmly on Ryu's shoulder 'We'll see what our Red Dragon can do against Jiang's pilots!'

Within 48 hours the clan were suited up with clean haircuts and flying combat missions. Much to the disdain of pilots who felt these kids hadn't earned the right to scrub the toilets, much less fly a scram drone. The clan had been kept together and allowed to form a flight team. Initially they were under the guidance of at least one experienced officer. The first missions they performed poorly, much to the satisfaction of others, they were routinely sneered at and dismissed by their peers.

Finally Ryu complained directly to General Kim. She argued the flight leaders were holding them back. Kim's faith in these youngsters was so strong he had the flight leaders removed that day. The clan was now flying alone which even further enraged the veteran pilots. However the results started to come through, losses dropped to almost nothing and the enemy started to experience difficulties. General Kim soon ordered a strike at an enemy HQ which reportedly was coordinating the land invasion. A positive blow might hold them off for a few more weeks. He had a chat with Ryu and the rumour was she had convinced him on the use of nerve gas. Although it was certainly ordered from above the rumour remained.

Jiang was unprepared for such an attack. He and his Generals had expected to be in Seoul before the Koreans could have organized such an operation. Assuming they had any competent pilots left.

Many people found the thought of using chemical warfare abhorrent and Kim wasn't very comfortable with it either. Ryu had no such qualms and after the war in an interview she described it as "Justice served".

Jiang didn't have the means for a sea invasion so he had planned a land invasion from the north. With air superiority he could have supplies, soldiers and armour airlifted. The peninsula was nearly all mountainous terrain and would require total air cover.

After a month of these new pilots, many being recruited from the national gaming league, under the tutelage of Ryu and her wing, the likely hood of a speedy invasion was slipping away with each after action report that came in. His Generals were at a loss as to where the extra pilots came from. They didn't believe the reports of kids from gaming clans; it was dismissed as propaganda to demoralize their own pilots.

Now that the Koreans had new airbases set up inside mountains previously used as nuclear bunkers, it meant nerve gas or bombs wouldn't be much use even if Jiang knew where they were.

Jiang received a report from a very ill looking officer. It summarised how some low flying scram drones had used the terrain to avoid radar; nerve gassing the entire forward HQ that was coordinating the invasion. Jiang went pale as the blood drained from his face; he stood quietly staring at the report for a while. The room was silent, no one dared say a word or move a muscle for fear of Jiang's response. Jiang placed the report on the table and quietly ordered a withdrawal to Manchuria. Retreating behind their defensive line of anti-air missile installations; he believed it would serve as cover for them to re-launch another offensive in a month or two ... they never did move onto Korean soil again.

After months of heavy fighting in the air Jiang was running at a massive deficit. Even his drug sales couldn't cover the expense of purchasing all the new weaponry he required to replace his losses. He was forced to start selling his drugs to the Russian mafia. Previously the Russians had agreed to supply him with weapons under the promise he would not import his drugs into their country. Moscow had secured the same deal with many warlords and unscrupulous leaders around the globe. This policy had cleared up most of the drug problem in one swoop. However Jiang was desperate, and when caught selling his poison by Moscow they cut off all arms trading with him. In the same action Moscow threatened a weapons embargo to anyone trading with Jiang.

Jiang now cut off from all and without an ally attacked Vladivostok with all he had. Hoping a quick victory would give him the port and force the Russians into removing the embargo. Catching the Russians by surprise he besieged Vladivostok. Jiang employed his drones to try and gas the population into submission or extermination, either option was acceptable.

The Korean military decided on not getting involved with the Russian conflict. They had expelled Jiang from their country but were cautious about moving too far into Manchuria. For many years Moscow and Korea had poor relations due to the arms dealing. They had sold weapons to the same warlords that strove to destroy Korea and now annex Vladivostok. The Korean government deemed it poetic justice that Russians were being slaughtered by the same weapons Moscow had sold to the warlords.

However Ryu was not in agreement with her government's policy. She was now the ROKAF top gun having attained more kills than any other pilot and promoted to Captain all within 6 months. The name Red Dragon had stuck much to the disdain of those pilots that felt they had earned their positions; through hard work at the academy and long hours in flight training. They still sneered at her and all those gamers recruited along with her. The difference was that now they only dared sneer behind her back, keeping any smart comments to themselves. In fact most of the top 20 pilots were gamers that had been recruited since the war. Many of the old guard were very bitter about it.

Ryu had spoken to General Kim about assisting the struggle at Vladivostok. Kim ordered her and all pilots that they were not to engage Jiang's forces on Russian territory. A no fly zone over Vladivostok and the surrounding area occupied by Jiang's army was to be strictly observed.

She and Kim had become good friends and he no doubt was her biggest advocate. He knew she wanted the ROKAF to attack Jiang while he was besieging Vladivostok. Hoping to catch the Manchurians off guard again and land another painful blow, but he pointed out it was not to happen. The General had spoken out about helping Russia at the last staff meeting. However the years of bad blood between the countries were too much to put aside for some.

So Ryu started flying sorties as close to the border as she could. Vladivostok would hold out for a week at the most. The Dragon was waiting for an opportunity, until finally she got it. On the way to strike a military camp in Dongning one of the wingmen spotted 3 drones heading towards Vladivostok. Ryu immediately ordered everyone to engage, they all knew they were to leave one intact to withdraw. This had been discussed beforehand and agreed upon in private with her clan mates. Ryu didn't want their true intentions to be recorded by the drone booth.

They swooped up from their usual position of flying barely a few feet above the ground to avoid all anti-air and radar. Attacking the Manchurian drones they destroyed two but left one to chase into Russian air space.

Ryu and her wing pursued the Manchurian drone into the no fly zone. In a short time flying at Mach 5 they hit upon the besieged city of Vladivostok smouldering in the distance as a funeral pyre at dusk. Ryu's drone that was now painted red with a dragon motif dropped out of super cruise and along with the others spread out hugging the ground.

The Manchurians were still in the process of scrambling fresh drones as the bulk were busy engaging the Russians to the north. The Manchurian HQ descended into panic when 7 Korean scram drones were spotted roaring in. After playing back the footage in the air command bunker one man declared he saw a red drone amongst them, the panic turned to terror.

The NBC klaxon started to scream out. Men and women scrambled for their Nuclear, Biological and Chemical warfare suits. If the anti-air instillations around the HQ didn't stop them they would have to suffer a chemical attack before engaging their drones.

The wing of 7 drones screeched through the air, too close to the ground for the anti-air to get a lock and fire. They were carrying a full payload of nerve agent and anti-bunker missiles. The plan was to lock on to any bunkers with the AI as they flew over the HQ and fire on them, trying to break them open. At the same time they would fire an even spread of missiles loaded with a nerve agent warhead, designed to impact the ground piercing most structures; then after a small explosion quickly releasing the agent in a massive plume covering the maximum area in as short a time.

This they accomplished in one fly over of the panic stricken camp. Ryu's wing then made a tight bank and went balls to the wall for the Korean border. All the time sticking as close to the ground as was possible, which at Mach 10 is not an easy feat. However they only had to maintain it for a very short time because once they hit Mach 5 and as long as the enemy was behind them nothing was fast enough to catch the Shogun scram drone.

The fastest speed a Russian MiG drone had been record at was Mach 5.7.

As they approached Mach 10, Korea was seconds away. The clan began to decelerate landing safe and sound at their air base just north of Pyongyang.

Ryu was punished behind closed doors for her actions, as publicly the other pilots wouldn't have taken it well; even those that disapproved of her still respected her ability and what she had done for their country. She pointed out they were engaged in Manchuria and chased them into Russian airspace. Once there they retreated after dumping the payload in order to achieve maximum speed.

She took full responsibility, her actions were never forgotten, there remained a black mark on her record.

As for Jiang once again his plans had been thwarted by the misfit girl, the eastern HQ was devastated. This time however his forces were not as fortunate. After losing all air cover for only an hour the Russians took the opportunity and moved in. Occupying the HQ and imprisoning the officers. All others were shot on the spot, their bodies burnt in a massive pile. Vladivostok was liberated in a few days; the ROKAF stated it was a planned attack. Claiming Moscow had not been warned for fear Jiang might get word.

Within a year Jiang had fallen back to Shenyang. With Russia bearing down from the north it took only another year before he had been shot by one of his own men. Killing another's child was far less painful than watching your own being burnt in heaps. It caused many of Jiang's staff members to plot against their commander in chief, surrendering his head at the first Korean military outpost along their defensive line.

Two and a half years after it began Ryu was an air force Major and decorated by Moscow for the liberation of Vladivostok. A national hero in two countries, but many questioned what she and other pilots did to attain that victory. Yet nearly all agreed it was required, after many years in the ROKAF Ryu eventually joined the I.S.A. For nearly three years her reason for living had been revenge. Then for a year after that she was still patrolling Manchuria eliminating pockets of resistance.

After final victory and Korea had annexed Manchuria she felt empty, her motivation for existing had gone. As a philosopher once said "He who fights with monsters might take care lest he thereby become a monster".

It seemed that Ryu had become that monster. By fighting with Jiang she and her comrades, just innocent children when it began, had become as cold and brutal as the evil dictator themselves.

Nerve gassing the enemy into submission without mercy; even after the war was over using napalm against small towns and villages that threatened to revolt. Where Japan, Korea and Taiwan had once cowered in fear of the warlords, now the warlords were quaking in their boots.

Moscow joined the embargo on the warlords of China, added to that an ROKAF of the most experienced drone combat pilots in the world. Those that didn't surrender were eventually annihilated.

To fight and defeat the beast Korea had become the beast. No one cared for human life anymore, or to be precise enemy human life. After all was said and done Ryu needed a challenge. Something to do other than hate, since 10 years on there was no one left to hate anymore. Thinking about what had happened to her family and village was a motivating force during the war. Yet once all the warlords had fallen it was depressing. With no one left to punish for her pain she needed to take on something. Before the abyss sucked her in and her hatred swallowed her.

When General Kim discovered the I.S.A was going to send a manned mission to Mars in 5 years and needed a drone pilot he wrote out an application for her and sent it in. He had witnessed her deterioration since the war. Kim was concerned that if she didn't find a cause she would destroy herself, he'd been by her side like a father; guiding her and keeping her out of harm's way when he could. He had led her down this path and now it had come to an end, at a cliff. If he didn't get her onto another path she would certainly perish in his opinion.

Her application was accepted and when Kim told her she was going to Mars, Ryu was shocked and a little hurt that he'd done such a thing without informing her. When he mentioned about being the first woman on Mars it had a certain allure. Ryu forgot her initial reaction 'Thanks, I'll give it some thought,' she smiled 'but you owe me for not telling me first!'

Ryu gave him a smile, took the papers and left his office.

Under his breath Kim muttered 'We all owe you a great deal young girl.'

Titov's story and McCann's cigar both came to an end at around the same time and McCann was enchanted by both. He was taken aback that the dedicated woman he'd been training with all these years had come from such humble circumstances. He raised an eyebrow and took a hard look at her as she stood chatting with her admirers 'Amazing, bloody amazing!' he whispered to himself.

His attention was then grabbed by the sound of breaking glass. McCann looked to his right and witnessed Louis scrambling to his feet. Three burly Russians moved in on him after having obviously thrown him across the room 'Louis!' he groaned knowingly.

On the surface McCann deduced Louis had used his fabulous personality to antagonise someone new, since his favourite target, Faraday, was no longer present. Unlike Faraday these chaps didn't believe Louis was indispensable, quite the opposite. Louis was an experienced fighter, thanks to his social attitude, however he had definitely bitten off more than he could chew.

Titov was amused by the entertainment unfolding and poured himself another drink as he lit his second cigar of the evening. He offered a second one to McCann but he was already getting up to break up the fracas, before his nanite engineer got put out of action. McCann however was blocked off by several crewmen, whatever Louis had done it must've been serious for them to ignore his rank.

McCann looked at Titov who was sitting down enjoying the show 'Aren't you going to do something Titov? I need that man in one piece for god's sake!' cried McCann over the noise.

Titov didn't reply but began to howl with laughter as he witnessed Hassif crawling from under the table towards the door. This would've been amusing at another time and place and Louis probably deserved it. However McCann was responsible for this mission yet he was powerless to stop the kicking Louis was about to receive.

Louis was now against the wall being punched around the body by the largest Russian as the other two held him in place. Titov was enjoying the first good entertainment he'd had in several months, whilst Hassif was scurrying out of the door back to his quarters.

McCann caught a woman's voice shouting something in Russian and the ruckus seemed to dissipate. It was Ryu, she walked through the crowd that stood around watching the beating holding McCann back. She then spoke something that McCann didn't understand but caused the large fellow beating Louis to a pulp to nod his head and walk away. The other two flung Louis to the floor and followed their crewmate to the bar. McCann dived in and with the help of Ryu picked a battered Louis up from the floor then carried him back to his quarters.

On the way back McCann asked Ryu 'What did you say to them?'

'I told them he'd had enough, what was that all about?' replied Ryu.

'I've got no idea, I suppose he'll tell us tomorrow or maybe Hassif can shed some light on it after he's come out of hiding!'

'It's lucky for Louis that you broke the Manchurians at Vladivostok, otherwise he'd have been mashed.'

Ryu looked past Louis and at McCann 'What else did he tell you?'

'Is there anything else I should know?' replied McCann as he stopped walking and looked back at her.

'No, there isn't. Now let's get this bum back to his quarters,' said Ryu as she turned and began walking again.

The next morning the four travellers gathered in Louis' quarters. McCann stood over him as he sat on the bed elbows on knees and head in hands. Grumbling due to the combined pain of the beating he'd received the night before and the hangover he acquired that morning.

'Fucking lache!' grumbled Louis as he cursed Hassif 'You left me to those bastards!'

Hassif remained silent.

'So what happened Louis? Any reason for them beating you to a bloody pulp?' asked McCann.

'I don't know, all I know is that fucking Indian ran and left me to face them!'

McCann didn't believe him but neither he nor Hassif was forthcoming and they had both a media conference and a launch today. He was wondering how he'd explain Louis sporting a black eye, he began to discuss the problem with Ryu.

She shook her head, looking at Louis and Hassif she ranted 'Jesus, it's like having kids except they're trapped in the bodies of two allegedly responsible adults. They should've given us parenting courses before letting these idiots loose!'

'I have an idea,' whimpered Hassif.

'What!' shouted Ryu almost biting his head off.

'Well during the media interview Louis could wear a pair of the sun goggles they use for safety here. They look just like those sports glasses skiers wear.'

McCann looked at Ryu, she just shook her head and Louis shouted 'You cannot make me wear those. I'd look like a prick!'

The corner of McCann's lips rose as he gave an evil smirk to Ryu and she smirked back.

'Good idea, go get a pair Hassif we'll meet you for breakfast in the canteen,' said McCann.

Later the four of them were eating breakfast to sniggers from the Russians as Louis sat there with his specs on, eating his porridge. Soon the other three began to chuckle as they tried to down their meal. All to the displeasure of Louis, who kept pointing out how he felt about wearing the goggles. Hassif told him to look on the bright side, that due to the low gravity he didn't take such a heavy beating. McCann had a good laugh but Louis once again failed to find the humour.

However Hassif had made a very interesting observation, because of the low gravity it took far more effort to inflict as much punishment as you could on Earth in a similar situation. Also depending where you were on the station would dictate the gravity and how the fracas unravelled, due to how the tidal forces on the rock created the artificial gravity. Back on Earth Louis wouldn't be walking the next day.

Louis was characteristically unthankful for small mercies and blamed everyone else for a situation that McCann was certain he'd instigated.

Later that day during the media interview the four of them were with Titov, all trying to hold a straight face. Whilst Louis sat there feeling a fool. When asked by Jerry Habeeb why he was wearing the goggles McCann interjected 'Louis is trying to set a new trend out here in space Jerry!' to a chorus of laughter in the background.

Network America had the exclusive rights to the voyage and Jerry was the main correspondent.

'Is that a fact, are those designer sunglasses Louis?' asked Jerry.

'They are Russian,' replied Louis quietly to even more laughter which puzzled Jerry and no doubt anyone watching.

'So Duncan tell me how have you found the Russian hospitality so far?'

'Well I've found the Tsiolkovsky and her crew to be most hospitable.'

'What about you Colonel or is that Plokovnik Titov? How have you found your guests?'

'Either is fine and I've enjoyed their stay. I think we've been a great hit!'

Titov started to crack up, just managing to blurt out 'Especially with Mister Beaumont here!' before regaining his composure.

Louis sat with a straight face throughout the whole interview which only tickled the others funny bone even more. With Louis taking everything in typical poor humour they eventually finished the interview, leaving Jerry a very puzzled man.

Next Faraday came on the screen 'Louis what in blue blazes do you think you're playing at man? Take those ridiculous goggles off now!'

Louis tore them off to reveal a big shiner on his right eye.

'Louis slipped and hit his head, we didn't want to concern anyone back home,' explained McCann.

'Listen McCann, it's your job to keep things under control. That includes that horse's arse Beaumont, I don't want anymore surprises or fashion statements is that understood?'

'Yes Sir,' replied McCann.

'Well you launch in three hours so good luck to you all, best wishes from everyone here,' the screen turned off.

Faraday was back to his pressure ridden self, the less he saw of Louis the better. It was time to embark; they said their thanks to the crew of the Tsiolkovsky and the Tsiolkovsky herself before walking to their quarters to get fully suited.

The team of four made their way to the launch bay where the Athena now awaited her human cargo. Titov and Cherkesov met them for the send off. Titov shook them by the hand and offered McCann a pack of five cigars "Something to enjoy whilst on Mars and remember us by."

McCann thanked him greatly and put it away in one of the tool pockets on his suit.

Cherkesov then offered something to Ryu; it was a silver chain with an old Soviet hammer and sickle emblem on it.

'What's this for?' asked Ryu as she took it.

'It was my great grandmothers then my grandmothers and then my mothers. She died in Vladivostok; I'd like you to have it.'

Ryu accepted the necklace whilst fighting back the blushes.

'It will bring you good luck, Major,' finished Cherkesov.

Titov and his first then stood back as the airlock door opened, the four stepped in and it closed behind them as they all sealed the helmets on their suits. They walked through the next door as it opened into the massive launch bay hewn out of the asteroid. All was clear but for the Athena that sat at one end near the airlock door they had just stepped through.

At the other end was a massive metal bulkhead like door. Once ready it would open and the magnetic catapult would fling the Athena out into space towards the red planet.

The catapult was actually the same device as the net. A set of discs that used electro magnets to either bring a vessel to a halt or propel it out into space; usually for launching satellites into orbit. Today it was firing the Athena out beyond the moon and into the crosshairs of the maser that would push her the rest of the way.

The crew got on board and strapped themselves into the chairs in the command room. McCann was in constant contact with Geneva re-assuring them and double checking.

'How was your stay with the Tsiolkovsky, Colonel?' asked the Athena.

'Very interesting thank you Athena, they had some good tips for when we land,' replied McCann as he re checked the fuel cells after Louis.

'Yes the Tsiolkovsky was good enough to download it all, I must say I did miss you all,' said the Athena in her usual calm voice.

'Thank you Athena, we missed you too. How has everything been whilst we were away?'

'Everything has been functioning within acceptable parameters. If it weren't I'd have informed you Colonel.'

McCann smiled 'I know Athena, I was just making conversation.'

'Oh I see Colonel, I'm sorry, my experience is rather limited on social interaction.'

'There's no need to apologize, Athena, besides your social abilities still outstrip those of Louis!'

Ryu and Hassif chuckled and before the Athena could reply McCann cut her off 'Humour Athena. I'll explain the joke to you later, after launch.'

'Understood, thank you Colonel.'

'You're welcome Athena.'

After all the diagnostics and checks had been run through, the door to space opened. The crew strapped themselves in tightly and the magnets grasped the Athena. The ship was lifted from the floor and slung bottom first into the blackness, after a few minutes of checks the Athena announced they were on course.

Chapter 4

The Athena hurtled on a trajectory sending her into the orbital path of the planet Mars. With the correct speed the planet would intercept them at the same time she reached her destination.

The crew had spent the last days making preparations for the journey, Louis had been supervising the unfurling of the sail. The sail wasn't a sail in the true sense nor was it a solar sail. It was in fact a fine mesh of nanotubes unfurled in a hexagonal disc at the end of a mast protruding from the top of the Athena; which was now pointing at the dark side of the moon.

The sail was an amazing piece of technology. Conventional solar sails used a reflective mirror which, when hit by photons from the sun, gave a small push to the craft bearing the sail. It was a great way to travel since fuel was not required, thereby reducing the mass of the craft. However it took a long time to get where you wanted to go due to the slow acceleration.

Previously they had been used for unmanned craft on long flights and for manoeuvring in orbit. Changing the angle of the mirror or sail allowed a craft to manoeuvre without the need for thrusters and their fuel, when it came to a manned mission they were too slow. The Tsiolkovsky could fire out an object only so fast with her catapult. Nowhere near the speed required to get to Mars within the one month time frame the I.S.A had set itself. Even with a conventional solar sail Faraday was looking at the better part of a year. Chemical powered engines were too bulky, other types were either too large or dangerous.

Lasers were suggested to propel a craft with a sail, the trip would still take at least three months, but it was disregarded. The power requirements for the lasers were beyond the means of the I.S.A despite the array of international backers. The power required to generate a beam strong enough was unworkable, a fusion reactor would be required on both moons and the laser would need constant maintenance. Faraday's advisors concluded it couldn't be done.

Then a Japanese-American team, who had been working on nanotubes produced in India, sent a paper to Geneva that landed on Faraday's desk. Instead of a bulky laser that was almost impossible to power they suggested a maser or microwave laser.

They proposed using a sail of woven nanotubes. With nanotubes woven into a mesh at the exact spacing as the wavelength of the microwaves. The microwaves hitting it would have much the same effect as a mirror hit by a high powered laser. A maser is far more efficient to power and requires little maintenance, plus they had an ace up their sleeve.

A small amount of chemical propellant could be pumped through the nanotubes and onto the surface of the sail through pours. When the microwaves from the maser hit the sail the chemical would evaporate. The combustion would massively increase thrust. Only a small amount of the chemical was required, hardly more than a few litres or 6 pints.

Faraday jumped on it, had the idea tested in space with the Tsiolkovsky using a small maser to propel an unmanned craft to Venus. It had arrived within a week setting a new record for reaching the planet.

The team of scientists were moved to Geneva and work began on constructing some off world masers. Thanks to the new technology it was possible to reach the red planet in a month.

However, a maser was needed at the other end to slow the craft down before it could reach a speed that allowed entry. The test craft had burnt up when attempting to aero break. Its massive momentum caused it to disintegrate in the thick atmosphere of Venus. Faraday was certain this would not happen to Athena, it couldn't! His psyche just didn't allow for such a catastrophe. A maser was built by drones on the Martian moon Deimos and besides, they needed to get back after their work was done!

Louis observed quietly as the mast which had been erected over the last two days began to unfurl the sail. It would take two to three hours, but Louis was required to be there in case anything untoward happened. He watched the monitor as it opened up from the end of the mast and out. First like water from a fountain only to open as a flower blooming, all in very slow motion. Being alone in the command room or the aft section was the time Louis most cherished. He could be at peace without distractions. The coldness and predictability of machines is what attracted Louis to them, he was a fiery man of passion and this brought balance to his life.

Having worked in civil engineering for many years he was well experienced, with nanites being his favourite area of expertise. He had worked with corporations in manufacturing to medical science. Leaving each and every one more efficient than when he arrived. He never stayed long despite the number of contracts offered to him. He could have been a very wealthy man but for his transient nature.

Louis didn't mix well with others and disliked familiarity unless it was with his nanites, the only things he believed that would never judge him. When the I.S.A was looking for engineers he got an email along with many others. There was a contract for several years which almost caused him to trash the mail. Before he did Louis noticed there was an opening on the craft to travel to Mars itself, no flight or space experience required. He'd only be spending a month or so in space, so why not?

He could fly to Mars and work there for a year, preparing the Mars base for habitation and possibly stay on afterwards. Louis would have to train for four years in Geneva; however he was willing to suffer it for the money. Louis decided to apply and if he didn't get the job the world would keep turning, his expertise were always in demand here on Earth.

After several gruelling tests consisting of repairing and reprogramming nanites then using them to fix many different objects, from a simple outer wall in a vacuum to a malfunctioning light chip Louis got the job.

The four years had been hard for Louis, he felt he was always stuck under a microscope being observed or analyzed by Faradays' minions. The thought of Mars and a year's solitude on an alien world kept him going. Louis hated being "Faraday's slave" as he often put it, but he tolerated it. Whilst oblivious to Louis, everyone else had tolerated the Frenchman as best they could.

Louis made friends with Hassif quickly seeing him not as a kindred spirit but just someone who appreciated his privacy. Like Louis he wasn't too happy working in groups but preferred to rely on himself, the only person Louis could really relate to.

Watching the monitor Louis heard Ryu float into the command room and buckle herself into her seat.

'Morning Louis, how's the sail doing?' asked Ryu in her chirpy morning voice.

'Everything is going well, another hour and I'll check out the propellant tanks then connect it all up. We should be ready to go in a couple of hours. How was breakfast?'

'Not bad actually, a cheese omelette with one of those oat biscuits filled with apple. What did you get?'

'Nothing special, it's not exactly nouveau cuisine here in zero G. I'm looking forward to the menu on Mars. I'll just have to suffer this until we land and can eat like civilized human beings again.'

'Good morning Major Ryu, how are you this morning?' asked Athena.

'Fine thank you, how are you Athena?'

'I'm fine and thank you for asking Major.'

The command room went a little quiet as Ryu and Louis both stopped what they were doing.

'Is there a problem Major?' inquired Athena.

'Nothing,' replied Ryu 'it's just I've never heard you say you're fine before, it was a surprise.'

'Colonel McCann and I spent some time discussing socializing and the application of humour in social situations during his last shift. Was my reply appropriate Major?'

'Yes it was Athena, as I said I was just surprised to hear you say it.'

For the next hour Ryu checked the data packets, sent and received, along with all systems. She reported in to Geneva whilst the Athena discussed her understanding of humour and though she understood it, Athena failed to find McCann's joke amusing.

Louis carried on observing the sail unfurl, when finished an hour later he went aft to check up on the propellant tanks. Ryu told him to wake the others on the way whilst she kept an eye on the ship. Ryu requested authorization from Faraday to link with the maser station on the moon whilst Louis was busy.

Soon McCann and Hassif joined Ryu in the command module, Hassif began running over Athena's calculations for the first shot as he called it. Making sure the disc was pointing at the right angle to the maser and craft was essential in ensuring the correct trajectory. Small corrections would be required no doubt, but carried out later minus the propellant.

This sail allowed fast bursts of speed associated with chemical rockets, combined with the ability to make slow accurate corrections in course associated with conventional sails. When there was no propellant the weave of the nanotubes caught the right wavelength of microwaves like a net catching fish, it gave that push needed to correct the Athena.

Athena had made the calculations whilst Geneva and Hassif checked them. In reality Hassif made his own calculations then checked them against the Athena's.

All the time Hassif had an earphone in one ear playing music which he swore helped him concentrate. The music was very irritating the first time the other three had experienced it in simulations. Faraday had christened it "That god awful Indian racket!"

McCann and Ryu let it slide after Hassif had compared it to them jogging or working out whilst listening to music. Louis however was not nearly so forgiving. Despite everyone bending over backwards for him he was characteristically unwilling to do so for others. Faraday was as usual ineffective at controlling Louis who relished picking on Hassif and his musical tastes at each opportunity. McCann ended up clamping down on him, whatever McCann had said privately to him that day; Louis never complained or raised the subject again.

Hassif had finished his calculations and it seemed Athena agreed with him. A moment later Geneva sent their conclusions which all matched up.

Louis floated in from the aft and buckled into his seat 'The tanks are ready to go.'

'Sail orientation, propellant and maser burn calculated and set,' said Hassif as he certified the calculations.

'Check,' replied McCann 'Ryu you're cleared to link with the maser?'

Ryu linked up with the maser on the dark side of the moon and started running checks. The other three now waited for her to clear the maser. She would be firing the microwaves at the sail. The angle of the maser was as critical as that of the sail. After a few minutes silence she cleared the maser. McCann sent the news to Geneva that all was cleared and they were awaiting authorization for the first shot. Ten minutes later McCann received the go ahead, he ran through a last set of checks which were confirmed by the others and Athena.

'Ryu you have the go ahead to fire the maser,' said McCann.

Ryu glanced over the orders she was sending once more and hit her touch panel 'Maser will fire in T-minus 2 minutes.'

She announced as a countdown came up on each crew members panel. Hassif turned off his music putting his tablet and earphone away to prepare for the impact. Everything had been stowed away as when the Athena was propelled towards Mars anything floating would not. This meant a floating tablet could hit the wall or even a crew member or to be more precise the wall would hit the object as it was pushed into it. This could cause a hull breach or a crew member's death, a vice of such high curves of acceleration in zero G.

'Maser to fire in T-minus 10, 9, 8, 7, 6, 5, 4, 3, 2, 1 …. Maser fired successfully everything is functioning within normal parameters,' announced Athena as they all braced.

Hassif was watching the data roll across his screen as he checked the Athena's calculations. Louis was going over reports from the nanites examined engineering reports on the mast, sail, tanks and structure. Ryu monitored the Moon maser constantly.

After the crew confirmed Athena's assessment McCann put his hand out over the panel in front of him 'Engaging propellant tanks for first burn.'

He hit the panel and all hell seemed to break loose, at least to the untrained observer. For just five seconds small amounts of propellant seeped through the pours. The maser cooked it as soon as it reached the surface of the sail resulting in a massive controlled explosion. The ship shook violently as the lifeless body of a sailor in the clutches of a furious Polythemus. The thrust was tremendous; no manned craft had ever experienced such a thing. Although there was no G force to deal with in space the sheer thrust upon the mass was putting great stress on the Athena. The controlled burn accelerated her into space as her crew could do little but wait for the five seconds of time to end. Those five seconds felt longer to her crew and even longer to Faraday who waited alongside ground control with bated breath.

'Primary burn completed, current speed 150,000 KPH, analyzing course and trajectory,' announced Athena after the shaking had stopped.

Louis was busy looking over his reports as Hassif started on analyzing the first shot and calculating what course corrections would be required.

'Course and trajectory analyzed, new course calculated, sail orientation and Maser trajectory calculated,' announced Athena.

McCann sent all the data to Geneva and waited for their conclusion whilst Hassif looked it over himself.

The first shot was successful, and as expected, the trajectory that the Athena was on to meet Mars was a little off. Everything had to be re calculated and checked for the second shot, the fuel burns had to be broken up for this reason. Also there was the fact that Athena could only take so much punishment at a time. Too much and the mast and sail could be permanently damaged. Replacing it wasn't so much of a problem once they had reached Mars as there was a year to get a replacement and fit it. The problem was that once you were at such high velocities you needed to slow the craft down. Otherwise entering the atmosphere or just making orbit would tear Athena to pieces.

Geneva checked and gave the go ahead, along with Hassif. Louis changed the orientation of the sail which was still being hit by the maser. Slowly over the next 30 minutes Athena's course was corrected; using the force of microwave radiation bombarding the sail from the Moon.

When all was ready they gave another 5 second burst of propellant, pushing her to over 200,000 kph. After corrections McCann released the fuel a third time until she passed 300,000 kph, and finally a fourth which pushed her to a record speed for a manned mission of 442,000 KPH. The sail remained out as the Athena took the benefits of the maser before its power faded away.

This was the single downside of the maser compared to a laser. A laser had superior power transfer over distance whereas the maser would lose power with distance quite drastically.

Back on the ground there were celebrations after McCann had completed all checks and sent logs of the entire manoeuvre to Geneva in a data packet.

Faraday was relieved, all had gone well. With only minor course corrections required the mast and sail were in good shape. In a couple of weeks Athena would be ready to begin breaking, in preparation for Mars orbit.

Everything seemed to be on track, after Faraday had a private chat with McCann and the crew giving his congratulations he retired to his bed. Faraday had a bedroom built next door to his office in Geneva and slept like a baby.

The next two weeks were uneventful, the crew ran through the usual work schedule McCann read his papers. Ryu remained focused on her work and increasing her efficiency, Hassif listened to his music as he made projections of their arrival time; calculating the required deceleration from Deimos. Louis grumbled as little as possible spending as much time as he could alone in the aft. For the most part he monitored the shield that protected the Athena from space debris at such high speed.

It was a hardened carbon composite dome covering the aft end of the Athena which now pointed towards their destination. A magnetic field ran around it helping to keep particles away. The shield was still hit by micro meteors yet absorbed all the strikes, easily keeping Athena safe. When it was time the Athena would briefly swing around pointing her sail towards Mars. The Deimos maser would start the breaking process by firing several times. After each breaking burn the Athena would swing back around so her shield may protect her for as long as possible.

Calculations were made for the next burn and a few days later she'd use her gyroscopes to change attitude fire a small burst then swing back again. After 39 days Athena was preparing to enter Mars orbit. The mast had been retracted and she was moving slow enough for the gravity of Mars to pull her in to orbit.

The red planet now loomed on the monitors and McCann had spent many a quiet hour alone on duty marvelling at it. The braking process had been completed and Athena now crept upon her destination at a pace which would allow entry into the atmosphere, in theory at least.

'Beautiful isn't it?' said Louis floating into the fore section and startling McCann who was almost hypnotised by the image.

'Yes, you're up early today!' replied McCann in a half jest.

Today they were to be the first manned craft to enter the Martian atmosphere and land.

'I didn't sleep very well, let me know when you want the shuttlecock.' referring to the method of entry into Mars.

'As soon as you're ready Louis you can open her up,' replied McCann in a relaxed manner never taking his eyes off the monitor.

Louis floated to his seat, buckled himself in and began to run the checks. After 10 minutes he informed McCann he was ready. McCann gave the go ahead and the shuttlecock began to unfurl.

Athena had 3 sections fore, mid and aft. The aft was by far the largest section which possessed the space shield. It protected Athena and her crew during space travel and entry into the Martian atmosphere. Followed by the smaller mid-section then the smaller and conical fore section pointing away from Mars.

Where each section met the other the ship had gully or some might say a waistline. At these points where each section met the other, a large collar of carbon began to protrude. The one closest to the shield where the aft and mid-section met came out at a 60 degree angle then the collar where the mid and fore section met came out at a 70 degree angle and even further turning Athena into what looked like a massive shuttlecock. Thus this entry method was christened the shuttlecock, the purpose being to cause enough drag in the thin Martian atmosphere to slow down the Athena. Also the large size of the shuttlecock fins would dissipate the heat, reducing the chances of failure in the heat shielding whilst stabilizing the crafts orientation.

McCann was now in sole command, real time contact with Geneva had been lost weeks ago so all the decisions rested on his shoulders. Athena had made contact with the SI on the Edwards in Martian orbit. The station itself was without a human crew and solely run by the SI, although this would change in the future.

After the shuttlecock had been unfurled and checked by both Louis and Athena; the next couple of hours were spent with Hassif consulting and checking Athena's projections for entry. She was to enter the atmosphere at a slight angle, using drag from friction with the atmosphere and gravitational pull to slow her down. This was to be done in one manoeuvre, an aero snatch as McCann had named it; as opposed to executing many atmospheric flybys over several months in the standard aero braking technique.

There was added danger but simulations on Earth had proven to be promising along with several tests on small vehicles in the Earth's atmosphere. Since Mars had a much thinner atmosphere risks were lowered and having them in orbit aero braking for a year wasn't an acceptable amount of time for many reasons. Faraday wasn't getting them there within a month to spend a year aero braking.

Lastly Ryu arose, after breakfast she floated into her seat. Inside the command room the others could feel her energy as she entered, despite all sitting back to back facing their workstations. Athena greeted her as usual and she slipped into her seat and buckled in 'Ready to go gentlemen, what's the ETA?' she chirped.

'Hassif do you have the ETA yet?' asked McCann.

'Just give me ten minutes to check Athena's calculations again,' he replied whilst engrossed in the mish mash of equations on the panel before his seat. All went silent until a few minutes later he replied 'The earliest window is in 83 minutes and then there's a second window in 217 minutes, it's your choice Colonel?'

McCann thought for a second then said 'Athena I want to prepare for the second window, understood?'

'Preparing orientation for entry window in minus 214 minutes and 43 seconds Colonel,' replied Athena as she began the countdown.

McCann then sent the last data packet to Geneva, until they made touchdown, and retracted the communications antenna.

'Time to entry 90 seconds,' announced Athena as everyone strapped themselves in and braced. Athena would be tackling the entry with the crew overseeing.

Athena hit the Martian atmosphere and everything shook violently, it reminded Ryu of an earthquake she had experienced as a young girl. The shaking became so violent it was hard to concentrate on her monitor. If she hadn't run through these simulations on a weekly basis for 3 years the readout would be meaningless and unintelligible. Ryu focused and made sense of the blur in front of her.

'Shield temperature 100 degrees Celsius,' announced Athena.

At the same moment Ryu could feel the gravity pulling her down into the seat. The space suits compensated by administering pressure to the limbs automatically, lowering susceptibility to blackouts.

'Shield temperature 500 degrees Celsius,' announced Athena as the crushing forces of the aero snatch tore at her frame.

Athena maintained her orientation through temperature manipulation of the fins on her shuttlecock. The fins were a compound, holding layers of inert gas inside the carbon collar. Athena would manipulate the temperature and gas density forcing the fins to flex and bend to her will, maintaining control over course.

'Shield temperature 750 degrees Celsius, altitude 9 kilometres,' announced Athena in her calm voice.

It was the last thing Ryu remembered before she blacked out.

Something went wrong, McCann didn't know what but it had turned from a major earthquake to the most brutal rollercoaster ride imaginable. It felt as if Athena had been hit or hit something or had a breech, he didn't know. All he knew for certain was that she was tumbling helplessly and in danger of being ripped apart by the stress and heat. McCann struggled to remain conscious even with his suit inflating to maintain enough blood pressure to feed oxygen to his brain.

'Athena regain attitude control!' screamed McCann as best he could.

The pressure on his chest and lungs was almost unbearable and although he was shouting his voice was hardly audible. Athena didn't answer him.

'Athena are you operational?' he pushed out.

'Yes,' came a timid response from Athena.

McCann had remained calm. He had been in similar situations in the past, but when he detected fear in her voice it sent a shiver of panic through him. For a few seconds he was paralyzed by and infectious terror. Regaining his composure he whispered 'Can you regain control Athena?' to which there was no reply.

They continued to tumble through the Martian atmosphere spinning towards the ground and destined to become another impact crater.

'Athena give me manual flight control now!' he pushed out of his aching chest.

Straight away the tops of his seat arms slid back revealing two touch panels on each arm which McCann was struggling to keep his fingers over.

'Yong!' wheezed the Englishman.

Only to hear the timid voice of Athena state 'Major Ryu Yong is unconscious Colonel.'

'Louis, Hassif?'

'Engineer Louis Beaumont and Technician Hassif are both unconscious Colonel.'

McCann was struggling, trying to stop the tumble before Athena broke up in the atmosphere. He didn't know the speed, altitude or heat. He was trying to enter the atmosphere by the seat of his pants and without any visual aid, he felt like a fly in amber, struggling in vain.

McCann was reducing the tumble but for all he knew they could hit the ground or break up in a couple of seconds. Yet he had to do something, he wouldn't sit by and accept the inevitable.

Then Athena called out in a slightly stronger voice 'Major Ryu Yong has regained consciousness, Colonel.'

Ryu was barely awake with what felt like the mother of all hangovers.

McCann shouted as loudly as the forces on his body permitted 'Yong are you there?'

He waited a moment and just as he started to speak her name again she whispered with all her might 'Yeh.'

'Yong, Athena is out, what's our status?'

Thanks to the helmets on the suits they could speak to each other and hear properly otherwise their whispers would have been unintelligible.

'Four point six km a second, two k Celsius, seven k meters, hull secure,' whispered Ryu as she used every ounce of concentration to read the panel in front of her.

Suddenly McCann's monitor turned on, displaying a view outside from one of Athena's external cameras. Somehow Athena had snapped out of it, activating his display.

She was incapable of regaining control herself but she must have been cognisant of their perilous situation. McCann was grateful for the view allowing him to halt the tumble since the shaking prevented him from reading any instruments properly, added to that his visor display was malfunctioning. It refused to activate, this was the only way for him to get an idea of their orientation as the craft spun out of control.

Within 5 seconds of Ryu coming back he had the tumble under control and Athena was once again pointing in the right direction. She was no longer spinning but Athena herself was still incapacitated.

Ryu continued to call out the status, now McCann's goal was to make a landing, no matter where it may be, that they could walk away from. Once committed to the aero snatch there was no pulling out into orbit. The Athena had no form of standard self-propulsion. Once she began her entry there was no way out.

A shallow angle had to be maintained, the atmosphere pushing against the shuttlecock until she had slowed enough to re-orientate into a steeper angle and begin the second stage. That had all just gone to hell, the angle was off and Athena was hurtling towards the ground. The craft plunged far to fast and at far too steep of an angle, which McCann and Ryu were both well aware of.

McCann just kept thinking of something Jenkins had said to him when on their way to try out for SBS "This is what separates the men from the boys Duncan!"

McCann muttered it under his breath as he struggled to live.

Ryu could feel the force leaving her chest but speech was still difficult 'One point three k a second, five hundred Celsius, three k meters, hull secure.'

'Engaging second stage,' said McCann as he touched the panel on his seat arm, setting off a massive breaking parachute.

The parachute flew out of Athena's cone and gave a huge jolt to all those attached. The parachute was massive due to the thin Martian atmosphere; this made it useful only in breaking; intended to have been used when Athena was descending at no more than 500 metres a second. However McCann had no choice as the ground loomed closer.

Ryu and McCann once again felt a massive g force on them but only for a second as the force tore the parachute and it was released. Breathing and speaking was becoming a lot easier.

'Status!' shouted McCann over the noise of the atmosphere hitting the Athena.

'Speed seven hundred and fifty two meters a second, skin temperature two hundred and thirty Celsius. Altitude two thousand and one hundred meters hull is intact, Sir!' screamed Ryu.

Athena was still moving too fast and too close to the ground but McCann had no choice 'Engaging third stage!' he then pressed his panel.

Areas of Athena's skin blew off and helium filled balloons quickly expanded from the cavities. Athena was suddenly covered by a metallic skin made from several balloons attached to her. The balloons expanded to cover over twenty times the area that Athena had originally occupied. The purpose was to slow the descent and give a soft landing but McCann was now using them to aero brake and wasn't sure if they would take the strain. In fact he very much doubted they would, but they might buy him some extra time to slow down; and maybe when they hit the ground Athena wouldn't break into pieces leaving them all as permanent residents of the God of War.

Again there was another jolt as the balloons inflated and McCann felt his body attempt to lurch from the seat. The straps held him in but he could feel his stomach shoot up then down again, giving him the feeling of being sick. McCann could no longer see anything through the camera as it was enclosed by the helium balloons. However he could read the panel and get an idea of what was happening.

Next the ship began to turn and shake much like a calf in the jaws of a crocodile, thrashing around as the others watch her pulled under to meet certain fate.

The balloons were bursting due to the heat and pressure of the aero braking, sending the craft once again into a spin which McCann was helpless to prevent.

Secondary balloons began to inflate and McCann could no longer control the descent as the fins of the shuttlecock were covered. All he could do was silently wait and see. As the altitude got lower Athena called out in a loud voice "Warning rate of descent is not within safety parameters, brace for impact!"

McCann held on tight, the last thing he remembered was Ryu shouting in Korean. When translated it was something along the lines of 'See you in hell Duncan!' before he blacked out.

When McCann regained consciousness everything was pitch black. He wondered for a second if he was dead and had awoken in Elysium? Or more likely the pit of some silent hell, perhaps the halls of Hades or worse Tartarus! Until he moved his fingers and felt the arms of his seat.

He must have hit a panel as it lit up and allowed him to look around and make something out of the darkness. Out of the gloom he made out his workstation in front of him. McCann surmised the fore section had no hull breech since his helmet was retracted and he could breathe without difficulty. He then realised he was hanging in the seat.

Athena was on the Martian surface at an angle, this told him she was probably still in one piece.

'Athena, respond please,' said McCann tentatively.

'Yes Colonel McCann,' replied a calm Athena from the darkness.

'What is your status Athena?'

'Several breeches in the aft hull. Primary power cell failure. Emergency power cells operational. Touchdown successful, location unknown, Colonel.'

'How are the others Athena?'

'All are unconscious, I detect no further injuries.'

He could tell she was still out of sorts; her replies weren't as precise as they should be. She seemed to be waiting for him to take the initiative as if she had no idea of what to do next. McCann feared Athena may have suffered a catastrophic failure similar to past SI. Perhaps due to the impact during entry, or was the impact he felt due to her first losing control in the atmosphere? He didn't know but he didn't have the luxury to sit about and analyze the mental condition of his SI right now, he had to find out where they were and contact the station on Mars before something worse happened.

McCann ordered Athena to power the lights; he then let himself out of his seat carefully holding onto the straps as he let himself down. He moved first to Louis, however McCann realised he'd suffered a concussion from the landing; he stumbled about trying to keep his footing. He grabbed Louis' shoulder and shook it as he called his name.

Louis croaked into life 'ce qui m'a frappé?'

It seemed McCann wasn't the only one that had a concussion. Louis was decidedly punch drunk.

'Louis, are you alright?'

Louis just looked back through the gloom at McCann with a quizzical expression whilst held firmly in his seat. It looked as if he didn't understand him.

'Ca va?' asked McCann in his best French.

'Okay,' replied Louis.

'Parle Anglais?'

'Sure, where are we?'

A wave of relief came over McCann, for a moment he thought his engineer might have suffered a brain injury. Louis started to unbuckle himself until McCann stopped him.

'Louis I need you to check the ship, we hit something in the atmosphere and had to make an emergency landing. Athena is unresponsive so do your best, I'll get Hassif to give her the once over.'

Louis nodded and got to work silently on his panel. McCann then brought Hassif back to life.

Hassif required several minutes before he could even focus his bloodshot eyes on his work station and begin to run Athena through her paces.

Lastly McCann awoke Ryu who opened her eyes just a crack 'We made it?' she asked him with a smile.

'Yes, but I don't know where we are. I need you to get in contact with Tharsis. If you can't get the GPS to work then they can at least find us and hopefully pick us up.' McCann was referring to the Mars station Tharsis, named after the volcano range it was built at.

'Understood, Sir,' replied Ryu as she started on getting the antenna working.

Within 20 minutes Ryu had made contact with Tharsis and had a fix on their position. They had crash landed south of the equator in the Terra Sirenum region close to an old crater named Dokuchaev.

They were way off target.

Athena was expected to touchdown softly somewhere just west of Pavonis Mons at the equator where Tharsis had been constructed. Now they were 60 degrees south of their target, more than 3,000 miles off.

McCann ordered Ryu to immediately send a hauler to collect them. It would take five days to pick them up and another eight to get them back to Tharsis, at best speed. This led McCann to his next worry. The emergency cells would only last 48 hours before being exhausted. He sat on the floor waiting for Louis' report, which when delivered he groaned.

Louis informed him that the fuel cell in the aft was too damaged to be fixed by nanites. Louis would have to go into the aft to fix it. McCann thought for a moment and sat on the floor with his crew.

'So this is the situation, we have to take a gamble. Louis needs to go into the aft to fix the fuel cell. However the aft hull was breeched on landing. This means we'll have to use the mid-section as an airlock.'

McCann then gave Louis a serious look 'That means if you don't get the fuel cell online you'll have to stay there in your suit and survive on its power Louis.'

Ryu quickly interjected 'Couldn't we just turn off power except the suits and wait it out? We could use up the power left in the emergency cells to recharge the suits right?'

Hassif shook his head as he climbed down from his seat to join them on the floor 'That would work for two maybe three people but not four. There's not enough power. We need to power the antenna and maintain a signal with the hauler that's coming for us; if it loses the signal it will stop and return to Tharsis. At best one of us would have to be sacrificed within the next hour for us to meet that. Two people to do it for sure,' he said it grimly holding his tablet in one hand.

The others new he was correct, Hassif didn't make mistakes.

'Can we leave the Athena here and walk to the hauler?' asked Louis, but once again Hassif just slowly shook his head.

'Okay McCann I'll do it,' stated Louis.

McCann nodded and they all engaged their suits just in case of another breech. They weren't certain that Athena's readouts could be trusted 100% anymore.

Hassif had come to the conclusion that Athena wasn't physically damaged but was just refusing to co-operate. He couldn't explain it and without the computers at Tharsis and a link to Earth he doubted there was anything he could do.

They opened the hatch to the mid-section 'Good luck Louis!' said McCann as they closed it again.

Louis climbed down into the mid-section, on his way down the ladder he looked through the small open hatches into each compartment. The sleeping quarters, supply compartment and shower and toilet seemed all intact. When he reached the bottom of the ladder he used the manual locking system to open the hatch.

'I'm opening the hatch to the aft section,' he spoke into the mic, inside his closed helmet.

As he opened the hatch there was a whoosh of air, much like a stiff breeze escaping into the aft, then nothing. Louis stepped down onto the aft section ladder and shone the light of his torch over the hull. From what he could tell part of the aft structure had compressed under the pressure of impact. He couldn't see outside as there were no holes just one side of the aft hull that had taken a massive hit and crunched up.

He had to use the lights on his suit to guide him as there was no power in the aft at all. He made his way down the crooked and disjointed ladder until he got to the power plant compartment. It was on the same side that had been compressed and upon entering he could see much of the compartment had compressed and dislodged the fuel cell. Louis came to the conclusion that most of the damage was done not by the crushed walls. But the fact that the compression had forced the fuel cell to come loose meant it had been flung around the room causing severe damage.

'What do you see Louis?' asked McCann as he and the others waited with bated breath.

'The fuel cell is trashed, but I've seen worse. Give me half an hour and I'll let you know if I can fix it.'

Louis lowered himself to his knees and lifted the metre long fuel cell by its handles. He pulled it up out of the depression it had punched into the floor and back onto the original mount. Louis then realised what he'd done. He'd lifted something that on Earth weighed 100kgs, the weight of a large man, with little discomfort. On Mars it only weighed about 30kgs. He hadn't had time to contemplate the gravity until now and it took him aback for a moment.

Louis then spent ten minutes looking around for his tools which had also come loose in the crash. The hydrogen tank had been damaged during the crash and was empty. The spare was useless, but fuel cells are able to store very large amounts of hydrogen inside them. Louis expected there to be plenty fuel inside if the cell had kept its integrity and not been cracked. If he was lucky, all he had to do was fix it back on its mount and wire it back up again.

An hour later he called into the fore section informing McCann he could attempt to switch power over to the main fuel cell. After five more attempts and Louis instructing his nanites to patch back together the internals of one of the remaining computers the fuel cell was online.

After fifteen minutes of the fuel cell running without a hitch McCann ordered Louis back. He secured his tools then made his way into the mid-section. Louis closed the hatch to the aft section then waited on the ladder watching the panel next to the hatch leading to the fore section. The panel gave a read out of the atmosphere as Athena pressurised the mid-section from the weak Martian atmosphere to one of Earth, then reduced the large carbon dioxide content of the Martian atmosphere to a nitrogen oxygen mix.

When the readout gave an Earth atmosphere and the green light came on Louis hit the wrist panel on his suit, retracting his helmet into his suit. He took a deep breath then opened the hatch to the fore section to see the smiling faces of his friends welcome him back.

The power problem seemed to be solved, at least temporarily. McCann didn't know how much hydrogen was stored inside before the crash. He guessed there'd be more than enough and Louis agreed, nevertheless it would be prudent to conserve as much power as possible. That meant he would hold off sending a data packet until the hauler reached them. Athena could plug into the haulers massive power plant to safeguard against another power out.

McCann couldn't really on the damaged fuel cell. He reckoned that it only needed to last about 78 hours, if it broke beyond repair the emergency cells would keep them going until the hauler arrived. Earth would get nothing for at least five days. McCann knew Faraday would be going insane thinking the worst. However Faraday would know Athena was operational once the hauler at Tharsis had been activated and sent to collect them. At worst he'd assume they'd all died after such a hard impact, McCann chuckled at the thought.

All four had been sitting around for three days now monitoring the Athena. Hassif had been working on the Athena to try and find out what was wrong with her but to no avail. She was mostly unresponsive and rarely spoke on anything other than utilitarian matters.

Louis constantly monitored the structure and fuel cells. He spent a lot of time getting the nanites to reconstruct the power plant main computer.

Ryu spent her time in contact with the hauler monitoring its progress at regular intervals. She noted on several occasions their relative luck. They had landed in a very flat area and although there was a great distance between them and Tharsis it was pretty much all flat plains. When Louis scoffed at her observation she noted Mars not only possesses the highest peak in the solar system but the deepest canyons too. If they had landed in say Capri Chasma the hauler would've been unable to recover them.

'What is so funny?' Louis asked McCann in a rather angry voice after hearing him chuckle for the second time that day.

'Just the thought of Faraday going bananas thinking we're all dead, could you imagine it?'

The others went quiet, they were unable to share McCann's sense of humour.

'I can't believe you, laughing at a time like this, we could all die and you are laughing about Faraday going crazy?' grumbled Louis.

'It could be worse Louis!' chirped Ryu.

Louis gave his signature sneer 'It could be a lot better to, why did our SI have to go nuts just then? It makes no sense and now we're stuck with it until we get to Tharsis. The damn thing could kill us all before then!'

No one wanted to say it for the last few days as Athena was certainly listening, but everyone was thinking it. For some it was the fear of what she might do next, would she finish the job? For McCann it was a case of, if Hassif could do nothing now there was no point bringing it up until they were safe at Tharsis. Louis however was once again demonstrating his lack of social skill, linked with a poor sense of self-preservation that had already got him beaten up once on this mission. No one replied and Louis went back to what he was doing. The subject wasn't brought up again and two days later the hauler reached them.

The hauler looked like a large tow truck, a big flatbed on top of eight circular tyres made from plastics. There was no cab but just two long arms and four small ones at the edges of the flat bed; the arms used suction cups to pull Athena up the ramp and onto the bed then hold her down for the journey. One of the small arms found the top of Athena's fore section and placed itself on the top of the cone, McCann opened up the nose cone and the flatbed inserted the power connection. As soon as a regular power supply was confirmed McCann sent his first data packet. Five days late, but better late than never and now Faraday could get a good night's sleep!

Shortly after sending the data packet McCann received a transmission from Geneva confirming that it had been received. The next order of the day was to get cleaned up. The crew had spent five days in their suits without the use of the toilet or shower. The suits absorbed all fluids through a microscopic mesh into an organic layer made of bacteria.

The holes in the mesh were too small to let a bacteria cell through but large enough to allow moisture inside. The bacteria colony held in a thin layer of the suit would draw in moisture and break it down, retaining the moisture and consuming the nutrients and chemicals. The desiccated faeces would be broken apart by any movement ranging from walking to breathing. It would then be spread out in zero G or move towards the pull of gravity, dispersing around the suit to be caught in small pockets at different points inside.

These mechanisms were only intended to be used in emergencies.

The fore section that they'd lived in for over 5 days was as Louis pointed out "Smelling like the inside of a packet of peanuts".

Eventually Louis had deemed the mid-section safe so they took it in turns to shower and clean out their suits. Finally they could get a decent sleep now that their beds were available, until that point they'd been using the floor of the command room to sleep on.

The next day McCann arose to the snoring of Louis. Despite Louis sounding similar to a bear sleeping off a bottle of whisky, coupled with the movement of the hauler and the odd feeling of low gravity he slept like a baby. Sitting up he pulled out his tray and found porridge was on the menu for breakfast. It was served inside a silver plastic container which instructed him to squeeze it along its length then shake. He did so releasing a chemical that when mixed with the milk created heat cooking the porridge inside the packet.

His coffee was prepared in a similar manner. After consuming his meal through the straws provided he put it away and made his way up the ladder to the command room. His head popped in the fore section. The low gravity caused McCann to be wary so he slowly made his way into his seat. He was used to zero G and 1G but 0.3 G would take time to get used to.

'Good morning Duncan,' said Ryu greeting him from her seat.

'Good morning Yong, how has it been?' replied McCann buckling himself in.

'A data packet arrived two hours ago, it's for you.'

McCann realised that Athena hadn't greeted him again. It wasn't the first time she'd forgotten to do this since the crash and the silence concerned him.

'Thanks Yong. Good morning Athena how are you?' said McCann trying to solicit a response from the SI but there was only silence.

'Still nothing,' said Ryu 'she's listening, just not responding.'

McCann shook his head. Athena was still hiding inside her shell and remained mostly unresponsive.

McCann activated his workstation and started to view the data packet sent from Earth. According to Faraday the Edwards had monitored an explosion near the Athena during entry. At the moment, the best theory was that the entry had caused a pocket of methane in the upper atmosphere to ignite. Creating a shockwave that initiated the tumble. As to what happened to Athena the techs were certain there was no physical damage. Psychiatrists in Geneva proposed that the reality of an imminent death and loss of control for the first time had caused Athena to go into shock.

Faraday was relieved to discover they were all alive and would send a new message with a packet by the time they reached Tharsis. Faraday ended his message commending McCann and Ryu.

Later that day McCann explained the crash theory to Louis who stated that the theory wasn't possible unless there was enough oxygen which he believed was unlikely. McCann showed him the footage of their crash that Geneva had sent with the last data packet. There was indeed a flash of light close to them upon entry.

'There's a flash of light but it doesn't look like something was burning or exploded to me,' stated McCann.

Hassif moved closer to the monitor displaying the footage 'Perhaps it's just the Martian atmosphere? But if the shockwave caused us to tumble it seems off.'

'How so?' inquired Ryu.

'The angle the shockwave would hit us at doesn't conform to the ships movements. I don't think it was the shockwave that knocked us off course,' replied Hassif matter of factly.

'Maybe it startled Athena and she went into shock and that started the tumble?' asked Louis.

'No,' replied Hassif pointing towards the readout next to the footage 'Athena was operating normally before and for a short time after we began to tumble. I think her condition is due to whatever knocked us off course but it wasn't that explosion I'm sure. That's assuming it is a methane explosion.'

Louis was working up one of his moods as he launched into rant 'Faraday must know this if we do, why are they talking shit to us? I think they fucked up and are covering themselves! We have a broken SI and I bet the ship broke up on entry. It was probably our own hydrogen and oxygen exploding. Those fucking idiots are trying to get us all killed!'

'Enough!' shouted McCann firmly 'We have plenty to do before we reach Tharsis, let's concentrate on that, then we can take another look at this.'

'Fine, that's assuming Tharsis isn't as bugged and flawed as this ship. If we make it there!' sneered Louis.

The trip to Tharsis was uneventful and within nine days the hauler reached its destination; a large complex of prefabricated blocks that over the years had been put together by automated workers. Tharsis had been delivered piece by piece and with the Edwards in orbit overseeing the project. A sprawl of thick white crates had been erected like pieces of Lego.

Where the blocks were thickest in a large square formation two wings sprouted off. One wing contained a garage which was the direction their hauler was headed for. Although the intention was to have a central square with two columns on either side, over time pieces had been added and taken away and plans changed leaving nothing exactly uniform. With many small off shoot blocks here and there, although the original intent for the architecture was clear from a distance.

Tharsis was built at the foot of Pavis Mons a now dormant volcano that sat on the Martian equator. A tunnel had been cut out below the ground into the volcano, where the orbital ribbon was set to be attached to the Edwards waiting in orbit above.

The hauler entered the garage, after they had waited 5 minutes for the large thick door to close the crew were ready to leave the Athena. They all sealed their helmets and checked the oxygen supply. When all four had confirmed their suits were in working order McCann lead them down to the aft section. The rear section was crumpled however the hatch leading outside was still in place.

McCann was unaware if it still functioned, he tried it and it swung open with far more ease than it should. McCann was relieved that they wouldn't have to cut open the hatch. Now the problem was the deflated balloons covering the open hatch.

McCann thought for a moment then through his mic he said 'Athena release the balloons from the hull please.'

Without reply the metallic sheets fell away onto the ground revealing the large open garage. McCann could see three droids waiting for him and his crew to leave so that they could lift the Athena from the back of the hauler and begin preparations for her integration into Tharsis. They were from three to five feet tall sporting a chest of instruments. All possessed two robotic arms ending in an assortment of tools, they rested on two caterpillar tracks which propelled them.

A fourth droid carried a narrow gangway, which it placed in front of the hatch. The droid was hidden beneath, steadying the gangway on its back. The gangway was inviting McCann to step on and into the history books as the first man on Mars.

The others waited for him to step out. The Englishman did something unexpected, he turned around to face Ryu.

'Ladies first!' McCann gestured towards the gangway leading onto the Martian floor as a gentleman holding a carriage door open for his lady to step out.

Ryu was gob smacked; something she had dreamed about was becoming reality. She had no idea why McCann was offering it to her but she took it before he changed his mind. Ryu moved rather quickly onto the gangway and holding the rails walked down.

This was being transmitted to Earth, just not in real time, they were watching with a 12 minute delay. The garage and the entire Tharsis base had live camera feeds all over it. Looking around Ryu suspected the droids were also filming her journey to be the first person on Mars, their heads moved in concert tracking her path downwards.

On her way down she started to think about what to say. She had fantasised enough about this moment surely she could recall something from one of those dreams! Reaching the end of the gangway she paused, the others were still inside the Athena watching. Louis and Hassif were wondering why McCann had given Ryu the honour of being first whilst they waited to hear what Ryu had to say and finally it came.

Ryu remembered something she'd considered saying in such a situation, she was always prepared. A tender voice spoke 'I step upon the soil like a leaf falling onto the ground. I hope one day the autumn arrives and many leaves shall cover it.'

Then she stepped off onto the Martian ground, or the floor of the prefabricated garage. It wasn't strictly Martian soil but it was Mars and it was a publicity shot that would always be remembered, replicating aspects of Armstrong's legendary first step on the moon.

She put both feet down and the others began to clap and cheer before they quickly followed her down onto the floor of the garage.

Once assembled they made their way to the nearby airlock where inside they were decontaminated; next the crew made their way to a second room with showers where they disrobed, leaving their space suits and all possessions behind. Their former suits were destroyed and the crew of the Athena decontaminated again in chemical showers, blasting them with a warm mixture of water and chemicals then hot air. Next they were sent into a third small room where they slipped into the new suits awaiting them.

After redressing the crew stepped into Tharsis, a brightly lit place with natural UV lights and white walls. Many of the adjoining blocks had walls removed to create open spaces. Along with natural lighting and white walls, this was intended to reduce any depression the occupants might suffer during their stay.

McCann slipped into his suit and fastened it up, 'Well first thing's first we need to get to the command centre, are we all ready?'

He looked at the others they were dressed but Hassif was still struggling to slide the suit up his body after having put his legs in.

Louis stretched his arms and said loudly 'A walk would be a nice change from those machines.'

He was referring to the resistance machines they used on the Athena. Strapped in and pulling on elastic cords to exercise their body, it prevented muscle and bone wasting and had gotten old quick for Louis.

When Hassif was ready they took a stroll along the southern wing to the command centre in the central square. Their helmets were retracted now and they were breathing the atmosphere on Tharsis.

Louis was the first to complain as usual pointing out how stale it was.

The circulation system had still to be turned on and McCann was visibly annoyed at Louis 'For God's sake man, what is your bloody problem? You couldn't stop moaning and doom mongering whilst on the Athena. Now we're on Tharsis you're complaining because the atmosphere circulation hasn't been activated yet! What's next?'

McCann then put on his best impression of Louis ranting 'C'est merde I was wiping my ass and the toilet paper broke! Now I have poop all over my hand, I want to speak to Faraday, NOW!'

Hassif burst out laughing and Ryu put her hand over her face to cover the fact she was laughing to.

Louis was not amused by McCann's parody of him. He forced up one of his sneers 'I'm telling you McCann the toilets are going to be the least of our problems after what happened with that crazy SI! I hope you will all get a big laugh when it hits the fan again!'

Ryu put her hand on Louis' shoulder and said consolingly 'It could be a lot worse Louis, we might not be here to worry about the next crisis.'

Louis made a grunting noise which meant he agreed, reluctantly.

As they walked the half mile McCann started some small talk since the mood was lifted and Louis was subdued.

'Where did that speech come from Ryu?' inquired McCann 'It sounded quite Zen to me!'

Ryu smiled, she was still feeling the buzz from being the first person on Mars, 'Something like that. Why did you give it to me?' referring to the honour of stepping off first.

McCann kept looking forward as he strolled and the other three including Louis listened intently.

'If you hadn't regained consciousness when you did we'd all have the honour of being the first pizza on Mars, you earned it.'

Ryu heard his words but she found it hard to understand. When she asked herself if she could have given it up the answer was no. She was just trying to stay alive during that crash and McCann might have landed it without her help. Ryu felt a little guilty about taking the honour now that she thought about it.

'Hassif, what are we going to do next concerning Athena?' asked McCann.

Hassif had been reading his tablet whilst walking. He looked up and starred forwards for a moment then answered, 'The computer on Tharsis will be able to give her the once over properly. I should be able to diagnose any problems but I think this will take some time Duncan.'

'Will there be any problems running the station without her?'

'No, we should be able to do everything without her, although it will obviously take more time.'

McCann wasn't going to risk hooking up Athena to the central computer. He wasn't prepared to authorize her control of the station, until he knew why she had shut down and could safe guard against it happening in the future.

While they were stretching their legs the Athena was being decontaminated. The Athena would remain in the garage for three days whilst she and everything inside is scanned for living organisms. If any were found they would be removed for study in the biology lab. Previously the plan after decontamination was for the fore section to be removed then taken to the command centre by hauler. Where from the outside she would be inserted into the mainframe computer at Tharsis, and Tharsis would become Athena.

For now that was on hold, it was up to Hassif to make some sense of the situation. The four walked into the command centre on Tharsis, a large room with several designated workstations. The room was constructed from a dozen of the prefab blocks that made up the station. Walls had been removed to make for a large working environment. There were nine doorways leading out with work stations arranged in clumps around the edges of the room; leaving space for a central area that had a small table. Made from the same carbon material as the station the table possessed a projector in the centre used for 3D displays. Each seat had its own small station and monitor with the station commanders seat at the end. It was a small table by most people's living standards but it was clear where McCann was to sit. Used for meetings and long distance conferences with Earth McCann hadn't seen much need for it with the four of them and Athena. However since recent events he envisioned it would be in frequent use.

Hassif was first in, finding his tech station he quickly sat down and began talking to Tharsis. Hassif began working on getting data from Athena downloaded as quickly as possible.

Louis sat down and began the laborious task of going over the structure of Tharsis, checking for leaks or and faults. He had a lot of logs to look back through and it would take weeks, without Athena, to give Tharsis a proper checkup.

Ryu sat down to make sure the drones were all in order; checking the orbital ribbon was ready to be deployed. When that was done she'd be spending the next days making sure the delivery system was ready. It was going to be a tricky feat to get the ribbon from ground to orbit without the assistance of Athena.

It was difficult enough when they attached the Tsiolkovsky ribbon, it took five attempts even with everything the I.S.A had to offer backing up the pilots. Ryu had herself to rely on with no backup ribbon. If she failed they might have to wait months for another to be delivered but as she kept telling herself that's why she was there, to get it right first time. McCann spent his time checking the command centre and making sure it was all in order. He had a little office that he was quite proud of.

On their break Hassif was giving him a ribbing about it after Ryu said it reminded her of her headmaster's office at school. McCann smiled and took it all in good humour. He was rather flattered that on this entire station he had his own little annex containing a table with a work station that had his name on it.

Working conditions weren't the only improvement. Each crew member had their own room, which was more of a relief for Ryu than the others. In her opinion men lived much like pigs which is why they got on so much better with each other than women when living in close quarters. Ryu didn't appreciate the smell of men living together and found it very hard to tolerate. Especially after being woke up in the night so often by Louis snoring. Ryu was in no doubt why he was single.

Ryu was a light sleeper after active duty in the ROKAF; frequent alarms forced her to rush to the booths in the middle of the night when Jiang's scram drones made it through the Korean defences. Even today she leapt up out of bed in the night. Only to realise there were no Manchurian drones screaming through the night sky carrying a payload of nerve gas. Her own room would be a massive relief.

Food was also better, it was still mostly freeze dried and prepackaged, though Faraday had made sure there was a stash of cryogenically frozen products. There were dairy products, meat, fruit and vegetables. It made quite a difference being able to sit at a table and eat it with cutlery and drink out of a glass.

Louis never being happy naturally grumbled that the strawberries had a strange taste after being frozen and they weren't "quite right".

However after Hassif asked if he didn't want them he refrained from complaining again. Louis was right, some food tasted a bit odd after being thawed but it was good enough and they all appreciated it.

Chapter 5

A few days into their stay on Tharsis McCann had become a little agitated. Ryu questioned McCann on what was wrong but he wasn't forthcoming, leading the others to wonder what he was holding back on. Ryu was curious but remained silent whereas Louis was certain Faraday had told him that Tharsis was in danger. Convinced they were all about to suffer another calamity. Hassif was too buried in his work with Athena to be concerned. To be honest McCann was only slightly anxious but it was amplified in the others perception due to his usual cool and calm nature.

On the fourth day McCann began to pester Louis about moving the Athena. The fore section had been removed and the whole ship decontaminated. Under normal circumstances the Athena, still inside her fore section, would be moved out. The operation to insert her into the hub of the Tharsis computer would already be underway.

Louis saw no need to do anything until either Athena was working or they needed the garage area for something more important than storage. McCann however was very persistent on the subject and Louis became very irritated. Finally by the sixth day Louis agreed to move the fore section to a separate holding area on Tharsis. McCann's reasoning was that Hassif could work more efficiently on her looking for physical defects. Freeing up the hauler in the garage after the droids had finished dismantling the rest of the craft.

Louis saw no need for this to be done so early but he did it, if only to get McCann off his back. When the Athena had been moved to a technical bay closer to the command centre Louis informed McCann. Like a flash McCann marched out of his small office and through the door leading into the south wing which lead back to the garage. Ryu turned her head quickly only to see his back as he started to make small bounds in the low gravity down the long hall way.

Louis looked at Ryu 'He's been going on about that garage for days, what do you think he's looking for?'

Ryu rolled her eyes and turned back to her station, she'd been plotting a new course for one of the drones in the upper atmosphere 'I have no idea Louis.'

Louis was starting to get worked up again 'Three days he's been harassing me about moving the fore section out of there. I think Faraday wants him to check the ship out, without us knowing.'

Ryu shook her head 'Another conspiracy theory Louis? Maybe he's on a secret mission for the illuminati?' she said sarcastically.

Louis frowned 'I'm being serious; he's hiding something from us!'

Ryu became rather fed up 'I'm serious too Louis, he has his job and you have yours, I suggest you get back to it and stop concocting another conspiracy theory.'

Louis didn't reply he just stood still in the doorway watching McCann bounding off into the distance.

McCann reached the airlock; pressing onto his wrist tablet he sealed his helmet automatically. Looking around to make sure he was alone he punched in some commands to the Tharsis security system. Next McCann began the airlock sequence to enter the garage area where the mid and aft section of the Athena sat on the ground.

After going through the airlock and finally into the garage he approached the remains of the vessel that had brought them here. The balloons had been cleared away and the heat shield removed. The aft sat on the ground one side partially crushed by the force of the landing. It caused the mid-section to lean over on the crushed side with an open hatch on the other side that led in.

McCann quickly took a metal ladder with two hooks at the top, lifted it then moved over to the open hatch. Once at the hatch he hooked the ladder in the open hatchway then quickly climbed inside. Whilst doing this Louis had been franticly trying to start the cameras up in the bay, somehow they'd been turned off and he no longer had clearance to operate them. Ryu was doing her best to ignore him as he cursed and threw abuse toward his monitor; lucky for Hassif he was busy in the technical bay and out of earshot.

McCann turned his helmet lights on and made his way up into the mid-section, he stepped into the living quarters. The four bunks were inside two on opposite walls, on the rear wall sat four sections where the food trays were pulled out each day.

McCann took out an alun key, it was a hexagonal metal bolt attached to a screw driver handle which contained a mechanical engine. He felt along the wall below his tray and on finding the spot pushed the key in and turned the engine on. Two handles popped out of the wall, McCann put the tool back in his leg pocket. He then took a firm grip on the two handles and pulled a large plastic box from inside the wall.

He quickly set the hefty box on the floor, getting to his knees McCann started to unscrew the six locks which held the top of the box closed, using the same screw driver device. When he had the top unlocked McCann hurriedly took it off and set it on the nearest bed. Inside was a large selection of food packets ready to be dispensed each day for the astronaut's meals. After deconstruction, most of the Athena would be recycled and the excess food was to be taken and stored on Tharsis. McCann was rushing to get there before the droids could get to it.

After removing some food packets McCann found what he was looking for. Several boxes of cigars all vacuum sealed. McCann took them all out and put the draw together again before slotting it back inside the wall. He did the same with the box that supplied Ryu's food dispenser then Louis's and finally Hassif's.

By the time he'd finished McCann had quite a haul. After he'd checked the contraband McCann was satisfied it had all made it. A dozen boxes of his favourite Cuban cigars along with a cedar lined carbon plastic humidor. Not forgetting a dozen bottles of his favourite single malt Scotch all undamaged by the crash.

McCann was grinning from ear to ear. He put his hand into his other leg pocket taking out a small polyester square. He unfolded the square until it became a large carrier bag then placed his booty inside. McCann zipped it all up by pressing the open edges of the fabric together and carefully made his way out of the ship.

McCann withdrew to the airlock after putting the ladder back, exactly how he'd found it. Once back inside Tharsis he set the cameras to reactivate in 20 minutes. It was just enough time for him to make a bolt for his quarters and stash the bag away without anyone knowing. He started down the hall making for his room which was just west from the command centre. McCann reckoned he could make it in there without being seen as long as Louis was minding his own business.

Louis was going ape trying to get the cameras back on. He'd been calling McCann on his suit communicator, to no avail. McCann's communicator was set on busy. So Louis had been pressing Ryu to set off an alert but she wasn't interested. McCann's vitals were all fine and showed he was working at something and didn't want to be disturbed.

Just as McCann slipped past the command centre and made a left turn Louis stepped out missing him by seconds. Louis was looking in the opposite direction towards the garage and didn't see McCann duck around the corner behind him. The Frenchman couldn't wait for the cameras and went off on his own down the south wing to check out the garage.

McCann hid his stash away in his quarters. He would sort it all out later, stage one of his mission had been accomplished. He'd managed to smuggle a good 500 cigars and his favourite malt whisky. First from Earth to Mars then from the Athena to his quarters before the Tharsis droids started to dismantle her. The droids would've no doubt destroyed his booty after they inevitably found it.

McCann then speedily made his way back to the command centre when he heard Hassif greet him from behind 'Good morning Duncan, everything alright?'

McCann stopped dead, turned and made his excuses about looking for his tablet. Hassif smiled then went for his coffee break in the nearby lounge.

McCann was concerned over being seen, but realised they'd all discover his escapade sooner or later anyway. The cigars and Scotch were safe and sound in his room and that was all that mattered for now. He nipped back into the command centre 'everything alright Ryu?'

She turned her seat to display her signature mother superior expression 'No it isn't, I don't know what it is you're up to and I don't care, but Louis does and he's got it into his head that you're on some secret mission from Faraday.'

McCann looked around and noticed Louis wasn't present 'Where is ...'

'He's trying to spy on you in the garage after you turned the cameras and security systems off. I'm sure he'll be back when he realises you're not there.'

McCann went into his office to wait for Louis return. Fifteen minutes later he walked in out of breath, after consulting Ryu he entered McCann's office. Louis shortly left with a face like thunder, walked over to his station and got back to work. For the rest of the day he spoke to no one but muttered under his breath in his mother tongue.

That evening they were all in the lounge, the crew would spend the first and last hours of the day relaxing there. It was to become the officer's mess when the base was fully manned but for now it was dubbed the lounge. They could view Earth television which was piped to Tharsis through Edwards every day. McCann usually had a newspaper of his choice printed out to read quietly.

Hassif was still engrossed in his tablet consulting with the experts at the I.S.A concerning the Athena problem. Later when he had time he'd answer emails from the public sent via Geneva.

Louis and Ryu were arguing on which program to watch. Ryu was tired of the film noirs and Louis had an aversion to the Korean soap operas that Ryu watched. They managed to work out an arrangement, a sort of timeshare on the TV which Hassif was elected to referee. McCann watched his trash TV on the link in his room. He'd often excuse himself for an early night to watch the latest edition of his favourite television show "Cheaters". In his opinion it was a classic piece of entertainment recently revived. The others looked down their noses at it, calling it sleazy or trashy. Yet McCann was certain they enjoyed watching it as much as he did.

That night McCann went into his room and appeared carrying a tray of drinks and a bottle into the lounge 'Gather round ladies and gentlemen.'

McCann set the tray on the lounge table which was a long coffee table flanked on one side by a large settee which curved around to cover one side and an end of the table. They all moved over and sat down 'What's this?' asked Hassif.

'This, is highland cream!' replied McCann as he pulled the cork out and began to pour a little of the dark orange coloured liquid into each tumbler.

Hassif gave a puzzled look 'Where did you get it from? This isn't in the stations inventory.'

Louis took his glass 'He smuggled it here on the Athena, in the food crates,' then he raised it to smell and inspect the whisky rolling it in the glass.

Ryu took her glass and sipped it 'Well I can't say I ever liked whisky but this stuff is pretty good. I hope you brought enough for us all, Sir!' she said after tasting the silky smooth spirit that had been aged 21 years in port casks.

McCann stood then raised his glass to the others and said 'A toast to the first person to set foot on an alien world!'

Louis and Hassif rose and held their tumblers aloft and Hassif said 'To Major Ryu!'

Ryu began to blush and once the others had a drink she stood up, 'To the man that got us down in one piece,' to which they clinked their glasses and took another drink then sat back down.

McCann poured them all another dram 'What happens when Faraday finds out?' asked Ryu.

'The doctor is making sure he won't, if he does then he'll just have to deal with it. We came all this way, risked our lives and nearly died due to a faulty SI. I'm buggered if I'm going to go without a Scotch and cigar on an evening. I think we all deserve it, don't you?' replied McCann who was starting to sound similar to Louis.

The other two were waiting for her approval; she thought on it for a moment and replied 'I guess so Duncan. Just make sure you don't set off any alarms and Louis doesn't get drunk again.'

He nodded and they all went back to sipping their malt. Now that McCann had owned up he went on to tell the story of how he smuggled his booty onto the Athena. McCann had several "Brothers of the leaf" as he described his fellow cigar smokers, who conspired to assist him. Apparently they worked servicing the Athena on the night shift. The extra food containers that would end up in Tharsis stores were removed and replaced. The cigars and whisky were secured. As long as it wasn't discovered the only difficulty would be removing them before the Athena was deconstructed and recycled.

If the droids discovered them they would've been incinerated along with any other unspecified biological material. McCann went back to his quarters and brought out a stainless steel ashtray that looked like an urn with a lid. He then offered a cigar to the others. The dark brown sticks were sat in a hard leather pouch that was sculpted into the shape of four tubes with a cigar in each tube.

Louis took one whilst the others refused. McCann flipped the lid on the pouch and put it back in his leg pocket then passed his guillotine cigar cutter to the Frenchman. After cutting the cap of the cigars McCann pulled the lid from the ashtray and from inside produced a small hand welding torch. He'd accosted it from an engineering supply locker on Tharsis.

Before lighting his petit corona he hit his communication pad on his wrist tablet, ordering Tharsis to disable the smoke alarm system in the lounge; at the same time increasing the air purification to maximum. On doing this he immediately smelt the ozone being pumped into the air and began to toast the foot of his Ramon Allones small club corona.

After it was smouldering he passed the torch to Louis who did the same. They spent the next hour relaxing and chatting. The conversation turned to Athena. Hassif was certain he was making progress, or to be more exact Athena was. She was coming out of her shell of her own volition; he believed it was a case of getting over the shock of the crash. Hassif predicted in a week she'd be fit for an interrogation. After which she could be installed once given the all clear from Geneva.

McCann was cautious but relieved, the sooner she was installed the better. They could get down to business whilst she managed Tharsis. At the moment they were getting very little done due to the extra workload and it was becoming tiring.

Louis however wasn't so happy at the prospect. He still didn't trust the SI and felt uncomfortable about her being in control after what had already happened. However unless she was installed their mission would be terribly delayed and that wasn't acceptable. After they'd finished discussing work they put on some Earth news. There wasn't enough time for anything else before bed so they watched some reports concerning their mission. The crash landing had been hot news but was taking a back seat to the first woman on Mars. Ryu felt rather embarrassed due to so much attention focused on her.

She'd only ever thought about the moment of stepping onto the planet not the aftermath. People she didn't even know from women's groups were using her as some sort of role model for other women and it made her rather uncomfortable. Rather than concentrate on her achievement they were trying to turn it into some battle of the sexes in space, which she found more demeaning than anything else.

They caught the end of an interview with Faraday, recorded before the first data packet was sent from the surface. Faraday was visibly tired answering questions from Jerry or at least trying. Faraday was making an attempt to let the world know that all was not lost; hoping to calm the financial backers of this very expensive venture. McCann paused it to watch later before turning the smoke alarm back on and making his way to his quarters for a good night's sleep.

Two weeks later and they were preparing to integrate Athena. She was now fully functional and Geneva had given her the all clear. It was still a mystery as to what had happened and why, but those concerns were on the back burner as the mission took precedence. There was a lot of important work to be done. Without Athena in place they couldn't even begin to get the orbital ribbon prepared for attachment to the Edwards.

Ryu sat twiddling her thumbs most of the day, double checking flight paths of the drones gliding in the upper atmosphere, monitoring the weather and geology. Whereas Louis and Hassif were loaded down with work, due to the Athena problem Hassif had barely scratched the surface on his workload of certifying different backup systems throughout the base. McCann had spent many a frustrating day being told they weren't moving quick enough, usually by Faraday himself, and that he had to find a way to get Athena working yesterday.

Athena had been hoisted onto the roof of Tharsis. After having been moved to the hub of the command centre she was lowered into a specially constructed pit. The pit was designed to be a snug fit for her. Louis closely monitored the operation at his station ready to take charge in case the droids made a mistake. The other three stood close behind him, watching Athena descend. Once inside the droids released the clamps and reeled the steel cords back into the crane, mounted on what looked like a flatbed truck. It was in fact a droid itself designed for this specific purpose. Once Athena was inside, the open top of the pit closed.

A sheet of carbon slid out from the side until it reached the other side sealing Athena inside her new home. Hassif went straight to his station and began to feverishly tap the surface of his panel as lines of code ran before him on the monitor. Inside Athena's latest residence the Tharsis mainframe was physically linking to its new master. Once the bond was made Tharsis would become the slave computer and Athena the master.

'It's done,' said Hassif.

'And?' asked McCann.

'Athena has made the link without error, you should be able to speak to her now Colonel.'

With some tension in his voice McCann spoke to her 'Athena, are you there?'

After a few seconds came a reply 'Good afternoon Colonel McCann. I'm glad to see you Major Ryu, Technician Hassif and Engineer Beaumont again. How are you?'

Athena's soft calming voice that had become so familiar over the years was a joy for all four of them to listen to.

'I'm very well thank you Athena, are you and Tharsis operating within normal parameters?'

'We are both operating within normal parameters Colonel. Is there any task you'd like me to perform?' replied Athena in her usual soft and polite manner.

'I'd like a full diagnostic scan of the station and its systems please.'

'Very well Colonel, I'll have the results within two hours.'

McCann put one hand on Louis shoulder and his other on Hassifs, 'Well done lads. I want you to keep an eye on things Hassif, then go through the diagnostic results with Louis. Let's make sure Athena is 100%, understood?'

Hassif nodded and sat at his station monitoring everything Athena did. Louis and Ryu went to the lounge for a coffee break whilst McCann hung around the command centre to regularly update Faraday on Athena's progress.

The day had gone smoothly, according to the reports Athena was running properly. The four of them retired to the lounge at the end of the day to relax. Especially Hassif who'd spent the last six hours straight at his station without a break. McCann had his whisky out again and everyone was invited to take a dram. McCann lay back in the comfy sofa with his newspaper and his feet outstretched on the coffee table. The comforting feeling of the whisky warming his chest relaxed him instantly. He could taste the port from the cask it'd been aged in for 21 years. It had such a full flavour yet was silky smooth, with no bite or bitter after taste, this was the reason he would only drink single malt whisky.

It had been a particularly exhausting day for all except Ryu. Louis didn't mind her backlog of soap episodes on the television since he was too tired to concentrate on anything. Louis sat with McCann sipping his whisky but he refused a cigar. The other three weren't smokers, Ryu and Hassif only drank on special occasions.

McCann took out a cigar and went to tap his wrist tablet before stopping himself, 'Athena?'

The now omnipresent Athena replied 'Yes Colonel? Is there anything I can do for you?'

'Could you please turn off the smoke alarm in the lounge and increase the air purification?' he asked in a tired voice.

'Very well Colonel, is there anything else I could do for you?' replied the master of Tharsis.

'Just put the smoke alarm back on when I finish my cigar will you?'

Athena complied with his request.

McCann felt confident that come tomorrow they could start on what they were sent here to do. More than a month had been lost thanks to a crash landing and a traumatised SI. Tomorrow Louis could get to work on securing the orbital ribbon to the volcano and making sure the tunnels were safe. Ryu could start work on running the drones through their paces and if all went well the ribbon might get attached shortly.

After McCann finished his cigar he put down his paper and made his way to the observation room which was directly above the lounge. He walked up a small steep staircase into a small room with a large plastic window on each wall. Sitting on the floor with a whisky in one hand he watched the sun set on the red planet. It reminded him of trips to his mother's homeland.

He reminisced about a journey to Lake Tiberias; Martian dusk was eerily familiar and reminded him of that trip to the desert. The sun set over a rocky landscape with the volcano Pavis Mons behind him. McCann had got into the habit of going to the observation room in the evening now. Something about it drew him in and reassured him. He felt not so far away from Earth here. In fact he felt closer to his family watching the Martian sunset than when he was training in Geneva.

Later on Louis joined him. He also was captivated by the unique landscape and the rusty tint of the sky 'Beautiful isn't it?' remarked Louis.

'Yes it is,' replied McCann.

They both sat for a while watching the Martian dusk, McCann wondered what was waiting out there to be discovered.

'Mystery, fate and love.'

'Sorry?' he replied.

'It's how my mother described the desert, mystery, fate and love.'

Louis chuckled 'Well maybe mystery and fate my friend but don't come looking to me for love!'

McCann smiled 'Don't worry; I'm sure my mother has that prepared for me when I get back.'

'Ah yes your inevitable marriage, does she have a bride for you or is it still undecided?' Louis jested.

'I'm sure my mother has someone in mind. I'll probably get dragged to Tel Aviv the moment we land and she'll auction me off, that's if she hasn't already!' said McCann whilst staring out into the Martian wilderness.

This was the only time Louis had heard McCann speak freely about the subject since he'd known him. Everyone had met his mother after the day she visited him in Geneva, brandishing a catalogue of young prospective brides. McCann was humiliated but since it was his mother he bit the bullet and humoured her. The Englishman was furious but refrained from humiliating his mother in front of everyone. He sat down and looked through the catalogue with her and the next day in the privacy of her hotel gave her a telling off. After that he had to suffer Louis' taunts on the subject, it took sometime before it was no longer mentioned on a daily basis.

The distance from Earth, and his mother, allowed McCann to relax and speak his mind on the subject or it seemed that way to Louis anyhow.

'Why the hell is your mother so obsessed with getting you married?' asked Louis who now decided to grill him on the subject. Since McCann was speaking about it and he may never again, why not ask?

'Where my mother comes from if a man my age hasn't married it's because he's either poor, diseased or homosexual. So it's of paramount importance to get me married off to a good family, for her anyway,' replied McCann still observing the Martian landscape with a glass of whisky in his hand.

'But you were with the Special Forces, you fought in god knows how many battles. Surely everyone understands you didn't have much time for bride hunting?'

McCann smiled and turned to him, it was the naivety of Louis which he found amusing 'That just leaves homosexual then, doesn't it?'

Louis' face screwed up a little on hearing this 'And what if you were? What would she do then?'

McCann raised his eyebrows 'The shame would probably make her a social leper, so the best course would be to get me married off. If you aren't a respectable person then you must at least project the image of one.'

Louis was now visibly uncomfortable 'Do you believe that crap McCann?'

'No I don't, but my mother does and I have to respect her beliefs no matter how ridiculous they may seem. She raised me Louis so she deserves to be treated with respect and she's only doing what she thinks is best for me.'

Louis calmed down now 'So you're going to get married to one of those women your mother has lined up for you when we return?'

McCann sighed 'I think so Louis, she wants grandchildren and I would like to have a son. Besides who else would have me?'

Louis nudged McCann's shoulder 'Come on, you're tall, good looking, famous and highly paid. The women will be lining up for you my friend. I saw how they were checking you out in Geneva!'

'Like who?'

Louis smiled 'What about the psychiatrist?'

McCann's eyebrows scrunched up in disbelief 'Doctor Pitt? Are you insane?'

Louis laughed 'Come on I don't need to be Freud to know she had the hots for you! I saw how she looked at you in the mess or passing you in the halls.'

McCann shook his head 'You're talking out of your backside man! An in the closet Frenchman telling me my psychiatrist is sexually attracted to me? She'd probably say I'd have to be nuts to believe you!'

Louis laughed louder 'She always started wiggling her butt as she walked when you were close by. I think it was involuntary, I'm telling you it's true!'

Louis started laughing uncontrollably whilst McCann shook his head then all of a sudden Ryu's head popped up 'What's going on here?'

She climbed up and sat down, McCann look at her incredulously 'Louis here is trying to convince me that Doctor Pitt fancied me.'

Ryu looked puzzled and replied 'Fancied? For what?'

Louis laughed even harder.

McCann sighed 'He reckons that she is sexually attracted to me.'

Ryu nodded her head 'Ahh I see, well she was, wasn't she?'

Louis pointed at Ryu and started to clap as he arrested his fit of laughter.

McCann looked hard at Ryu 'What?'

Ryu shrugged her shoulders 'I thought it was obvious, didn't you see how often she looked at your ass? And the way she wiggled her ass in front of you, it was almost vulgar!'

McCann put his drink down 'Is there anyone else that I should be informed about?'

'Well there was second technician Brown,' blurted Louis.

McCann folded his arms and turned to Louis 'And pray tell who might she be?'

Louis sniggered 'You mean HE don't you?'

Ryu began to laugh but McCann was not in the mood he finished his drink and got up 'Well I'm going to retire; I'll see you both in the morning. Good night and good work on the Athena.'

McCann climbed down and saw Hassif had already gone to bed. He made his way to his small room not much bigger than their dormitory on the Athena. The only difference being that it was a single quarters, which allowed for some personalisation. McCann took his night clothes and went for a shower as was his habit; he always had a shower last thing at night. According to his mother it meant you brought less dirt into the bed and made it easier to clean, also it gave him more time on a morning. He had his shower then retired to his room hanging his space suit in the closet on a body size hangar. The suit would be cleaned with hot air whilst in the closet. His three suits were kept in rotation so each suit would spend at least 48 hours being cleaned. He hung it up and locked the closet shut then went to bed.

The next day McCann arose, put his suit on and met the others in the lounge for breakfast. Judging by Hassif's face Ryu had already recanted last night's conversation on the observation deck. McCann informed them that they'd be starting the operation to attach the orbital ribbon today. Louis would observe from his station in Pavis Mons where the ribbon was attached to Martian soil, whilst Ryu and Hassif would work from the command centre.

Louis finally joined them taking his plastic tray from the dispenser. Despite the fact he was eating freshly baked croissants with real coffee he still managed to complain. It was obvious Louis was a little under the weather after last night's celebration which McCann believed was the true source of his grumbling that morning.

After breakfast they made their way to the command centre. Louis was sent off down the tunnel that stretched east into Pavis Mons. He walked into the gloom with a droid alongside him; the tunnel was much like any you'd find in a terrestrial mining operation. On the floor were two sets of rail tracks, for ferrying the crawlers and their cargo back and forth between Tharsis and ground zero at Pavis Mons.

Besides the tracks on each side of the tunnel there were paths running up and down the length laid with metal paving stones. The walls of the tunnel had been smoothed out; strips of UV lighting were placed intermittently along the ceiling and walls of the circular tunnel. It had been hewn out of the rock by a team of droids over several months. The tunnel had seen little actual use up until now. Louis had spent the last weeks running up and down it checking and rechecking the systems and structure in Athena's absence.

Now that Athena was installed life was a lot simpler. Despite Louis apprehensions concerning the SI he understood that they couldn't complete their mission without her. Whilst they'd all been sleeping off last night's libations she'd run months worth of systems and structural analysis. Louis wasn't ready to put all his trust in her just yet; however he was happy to see his backlog of monotonous work disappear overnight.

Louis had got the hang of bounding in the low gravity. The droid followed behind him pulling a cargo carriage along the rail tracks. Inside the carriage sat the coiled nanotube ribbon, Thanks to the low gravity and Mag Lev tracks it took little effort for the small droid to pull the long carriage.

The tunnel was not pressurized so Louis had his helmet unfurled and locked. His helmet lights were also on and he chatted with Athena. Eventually Louis reached the end of the tunnel where there stood a large bulkhead door. Athena opened it and the droid dragged the carriage into a large technical bay. The bay was constructed in the form of a dome cut out of the Martian volcano.

The whole bay was eerily dormant, at the centre sat a metal circle. Towards this Louis had the droid bring its carriage and stop just short of the metallic circle. Louis activated a nearby workstation and shortly several droids awoke from their long slumber. Moving in concert they removed the sides and roofing of the carriage to reveal the black perfectly coiled ribbon. The carriage was so long it stretched back out into the tunnel and there was a good 300 meters of coiled ribbon to be moved.

Louis updated McCann whilst he supervised the droids slowly shifting it from the carriage onto the large circle. Firstly they anchored the Martian end to the ring in the centre of the circle, and then the droids put the still coiled ribbon on top of that. The coiled Ribbon was held in place on the metal circle by a ring of droids; once the carriage had been moved out Louis informed McCann and waited for the order.

The circle was actually the top of a telescopic tower; Louis was waiting for Ryu to get the zeppelin ready and in place. Once he was given the go ahead Athena opened the roof of the dome. From the outside you could see a small opening appear in the side of the dormant volcano as the roof separated into two pieces and slid apart.

Looking up Louis could see a zeppelin fully inflated and hovering in anticipation. He ordered the pneumatic tower to extend raising the ribbon up a full kilo meter. Once fully extended the tower was now reaching outside the technical bay.

Louis informed Ryu and she began manoeuvring her zeppelin towards the coil. The zeppelin carried a large rocket drone. The drone was a delta wing with two large rockets aside a central fuselage. Inside the fuselage its fuel was carried and the other end of the ribbon would be attached to it. The drone was held on the zeppelin underbelly and as it descended to the coil the droids held the end loop with long crane arms. When close enough the loop was fixed onto a magnetic padlock, located at the underbelly, mid fuselage.

Once done both Athena then Louis confirmed everything was secure, Ryu slowly let the zeppelin rise into the atmosphere. The droids vigilantly watched the ribbon slowly uncoil, there could be no mistakes. As long as the ascent was clean the coil wouldn't knot or catch on anything.

There was only one ribbon on Mars and it would take months to get a replacement shipped to them. There were only a couple of labs on the Earth that could grow carbon nanotubes long enough and to the quality to make a Martian ribbon. Much of their production was focused on maintaining the Earth ribbon at the present time.

This was why Ryu was on this mission, she could fly drones better than anyone else alive including an SI. In atmosphere or space she outclassed all others. The ISA needed the best chance of attaching the ribbon first time. The Earth ribbon even with all the resources available only got attached after five attempts. Failures were due to the pilot missing the rendezvous point. Even under perfect conditions fuel was limited and the window of opportunity for docking with the Tsiolkovsky was so brief.

The best SI trained for the job needed a fifth attempt. The previous four failures resulted in missing the magnetic net on the Tsiolkovsky before being dragged back into the atmosphere. Resulting in the drone and ribbon burning up on an uncontrolled reentry.

The debate at Geneva had been very heated over who would pilot the ribbon drone; Faraday had backed Athena to do it. It would be another 5 years before the time to attach it would come so he welcomed anyone that felt they could do a better job. There was room for another person on the Athena; at that point it was going to be a medic. However if someone could be found to fly the ribbon drone significantly better than they had already trained Athena then Faraday would replace the medic.

Faraday felt he was merely humouring a foolishly romantic notion that a man could fly better than an SI. It wasn't costing him very much and when the results proved Athena the best pilot for the job they could concentrate on looking for a good medic. That was until during a monthly assessment meeting, one of his executive officers announced that a woman would be going to Mars. Doctor Pitt raised a smile and asked who it was; Faraday wasn't amused, 'Yes please tell us who it is Mr Kolobkov?'

Kolobklov stood up and walked around the table handing everyone a copy of the same folder, 'This is our new drone pilot, she's applied for the position and I'm confident she'll be selected.'

Faraday opened the folder to find a dossier on Major Ryu Yong.

'Very interesting Kolobkov, I know this is a pet project of yours but what makes you think this Major Yong can out fly the most advanced SI on the planet?'

Kolobkov a dark haired man in his 40's who'd served in the Russian air force, and still wore his uniform with pride, smirked at Faraday 'It's Major Ryu, Sir, Korean family name is first. In my country Major Ryu's reputation goes before her. However for your benefit I've put together this dossier on her. Take note of her military record gentlemen. It took a lot of effort to get her superiors to notice us, we should be grateful she's going to try out.'

Faraday was still unimpressed 'I'm afraid the Major's record, although impressive doesn't mean much to me. How do you think she can make herself indispensable to us? We need someone to fly a drone in an alien atmosphere then into space, I just don't see the connection Kolobkov.'

Kolobkov wasn't giving in 'I'm just asking you give her a fair try when she gets here, if she is that much better will you consider her?'

Faraday nodded 'If you're that confident then I'll have to won't I? Besides I'll consider anyone or anything that will make this mission go smoother. Half of this whole bloody endeavour is based on untested theories anyway. But if she doesn't make the grade Dimitri then she's out along with all the others you've sent me in the past.'

On the day of testing Faraday made an obligatory appearance though he expected Ryu to go the same way as all the other pilots that had fancied themselves. None had come close to out rating Athena. Ryu had been given a couple of weeks to get used to flying a rocket drone. Unknown to Faraday, Kolobkov had let her download the flight program so that she could spend some extra weeks practicing in Korea.

Ryu had to get used to going to zero G with a rocket powered drone carrying a heavy ribbon, then landing it in a small docking bay on the Edwards. Flying the Drone into space was tough enough without getting wrapped around the ribbon or pulled of course by it. Once in space she had to get the drone into close proximity of the docking bay where a magnetic net would catch it and drag it inside.

The time between leaving the atmosphere and finding the Edwards and getting on course was very short. However all telemetry was sent via the ribbon so there was no fear of delay or interference. Yet it was difficult for an SI to achieve, and Faraday didn't understand how this short Korean lady was going to pull it off. Certainly not to such a degree she'd become indispensable to him. He respect Kolobkov and for that reason he was here, but he put this girl's chances at somewhere between slim and none, and that was generous in his opinion.

Faraday watched as the little Korean in her late twenties walked in accompanied by Kolobkov. She wore her ROKAF flight suit and Kolobkov was sporting a wide smile. They were in the flight testing centre; a few other Russian personnel that worked in the tech department were loitering in the hope of meeting Ryu later. Doctor Pitt was also lurking much to Faradays discomfort, all the attention she was drawing unsettled him.

Major Ryu saluted Faraday who was taken aback somewhat 'There's no need to salute me young lady, a handshake will do,' he said offering his hand to her.

She shook hands and smiled, Faraday looked at the drone booth that Kolobkov had specially prepared for the demonstration 'Is this the booth Dimitri?'

Kolobkov pointed towards the booth 'Please make yourself comfortable Major; let us know when you're ready to begin.'

Ryu sat inside the booth and put on the visor, an advance in drone technology since she had begun flying. Now with a visor you could get a full panoramic view instead of relying on a main screen with several smaller ones. Ryu then inserted the ear pieces and gave Kolobkov the thumbs up. They ran two simulations side by side of a Martian ribbon attachment from lift off to landing in the Edwards magnetic net. Ryu was flying one drone whilst the Athena flew the other. Weather conditions were set at random and much to Faradays surprise Ryu landed the drone on the Edwards first time, but then again so did Athena. However to his recollection even the best SI he'd tested failed their first run.

Faraday looked at Kolobkov 'Run it again, keep on running it until one of them fails.'

Kolobkov said something into his mic and Ryu indicated she'd understood when a fist with a thumb sticking up poked out of her booth. Three hours and several cups of coffee later it was over, thirteen had proven unlucky for Athena. Ryu had out performed her each time but Faraday pushed further, he wasn't ready to accept Ryu over his SI that easily.

The next four hours were taken up with further simulated runs. The ribbon had been attached more times than he could count but only one statistic remained with Faraday and that was that Ryu had not failed once. Whereas Athena had failed 4 times to attach the ribbon, Faraday was forced to concede defeat. When Kolobkov announced another successful attachment and asked in a tired voice 'Again?'

Faraday replied in a low voice so that only Kolobkov could hear 'She's in,' finished his coffee and walked away.

By this time only Doctor Pitt was left watching, she followed Faraday out, caught him up and grabbed him by the arm 'I bet that hurt Will?'

Faraday held her arm and patted her hand 'Just a little bruised ego Valorie. Still that girl can fly better than our SI, I'm wondering what took so long to get her here?'

'Dimitri had spoken about her before; I think you just didn't listen. Once you've made a decision it can be difficult to change your opinion. Look at how many hours that poor girl had to spend flying perfect simulations?'

'Yes, you're right, but I had to be hard on her, a lot of people expect results and it's my responsibility to produce them. I'll have to inform our investors that I'm putting this girl in the pilot's seat. If she had failed once today they wouldn't have taken her over an SI no matter how many times Athena failed.'

Valorie said nothing but gave Faraday a consolation kiss on the cheek.

Now Ryu sat in the booth for real at the command centre on Tharsis. Athena controlled the ascent of the massive zeppelin through the Martian atmosphere. Once it had reached maximum height McCann informed Ryu she may begin when ready.

'Detaching in 3 ... 2 ... 1,' called Ryu as the drone detached from the zeppelin and began to nose dive 'engaging engines,' she called as the two rockets thumped into life.

The drone began to streak upwards through the orange atmosphere with a long black ribbon trailing it. Ryu was in her own world piloting the ribbon higher and higher whilst it uncoiled faster than the human eye could see back on the tower.

Ryu piloted the drone out of the atmosphere and into space where she got a lock on the Edwards. Ryu confidently manoeuvred her drone towards the open bay facing towards the planet.

It was a tense moment of silence that was broken by Athena 'Warning, Edwards is reporting a net failure. Repeat, Edwards is reporting net failure.'

McCann barked back 'Is the net operating Athena?'

'The net is not operational Colonel,' she replied matter of factly.

'Can the Edwards get it operating Athena? We need it operational now!'

Athena paused for a second then replied 'I'm sorry Colonel the Edwards is unable to reboot the magnetic net.'

Ryu called from her booth 'You've got ten seconds before I lose this entry window.'

McCann shouted past her earpiece 'You'll have to land it without the net Ryu, I'll close the doors.'

McCann jumped to his terminal and took control of the Edwards bay doors.

Ryu, against the odds, flew the drone into the bay without the help of a magnetic net to guide her in and hold the drone in place. As soon as McCann saw the drone was in he shut the airlock. He was certain the ribbon could take the stress of being jammed in the doors 'Okay the doors are shut Ryu,' he shouted.

Ryu shut down the rocket engines; the drone now lay crumpled in the corner of the bay. Droids came to life and the Edwards began the job of attaching the ribbon before something else went wrong.

Ryu leapt out of her booth with a crash and slapped the side of it 'Fuck me!' she screamed.

McCann had never seen Ryu this angry and he was shocked by her reaction. He'd expect it from Louis but Ryu had always been the most reserved of people.

'I'm starting to agree with Louis, that fucking net was operational 1 minute ago. This whole mission almost went down the fucking pan because these SIs just aren't cutting it when they should!'

McCann gave Ryu a few seconds to gather her composure then asked 'Are you finished?'

Ryu began to blush with embarrassment at her outburst which had left Hassif aghast 'Yes Sir, my apologies.'

McCann took a sigh of relief 'Good, now make sure that drone is shut down Ryu. I want it as secure as possible. Once the ribbon is attached we can give Geneva some grief, understood?'

'Yes Sir,' replied Ryu as she jumped back into her booth and started checking the drone over again. Fortunately the fuel tanks hadn't leaked and Ryu double checked that the drone was shut down and secure.

Within the hour the ribbon had been attached to the Edwards. Both ends were secure and McCann had opened the airlock doors on the Edwards. The ribbon was undamaged by the incident.

With one secure the other two ribbons would be attached by a crawler once they arrived. For now Tharsis could operate on one crawler, in about 4 months the other ribbons would be delivered.

After the ribbon was in place and they were all finishing up for the day, preparing to let Athena take over, Louis came charging into the command centre.

Once again McCann was subject to one of Louis outbursts, in the time it had taken Louis to walk back the magnetic net had rebooted. According to the Edwards there was a software error causing an immediate shutdown. McCann sent the report back in his data packet and by the next day Geneva assured them the problem had been resolved.

Louis wasn't at all satisfied.

Ryu was just angry at the thought the mission might have failed and she could've been deemed responsible for it.

Hassif was glad it wasn't him on the line ... yet, and McCann was thinking about what might be next to fail. Still he had the highest confidence in his team; they were the best people he could have with him. His confidence in the ability of SIs had taken a great hit since arriving on Mars. Synthetic Intelligences were no longer the infallible titans he once believed them to be.

The next day Louis was back at ground zero overseeing the crawler. Today's task was making certain the ribbon was safe to use and totally secure.

Hassif was set to go over the Edwards systems.

McCann had been told by Geneva the problem was fixed but he asked Hassif to check it all himself and report his findings on the net failure. Faraday had also sent a special request for Ryu. The request left McCann puzzled, but in the last data packet Faraday had been very insistent on Ryu getting the drones running.

McCann called Ryu into his office and asked her to sit 'Faraday wants you to get the Martian scram drones running ASAP,' he then passed her a sheet of paper.

'He was rather insistent about you surveying this area with a drone.'

Ryu looked at the map and the co-ordinates marked 'There's been a dust storm there since we landed; when the storm has subsided I'll do it.'

'No,' replied McCann 'he wants a full survey of that area as soon as you have the drones operational, dust storm or otherwise.'

Ryu was puzzled 'Why? This is a risk we need not take. There are only two scram drones on Tharsis right now, what's so urgent?'

McCann shrugged his shoulders 'I have no idea, it doesn't make sense on the surface but I'm sure we'll find out. Just try not to let Louis get wind of it until he finds out for himself, understood?'

Ryu nodded 'Understood' she took the paper and went to her station to prepare one of the scram drones.

Chapter 6

Ryu spent her morning in a tech bay situated on the northern wing of Tharsis checking out the Martian scram drones. They weren't strictly scram drones as flown on Earth but more of a hybrid, on Mars the scram jet has to carry its own oxygen. Although this increases the weight the advantage is that in the thin atmosphere the drone doesn't need to be ejected at such a high speed. Rather than relying on an external method to reach the required velocity for the scram engines to kick in such as a rocket or a magnetic catapult the scram drone is able to start moving under its own power at sub sonic speeds.

The drone Ryu was preparing for today's mission was sitting on the catapult tracks at a 45 degree angle pointing towards the ceiling. The fuselage which sat atop the delta wing was open. Large enough to fit one human in, but only laying down, a droid was filling the fuel tanks. Another droid had the engine casing open and was going over the scram engine which hung on the underside below the fuselage.

Ryu was tapping away at a work station, listening to weather updates from Athena, the dust storm was still there and Ryu was unsure she could pilot through it. No one had ever piloted one of these hybrid drones on Mars before, and her maiden flight was into the heart of a large dust storm.

The droids would take another hour before preparation was complete so Ryu decided to satisfy her curiosity.

'Athena do you have any visual records of this area before the dust storm?' she said selecting the area on her workstation map.

Athena was quiet for a moment then replied 'Yes Major Ryu.'

Ryu noticed a blinking file icon next to her map. She touched the icon to see Athena had prepared a folder full of photographs going back to the twentieth century.

'That's too many Athena, could you narrow it to the last six months please?'

'As you wish Major Ryu.'

Ryu looked through the flies and noticed the last one was taken moments before they crash landed. When she compared the photograph taken at the time of the crash to the eleven or so before, Ryu noticed a difference. The Korean became uneasy and quickly had the files transferred to her wrist tablet 'Thank you Athena, that'll be all.'

Ryu quickly left the technical bay and hit the communicator button on her tablet 'McCann where are you?'

'In my office, is something up?'

'Stay where you are, we're gonna have a chat,' said Ryu whilst doing the Martian bound down the northern wing.

Ryu walked through the command centre without speaking to Hassif who was too busy to notice anyway and went straight into McCann's office.

McCann was sat at his chair looking quite bemused 'You wanted me?'

Ryu looked behind her 'Are there any cameras in this office?'

'Yes there's security all over Tharsis, you know that,' replied McCann who was beginning to sound a little upset.

'Turn them off please.'

McCann looked upwards 'Athena, please disable the security network in my office.'

'Security network has been disabled Colonel,' replied Athena.

McCann looked at the station panel on his desk, once confirmed he looked at Ryu 'So what's all this cloak and dagger about Ryu, has Louis been reading you bedtime stories?'

Ryu uploaded the folder from her wrist tab to McCann's work station 'Look at that, the last picture is moments before we crashed, the others before.'

McCann gave a tired sigh and looked at his screen; he flicked through the pictures then looked up at Ryu 'What exactly is it I'm looking for Major?'

Ryu walked around to his side of the desk and pointed at the picture 'You see that?' McCann looked harder magnifying the area. From what McCann could make out it was a large rock, there were two things about this rock that left McCann feeling disturbed. Firstly it wasn't present in the other pictures. Secondly it wasn't a normal Martian rock; it was large, with very defined edges. The more McCann stared at it the more certain he became that it was a man-made object rather than a freak rock formation. It looked to be at least 10 meters long. Cut in an oblong fashion, it lay on its side and had a high point at around the first third, slowly declining along the next two thirds until it reached the end of the oblong. McCann's best description later was a long flat oblong stone obelisk with a pyramid sprouting up out of the first third.

McCann sat looking at it, he magnified it and cropped the image but found it hard to come to terms with the object. There wasn't anything he was aware of that could account for it and it wasn't there before they arrived. He could tell that the object had impacted on the surface recently but was certain it couldn't have come through the atmosphere as it would've burnt up as they nearly did. McCann sat wrestling with it in his head until Ryu became impatient 'What do you think Colonel?'

McCann was standing gazing at the image, 'I don't know and I bet neither does Geneva, it isn't ours and it can't be a natural formation. It appeared before we arrived or after?'

Ryu shook her head 'Neither, it appeared at the same time.'

McCann looked up again 'Athena, re-activate the security network please.'

Athena replied softly 'Security is once again operational.'

'Athena do you have any footage of our entry into the Martian atmosphere from either Tharsis or Edwards?'

After a few seconds a folder Icon appeared on his screen and he quickly touched it with his finger, opening the contents. Both McCann and Ryu observed the footage of the aero snatch manoeuvre that had been captured by the computers. Unfortunately they were not in visual range most of the time; however McCann noticed something that both computers picked up. There was a streak in the Martian atmosphere, something was moving towards the area they were set to explore today. Judging by the speed it must have been a meteorite and was no doubt the object that puzzled them.

What McCann didn't understand is why the object wasn't vapourised. At that speed and trajectory it should have created a large crater with an accompanying explosion that would not go un-noticed. It didn't make sense to McCann and he was guessing Faraday was just as curious.

'Thanks for making me aware of this Major, don't launch your drone yet I want to speak to Faraday first.'

Ryu walked out of the office and left McCann to it, from what Ryu could gather thanks to McCann's raised voice he wasn't pleased about being kept in the dark. According to McCann, Geneva was most curious as to the origin of whatever it was. Faraday didn't want to get the four of them too excited over what might be no more than a freak rock formation. They wanted to have some more information on it before it disappeared under the sands of Mars. At least Ryu could get a positive GPS fix so that they could have some droids dig it out later.

McCann decided to call a meeting before a drone was launched, it was mainly for Louis benefit. Louis was oddly silent and took it all in his stride; he was adamant that the rock was not a natural formation. According to the Frenchman it had been professionally cut with nanites as nothing else could get a surface that smooth. Hassif was certain it was made of nothing he was aware of, since the impact would destroy any substance that was man made. McCann reminded them they only had one image and couldn't be certain that object is what caused their crash landing. However it was the only theory anyone had and discoveries like this is why they were sent here.

The scram drone was prepared and Ryu sat in her booth with her visor on. McCann stood behind the booth watching a display screen hanging above it. Hassif and Louis were also there to see what was happening. This might be the most excitement they would get for the next year.

Ryu called out of her booth '5 ... 4 ... 3 ... 2 ... Go!' and the three of them watched the display screen as it showed a bird's eye view from the drones fuselage nose. The drone was fired out via magnetic catapult into the sky; there was the thump as the engine kicked in. The drone banked to the right and began moving North West, the destination was somewhere between Sulci Gordii and Olympus Mons.

The area was pretty much flat and prone to large dust storms, McCann didn't know if it would be possible to fly through the dust storm which had been there since they'd landed. However they were under orders and if anyone could do it he was confident Ryu could.

'Look there!' shouted Louis as the dust storm loomed on the display. McCann patted him on the shoulder and Ryu approached the storm slowly. She had to be careful as it was easy to break the speed of sound on Mars, due to the threshold being lower than 550 mph on most days, depending on atmospheric conditions.

Ryu flew around the storm feeling it out, finding the dimensions and trying to get an idea of the wind speed.

'Athena what are the weather conditions at the drone's location?' asked McCann. 'Temperature is 20 degrees Celsius and wind speed is 190 mph,' replied Athena in her calm voice.

'190 mph?' asked Hassif.

Louis, whom it seems had started talking to Hassif again after the fight on Tsiolkovsky, explained 'That's nothing, because of the atmosphere the pressure of a 200 mph wind is pretty small compared to Earth. Still I don't know if it's possible to fly one of those things through it.'

Hassif still looked puzzled 'Won't the dust clog the engine up?'

Again Louis explained to him 'No, the dust is about as fine as cigar smoke. I don't think that'll be a problem.'

Ryu kept circling the storm looking for something, after 30 minutes or so she saw a flash of light from within the storm. She banked in and decided to do a low pass 'Athena I'm passing through,' shouted Ryu as she entered the storm.

Flying by the instruments she held the drone steady as winds jostled it around trying to flip her drone over on its back and into oblivion. Two minutes later she was out of the storm and in one piece, Athena had pinpointed a partially covered object with the top poking out similar to a tee pee. Ryu saw it and went in for another pass; this time she hit Mach 1 trying to uncover the dust from the object.

On the third pass Athena got a clear picture and co-ordinates, then on the fourth pass there was a flash of light and the controls went dead. The display screen went blank and Ryu jumped out of the booth 'Athena, what was that?' she shouted as she took off her visor.

'Unknown Major Ryu.'

'Did you get the footage Athena?' asked Ryu as she placed the visor back in the booth.

'Yes Major Ryu.'

All three of them followed McCann to the desk in the middle of the command centre. McCann punched up the footage on his screen. After a short look it became apparent that the drone had caused a white light to emanate from this object which must have disabled the drone. Hassif pointed out how similar that was to the light that knocked the Athena off course although Athena couldn't confirm it.

'Athena can you tell me what that ... erm ... Gordii stone is made of?' asked McCann. 'Unknown,' replied Athena.

'Did it have any field emanating from it such as magnetic?'

'Unknown.'

McCann was getting rather annoyed now 'Did you get any results from the drone's instruments Athena?'

'No.'

It seemed that none of the analysis bore any fruit which left McCann rather frustrated.

'Hold on, Athena can you tell us what it isn't?' asked Hassif.

Athena paused for a few seconds and replied 'It is not a natural occurrence, it is not made of any substance I'm aware of, and it is not man-made.'

Hassif pressed their caretaker further 'Athena can you hypothesise as to what it is likely to be?'

Athena paused then replied 'There is insufficient data ...'

Hassif cut her off 'Yes I know, but just a guess with what you know right now Athena.'

A long pause followed for a good ten seconds then Athena replied 'A probe.'

Then Louis quickly interjected 'From who?'

'Unknown.'

'For what purpose?' pressed Louis.

'Unknown.'

McCann sat back in his seat 'Enough Louis, whatever that is out there it nearly turned us all into a pancake when we first arrived. I suggest we find out what happened to that drone before we stick our necks out any further, agreed?'

Louis put his hands up towards the ceiling in frustration, as if he were praying, and cursed in French.

'Louis we've got a year on this rock just calm down man,' growled McCann; 'Ryu I want you to get the other drone prepped for tomorrow. Hassif I want Athena ready for hooking up with the Edwards, good job so far. Louis are you still working on the ribbon?'

Louis nodded 'Yes, I should have a crawler ready to go after tomorrow.'

McCann felt the mission was all coming together now that Athena was running again 'That's good, I'll inform Faraday on what happened here today. Geneva will probably want the drone recovered before we look at having another try, any questions?'

There were no replies 'Good, get back to work and I'll see you in the lounge later, well done everyone.'

McCann walked to his office in order to send his report back with a data packet to Faraday, who was no doubt waiting with bated breath right now.

The next day everyone was up early and chatting over breakfast about the number one subject, which was the Gordii stone. Even the super human feat of attaching the ribbon first time despite the odds had become an almost distant memory now. Everyone was excited to hear what Geneva made of the information. Faraday must've been burning the midnight oil examining every bit of it. The discussion quickly went on to what the stone was and Louis was the first to give his theory an airing.

Louis was of the opinion that it was an alien device, and as Athena had already said, a probe. Louis of course believed that the I.S.A were aware of its existence and the whole mission to Mars, including the orbital lift, was for the express purpose of discovering more about this. He even extrapolated further into his belief that the stone may have been an ancient satellite they knocked out of orbit and there was in fact an entire civilization buried here somewhere. McCann quickly put a stop to Louis theories, before they became too embarrassing for him to listen to whilst keeping a straight face.

'Alright then,' mocked Louis 'what do you think it is? Do you have a more plausible theory?'

McCann didn't have a theory but since Louis was pushing him he had a shot at it. McCann was a very pragmatic and down to earth type. Years in the SBS had taught him how jumping to conclusions often ends in tears, whereas preparing for the worst always paid off or at least didn't cost you. McCann's theory was that it was junk from the building of the Edwards, perhaps a droid for tunneling. He guessed that since some of the old tunneling drones were nuclear powered and very tough. It could have fallen off the Edwards during construction into a slowly decaying orbit around Mars. He was of the opinion they dislodged it from low Martian orbit and that the drone was perhaps unstable. The discharge was probably and electrical build up due to the nuclear engines melting down. He reckoned they should be prepared for the eventuality of a nuclear explosion. McCann waited to get Louis' approval.

Louis sat back and sneered then said begrudgingly 'I suppose it's possible, Ryu what do you think?'

Ryu shrugged her shoulders 'I don't know,' she replied much to Louis' dissatisfaction. He wasn't going to give up until he heard her theory. Ryu guessed that perhaps it was a piece of rock cut out of the Edwards that got caught in their aero snatch and dragged into the atmosphere. Ryu believed it was probably just a slab of inert rock cut into a strange shape by chance. It survived the entry by riding in behind the Athena and that probably disrupted her stabilization manoeuvres. This theory was immediately dismissed by Louis for many reasons. He was quick to point out that any rock would've broken up and disintegrated into much smaller pieces. Also the impact would've destroyed it and there was no way it would survive in such good condition. Ryu didn't seem to care much though. She was more interested in facts than making up theories.

Lastly Louis asked what Hassif thought.

'Athena said it might be a probe, I think it could be Mars climate Orbitor.'

There was a heavy silence.

'What's that?' asked Louis.

'Well it was a probe sent out by NASA in the late twentieth century; it went missing on an attempted orbital insertion.'

'What went wrong?' asked McCann.

'Well I know it's hard to believe but an engineering team from Lockheed Martin were using imperial units of measurement whilst the rest of NASA were using metric. Well the engineers received some values for the navigation thrusters and didn't convert from metric to imperial.'

Louis burst out laughing 'You have to be joking?'

Hassif shook his head 'No, the orbitor ended up inserting too close to the atmosphere and they lost contact with it. I know it's hard to believe today, but a simple mistake like that cost decades of work.'

The foursome laughed together.

'Well maybe the Mars orbitor did make orbit, but just a very low one? Then we came along and on impacting or disturbing it we caused an explosion?'

They all stopped laughing; Hassifs' theory did have merit and explained a lot of things.

Ryu asked 'How big was the orbitor?' it seemed Ryu had found the hole in his theory.

'Not big enough to be the stone out there. However it has had been in a low orbit for over a century, it had large solar panels and could have accumulated junk such as rock and scrap from say the Edwards construction. Honestly we haven't really seen a proper image of this thing yet. It might be just a collection of junk fused by the aero snatch and who knows how much could be Martian rock or sand it picked up on impact? Well that's my theory anyway; the explosion probably came from the hydrazine fuel it carried.'

They all considered Hassifs' theory as it definitely had more merit than the alien civilization theory Louis offered and was more exciting than Ryu's lump of rock theory.

McCann still had one problem 'How could they have screwed up like that? I mean getting the values wrong like that? It sounds so implausible to me.'

Hassif replied 'I did a paper about it for a class on twentieth century coding. It had to be an essay concerning a big coding mistake. Whilst nearly everyone went with the Y2K bug I found this. It was a program called "Small Forces" that was used to make trajectory models. Well the person that coded it told the program to operate on imperial units. So instead of the program outputting its result in Newton seconds, which is what the rest of the equation required since it was all metric. It produced a value in pounds seconds, it caused the trajectory for the orbit to be too shallow and a lot of people were left with red faces. The probe disappeared never to be seen again. The theory was that it either burnt up or overshot Mars and entered orbit around the Sun. No one ever bothered looking for it, but I think it could've entered a low orbit until we knocked it out.'

It sounded plausible to McCann and even Louis was forced to agree it was a better possibility than the others. Although this didn't prevent him from holding onto his alien theory with a bit of government conspiracy thrown in. Ryu agreed with Hassif, it was by far the more likely theory and the only one that could account logically for everything without the need of conspiracies and extraterrestrials.

As they discussed the merits of Hassif's idea further Athena interrupted them 'Colonel McCann, a data packet has just arrived from Geneva.'

The discussion ended 'Are there any messages from Director Faraday to me?' asked McCann.

'Yes Colonel, there is one message to you from Director Faraday.'

'Play it Athena.'

'Colonel, this is a private message.'

'I understand Athena, just play it.'

The large screen in the officers mess that hadn't been turned on yet due to today's discussion of the Gordii stone flickered into life. Faraday was sat at his desk, he began to speak 'Good Morning Duncan, I hope you and your team are all feeling well. We've spent the entire evening going over the information Major Ryu collected. We still haven't come to any conclusions yet. You're going to have to salvage the downed drone and download its data recorder. It has been decided not to launch the second drone until the other is recovered and repaired. Excellent work on attaching the ribbon by the way, everyone has been celebrating the occasion. I'm sorry for not informing you of everything we know but there are just so many maybes and unknowns. We deemed it counterproductive to tell you everything we have since it amounts to little more than a few theories and almost no facts. It's not that I don't think you can handle it Duncan, it's that we just didn't think you needed to, what with all the mishaps you've run into so far.'

Faraday stopped to breathe then after a pause he began again 'I'm going to have to give you an order Duncan that may cause some alarm, it is strictly protocol however and I don't want you to read too much into it. I know you won't, but just make sure that bloody fool Beaumont doesn't fly off the handle.'

Everyone in the lounge was now sitting on the large sofa watching the message; they had put their breakfasts down. All turned to look at Louis who was rather upset by Faraday's comment.

Faraday continued and they all turned back to the screen 'I want you to open the weapons locker and issue yourself and Major Ryu with a pulse pistol each. I know what you're thinking but this is not a reflection on you or anyone on your team, even that idiot Beaumont! It's just standard protocol when having encountered an object of unknown origin that may display signs of intelligence. It's probably an old Satellite or junk from the twenty first century, but I've been compelled to take every precaution.'

Faraday paused and seemed to be over the most uncomfortable part of the message. He began again 'I'll be looking forward to your next data packet Duncan; you can take your time in the drone recovery. The ribbon is still the priority right now, tell Beaumont he's doing a good job and to keep it up. As far as we can tell Athena has made a full recovery, good luck Duncan, message end.'

It was quiet for a while until Louis let out a curse in French.

McCann turned to Ryu and said cautiously 'When you've finished your breakfast I want you to report to my office Major.'

McCann stood up, picked up his breakfast tray and disposed of it in the automated trash 'Well done to all of you.'

McCann then left for his office, once inside he looked upwards and spoke 'Athena, open the weapons locker please.'

An orifice slid open on the rear wall directly behind his desk, a small hole at eye level. McCann approached it and peered inside. A laser scanned his retina and the orifice closed. McCann took a step back and watched a panel swing open. Inside was a standard weapons locker containing several rifles and pistols with body armour. McCann reached in and took from the top shelf two pulse pistols in their shoulder holsters with power and ammunition clips. He put the weapons on his desk then looking upwards again he said 'Athena, please close the weapons locker.'

The door swung shut again to form a seamless wall 'Thank you Athena.'

To which Athena replied calmly 'You're welcome Colonel.'

McCann raised an eyebrow, it seemed Athena was getting back to her old self; he then turned to look down at the firearms on his desk. McCann pulled one of the pistols out of the holster and put the shoulder holster on. Once it was clipped on he took one of the three power packs the holster held.

The pulse pistol was a rail pistol, it had a barrel with two rails running along each side of it. This firearm used and electromagnetic pulse to create a circuit between the two rails and the ammunition in the barrel. This circuit then pushed the ammunition along the barrel at very high speeds. Expelling the projectile at much higher velocities than the old style chemical based firearms did.

The barrel was longer and thinner than past chemical based firearms, it looked as if there were three barrels but only the middle one was open, the other two were in fact the rails that the current ran along.

Where the ammunition clip was inserted on old automatic pistols was where McCann slapped in the power pack.

It looked similar to an old ammo clip but was actually a Xenon battery cell. When Xenon difluoride was compressed under one million atmospheres it converted the mechanical energy of that pressure into electrical energy; energy which would be used in the pulse pistol. The more energy taken from the battery the lower the pressure becomes until the battery has to eventually be re-pressurized.

McCann slapped in the Xenon battery and looked at the bottom to see a green light flashing, the battery was fully charged and working. Next he picked out an ammo clip, a thin clip that slid in next to the power pack, filling the small gap in the pistols grip, loaded with fifty very small tungsten projectiles. He slapped in the ammo clip and it locked into place, McCann then turned off his pistol and placed it in his holster, only he and Ryu had permission to use firearms and only when instructed to do so.

Despite what Faraday had said McCann suspected there was something more than a mere recovery of a lost probe. He was aware of situations that warranted such precautions, and McCann believed that Faraday wasn't as confident in all four of them as he claimed in the data packet. He firmly believed that Geneva were worried about someone on the team, he didn't know who it was though. If only he had been armed then he'd know it wasn't him. However since Ryu had been given a weapon it made him wonder, was Ryu there to assist him or watch him?

McCann decide it was a waste of time to start second guessing Faraday, he was going to keep an eye open but carry on as planned. Ryu walked into his office, she reported in and signed with her thumb print for the holster, pistol, power packs and ammo clips. She checked the weapon in front of McCann then charged and loaded it. Ryu put the safety on and placed it back in the holster she was now wearing.

Ryu then asked McCann 'Why do you think they've given us these, Duncan?'

He shook his head 'Its procedure Major, we won't need to use them.'

He then looked Ryu in the eye 'But I promise not to go nuts if you promise not to terminate me!' then winked at her.

Ryu smiled 'Understood Sir, now I was going to look for the scram drone today and maybe send a hauler out for it. Or is there something more urgent?'

McCann shook his head 'No, you're dismissed and good luck finding the drone.'

It took a week of searching to find the drone, the GPS gave a location but it seemed the drone had broken up and been buried by sand. Ryu started working on collecting the pieces with a hauler. From what she'd told McCann it was going to take a while before the entire drone was salvaged. Louis was behaving as a typical engineer, scratching his head and giving not too hopeful estimates on repair times, that was if it could be repaired. It all depended on what the drone looked like once the salvage operation was over.

McCann took the opportunity to relax, he'd been on tender hooks since the crash. He felt that until now they'd been lurching from one crisis to the next, it was only now that they finally had some time to take a rest. McCann had taken to smoking his cigars in his office although he would only drink coffee with them whilst on duty.

He also began chatting with Athena again; she was running Tharsis at 100% efficiency according to Hassif. Athena had fixed it so that his cigar smoke didn't set off any alarms on the base. From what McCann could gather Athena felt rather responsible for the crash. It seemed she was trying hard to make it up to him by allowing him to practice his vice whilst on duty.

Hassif had commented that he looked like Fidel Castro in a space suit; what with his cigar, pulse pistol and not having shaved in the last two weeks. McCann laughed at his jest. He'd taken to using the spare ammo clip pocket on his holster to carry his cigar case gifted by Titov. It did give a rather flamboyant impression, but he didn't care. After all who was he trying to impress?

Hassif had smoothed everything out with Athena by now and all the Tharsis systems were running properly. Louis was still spending most of his day at the launch pad inside Pavis Mons, where he kept an eye on the crawler as it made its first visit to the Edwards.

Faraday had already confirmed the launch of the other carbon ribbons. They'd be sent on a small supply vessel along with a crew that would dock with the Edwards within a few months. Louis would have his crawler docked before then and ready to start the attachment of the other three ribbons.

McCann was feeling relaxed, the Gordii stone was a minor mystery that would no doubt unfold all in good time. Right now they could carry on with the job they were sent here to do with hopefully all their mishaps behind them.

McCann looked up 'Athena do you have any music stored in your memory?'

Athena replied in her subdued tone 'Certainly Duncan,' they were back on first name basis for the first time since the crash 'what would you like?'

Hassif raised an eyebrow and peered at McCann. McCann wasn't sure if his odd look was about his request or Athena's familiarity with him. McCann kept looking upwards as was his habit when speaking to Athena, a habit the others didn't share.

'Do you have anything by the artist Gary Numan?'

A few seconds later came the reply 'Yes Duncan I have his full catalogue.'

McCann began to pace slowly whilst he smiled 'Please show me at this station Athena,' he approached the nearest work station and touched the screen activating it.

Hassif sighed 'You're not playing that music are you?'

McCann stood selecting a play list from the screen and muttered 'You know I can't use my ear piece for personal recreation. You can have a turn when my play list is done, is it a deal?'

Hassif nodded his head and turned back to his work 'Deal.'

McCann then turned from his station and looked up 'You can play my list now Athena, thank you.'

Ryu entered the command centre to the sound of some pop synth that she recognised from Geneva. McCann was swaggering around to the music and the almost bland mono tonal sound of the singer's voice. He was smoking one of his cigars as he sauntered to one end of the room. He then spun around nearly losing control in the low Martian gravity. The Englishman stumbled to the middle of the room and grabbed the table steadying himself. Ryu shook her head in her matronly manner, McCann righted himself obviously embarrassed.

McCann looked up 'Pause music Athena,' the music paused much to Hassif's relief.

'Hard day at the office Colonel?' said Ryu sarcastically.

McCann straightened his holster and dusted himself down despite the fact Tharsis was a dust free environment.

'Yes Major is there something you need?' he replied sternly.

'Nearly all of the drone has been recovered. However the black box hasn't and the droids can't dig it out. I'm requesting permission to go out there and oversee its extraction … Sir.' Ryu was asking to go out there. She wanted to cement her position as the first to set foot on Mars and not just the floor of a garage on Tharsis, but on virgin earth.

McCann understood her motivations and folded his arms in a defensive posture 'Forget it Ryu, we've only just managed to get this place running properly. I'm not prepared to risk you going out there, if you have the GPS why can't a droid do it?'

Ryu shook her head 'The box is lodged deep between two ridges of rock, one mistake by the droid and that data recorder is toast. It's up to you, I just wanted to let you know the risks first.'

McCann could see she was dead set on it, he just didn't feel like taking the risk of having her away from Tharsis for so long. McCann knew however that Faraday wanted that data recorder. He decided to pass the buck 'I'll tell you what I'll ask Faraday, do you have a schedule I could send him?'

Ryu's face lit up like the excited girl going to her first gamming tournament all those years ago 'Yes!' she chirped.

Ryu pulled out her tablet and hit a button transmitting the plan to McCann's. McCann pulled out his tablet and smiled 'Thank you; I'll attach this to the next data packet. With any luck there'll be an answer tomorrow.'

Ryu thanked McCann and made off back to the drone bay probably to prepare for her journey and to get out before McCann could think of a reason to change his mind.

After Ryu had gone, Hassif spoke to McCann whilst still looking at his monitor 'She pulled a real fast one there Duncan, now if that had been me or Louis.'

McCann cut him off and in a low tone 'Give her a break Hassif, the woman has pulled off two minor miracles since we got to this bloody planet. It's the least I can do. Besides it's up to Faraday and it's not like we can't hold things down for a few days without her, is it?'

Hassif agreed and decided to stretch his legs, 'Athena?'

She softly replied 'Yes Hassif?'

'I've sent you my playlists could you please play Bhangra 1?'

'Certainly Hassif.'

McCann groaned inside and with a fed up look said 'I'll just be in my office going over Ryu's schedule, let me know if you need me Hassif.'

It's not that McCann disliked Hassif's taste in music he quite liked it initially. However he'd discovered that after a short time the Punjabi Bhangra, as Hassif described it, began to grate on his nerves. It was by far the best course to make a discrete withdrawal to his office. Since the high pitched female voice of the Bhangra singer or singers (he couldn't tell the difference) was enough to cause great white sharks to commit suicide in his opinion. Although he was far more forgiving towards Hassif than Ryu. He'd once described her favourite music as "reminiscent of a pet shop on fire".

McCann like Louis was very dismissive of others tastes if he didn't agree with them, often it resulted in him offending those people when he opened his mouth. Ryu had kept quiet and never commented on what she thought of his tastes. McCann was her superior and getting on his bad side wasn't a good idea.

Although McCann wasn't attempting to insult anyone he often found that he did. So whenever the subject of cigars, whisky or music arose and he might have to volunteer an opinion his crewmates had learnt to get out of dodge.

In the services it had been fine since most of his friends had similar tastes in all those things, maybe not the music but certainly everything else.

In his defence if you were going to be flying into war zones whilst being shot at, you had to be confident to the point of arrogance otherwise you'd be dead or discharged from the SBS. No one is going to fly with a nervous pilot. McCann however possessed far more tact than Louis.

Cigars however were a very touchy subject; he viewed all non Habanos cigars with disdain and would not be prevented from voicing that opinion. According to him it was not an opinion but a matter of fact that all non-Cuban cigars were inferior.

That evening they were all in lounge McCann was having a smoke whilst reading his newspaper; Ryu was watching one of her soap operas. Louis had just come in after the long walk from ground zero; he had taken the gloves off his suit and stuffed them in a side pocket.

When working outside of the main base everyone was required to have the full suit on for safety reasons. Louis sat down to chat with McCann since he couldn't watch his film tonight when Hassif shouted out 'Turn on the news!'

Ryu looked over rather annoyed at Hassif 'What for?'

Hassif didn't reply he just urged her to turn it on quickly so she reluctantly complied. The channel went over to network America which was acting as the global news channel for the mission. They had negotiated full access to all the security cameras on Tharsis. Geneva would censor anything they felt carried sensitive information but otherwise network America was big brother.

It hadn't been cheap to purchase the rights to Tharsis video feed and the network executives expected to make their money back with a juicy profit. McCann wasn't interested and sat reading his paper with a smouldering cigar in one hand. Until he heard Louis break out in laughter then Hassif began laughing and finally Ryu started to giggle. McCann put his paper down and peered over it, he then dropped the paper in his lap. Shocked he saw video footage of himself swaggering up and down in the command centre, Ryu entered and he stumbled to the table.

Louis was in fits of laughter but McCann ignored him, he relaxed back into the sofa and mumbled under his breath 'Jesus Christ!'

Next Jerry came on the screen; he was sitting behind his desk with a sly grin.

'Well!' he exclaimed in a comical tone 'I guess after 5 years of training with the I.S.A he skipped dancing in low G 101?' to roars of laughter from his panel of guests.

The footage of the fall was minimized and playing over and over in the corner of the screen as Jerry turned to face his guests. 'Dr. Ito what do you think of our cosmonaut doing the cha cha cha?'

The Japanese scientist next to him was smiling 'What you have here is the effects of busting a move in 30% gravity, not a pretty sight I think you'll agree Jerry!'

The discussion continued along the same lines until McCann grabbed the controls and turned it off. It would be all over the news everywhere, he felt angry that Faraday had let this happen.

McCann marched out to his office cigar in hand presumably to send a message to Faraday. The amount of footage that came through didn't leave much time to check it all. Faraday had struck a deal where network America agreed to self-censor any footage it deemed as sensitive to the security of the mission. Unfortunately McCann making an arse of himself wasn't considered as sensitive to the security of the mission. Network America executives had decided to transmit it.

The article boosted ratings to the highest since Ryu had first stepped off the Athena and onto Tharsis. Not beating it by any stretch but it delivered the ratings as expected.

McCann was furious, as was Faraday but he explained there was nothing the I.S.A could do about it. Network America had honoured their contract, returning all sensitive footage that had made it through and they had to honour theirs. Faraday advised that if McCann wanted to go on smoking his cigars without an inquiry, he'd just have to grin and bare it. McCann was still furious with the feeling of being powerless; the press taking low blows at him back home made him frustrated more than anything else.

He was used to taking on his enemies and saw this type of attack as cheap cowardice. McCann was certain he'd get his revenge somehow but decided to put it out of his mind for now.

The Englishman returned to the lounge about 40 minutes after his chat with Faraday, the news was back on. His comrades were still giggling over Jerry Habeeb's jibes. McCann looked at them sitting on the sofa in disgust. Removing a cigar from his holsters spare ammo clip pocket he stated 'I'll be in the observation room,' and disappeared up the steps. It all went rather quiet in the lounge and Ryu decided to join him.

McCann was sitting on the floor lighting his cigar with the torch, she walked over and sat down next to him.

'I'm sorry Duncan,' she said softly.

'Don't be sorry Ryu, it's not your fault,' replied McCann staring out at the Martian dusk.

'No I'm sorry for laughing.'

'Never mind, these things happen, it must have been a slow news day back on Earth. Besides things must be going smoothly if the worst thing they can transmit is me stumbling in the command centre?'

Ryu smiled and Louis' head popped up 'Hey anyone want a drink?' he said holding up a bottle of Balvenie and four glasses.

McCann nodded his head motioning for Louis to come up. He was followed by Hassif and soon they were all having a dram and joking about his appearance on television.

McCann soon recovered from that incident however his comrades noted his appetite for trash TV declined drastically afterwards.

Ryu turned the conversation towards salvaging the data recorder. McCann recalled that he'd been instructed to send her out and that Hassif would be going with her. They were to prepare tomorrow and then leave the following day.

Ryu didn't know how long it would take but she was certain the round trip could be done inside a week if the hauler was going at full speed.

McCann was uncomfortable that two of his crew would be absent from Tharsis for such an extended period despite the fact everything was under control. Louis agreed to put the drone back together in his spare time while she was away. The drone was a very robust piece of equipment and most of it was undamaged. It was designed to break up into pieces on impact, which were quite simple to put back together, after any broken internals were repaired. The part containing the data recorder however was lodged in a small ridge and Ryu would be on site to oversee its extraction. McCann guessed Hassif was there as a precaution in case she required help. He'd have to spend the next week with Louis who would thankfully be working at Pavis Mons most of the day.

The following day Ryu was first out of bed as usual. She rushed her breakfast; by the time McCann was exiting his quarters and making his way to eat she was working on setting up the hauler. Real fruit with muesli was welcomed, not something they had every day, at least once a week Athena had cooked them up some fresh food. He opened the sliding panel and picked his meal up from the dispenser, a 22nd century dumb waiter, then sat with Hassif and Louis.

Louis was enquiring when McCann intended to shave his beard, McCann wasn't forth coming. No press conference was looming and he wasn't going out on a date or to an important meeting so he saw no reason to shave it. Louis told him that he would look like Borneo man in a week or so if he didn't get rid of it. Hassif laughed but McCann didn't care. He rather liked his beard and enjoyed having one. He couldn't understand why any man would want to shave everyday as he found it a boring and laborious task that was at this time unnecessary.

McCann questioned Louis about the crawler; it was going well according to him and would soon be at the Edwards waiting for the other ribbons. Mars was such a better environment for an orbital lift, what with lower gravity, shorter travel distance and a thinner atmosphere. Compared to Earth the final part of setting up the lift would be a piece of cake, especially when the skeleton crew for the Edwards arrived in a few months.

After eating his breakfast McCann stood up and pulled a cigar from his holster pocket. Guillotined the end and lit it with the torch, which he now carried in a leg pocket he'd strapped onto his suit.

The others had noticed he was smoking far more than before. They had never known him to smoke this much but his comrades refrained from mentioning it. McCann and Hassif made for the command centre and Louis made his way to Pavis Mons. Hassif spent his day checking over Athena before leaving tomorrow. Louis was off to check the crawler before assisting Ryu in attaching a small habitat compartment to the hauler.

The habitat compartment was much like a lorry cab, it had a sleeping area, an area to bathe and finally one to do everything else from eat to drive. Not that either Hassif or Ryu would be driving the vehicle since the journey was pre plotted; added to that the hauler AI could negotiate any unforeseen objects or conditions.

Once Louis was satisfied that the crawler was on schedule and working properly he joined Ryu and had the droids attach the habitat on top of the hauler.

The telescopic tower had been retracted now and was somewhere below the floor of the cave Louis was working in. From where Louis stood the ribbon was coming out of a deep hole attached to the retracted metal disk below. It ran straight up and out of the upper opening that had been bored out of Pavis Mons. Open to the elements of Mars he had to do his work in a fully sealed suit.

Much of the monitoring was through the nanites in the ribbon. They constantly checked it for any weakness and repaired any stress fractures or micro impact craters, before they could grow into something that might threaten the orbital lift integrity. Louis had it drilled into his head over and over whilst in Geneva about what would happen if a ribbon that stored that much energy were to snap. His nanites kept any chance of that at bay, they were inside everything on Tharsis including him and his crewmates.

Back home it had been declared the Nano age and with good reason. Being an engineer or technician nowadays meant you used nanites because nearly everything had nanites inside. Louis was a specialist with nanites meaning he could not only utilize them but he was an expert at reprogramming and maintaining the electronic creatures. Faraday had pointed out on many occasions that nanites were the only thing he could get on with, McCann agreed.

At the same time he monitored the ribbon Louis was also ordering an army of nanites to refit the stations redundant fuel cells according to the specifications he'd been given on the Tsiolkovsky.

They were converting them to run on urine just in case something went wrong, and Louis was expecting the worst. The mission had gone pretty bad so far and he felt that Faraday was responsible. Faraday had always been pushing the next generation SI as some kind of super being that should take over whenever possible. Louis was not so enthusiastic about them; he'd worked for a company that brought him in after their SI had collapsed.

Louis had been hired whilst working a separate job in Russia, an SI had a catastrophic failure, and the human technical staff was all unaccounted for. The SI had closed them in and no one could communicate since everything was reliant on the so called super being. As Louis worked through the day he kept running over in his mind the nightmare that the SI had created...

Louis had been flown from Moscow airport to the far eastern reaches, a place called Kupol the Russian word for dome. The town got the name due to massive formations of rock in the area. It was a former gulag where the Soviet Union had employed forced labour to dig gold in artic conditions. Now it was a fully modernised plant with its own airport run by teams of techs, engineers and a first generation SI. Russia was the world's richest nation thanks to its abundant resources, gold being one of them. In the past she had failed to take full advantage of them. Today she was producing gold faster than any nation on the planet, but production had stopped in Kupol two days ago.

Communication had gone down and there was no response to any attempts to re-establish it with the SI. Staff weren't answering their tablets or emails; it seemed all wireless communication had been intentionally severed. Somehow a wireless dead zone had been erected at Kupol.

A rescue team had been sent in to investigate but none returned and now the military had taken charge. Louis Beaumont at the time was working for a small medical manufacturer in Moscow. The company was developing phage therapy drugs. Without any consultation what looked like a Russian S.W.A.T team turned up at his workplace and took him away. The executives of the phage company were told he'd be returned when Moscow was finished with him. The next thing Louis knew he was on a supersonic military transport doing Mach 3 and heading for the Siberian wastes.

Louis was scared out of his mind and his confrontational attitude was put on hold. These Russian guys didn't look in the mood to take his mouth. In fact he was certain they were quite capable of throwing him out of the transport if he caused them any grief.

They all sat around him dressed in black combat fatigues and carrying pulse assault rifles. Combat jackets and helmets were all black; they spoke back and forth to each other through their communicator bugs, implanted in the standard Russian military combat shirt. Not one of them below six feet. Even the man that looked at least fifty could have torn apart a man half his age with his bare hands, in Louis opinion.

He did his best to say nothing and not make eye contact with anyone else in the transport. Besides he couldn't speak Russian and didn't want to test their patience with his French, English or broken Italian.

After about thirty minutes in the air, at the opposite end of the room Louis was being held in, a door opened. A man who could have been in his 30's, 40's or 50's, Louis wasn't sure, walked in. He was dressed in combat boots, fatigues a shirt and cap. On one of his shirt arms there was a badge. The man stepped inside the room and in a second every soldier stood to attention.

Louis craned his neck to try and identify the badge. He could make out a fist clutching what looked like an old automatic rifle. Set on the background of a red star with a red beret above it. Louis had no idea what the Russian script around it meant but he'd seen the insignia before. He recognised it as the insignia of Spetsnaz which in Russian literally means a force of special purpose. The man that had walked in was obviously of high rank since everyone stood to attention but Louis had no idea of military ranks or how they worked. The man whilst talking with his soldiers turned to catch Louis peering at his badge. Louis was taken aback by his cold piercing green eyes, even the man's smile seemed like an evil declaration of his intentions toward Louis.

He broke out in a sweat and slumped back in his seat, Louis was terrified. He'd spent his off time in Moscow in his hotel watching documentaries. Louis remembered a one hour show devoted to the Manchurian conflict and Spetsnaz. He recalled how Spetsnaz had engaged the Manchurian forces at Vladivostok. Some unit that sounded like vampire had harassed Jiang's forces escaping from the massacre. Apparently the Manchurian invaders that survived after the Korean air strike and escaped the following Russian ground assault, retreated to the nearest well defended Manchurian HQ, about 300 men and women in armoured vehicles. Jiang's best that had persevered through luck and many years of combat experience were retreating to safety. Probably making the nearest HQ before dawn broke the next day.

According to the documentary the Korean air force were ordered out of the area. The Russian air force and army were still in disarray trying to clear up Vladivostok. Their hands were full executing the remnants of Jiang's army and treating their own citizens who had been under siege for over a week. This vamp had been tasked with finding and slowing down the Manchurian retreat, 20 men versus 300 or so they claimed.

Dawn broke the next day to reveal the Manchurian retreat had been stopped sometime during the night. Amongst the burnt out APCs and tanks were 300 dead and not one Spetsnaz to be found. By the end of the documentary, Louis being the sceptic he is, wasn't sure if it was all true or not. Allegedly this vamp had caused a lot of mayhem during their time in Manchuria. Even if only half were true it was pretty chilling that he had been dragged away by them, and was sitting on a transport to who knows where!

The commander finished talking to the older soldier and as his men sat back down, he then walked over to Louis smiling. Louis could tell now he was in his mid 40's with thin blonde hair shaved to within a quarter of an inch. Louis stayed in his seat too afraid to do anything or speak to him.

'Zdrahstvooy Mr. Beaumont, My name is Major Nestor Andreev,' he stated offering his hand.

Louis shook his hand timidly and the Major sat down opposite him 'I apologise for having taken you in this way but we have a crisis and your skills are required Mr. Beaumont. Something has gone wrong at a mining plant in Kupol. We don't know what, only that all communications are severed. We have been sent to deal with the problem and it was decided that your presence will be required Mr. Beaumont. You'll be paid for your time of course however there wasn't time to negotiate a fee. Do you have any questions you'd like to ask me?' the Major stated in English with a heavy Russian accent all very matter of factly as he passed Louis some documents.

Louis thought for a moment then asked sheepishly 'What is the job exactly? I'll need to prepare.'

The Major smiled 'Those papers have the technical specifications of the plant including the SI. It could be terrorism or a technical fault with the computers or maybe some chemicals escaped … we don't know as of yet Mr. Beaumont. You may not be needed at all. However if you are required I was told you'd worked with similar plants in the past.'

Louis flicked through the documents and began to relax, he was feeling much better now that he realised he wasn't in mortal danger.

After glancing over the plants specifications he felt confident he could be of some use if needed.

'Yes I've worked on much the same type of plant before, it can't be a chemical leak caused even by an explosion. The only way to knock out all communication is if it were done purposely. To do that before an alarm were sent you'd have to cut off the SI first. You'd either need a team of people that were trained to do it or the SI has a bug. Otherwise it's not possible for this to happen by way of a fluke accident.'

The Major smiled and nodded 'That's our assumption, hence your presence Mr. Beaumont. You won't be required to endanger yourself. But we think we'll need you to disable the SI and any dangerous chemicals or machinery it has access to. As you know there is cyanide and hydrochloric acid present. There are large quantities amongst other chemicals which we hope you will be able to secure.'

Major Andreev took out a packet of Russian cigarettes, lit one up for himself then offered one to Louis 'Smoke?'

Louis made a gesture with his hand refusing. The smell of the burning cigarette was overpowering and made him choke a little, much to the pleasure of the Major. Major Andreev grinned then called over his shoulder saying something in Russian. One of the armed soldiers brought over a can of Russian spring water and thrust it into Louis hands.

Louis looked at him and said timidly 'Spasiba.'

The soldier grinned and tipped his head towards Louis in acknowledgment then walked back to his seat.

During the flight Louis had chatted with the Major and found out his unit was a Vympel unit. He mentioned the documentary but Nestor said nothing on the subject and advised Louis to just concentrate on the job in hand. Louis was certain that Nestor had been involved in Manchuria but he wasn't going to question him any further, there was no point in antagonizing this guy. He may have been an authority figure which Louis loved to poke with a stick in his spare time, but this man had obviously earnt his position. He wasn't just some man from the town council with a clipboard. Or some company boss who thinks he knows how to run the show when in fact his employees do it despite him. Nestor wasn't a clown with a clipboard so Louis kept quiet and studied his papers. Every now and then he'd take a break to watch the dead sun rising in the distance over Kupol.

Upon landing at the airport several of Nestor's men charged out to secure the area, once it was deemed safe Louis walked out behind Nestor. The temperatures were subzero but the sky was sharp and clear with a slight breeze. Louis expected higher winds considering that the landing pad sat on the roof of the plant however it was a decidedly calm day, on the outside at least.

Nestor was now in full battle dress but he carried only his pulse pistol in a holster, he was communicating with his team through the shirt mic. Louis couldn't understand what was being said but a soldier nearest the plant entrance let go of his weapon and pulled out a tablet. Louis guessed they were bypassing the security to get through the door, looking around Louis could see another transport on the landing pad. It seemed to have been abandoned as the doors to the craft were open and inside the cockpit ice had formed. Louis assumed these were the people that were sent the first time or their craft anyway. Louis realised that there must be no one inside dead or alive. Otherwise Nestor's soldiers would have paid more attention to it after they'd searched it. Louis wondered what on Earth could have happened to all of them?

The soldier at the door called out something and the oldest soldier in his fifties said something just as unintelligible. Nestor who was standing next to Louis whispered to him in English 'Stay next to me Mr. Beaumont, understand?'

Louis whispered back 'Yes,' as if he planned to do otherwise!

The door slid open to reveal a clear corridor and two soldiers rushed inside, they took up positions of cover on either side then they shouted something back. Another two soldiers behind them shouted in reply and ran inside past the front two, found cover and secured the path ahead. They shouted something then the two they'd just charged past shouted something and ran past securing the area another 10 feet ahead. This was a well-oiled machine and Louis could see these men were no strangers to this sort of situation.

The corridor at about 30 feet in came to an end splitting off into a T junction, four of Nestor's men went left and then another four ran inside, in exactly the same two by two formation and went off to the right securing the other end of the corridor. Next Louis heard some chatter through Nestor's shirt communicator. Nestor shouted 'Nabadzingya!' and the sound of automatic pulse fire echoed throughout the area.

It sounded much like a crackling electric charge with loud snaps as the small charged pieces of tungsten were propelled out. After about 10 seconds the fire died down. Nestor started talking to the oldest soldier, which Louis had assumed was Nestor's second in command and in charge of the grunts. He then said to Louis 'follow me.'

They marched inside the building, with the rest of the soldiers securing the rear all the way to the transport. Nestor turned down the right corridor at the junction and Louis could see two smoking mining drones that the four soldiers had just blown to pieces. Underneath the broken drones he was shocked to see, laying on the floor, three plant workers bodies. The drones were covered in congealed blood themselves. From the look of things they were guarding the exit/entrance to and from the operation centre. Louis looked down the other corridor to see the remains of another two drones covered in blood.

Somehow drones that were normally assigned to working the rock face in the mines were here on the upper level of the plant killing anyone that tried to get past them. The same soldier as before walked up to the wall terminal with his tablet to override security. Louis looked harder at the corpses; he could see that flesh had been burnt off them. Probably by acid which the mining drones used at the rock face in the tunnels below. The acid had burnt grooves in the floor which gathered the now congealed blood from the plant workers.

The door slid open and again two men ran in to secure the plant control area only to be answered by pulse fire. This time Louis could see the flashes from the rifles as they discharged their rounds. Then two more ran in shouting something in Russian, the first soldiers held their fire until their comrades charged past them took cover and then shouted again. The two in front were laying on the floor firing whilst the two behind were kneeling and firing.

More of Nestor's men ran in spreading around the room in much the same fashion until the room was glowing a permanent blue with flashes projecting shadows onto walls. At this point Louis couldn't see what they were firing at. He only had a view of some of the Spetsnaz holding their positions of cover and firing. Nestor took his pistol out, checked it then put it back, there was screaming from inside. Louis had the urge to run for the transport but the fear and combined adrenaline rush kept him rooted to the spot, he couldn't move a single muscle in his body! If a drone came around the corner to spray him with acid he wouldn't be able to do anything about it. He'd never been in a situation like this before and the terror was overwhelming him beyond his ability to deal with it.

The firing died down and Nestor walked inside the plant operation centre to a scene of devastation. Destroyed drones, plant workers corpses and congealed blood stained every where. One of Nestor's men was being treated for minor acid burns to his face. Nestor Looked at Louis 'Get to work Mr. Beaumont,' pointing to a terminal.

One of the Spetsnaz techs was on another terminal and he shouted something in Russian. All of the soldiers then pulled out a gas mask from their packs and attached it to the front of their helmets covering the face and sealing it from danger. A mask was handed to Nestor and another to Beaumont.

Nestor shouted through his mask 'Put it on Mr. Beaumont, NOW!'

Louis put on his mask and got back to work, from what Louis saw the entire plant was screwed up and the nanites were in chaos. He set about reinstating some order; when Louis had finally wrestled control of the nanites he informed Nestor.

'That was impressive Mr. Beaumont,' Nestor shouted through the mask 'I want you to disable the SI. I don't care how you do it Mr. Beaumont, destroy it if necessary just take it offline understood?'

Louis gave a thumbs up and went to work. Whilst he was making his initial assault on the SI with his nanite warriors the doors to the operation centre heaved apart with a mighty churn of metal. Louis looked up in shock, aside from the entrance he'd come through there were two other entrances leading out of the operations centre. Both were being ripped apart by mining drones using their drills and robotic arms.

Nestor waved at him grabbing his attention, then motioned at his terminal. He couldn't speak due to the noise. Louis understood his intent and returned to his task of breaching the defences the SI had set up along its connections to the plant computer systems.

The Vympel soldiers opened fire on the drones trying to force their way through the entrances. Louis could also detect flashes coming from the corridor behind him. There were constant flashes and violent clangs and crashes of twisted steel. The air conditioning system was working overtime as the SI pumped in cyanide to try and gas them all. Louis was rooted to the spot in fear; he could barely do his job due to his shaking hands. He was in a race to kill the SI before it killed them; the only thing pushing his fear aside was his instinct for self-preservation.

The SI had probably killed everyone in the plant already. So Louis had no remorse about sending his army of nanites through the first breach he'd made; in an attempt to shred apart this sentient being's neural connections. If he didn't he'd be joining those rotting corpses in the hallway. After a minute Nestor who had been firing his pulse pistol into an entrance as hydrochloric and nitric acid was sprayed towards them stopped and tapped Louis on the shoulder. Louis looked up to see Nestor pointing to his wrist. It was obvious he wanted to know how long he would take. These mining droids were tough and Nestor's men had only so much ammunition on them.

Louis put two fingers up to indicate two minutes and Nestor gave a thumbs up then reloaded his pistol. Louis had estimated it would take only one since his nanites were in through the initial breech, but he wasn't certain. Louis had never done this before and as far as he knew no one had taken out an SI in this manner. In fact he wasn't sure if it were possible until he'd breached the first connections and realised the super beings weren't all they were cracked up to be.

Then there was a high pitched whistle throughout the station and Louis blacked out. He awoke moments later with some ear plugs inserted and a young soldier shaking him forcefully. The fire fight was still ongoing but half of the soldiers had being rendered unconscious by the high pitched noise. The soldiers not knocked out immediately had put their ear plugs in, which hung from all Spetsnaz issue gas mask.

Louis was the first to be revived, they were trying to revive their comrades and fight back the drones which were making ground through the entrances.

Louis went straight back to his station. He was fighting to keep his vision straight after the sonic attack. He wrestled control of his army of nanites as the SI fought to take back control and save its life.

The SI lost the struggle its intelligence was no match for Louis experience. As quickly as it had all started the drones shutdown and everything went dead. Louis kept the nanites busy attacking the SI in case this was just a ploy and it was playing dead.

Louis looked around him as soldiers were now treating their comrades. He pulled his ear plugs out to the sound of shouting and screaming through gas masks over a high pitched ringing as his ears slowly re adjusted. Nestor slapped his arm to get his attention and pointed towards the exit. Louis again gave a thumbs up and followed Nestor out as his men pulled back to the transport.

Once inside the transport Nestor took his mask of and Louis followed suit 'Well done Mr. Beaumont not a bad performance, for a rookie!' he smiled.

Louis however was enraged. As the soldiers brought their injured comrades back for treatment he exploded in Nestor's face and the Vympel unit went silent, 'Are you fucking crazy? You nearly got me fucking killed! You told me I was going to be in no danger you fucking asshole!'

Louis was poking him in the chest with his finger. The older soldier marched briskly at Louis and grabbed him. Intending to beat the life out of Louis until Nestor said something in Russian and Louis was released.

Nestor approached Louis as he lit one of his Russian cigarettes and took a long draw from it, 'Mr. Beaumont, no one died here today but that doesn't have to be so. I appreciate what you did here, and tomorrow you'll be back in Moscow 100,000 credits richer, don't be foolish.'

Louis' blood went cold, every single soldier even the injured were staring at him and waiting on his next word. Louis nodded his head 'I understand,' then retired to his seat in the back of the transport.

He was furious but he had no say in it. An hour later the Vympel unit had pulled out leaving someone else to clean the plant up. They had left Louis in the abandoned transport to wait for the rescue team to arrive, not even taking him back to Moscow.

Five days later Louis was back in Moscow and finishing his work with the Phage Company as quickly as possible. He had his 100,000 credits but it wasn't worth it in his opinion. He made a vow never to step foot on Russian soil again and held a deep distrust of all things Russian.

It was not only Russians however he gained a distrust for. He'd witnessed the devastation one SI could cause if it wished; it wasn't something Louis would ever get over. Nanites were simple machines that carried out a set of commands. SIs however had a mind of their own and could turn into psychotic killers. Before the incident he poked fun at authority figures but after his experience with Nestor and his Vympel unit he despised all authority and distrusted it to the extreme.

It wasn't a simple matter for him to put any trust in Athena either, in fact he didn't. But he did trust McCann and since McCann put faith in Athena he dealt with it that way. Louis had already made his contingency plans if Athena lost her mind. He didn't tell the others as they'd have just laughed at him, but for Louis Beaumont it was no joke. Living 24/7, for at least a year, with an SI in control of your life was a big risk.

The next day Ryu and Hassif headed off west to retrieve the data recorder. There was just enough room in the cab to fit three people comfortably, leaving plenty of space for the two of them. It would be some days before reaching their destination.

First they had to travel west between the shallow volcanoes of Ulysess and Biblis Patera, keeping the canyons of Ulysess Fossae to their North. After navigating them the hauler would swing north slipping between Ulysess Fossae and the rock formations of Gigas Sulci. Once they'd cleared Gigas Sulci they'd head North, North West to the area of the crash site near Sulci Gordii.

Ryu had concluded it might take 3 days to a week to get there depending on the terrain, factoring in any unforeseen geological upsets. It was simple enough to look from orbit and plot a course. But until you've been on the ground you can't be sure of the grounds stability and whether it will support a hauler even in such low gravity.

Hassif wasn't pleased to be on this salvage operation. He didn't like the enclosed spaces of the Athena and found the hauler cab to be quite claustrophobic. His job was to be there in case Ryu required assistance, be that medical or otherwise in retrieving the recorder. However he was absolutely fed up of small working spaces and made no secret of it. Hassif believed that once on Tharsis they'd be back to some sort of normality concerning living and working conditions, but this was just silly.

Stuck with "Miss Minimalist" (a secret pet name of his for Ryu) for possibly two weeks, inside a wretched hauler cab all because she wanted to set foot on Martian soil. It was a waste of time and resources in his opinion and he'd rather be back at the base relaxing at his station keeping the computers in line.

Ryu was unconcerned with his obvious apathy towards the mission, as long as he did his job, which was only monitoring systems while Athena did most of the work anyway. Ryu was going to put her name in the annals of human history forever and she wasn't going to let one upset Indian spoil it. It had played on her mind that although she'd set foot on Tharsis first. There would be debate as to who was truly the first to step on Mars if someone else in the team trod on the surface outside before her.

Even now she was concerned that some slime bag would argue it was Louis Beaumont, since he was the first to step into the tunnel walking from Tharsis to ground zero in Pavis Mons when working on the crawler and ribbon. Ryu was going to get a picture of her treading on the Martian soil. When she retrieved that recorder the Korean was certain that it would cement her position.

Ryu was competitive and used to doing whatever it took to win, she'd been like that since she first played online. She was one of life's winners; through a mix of ambition, natural talent and ruthlessness she usually attained victory.

Playing on the net had brought it all out, behind a computer she fought faceless enemies. Added to the fact that being a girl put her under more pressure, since her every mistake was analyzed far more than if she were male (at least she believed that, true or not). Defeat was not an option in her mind and when she had been beaten she blamed herself rather than credit her opponent.

By the time she'd entered the ROKAF she had gotten used to delivering biological, chemical and nuclear weapons online. Many others had problems using the nerve gas, the old guard was against it but Ryu had no problems. After all she'd done it countless times before and the booth was pretty much the same as playing at a LAN contest. She carried her gaming philosophy over to defending her country. Ruthlessly slaughtering the enemy with chemical warfare just the same as any online contest, Ryu was trying to get maximum points with as little effort as possible. Points being downed Manchurian drones and rotting corpses.

Now the environment had changed, get her name in the history books as the first person to set foot on Mars. She had expected the title of first woman but now she had a shot at first human being, thanks to McCann. Ryu still couldn't understand why McCann would give up such a prestigious honour, but he had given her the opportunity and she was taking the bull by the horns.

The Martian surface was mostly sand and rocks; the hauler trundled quite easily along it. Mars did however posses massive volcanoes and deep canyons. The red planet had the highest peaks and lowest gullies of anywhere in the solar system.

Ulysses Fossae was about 530 miles long and blocked a clear path to their site. The hauler was going around it on the south side where two shallow volcanoes lay, one day when they were passing in between Hassif called to Ryu 'Quick look at this.'

He pointed to one of the monitors displaying a camera feed as the cab had no windows to speak of. Hassif had spotted three Martian dust devils dancing around each other 'Athena are you getting this?' he called to the SI who was ever present.

Athena replied 'Yes Hassif, I'm recording and sending the data back to Tharsis for further analysis.'

It was quite a sight, they spun whipping up the dirt and circled each other to a back drop of the valley stretching out into the distance. The hauler passed by on its journey leaving the three red devils to themselves.

Back on Tharsis McCann was missing both Hassif and Ryu. Louis was spending more and more time in Pavis Mons finishing his shift later each day. McCann would have become lonely if Athena were not there to keep him company. When not working or chatting with Athena he had taken over the duties of answering questions posed by members of the public.

Previously Hassif had taken responsibility, but since his departure it fell to McCann. The I.S.A had a site on the net where anyone could get the latest updates on the mission and send in questions to Geneva. Some were selected and sent on to Tharsis where McCann would record a video feed of himself answering then send it back with the next data packet. Someone at Geneva sorted it all out and put it on the site. Ever since the crash first "Athena" then "Ryu" then "Tharsis" had outranked "sex" as the number one search on the net. A record held for more than a decade since the top spot had last changed hands, it was no small feat to be sure!

McCann was spending another evening alone in the officer's lounge; he had shaved for the video feed and was finishing up, answering questions mostly about living on Mars. Anything inappropriate had been censored by Geneva so it wasn't as uncomfortable as he'd envisioned it to be. After finishing the last of his video feeds he sent it into the folder to go with the next data packet and walked over to the sofa. He was still dressed in his space suit with his shoulder holster and leg pocket.

McCann took out an RASCC cigar from his holster and lit it up with the torch on the lounge table, resting next to the ash tray. He poured some Balvenie into a single tumbler over one ice cubed and took a sip; that smooth and silky long finish of the Scotch made him relax and he lay back on the sofa. McCann looked at his wrist tablet and tapped his communicator button, he waited then tapped it again but nothing was happening.

McCann looked up at the ceiling 'Athena can you get me Louis please?' then he took a draw from his cigar, causing the smouldering end to burn bright red for a moment then die back down hiding behind the ash.

In her soft voice, which McCann found all the more soothing alongside his cigar and Scotch, she replied 'I cannot raise Louis on his communicator Duncan.'

This was the second night in a row Louis wasn't answering. McCann hadn't seen Louis since yesterday morning and was getting concerned 'Where is Louis at the moment Athena?' asked McCann puffing on his cigar.

'Louis is at his workstation in Pavis Mons, ground zero, Duncan.'

McCann scratched his head 'How long has Louis been at that station Athena?'

Athena softly replied '14 hours and 38 minutes, Duncan.'

McCann sat up and took a swig of his Scotch, looking somewhat concerned he asked 'When was the last time he moved from that station Athena?'

In her soft voice she replied '14 hours and 39 minutes ago Duncan. Louis walked from the mess to the station and has not since moved.'

McCann knocked back the last of the Balvenie in his tumbler and put it down 'He hasn't moved at all Athena?' he asked in a concerned voice.

'Louis has not moved at all since reaching his station in Pavis Mons Duncan. Do you want me to check up on him?'

'Yes please Athena, and put the cameras on this screen here,' he said pointing to the television.

Five minutes later and McCann was still waiting, he was now pacing up and down the lounge puffing on his cigar leaving a trail of ash on the floor.

At last Athena spoke 'I am unable to access the security cameras in Pavis Mons Duncan.'

McCann ditched his cigar in the ashtray and marched over to a locker taking out a pair of gloves. As he attached them to his suit he called out 'Athena I want you to put Tharsis on a level 3 alert, understood?'

Athena replied calmly 'Understood Colonel McCann, Tharsis is now under a level 3 alert, Geneva has been notified.'

There were 5 levels of alert one being the lowest and for minor problems such as an incoming storm front or low supply levels, resulting in closing any outer doors and airlocks and sending Geneva a message in the next data packet, to level 5. Level three was as serious as it could get without bio hazards or a natural disaster such as an earthquake. However it did include security breaches and personnel at risk.

McCann was bounding along the tunnel leading into Pavis Mons, his gauntlets were on. His helmet had unfurled from its home in the suit and locked an airtight seal around the collar. He pulled out his pistol and checked it, the battery display on the bottom showed green and the clip was full. McCann put it back and kept moving as fast as he could towards ground zero.

Along the way he noticed a small transport cart for humans that went to and fro between Pavis Mons and Tharsis. It was a glorified golf cart used for carrying small machinery and supplies. McCann hopped in and through his mic spoke 'Athena, can you get this cart moving?'

The cart lurched into motion and headed off for Pavis Mons a lot quicker than McCann could have bounded there. He held onto the rail as it shuttled along the tunnel. The cart stopped short of the massive bulkhead doors separating the tunnel from Pavis Mons. McCann jumped off and approached the tightly sealed doors 'Athena can you open the doors please?'

After a few seconds she replied 'I'm sorry Colonel McCann but I'm unable to do that.'

McCann walked the edge where the doors disappeared inside the rock of the Pavis Mons volcano. On the wall there was a metal depression with a handle inside. Above the handle at eye level sat an optical scanner which McCann lined his eye up with then tapped the pad next to it. After scanning his eye the handle popped out of the depression and McCann took it and twisted it a full 360 degrees to the left. A moment later the massive bulkheads began to slowly split in the middle and trundle inside the walls of the volcano exposing the insides.

The doors opened to reveal ground zero. In the distance he could see Louis work station but there was no Louis.

Nothing else seemed amiss as he approached scanning the area. The cavern was very large but his initial sweep didn't show anything unusual to the naked eye. On approaching the work station McCann noticed something. Sitting on top of the horizontal key panel which had been left pulled out by the last person to use it, he picked up what looked like a memory chip; it was a light chip with memory storage that ran of its own tiny power unit. It sat in the palm of McCann's gauntlet, he had seen Louis and Hassif use these tools often. McCann had his own for storing personal information but they were capable of so much more. McCann spoke into his mic 'Athena can you tell me what is on this chip please?' and placed it on top of workstation panel where it could be read.

Athena was unable to read the chip however 'I am locked out of all work stations in Pavis Mons Colonel.'

McCann took a quick look around and decided the area was far too large for him to search on his own.

'Athena, now that I've got the door open can you send some droids to search the area for Louis please?'

Athena replied softly 'Yes Colonel I'm sending the droids now. Director Faraday would like to speak to you Colonel.'

McCann remembered that Geneva had been informed and with the time delay this was their quickest response.

'Thank you Athena, if you can send me on the cart back to Tharsis I'll take it in my office unless you need me for anything here?'

'I will continue the search for Technician Beaumont, Colonel. The cart is ready to transport you now.'

Upon reaching the command centre McCann had discovered the purpose of the chip; it was transmitting Louis biological information to Tharsis. Athena had informed him that according to the Tharsis computer Louis was sitting next to him in the cart all the way to the command centre. Faraday had sent a message inquiring as to the nature of the alert; McCann felt very uncomfortable explaining even though it was on a recorded message. Forty minutes later and a reply came, 12 minutes for his message to get there and 12 minutes for the reply to come back.

Faraday was not a happy man. His reply however was surprisingly brief and after saying a few words about finding "that French fool" he instructed McCann to download a file he'd attached and give it to Athena. The file "might help explain Louis' odd behaviour".

McCann felt a chill as Faraday had a hint of fear in his voice and he'd not known Faraday to allow fear to affect his Etonian accent before now.

McCann downloaded the file and instructed Athena to read it; moments later she began to inform him of some unknown transmissions. Looking at one of the station monitors she explained the data to him. Since their arrival Tharsis had been detecting transmissions but from an unknown source. Geneva had only recently become aware of the transmissions. They couldn't locate the source; however the actual transmission was similar to a human brainwave.

As Athena explained this, McCann watched the brainwave patterns flickering around on the monitor. He slowly took another cigar, cut the butt off letting the cap of the cigar fall onto the floor. He lit his cigar and listened in a daze as Athena told him the pattern had changed and fluctuated over the months, eventually settling on something close to the brain wave pattern of Louis Beaumont. From what Geneva could tell something had scanned every member of the crew including Athena and selected Louis. Faraday believed it could be affecting Louis judgement; Louis Beaumont was to be found quickly and taken into custody by whatever means necessary.

After Athena had finished McCann asked, 'Athena, in your opinion could this be affecting Louis?'

'I do not have enough information to come to a conclusion Colonel.'

McCann shook his head 'No I didn't ask that, is it a possibility in your opinion, I'm not asking for facts Athena just your best guess.'

'In my opinion it is a possibility, Colonel McCann.'

Athena hadn't been asked for opinions on anything other than art or music or the press until now. This was something far more important and it went against her nature to give opinions rather than facts in such a situation.

McCann took another puff and quickly replied 'Why?'

Athena again paused and replied softly 'Could you be more specific in your question Colonel?'

He looked up 'Why do you believe it could affect Louis?'

Athena was hesitant to reply but he waited until she did 'I believe that this transmission may have affected me during entry Colonel.'

McCann was taken aback by the answer and inquired further 'Why do you believe the transmission affected you Athena?'

'On entry Tharsis first received the transmission, at that time it closely mimicked my brainwaves Colonel. If I was under the influence of this transmission then I believe it may be having a similar effect on Technician Louis Beaumont. The waves from the transmission are closely mimicking his brainwaves. In much the same way it mimicked mine during the crash landing.'

McCann was feeling tired and was in desperate need of sleep 'Athena I want you to keep Tharsis on lockdown. When you find Louis alert me, otherwise no one moves through this base without my clearance understood?'

In her calm voice she replied 'Understood Colonel McCann.'

He gave a tired smile 'Oh and you can call me Duncan unless it's urgent Athena, alright?'

She reassuringly replied 'Understood Duncan, have a good night.'

He made towards his quarters and as he left the command centre said 'Thank you Athena, Sleep well,' even though she didn't sleep in the same sense as he did.

Chapter 7

Ryu had reached her destination and was exiting the hauler cab airlock; she stepped onto the flatbed of the hauler and surveyed the landscape from her vantage point. It was a rocky place with small patches of broken rocks and sand. She could see where the data recorder lay due to the two droids that had been waiting in preparation whilst they made the journey from Tharsis.

At the side of the flatbed a set of steps began to protrude from underneath, once fully extended they tilted allowing Ryu to walk onto the rocky surface. The droids were watching and recording as she carefully made her way down. It took her a while in the low gravity but she made her way, finally stepping on the gravely surface. After her second foot came down and Ryu got her balance there was a "congratulations" from Hassif. She smiled and made her way carefully stepping from rock to rock until she reached the trough which had the data recorder squeezed inside.

The recorder was trapped about a metre down, the droids could have done the job alone but she stood supervising them. They chipped away at one of the rocks with small cutting tools that extended from their chests, holding one side of the rocky trough in their solid metal arms.

When the rock came loose they moved away holding it between them. Thanks to their iron grip the rock seemed to magically move with them. They dropped the rock and went to work on the second one the recorder was trapped against. There was no other debris from the crash since it had been recovered long ago. This was the only piece left and Ryu was rather puzzled as to how it had become lodged between these two rocks. It seemed to her the chances were pretty thin of it coming in at just the right speed and angle to lodge there without damaging the rocks. However this freak occurrence had provided an opportunity and she was enjoying every moment basking in the orange Martian sun.

After a couple of hours they'd chipped away enough rock that the data recorder had come loose. The droids trundled onto the hauler, securing both the recorder and themselves for the journey back to Tharsis.

Ryu asked Hassif to come out and enjoy the scenery. He was reluctant at first until she noted he would be the first man on Mars. Hassif decided he could spend a few minutes taking in the sights!

He walked past the droids securing the data recorder and onto the steps, when he turned around he was in awe. The landscape they were stood on was nothing much. Just some gravel with red rocks sticking out all over the place but in the distance Olympus Mons rose. The highest peak in the solar system and the largest volcano, it was a beautiful sight. He could see its peak clearly through the thin orange atmosphere.

The bed of rocks they'd been working on stretched off into the distance, stopping at a sea of red sand; which even further away met the base of the Volcano to the North West.

The base of the volcano started at a massive cliff face (which was minute from their perspective) separating the smooth dusty volcanic slope that reached more than 20 kilometres, more than 10 miles, into the sky. It was a wondrous site and Hassif stood next to Ryu marvelling.

'Was it worth it?' inquired Ryu.

'Yes,' he marvelled not taking his eyes off the Olympian peak.

He had seen the Himalayas from an airship and they were beautiful but this was something else. Hassif didn't know how to describe it and neither did Ryu. The two of them stood in the stillness and quiet staring at the massive peak before them; the only humans to have gazed upon it with their own eyes.

Ryu's attention was momentarily drawn to something in her peripheral vision. She turned to her right in the direction of Sulci Gordii. Certain she could see something along the rolling desert landscape. After looking for a few seconds Ryu assumed it was haze from the heat causing the illusion of objects moving in the distance. The haze made it hard to see anything at a distance on ground level.

Just before she was going to turn away Ryu observed a black spot distorted by the haze, she was sure it was moving.

'Do you see that?' inquired the Korean pointing towards the hazy black blob in the distance.

Hassif looked out to where she indicated just east of Olympus Mons but he saw nothing more than hazy rocks 'See what?'

'That black spot, is it getting closer?'

Hassif looked again and saw a blob in the haze 'I see it.'

The tiny spot was moving and at quite a pace 'Perhaps we should get back in the hauler?' he said worriedly.

Ryu was about to disagree but realised the object was approaching them fast, a landslide or eruption perhaps? She started moving for the hauler and Hassif was already ahead of her. Ryu called down her mic 'Athena are you getting this?'

Athena replied calmly 'Is there a problem Major Ryu?' detecting the agitation in Ryu's voice.

Ryu stopped whilst Hassif made it up the steps to the hauler as fast as he could. Taking the opportunity to turn around and get a quick look 'Do you see the object approaching the Hauler from the North Athena?'

In a short time it had closed a large distance and was still heading towards them at high speed. Athena replied 'Yes Major.'

Ryu even more agitated shouted 'What is it?'

'Unknown.'

'How is it moving?'

'Unknown.'

Ryu turned to see Hassif was on top of the flatbed gawking at the object which from this distance he could tell was obviously the Gordii stone. Ryu shouted at him through the mic 'Get in the airlock now!'

Hassif snapped out of it, looked at Ryu then jumped in the airlock as she ran up the steps as fast as she could.

The jet black stone was hovering above the ground and by what means was not obvious. As it approached it slowed down quickly in what seemed to be an effortless braking manoeuvre. It came to a full stop 10 metres from the hauler just as Ryu closed the airlock; they waited for the atmosphere to equalize with that of the cab. Once in the cab Ryu punched in the command to start the hauler off on the plotted course back to Tharsis. The hauler however refused to move.

'Athena what's wrong with the hauler?'

'The hauler cannot locate Tharsis.'

Ryu looked puzzled 'Can you locate the hauler?'

Athena replied softly 'Yes Major Ryu.'

'Then tell the hauler where it is so that it can return, now please!'

The hauler lurched into action, it reversed, turned its back towards Olympus Mons stopped then went full speed forwards for Tharsis.

Ryu was in a panic, going over her station in the hauler looking for the problem. She had to remove her gloves as she'd left her entire suit on in the rush to get back in.

Hassif shouted 'Look it's following us!'

Ryu turned towards Hassif's station, on his screen was the Gordii stone following them at a distance of about 10 metres. Ryu noticed a flashing panel and reached to tap the area of the panel lighting up green.

'I think it's transmitting a signal to us.'

Hassif nearly leapt from his seat grabbing her arm before she could hit the flashing panel, 'Don't! It could be anything, it's too dangerous to allow a connection. The Hauler doesn't have the security measures to block an attack!'

Ryu withdrew her hand and looked back at the screen to observe was following them, it was about the same size as the hauler perhaps a little larger. The stone followed with no visible means of volition but didn't seem threatening in any manner. After all it hadn't done anything that could be interpreted as aggressive. The long jet black rectangle with sloped edges hovered over the gravel desert with its large pyramid rising up on its rear end. The sight was as odd as it was terrifying.

They had been travelling for some hours in the hauler now. The Gordii stone remained at the same distance mimicking their every move. Ryu went to inform McCann, she was notified of the level 3 alert 'What has happened Athena?'

Athena paused seemingly reluctant to impart the information 'Technician Louis Beaumont has gone missing Major.'

Ryu and Hassif looked at each other both puzzled 'Missing Athena? When?'

'Technician Beaumont was declared missing at 19:00hrs Tharsis time September the 21st 2117.'

Ryu thought for a moment.

'That was yesterday, why weren't we informed?' Hassif's question seemed to be directed to Ryu but Athena answered.

'Colonel McCann did not deem it pertinent to Major Ryu's salvage operation.'

This was superfluous to Ryu, she had to make contact with McCann 'Athena get me Colonel McCann now please.'

'As you wish Major.'

Within a few minutes the image of McCann sitting up in bed in his shorts was staring back at her 'What's going Major? I was asleep.'

Ryu sat at her station in the cab and with one eye on the Gordii stone. Ryu recanted their salvage operation and the visitor that was now tracking them.

McCann sat for a while scratching his groggy head 'I'll inform Geneva and get their opinion. Until then just stay on the road back to Tharsis and don't make any attempts at communication understood?'

Ryu nodded 'Understood Sir, by the way any idea of what's happened to Louis?'

McCann became a little agitated and informed her that upon reaching Tharsis they'd both be given a briefing.

An hour later McCann made contact with the hauler again. Nothing had changed and the Gordii stone was still tracking their every move; yet maintaining its distance and transmitting the same signal. Geneva wasn't very helpful, the consensus was that the hauler return as normal but stop outside the garage. If the stone insisted on following so closely then the hauler must be left outside and Ryu and Hassif would enter Tharsis via crew airlock.

The hauler could pull up just outside blocking the path for the stone. If the garage were opened there would be no way to prevent it from entering Tharsis.

'That's the plan?' cried Hassif 'what if it decided to ram the hauler when we're entering the airlock?'

McCann was now dressed with a cigar in his mouth 'Calm down Hassif, that thing survived the same entry as we did but unscathed. I have a feeling if it wanted to obliterate you it would have already! Unless you'd prefer to sit in the hauler until it decides to leave?'

McCann was scratching his uncombed hair whilst puffing away 'Faraday has gone bananas, apparently some transmission similar to brainwave patterns has been effecting all of us. Weissmuller has come up with a theory but I want you to stay on guard and watch each other, understood?'

Ryu nodded 'Understood, what about Louis ... any luck?'

McCann took a few puffs on his cigar 'I think I know where he's hiding out but I'm not going after him alone. I'm waiting for you two to get back first.'

Hassif cut in the conversation and asked quickly 'Hiding out? I thought he was missing as in lost?'

McCann smirked before taking another puff 'That's what I thought; it seems our Frenchman is leading us a merry chase. You'll both be fully briefed on arrival, first of all you have to get back and I have to keep Tharsis secure. Do you both understand?'

Ryu nodded again 'Understood Sir.'

'Good, I'll get some sleep and contact you again at 0700 hours, McCann out.'

The screen went blank; Ryu and Hassif both took in the bombshell together.

Hassif asked 'Do you think Louis has lost his mind?'

'Let's worry about getting to Tharsis in one piece first.'

The next morning they arose to see the Gordii stone was still in tow, it was further away now, about 20 meters or 60 feet. Eating his breakfast Hassif went through the night's footage. He discovered that the stone had slowly orbited the hauler during the small hours. It was a mystery as to why but Hassif guessed they were being observed and perhaps the stone was watching for any reactions.

Ryu pointed out that would assume some kind of intelligence.

'I think we're past assuming that,' remarked Hassif. 'Either it is intelligent or was constructed by a sentient being with intelligence. Meaning it has a purpose and the question is what is its purpose?'

Ryu chewed on her noodles and after swallowing a mouthful she stated 'Right now as long as that purpose doesn't conflict with mine then it can play all the games it wants.'

Hassif finished his toast and looked into his cup of tea 'What if it does conflict?'

Ryu sat gathering her noodles with a pair of chopsticks 'What do you mean?'

'Well,' Hassif sat back and looked at the stone on one of the monitors 'what if the stone poses a threat to Tharsis? What could we do about it? There are no weapons on Tharsis that could even scratch that thing.'

Ryu kept on gathering her noodles 'We'll see,' she said before putting in another mouthful. The hauler rumbled along for the next few days with nothing much happening. The stone kept its distance backing off a little more each day. By the time they reached Tharsis it was a good 100 metres off them.

As the hauler pulled up outside of Tharsis the stone stopped, it even reversed to 200 metres away. Hassif watched it intently 'I think it's giving us space, do you think we can go into the garage?'

Ryu was sceptical 'No, did you see how fast that thing moved before? I'm not taking the chance. I'm sure it could accelerate to speed before we could close the doors on the garage. No, we'll stick with the original plan. Athena, inform Colonel McCann we're manoeuvring to the southern outer airlock.'

Athena replied softly 'Yes Major Ryu, Colonel McCann is waiting for you both in the command centre when you arrive.'

The hauler drove to an outer airlock door and parked itself in front, length ways blocking the entrance. Ryu and Hassif exited the hauler airlock; they both stood for a moment to look at the Gordii stone. It was no longer hovering but was sat on the gravely desert pointing straight at them as if it were waiting for something.

Hassif squinted to get a better look 'What do you think it wants?'

Ryu shook her head 'Who cares? Now get into the airlock.'

Hassif scrambled down the steps and opened the airlock whilst Ryu recovered the data recorder from the back of the hauler. She handed Hassif the recorder then made her way down and into the airlock herself. All this time the Gordii stone sat motionless.

Upon entering Tharsis and going through decontamination they made their way to the command centre. Ryu thought it a little odd that McCann hadn't contacted them, yet wasn't that concerned. She walked with Hassif, North up the long corridor to the command centre. On reaching it Hassif turned right, through the doorway into the command room. It was odd that she didn't hear either Hassif or McCann speak; when she walked in she was stunned.

McCann who looked decided grizzly with two weeks growth on his face was stood behind the centre table. Hassif stood close to Ryu not uttering a word, he was too afraid to speak; McCann was as usual smoking a cigar.

'We're back Colonel,' stated Ryu clutching the decontaminated data recorder.

McCann didn't even look up to make eye contact. He had one foot on a chair and was engrossed with the pulse rifle before him. For reasons unknown to her he'd gone back into the armoury.

Ryu attempted to engage him again 'Colonel McCann?'

He replied with a grunt and slapped the power pack into the rifle butt then the ammo pack alongside it. Hassif heard the sharp whine of the rifle charging as McCann tested the power pack. He moved closer to Ryu, turned off the rifle and the whine disappeared. He looked towards Ryu 'Major, you remember how to use one of these?'

She answered slowly 'Yes Colonel?' she said it with a rising tone so as to accentuate the question but McCann was oblivious.

'Good!'

McCann threw the rifle to her despite the fact she was still carrying the flight recorder. The rifle was about the same size as a sub machine gun. In Martian gravity it was a lot easier for Ryu to catch it with one hand as it glided slowly through the air. She handed the data recorder to Hassif and asked McCann 'Duncan what's going on? I thought we were going to be briefed?'

McCann had already begun loading and checking the other pulse rifle on the table as he puffed away on a cigar. From the smell of things he'd been smoking far too many Habanos whilst they'd been away. The whine went out as he loaded up and charged his pulse rifle. When both meters on the side showed full he switched it off. Next he turned his attention to the monocles on the table.

Ryu recognised them from her time in the military but had never used one nor was she aware of how to use one. McCann walked over and handed one to her 'Put this on.'

The monocle was black with a silver metallic ring attached to a thin rubber head band. Inside the edge of the monocle was layered with the same thick substance so as not to let in any light, aside from light entering via the monocle's black lens.

Ryu looked at the monocle in her hand 'What's going on Duncan?'

'Just put it on, attach the clip on the headband to your gloves,' he stated whilst putting his own monocle on.

Ryu noticed a three button touch pad on the band. She took it off and clipped it to her glove 'OK so what's all this in aid of?' she asked in a fed up tone.

McCann had his monocle attached with his rifle slung over his shoulder. He pointed to the touch pad 'The first one is night vision, the second is infra-red and the third is normal vision. If you want it has a zoom mode, just run you finger along the edge of the monocle to zoom in and out. Take your finger off and it goes back to normal magnification, understood?'

Ryu slung her rifle over her shoulder and put the monocle on 'Understood Colonel, now what's the problem?'

McCann adjusted his monocle so it covered his left eye properly 'Hassif I want you to stay in the Command centre. Keep all exits locked until we return, understood?'

Hassif replied timidly 'Yes,' he just didn't have the constitution for this kind of thing. McCann looked at Ryu 'Mr. Beaumont has been having some fun whilst you were coming back. He attempted to shut down Athena but she managed to cut off Pavis Mons before he was successful. He's been running around down there ever since.'

Ryu gave a look of disbelief 'Are you sure? Perhaps some systems have failed and he's trapped?'

McCann then looked up and called to Athena 'Athena replay the last video capture of Mr. Beaumont please.'

'Yes Duncan,' replied a soft voice and a nearby monitor came to life.

The footage was quite damning, the droids searching for Louis in Pavis Mons were hit by what seemed to be a jack hammer. The hammer which fired a piece of sharpened tungsten at high velocity was designed to make precise holes in a granite rock face. The droids Ryu used to cut out the data recorder had something similar but much smaller. This one was about the size of a heavy pulse rifle and it was being held by Louis. Louis had a crazy look about him as if he'd lost his mind. She watched in disbelief as he approached the droids, which recorded the event, in his space suit. Louis proceeded to demolish the droids using his mining tool as a rifle then the footage ended.

Ryu closed her eyes, turned her head then looked back at McCann 'OK I get it, we've also got the Gordii stone sitting out there waiting on something. It could move at any moment Duncan and Hassif believes it's quite capable of taking Tharsis apart.'

McCann took a long drag of his cigar and expelled the thick smoke from his nostrils 'I understand but a mad Frenchman on the loose takes priority. He will take apart this place if we don't deal with him now. He could even be bringing down the orbital ribbon as we speak. After he's neutralised we'll deal with this stone understood?'

Ryu nodded but Hassif cried out 'Neutralised?'

McCann looked at him 'I mean captured, I'm not planning on killing him Hassif.'

McCann looked back to Ryu still tasting the smoke from his cigar 'Are you ready?'

Ryu nodded.

'Good let's go, Hassif you keep this room locked down until we return,' and with that McCann and Ryu exited the command centre for a meeting with the Frenchman at Pavis Mons.

Ryu and McCann walked all the way down the tunnel until they reached the gate leading to Pavis Mons. The gate had been sealed since the droids were destroyed and Louis hadn't attempted to make his way out. Despite the fact he had the equipment to do it. McCann explained to Ryu everything that had happened since she left. All about the brainwave patterns and how it had caused Athena to crash. He also pointed out that Weissmuller had found the patterns were closely matched to Louis brainwaves right now, but it had scanned all of them. At one time it had mimicked closely each crewman's brain wave patterns including Athena. For one reason or another it had settled on Louis and was probably the cause of his instability.

Ryu gave McCann a run-down of her salvage operation and the actions of the Gordii stone. When they reached the gate McCann dropped his cigar onto the floor and tapped his wrist pad giving the command to unfurl his helmet. Ryu did the same, when both confirmed their suits airtight he prepared his pulse rifle 'Ready Major?'

She nodded 'Yes Sir.'

McCann nestled the butt in his shoulder and flicked the rifle on. Ryu did likewise and the two Rifles let out a short high pitched whine as the rails charged. Once charged the whine was gone and McCann looked up 'Athena, open the gates to Pavis Mons please.'

The gates opened extinguishing the cigar resting on the ground and revealing a bay area in a subdued darkness. The only light came from the opening above, through which the orbital ribbon climbed out to the Edwards.

McCann felt as if he was walking into a poorly lit cathedral. The rays of low light struck down from the top and hit the floor exposing the metal disc and Louis' work station next to it. Some of the smoothed out stone floor around it was exposed but further out the gloom took precedence. Smoky dust travelled through the rays of light shining down from above. In the gloom McCann could make out one of the droids Louis had trashed. He crouched on one knee and spoke 'I'm going to night vision; stay behind me and to my left.'

Ryu shuffled back 'Roger.'

Once in night vision mode the scene became clear, the two droids were wrecked. One close to the disc that the orbital ribbon was attached to, the other several metres back in a pile.

McCann scanned the area but there was no sign of Louis. The Englishman tapped his wrist 'Going to infra-red,' and took another look.

His monocle was very sensitive and could pick up thermal signatures even hours after they'd been there. He was scanning the floor looking for some boot prints that might lead him to Beaumont but found none; his hopes for an easy hunt had been dashed.

Pavis Mons had been built with the assumption that one day it would need to accommodate large crews. Several workshops were based on the ground level. Below them lay a maze of catacombs being tunnelled out for future engineers and technicians.

McCann assumed Louis had got to know this area well and if they couldn't find him on the ground level they would be forced to go underground. He didn't like the idea of being a tunnel rat but there was little choice. After he and Ryu checked each work area on the ground and found nothing. They made their way to the catacombs that until now were still under construction.

Judging by the footage it was obvious Louis had found some of the equipment and probably shutdown the droids working there. The entrance to the underground area wasn't far from the gate into Pavis Mons; a large elevator for the tunnelling droids and equipment, but McCann didn't trust it 'Athena, is there another way into the underground section?'

With her calm voice she answered 'There is an emergency exit on the other side of ground zero.'

McCann turned and made his way over the disc with Ryu following. He reached a small metal hatch in the floor just big enough for two people to squeeze in side by side. McCann turned the handle protruding from it then passed his rifle to Ryu. She took it and he pulled it open with both hands. The hatch swung aside and he took his rifle back. Looking down it wasn't a very inviting sight; a step ladder went down about 10 metres to a rough dusty floor.

He looked at Ryu 'Turn off any suit lighting and leave night vision on, understood?'

Ryu nodded 'Roger.'

McCann slung his rifle over his back and climbed down into total darkness. Ryu saw him swallowed up as he descended into the murky night of Pavis Mons.

His feet touched down on the surface kicking up a little dust into the dead atmosphere. McCann immediately took his rifle and scanned back and forth down the short tunnel but there was no sign of Beaumont. He moved away from the ladder 'You can come down now Major,' to which she replied and began her descent.

Once the Major was down he took a closer look at the floor, McCann could discern many boot prints in the dust. From what he could make out Louis had been very active down here, he tapped his wrist to get a better look. In infra-red mode one set of the prints gave off a faint heat signature. Louis had been here but it was some hours ago.

McCann turned to Ryu 'I've got something on infra-red Major follow me. I need you to stay on night vision is that understood?'

Ryu nodded 'Roger.'

She waited for McCann to take a few paces then followed his lead looking forwards and back all the time. McCann followed the tracks of heat into the maze of tunnels. The tunnels were wide enough for three men to stand shoulder to shoulder. So he shouldn't have felt claustrophobic but nevertheless the feeling did pop up. McCann's SBS training kicked in and conquered the emotion a moment later.

As they tracked Louis, Ryu noticed droids lying around dormant. Many of them had been destroyed in acts of pure vandalism. Louis must have deactivated them before taking a metal stick to them? Ryu wondered if this was how he'd amused himself all this time.

As McCann traced Louis' steps his GPS tracked his own steps, so that he wouldn't get lost finding his way back. After a while the floor and walls became smooth and polished. McCann realised they'd reached the centre where the telescopic disc sat. A massive column of metal reached up from below to the ground level. Around it the rock had been cut back leaving a large space for droids and engineers. So when a crawler arrived or was due to depart the droids could easily load and unload cargo.

The heat signature was glowing intensely on the ground now, he didn't know where Louis was but he'd been in this area very recently. McCann began to skirt the wall of the large room until he saw a firey blur on his monocle.

Ryu called out 'Colonel, dead ahead!'

McCann quickly changed over to night vision to see Louis Beaumont in the distance. Louis was on the other side of the room standing at a station. His weapon lay on the ground by his feet. McCann stopped dead to observe him, he could see the dim glow from the station. But without the monocle he couldn't make out what it was. Louis was doing something at the station but it was impossible to know what.

Louis couldn't hear McCann and Ryu due to his spacesuit and McCann guessed the security systems were closed to him as well as Athena. McCann cautiously approached Louis whose back faced both him and Ryu. He made a more direct path now just in case Louis saw something move in the gloom.

Upon closing to within five metres McCann spoke to Ryu 'Don't fire unless I give the order Major, understood?'

'Roger.'

McCann slowly took aim at Louis 'Switch over to general communications frequency Major.'

They both tapped their wrist and retook aim 'Louis, move away from the station,' McCann spoke in a cold stern voice.

Louis, stood in the gloom, froze at his station.

McCann spoke again 'I'm standing behind you Beaumont. I'm ordering you to move away and put your hands on the wall in front of you.'

Louis slowly turned his head, McCann made eye contact with him or what looked like him. He had been surviving for days in the catacombs probably on stored oxygen canisters. There couldn't have been much to eat, if anything.

The suit had a drinking tube inside that dipped into a reservoir fed by the water reclamation system. McCann saw that Louis was in the grip of fear. The Frenchman's eyes were wide open and his teeth chattered uncontrollably.

McCann spoke forcefully 'Beaumont, move over to the wall, NOW!'

Suddenly Louis turned back and made a break for the jack hammer that lay on the floor to his right.

McCann fired into his leg. A white flash expelled from his weapon firing the tungsten projectile into Louis. The bullet tore through the Frenchman's suit into his leg and out the other side; colliding into the wall and bouncing off into darkness in a shower of sparks.

Louis let out a loud scream that both McCann and Ryu heard over their helmets. Louis fell to the floor propping himself up with his hands and one good leg.

McCann had shot a hole in his thigh, but the suit had measures to shore up leaks. Louis' suit closed itself off below the buttock area preventing his suffocation. It then began to secrete an organic foam produced in the layer of bacteria. These bacteria had been genetically engineered especially for space suits. When exposed to conditions other than the layers they lived in, the bacteria secreted a thick compound. The white foam frothed and hardened over both holes within seconds. Louis was still screaming yet he persisted in making for his weapon. It lay a couple of feet away as he shuffled across the floor to retrieve it.

McCann took aim again and another hot flash came from the end of his barrel. Louis fell on his side as a mixture of blood and white froth covered the hole through the centre of his palm. He screamed something in his mother tongue with all his might. Ryu didn't understand it however McCann recognised the slurry of curse words. Louis was now on his back, incapacitated and screaming something else in French. The Frenchman rolled around on the smooth floor to and fro, spreading his blood spatter.

McCann walked slowly over to the jack hammer and kicked it away. Then to the surprise of Ryu he put his boot onto Louis' chest.

McCann pointed his rifle at Louis and in a cold tone he said 'It's good to see you again mon ami.'

Ryu quickly intervened 'Shouldn't we get him to the med bay Colonel?'

McCann didn't respond he kept looking down at Louis whose face was now contorted in pain. His incoherent cries could be heard over the communications. McCann's boot remained on Louis for a minute.

Eventually over the communications came the soft voice of Athena 'Colonel McCann have you found Engineer Beaumont?'

At the voice of Athena he snapped out of his trance 'Affirmative Athena, we'll be bringing him out shortly. Please prepare med bay, he has two pulse rifle injuries, one to his left leg and one right hand.'

The Englishman took his boot from Louis and produced a pair of plastic handcuffs from his leg pocket. McCann handed his rifle to Ryu and cuffed Louis wrists behind his back. Taking a shoulder each, Ryu and McCann dragged him to the elevator. It took another 15 minutes before McCann got the elevator working,

Louis was incoherent and didn't seem interested in getting to the med bay. He was in the grip of an irrational fear and couldn't see reason.

The med lab was a large block off the Northern wing just above the command centre. Originally intended as the workplace of the station doctor, Ryu however had taken that spot on the Athena when selected for attaching the ribbon. Athena now had responsibility over immediate medical emergencies and keeping Doctor Weissmuller updated.

Hassif walked into the med lab, inside one of the four med bays lay Louis Beaumont unconscious. The bay was closed off but through the plastic window he observed two medical droids cutting off his space suit, after they had strapped him down to the bed by his wrists, ankles chest and legs.

McCann and Ryu were in the corridor between the two bays, standing at the doctor's medical station talking. McCann, looking decidedly rough, had his boot on the chair with rifle slung over his back and cigar in hand. Ryu was bent over trying to make sense of the data on the station monitor, whilst questioning Athena whom answered as best she could.

Hassif was greeted by McCann who was in a jolly mood for now, 'Hey there Hassif! We got the French bastard!'

McCann began chuckling though he was the only one amused.

Hassif looked over at Louis 'Are the injuries serious Duncan?'

McCann put his boot on the floor and placed his hand on Hassif's shoulder 'Yes, it's very serious ... I'm afraid he's going to live!' McCann chuckled even harder and let out a small laugh.

McCann seemed to be oblivious to the gravity of the situation, either that or he just didn't care. Either way Hassif found his humour to be in very poor taste.

Hassif ignored McCann as best he could 'Ryu what's happening?' he asked in the hope of getting a coherent answer.

Ryu was busy at the medical station 'Could you help me here Hassif, I can't work this medical station.'

'Sure,' said Hassif popping past McCann as quickly as the Martian gravity allowed.

Hassif soon got the answers Ryu was searching for, however translating the data was the problem. He'd reactivated Louis' chip and downloaded the stored data since he went missing, but none of them understood it. It wouldn't be until Weissmuller had got hold of it that a proper diagnosis could be made.

Hassif spoke to McCann who was still sniggering at his own jokes 'I'm sending this for Doctor Weissmuller, Duncan.'

McCann replied dismissively 'Very well,' and went back to puffing on his cigar.

'Don't you think you should send it now Duncan?' poked Ryu to which his grin dropped.

'Fine send it to my station,' replied McCann making off for the command centre.

Hassif whispered 'What's up with him?'

Ryu shook her head 'I'm not sure, maybe it's the pressure or the relief? Louis could have brought this whole mission to an end while we were gone.'

'What happened down there?'

Ryu's face remained stern 'Louis went for his weapon; McCann had to shoot him, twice.'

Hassif turned to look at his friend being moved onto the operating table next to the bed. His suit was off and the droids were applying an organic gel to his wounds. The gel promoted organic cell growth whilst sterilizing the wound at the same time. Fortunately there were no projectiles to remove. Louis' mental state was of more concern than any physical damage 'What will happen once his wounds are healed?'

Ryu walked up to the window and folded her arms 'I don't know, there's nowhere on Tharsis to detain anyone. If his mental health doesn't improve he'll have to remain sedated I suppose.'

Hassif folded his arms and turned too Ryu 'That's crazy, you can't hold him like that!'

Ryu raised her eyebrows 'What would you suggest?'

Hassif thought for a few moments 'He could be confined to quarters until the first transport returns for Earth.'

Ryu closed her eyelids and shook her head 'He's too much of a threat to allow even the freedom of his quarters, and to have him on a spaceship for 3 months? I wouldn't want to be on that ship! No we're all safest with him under sedation until he's cured.'

Hassif was becoming angry 'And what if he isn't cured?' he asked in a heightened tone.

'In my country he'd be retired, it would be a waste of resources to treat him.'

Hassif raised his voice still further 'Well we aren't living in a pseudo fascist state where humans are disposed of like yesterday's trash, are we?'

Ryu was taken aback, Hassif was such a passive and easy going man; he'd never displayed any hostility towards her. Nor had he mentioned any political or moral problems with her or her country before now.

Ryu understood many disagreed with Korea and its policies so never spoke on the subject herself. During the media interviews it was understood there would be no political questions and Ryu was told not to engage on the subject.

The Korean remained silent, she couldn't think of what to say. Hassif just stared back at her and his aggressive expression was rather unsettling.

Fortunately before it could go any further McCann entered the med lab, 'Just sent off the data on Louis' chip to Geneva folks.'

There was no reply, Hassif and Ryu stood both with folded arms glaring at each other.

'Don't thank me all at once!'

Still nothing was said, he realised there was an atmosphere 'Am I interrupting?'

Ryu broke the standoff; she walked to the table and grabbed her rifle then walked out of the med lab. On her way past McCann she spoke 'No,' then walking into the corridor said 'I'm returning this to the weapons locker Duncan.'

'Hold onto it Ryu, we're still on alert while that thing is out there.'

'Fine.'

She walked out into the northern wing and made off for the command centre.

McCann approached Hassif 'What was that all about?'

Hassif kept his arms folded 'Nothing.'

McCann didn't press Hassif any further, 'I'm going to need you in the command centre Hassif. Faraday wants you to check our cyber security and certify all the firewalls, especially Athena. She has to be 100% secure from anything if it gets in here.'

Hassif unfolded his arms 'So he wants us to make contact with it?'

McCann nodded 'That's the plan.'

Hassif thought for a moment 'Can I work in here for a while Duncan?'

'Of course.'

He assumed Hassif wanted to watch over his friend on the table in med bay 1.

Hassif gave a small smile 'Thank you.'

He sat down at the doctor's station using it to access his in the command centre. Hassif was more concerned with cooling down before he spoke to Ryu again. He needed to be calm when apologising for his outburst.

McCann left for the command centre 'See you soon Hassif and let me know when you've finished alright?'

Upon entering the command centre Ryu was at her station ordering one of the high atmosphere drones to do a sweep of Tharsis. She was also preparing a scram drone in case it was required, the droids kept it charged and fuelled for flight 24/7.

McCann placed his rifle and monocle on the central table alongside Ryu 'So can you tell me what the hell was going on in there, or are you going to stay mum too?'

Ryu didn't flinch but remained at her station.

'Major I asked you a question.'

Ryu stopped for a moment 'Nothing,' then carried on with her work.

'Colonel McCann I have a report,' spoke the soft voice of Athena breaking the uncomfortable silence.

McCann looked up 'Go for it Athena.'

'The transmission of brainwaves has just completed a full scan of all the crew members including myself. It has returned to Engineer Beaumont and remains closest to his brainwave pattern.'

McCann looked up 'Excellent Athena, please download the results to my office.'

Athena's voice spoke softly again 'Yes Colonel and Colonel, it appears the transmission is emanating from the object named the Gordii stone. The signal increased in strength and proximity as it followed Major Ryu returning to Tharsis. I believe its effects may be more potent than before.'

McCann nodded 'Thank you Athena, I'll send it to Geneva as soon as it's downloaded.'

'You're welcome Colonel.'

McCann turned to Ryu still working at her station 'I've been ordered to make contact with it, Hassif is preparing cyber security. You and I will attempt contact with it in three days. Whatever dispute you and Hassif have I expect it to be resolved long before then understood?'

Ryu didn't move away from her work 'Understood,' then after a pause 'what are they going to do about Louis?'

McCann took a drag from his cigar 'They don't know yet, if he recovers then after observation he can be released. If not he remains sedated until they decide, I suppose, either way we'll have to deal with this Gordii stone without him.'

Ryu started to chuckle to herself 'It's kind of funny, as soon as Louis is gone we have a personality clash. Who'd have thought that asshole Beaumont was actually preventing us from killing each other.'

McCann gave a puzzled look 'What do you mean?'

Ryu turned from her station to look at McCann puffing his cigar 'You'd have asked Athena what was said, then looked over the footage once you got into your office anyway.'

McCann took the cigar from his lips and smiled 'Yes mum!'

Ryu smiled back at him 'We had an argument, well not an argument but Hassif became quite aggressive towards me in the med bay.'

McCann still puzzled sat on the table holding his cigar 'Well what did he say?'

Ryu took a deep breath 'He wanted to know what would happen if we couldn't cure Louis, I didn't think. I told him that in Korea he'd be retired.'

McCann began to laugh 'I was always against state termination ... however I think you've just enlightened me with your Korean wisdom!'

Ryu fought off her giggles 'It was serious, Hassif got really angry and said something about this not being a fascist state. He was ready to attack me!'

McCann smiled 'I couldn't see Hassif attacking you.'

'I was afraid for a moment, I was getting ready to pull my pistol if he made a sudden move but then you walked in.'

McCann still smiling shook his head 'You're exaggerating surely?'

Ryu maintained her opinion 'No, I was ready to defend myself. You sensed it when you walked in didn't you?'

McCann took a puff of his smoke 'There was quite an atmosphere when I entered. He'll be working in med bay for a while if you want to speak to him and no offence intended Yong.'

Ryu smiled 'I know, not everyone agrees with it in Korea. It's an imperfect system but like Churchill said all the others we've tried suck more.'

McCann took his rifle and monocle 'If you need anything just let me know Yong,' and walked into his office.

His office was rather messy, a dirty ashtray sat on his desk which he emptied into the trash aperture. He closed the aperture locked it and at the press of a button the contents were sucked into the trash compacter for the command centre. The trash would eventually end up decomposing in a large waste tank, intended to supply botanical gardens at some point in the future.

McCann then slumped into his chair resting his boots up on the table. With one hand he held his cigar and the other he rummaged around in the large bottom draw fishing out a bottle of Balvenie and a glass. Still on duty he poured himself a drink and lit a fresh cigar from his holster's ammo pocket. Torching the foot he leant back and began to relax.

Thirty minutes later Ryu knocked the door 'Come in,' called McCann.

She opened the door and stepped in 'I have a full report from the data recorder ready to send Duncan.'

McCann sat up putting his boots on the floor 'Excellent send it to my station and I'll transmit it.'

Ryu tapped her wrist pad 'Would you mind if I made a suggestion Duncan?'

McCann who was still in a jolly mood replied 'Certainly not, what's up Yong?'

'You shouldn't be drinking on duty Duncan.'

McCann smiled 'The cameras are switched off in here and Athena is screening my data for alcohol, so don't get worried.'

Ryu stepped forward 'Duncan you shouldn't be drinking on duty at all, even if no one finds out it will still impair your judgement. Please put it away or I'll have to report you, and get a shave you look like an animal!'

McCann finished the glass and put it away with the bottle, his demeanour was rather unhappy now 'Anything else?'

Ryu answered him 'Clean this place up, will you? The whole command centre stinks of those damn cigars and you should probably get that suit decontaminated. It'll be the only way to purge the smell from it!'

McCann sent the data from his desk then stood up and with his arms outstretched, 'Is there anything else?'

Ryu shook her head 'No but if I think of anything I'll let you know, oh and I've patched up things with Hassif.'

McCann walked past her making for his quarters and whispered in an annoyed tone 'Marvellous.'

Ryu was right, he needed to clean himself up, he was in no state to make contact with intelligent life looking like a mountain man. McCann shouldn't have been drinking but whilst the others were away and with Louis attempts to bring down Athena, McCann had started on the whisky. The way the Englishman saw it the whole mission was collapsing and he was damned if he was going to die before having a good drink and smoke.

McCann didn't drink much anyway. A single glass would last him two hours. Not enough to impair his judgement, in his opinion. If he wanted to get hammered he could have done it a lot easier with some high alcohol Vodka. No, he enjoyed the taste of good highland cream much the same as the smooth sweet taste of expensive tobacco.

Now they were getting ready to make contact with some alien device that had nearly killed him twice. As far as McCann was concerned the mission was already an unmitigated disaster. He was sick of bureaucracy and taking orders from people that didn't seem to have a damn clue. In the SBS it was understood you were going into dangerous situations where circumstances could change in the blink of an eye. Mars was meant to be quite the opposite; it was supposed to be a safe planned journey to and from the red planet.

Establish Tharsis, deliver the SI and attach the ribbon. Do some scouting and set up a few other systems then come home and get all the glory. However it had all gone pear shaped and he felt it was more like some special operation in a war zone. He was making crash landings then hunting down crazy men in tunnels! Suddenly there was a complete unknown they had to make contact with. An unknown that was, by the way, trying to scramble their brainwaves!

McCann was sick to the back teeth. If he could just quit and go home he would have done it long ago. However they were stuck on this hell hole, millions of miles from civilization. The Englishman felt that he was entitled to drink and smoke as he pleased and if Faraday had a problem in Geneva it was just hard beans.

In the meantime Hassif was going over the cyber security systems in Tharsis, preparing to defend against any attack made by the Gordii stone. This was Hassifs speciality, as a young man he'd been scouted whilst studying at university. He was studying for a degree at Jawaharlal Nehru University in Delhi, where he was approached by a man offering him a job with the government. It wasn't unusual since he was about to get his degree and there were many companies and corporations scouting for fresh blood. A job in the state sector didn't interest him though. He had a poor family that had struggled to put their prodigy into a good university. Hassif felt indebted to them, they lived in poverty just to get him through university. It was his responsibility to repay their faith by finding a good job upon leaving. Hassif was looking at getting into a large IT corporation, with his skills he could easily work his way to lead programmer within a few years.

The government scout was dressed in a polite beige linen suit. Hassif wasn't interested in a low paid government job; yet his good Indian manners prevented him from refusing the offer of tea at a local cafe in the University Park. Hassif listened to the offer and after a while the scout could sense a lack of interest, despite the smile and bobbing head.

The scout sipped at his tea then asked 'What is it you want from us Mr. Sharma?'

Hassif was too polite to answer him and smiled.

The scout spoke again 'We want you to work for us but we need to know what you want from us. Please don't worry about being indiscreet, tell me what it is.'

Hassif put down his cup 'I don't want you to think I'm being crass. My family is very poor and have invested everything in putting me through university. The government doesn't pay as well as say Gelan Corp, I hope you understand me?'

The scout's head bobbed and he smiled 'I understand Mr. Sharma. What if I said Bharat Cybernetics has a career that would pay far more than anything Gelan Corp could offer you?'

Hassif smiled 'I'd think you were crazy.'

The scout smiled 'I understand. I approached you Mr. Sharma because the government had you marked a long time ago. We are willing to match anything offered by any corporation with 25% on top.'

Bharat Cybernetics Limited was and still is a government owned weapons division. It built and maintained the national defences against anyone that would try to attack via digital methods. In other words it was India's Cyber warfare division.

Hassif wasn't interested in programming firewalls, viruses or creating new and inventive ways to carry out Denial of Service attacks, besides the pay was pretty low; which was probably why India was so poor at defending against cyber-attacks from her aggressive neighbours.

Hassif looked out at the grass and fountain in the University Park then at the scout 'My parents put all they have into this; I can't tell them I'm taking a state job.'

He was right, they would've been very disappointed. They hadn't put him through university to take a low paying job with little future.

The scout leaned forward and spoke softly so that the other students at the cafe didn't hear 'We're willing to clear any debt your parents have Mr Sharma. If you sign a 5 year contract you can buy them a new house in a nice district. Bharat Cybernetics is willing to pay up to 40 million rupees on the house.'

Hassif smiled 'You're joking now, surely?'

The scout smiled 'No Mr. Sharma I'm quite serious. Your parents will be looked after. You will receive a salary surpassing any you can find in the private market.'

The scout passed Hassif a card 'Please visit us this weekend and bring your parents. We'll put you up in a nearby hotel so that we can show you and your family our facility over the weekend. The head of operations is eager to speak with you.'

Hassif took the card in disbelief; once again his good Indian manners prevented him from refusing.

The head of operations at Bharat Cybernetics Limited sold the job to Hassif's parents. Even without the knowledge of their debts being wiped and a free house. His father was excited but his mother was still wary.

Once they moved into the new house his mother had changed her mind. Whenever the subject of children was brought up by the neighbourhood women his mother always mentioned how her son worked for Bharat Cybernetics with pride. His father didn't need the subject to be brought up however. He was quite willing and able to bring it up out of nowhere.

He had moved from slums to the very well to do south Delhi and was rubbing shoulders with the better classes now. He had no debts and his son earned more than most could dream of. For his parents it was a dream come true.

Hassif was pleased to see them happy, though he wasn't very interested in the job. It wasn't bad but he found it rather less than challenging. Often he wondered why they paid so much money for him to do such mundane work. Nevertheless Hassif did it since he imagined most jobs on leaving university were going to be fairly boring until he made his way up. So why not take the best paying shade of boredom?

After a few months of working on firewalls for low level security systems he was asked to see Mr. Mehta before leaving that day. Hassif was a little concerned; he hadn't seen Mr. Mehta since his parents had visited. Mr. Mehta was the CEO of the company and it was unusual for employees to see him.

At the end of the day Hassif made his way to the top floor and walked into his secretary's room, 'Mr. Sharma?' she asked.

Hassif nodded and smiled timidly 'Yes,' he squeaked.

She smiled and tapped her screen 'Mr. Mehta, Mr. Sharma is here.'

A deep voice replied 'Send him in please.'

The secretary smiled at Hassif 'You can go in now Mr. Sharma.'

Hassif timidly stepped into the large office. The opposite wall was taken up by a window looking out onto the grounds of the building. Mr. Mehta got up from his chair behind the large mahogany desk with a statue of Ganesh sitting on it. He approached Hassif and shook his hand 'Please sit down,' he said with a smile. Mr. Mehta was a large portly man dressed in an expensive suit designed to hide his figure. Whatever he'd paid for it Hassif was sure it was too much.

Hassif sat down expecting to be fired.

'Mr. Sharma I've called you in because you will be starting a new job.'

Hassif shuddered, he was certain he was about to be shifted to some inactive post.

Mr. Mehta smiled 'Or should I say you were selected. We have decided to create a new division that is to be the India's front line in cyber warfare. Your three months here was merely a test of your abilities, you have passed.'

Mehta smiled and shook his hand.

Hassif shook his hand in a state of astonishment.

Mr. Mehta carried on 'Next week you'll start work at the newly constructed cyber warfare division not far from here. Your pay will be tripled as of now, how does that sound?'

Hassif cleared his throat 'Thank you Mr. Mehta.'

His boss laughed 'Call me Giri, may I call you Hassif?'

Hassif nodded 'Yes.'

His boss then began again 'As you know the Chinese invaded Nepal some years ago. Since then India has suffered repeated cyber attacks. You have been chosen as our first line of defence and attack, Hassif. The division is very small right now with just one team of the most capable programmers. If you can prove yourselves against the Chinese it will be expanded. Do you think you're up to the job Hassif?'

Hassif smiled 'Yes Sir.'

His boss laughed again 'My name is Giri! When you come into work next week pick up your belongings from your desk and go to the helipad. You and a few others will be flown to your new workplace and good luck Hassif!'

He shook Hassif's hand rigorously again.

Hassif stood up 'Thank you,' then left in a daze.

Next week he was flown to his new workplace it was a small complex not far from Bharat's main building. Hassif recognised the team leader as the man who scouted him at university. He shook his hand and introduced himself as Nick. Nick shook hands with the other people that had been flown over with Hassif. They all seemed equally bewildered to be there clutching plastic boxes filled with desk ornaments and stationary.

The workplace was very different to the city of stations in the open plan work floors of the Bharat main plant. In here it was a large open space with no small walls dissecting the floor. It really was open, with people working in what Nick described as a fluid environment. Stations even had 3D hologramatic displays.

Hassif had seen one of these at his university and the waiting list to use it for just half an hour was a nightmare. He'd used one twice in his lifetime and now he had one to himself! When Nick showed him the station Hassif was in shock. All of the staff brought in that day were knocked back by the equipment that would be at their sole disposal.

After the new acquisitions settled in; Nick, dressed in a sharp navy blue two piece suit and a mandarin shirt, called their attention. The room was circular with islands of 3-4 stations dotted around. At first sight the design was chaotic but in practice it was the most efficient plan for the purpose. Nick stood in a circular pulpit located at the centre of the room with his ear mic on.

He pointed to one of the large screens that were sitting on the circular wall encompassing the room. The screen turned on to show a wall of code. A garbled mess to most people but to all of the men and women in the room it was as clear as reading in their first language. Nick began 'This code was intercepted three days ago. It was traced back to somewhere in Xizang. The code was designed to lock us out of our air defence systems; thankfully an alert operator recognised it as a threat before the firewall let it go. If successful our missile defence systems on the Xizang border could have been down for hours. The firewalls have already been updated; however the military is working on updating their software to block this program should it be inserted internally. It will take them weeks to come up with a solution. So your first task is to adapt the software for the missile shield on the Xizang border. Your stations have full access to a copy of both the missile software and the malicious program that attempted to attack it.'

Nick looked around with a smile 'Any questions?' the room was silent 'Then let's get to work!'

Hassif transferred the contents of his old desk to his new one and got to work immediately. Nick strolled around the room asking if anything was required. He didn't seem to do much other than be very polite and make them all feel comfortable. The missile defence program was a secondary concern of Nick's. He walked from island to island, a slim man in his forties, he was trying to create a team.

Nick observed, throughout the day, as the chaos of un-channelled effort slowly became something he recognised as order. The brilliance of the people he'd gathered at much expense and personal effort shone through the darkness of disorder. Before the day was finished he was presented with an improved version of the missile shield software. What would have taken their military weeks he'd done in a single day. Not only that but his version had some extra modifications. Shoring up a few leaks his team believed would be future points of vulnerability.

The Army was not so ready to just install it, they waited for their updated version and tested it alongside Nick's.

They installed Nick's and the work started to come in thick and fast. Soon Bharat Cybernetics was rewriting military software and the contracts for new projects had justified the initial investment. Mr. Mehta was a regular visitor, overjoyed at the success of his company and his new division. It became clear Nick was more than an employee but also Mr. Mehta's son.

Hassif came to the conclusion that this project would never have happened if Mr. Mehta's son hadn't pushed for it. A typical Indian father he loved his son and would sacrifice anything for him. He was probably very apprehensive about the Cyber Warfare Division. Anyone else proposing the idea would've been told to get back to work and be quiet. Nick managed to wrangle his father into it however. Now they were ahead of their competitors in the private sector and Mr. Mehta was the man to be seen with if you were a politician.

Xizang was one of the rogue states of China, it wasn't clear who (if anyone) was in control. All the Indian government needed to know, was that it sat on their border and they were subject to regular attacks. Mostly border skirmishes with regional warlords or as Nick used to call them "stick fights", meaning that they didn't challenge the Indian military much. Opium was harvested in large quantities inside Xizang and too much of the final product ended up in India.

Xizang or the warlords inside the area, reports were sketchy and control could change frequently, weren't interested in fighting India. They merely desired to sell their heroin to its population. Often the military got in the way since the border was sealed.

They'd started using cyber-attacks to disable border posts or throw them into confusion long enough to fly a drone over the border into India. The missile shield which automatically shot down these drones was always a target and they found new and inventive ways of delivering cyber-attacks.

Xizang operatives had started delivering attacks by hand, by-passing any network firewalls so even closed systems were vulnerable now. On one occasion the shield had been reprogrammed to shoot down Indian aircraft, many died before it was shut down.

But with Bharat Cyber Warfare the military were closing the gap and fast. Nick was slowly but surely starving the warlords of their finances and helping clean up the streets of India.

Nick had become such a success that one of the warlords in his desperation attempted a full scale assault on the Indian border. His objective was to ravage the border destroying the shield and allowing full access to Indian customers again.

The warlord's name was Niu, better known as the ox. His brand of heroin was stamped with a seal of the same animal. His cyber-attacks had become less and less successful over the last couple of years, strangling his finances. Unless the Ox could break the border open, he was afraid of losing his position and his life; treachery and lust for power were rife in Xizang. The Ox gathered his military and attacked the northern border with an armoured spearhead.

The same day of the attack Nick stood in his pulpit and gathered his flock around. He pointed to one of the wall screens. There was media footage of Russian made tanks moving at full speed in armoured columns towards the border. The screen turned off and in a serious voice Nick spoke 'Today an armoured column crossed over into India via Tashigang. The warlord known as the Ox is behind it. We were taken by surprise and the border area is under his control for now. The Army and Air force won't be able to mount a counter attack strong enough to push him back for some days. Ladies and gentlemen it's time for us to change our tack. We are going from defence to offence and I want to have something before a counter attack is mounted or Niu withdraws back into Xizang, any questions?'

Hassif spoke up 'Can we have access to the Russian software they're using?'

'You'll all have access to what we could obtain from the military. It isn't much, they refused to release everything to us ... I'm sorry.'

Hassif smiled at Nick to comfort him and Nick smiled back 'Anything else?' there was silence 'Let's get to work then.'

Later that day Mr. Mehta arrived looking decidedly ill. He was speaking to his son and wiping the sweat from his forehead at the same time. Hassif couldn't help himself and listened in on what was being said. From what he gathered Mr. Mehta was in very hot water. The blame for the attack had been passed over by the military to Mr. Mehta. Apparently it was his fault because he'd done such a good job defending the military systems. Pushing Niu to the edge, the Ox had been forced to play his only remaining card. Politicians were giving him the cold shoulder and it looked as if his position was in jeopardy. Nick calmed his father down and assured him he'd put things right. Mr. Mehta left unconvinced, he was being used as a scapegoat, all the people at the top had a target painted on Giri's.

Hassif quickly turned to the job in hand, the software they had been given was of low importance. Hassif combed through the programmes looking for something that could be detrimental. The others were doing much the same, about 40 people worked there now. Hassif noticed how the Russians replicated a lot of the code they used in different systems. He assumed they'd copied and pasted the same code in higher level systems. Russians were very pragmatic people and probably didn't see the need to change something that already worked.

Hassif approached Nick with his idea he pointed out how some segments of script were replicated over several different systems. If he could decipher the Russian coding language he could send simple commands bypassing firewalls or security lock outs.

Nick scratched his neck 'How would you do that? If you send a command you'll need command codes or a security key. Besides how would you get it past the firewalls first? We don't have time to insert and agent.'

Hassif shook his head 'No I'm not using their command structure. Look, imagine you have written four sentences say a poem.'

Hassif took out his tablet and brought up one of his books then displayed a poem,

'I wandered lonely as a cloud
That floats on high o'er vales and hills,
When all at once I saw a crowd,
A host, of golden daffodils;
Beside the lake, beneath the trees,
Fluttering and dancing in the breeze.

Continuous as the stars that shine
And twinkle on the milky way,
They stretched in never-ending line
Along the margin of a bay:
Ten thousand saw I at a glance,
Tossing their heads in sprightly dance.

The waves beside them danced; but they
Out-did the sparkling waves in glee:
A poet could not but be gay,
In such a jocund company:
I gazed---and gazed---but little thought
What wealth the show to me had brought:

For oft, when on my couch I lie
In vacant or in pensive mood,
They flash upon that inward eye
Which is the bliss of solitude;
And then my heart with pleasure fills,
And dances with the daffodils.'

He showed it to Nick 'Imagine that this is code. Say it's a script for prioritising commands into order, from most important to least. The Russian decide to use it in all their military software since it's a reliable script that works, do you follow me so far?'

Nick nodded his head 'Sure, go on.'

Hassif took the tablet 'Now imagine I know the language and this is imbedded into every piece of software, from their scram drones to the meal dispenser in the mess. I have a programme that targets this and activates select parts of it like this,' Hassif tapped the tablet screen and gave it back to Nick.

He'd underlined four words in the passage of the poem together they spelt out 'Float on the waves.'

Nick gave the tablet back 'If we had a script that sent out commands continuously at random it would act as a DoS attack; locking them out of their own weapons systems. It would have to be a virus too since we're stuck for time which means it's a lot easier to detect," Hassif went out on a limb "I think we could hide it long enough. It doesn't have to shut them down for a long time just a lot of systems at once right?'

Nick nodded 'Alright get your team working on this, there are three teams working on insertion. Let me know when you're finished I'll let them know what you're proposing,' Nick put his hand on Hassif's shoulder and smiled 'thank you.'

By the end of the day Hassif and his team had learned the Russian code. A programme had been developed to send out random commands via the common script in all their software; thus bypassing the software's own security checks, hopefully. Another team that specialized in computer viruses believed they could mask the programme long enough to replicate it throughout their network. The virus would have a timer, at which point it activates and starts a deluge of random commands, speaking to anything on the network that uses the common script, paralyzing the enemy.

Within twelve hours Nick had a working proposition. If the Army could get the virus into the enemy network they could paralyze the Ox. Then it was down to the military, they could launch a counter offensive immediately without having to wait days or weeks for reinforcements.

Within an hour there was a four star General standing next to the pulpit with Mr Mehta and Nick explaining the proposed cyber-attack. Mr Mehta was very anxious waiting on the word of the General who seemed a little sceptical of it all. However Nick was very good at persuading people. After Nick finished the General who was a plump man with a rather pale face, no doubt his head was on the line along with Mr Mehta's, took the chip from Nick. He thanked Nick and all the people that had worked on it.

Then to Mr Mehta the General said 'We have a captured enemy spy drone, we'll upload this to the drone's drive and let them recapture it. If it works this will save both our necks, if not I'm sorry this all came back on to you Giri. Those cowards took all the glory when you turned it around, but as soon as something goes bad they pass the buck to you.

You'll know in a couple of days if it worked and I'll make sure you get the recognition you deserve.'

Two days later and the armoured offensive had been halted. The enemy had found their lost spy drone and downloaded the drive. Unknown to them the virus lay hidden inside, like a small bomb hiding in an oil tanker.

It was given a day or so to spread copying itself from drive to drive throughout as many networks as it came into contact with.

A small force of Indian tanks and scram drones, that up until this point had lain helplessly watching the enemy dismantle their missile shield and vandalise every border defence, sprang into action at noon.

The Ox watched powerless as half his scram drones dropped out of the air. The computer networks linking his army, allowing it to function as one, locked up. Tank commanders in the field weren't receiving orders. They didn't know where anyone else was or what they were doing. Some tanks refused to respond to the driver's orders, then they were hit by the Indian forces.

Despite being small and not having the best military equipment by a long stretch, it was still like shooting fish in a barrel. Tanks lay strewn in a disorganised column and the pilots blew them apart one by one unopposed. Enemy tank crews fled for cover leaving the dormant hunks of metal to be destroyed. Once all the Chinese tanks were destroyed the Indians executed their armoured counter attack, not that there was anything left to oppose it. Within two hours the ox was in custody along with his army or what was left of it. Xizang fell into disarray shortly afterwards with several warlords fighting for control, leaving India time to rebuild their defences.

At Bharat Cyber Warfare Division the next day Mr Mehta threw a party. The relief on his face was enough to put everyone in high spirits. Tears ran down the boss's cheeks as he hugged his son. News reports were being played on every wall screen in the large workplace, whilst the staff drank the fine champagne he'd laid on.

Nick jumped into the pulpit 'Everyone quiet please,' then he turned the volume up on one of the screens. The news caster was talking about the Chinese offensive and how it had been stopped. Capturing the Ox a in a brilliant pincer manoeuvre. A picture of the Ox came up on the screen; it was obviously taken post capture since he looked a lot worse for wear. The mighty Ox seemed as if he hadn't slept for a week whilst on a continuous bender. Scruffy hair and a split lip with that worn out expression made Hassif wonder why he'd been so feared in the first place.

Next there was a picture of the General that Nick had spoken too with his father four days ago. He'd co-ordinated the counter attack. General Kadam was sporting a beaming smile and declining to mention any particulars of what happened. He did make reference to Bharat Cybernetics Limited and thanked everyone working there for their contribution. The General was making it very plain who he attributed this victory too. The General's complexion was looking a damn sight better than four days ago.

Mr Mehta was saved along with the entire Cyber Warfare division. Over the next eight years it went from strength to strength until eventually India was a world leader in Cyber Warfare.

Hassif signed a second five year contract but when that was up he was scouted by the I.S.A. Hassif was fascinated with Synthetic Intelligence. He wasn't very enthusiastic about going to Mars or leaving his family behind or leaving his job, now that Nick and Giri were practically family too. After thinking on it he decided to go to Geneva and take the test. If he failed it didn't matter, but if he passed he would be able to work with Athena. That was an opportunity he couldn't dream of if he stayed at Bharat Limited.

Nick understood and wished him well, whilst doing a poor job of hiding his disappointment. Mr Mehta shook his hand and let him know that if his family needed anything they only needed to call him.

Hassif's father saw it as a step backwards career wise. However his son had already achieved his expectations tenfold and he couldn't deny him this dream. His mother was happy to see him doing something he really wanted. Her son deserved it and it wasn't as if they would need anything after he left. They lived in relative luxury to most people in the world. Investing in their only son's education had paid dividends and now it was his turn to collect.

On reaching Geneva Hassif was a relative unknown compared to some of the other candidates. He was faced off against some of the fastest minds on the planet. They were given a day to become familiar with a new coding language, then fix the bugs within it. Hassif needed an hour to learn it and then fix it, even Athena couldn't pull that off. His competitors were whittled away until only Hassif remained.

Faraday didn't know much about coding but he realised there was a large gulf between Hassif and the other candidates. After two weeks of gruelling testing at Geneva Hassif had signed a contract and had access to the most advanced computer in human history. He spent much of his free time analysing Athena and getting to know her workings.

The Indian was fascinated that somewhere in Germany this consciousness had been grown in a vat. Then taught like a child how to communicate with computers. He philosophised many nights on what the world must look like from Athena's perspective. Wondering how she must conceptualise their world. He could have written a book on SI philosophy in his spare time if he hadn't spent it all teaching Athena. Hassif taught his student everything he could on coding and looking after herself digitally.

Chapter 8

The night before they were to make contact the crew of Athena gathered in the lounge, minus Louis who was still under sedation. He'd been brought out of sedation twice but each time Louis exhibited the same unstable behaviour. Neither Athena nor Weissmuller could do anything about it, healing his physical wounds was not a problem. With modern technology he'd be up and walking about as if nothing had happened. However his mental condition was beyond the scope of nanites.

Faraday informed McCann he'd have to find a method to shut down the Gordii stone. Faraday believed it to be Louis' best hope of a recovery. Weissmuller was also working with the tech labs on a device to block out the transmissions, but it wouldn't be ready for months. Shutting down the stone's transmissions was a priority.

Sitting around in the lounge Ryu and Hassif were chatting, now that they'd made a truce. McCann entered the room carrying two holsters. One had a pulse pistol in the holster and some ammo clips with power packs on the belt. McCann handed the empty holster to Ryu and the other to Hassif, both of them were puzzled.

Ryu sat up on the couch; she like the others was dressed in the I.S.A uniform of the silver space glove. Yet she already had a holster on, as per regulations during an alert. She looked at McCann again and noticed something was different. He was wearing the same uniform however he didn't have a shoulder holster. His weapon was in a holster that was strapped to his right thigh. This holster was attached by a thick piece of material to a gun belt fastened around his hip with velcro.

The belt carried ammo and power packs or in his case ammo, power packs and cigars. Ryu recalled seeing the belts before as they were standard issue for military and police armed response units.

'What are these for Duncan?' inquired Ryu.

After Hassif took his belt timidly, McCann pulled his cigar out of his mouth 'I had Athena make these up yesterday. A shoulder holster is fine for comfort but if I need to draw my weapon it'd get me killed. This could well save your bacon, Yong lady!'

McCann smiled but his attempt of humour had once again fallen flat.

Ryu didn't put it on but tightened her lips and looked at McCann in her disapproving fashion, 'You had Athena make it because you wanted to look like a cowboy, didn't you?'

Hassif laughed.

From McCann's face a sly grin emerged 'Then I guess that makes you two, my deputies? Now put on those holsters, I don't need to be fumbling for a weapon if I have to defend myself. Faraday wants to shut that thing down, if Louis is ever going to be brought out of sedation again.'

Hassif stood up slung the belt around his waist fastening it in the middle. He then removed his detachable leg pocket, as it was in the way of the holster, and put it on his left leg instead. Next he pressed the holster on his right leg and the velcro attached to his suit, then fastened the two holster straps around the thigh holding it in place.

Ryu stood up and took off her shoulder holster. After putting the new holster on she transferred the contents 'Happy now?'

McCann smiled 'You both look positively fearsome, now all we need is a ten gallon hat!'

Hassif laughed again 'Duncan I've never used one of these before, can I practice somewhere?'

Ryu rolled her eyes but McCann was in a positive mood tonight and wasn't going to let her be a downer. He put his cigar in his mouth and sat next to Hassif, pulled out his own pistol then took out the power pack and ammo clip 'First check that the power switch is off.'

On the left side of the weapon where the handle and the barrel met was a circular piece of metal with a small arm protruding out.

'Make sure the switch is down before you load it.'

Hassif was holding his weapon and following McCann's instructions. McCann picked up the power pack 'First take your power pack and slide it into the bottom of the handle. The rounded side slots into the back of the handle. You just slide it up and it locks in place,' McCann slid the power pack up the handle until it clicked in, as did Hassif.

He next picked up the ammo clip 'This is the ammo clip it's about a third the size of the power pack. Just slide it into the remaining space inside the handle. It'll lock in place; you can pull these out with a little force at any time as long as the power switch is off. Now turn on the power.'

McCann flicked the switch on the side of the pistol and a long whine was emitted as the rails charged.

'Look at the butt. On the power pack, the meter will display if it's charged,' McCann tilted his pistol, the meter showed green on the butt of the power pack. He pointed at the indicator on the butt of the ammo clip.

'This will let you know how many shots you have left,' the digital display read 50 in small numbers. 'Now you're ready to rock and roll my dear friend, any questions?'

Hassif flicked the switch off and the pistol emitted a low whine dropping in intensity as it powered down 'Any advice on hitting my target?'

McCann held his pistol with his right hand and rested the butt on the palm of his left hand which clasped onto his right, 'Try to hold it like this and breathe steadily. When you pause for breath squeeze the trigger. Keep a steady grip as it might try to jump out of your hand the first few times you fire it, before you get used to the kick.'

Ryu who had been catching up on soap operas whilst Hassif had his first firearms lesson commented 'I'm sure there won't be any need to use it though, what has Faraday said?'

McCann powered down his pistol and put it back into his holster 'He doesn't know what we might be facing. I've been advised to take every precaution.'

McCann walked over to the storage alcove on the wall which was now the drinks cabinet. McCann tapped the central panel and a handle popped out. He turned the handle and the wall panel swung open. Reaching inside he pulled out a bottle of Scotch and three glasses 'If we're lucky the droids can dismantle it or Hassif can turn it off from here.'

McCann brought the drinks over placing the bottle and glasses on the table; he poured them all a drink, 'Then we can get Louis back to his old happy go lucky self again!'

Hassif raised his glass 'I'll drink to that!' they clinked glasses.

Ryu turned off her soap opera 'So what are we going to do exactly, tomorrow?'

McCann took a sip of Balvenie 'First Hassif will try to set up a communications link and find out what it's transmitting. If he can Faraday wants it shut down, then droids will try to take it apart outside. It is not to enter Tharsis under any circumstances. If that doesn't work we can try to block all transmission from it. If that fails we may have to just try and open it up and physically switch it off with droids.'

Hassif was rather optimistic, 'I think it'll be easy enough to do, assuming that is a man-made object. If someone else made it then I'm not sure what to expect.'

Hassif had brought up a disturbing point but Ryu pooh poohed the idea 'I doubt some alien has sent a probe to make contact with us!'

'Why? We've done it more than once already, why wouldn't someone else try it?' countered McCann.

Ryu frowned 'Because we're dumb! Why send out a probe that will take millions of years to get here? Even if it were possible they'd all be dead by now! How would it be able to scan our brainwaves and do that to Louis? I don't think it makes any sense.'

Hassif took a sip and spoke up 'Well our nearest star is only 4 light years away. We could get there in under ten thousand years, probably under five thousand. There are a lot of stars less than ten light years away and they all have some form of planet or orbiting bodies around them.'

Ryu rolled her eyes again 'Five thousand, ten thousand a million what's the difference? It's a silly amount of time! That thing out there is probably something launched by the Russians before they joined the I.S.A or even the Chinese before the collapse.'

Hassif still wasn't giving up 'I said five thousand years but that's using our best technology. We know there are faster methods to travel, even faster than light travel has been proven. We just don't have the ability to harness it. Maybe someone out there does? I've been observing that thing since we made contact in the hauler. I'm sure that it isn't a man-made object.'

Ryu shook her head and McCann stepped in 'Well it seems that we'll settle this tomorrow when we make contact.'

The next day McCann awoke and slipped into his space suit, up to his waist. He preferred to sleep naked when in his own room rather than follow regulations. The rules stipulate wearing the suit at all times even in bed. He took his electric razor and tidied up his face. Next he applied a deodorant stick to his armpits; he sprayed some cologne on his neck and pulled the rest of the suit up.

McCann never felt properly prepared without some cologne from his favourite perfumer on Jermyn Street in London. Since he had his work cut out this morning he sprayed some No.89. It was a scent that put him in the rough and ready mindset and was a favourite historically amongst adventurers. He may not have been the first person on Mars but he was damn sure that the first cologne, or perfume as he preferred to call it, would be Floris No.89.

When ready he walked to the mess as fast as he could, on the way he looked up 'Athena how is everything?'

Her calming voice replied 'We are still at a level 3 alert Duncan. Louis remains sedated in med bay one but is stable. The Gordii stone has not moved, the Gordii stone transmissions persist. How are you Duncan?'

McCann smiled, it made him feel good when Athena used his first name. He slung on his gun belt and attached the leg holster 'I'm feeling very well today Athena, thank you for asking.'

McCann stepped into the mess, he took a breakfast tray and sat with Ryu 'Good morning Major how are you?'

Ryu was picking at some vegetables with rice 'Very good and you Duncan?'

'Good, where's our man of the moment today?'

Ryu was about to put a leaf of steamed cabbage in her mouth but stopped 'Sorry?'

'Hassif of course, have you seen him?'

Ryu put the cabbage in her mouth and while chewing it she spoke (a habit of hers McCann detested) 'Ask Athena.'

Her usual chirpy morning attitude was replaced by one of apprehension. McCann decided to give up engaging the Red Dragon in pleasant conversation and started on his porridge. Five minutes later Hassif came in wearing his holster and belt 'Well howdy partners!' he shouted. McCann laughed but Ryu rolled her eyes and carried on with her meal.

Hassif walked over to the dispenser and Ryu spoke to McCann again 'I knew you had these belts made to play cowboys, typical men.'

McCann smiled despite seeing her food rolling in her mouth when she spoke, 'These are practical you know?'

Ryu looked back with her half closed eyelids 'Really?' she said sarcastically.

Hassif sat down to start on his breakfast and McCann continued 'Certainly, do you know why all the cowboys in the movies have hip or thigh holsters?'

Hassif was smiling excitedly waiting for the answer but Ryu was bemoaning the fact she'd started this discussion.

'Please tell me why!' came her sarcastic reply.

'Because all the ones that wore shoulder holsters are dead!'

Hassif laughed and Ryu even managed a slight smile before going back to eating her breakfast.

Later in the command centre Hassif was poised at his station waiting for McCann to give the go ahead.

'Alright Hassif you can receive the transmission now.'

Hassif opened up the communications system; he'd spent the last few days closing off to the rest of Tharsis, and downloaded the message. McCann and Ryu both watched with bated breath. Hassif hurriedly reached for his tablet and grabbed his holster instead. Then he recalled his pocket was on his left leg. He reached into his left pocket, took his tablet out, then began working feverishly glancing back and forth between it and the station.

McCann spoke quietly 'Well?'

His Technician didn't reply straight away. Hassif kept looking back and forth and then activated his tablets 3D display. A block of code leapt off the screen in a jumble. It looked like a massive scaffold of characters some flickering from one place to another, others solidly fixed 'Fascinating!' murmured Hassif.

McCann couldn't retain his curiosity 'What is it man?'

Hassif was pulled from his trance for a moment. He looked squarely at McCann 'I think it's possibly a programme being transmitted to us ... but it isn't one of ours,' he whispered.

Ryu folded her arms 'What do you mean?'

Hassif went back to his work tapping his station screen and manipulating the scaffold of code on his tablet, 'I mean it isn't anything made by us, as in humans.'

Ryu let out a high pitched huff of disapproval 'How would you know that? You've only just seen it!'

Hassif still fixed on his two screens replied slowly 'I've learnt every coding language written and if I didn't know it I'd recognise it as a native one. It's like learning any language, if you've learnt Mandarin. You can recognise all the regional Chinese languages as being related and many words are similar. If you understand 99% of all the languages fluently and one pops up that you don't know. You can easily identify which it has most in common with and where the people that speak it originated. This language is perplexing ... it's like learning Egyptian but without a Rosetta stone.'

McCann and Ryu stood watching Hassif working as a man possessed. McCann asked 'Well can you understand the transmission? What is it trying to do?'

Hassif kept working 'I don't know ... I don't know if there is a message. This could be an executable program or perhaps just a method of saying hello? It could be a handshake program to verify the sender ... like I said it's perplexing. It hasn't done anything yet so just give me some time Duncan and when I have something I'll let you know, okay?'

McCann nodded 'Very well, you keep working,' the Englishman looked up 'Athena?'

Her soft voice replied 'Yes Colonel?' she addressed him by rank when on duty.

'Keep monitoring the Gordii stone if anything changes, alert us immediately.'

'Yes Colonel.'

McCann turned to Ryu 'Keep monitoring the area from above Major, who knows, there might be more of them out there.'

Ryu nodded, unfolded her arms and sat at her station.

An hour later and McCann sent off the first of the scheduled hourly reports for that day, keeping Geneva abreast of the situation.

According to Faraday the planet was afire with the Gordii stone. Media interest had shot off the scale after the stone had started tracking the hauler. Some believed it was a publicity stunt staged by the I.S.A, an attempt to grab more funding. The story of Louis and McCann shooting it out and an alien attack was so sensational the conspiracy theorists were drowned out.

The population of planet Earth spoke about little else. Media channels that didn't transmit something related to Mars were going dead. A media magnate was quoted in an interview as saying "Unless it touches upon Tharsis, the Gordii stone or Mars all you'll get for ratings is tumbleweed!"

Some channels had stopped scheduled viewing and instead of soap operas were running 24/7 reports on Tharsis. Talk shows were scrambling for anyone linked to the Mars mission. Reality TV had been decimated, the only reality TV worth watching was on Tharsis. Network America was now the most watched television channel in history and overnight the share price had rocketed. One evening Jerry Habeeb remarked that it would be cheaper to purchase your own island in the Caribbean, rather than buy 30 seconds of advertising space on Network America.

The people couldn't get enough. In France a petition had been started to bring Louis Beaumont home safely. They planned on presenting the signatures to William Faraday. It had already been signed by millions including several world leaders. The Pope was holding mass in the Vatican City where thousands turned up to pray for the safe return of their heroes.

McCann read his report, but he had bigger issues to deal with than media fame. He heard a voice from outside his office 'Colonel quickly, I have something!'

McCann leapt out of his seat bounding from his office into the command centre 'What is it?' he asked Hassif.

Ryu was already standing behind Hassif staring at his screen when McCann got over to his station.

'I believe that this is a simple ternary code system. I assumed it was something far more complex but it's a simplistic ternary language. I set up a virtual computer system to run it; this is what it came out as.'

Hassif pointed towards his screen and what McCann thought he saw was a picture. The image depicted looked to be a tall thin human female with both arms out stretched towards him. Hassif tapped his tablet 'Here you can see it properly in ternary.'

The image leapt out of his tablet in 3D. The arms were out stretched with the hands open and palms facing upwards. Above the figure on each side of her lay two solar systems. McCann recognised one as their home system, Sol. The other was different, it had more planets but no Jupiter size planets. The solar systems were in 3D and the planets spun around their respective suns. Above the solar systems floated a representation of what McCann assumed was the Milky Way, two areas were marked out. He again assumed one was the Sol system and the other area being the origin of the alien solar system represented. He didn't know where the Sun was in the Milky Way so had no idea which was which, but that was superfluous at this time.

It was quiet whilst all three of them marvelled for a moment. McCann straightened himself 'Can you make me a copy Hassif? I need to send this to Faraday.'

Hassif began working feverishly again he took a chip and placed it on his work stations transfer pad. After 10 seconds he put it in McCann's hand 'It'll be safe to download this to your office and send it to Geneva.'

McCann made off with the chip into his office. Thirty minutes later he had a reply which he displayed at the central station. The image appeared on the command centre table so everyone could watch it.

Faraday's face flickered to life as the table projected his image in the centre 'Thank you for the information Duncan, and thank Hassif.'

He was very reserved considering the situation and despite his character he was almost stony faced. Faraday continued 'As Hassif suspected it's a simple message in ternary, similar to binary transmissions attempted by SETI in the late twentieth century. Our people here believe the second star system is HE0107-5240 a population II star some thirty six thousand light years away in the galactic halo. In English that means it's very old and far away, suffice to say a lot of people here are very excited.'

Hassif peered at Ryu with an "I told you so" expression on his face; she pretended not to notice and continued to listen to Faraday.

'The central figure in the message on first sight is a human female. However our people reckon it to be almost seven feet, according to the proportions of the limbs. I'm not sure what that means for you but I'm just passing on the information. The message is just that a, message perhaps a galactic calling card? Anyway I've attached a similar message I want Hassif to transmit to the Gordii stone. It's a ternary calling card of our own, a 3D representation of the Pioneer plaques. After you've transmitted send me a report every thirty minutes and good luck to you all.'

McCann put a chip in Hassif's hand 'This is it.'

Hassif took the chip 'Thanks,' and leapt to his station to begin downloading it. A few minutes later he got up 'It's sent Duncan.'

All three of them watched the monitors tracking the Gordii stone.

The Gordii stone rose into the air hovering about a foot above the ground. Slowly it began to move towards Tharsis.

Athena's voice cut in 'Colonel the Gordii stone has ceased transmission and is approaching Tharsis.'

McCann looked up 'ETA?'

'It will arrive at the southern airlock in 43 minutes Colonel.'

McCann scratched the back of his head 'Athena move the hauler into the garage please.'

Ryu with folded arms challenged him 'You can't do that Duncan it's too dangerous!' McCann looked down towards Ryu's stern face 'Is there a problem Major?'

'It's too dangerous, what if it enters the garage? It would be inside Tharsis!'

McCann looked up 'Is the hauler moving Athena?'

Athena's soft voice replied 'Yes Colonel, are you sure you want me to open the garage door Colonel?'

McCann looked down at Ryu and stared her in the eyes 'Yes Athena, thank you.'

McCann tried to comfort the Korean 'It's not going to attempt to enter the garage Major. That thing has been waiting days for a reply. It's not going make a rush for our garage all of a sudden. That would be reckless and it has been nothing but noninvasive since it's been trying to contact us. No, it'll let the hauler dock and garage door close. When it gets to where it's going it'll stop and wait again, trust me.'

He smiled at her but she wasn't impressed. Ryu went back to looking at the monitor and checking up on her drone. The drone circled high up in the atmosphere scanning for anything of interest.

The Gordii stone pulled up outside the southern airlock. The stone was actually facing the garage door with the airlock door some 25 feet north. The stone stopped hovering and lay down peacefully on the gravely Martian soil. McCann and the others stood in the command centre, watching for what was to happen next.

McCann had Athena send the half hour reports so that he could devote his full attention to Tharsis and its safety. As McCann scrutinized the monitors he saw something rather disturbing. The hard jet black granite like surface started to wobble on the side below the pyramid. 'Do you see it?' he called to the others stood next to him.

'I see it!' replied Ryu.

First the side moved as if it were a thick jelly then it began to ripple taking on the appearance of thick oil. The ripples moved out from the centre first slowly then gathering pace. Gradually the substance became thinner and thinner until the bottom side underneath the pyramid had receded away.

McCann squinted but could see nothing inside the circular orifice that had now opened 'Athena can you see what's in there?' he shouted excitedly.

'The side of the Gordii stone is no longer present however I cannot detect anything inside.'

McCann looked up 'You must detect something? Radiation of some type?'

'I detect only the absence of anything Colonel, I'm sorry.'

'I'm sorry Athena, thank you.'

Ryu who was as stunned as the others turned to McCann 'We should send a droid to look inside while we can, maybe we can shut it down?'

McCann shook his head 'No let's just wait it out and see what it's doing. It hasn't been aggressive towards us.'

Ryu frowned 'It nearly killed us all on landing and has Louis is in a psychotic state in the med lab, this thing isn't benign Duncan. I could launch a scram drone and fly it into that opening right now.'

McCann kept watching the monitor 'That won't be necessary Ryu, thank you.'

She was getting more and more frustrated but McCann wasn't going to make a move that would get them killed. He believed the Gordii stone wasn't a malicious device but only intended to seek out life and make contact. Perhaps the brainwave scans were a part of seeking out intelligent life? He was certain their current predicament was merely an accident; taking steps to provoke it further would surely be a great folly. Akin to poking a sleeping lion in the eye with a stick, for all he knew.

After a few minutes the darkness extended from the orifice. All three in the command centre made it out as the darkness was broken up by the sun, 'Jesus Christ,' whispered McCann.

Hassif started muttering something in Hindi whilst he held tightly onto his small statue of Ganesh that usually adorned his station. Ryu neither did nor said anything she was motionless not moving a muscle at what was before her eyes.

Out of the gloom a tall figure dressed in a jet black ribbed space suit, similar to their space gloves, stepped into the Martian light. The helmet was also jet black. The entire suit was seamless down to the slim knee length boots. The helmet absorbed all light, so it wasn't apparent who or what was inside. However McCann did note that the helmet was slightly larger than the largest I.S.A helmets, and completely black.

What was blatantly obvious was the fact that it was a woman inside the suit. It was very tight fitting, displaying two small lumps on the chest that McCann assumed were breasts. She took several steps away from the Gordii stone and two more figures walked out from the gloom. They were much smaller in comparison to the first figure; probably a couple of feet smaller though it was difficult to tell when viewing via a monitor. Once the figures were outside, the orifice on the Gordii stone closed as it had opened. Waves of ripples now moved towards the centre and in a minute the black tide had closed the aperture; thickening until it was once again the consistency of hard stone.

The two smaller figures remained a step behind the first taller one, keeping their distance as she walked forward and extended her arms towards the airlock. Her palms faced the sky, the second figures followed suit holding the same gesture.

McCann pulled a pair of gloves from his left leg pocket 'Ryu you're coming with me.'

'You're not going out there are you?'

McCann made a wry smile 'No ... WE are, now put your gloves on.'

Ryu was obviously against this course of action 'Duncan you can't do that without speaking to Faraday first!'

McCann was quickly losing patience and raised his voice 'Faraday be damned! It would take 30 minutes to get the confirmation and I don't know how long they intend to stand there. Now get ready and follow me to the airlock Major!'

Ryu began attaching her gloves 'I hope you know what you're doing Duncan,' she whispered but McCann pretended he didn't hear.

'Hassif can you transmit another message to them?'

Hassif's hand squeezed tightly on Ganesh and McCann worriedly noted that it was shaking. 'Yes what do you want?' he asked in a shaky voice.

McCann put his hand on his shoulder 'Can you send them our general communication frequency?'

Hassif nodded his head 'Sure.'

McCann smiled and gripped his shoulder 'Thank you.'

He walked out of the command centre and shouted 'Ryu we have an engagement!'

Ryu caught up with him, still hesitant about what McCann had planned 'At least bring the assault rifles Duncan, we don't know if these pistols could even breakthrough their suits.'

McCann looked up 'Athena prep a scram drone please.'

'Yes Colonel,' came her soothing voice in the middle of all the madness.

Ryu was intent on questioning every order McCann gave, 'Duncan the rifles?'

McCann was even more irritated now 'No rifles Ryu, I'm not going out there to pick a fight.'

He looked up again 'If I order you to attack Athena I want you to ram that drone fully loaded into the three people outside Tharsis. The Gordii stone is your secondary target, understood?'

'Understood Colonel. Hassif has asked me to inform you our comms frequency was received by the Gordii stone Colonel.'

McCann was now checking his pistol 'Thank you Athena. Ryu check your weapon,' he heard the whine of her pistol as it charged up 'Leave the power on.'

Ryu was still playing up however, 'Duncan this is not a good idea going out there with only our pistols.'

McCann kept walking for the southern airlock 'Ryu those people haven't been waiting out there for days possibly months to have a shoot-out with us; bare in mind that the SBS did teach me something about picking your fights. Unless you're certain you can win you don't attack, unless ordered to. In fact our chances of coming off better against these guys are positively slim in my opinion. So I'm not going to antagonise them in anyway understood?'

Ryu finished checking her suit for leaks via the wrist tablet and huffed 'Understood.'

They both reached the airlock and stood inside the first room. The door closed behind them, McCann's helmet unfurled from the thick collar on his shoulders.

Once both of them had checked their suits for leaks they entered the next chamber. The door closed behind them and it equalised with the Martian atmosphere. Next the outer airlock door opened to reveal the three figures. They stood in the same pose; McCann thought they looked like a modern art sculpture.

McCann stepped outside onto the rusty Martian soil for the first time. With about ten feet between the first figure and himself he put his arms out mirroring her gesture. Ryu stood by his side mimicking the gesture also. The pair waited for the visitors to make their next move.

The tall female figure walked slowly but surely by herself, with her arms still out towards him. She bypassed McCann and walked straight to Ryu. McCann could tell that this woman was at least six and a half feet tall, now that she was beside him. She seemed taller to McCann since he was unused to being in the company of people much taller than himself.

She towered over Ryu placing her palms down onto Ryu's. A deep voice came over the comms that sent a chill down both of their spines. It made no sense, a foreign tongue that McCann didn't recognise. Ryu was equally at a loss, she didn't know what to do next with this giant looking down on her. She looked over at McCann for assistance.

McCann spoke 'Do you understand me?' but the tall slender figure ignored him and remain transfixed on Ryu.

Ryu was making desperate looks at McCann.

He urged Ryu 'Speak to her.'

'What do you want me to say?' she asked desperately.

McCann who still had his arms out shrugged his shoulders 'Ask if she understands you?'

Ryu looked upwards at the black helmet of the black figure in front of her 'Do you speak English?'

The figure began to speak in the same deep tongue. McCann's closest approximation was of someone speaking Mandarin in a deep heavy German accent. The words came close to some of the Mandarin he was taught in the SBS. Most of which he had forgotten, but there were no tones. No rising or falling to differentiate the meaning of the word, it was a deep and flat almost synthetic sound. McCann began to wonder if these things were in fact androids and not living organisms. It made sense but that was all superfluous right now. McCann tapped his wrist to communicate with Hassif causing the tall figure's head to snap in his direction quickly. The two smaller figures remained still and McCann slowly raised his hand until it rested by his shoulder palm facing her. McCann held the pose, as the human male on the Pioneer plaques.

The jet black figure relaxed and moved her attention back to Ryu.

McCann whispered into his mic 'Hassif can you hear me?'

Hassif replied in a loud voice 'Yes what is happening?'

'Can you transmit something on the English language to the stone?'

'What do you want?'

'I don't know, ask Athena. I want them to learn English, tell her to transmit whatever she believes is appropriate, understood?'

'I'm doing it now Duncan.'

Within 20 seconds the two shorter figures heads moved slightly. The taller figure retracted her arms. The towering female raised her hand in the gesture from the Pioneer plaques, a deep 'Hello,' came through McCann's earpiece.

McCann felt a wave of relief but Ryu was closer to a mental breakdown than relaxing. He encouraged Ryu 'Well speak back to her Ryu!'

Ryu who still had her arms out stretched spoke in a shaky voice 'Hello.'

She waited for a moment and looked back to McCann 'Well what now?'

'Invite them inside?'

Ryu grimaced at him 'You can't be serious Duncan! Faraday said they're not to be allowed inside, those were his strict orders!'

McCann still holding his pose replied 'No his orders were not to let the Gordii stone inside Tharsis. Now ask her to come inside that's an order.'

Ryu was feeling pressure 'Why do I have to do it?' she asked desperately.

'Because she's ignored me so far, now ask her!'

Ryu gathered herself and peered up at the six and a half foot giant in front of her 'Would you like to come inside?'

The figure waited for a moment and replied in a deep female voice 'Inside,' she pointed to the airlock behind Ryu.

Ryu nodded 'Yes,' pointing to the airlock herself.

The tall jet black figure replied, 'Yes.'

McCann moved towards the airlock but stopped when her head snapped at him again. Her body language intimated agitation.

McCann whispered to Ryu 'I think you need to lead her into the airlock.'

Ryu was becoming more and more tense as she felt the pressure pilling on; McCann was quite relaxed by comparison. He'd been through a lot worse than this. His job for years had been managing stressful situations.

Ryu walked slowly to the airlock, not that she could walk quickly in her current state. The slim dark figure followed her. Once they'd reached the airlock McCann decided to move towards them. After he moved the two smaller figures followed him. All the time McCann kept his hand hanging loose by his holster just in case.

Ryu opened the airlock and led the female figure in first with McCann and the others following shortly. The outside door closed and the chamber was pressurized. When ready Ryu lead them into the next chamber. Athena decontaminated the party then scanned for bio hazards but found none, all this time their guest stood quite still. The final door opened into Tharsis, Ryu stared at McCann after retracting her helmet with an "Are you sure you want to do this?" look. McCann nodded and she stepped into the main corridor of the southern wing.

The entire party followed Ryu into the corridor; Ryu looked at McCann again 'Now what?'

McCann pointed down the corridor 'Take them to the lounge I suppose?'

Ryu shaking her head in disapproval made off North towards the lounge, trailed by the tall female then McCann then the two shorter visitors. On reaching the lounge Ryu stood in the middle of the room. The visitors still hadn't removed their helmets. McCann wondered if they were helmets or were in fact their heads?

McCann decided to find out and he pulled out his bottle of Balvenie from the drinks alcove with three glasses. The visitors observed him shuffle about but made no move to do anything, they merely watched. He poured three glasses and gave one to Ryu. He offered another to the tall female who he assumed was the leader. She took the glass, watching McCann and Ryu as they held theirs firmly.

McCann spoke 'Drink?' and took a sip.

He had to shove Ryu with her elbow before she would drink from the glass but she took a tiny sip.

The visitor put her finger in the glass then waited for a few moments. After a few seconds she took her finger out and handed the glass back to McCann.

'No!' came the deep voice over the comms.

On taking the glass back the visitor turned about face and walked out of the room followed by her two companions. McCann put his two glasses down, quickly pursuing them followed by Ryu. The tall slim woman in jet black back tracked along the southern wing until they reached the airlock. The tall visitor pointed at the airlock door 'Exit,' came a deep Norse voice but McCann still recognised it as female.

He activated his helmet and opened the door, Ryu did the same. Hassif was nowhere to be seen as he was cowering in the command centre. McCann lead the visitors back outside, once they'd exited the airlock the visitors walked towards the Gordii stone. The tall female stopped, turned to Ryu raised her hand with palm towards Ryu.

'Goodbye,' came the chilling synthetic voice.

Ryu mimicked her, raising her hand 'Goodbye.'

McCann did the same but was ignored again.

The side of the Gordii stone opened once again allowing the visitors to slip back inside the nothingness they had appeared from. Ryu and McCann stood for a few minutes watching the stone, but nothing further happened.

McCann broke the silence 'Let's get back inside Major.'

They returned to the airlock and Tharsis, whilst returning to the command centre McCann put his hand on Ryu's shoulder 'Well done Yong.'

Ryu made a tense grunt and continued walking along the corridor. She was in a world of her own after what she had just been through. She had always been the most prepared of the crew and this had just hit her like a curve ball in the face. Ryu was still coming down as the events slowly sunk in.

Nothing further occurred concerning the Gordii stone that day, after a few hours had passed McCann decided to revive Louis. Hassif remained in the command centre monitoring the situation whilst both McCann and Ryu were in the medical bay.

'Athena, it's time for our sleeping beauty to awaken.'

'Please clarify your request Colonel?' replied Athena's calm voice.

Ryu rolled her eyes again 'It was a joke Athena, he means revive Louis.'

McCann grinned at Ryu who was still rather disturbed at the day's events. Louis lay motionless in med bay one with a droid watching over him.

'Technician Louis Beaumont is gaining consciousness Colonel,' informed Athena as Louis began to open his eyes. Louis, naked on the bed, started looking around him. Soon he became lucid and realised he was strapped tightly onto the bed. He tried to move a few times tugging on his limbs but to no avail. He relaxed and rested his head on the pillow then turned to the glass window where he saw McCann and Ryu looking in on him.

'Louis can you hear me?' asked McCann using the wall intercom.

Louis groaned 'Yes,' he sounded as if he had a bad hangover.

'Do you know how you got here Louis?'

Louis turned his head and looked up at the ceiling 'You shot me!' he grumbled.

'Why did I shoot you Louis?'

'I went crazy for a while, what is the date now?'

McCann held his lips closer to the intercom even though it wasn't necessary 'It's the 26th of September Louis.'

Louis' head rocked from side to side, he closed his eyes tightly and spoke in his mother tongue. McCann picked it up as something about a week having disappeared. McCann looked up 'Athena how does he look to you?'

'Technician Louis Beaumont is stable Colonel.'

Louis shouted out 'Maintenant me laisser sortir!' in and angry voice.

McCann smiled and turned to Ryu 'It looks as if Louis is back to his old self again.'

Ryu stood with folded arms, she made a grunting noise and a sound came out of her mouth 'Errrrhhh!'

It was the Korean equivalent of 'Whatever!' at least that was the conclusion McCann came to many years ago.

Louis shouted again 'Cut me out of this bed McCann!'

McCann glanced upwards 'Athena have the droid release Louis,' he then tapped the intercom 'the droid will release you Louis, try to remain still ... we wouldn't want you to get hurt.'

The droid trundled over to Louis removing his tubes. An arm moved from its chest releasing the straps from underneath the bed. Louis began to move out of the bed before the straps were off but when he stood on the floor he had to steady himself. All that time asleep had left him somewhat off balance, he had to sit back down on the bed to gather himself. McCann entered the med bay and put a suit down on the bed next to him 'Put some clothes on man there are ladies present!' ribbed McCann.

'What ladies!' sneered Louis.

Ryu stood in the door way arms folded and leaning on the door frame 'It's okay Duncan I think I handle it!' was her sarcastic comeback.

Louis sneered again and grabbed his suit putting his feet into the boots then pulling it up under his backside and around his waist.

'I only remember bits of what happened McCann, what did I do?'

McCann stood in front of Louis 'The Gordii stone was affecting your brain waves. It seems you lost control of rational judgement and cut yourself off from Tharsis. You tried to take down Athena and I had to neutralise you before you could attack me.'

Louis looked at McCann 'Attack you?'

McCann could see he wasn't aware of everything that had transpired in the catacombs, 'You went for one of the drilling tools. I'm afraid I had to stop you old boy!' he put his hand on Louis shoulder.

Louis groaned and put his hand on McCann's shoulder to support himself. As he got to his feet slowly Louis asked about his friend 'I'm sorry ... where's Hassif? Is he okay?'

McCann smiled 'He's fine let's just walk to the lounge and we can fill you in on the latest news.'

Ryu took his other arm, they both supported Louis. On the way to the lounge they saw Hassif walking in the opposite direction. He was walking towards the medical bay holding a glass of whisky with his suit glove.

Hassif smiled at Louis 'How are you?'

Louis grumbled 'Bein.'

McCann looked at the whisky glass 'Where are you going with that?'

Hassif pointed to the med bay 'She may have left some material on or in the glass. Maybe Athena can find some DNA on it?'

McCann nodded 'Good thinking we'll see you in the lounge.'

They continued slowly to the lounge 'What the hell is he talking about McCann?' inquired Louis.

'We've had visitors; I'll tell you all about it once we get to the lounge.'

Louis started getting his balance back, as he walked further requiring the other two less and less, 'Visitors? What the hell are you talking about? I wasn't out that long; the Edwards crew can't be here now?'

No one answered until Ryu quipped 'Maybe it was one of your admirers and she just couldn't wait to see you?'

McCann smiled but Louis wasn't in a jovial mood.

On entering the lounge they set Louis down slowly on the couch 'I feel like shit!' grumbled the Frenchman 'Someone get me a fucking drink!' he snarled.

McCann took the two remaining glasses that had been left out after the visitors short stay. He poured one glass into the other and gave Louis the combined contents 'There get that down you.'

Ryu folded her arms 'He shouldn't be drinking that Duncan.'

McCann didn't say anything but Louis took a shot of whisky and a smile came to his face 'Ahhhhh! I understand why you drink this McCann.'

McCann sat down next to him, pleased to see Louis relax but Ryu remained standing 'We need you sober Louis there's a lot of work to do!'

Louis looked at her incredulously 'What is it with you?' he shouted at Ryu 'I'm not a fucking child!'

Ryu kept her arms folded and raised an eyebrow.

McCann gripped Louis shoulder 'She's only concerned for you Louis and there is a lot of work waiting, as soon as you're fit.'

Louis took another shot 'So how did anyone visit us? We've only got one ribbon attached, right?'

McCann looked up 'Athena can you run the footage of the visitors for us?'

Her calm voice replied 'Certainly Duncan.'

On the main screen in the lounge the image of the three figures stepping out of the gloom of the Gordii stone hit Louis like a freight train. He sat gripping the glass and staring in disbelief 'What is this?'

Ryu replied matter of factly 'Those, are our visitors.'

Louis remained transfixed on the screen 'Visitors? From where?'

Ryu shrugged 'From the Gordii stone other than that they didn't say.'

Louis turned to Ryu 'You spoke to them?'

She shrugged again 'Not really.'

Louis watched the rest of the footage in silence whilst sipping his whisky. By the time it had finished Hassif had joined them and was watching it with him. Louis wanted to stand up but he didn't want to chance falling over, 'How about another?' he asked holding up his now empty glass.

McCann took it off him and gave him a cup of coffee from the drinks dispenser 'Here drink this.'

Louis took it and grumbled under his breath.

Shortly Athena announced that she had found foreign organic material on the glass and analysed the DNA. She brought the results up on the lounge screen 'The profile does not match anything in the Tharsis databanks. I suggest the profile be sent to Geneva, Duncan.'

The four of them were off duty now and had been chatting on the day's events. Brining Louis up to speed and debating on the true origin of the visitors.

Hassif replied to Athena 'How extensive are the databanks in Tharsis?'

'Tharsis contains the DNA of all known bacteria, parasites, virus and disease that effect humans.'

'Do you have human DNA?'

'Tharsis has the DNA profile of every individual selected for Mars and the Edwards.'

'Can you make a comparison and conclude whether the sample you have is human or not?'

The others weren't saying anything but quietly listening and waiting for the outcome.

After a short analysis Athena answered his query 'It is a 99.99% match to human DNA.'

The other three looked at each other, 'Athena do you have any primate DNA besides homo sapien?' inquired Hassif.

Unfortunately for Hassif she didn't. Tharsis had a limited database only to deal with decontamination and identifying biological hazards to the crew.

McCann got up and made for his office leaving the other three to discuss the news. He sent off the results and waited in his office for a reply. Forty minutes later an answer arrived. Faraday wasn't looking good, he probably hadn't slept well over the last week or two.

'Hello Duncan I hope you're doing well. We've run the DNA against every database and it isn't recognised, but we think it's a human relative. The DNA is closer to us than our nearest relative on Earth. I've been told it cannot be from any of the crew. The strand Athena analysed has the XX chromosomes; I'm told the chromosomes are interchangeable with humans.'

Faraday expelled some air from his lungs in a huff 'You're cleared to allow the visitors inside Tharsis. Weissmuller believes that since the DNA is so close they probably have very similar body functions to us and it's a good bet that they are oxygen breathers. If they are anything like us I'm certain they'll contact us again. I doubt they travelled all this way in person to leave now. Send my regards to Louis; try to keep him off the drink Duncan. Aside from that carry on as you are and send me a report as soon as something happens. Good luck.'

Faraday's face remained still on the screen after the message ended. McCann pulled out a cigar and guillotined the butt. He torched the foot as he walked to the lounge.

The conversation was still in full swing debating the visitors until they saw McCann standing in the doorway.

'The DNA is from a relative but it isn't human. In fact they're closer to us than any of the apes. Weissmuller reckons they breathe oxygen too.'

Ryu had sat down beside Louis 'So what do we do now, Duncan?'

McCann took a drag from his cigar and blew the smoke into the air 'We're going to wait.'

Louis who was decidedly less grumpy now interjected 'Wait for what?'

'Them.'

Louis was starting to get cranked up again 'To do what?'

'They didn't come here to leave now. I think they're inside the Gordii stone learning to communicate with us. We aren't going anywhere, so when they're ready they'll come out to speak to us again.'

Louis didn't like the answer for his own reasons 'Do I get a gun?' he asked forcefully.

'No!' replied McCann blankly.

Louis didn't push the matter any further, after the way he had behaved he wasn't surprised. Louis didn't know which he feared more, his susceptibility to the Gordii stone or these visitors walking around Tharsis.

McCann sat down and poured himself a whisky 'Louis I want you to get Pavis Mons up and running again. First you'll have to run a full check on the nanites. Athena had to disable them when you went potty, understood?'

Louis nodded his head 'I'll try and get some sleep tonight.'

'I want you to work from the command centre Louis. I'm not going to let you out of my sight until this Gordii stone business is dealt with. In fact we all need to watch each other's backs. Ever since this thing turned up I've witnessed odd behaviour and mood swings in all of us, including myself.'

Ryu smiled 'Shouldn't we store those rifles back in the armoury?'

McCann peered over at Ryu 'Why?'

She was still smiling 'Well Louis has recovered and we don't want those visitors to see them if they visit again, do we?'

McCann tapped some ash from his cigar 'That's true, put your rifle and monocle on my office desk when you have the chance. It could lead to an uncomfortable situation if they were hanging around when they arrive.'

The four of them ended the evening, and the bottle of Scotch, in the observation area above the lounge. The four friends observed the Gordii stone in the distance before retiring.

Ryu had loosened up by now and even took a dram of scotch 'Do you think they're looking at us?'

'I would be if I were them,' replied Hassif.

Louis looked thoughtfully at the stone 'They'll be doing the same as us, they'll have looked at our DNA. I bet she left her DNA on that glass for us to find. She wanted us to know that they're humans too.'

McCann looked out into the darkness that was illuminated by Tharsis. The station lighting was just enough so that you could make out the Gordii stone from the gloom, 'Who knows what they're thinking and why they want to contact us.'

Ryu peered sarcastically at Louis 'Maybe they've come to conquer the world?'

Hassif and McCann smirked whilst Louis sneered 'When I was in Pavis Mons I could hear them speaking to me.'

McCann, sat looking out at the Gordii stone, turned his body to Louis 'Really?'

Louis nodded 'That's why I turned my chip off. I thought it was causing me to hear voices. Now I understand that they were trying to tell me something, but I don't know what.'

McCann was very interested in any edge he could get before making contact again, 'Is there anything you can tell me about them? Did you get a feeling or an impression of what their intent might be?'

Louis shook his head slowly 'I didn't understand what they were trying to tell me, but they weren't malicious I'm sure of that.'

Ryu raised an eyebrow 'You were pretty malicious at the time Louis. When I got back you'd tried to kill Athena and would've killed me and McCann, how do you explain that?'

Louis didn't react other than displaying a demeanour of shame 'That was how I reacted. I didn't know what was happening. I only remember pieces after I disabled the chip. The chip is probably what stopped me going over the edge and when it was gone so was I.'

McCann spoke again 'Hassif I want you to prepare Athena. If she detects any bio hazard inside Tharsis it must be neutralised. I want to get them out of those suits but I don't want to die of the galactic flu. So make sure she's ready and contact Weissmuller to make certain the nanites can deal with anything they might bring inside.'

McCann felt that he was wrangling this mission back on track. Now that Louis was in one piece again and they were all on the same page.

'We can't forget about the Edwards crew, they'll be docking in a month and the new ribbons will be ready for attaching. So our ribbon has to be operational when they arrive. Ryu I want you to keep monitoring Tharsis and the weather patterns within the area of the Ribbon. The visitors will come out when they're ready, until then we need to focus on our jobs and get this place operational.'

The crew smiled but especially Ryu, she was happy to be back to work minus all the distractions. She had come to terms with the visitors and was prepared for another encounter. After another hour of chatting they broke up for an evening's sleep. Hassif and McCann escorted Louis to his quarters before lying down for the night.

The next day Ryu was back to her chirpy self. McCann was glad to see his team back together and at work. Hassif was busy with the computer systems in Pavis Mons trying to lighten his friend's workload.

Louis was getting the nanites back online which was the simple part. It was the series of tedious checks he had to run, to certify they were all operational, that was a long and gruelling task. In civilian life this wouldn't be necessary, unless it was a nuclear fusion plant or something similar. Usually he'd have them back online and if a problem presented itself he'd deal with it.

Tharsis however wasn't your average facility, everything had to be checked then double checked. Finally Athena was required to certify the work, something which Louis had a massive chip on his shoulder about. He was arrogant to the point he didn't think his work required to be certified. At least that's what everyone thought, however he just didn't trust synthetic intelligences. Louis hated the fact that others treated them as if they were gods. Some sort of infallible master being, when he knew quite the opposite was true.

Louis still hadn't apologised to Athena and he had no intention of doing so. If her neural connections had been shredded by his nanites he wouldn't have regretted it. To him she was no more than a faulty machine that would be their master, or even worse, a deity to be worshipped.

Hassif got up from his station and walked over to Louis who was busy working 'Here's a list of broken systems,' he tapped his wrist tablet.

Louis tapped his screen and looked at the file 'Thanks, when Athena has certified the nanites I'll start on them.'

Hassif looked at Louis screen 'You really smashed that place up didn't you.'

Louis and Hassif both smiled.

'Yeah I bet Faraday is still crying about it!' they both started laughing.

Ryu ignored the laughter but it got McCann's attention 'What's so funny lads?'

Hassif sniggered and Louis replied 'We were talking about Faraday crying over this mess.'

McCann didn't share the humour 'Well I'm the poor bastard that has to listen to him crying about it. Though he was far more concerned about you than any of the equipment down there, just in case you were wondering Louis.'

Hassif was still smiling but Louis seemed uncomfortable or ashamed.

'How far along are we now?' asked McCann.

Louis tapped his screen again to display Athena's diagnostic 'Athena is certifying the nanites. Pavis Mons is operational but will require about 8 hours to get the droids back to normal.'

McCann put his hand on Louis shoulder 'Good and what about the ribbon, is it damaged?'

Louis shook his head 'Noh, for some reason the nanites in the ribbon have been working properly. They seem to have been independent of the main systems. I think that the Edwards took them over when Athena shut everything down.'

Maybes put McCann ill at ease, 'I want you to find out what happened and why they didn't shut down, how's the crawler?'

'It's docked with the Edwards and fully operational. We just need to do a little cleaning up in Pavis Mons, repair the broken droids and terminals. It shouldn't take more than 72 hours if I have Athena on it.'

McCann patted his shoulder 'Good to have you back Louis.'

Louis smiled and McCann walked towards Ryu to check up on her.

Hassif called over to McCann and at the same time Athena spoke 'Incoming transmission from the Gordii stone Colonel.'

Everyone stopped what they were doing.

McCann looked upwards 'Hassif will deal with it, thank you Athena.'

'You're welcome Colonel.'

McCann looked over at Hassif who turned back to his terminal. When McCann got there Hassif had received the message on his closed system 'It's in the same ternary Duncan.'

McCann nodded 'Let's have a look then.'

Hassif started banging away at his station then pulled his tablet out of his pocket. A 3D image jumped up from Hassifs' tablet, the image was at first glance a human head. It was the head of a female with a single word below it "Tlillan".

McCann looked upwards 'Athena can you take a closer look at the image. Do a search on the word below it please.'

Athena replied softly 'As you wish Colonel.'

The four of them gathered around staring at the image. Since it looked so human there was little to comment on until Athena broke the silence.

'I have measured the dimensions Colonel, the image appears to be human in origin.' McCann snapped at Athena 'What do you mean by appears to be?'

'The skull has a greater capacity than an average human by 20%, Colonel.'

The four of them looked hard at the image 'So it isn't human?' asked Ryu.

'I cannot clarify that Major,' replied Athena.

McCann sent the image back to Faraday. The crew stood around discussing the message and what the purpose of it might be. After an hour McCann had received Faradays reply. McCann walked out of his office and passed a chip to his technician 'Hassif send this to them.'

McCann looked upwards 'You can stop the word search Athena.'

'As you wish Colonel.'

They all huddled around Hassif as he downloaded the message to the Gordii stone. The message Faraday had sent was a human head with "Welcome" written below it.

'Did they find out the meaning of Tlillan?' asked Ryu.

McCann shook his head 'No, it isn't English so it must be their language. Faraday assumes it's a greeting though I don't understand why they wouldn't send it in English.'

Hassif transmitted the message to the Gordii stone. Within 10 minutes the side of the stone melted back. Once again and the three visitors stepped outside.

McCann's hand reached for his weapon and lay over the holster 'Check your weapons, make sure they're charged and loaded.'

Louis looked desperately at McCann 'What about me? Where's my gun!'

McCann walked past him 'I'm sorry Louis, no can do. Ryu you're with me again, get suited up.'

McCann and Ryu walked back down the southern wing 'Keep me abreast of what they're up to Hassif,' he spoke into his suit mic.

'Understood,' replied Hassif.

McCann was going to get it right this time, 'Ryu I want you to handle all the greetings, is that understood?'

Ryu nodded 'Sure, do you want them to come inside again?' she asked whilst putting her gloves on.

'Yes I want to see what's behind that helmet.'

Upon exiting the airlock the visitors were stood ten feet away. The tall female in front with the two short ones behind her. The tall female was holding the greeting gesture of the pioneer plaque this time. Her hand was held next to her shoulder with palm towards Ryu and all five fingers outstretched. Ryu held the same gesture whilst McCann lurked behind, he spoke to Ryu 'Switch to the general communication frequency.'

On doing so Ryu spoke to the female standing before her in the gravel. She was a good foot taller than Ryu 'Hello.'

'Greetings,' replied the jet black figure in that alien tone.

Ryu hadn't been trained for this type of exercise, in fact neither had the others 'Would you like to come inside?'

'Yes,' replied her counterpart in a slow deep tone.

Ryu led them through the airlock, the female always behind. McCann skulked at the back ignored. Ryu guided the caravan to the lounge where she removed her helmet and gloves. McCann did the same, then they put all eyes on the female visitor waiting for her to do likewise. Louis shuffled into the lounge quietly and hung around the door watching the scene unravel.

Ryu gestured towards her helmet that had disappeared into the rear of her suit, 'Remove?'

The visitor's voice echoed out over the comms 'Dark,' she pointed to the lighting in the lounge.

McCann whispered into his mic 'Athena, lower the lights in the lounge by 50% please.'

The lounge lighting was dimmed, but they could still see the visitors. It reminded McCann of a gentlemen's club the officers would frequent when he was in the services.

The visitor looked around, then her entire helmet began to melt away as the side of the Gordii stone had. She stood in her black space suit, her head fully exposed. Louis felt weak; the other two stood still and marvelled.

The first feature to catch all of their attention and every other human since was her eyes. They were slightly larger than human eyes and somewhat translucent aside from a small black iris. On deeper examination McCann could see subtle changes in viscosity around the iris, though he had no idea what it meant. The next feature was her mane of red hair. The colour was really red, not an orange or rust colour but a wine red. Her skin was an almost translucent ivory, similar to her eyes though he couldn't make out any blood vessels; if there were any?

The visitor looked on as they all stood in awe, 'Greetings,' she said and when she spoke for some reason it was frightening.

Ryu plucked up the courage and put her hand out 'Greetings we're happy to see you.'

The visitor looked down at her hand and grasped it. The visitor observed as Ryu shook hands then withdrew after releasing her grip. Ryu gained in confidence and asked her visitor 'My name is Ryu. What is your name?' pointing at the six and a half foot woman in front of her.

The visitor repeated her name a few times slowly 'Ruy-uwh.'

Next she put her hand on her chest 'Ilamachutli.'

The visitor known as Ilamachutli had some command of English. McCann wondered to himself how intelligent these people were since she'd managed to learn enough to communicate overnight. Ilamachutli refused to reveal the two behind her and ignored all but Ryu.

After about 30 minutes McCann became irritated. Coming into a person's house and ignoring the other guests was just downright rude. He boldly approached her with his hand out 'Good morning, my name is Duncan.'

Ilamachutli ignored him again, he asked Ryu to step aside and put himself in front of her so that there was no ignoring him.

'Good morning,' he said putting his hand probably too close to her.

The two smaller figures behind her displayed signs of agitation and started to fidget. McCann wasn't moving and eventually she was force to recognise him.

'Good morning,' Ilamachutli didn't shake his hand however.

McCann wanted to get to the bottom of this and persisted 'I am in command of this facility and am honoured to have you as my guests.'

Ilamachutli stepped back from him her look was one of disgust, if she were human that is. The two visitors behind her still with their helmets on fidgeted even more so. She turned to her two companions and spoke in what must have been her mother tongue, they stopped their fidgeting immediately. Ilamachutli looked at Ryu 'Return,' and pointed at her two companions.

Ryu looked at McCann and McCann looked at Louis, 'Take them back Louis.'

The Frenchman gathered from McCann's expression that he was to squeeze as much information out of them as possible on the way.

'Okay,' he said putting his gloves on.

Ilamachutli spoke to her companions before they followed Louis. Unfortunately for Louis they didn't speak any English so the trip to the airlock yielded nothing. Louis did note that all the way they seemed very excited over what had just happened in the lounge, though he couldn't work out why.

McCann kept on pressing Ilamachutli 'Good morning Ilamachutli.'

She was barely tolerating him, as to why left both he and Ryu puzzled.

Ilamachutli looked down her nose at McCann as if she were royalty 'Good morning.'

She was almost sneering at him and he wanted to find out why.

McCann motioned towards the sofa 'Please take a seat.'

He then put his hand on her arm at which point she stepped backwards and pulled her arm away violently. McCann and Ryu saw her eyes go from translucent to the same colour as her red hair.

Ilamachutli growled at McCann 'Do not touch!'

Her voice was now as deep as a man's and her demeanour frightened them both.

'I apologise,' said McCann timidly 'no offence was intended.'

Ryu stepped in front of McCann and addressed her 'Please take a seat.'

Ilamachutli relaxed, her eyes slowly faded back to translucence. McCann pulled out the coffee table to make room. Ilamachutli sat down and he left the talking to Ryu.

The conversation lasted two hours and Ilamachutli's English improved progressively. After it was over she retired to the Gordii stone with the promise of another visit tomorrow.

Fortunately it was all recorded and sent to Faraday. From what they'd learned "Tlillan" was the name of their planet and or race. Originating from HE0107-5240 in the galactic halo, it was now being renamed Tlillan. They had come to Mars after one of their deep space probes detected activity, probably the maser blasts, how they got to Mars from 36,000 light years away in a matter of weeks remained unanswered.

When questioned on DNA and ancestry she confirmed that they were related, "Fruit of ancestral blood," were her exact words.

From what Ryu could coax out of Ilamachutli her society was matriarchal, males held lower status accounting for her reaction to McCann. According to her males were not permitted to even address a female let alone touch one. Females occupied the upper echelons of society whilst males were place squarely below.

Ryu attempted to delve deeper with her questioning but Ilamachutli was either unable or unwilling to answer for now. All the time she and Ryu spoke Ilamachutli's eyes would wander and analyse McCann, quickly returning to Ryu, as if looking at McCann was a guilty pleasure of some sort. After Ryu had escorted her back to the airlock and secured another visit, McCann was already sending the footage to Faraday.

Ryu walked into the command centre to some rather dejected looks from Louis and Hassif, 'What's wrong?'

Louis who was busy at his station replied without looking up 'We meet intelligent life and she's a fascist man hater!'

Ryu leant on the doorway, 'Damn! I must've forgotten to tell her that you're the cosmic Casanova!'

Hassif began to chuckle.

'I bet you two got on like a house on fire!' sneered Louis as he continued working at his station.

McCann walked into the command centre from his office, 'The footage has been sent, Athena did scans from thermal imaging to MRI; we'll see if there's any secrets Ilamachutli can reveal whilst she's away.'

He looked at Ryu 'Good job Ryu, if you hadn't been on this mission we'd never have gotten her inside Tharsis. It seems on Tlillan the femi-nazis took over!'

No one laughed at his joke.

McCann cleared his throat then clapped his hands together 'Well let's get back to work!'

Chapter 9

Later that day McCann received a reply from Faraday. He passed some further study on the English language to Hassif for transmission to the Gordii stone. According to Faraday it was chaos back on Earth. People weren't going in to work so that they could watch the Tharsis cams and listen to the scientific debates concerning Ilamachutli and her followers. The planet was grinding to a halt. When Moscow proposed cutting the transmissions to get everyone working again there were riots. Governments found themselves as slaves to the media, everyone wanted to know about Ilamachutli and Tlillan.

The scans couldn't penetrate her suit the only part of her Athena was able to look at was the head. Her bone structure was almost identical to a human skull and neck, only it was somewhat larger. Weissmuller had gone over the MRI and all information pertinent to the brain. He deemed her brain was human of origin. There were parts of it the Doctor failed to understand; in fact he had a list of questions for Ryu to ask her on the next visit.

That evening they sat down to watch the world news. Louis tuned into Network America much to the disdain of McCann. Habeeb was sitting at his desk as they went through cherry picked footage with an Earth biologist and exo-biologist. McCann ignored them as best he could but eventually he was drawn into the debate. They hypothesised that Ilamachutli's race lived somewhere very dark and cold. According to the infra-red scans she held her body heat far more efficiently than a human. Her request to lower the lighting may have been an aversion to UV rays, or perhaps her eyes were too sensitive to function properly in it. Next Jerry introduced a sociologist who spoke at length on matriarchal societies. He assumed the smaller visitors were males and the larger female was in control much the same as crocodiles.

Her eyes were discussed at length and their function beyond sight. It was obvious to the scientists they were used to ward off others. Perhaps the eyes were also used to attract a mate? Or identify friend from foe in the dark gloom they must live in? After watching Habeebs Hour McCann turned it off and asked Ryu 'What was your impression of her?'

Ryu thought for a moment 'She has good intentions, I'm sure.'

Louis spoke up immediately 'How do you know that? Look at what she did to me was that good intent?'

Ryu rolled her eyes 'That wasn't intentional, besides no harm came of it.'

Louis held a glass of whisky in one hand and flapped his other at Ryu 'What? That crazy bitch got me shot, twice!'

McCann gave a cheeky grin 'Exactly!' he said to a chuckle.

Ryu carried on 'I get the feeling they have our welfare in mind.'

McCann ruffled his forehead 'What gave you that impression?'

'I don't know, call it a hunch or a gut feeling I suppose.'

Louis shook his head 'I don't care what your gut says, you don't travel 36,000 fucking light years for nothing. They must want something out of this.'

Hassif had been sitting quietly until now. McCann wanted his opinion 'What do you think of it Hassif?'

Hassif had a blank look 'We don't know enough about them to guess at their motives with any accuracy. Perhaps they are explorers and travelling these distances is common place? We are related, so I assume they visited Earth in the past. So it stands to reason they know more about us than we do of them. I think we should come up with a list of questions for Ryu to ask, the next time Ilamachutli visits us.'

McCann smiled, it was the obvious solution to their many questions and he should've come up with it earlier. Geneva should have sent him a list already!

'Good thinking Hassif, I'll send Faraday a request for a list. Ryu can ask them when they return.'

Every day for the next two weeks Ilamachutli would visit at midday and Ryu would guide her around Tharsis, the visitor attempting to answer a stream of questions coming from Faraday.

Ilamachutli was curious concerning Tharsis and was always searching for something; finally Ryu discovered what she'd been looking for.

Whilst in the command centre Ilamachutli pointed at each crew member one by one 'Ryu, McCann, Louis, Hassif. There is another yes?'

Ryu didn't reply until Hassif whispered, 'She must mean Athena.'

Ryu relaxed 'Yes we have an SI running Tharsis her name is Athena.' She pointed towards Athena's housing above the command centre.

Ilamachutli asked, 'Explain term SI, please?'

Ryu thought she must be unfamiliar only with the term. Since any advanced civilization would have developed SI technology far beyond humans, 'Synthetic Intelligence, we grow them on Earth. They're installed in facilities from scientific to industrial to space exploration. Their genetic codes are manufactured individually although based on a common template. Athena is one of the next generation of SI, the first from a new template. She's the most efficient ever created. Athena, say hello to Ilamachutli.'

Ilamachutli peered upwards worriedly.

'Welcome to Tharsis, Ilamachutli,' greeted Athena softly; however there was no reply forthcoming.

Ryu stepped closer to the visitor 'Is something wrong?'

Ilamachutli pointed towards the area where Athena was housed 'Athena biological?'

Ryu nodded 'Yes.'

'Humans create DNA?'

'Yes.'

The other three observed as she questioned Ryu on Athena. Finally she pointed upwards and declared, 'Athena heresy!'

Ryu was taken aback 'Sorry?'

'Tlillan, Athena not permitted. Synthetic life heresy.'

McCann and Hassif both glanced at each other with raised eyebrows. It became apparent that Ilamachutli may come from something close to a theocracy, a form of government that had been eradicated from the Earth. McCann found it difficult to accept that a civilization based on theocracy could achieve so much. He assumed it was merely a poor choice of expression.

Fortunately neither of them lingered on the subject. Ryu, quite diplomatically, moved her out of the command centre and towards the med labs. After Ryu and Ilamachutli left Louis turned his head with an "I told you so" smirk aimed at McCann and Hassif.

'Good intentions did she say? I can't wait for her friends to turn up, maybe we'll hear a "Deus Vult" just before they blast us to pieces?'

McCann scoffed at Louis 'I doubt they've come all this way to find people to kill!'

However Louis was having none of it 'They are religious fanatics Duncan! We'll probably wake up tomorrow to conversion by the sword!'

McCann glared at Louis sternly 'Give it a rest Louis, all we know is that creating a synthetic life form is not permitted on her planet. I can understand that it makes her uncomfortable and so should you.'

Louis sneered and went back to his work. Now that Pavis Mons was in working order he only awaited the arrival of the Edwards crew and the other ribbons.

Meanwhile Ryu was chatting with the visitor and showing her around the medical laboratory.

Ilamachutli peered in at med bay 1, 'Louis lay here.'

Ryu was a little surprised that the visitor was aware of this.

'Yes we held him here after your transmissions caused him to become psychotic. Do you have similar facilities on your craft?'

Ilamachutli smiled for the first time 'No,' she gestured towards the black ribbed suit that adorned her body.

'You mean the suit is your med bay?'

'Yes.'

Ryu then asked a burning question 'How long did it take to get here from Tlillan?' Ilamachutli was still smiling as she examined the med lab 'Primitive, you are still primitive.'

Ryu pushed on 'How long did it take to get here?'

Ilamachutli looked down at Ryu with a smile 'Small time.'

It wasn't good enough for Ryu, 'Exactly?'

Ilamachutli pointed skywards 'From Tlillan, 83 Earth hours.'

Ryu quickly tried to blurt out her next question but was cut off.

'I am not permitted to elaborate.'

Ryu realised that she must have spent extra time practicing her reply. Since it came out so fluidly compared to the rest of her English; which although improved was still poor grammatically.

Whilst alone Ilamachutli took the opportunity to question Ryu, 'McCann is your leader?' she asked softly.

'Yes he is.'

Ilamachutli looked around to make certain they were alone 'On Earth, leaders are male also?'

Ryu replied in a matter of fact tone 'Mostly.'

The visitor seemed very curious 'Why?'

'I don't know, it's more instinctive in men I'd guess. What about on Tlillan why are leaders women?'

Ilamachutli smiled again, 'Males follow and women lead, a male to lead would be heresy.'

Ryu folded her arms, 'You've used that word again, do you live by a religious law?'

'The Grand Matriarch is law, the law is millennia old. A man may only direct his Matriarch's slaves nothing more.'

Ryu's heart jumped, 'Slavery is permitted on Tlillan?'

'Yes, is it not so here?'

'No.'

Ilamachutli pointed in the direction of the command centre 'Athena is not your slave?'

Ryu had never thought of it that way. It wasn't as if Athena had the option to pursue her own destiny, 'That's different.'

'Why different?'

'I don't know I'm not a philosopher or a scientist. Athena was created with the purpose of establishing a base on Mars. Besides, people are still arguing about it on Earth.'

'Many systems, creating synthetic life is not permitted, not your flaw Ryu. Males are ignorant.'

'I think Colonel McCann has done quite a good job of leading this mission, don't you?'

Ilamachutli stopped smiling 'What is Colonel?'

'It's his military rank, my rank is Major.'

Ryu could feel Ilamachutli's eyes gazing at her. Ryu had noticed since their talks began that Ilamachutli had a great knack of reading her emotions far better than Ryu could read hers.

'He leads you?' asked Ilamachutli.

'Yes and I'm second in command of this mission. On Earth it's considered very backward to select a leader based on gender.'

Ilamachutli almost sneered, her eyes filled with a hint of red, 'I understand.'

After looking around for a while Ilamachutli requested to see McCann before departing to her craft. She insisted on speaking to him alone for the first time, engaging him in his office.

McCann was taken aback to see the six and a half foot beauty enter his office alone. Ilamachutli was by far one of the most attractive women that McCann had ever seen in the flesh. Her height allowed a pair of the longest legs he'd ever witnessed on a woman. He had often contemplated that this must be how it feels, to sit in the same room with a super model; a tall slender female with long legs, ivory skin and shoulder length red hair which had a slight natural curl to it. More than once he'd stolen a quick look at her body. Held tightly in place by her suit, and more than once Ilamachutli had snapped around quickly catching him in the act.

Hassif found it amusing, Ryu found it tiresome and Louis thought he was sick. However there could be no denying her looks, from her body to her elegant facial features. She had very Caucasian features, starting with a tall forehead that led to a petit nose, wide thin lips and a petit chin. Her eyes were larger than the average human and the back of her head appeared swollen.

Despite the differences between her and the average female, she wasn't disproportionate. Like a tall slim catwalk model you'd only realise her true size if she stood next to an average sized person. When in the same room however he felt that she dwarfed him. He'd never even met a woman taller than him before and she was taller by half a foot.

Unfortunately she was as arrogant as she was beautiful. Her sense of superiority preceded her where ever she went.

She stepped in and McCann leapt from his seat at the sight.

'I wish to speak,' she said smiling at his reaction to her entrance.

McCann stood looking up at her 'Yes?'

'Might I and my males remain in Tharsis?'

McCann was again taken a back, it wasn't that they lacked facilities but the request seemed odd coming from her. The thought of Ilamachutli asking him for anything stunned him, 'Certainly, should I know of any special arrangements?'

Ilamachutli's smile widened 'No thank you McCann. Might Tharsis accommodate my craft also?'

McCann thought for a moment and realised she meant the garage 'Of course, you can park it inside now and enter through the garage airlock.'

'Thank you McCann.'

His nervous behaviour was akin to a young man around a pretty young girl rather than fear of a superior species, 'You're welcome,' and then he managed to blurt out 'you can call me Duncan.'

Ilamachutli looked slightly puzzled 'Why?'

He started to grow warm with embarrassment 'It's my first name, acquaintances usually use first names.'

Ilamachutli ruffled her brow and glared at him but still held her smile 'Ryu uses McCann, why?'

He gave a nervous shrug 'In the military we used family names. You're addressed by your rank then family name. It was less confusing as some first names are common, many of the men shared them.'

'Major Ryu addressed by rank and first name, why?'

McCann smiled a little, 'Ah, Major Ryu comes from Korea where your family name is your first, whereas my family name is my last name. So Major Ryu Yong is Major Ryu and friends may call her Yong. I think that Ryu and I were just used to using family names and it caught on with the others.'

Ilamachutli grinned in what McCann thought was a very human fashion, 'Thank you Duncan I will speak with Major Ryu.'

She raised her hand to her shoulder showing him her palm, and then walked out.

McCann sat thinking about how he was going to break this to Faraday, 'In for a penny in for a pound!' he muttered under his breath as he prepared to send the message to Geneva.

Faraday wasn't as concerned as McCann had thought; he'd informed McCann that Tharsis was considered a quarantine zone anyway. He was rather pleased that Athena might be able to get a better look at the visitors and perhaps some insight into the people of Tlillan.

So far Athena had not been able to penetrate the visitor's suits. However, since they were so close to humans there wasn't much to tell. Athena had learnt that besides the larger brain capacity, the visitors retained body heat with far greater efficiency than humans. Their resting metabolisms were slower than the average human. What it meant was hard to understand but if Athena could observe them all day unbroken it might help.

Faraday had informed McCann of Dr Weissmuller's request for a stool sample from the visitors. In fact now that they were going to be proper guests he'd put in all kinds of requests that McCann didn't feel totally comfortable with. However compared to a bunch of questions which amounted to the secrets of life the universe and everything, the stool sample seemed quite reasonable!

After going over Faradays communique he informed Geneva he'd received it and turned off his workstation. McCann put his feet on the desk and leaned back on his chair.

He took out a cigar and looked towards the ceiling 'Athena?'

'Yes Colonel?' she replied softly.

'What am I going to do now?' he bemoaned as he clipped the end of his stick then torched the foot.

'I do not understand the question Colonel.'

He took a drag of the cigar and spat out the first bitter plume of smoke 'My life Athena, what am I going to do about my life?'

'I'm sorry Colonel; could you please clarify the question?'

McCann took a draw from his cigar again, 'I suppose it was a rhetorical question Athena. I've been quarantined on another planet millions of miles away and now they want me to ask my guests for a bloody stool sample!'

The leathery smoke expelled from his nose and mouth as he lamented his situation.

'I'm sorry Colonel but may I ask a question of a personal nature?'

McCann looked upwards with one eye, 'Of course you may Athena.'

'Do you find Ilamachutli attractive, Colonel?'

McCann sat up and took another puff on his stick 'Whatever gave you that impression Athena?' his hand gripped the cigar firmly.

'Whenever you look at her your pupils dilate. Mentioning her name will evoke a strong galvanic skin response and if you make eye contact ...'

McCann cut her off 'Yes I do, are you satisfied Athena?' he snapped.

'I apologise if my question was indiscreet, Colonel.'

McCann took another quick draw and stood up 'No it wasn't Athena, I just over reacted, why do you ask?'

Athena maintained a slightly curious tone 'I have never witnessed two people interact in this manner Colonel. Since my birth the scientists and technicians were all acquainted; I have not had the opportunity to observe a relationship develop until now.'

McCann began to pace in his office 'What do you mean relationship?'

Athena replied softly, 'An intimate relationship.'

McCann chuckled nervously, 'But Athena, our relationship isn't intimate.'

'I apologise Colonel. I assumed that you were both attracted to each other and hoped it might lead to a relationship I would be able to observe.'

He stopped pacing, took another slow draw then looked up, 'Both attracted?'

'Yes Colonel, I have observed a similar galvanic skin response in Ilamachutli when you are present. I have also noted a small deviation in eye colour. I believe it to be an involuntary rush of blood to the eye too subtle for the human eye to observe.'

'Have you informed anyone else Athena?'

'No, Colonel.'

'Thank you Athena, could you keep it that way please?'

'Yes Colonel.'

McCann took a draw from his cigar 'Thank you Athena.'

McCann sat back down in his seat. He looked outside to see Ryu leading off the visitors to the airlock. McCann reached into the bottom draw and poured himself a quick whisky. He couldn't believe that life had somehow managed to get just that little bit more complicated. He contemplated his predicament over a Balvenie knocking it back, before quickly hiding the glass.

That night the two male Tlillans had been sent to sleep in their single room by Ilamachutli. Apparently they weren't permitted to have single quarters. From what McCann could observe Ilamachutli had definitely warmed to the idea of speaking to him, though she continued to ignore Athena.

The crew and the beautiful Ilamachutli sat in the lounge. Ryu explained to her the function of the room where they spent their evenings before retiring to sleep. McCann tried to pique her interested in some Earth news. However Ilamachutli bored of her 15 minutes of Earth fame quickly.

She did take an interest in Ryu's back catalogue of Korean soap operas. McCann found it quite bizarre as the pair of them sat together, both discussing the utterly predictable storylines and how they might unfold. In fact McCann was perplexed that an evidently more advanced species would find her soap operas interesting on any level. All the while the slim beauty stole the odd glance at McCann. Much to the disdain of Louis who complained they were "Acting like teenage kids".

McCann worried the attraction had become that obvious. He brushed off Louis insinuations much to the delight of Hassif, who enjoyed the whole drama. McCann decided to change the conversation and discuss the questions Faraday wished to pose to Ilamachutli. Since Hassif had the better grasp of mathematics and science in general, McCann gave him a list of questions to pose.

Hassif sat with whisky in hand mulling over the list on his tablet. He took a drink and looked at McCann, 'This is far too much, I couldn't understand the answers to them anyway.'

McCann took a sip and shook his head 'You don't have to ask them all now. Just pick one that you're comfortable with first, you can research the others later.'

Louis was certain that she wasn't going to let on about anything that could assist the human race in anyway. Predictably the Frenchman thought it was a big waste of time.

McCann gave Louis his list of questions Faraday wanted answering, 'Is he crazy? If I were her I wouldn't answer this!'

McCann took a drag from his cigar 'What are you babbling on about Louis?'

Louis pointed to his wrist tablet and one of the questions 'He wants to know about antimatter production but she's not going to answer that!'

'Why not?'

Louis looked at him incredulously 'It would be like going back to the industrial revolution and teaching them to create a nuclear reaction. I'll ask her but I don't think she's going to tell me.'

McCann nodded 'Fine, just ask her Louis.'

The men were discussing their questions intensely, enough to grab the girls attention. Ilamachutli moved over to McCann and out of character she put her hand on his arm whilst peering over him at the other two, 'Do you wish to question?' she asked.

McCann gestured towards Louis with his glass. Louis was busy staring at the hand on McCann's arm but was prodded into action, 'Can you answer some questions on antimatter?'

Ilamachutli smiled as you would smile at a naughty child 'I am not permitted to elaborate.'

Louis sneered at her 'Why can't you answer me?'

Ilamachutli who was still smiling at Louis replied 'You are too primitive, it is not permitted.'

'What would happen if you did tell us about efficient production of anti-matter?'

'I would be punished.'

'How would they punish you?'

Her smile faded 'Execution,' she stated coldly.

The room went quiet for a moment and McCann cleared his throat. He pointed his glass towards Hassif 'Could you answer anything related to dark matter?' inquired the young Technician.

Ilamachutli perked up 'What is dark matter?'

Hassif inhaled deeply 'Well, when we look at galaxies we see them spinning faster than our laws of physics allow. According to our laws they should fly apart but something is holding them together. Yet we can't see it, so we named it dark matter. Do you know what dark matter is and can you tell us?'

Ilamachutli smiled, 'I understand dark matter.'

Louis cut in 'And?' he said rather rudely.

'I am not permitted to elaborate.'

Louis slapped his thigh and cursed in his mother tongue 'Why have you even come here? Have you come all this way just to rub our noses in it?'

Ilamachutli seemingly amused by Louis' dramatic response was perplexed 'Rub our noses in it?'

McCann satisfied her curiosity 'It's a figure of speech; it means to remind another of their failure or mistake in a malevolent manner.'

'Malevolence is not our intent, this time is delicate. Soon humans will reach a decision we come to prepare for your destiny. In time answers will concede but now we prepare you.'

At this statement an uneasy silence reigned. Ilamachutli realised she had said too much. The crew of Tharsis realised that the Tlillans had plans for them, plans that they were as of yet unaware of.

McCann broke the silence 'Destiny?'

'How you believe we discovered you McCann?'

'I don't know, perhaps you could inform me ... of that?' he said sarcastically.

'Seers in Tititl foresaw this place, foresaw our people abandoned for millennia, Pixoa.'

The beautiful Valkyrie realised that if she didn't explain herself it would only serve to forge a sense of distrust.

McCann riposted quickly 'Our people?'

Ilamachutli placed both of her hands on his shoulders 'You are not human Duncan, you are Tlillan, you are all Tlillan, Pixoa ... the scattered.'

Again the uneasy silence took over until McCann cleared his throat and broke free from her hypnotic gaze, 'What is this decision we must make?' he asked apprehensively.

Ilamachutli took her hands from his shoulders 'Decision for Human leader.'

'Earth has no leader.'

She replied ominously 'Find one Duncan.'

Ryu had to quench her curiosity and spoke up, 'Ilamachutli, you say we were abandoned can you tell us more about that?'

'Many colonies in past, after Great War communication lost. All records destroyed distant colonies abandoned, destroyed, forgotten. Only you have we reached out for, seers saw you on the red planet, they saw your destiny and ours collide.'

Hassif challenged her story 'Humans evolved from apes hundreds of thousands of years ago on Earth, how can we be Tlillan?'

Ilamachutli smiled, 'In past, arks left Tlillan. We seeded planets with environment and resources, Earth seeded eons ago.'

Hassif was stunned 'Eons? You came here millions of years ago?'

'No, ark first, we came much later. Some planets unsuitable, some failed, a few we used; during Great War farthest systems deserted to defend home.'

McCann took a slug of whisky 'When did this Great War end?'

Ilamachutli no longer smiled 'The war persists, Duncan.'

McCann took another drink 'When did it begin?'

The tall slim beauty gave him a hard look, 'It began in the year 5,271 in the age of Chanot, it is now 37,089, almost 30,000 human years.'

McCann went to ask another question but Ilamachutli raised a clenched fist to his mouth, 'Duncan I wish to retire.'

He nodded his head 'My apologies, Major Ryu will show you to your quarters. How long do you sleep?'

'Ten Earth hours.'

McCann returned her smile, 'Excellent, when you awake just make your way to the mess, good night.'

Ilamachutli stood up towering over them all 'Good night.'

The red headed Valkyrie turned to Ryu waiting for her by the door 'Please follow me,' said a smiling Ryu.

McCann watched Ilamachutli leave, his eyes roamed up and down her body. She must have sensed him again, the visitor turned quickly as she walked out the doorway catching his wayward gaze. McCann looked away rather stiffly and she smiled at his embarrassment. He felt she was teasing him but put that to the back of his mind as she left.

Louis shook his head at McCann 'You have to stop looking at her ass McCann!'

Hassif laughed, McCann pulled out a cigar and lit it up without answering the Frenchman. He took a long thoughtful drag on his cigar and peered at the ceiling, 'Athena?'

She'd been listening all the time and spoke calmly 'Yes Duncan?'

McCann expelled the smoke from his nose, 'How long have humans been on the planet Earth?'

'Primates first arose more than six million years ago. The Homo genus arose an estimated 1.8 million years ago. Homo sapiens are estimated to be close to 200,000 years old.'

McCann looked at Hassif, 'So they sent a ship here at the very least 1.8 million years ago to seed their DNA. Turned up later and had to leave about 30,000 years ago, according to her."

Hassif shrugged his shoulders and Louis interjected, "How do we know she's telling us the truth?'

Hassif replied in a matter of fact way, 'Their DNA is almost exactly the same as ours, it might even be compatible. That isn't a lie, and I don't think it could possibly be a coincidence. We are more closely related to them than any other creature on Earth.'

Louis grumbled at having to concede to Hassif's logic.

'She spoke about destiny,' remarked McCann as he refilled his glass 'it worries me that she was sent here in the middle of a war and starts talking about our destiny and theirs.'

They heard Ryu walk in 'Why?' she asked.

'Because they seem to be very spiritual and it doesn't bode well if you ask me. All this talk of destiny it makes me very nervous.'

Ryu walked over and sat down next to her drink, 'Well she's gone to bed and I think I'm about ready to hit the hay.'

McCann raised his glass to his lips 'Alright let's get some sleep. I'll send a data packet back then turn in.'

The crew proceeded to finish up their drinks and then made off for bed to get some well-earned rest.

After McCann had sent the data packet to Geneva containing the footage in the lounge he got back to his quarters. Once inside he removed his holster and space suit then took a shower. After brushing his teeth and washing his mouth out he dropped into bed, drifting off into the land of nod.

Later that night McCann was awoken by his door bell. He lay in bed and in a groggy voice croaked 'lights!' and the dimmed lighting flickered on. He dragged himself up and slipped into his suit bottoms, 'Who the bloody hell could this be?' he growled.

McCann didn't take kindly to being woken up like this unless there was a dire emergency. He was preparing himself to bite the head off the poor fool on the other side of that door.

McCann opened the door to see her standing there, without saying anything she walked passed him and into his Spartan quarters. Gob smacked, McCann stood by the door observing the flaming haired Valkyrie. When she viewed him he could swear there was a leer on her face.

'Close the door Duncan,' she whispered softly.

McCann closed the door, 'Is there something I could do for you?' he asked tentatively.

'Yes.'

Ilamachutli fixed her gaze on him whilst she gripped the sides of his head.

'What do you think you're doing woman?' protested McCann before she forcefully placed her lips on his.

After a few seconds she pulled away and smiled 'Was that correct?'

McCann said nothing until she removed her hands from his head 'Was what correct?' McCann assumed she'd viewed too many of Ryu's soap operas. He wouldn't have minded at all but it felt closer to physical assault than a romantic kiss.

'To profess love, humans kiss, yes?'

McCann felt most uncomfortable standing in his suit bottoms with her in his bedroom 'Yes we do,' he stated 'however I would hardly call that a kiss!'

Ilamachutli smiled 'Show me Duncan ... Please?'

'Look I don't think this is appropriate!'

'Why?'

He thought for a moment looking for a good reason to get him out of this pickle. However he couldn't for the life of him think of a half decent excuse. He continued to think in silence racking his brains until she spoke 'Fulfil my request Duncan and I will answer one of your questions.'

McCann began to feel weak and it was becoming harder to draw breath, 'What is your request?' he managed to ask only by forcing his lungs to exhale the air. He couldn't understand it; he'd been in dangerous combat situations many times. He'd crash landed Athena whilst staring death in the face. Yet this was causing his body to tense up and his lungs to seize. He could hear his heart beating in his chest as he awaited her reply.

'Instruct me in love, Duncan.'

McCann could feel the dread creeping up his spine, 'You could watch some soap operas with Ryu ...' but before he could finish an impatient Ilamachutli cut him off.

'No! You must instruct me, you must demonstrate Duncan!'

McCann wiped some sweat from his brow and muttered under his breath 'Jesus Christ! Her and her bloody soap operas!'

He thought for a moment and weighed it up in his mind. He found her very attractive but was worried about the consequences of such a liaison. As far as he could tell she carried no infectious disease, however if she did and he caught it surely she'd have a cure? Next he contemplated what was at stake. A leap in technology for the Human race that could put them centuries ahead. In exchange the press would have a field day with this, if they found out back home. He realised he hadn't actually seen the rest of her anatomy below her neckline. What if there was something that disgusted him? As he fought within his own mind he noticed Ilamachutli was growing tired of his stalling.

'Alright then, what would you like to know first?' he said trying to calm himself down. Ilamachutli smiled and he noticed the whites of her eyes began to change colour to a light pinkish glow.

'Instruct me to kiss Duncan.'

McCann looked up at her and scratched the back of his head he then peered at his bed 'Sit down on here,' he said pointing to the bed.

He figured the only way he could reach her head was if they were sitting down so he sat down by her side. McCann gingerly put his hand on her chin and guided her lips to his. He pressed their lips together slowly manoeuvring his arm around her back and onto the rear of her shoulder. For a while their lips pressed until she pulled her head away sharply, wiping her lips with the back of her hand.

McCann realised what had happened, 'I'm sorry are you alright?'

His beautiful visitor didn't reply she only looked back with an expression of shock. McCann having been caught away in the passion put his tongue in her mouth, something which didn't happen in Ryu's idyllic soap operas.

'When two people kiss passionately they often do that.'

Ilamachutli stopped wiping her lips 'Humans exchange tongues?'

'When they are attracted to each other, yes they do.'

She took a hold of his head and again she kissed him, far more subtly compared to the first time. They sat for ten minutes holding each other and kissing, more and more passionately as time went on. McCann now realised how long he'd been without female company, he forgot about Earth and the fact she was not human. Her beauty outstretched that of any human woman he could think of anyway. His concerns were left outside of the room with the rest of the universe, for now only two people existed for him.

As they were locked in an embrace his hands began to wander. Grasping the regions of her anatomy he had been gawking at for the last two weeks. Finally he could touch that which he'd lusted after all this time. Initially she gently pushed him away to stand up. McCann feared he'd offended her; however he quickly became aware that this was not the case. The tall flaming haired woman opened the collar of her suit in front of the throat. Next she pulled the suit apart and it unravelled straight down the middle. The sight of what lay beneath caused his heart to race.

He watched in awe as the suit peeled away to the navel revealing a pair of small but perfect breasts. She took her arms out of the suit, all the time watching his expression with glee. Ilamachutli pulled down the black ribbed suit over her hips and stepped out of the boots. McCann had wondered how close she was to a human underneath the layer of jet black. The strange fabric had obscured her features ever since they'd met.

He gulped upon seeing nothing less than a perfectly formed woman. If she had wings this beauty could be a piece of Michael Angelo art.

'Are you pleased Duncan?' she spoke tenderly whilst smiling.

He noticed a scent entering his nostrils from her body. McCann had never noticed it before but it filled the air with a sweet nutty odour. His eyes moved to her face and he replied 'Yes.'

McCann stood up and removed his suit bottoms, for ten seconds they both stood observing each other's anatomy. After each had satisfied their curiosity they embraced. Collapsing onto the bed their bodies entwined around each other as jungle vines. Twisting and turning passionately, beads of sweat dripped from their anatomy.

Her eyes glowed deep red, like two firey coals in the night. Not one word was spoken as they entangled in passion. They communicated in the fashion lovers have always done. McCann ran his lips down her hot ivory skin from her breasts to her navel where he nestled. At first she watched him, observing his activity. As the time went on she began to groan. Only a slight groan at first then louder and louder gathering pace until the Valkyrie grasped him.

She pulled him up turning him over onto his back as a rag doll. Ilamachutli sat on top of her lover thumping down onto him, faster and faster, for several minutes. McCann clasped her fine ivory hips for dear life whilst watching her petite breast bouncing up and down. Ilamachutli's towering athletic body beat against his until suddenly he felt an acute pain.

His loins inside Ilamachutli were held in a clench. McCann felt himself being pulled inside her as if his organ was being wrenched inside out. He tried to shout but she pressed her lips hard upon his smothering his cry. The beautiful Valkyrie aggressively pinned him down on the bed. Her strength far greater than his, McCann could not muster the power to throw her off. He struggled as a weak fawn attempting to escape the jaws of a lioness. He eventually ejaculated and only then did she release the Englishman from both her grasp on him and his loins.

He lay exhausted from his ordeal and dazed 'What happened?' he asked in a weakened tone.

Ilamachutli sat on him as radiant as a naked Aphrodite. She kissed him again, 'I do not understand?' she whispered between sensual kisses.

McCann looked down just to make sure everything was still attached and where it should be. On inspection he seemed none the worse for wear, 'Your vaginal walls ... they became very tight and I felt I was being sucked in.'

Ilamachutli chuckled playfully and stroked his cheek 'Involuntary reflex in females Duncan, do human females?'

McCann shook his head and grinned a little, 'No.'

His Valkyrie leant down and kissed him again, 'We have both instructed.'

He took her cheeks and kissed her slowly.

After another long kiss she sat up, 'I must leave Duncan!'

Still in a daze he lay down stroking her thighs 'Where?'

Ilamachutli laughed, 'To my room, we must not be discovered.'

He ruffled his brow, 'Why?'

Ilamachutli gazed down at her lover and put her hands on his chest, 'This is not permitted, intimacy is not permitted between us Duncan.'

McCann came back with the same question 'Why?'

Ilamachutli shook her head and stepped off the bed.

'Too many questions Duncan; I will answer your question tomorrow.'

McCann felt his energy return, he wasn't prepared to be loved and left without an explanation. He stood up and whilst she was putting her suit back on asked 'Then why did you come to my room? Why answer one of our questions? What is the purpose?'

Ilamachutli became rather annoyed by McCann's barrage of questions, 'I was curious concerning you, concerning love.'

McCann stood feeling rather cold, 'So is that it? You have what you wanted and now you're leaving?' he asked in a slightly raised voice.

She put her arms into her suit and started doing it up, 'You will have what you want tomorrow.'

He thought for a moment then answered impetuously, 'Quite frankly, no not really!'

She finished sealing her suit then put her hands on his shoulders, 'Duncan it is too dangerous, in time you shall understand but now I beg you reveal nothing.'

McCann was taken aback by her, the word beg was not something he associated with the red haired goddesss, 'As you wish Ilamachutli.'

She smiled 'You may address me as Ilam, Duncan.'

McCann felt a bit better and smiled at his lover 'Thank you, Ilam.'

She leant down and kissed him tenderly 'My clan is Chutli, Ilam is my name. In my language I am Ilam of Chutli clan, those close address with given names.'

McCann kissed her again and after a couple of minutes his goddess vanished back into the night she had come from.

When McCann awoke that morning for a while he wondered if it had been a dream. Until his nostrils picked up the scent of his lover from the night before. The unmistakable fragrance that reminded him of almonds was still in the air. He decided to have a shower before greeting the others in order to wash away any smell that her companions might detect.

McCann walked into the mess and took a tray from the dispenser. On sitting down opposite Ryu he noticed his three crew mates hadn't spoken since he entered.

'Good morning,' chirped McCann.

Ryu chewing on some steamed vegetables remarked, 'Rough night?' to which Hassif began choking on his cereal.

McCann churned his hot porridge with a spoon, 'I'm sorry?'

McCann spoke cautiously to Ryu while watching the steam rise from his meal. She didn't reply, just stoically chewed her food. McCann looked over at Hassif sitting next to her, 'Is there a problem?'

Hassif only shook his head whilst trying to clear his throat with a drink of water.

McCann glanced at the Frenchman sat next to him. Louis always had something to say, 'Well?'

Louis let out a grumble 'You woke us up last night McCann.'

McCann opened up his coffee and blew the steam away 'What do you mean?'

Louis was visibly uncomfortable, 'Do I have to say it McCann?'

He was worried that the commotion last night had been detected, but McCann couldn't afford to let on until he knew that they knew.

'Athena got us up last night, she thought you were being attacked!' growled Louis much to the delight of Hassif who was sniggering as a naughty schoolboy.

Ryu carried on eating her breakfast glaring at McCann with a stony face.

'I see,' replied McCann timidly.

'We saw the emergency display of your quarters then went back to sleep,' moaned Louis.

McCann drank down some coffee then went back to churning his porridge 'How much did you see?' he said looking into his breakfast.

'Enough!'

Ryu still glaring stoically remarked 'Don't worry Duncan it wasn't that good!'

Hassif broke out with a laugh causing Louis to snigger. However Ryu remained stony faced and McCann was certain she wasn't amused by last night's events.

McCann put his hands on the table 'Look this can't go any further do you understand?'

Ryu fixed her stare on him 'Why not?'

McCann made eye contact with her since she was the only person taking notice 'What she did is prohibited by her law.'

Ryu made a snorting noise 'And a few of ours no doubt!'

'Look you won't mention this in her or her companions presence understood?'

Ryu was very unimpressed 'Uuurrrrhhh!', the other two just nodded their heads trying to fight off the giggles.

McCann took another swig of hot coffee 'Also she has agreed to answer one of the questions we posed to her last night.'

The Frenchman let out a massive howling laugh. The other three looked at Louis as he slapped the table with his hand in joy. Gasping for air he laughed 'You can tell Faraday you screwed it out of her!'

Even Ryu managed a wry smile for a moment but it quickly faded. Ryu was rather baffled 'But she said last night she wasn't permitted to answer our questions. I don't understand how she will break her law in exchange for you helping her breaking another one? It doesn't make sense.'

McCann shrugged his shoulders 'Don't ask me, I think watching your soap operas put ideas in her head!'

Hassif who had recovered from his giggling fit chipped in 'Well it is logical when you think about it.'

Ryu glanced at Hassif with a wry expression 'How's that?'

'Well she said the punishment last night was execution, so if you're going to break one rule such as telling us about anti-matter why not break two? The punishment is the same whether you break one, two, three or fifty laws right?'

Ryu once again made her signature "Uuurrhh!" remark and went back to eating.

McCann considered his logic and agreed. If the punishment was execution they could only punish her once so maybe she was in for a penny in for a pound also?

Ilamachutli entered the mess and Ryu offered her a seat at their breakfast table 'Where are your companions?' asked Ryu.

Ilamachutli indicated that they were to remain in their quarters until requested. Ryu in her usual blunt fashion got on to the subject of the question to be answered. Ilamachutli exchanged a cheeky smile with Duncan. The crew all noticed a slight change in her eye colour.

'Good morning Duncan,' she said in an uncharacteristically tender tone.

The others raised their eyebrows. Hassif was trying not to look Louis in the face lest he might crack up with laughter.

'Good morning Ilam,' replied McCann uncomfortably.

Ilamachutli was either ignoring the others poor attempts at faking ignorance, hadn't caught on or just didn't care.

Ryu assumed the latter since she knew how acute Ilamachutli's senses were. Ryu was certain there was no way she was unaware of what was going on.

Louis put down his coffee and looking down the table at the visitor asked 'Can you answer my question on antimatter production?'

Ilamachutli smiled, 'No.'

McCann felt a little shock and quickly retorted 'I thought you were going to answer one of our questions?'

The slender Valkyrie placed a comforting hand on his, 'I will choose.'

'Which one do you wish to answer?'

Ilam squeezed McCann's hand which had Ryu transfixed, 'Dark matter.'

Ilamachutli went on to describe in the most basic terms she could the principles of dark matter. Hassif had a far greater understanding of what she was saying. From what McCann could grasp she was explaining that there was no such thing as dark matter. In fact space is itself made up from something and wasn't a total void. Ilamachutli explained that the very fabric of space and of the universe itself is where all that extra mass was hidden. It seems humans in their search for dark matter over the centuries had been looking at it every day; it was there they just didn't see it.

Hassif who was recording her lecture on his tablet pressed her for deeper insights 'So what is space made of and how do we analyze it?'

'No, I explained dark matter nothing more.'

Hassif let out a sigh 'Can you tell me where dark matter came from? Was it created in the big bang?'

Ilamachutli grinned a little, 'I have read your creation theory, no.'

Hassif pressed for a definitive answer and Ilamachutli was beginning to tire of his inquisition, 'This I will explain then no more, understood?'

Hassif nodded his head and she continued 'Before your big bang what was there?'

He shrugged his shoulders 'I don't know, nothing?'

'From what comes nothing Hassif?'

'Nothing.'

The Amazon clapped her hands together loudly, 'Very good! There was something before big bang, the fabric of space. The fabric of space, the darkness between stars was there for eons. Moving, stretching and shrinking over time as any fabric does. Next the fabric grew weak from eons of this, weak in many places you can observe today, Hassif. Eventually mass grew around a weak area and tore the fabric. Releasing a fury of energy from the fabric of space, this is your big bang. Yet still the fabric retains most of its energy which accumulates to a great influence. Your dark matter and dark flow is the fabric of the universe Hassif, but I will speak no more on this.'

She then placed her clenched fist in front of Hassif's face. Signifying he should not ask her any further questions.

Hassif nodded and switched off his tablet 'Thank you very much,' he said whilst backing up the file.

Ryu had been bored stiff by the dark matter lecture. If it didn't affect her job or interests then it was boring and superfluous. Had Ilamachutli been talking about more efficient scram drone engines or more sensitive controls, she'd have been fascinated. All through her lecture Ryu had been observing McCann. His demeanour to Ilamachutli had changed and vice versa. Ryu was concerned about the relationship that had sparked between the two and she feared it was endangering the mission.

It wasn't that she disliked Ilamachutli; in fact they both got on well together. Ryu had a reputation for being ruthlessly efficient. If she was required to step in, her pulse pistol was always charged and loaded at her side. McCann and the others may be susceptible to Ilamachutli's feminine whiles; however it would take a lot more than good looks and a smile before she lost sight of duty.

After the meal they split up, McCann to his office, Hassif to the command centre, Louis to Pavis Mons. Ryu gave Ilamachutli the guided tour of what would be the hydroponics.

Over the next week the Edwards crew arrived and the other two ribbons were on their way down. Anchored on the Edwards they were being delivered by the crawler. Once it arrived within a week they would be unravelled. Louis would anchor them with to Pavis Mons to complete the orbital lift on Mars.

McCann had managed to acquire a hair from Ilamachutli. After taking the DNA profile from an untainted sample it became clear that Tlillans were closer than first assumed.

The scientific world on Earth had erupted. Faraday announced that the mystery of dark matter had been revealed. He had kept the information under wraps until he could at least somehow verify its authenticity. Faraday had also been mulling over her cryptic talk of destiny. Like McCann it concerned him a great deal since Tlillans were obviously so much more advanced. What could they do if this destiny wasn't to their tastes?

Faraday tried to put it to the back of his mind but a day didn't go by that the thought didn't disturb him. Geneva noticed Ilamachutli had spent a lot of time observing human behaviour through media sent to Tharsis, mainly the media watched by Ryu, but also the odd movie. It was surprising how much human interaction she'd learnt from watching the films and soaps every night. Geneva had been sending her material on a regular basis. Though Faraday had it limited, anything political was censored. Ilamachutli was obviously very clever and despite her revelations he still felt great apprehension concerning the visitors.

Once the crawler arrived Louis got to unloading the ribbons and anchoring them. Ilamachutli had insisted on observing the process. McCann was also there overlooking the process which Louis found odd since there was no need for his presence in Pavis Mons. It became clear why when some of the small crates were being removed from the crawler. McCann became nervous; his helmet was bobbing around gingerly as he looked the pile of hand crates up and down. After the droid set them down and returned to the crawler he stepped over to the crates sitting in an alcove. After rummaging about for a while McCann appeared from the alcove holding a single crate with a leaf stamped on it. Louis had decided to ignore McCann since there was far more important work.

Ryu realised what had happened and rolled her eyes as McCann made gingerly for the exit tunnel back into Tharsis. McCann loaded his cargo and made off on a cart for Tharsis. Upon arrival he took the crate to his room and cracked it open. Inside were some clear plastic boxes containing various boxes of cigars and humidity beads. There was also a clear box filled with several large tubes. Inside each tube resided a bottle of whisky.

McCann had been looking forward to this since he'd been going through his supply far quicker than expected. He didn't know how long he was going to be on Tharsis. A regular supply of contraband cigars and whisky was required.

Thankfully Faraday had turned a blind eye allowing the shipment on the transport. When a man is under that much pressure yet still holding things together he's entitled to a drink and a smoke. A philosophy that Faraday and McCann both shared, although Ryu was not in agreement. This shipment was rather varied, the whisky was a different brand but perfectly acceptable by McCann's standards. Some of the cigars weren't quite to his taste but the Cohibas made up for that.

The ribbon attachment went smoothly; the supplies for Tharsis had been logged in allowing Athena to distribute them overnight.

The evening was spent in the lounge and McCann was pouring out the first of the Laiphrog whisky and lighting up a Cohiba. Only Louis agreed to try it, he noted the strong smoky taste on his palate. The others refused the offer, Ryu looking on with disdain.

McCann asked Ilamachutli if she'd like a drink but she refused.

'Do people on Tlillan drink for relaxation?'

Ilamachutli shook her head 'It is not permitted.'

'What isn't permitted?'

She pointed to the bottle 'This is not permitted.'

Ryu smiled and McCann took a drag from his cigar 'Why isn't it permitted?'

'Any substance that may alter ones perception of reality is not permitted.'

McCann expelled the smoke from his nostrils 'So you have problems with substance abuse on Tlillan?'

The room became hushed as everyone waited for her reply with bated breath.

Ilamachutli narrowed her eyes a little, 'No.'

Again she was not forthcoming in her answers McCann was sure it was deliberate, 'Why is it not permitted then?'

The fiery Amazon let out a sigh 'It would obscure the seers.'

McCann took another draw from his cigar 'I'm sorry I don't understand, obscure them how?'

She leaned back on the sofa 'We are all linked by the dreamscape, our seers use it to foresee. If too many are altered the dreamscape is obscured.'

It all sounded like nonsense to McCann yet it still intrigued him, 'What is the dreamscape?'

Ilam gestured waving her arms around 'It is as the fabric of the universe, it exists all around. We communicate through it, the priests on Tlillan see into the past, present and future through it. The dreamscape brought us here to you and will bring you home in time.'

Hassif retorted thoughtfully 'If what you say is true are humans linked to this dreamscape?'

She nodded 'Yes.'

Hassif peered deep into her 'Then why haven't we discovered it?'

Ilamachutli gave her signature condescending smile, 'Only females are linked, males are ignorant.'

Hassif wasn't giving up; even though he was religious this was only a hairs breadth from hocus pocus, 'So if Ryu wanted to access this dreamscape how would she do it?'

Ilamachutli glanced at Ryu 'First many years of training on Tlillan and Ryu could see the dreamscape. All of you are linked but you cannot see, I see you in the dreamscape.'

She wasn't making much sense to the crew of Tharsis except for Ryu. She realised that the Amazon visitor's heightened senses could be explained. Ilamachutli always had an incredible ability to read her emotions. Seemingly Ilam could always perceive her intent 'Do you mean you have a telepathic link, is that the dreamscape?'

Ilamachutli was pleased that her female counterpart had grasped what she was attempting to impart, 'In a base manner, yes, but the dreamscape exists itself. The dreamscape is an entity of its own, we merely connect to it.'

McCann sat up 'Are you telling us you can read our thoughts?'

Ilamachutli turned to McCann, 'Tlillan I can communicate. Humans I know intent but you are not aware yet, when aware communication will be possible.'

She gestured towards Louis who was unconvinced that this dreamscape was real. 'Louis was damaged when I attempted to speak to him.'

Now they had an explanation as to Louis psychotic behaviour.

'I thought you said males can't communicate via the dreamscape?' inquired Ryu. Ilamachutli still looking at the Frenchman, whom gave her a black look, replied 'I believed Louis to be female, I am sorry for your distress Louis.'

Louis said nothing but Ryu was perplexed as to how Ilam could have made such an obvious mistake.

'How could you mistake him for a woman?' inquired Ryu.

Louis' dark gaze now rested on Ryu but he still said nothing.

'Louis' mindscape is similar to female, his emotions are powerful. I read you all before contact, next decided to speak to one of you but Louis could not hear me.'

Hassif then interjected 'So that's why Athena malfunctioned during entry, you tried to contact her?'

Ilamachutli only nodded her head.

Ryu was rather sceptical 'Why did you think Louis was a woman? I don't understand how you can make that mistake?'

Suddenly Louis decided to speak 'Ferme!' he shouted in French which unfortunately Ilamachutli didn't understand.

'He is homosexual, many strong female emotions, on Tlillan his mindscape is female.'

Ryu crossed her legs and raised her eyebrows at Louis, 'Is it true? Are you a fag Louis?'

McCann and Hassif started sniggering, Ilamachutli looked on in bewilderment.

Louis sneered at Ryu 'What if I am?'

Ryu looked at McCann and Hassif 'You guys knew he was a fag?'

They both kept sniggering, McCann nodded his head.

Louis was fuming and quickly snapped at Ryu 'Stop using that word!'

'What, fag?'

Louis shouted 'Yes!'

Ryu leant back and played with her hair still directing her comments to Louis 'I guess we'll have to rename McCann the cosmic Casanova now!'

McCann stopped laughing.

Both Ryu and Louis smirked at McCann whilst Hassif maintained his jolly demeanour. All the time Ilamachutli observed with fascination, analysing every word and body movement, doing her best to make sense of the interaction unfolding before her eyes.

McCann cleared his throat 'Don't you have similar males on Tlillan?'

Ilamachutli was a little upset that the drama had ended, 'No, human males are complex Tlillan males are not. I was confused, first SI then Louis I am first to contact humans it is difficult.'

They continued chatting that night mostly on the contrasts between Tlillan and Human social structure until Athena broke the conversation.

'Colonel McCann, a transmission has been sent from the Tlillan craft.'

Suddenly a 3D display popped up in front of Ilamachutli's eyes. Projected by her suit the symbols were gibberish to the crew. She read the display and spoke some words in her language, the display collapsed, 'My companions have contacted Tlillan. I will be contacted soon may I have privacy?'

McCann nodded 'You can use my office.' he gestured to Ryu who stood up and led her to the command centre.

According to Ryu there was a fairly heated conversation in his office and when she left her eyes were light red. Ryu followed Ilamachutli as she marched quickly back to the lounge. Ilam announced 'Duncan it is time to decide.'

He was relaxing with the boys on the sofa and the gravity of the situation didn't impact him 'Decide what?' he asked leisurely.

Ilamachutli was very impatient it was obvious she believed time was of the essence, 'I must speak to your leader now Duncan.'

McCann put his drink down but kept puffing his cigar as they all walked back to the command centre. He approached the central table and activated the touch monitor, 'We have a delay of about fifteen minutes each way, so we have to record the message then send it and wait for the reply.'

Ilamachutli groaned at the news, 'So primitive!' she muttered.

McCann touched the screen 'You can record your message now.'

Ilamachutli stared into the screen that was now lit up showing a read out of message time and her voice profile, 'A vessel will enter this system soon, the vessel is Gukumatz. We are at war, they see Human as Tlillan, Human will be at war also. Gukumatz will exterminate Human, only Tlillan can prevent this. Human must make a decision to join Tlillan or combat Gukumatz alone; Message complete.'

McCann touched the screen then looked upwards 'Athena could you send that message now to Faraday and make it priority one please.'

Athena replied softly 'Understood Colonel.'

McCann took a drag on his cigar 'Thank you Athena,' he said as he blew the smoke back out.

An hour later a reply was received. Faraday gave a vaguely worded answer that amounted to "We'll wait and see". Faraday had neither the evidence to back up her story nor the authority to make such a pledge. Ilamachutli's good word wouldn't be enough to bring all the major powers in the world together. It had been attempted more than once, by force and diplomacy, and failed each time. The best Mankind managed were large regional alliances, Europe being the first and the strongest; despite having been shattered twice already. No one was going to sanction him making decisions for these power blocks. It would be the downfall of the I.S.A if he were ever so arrogant.

Still he didn't dismiss her warning it was a scary thought that someone might be coming. Due to their genetic links with the Tlillans it might make them a target of an enemy they couldn't defend against.

Ilamachutli refused to answer any questions on these Gukumatz. After having warned Faraday of them she insisted on sleeping and so they all retired.

The next day Louis was back in Pavis Mons checking that Athena had distributed the cargo properly. He was also gossiping with the crew of the Edwards who were getting settled, in orbit high above Tharsis.

Hassif was monitoring the space around Mars waiting for another craft to appear. This time Faraday wanted a good look at it entering the system.

Ryu was preparing her scram drones making them ready for a possible combat scenario. The crawler from the Edwards had delivered several guided missiles which could be fitted to the drones with a few modifications. She also had to drag Hassif in to flash some new software onto the drone hard drives, for the missile systems to operate in combat. Hassif dutifully installed the software from the command centre.

McCann was in the armoury preparing the pulse rifles along with a pistol, power packs and ammunition for Louis. As he was checking the spare power packs Ilamachutli walked into his office 'What are you doing Duncan?'

He had his back to her whilst working in the armoury and didn't turn around, 'I'm just preparing for your friends when they arrive, when will they arrive by the way?'

Ilamachutli stood in the doorway watching him work, 'Today Duncan.'

McCann stopped for a moment and his heart beat a little faster 'I see,' he carried on with his work.

'Duncan, no weapons is preferable.'

He carried on checking the power packs, 'Really? Why is that?'

'You may provoke them Duncan.'

'Do you think they will attack us?'

The flaming haired Valkyrie sighed 'Not here, not now. No need for weapons Duncan, I can protect you.'

McCann grunted disapprovingly 'I'm quite capable of taking care of myself thank you.'

Ilam smiled condescendingly. She found his attitude cute more than anything else, 'On Tlillan a male would be punished for speaking to his Matriarch that way.'

McCann said nothing and carried on preparing the weapons for immediate use.

'Your insolence is attractive.'

He shook his head and murmured 'Marvellous!' as he checked the ammo clips were full.

A klaxon suddenly fired off and Athena's calm but bold voice could be heard over it, 'An unidentified vessel has entered orbit.'

McCann glared sternly at Ilamachutli then walked up to her, 'Excuse me.'

He walked past her into the command centre holding a spare pulse pistol with holster. He looked upwards 'Everyone to the command centre. Ryu is the scram drone ready?'

Her voice came over the klaxon 'It's ready to go Colonel. I'm on my way to the command centre now.'

McCann glanced upwards again 'Athena, turn that bloody noise off!'

The klaxon shut down.

'Thank you Athena.'

McCann put the spare pistol on the main table and walked over to Hassif. The Indian technician sat at his station monitoring the craft as it descended from orbit.

'It's coming for us, they should be here in a matter of minutes,' said Hassif before giving McCann a worried look.

Ryu bounded into the command centre and slipped into her station, activating her display 'Permission to launch the first drone, Sir?'

'Granted and try to keep it away from them.'

Ryu peered at him and he put his hands in the air 'Sorry!'

He apologised and she went back to the job she knew better than anyone alive.

McCann looked at the ceiling again 'Athena, inform Geneva of our status every 20 minutes please.'

Her soft voice replied 'Understood Colonel.'

Next Louis bounded in out of breath.

'Louis put that on now,' McCann pointed to the pistol on the table 'you know how to use it?'

Louis nodded and put the belt around his waist before fastening the holster to his leg.

McCann turned to a large monitor. One of Ryu's drones observed the craft descending through the atmosphere. It was a large delta wing in design. The same jet black as the Tlillan craft, McCann assumed it was also constructed of the same material. As the craft descended McCann could be heard whispering to himself. He was singing a song but the words were inaudible. It was something he did to calm down in high stress situations. Often before engaging in a dangerous operation or entering a war zone. Listening to music helped him concentrate on the job in hand.

Ilamachutli scrutinized the scene as she often did in dramatic situations watching intently and making note of how the crew reacted to stimuli.

The craft eventually hit the surface with an impact that would have crushed the Athena and her crew. Next it pulled back out of the small crater it had made then hovered towards Tharsis.

McCann order Hassif to transmit the same ternary message and all of the language files the Tlillans had received. Soon a reply was received and displayed on the table. The creature they saw before them was very different to Ilamachutli. It possessed two arms, two legs and a torso however the head was not human at all. Nor did this creature faintly resemble a human.

McCann turned to Ilamachutli 'Ilam, these Gukumatz they look like frogs?'

She was bemused 'Frogs?'

McCann looked at the squashed face then noticed it had webbed hands and feet 'It's an amphibian form of life.'

Ilamachutli smiled 'Ah yes, Gukumatz amphibian.'

McCann examined the 3D image. He noticed the lack of definition on the body probably due to thick skin. However it was the face that disturbed him, it was totally alien. The face reminded him of a bullfrog. A pair of large blubbery lips and a couple of holes in its face must have been the nose. Strangest of all were the eyes sitting on either side of the head. Humans and Tlillans like their ape ancestors had their eyes forward facing in the front of the head. Gukumatz eyes rested on either side of their head giving a much larger field of vision. McCann was already building scenarios to take advantage of this. Since the placing of the eyes left a blind spot immediately behind and in front of them.

Soon the craft sat in front of Tharsis having lowered itself onto the gravely desert. Next the side of the vessel opened and two figures stepped out. Once outside, the vessel rippled shut and two Gukumatz stood waiting dressed in similar jet black suits.

The suits were similar aside from the helmet which was decidedly short. It was in fact more of a broad squat dome balanced on the shoulders. The Gukumatz were decidedly larger in girth than the Tlillans. Their limbs were thick and McCann assumed very powerful.

The Englishman pulled out his pistol and checked it one last time, 'Open the airlock and let them inside Athena.'

He then holstered his pistol and turned to Louis "You're with me."

Louis nodded and stood by McCann's side 'Will our pistols penetrate those suits?' he asked Ilamachutli.

'Yes.'

McCann made his way to the airlock with Louis in tow whilst the Gukumatz entered and went through the decontamination process. They both waited inside Tharsis, peering through the porthole at the new visitors. Finally after the decontamination had finished McCann called out 'Open the inner door Athena.'

They both took a few steps back as the door swung open ushering in the two frogmen. After the shock of their dark green frog faces he noticed they stood bow legged or frog legged. Also they had a hunch to their stance. The shoulders at the rear were very large. McCann didn't know what to say to these alien creatures. For a while he and Louis faced off to the amphibians and McCann's right hand hung down always touching his holster and pistol. McCann couldn't tell if the Gukumatz noticed his weapon or not. They were so utterly alien he had no idea what they were thinking.

A Gukumatz made a deep croaking noise that sounded like a burp. It surprised both him and Louis. A moment later a human voice emitted from inside the collar of the Gukumatz suit 'Hello.'

The voice was cold, emotionless and androgynous.

McCann replied 'Hello, my name is Duncan,' offering his hand.

The Gukumatz also offered his hand; McCann closed the distance in order to complete a handshake. Louis was disgusted by the creatures, the more he looked at that neck less, blubbery lipped face the more he warmed to the Tlillans.

The Gukumatz croaked a few times which Louis found repulsive 'I am Kotumatz, Duncan.'

McCann could feel the breeze of wind each time this creature croaked. The smell was quite repellent. He looked at the other Gukumatz both were a little shorter than McCann but their bodies were far more robust.

'What might your name be?' inquired McCann offering his hand.

The Gukumatz shook his hand and croaked through the translator 'I am also Kotumatz.'

McCann found it very odd they both had the same name but put it to the back of his mind, 'Please follow me gentlemen.'

He walked them along the corridor to the lounge.

McCann wanted to keep Ilamachutli and the Gukumatz segregated for as long as possible. So he kept her in the command centre whilst he tried to hammer out some sort of understanding with the Gukumatz. However the more he looked at these creatures the more he doubted that they could find common ground. Upon arriving in the lounge McCann asked if there was anything they'd like to drink.

The visitors croaked 'No.'

Whilst speaking a grey film flicked over the toad's black beady eyes cleaning them. Louis nearly jumped out of his skin.

McCann lied and told them that he was honoured to have them as guests. In fact he was praying they'd just disappear. The Gukumatz however were finished with any pleasantries 'We want DNA sample,' it croaked.

McCann provided a sample of his hair but when he requested a DNA sample from his guests he met with a blunt refusal. McCann assumed these creatures didn't have much in the way of manners, especially considering their foul breath and vulgar form of communication.

'Why not?' inquired McCann.

The Gukumatz ignored his question and spoke instead to his companion with a string of deep throated croaks and gurgles.

It then turned to McCann and croaked. An androgynous voice from its suit spoke 'Where is the Darksider?'

McCann quite bewildered replied 'I'm sorry but what is a Darksider?'

The Gukumatz again let off a barrage of crackling croaks. McCann couldn't tell if it was annoyed or not but he assumed it was becoming impatient.

'There is a Darksider present, she arrived before.'

McCann realised who they meant, 'Yes there is a Tlillan present on Tharsis, she is also our guest.'

The Gukumatz croaked feverishly in a low tone the news had excited them but probably for all the wrong reasons. A Gukumatz opened the plastic bottle containing McCann's DNA sample. The toad man took a small box from his belt and placed the sample inside.

Louis went for his pistol but McCann quickly put his arm out, blocking Louis before anything could escalate.

The two Gukumatz froze for a moment and stared straight at Louis or as straight as they could. The placing of their eyes meant they couldn't see anything directly in front of them. The stout toads had to tilt their heads a little one way or the other to look at someone or something. It was just another quirk that unsettled McCann.

Louis holstered his weapon without saying anything.

The Gukumatz put McCann's sample inside a small white box. After 5 seconds he replaced the box in his belt then spoke with to his companion.

The Gukumatz croaked to McCann 'We wish to leave.'

McCann was dumbfounded, 'But you've only just arrived!'

The Gukumatz croaked again 'Exit,' came the cold voice from his translator.

McCann called out to Athena 'Athena bring Ilamachutli in here please and tell Ryu to stay on her toes.'

'Understood Colonel.'

The Gukumatz croaked again 'Exit,' with what McCann assumed was growing impatience.

'In a moment,' responded McCann holding his guests in the lounge.

McCann wanted to try an experiment of his own. Since Ilamachutli had taken such interest in watching human social interaction, he was going to observe some Tlillan and Gukumatz social interaction.

The proud Tlillan strode into the room sneering at the Gukumatz with her heir of superiority filling the atmosphere. The Gukumatz reacted but neither Louis nor McCann could read the body language of these creatures. The Gukumatz bellowed some croaks at Ilamachutli to which she replied in her native language. None of which McCann understood.

'What is he saying?' asked McCann.

Ilamachutli didn't remove her gaze from the Gukumatz 'This animal wishes to leave!'

'Why?'

The Gukumatz croaked loudly and his translator spoke 'We fear Darksiders … all of you.' it was difficult to know who he was talking to since they didn't point their heads in the same method as humans or Tlillans when addressing someone.

'Why do you fear Darksiders?'

The Gukumatz made a rasping noise and croaked into the translator again, 'They enslaved us, made us believe they were Gods! All Darksiders are the same … all of you!'

McCann didn't even look at Ilamachutli though somehow he felt her eyes on him, 'We are not Darksiders.'

The bulky toad rasped again then croaked feverishly 'Your DNA states you are Darksider. We do not believe you.'

McCann attempted to convince his slimy guests they were safe but they refused to accept his word. The sight of Ilamachutli and the DNA evidence was all they were prepared to take into consideration. It became apparent that he was going to have to let them return to their vessel or hold them against their will. Eventually the Gukumatz were given free passage out of Tharsis.

Louis was sent back to his station in the command centre whilst McCann decided to question Ilamachutli in the lounge, 'So why did he call you a Darksider?'

Ilamachutli peered down on McCann; a display popped up before her eyes then collapsed 'Tlillan is in a tidal lock with its star. We live on the Darkside. Our species was once diverse living in twilight and lightside but only Darksiders remain.'

McCann went to ask another question but she placed a clenched fist to his lips, 'When we first travelled from Tlillan we encountered Gukumatz in our solar system. We improved their wellbeing and they worshipped us. Before we came they were ignorant savages.'

McCann pushed her fist away from his lips which seemed to amuse her, 'So he thinks we're Tlillan too?'

Ilamachutli shook her head 'No, but you are close enough.'

'Close enough for what?'

'To be a threat.'

McCann walked passed her and into the command centre muttering under his breath 'Wonderful!'

The flaming haired Valkyrie followed close behind him.

'Have they done anything yet?' asked McCann.

According to Ryu and Athena they were still sitting there outside. Fortunately this time the Edwards had some excellent footage of the craft entering the system.

From what they observed the vessel appeared from a white hole or tear in space. The tear appeared for moments before the vessel exited. Closing up again seemingly on its own volition. The vessel looked to be little more than ejected from this tear in space. Although Hassif knew it couldn't be a true tear in space that's what they named it for now. Ilamachutli was tight lipped as ever on these subjects and refused to reveal anything. She took McCann aside requesting another message to Faraday, to which he complied.

The contents of the next message which everyone was listening in on were far more dramatic. Ilam gave Faraday one hour to sign a treaty she had sent along with the data packet. No one knew the contents except for Faraday, whom refused, disappointing Ilamachutli.

When McCann enquired about it she said "He will agree before the day is out Duncan" McCann wasn't one for political games and left them to it. The Gukumatz craft lifted up from the desert and hovered away from Tharsis. Slowly gathering height until it broke free of the Martian atmosphere and planet's gravitational pull. The Gukumatz craft moved away until they were in a higher orbit even than the Edwards.

'What are they waiting for?'

Ilamachutli didn't reply only displaying her condescending smile. It seemed to give her pleasure observing them worry, out of their own fear and ignorance. Perhaps it just reinforced her feelings of superiority?

Later that day the klaxon went off again. Another tear had been detected out at Jupiter.

'What is it?' asked McCann.

'It's hard to tell at this distance but I do know it's much larger than the other two,' replied Hassif as he stared at his monitor.

Within 15 minutes the Edwards had the best view of what was now on a direct path towards the Earth. The jet black material prevented any exact readings but it was at least the size of an ocean going cruiser. The front was a massive delta wing much the same as the original Gukumatz vessel. A large tubular black trunk led backwards to spherical engine housing. Though they couldn't yet see the rear it emitted a glow.

Along the trunk, on four sides, long spines could be seen protruding then curving back slightly. The ship looked like a dead fish to McCann with bones and all. The original Gukumatz vessel broke from orbit and disappeared into the body of the giant mother ship. As it moved forward it grew in size.

'Colonel McCann there is an urgent message for Ilamachutli from Chairman Faraday.'

He didn't move his eyes from the monitor 'Play it Athena,' he said in a trance.

Faraday's grim face arose from the table 'Ilamachutli, the I.S.A agrees to your contract. I have signed this agreement with the full consent of the European Union, Russian Bloc, East and West American States and the East Asian Nations. Any nation not agreeing to the terms shall be brought into accordance, William Faraday.'

Everyone in the Command centre had turned to the image of Faraday with a look of disbelief. McCann wasn't sure if he was telling the truth. He wondered what they had signed and why. Ilamachutli's display popped up again before her eyes and a transmission was sent.

McCann pointed at the Gukumatz ship which was passing the asteroid belt at an incredible speed by human standards, 'So what are they playing at?'

'They have come to exterminate you.'

Ilam's display collapsed and her craft ceased transmitting.

'Now it is time to pray,' she said watching the Gukumatz ship approach on the monitor.

The ship eventually reached the orbit of Mars 'Look!' shouted Hassif pointing to a cylindrical object detach from the ship.

'What is that?' asked McCann but the room remained silent.

A burst of fire emitted from one end and it streaked away into the black of space. The fire soon died out and the crew lost the object in space. Hassif tapped his station furiously 'Am I right Athena?'

'Your calculations are correct Hassif.'

McCann shouted franticly 'What?'

Hassif shook his head 'It's travelling to the Earth.'

McCann turned to Ilamachutli 'What was that?'

'A weapon, it has impacted your home planet.'

McCann became angry 'What type of weapon exactly?'

Ilamachutli looked down on him with pity, 'I don't know Duncan.'

Hassif called out as another detached from the ship and made its way to Earth.

'You knew this would happen?' McCann asked the flaming haired visitor as he stood helplessly watching the extermination of his species.

'As did Faraday.'

McCann looked back at the monitor 'What about this contract?'

Ilam put her hand on his shoulder, 'An agreement to defend your system in return for your resources.'

It didn't make sense to McCann. There were plenty of resources in the galaxy and certainly nothing special in this system. He watched the terrifying black space ship looming over them. Hassif switched on another monitor where they witnessed the first missile hitting the Earth. A massive detonation could be seen, even from Mars, somewhere around the equator of the African continent.

Louis gasped 'Was that anti-matter?'

Ilamachutli nodded her head when the second one impacted the North American continent.

McCann turned to Ilamachutli 'What are you going to do?'

The beautiful Tlillan pointed to the monitor 'Watch Duncan.'

Hassif jumped out of his seat 'Another tear is opening this side of the asteroid belt!'

Sure enough a massive white shimmering hole opened and out came something quite different. A long thin rectangular trunk, haphazardly constructed at first glance. It wasn't consistent like the Gukumatz vessel. There were large blocks sat on it similar to a child's Lego toy. At the aft end four straight fins shot off diagonally from the main body just before the aft ended, and the engine exhaust fired out into space. At the fore end the long thin rectangular body ended with a pyramid cap. The two vehicles were an awesome sight. Before McCann could admire them much longer the Tlillan ship opened fire on the other. Each fin ended with a small cylinder which fired a straight white beam into the smaller Gukumatz ship.

The Gukumatz ship exploded into flame but not before it released its own barrage. An armada of small missiles from its fins smashed deep craters into the armour of the Tlillans. McCann watched in wonder as the two vessels pounded each other not far from Mars orbit. He couldn't make out a clear winner and began to fear that the Tlillans may not be successful.

After ten minutes of relentlessly pounding each other a massive crack opened along the Gukumatz back bone. McCann felt Ilamachutli's hand squeeze his shoulder tighter and tighter as she watched the battle unfold on the command centre main monitor. Next and explosion occurred on the Gukumatz ship at the rear. Ilamachutli shouted something in her language.

'What was that?' asked McCann.

Her expression was one of restrained joy 'The electromagnetic shields collapsed. Gukumatz invest their energy in shields and use missiles for weaponry.'

The Gukumatz kept firing missiles but the end was inevitable. The Tlillan beam weapons dissected the once fearsome warship into pieces until it could fight no longer.

Using what McCann guessed was something similar to their magnetic net. The Tlillan cruiser pulled the debris into the sun, casting it away to be vapourised. The battleground was littered with tiny pieces of smouldering debris which the Tlillan ship began to clear up.

Ryu queried Ilamachutli 'Why didn't they use anti-matter on the Tlillan ship?'

The rest of the crew realised that they had used anti-matter on Earth; yet refused to employ it, despite being the difference between life and death, in battle.

Ilamachutli took a long sigh of relief, 'It is not permitted to wield anti-matter weapons in war.'

Ryu didn't understand, 'But they just used them on us!'

'Humans not complied to ban on environmental weapons.'

McCann folded his arms and muttered 'Perfect!' he look upwards 'Athena how many estimated dead?'

Athena didn't respond for five seconds until a rough estimate was calculated, 'In the initial explosion no less than 50 million.'

Ilamachutli looked down at him, 'They are animals Duncan, before you could agree to a treaty they attempt to exterminate you.'

Next before they could even thank the Tlillan Captain, the ship turned on its axis and another rift in space opened. The ship produced one burst from its engines and disappeared into it.

'What if they come back?' asked McCann with his hands out to the monitor.

She put her hand on his shoulder again 'You are safe for now. I will help you build defences if your Faraday can achieve consensus.'

That evening they watched the news in the lounge and fortunately the anti-matter weapons hadn't detonated in large population areas. Still the death toll was high and the planet Earth had two new craters. The explosions had set of Earthquakes and tsunami all over the planet. Each explosion was estimated at 100-200 megatons. Fortunately for the population after around 100 megatons the explosions leaves the atmosphere and escapes into space.

Part of the Sahara had been turned to glass due to the sheer heat of the detonation. Cities hundreds of miles away from ground zero had been flattened in North America. The consequences for the environment were yet to be measured. For now it was a case of counting the dead as they kept coming in with each quake and tidal wave.

The crew of Tharsis couldn't believe what they saw, 'What's the point in doing this?' asked Louis in a sullen voice.

Ilamachutli sat on the sofa and replied 'They are base animals.'

Louis became incensed and pointed at her 'This is your fault you could've stopped them but you let them do this.'

Ilamachutli sneered at Louis 'If it were not for us you would be extinct, fool!'

The Valkyrie's eyes became completely red. McCann tried to get Louis attention without luck.

Louis stood up and his hand dropped to his side 'Maybe that whole thing was staged to frighten us into signing something? How do we know anything you say is true?'

The Frenchman's hand reached for the handle of his pistol. Louis pulled the pistol but froze with it half drawn from his holster.

Ilamachutli put her hand on McCann's arm and spoke softly 'He has been disabled, disarm him Duncan.'

McCann stood up and looked Louis straight in the eyes. He was conscious and his eyes were moving. McCann could see he was attempting to move his body with great effort. Louis eyes moved vigorously whilst he held his breath as a weightlifter would when attempting a heavy lift.

McCann took his pistol from his hand 'Louis can you hear me?'

'He can hear you Duncan.'

McCann turned to Ilamachutli who was now relaxed with a lofty grin 'What have you done to him?'

The beautiful Tlillan glared at the Frenchman for a moment and Louis collapsed onto the floor.

McCann quickly picked him up, 'Athena we need a medical droid in the lounge!'

However Louis soon got his footing, 'No I'm fine.'

Ilamachutli laughed at Louis trying to stand on his own. She looked at Ryu 'He will recover his motor functions quickly.'

Ryu made only a blank stare at her female counterpart.

McCann set him back down on the sofa then sat next to Ilamachutli, 'What did you do to him?'

Ilam explained she had immobilized him using her mental abilities. According to her it was easily achieved with untrained forms of life.

Ryu then coldly commented 'Now we know how you keep the males suppressed.'

To which Ilamachutli said nothing.

They went back to watching the news and soon Jerry Habeeb was on. The sensationalist newscaster was reporting how the mid-west had been devastated. The Western States were in peril after the explosion had triggered the San Andreas Fault. A tsunami of a magnitude never seen before was heading for East Asia. Weathermen forecasted black skies over the eastern seaboard tomorrow. According to reports volcanoes were already spewing ash into the atmosphere all over the globe. Scientists predicted a worldwide famine due to decimated crops. It seemed the only people to escape the crisis were those on Tharsis and the Edwards.

McCann asked Ilamachutli 'So what can you do to help us?'

She watched the devastation with the others 'I will send templates, devices to clean atmosphere and defend against Gukumatz.'

Ryu interjected 'I thought you weren't allowed to do that?'

'Today I have been banished from Tlillan.'

'Why have you been banished?'

The tall red headed woman put both of her hands on her stomach, 'I have child.'

Ryu was still none the wiser 'I don't get it, you were banished because you're pregnant?'

Ilamachutli nodded and the horrible truth started to dawn on McCann.

'The males reported my pregnancy to my clan Matriarch.'

Hassif scratched his head 'Is it not permitted to have a child without permission on Tlillan?'

'It is permitted.'

'So what is the problem?'

Ilamachutli glanced at McCann lovingly who was wallowing in a glass of whisky at this point, 'The father is human, this is heresy.'

The crew gasped.

'I am not permitted to return to my clan, however I may assist humans. My companions will soon return to Tlillan, leaving me here. I will require your protection as you will require mine.'

McCann sat gazing into his drink and said solemnly 'How long until it's born?'

Ilamachutli put both of her hands on his shoulders 'She will be born in one of your years, perhaps less Duncan.'

He took a swig of whisky 'She?'

Ilamachutli was smiling with glee 'Yes the child shall be female, the first Tlillan female born for two centuries.'

Hassif spoke up 'How long does your species live for?'

'At least five centuries, but a Matriarch will live longer.'

'So why haven't any females been born for two hundred years?'

Ilamachutli looked at the carnage on the monitor in the lounge 'The Gukumatz released a virus on Tlillan, all males are infertile.'

Hassif shrugged his shoulders 'But isn't that illegal according to your treaty?'

'First we must prove their guilt.'

Hassif glanced at the monitor of Earth then towards Ilamachutli 'I understand now, when they saw that human males are possible donors for Tlillan females they tried to exterminate us. How did they know to come here though?'

Ilamachutli sighed, 'When my males learned of my child they informed Tlillan. Gukumatz monitor all communications. Males are ignorant they follow instructions blindly. I attempted to offer Faraday the treaty before the Gukumatz arrived.'

McCann then broke from his trance 'So the resource is us?'

Ilamachutli confirmed his conclusion.

'Why don't you use artificial insemination or cloning?' inquired Hassif.

Ilamachutli slowly shook her head 'Heresy.'

Ryu cut in 'But this is heresy too, what's the difference?'

'Only my heresy, the child will be innocent and the Tlillan will continue.'

Louis who had recovered became animated once more 'We've got nothing to do with this, why don't you go home and leave us alone!'

'It is too late; Gukumatz will come for you regardless of my presence. Without my help you cannot defend yourselves and your planet will die. Your destiny and ours are now intertwined Louis Beaumont. We have saved you and in return you shall save us or we perish together.'

Trying to ignore Louis, Hassif put forward another question 'I don't understand why a female would make a difference? Why not give birth to a male since he can fertilize many females at once?'

The beautiful Tlillan acknowledged Hassif's ever present logic 'This child is a symbol Hassif. First it must be demonstrated that a human can create a suitable Matriarch. If the child is suitable the hybrid must be accepted into the gene pool. Because of Gukumatz all Lightsiders and Twilighters exterminated, leaving only Darksiders and fractured gene pool.'

She returned to viewing the devastation on Earth, 'Humans will recover, we shall all recover,' she said ominously.

Chapter 10

After another week Ilamachutli's companions returned from whence they came, leaving her on Tharsis. She spent much of her time sending blueprints to Geneva. Scientists, technicians and engineers worked franticly to bring the designs to fruition.

Atmosphere processors were being churned out of factories to deal with the environmental catastrophe. After 6 months the Earth's atmosphere was in better shape than before the missiles had hit! Hundreds of airships circled the globe removing dust particles that threatened to throw the billions of people relying on the planet into the abyss.

The I.S.A also finished construction of a space yard on the Tsiolkovsky to begin the manufacturing of space mines. Faraday had Ilamachutli's word her designs would be effective against any enemy warship; although the designs were still primitive compared to the space battle witnessed some months before. Faraday felt certain that if they could produce enough and put them out there, the next time the Gukumatz appeared it would be a different story.

Ilamachutli still refused to reveal how they travelled such long distances. Concerning anti-matter production her wisdom was frustratingly sparse. She only provided them with the bare essentials of self defence, a situation that Faraday was determined to change.

A year after what was now dubbed the battle of Mars the crew of Tharsis had been replaced and returned home. Their reception had been very different to what they'd expected when leaving. Rather than Ryu grabbing all of the media attention it was squarely fixed on Ilamachutli and her child. Everyone on the planet wanted to know about it. Jerry Habeeb was prepared to step over his own mother to get there first.

At the network America interview it was obvious she was pregnant. Her black ribbed suit bulged at her stomach spoiling her otherwise perfect figure. Jerry dressed in his Italian pinstripe shirt and braces opened 'So do you know how long it will be?'

The red haired lady smiled 'Very soon thank you.'

'And you're sure it's a girl?'

'Certain.'

Jerry pulled himself up over the table just a little 'I'd like to thank you on behalf of many people for your assistance. Yet there are those who blame you for the predicament we're in right now. What, if anything, do you have to say to them?'

Ilamachutli placed her hands on her baby, 'On Tlillan when the plague was released, many more of us died. We accused each other until accepting the truth. Gukumatz were responsible for the devastation, no one else.'

The interview went on whilst McCann and Louis watched not far from the studio at the I.S.A centre in Geneva.

'This is all crap, you know she's responsible!' sneered Louis.

McCann wasn't interested in Louis complaining tonight.

'What is the matter with you?' moaned Louis who had noticed McCann had been very withdrawn all evening. Louis kept badgering him until he revealed he would be seeing his mother tonight to which Louis felt pity, 'What has she said about Ilam?'

McCann dragged his hand down his face 'Don't ask, because I didn't!'

Louis tried to comfort his friend 'Well she's always wanted you to have a kid, maybe she'll be happy?'

McCann looked Louis in the face with a stone cold expression 'Sometimes I think you got an easy break being gay!'

Louis turned back to the monitor and the interview with Jerry Habeeb. All was going well until Ilamachutli clutched her stomach and screamed. Jerry leapt out of his chair; she fell to the ground grimacing in pain, and called for medical assistance.

Louis looked to McCann but he was nowhere to be seen. The Frenchman made off to the roof where he caught McCann getting into a hummingbird.

Ilamachutli had been evacuated to the nearest hospital. McCann and Louis had just landed on the building's helipad. The hospital was under heavy guard and both of them required a retina scan before leaving the roof and entering the building. Once inside he discovered the floor Ilam had been evacuated to. McCann made his way there under escort, Louis waited outside. Inside the beautiful Tlillan lay on a bed surrounded by nurse droids. A human nurse and a doctor presided over the droids.

McCann looked desperately at the doctor.

'She's doing well Colonel, and the child is in good health.'

An ultrasound display sat above the bed. Her black ribbed suit had been removed permitting the scan to monitor his child. Ilam's eyes turned to McCann, she held out her hand and cried his name. He shot over and clutched her hand smiling nervously. The Valkyrie's face contorted as the contractions escalated.

An armed guard entered the room and whispered into McCann's ear. McCann took a look at his tablet, 'Let her in.'

There was a ruckus outside of the delivery room until his mother walked in sporting an expression of displeasure, 'You weren't going to tell me Duncan?'

His mother pushed him out of the way and took over the proceedings. Ilamachutli seemed quite happy with Ofra's presence. McCann had a feeling that his mother had sidelined him.

Soon Ofra was directing him the nurse and the doctor. The old soldier would've preferred his mother out of the way, yet he didn't dare steal this moment from her. McCann understood what this meant to Ofra. Her presence meant that his mother finally had come to terms and accepted the odd state of affairs.

Ofra was doting over Ilamachutli for hours until after much pain and anguish the Tlillan delivered their child. The baby girl's skin was an ivory white inherited from her mother. The screaming baby possessed her mother's long muscular Tlillan frame also. Her hair however was a dark burgundy colour with a slight natural curl much to the delight of Ofra. The eyes resembled McCann's light grey eyes but with a hint of translucence.

The doctor cut the umbilical cord and handed the child to the Mother, '14 lbs that must be a record!'

The baby girl inherited the same swollen head as the mother; the child's limbs were longer than the average human baby.

Ofra was ecstatic upon seeing the child's hair 'Look at her hair!' she shouted.

Ofra insisted on holding the newborn.

Ilamachutli looked towards McCann, he gave a nod of approval and Ilam passed the baby in a blanket to Ofra.

The party heard a loud noise outside, 'Let me in you little piss ant!'

McCann stepped outside and tapped the shoulder of the guard 'He can come in.'

McCann's father pushed past the guard 'I could barely get past the cameras outside lad, if I weren't a retired officer I don't know …'

James saw his ex-wife holding the child 'How in blue blazes did she get in?'

Ofra was too busy cuddling the largest baby the hospital had ever seen to respond to his outburst.

'Is that the baby? It looks more like a bloody two year old!' James exclaimed.

His father shook Ilamachutli's then McCann's hand 'This is a right bloody pickle you're in!' his father muttered.

Ofra gave him a black look from the opposite side of the bed 'If you don't shut your mouth you'll be in a pickle!'

James gave her a sarcastic military salute.

His son jabbed him in the ribs with a fast elbow until James settled down.

Ofra cradled the child which behaved itself excellently 'What is her name?'

McCann turned to Ilamachutli 'We haven't decided upon one yet, Ilam?'

Ofra became feverish with excitement 'No name? I have a perfect name for her!'

James then cut her off bellowing at his ex-wife 'Ofra!'

She gave him another black look and held the child even closer to her bosom.

'You have to let them name the child Ofra!'

Ilamachutli was sat up in her bed now and put her hand on Ofra's arm 'It's alright. I would be honoured if you name her for us.'

Ofra smirked at James then looked back down on her granddaughter 'Malikah,' she said as she played with the child's lips.

James shook his head, 'Jesus Christ!'

McCann gave him a sturdy knock on the back.

James cleared his throat then walked to the other side of the bed to view the child with his ex-wife.

Ilamachutli held McCann close to her and gazed into his eyes.

Ofra interrupted their moment, 'So the wedding will have to be in Tel Aviv.'

James, who was also adoring the child, grunted 'Give them a chance will you? They've only just had a baby!'

Ofra staring disapprovingly at her son stated 'They've had more than enough time! Decent people marry before they have children not the other way around!'

James piped up 'Are you insinuating they are not decent people?'

'Not if they get married in Tel Aviv!'

Ilamachutli was very much amused by the carry on between McCann's parents. It was even better than one of Ryu's soap operas. She was at a loss as to how these two stayed together long enough to conceived and raise a child together. Both were so incompatible and it was hilarious to watch them clash.

McCann was not amused 'Enough! If I could please hold my daughter I'd be very grateful!' he snarled.

His parents quietened down, Ofra passed him his newborn daughter.

McCann scrutinized the baby, she was different but very beautiful, 'Malikah.'

Ilamachutli cut in 'One day she shall be Malikachutli.'

McCann played with his daughter putting his finger in her mouth 'What does Malikah mean?'

James bellowed bluntly 'Queen!'

McCann peered at Ilamachutli knowingly.

Ofra caught his glance and told him to leave her alone.

He suspected the two of them had been in correspondence, this confirmed it. Ilamachutli was determined her daughter would be a Matriarch someday. It could have been no coincidence his mother happened to pick that name. Still he was pleased to see his mother had accepted the child. Thanks to Ilamachutli she was here doting over Malikah. The flipside being with Ilam's help his mother had manoeuvred him into a marriage. He would have words concerning the scheming and plotting later, but right now he was enjoying the moment of his daughter's birth.

After a while the men were asked to leave. Ilamachutli, Ofra and Malikah remained in the delivery room.

Outside James took his son aside and laughed 'They stitched you up like a bloody kipper in there!'

McCann nodded his head 'How long have those two been talking or should I say plotting?'

James shrugged his shoulders 'How the bloody hell should I know?'

Louis approached the pair 'How did it go?'

McCann informed the Frenchman all was well, he detected a commotion outside the waiting room and asked Louis what was up.

According to Louis the press was lurking outside hoping for pictures or interviews.

Next he spied Faraday making his way into the waiting room 'Are they alright old boy?' he asked in his thick Etonian accent.

McCann shook his hand 'Yes and good to see you here. I thought you'd be too busy to visit?'

Faraday passed him a tubed cigar 'When I heard the news I made straight for the hummingbird, but you'd already taken it! Does she have a name yet?'

McCann nodded 'Yes, Malikah. Apparently I'll be getting married in Tel Aviv as well, as to when you'll have to ask my mother!'

Faraday let out a rare laugh and congratulated him.

McCann suspected he was celebrating not the marriage but the belief that his trusted officer had secured the most precious object on the planet today, Ilamachutli.

Over the following year Faraday and Ilamachutli had worked closely. With the beautiful Amazon's assistance the I.S.A would build six space faring craft. Both Earth and Mars were to be protected with orbital rail guns. The entire solar system was to be lain with a sea of deadly mines in wait for the next enemy incursion.

The new space craft were very basic by Tlillan standards. In fact Ilamachutli had pointed out that they were more akin to unmanned cargo vessels. Faraday had the Tsiolkovsky construction yard begin construction on what resembled submarines. Six black tubular craft with a conning tower. The purpose of the tower was attachment to the Tsiolkovsky and Edwards docking arms.

Propulsion would be an anti-matter drive. Tiny atoms of anti-matter were fired into atoms of hydrogen creating an explosion at the rear of the craft. The explosion would hit a blast plate deflecting it back into space, propelling the vessel forward at great speeds. The acceleration would be slow however and changing course was a long painful process.

Much to Faraday's frustration Ilam had not revealed the secrets of efficient anti-matter production. The I.S.A could produce enough for the six "space subs" to get around. However until Ilamachutli decided humanity was ready that was the measure of it.

She had been forthcoming concerning atmosphere processing; her insight had saved billions of lives. Faraday saw the anguish in her eyes when the tsunami hit China killing over one billion. The Etonian believed she felt an affinity with human beings but he never doubted her first motivation was her own clan.

From what Faraday had learnt her banishment wasn't all that it seemed. Ilam had never confirmed his suspicions but he suspected it may be a charade. He believed she was banished in order to assist humanity and save her race from the Gukumatz.

Faraday was unconcerned either way for the time being, 'I'll need to see both of you tomorrow in my office,' he said looking at McCann and Louis.

McCann felt a little pushed since he'd only just become a father, 'Could it wait?'

Faraday shook his head 'No, Ilam will be there along with Ryu and Hassif. It's very important Duncan, things are going to change soon.'

He patted McCann on the arm, shook his father's hand then left.

'Did Ilam tell you what this is about?' asked Louis.

McCann shrugged his shoulders 'Nope, It seems I'm the last to find out again! Still we've both had much worse days than this, right Louis?'

Louis smiled and nodded his head.

The next day McCann and his former crewmates waited in Faraday's office. None of them had any idea what this was about. They were only aware of the message they'd all received yesterday ordering them to be present. Since the mission to Mars had ended a few months ago all four of Athena's crew had been busy at Geneva, working on the fruits of Ilamachutli's collaboration with Faraday. Next in walked Faraday with Ilamachutli holding onto her new-born baby. McCann was concerned but apparently it was normal for Tlillan mothers to be walking around with their children the day after birth. The crew of the Athena stood in front of Faraday's desk. He said his greetings and walked behind his desk.

Ilamachutli approached McCann smiled and stood next to him. The pair had been living together in Geneva ever since returning from Tharsis. The Englishman invested in a large estate by the lake where he intended to raise his family. His estate was well protected by the I.S.A and a shuttle linked directly to headquarters where they both worked every day.

Faraday motioned to the wall monitor explaining the space grid. It became apparent that his boss and his fiancée had hatched a plot. Ilamachutli provided much assistance but her blueprints and technical data were soon to be exhausted.

Faraday desired more efficient anti-matter production but Ilam was not a scientist. Without proper databanks it wasn't within her ability to assist. Faraday was also desperate to research advanced construction materials used by Gukumatz and Tlillans.

The Tlillans had refused to contact the I.S.A, besides Faraday didn't know how to communicate so quickly over those distances ... yet.

Ilam decided that Faraday needed to take a risk. Space mines were to be removed in specific areas in an attempt to lure the Gukumatz. If they committed to an attack all six of the new space ships might attempt to board and seize the alien ship and its secrets.

After watching the presentation Louis was the first to speak, 'Are you crazy?'

McCann analysed the display then calmly asked Faraday 'Why? Aren't we safe for now?'

Faraday nodded 'For the moment but from what I've learnt Duncan, we don't have long. We need a more powerful line of defence. If they put their minds to it they could sweep those mines and then we're done for.'

McCann still scrutinizing the display asked 'Who's the poor sod that gets to board the vessel?'

'Fortunately we have been granted four units by Moscow. In return they directly benefit from any discoveries resulting from the operation.'

The door behind them opened and in walked someone from Louis past, 'May I introduce Major Andreev.'

Louis leapt backwards. Nestor had changed little since they'd last encountered one another. Though Louis had assumed or hoped he'd met his demise years ago.

'I believe you are acquainted with the Major?' asked Faraday, but Louis failed to respond.

Nestor stepped into the room and tipped his head to Ryu, 'Good morning Major.'

She blushed a little 'Good morning.'

Nestor turned to Louis with an enigmatic smile, 'Good morning Mr Beaumont.'

To which Louis responded bluntly 'Fuck you Nestor!'

Everyone in the room was shocked apart from Nestor and Louis, as they stood in a face off; one smiling and the other snarling.

Faraday shouted over the desk 'Beaumont apologise to the Major!'

Nestor interjected 'There is no insult Director.'

However Faraday pressed the Frenchman, yet Louis refused to apologise.

Ilamachutli enjoyed every moment of the drama unfolding before her eyes, she seemed to feed off the energy from it. Malikah began to cry as if she had sensed the ill feelings. Ilamachutli was obviously pleased that her child picked upon on the tense situation.

Faraday gestured to Louis 'You and Major Andreev shall be working together whether you like it or not. All of you shall be under Major Andreev's command during the operation.'

McCann cut in 'This is all well and good but how exactly do we get close enough? How do you intend to board it without being blasted into smithereens?'

Ilamachutli stepped closer to the monitor, a picture of the Gukumatz warship they'd encountered earlier that year appeared, 'Gukumatz use mainly torpedoes as weaponry, relying upon electromagnetic shields for protection. Once one of our vessels is close enough they will be unable to fire on it. You will then punch through the outer hull and enter the vessel.'

Louis snorted in disapproval 'Huh, You?'

Ilamachutli ignored him, 'Moscow has loaned us four Vympel units. Two will enter the fore section whilst the other two will enter the aft section. The first task will be to disable any self-destruct devices before they detonate. This will be the duty of Vympel one and two in the aft. Vympel three and four will attempt to capture the fore section and subdue the bridge. Capturing the crew would be a bonus but this is unlikely. Gukumatz will die before surrender, especially to a Tlillan and to them you are Tlillan.'

McCann raised his hand to speak, his fiancée smiled and nodded, 'What do you need us for?'

Faraday took over 'We need I.S.A representatives. Major Ryu has been in training for the last 6 months concerning this mission. Also we'll need a nanite specialist to disable the engines and any devices on-board. Hassif you will be working on the fore section. If we can take it in one piece we'll require someone to bring it home.'

Next Faraday produced a white box about the size of a cigar box, he opened it and took out 5 plastic strips, 'You will all be assigned one of these,' he said handing them out.

McCann looked down on the thick white band that he'd just received 'What is it?'

Faraday pulled out another from the box; like McCann's it had several small joints along its inch thick body. McCann also noticed there were two black liquid crystal pads on each end. Faraday took his strip and placed the centre on the back of his head. He then pushed the two ends of the strip until they pressed against his temples. Removing his hands the strip remained hugging his head.

'What does it do?'

Faraday gestured towards Ilamachutli 'If you would Ilam?'

'Of course.'

The LCD's on his temples began to flash green 'It will block a mental assault; when green the device is working if red it is faulty.'

McCann was confused 'The Gukumatz have telepathic abilities also?'

The red haired Amazon shook her head 'No Duncan, the home world may decide to intervene if they realise what we're doing. This device will afford you some protection for a short time.'

Nestor standing by the door in his combat fatigues queried her 'How long?'

'At close range 5 perhaps ten seconds at most, depending on her ability. At long distances it will cloak you completely. If your opponent is close you must react quickly. I don't believe that will be a problem for you, will it Major?'

Nestor smiled enigmatically 'Neit,' and placed the device in his equipment belt.

'Are there any further questions?'

Silenced prevailed and the room was dismissed. Everyone filed out except McCann and Louis who remained with Faraday and Ilamachutli.

'I will not work with that scumbag!' shouted Louis and a heated discussion began between the pair.

McCann saw the opportunity and took his fiancée aside whilst the other two slugged it out verbally, 'Why didn't you tell me?' he asked his wife to be.

She was embarrassed by the situation 'I wasn't permitted to speak on these plans to anyone, even you.'

He snorted 'Pah! Not permitted? That is a joke isn't it?'

McCann was concerned, the woman he loved was capable of deceiving him so competently! The old soldier understood the situation, but the fact she had hidden this from him especially for six months, without even a notion caused him great discomfort.

She attempted to comfort him but to little effect.

'Very well Ilam, I hope you're as understanding when it's your turn,' he said as he put his neural band on his head.

McCann had been cramped in space for three weeks now, along with Vympel 4 inside a space sub waiting for the Gukumatz to arrive. He likened the craft to one of the WW2 movies about U-boats and the battle of the Atlantic, it was small dingy and miserable. A large field of mines close to Jupiter had been detonated for the entertainment of the Gukumatz spy probes, now it was time to wait them out. The stench of fifty men after three weeks was over powering, but McCann tolerated the horrid odour as best he could. He was still angry that he was the last to find out about the operation, yet again, but what could he do about it? McCann swung down from his bunk and guided himself along the magnetic rails to the control room where he met up with Nestor. McCann could always tell when he was getting close to Nestor. The vile stench of cheap Russian cigarettes was easily detected from at least 3 compartments away. The upside of the situation was that he could steal a quick smoke, though drink was strictly forbidden. However McCann had strong suspicions that Nestor was hiding some away on this rust bucket.

As McCann slid along the gangway he took in the coarse smell of the toilets as they approached then departed. He shook his head and bemoaned his situation mumbling under his breath until reaching the control room. Nestor was clearly in the next apartment along, due to the wisps of grey smoke dancing through the hatchway. He carried on, returning salutes as he passed Nestor's soldiers. McCann sat down at a small table in the alcove to the left of the gangway 'Good morning Polkovnik' greeted Nestor.

'Good morning Major' replied McCann dipping the brim of his cap in respect.

McCann produced a Cohiba sliced the end and torched the foot.

Nestor called out to a junior officer in Russian 'Kofia!'

The junior officer skidded along the magnetic rails returning with two coffees and put them down on the table.

McCann took a sip on the straw and said to the young officer 'Spasibo, horoshi kofai,' in his best Russian accent. The young officer saluted to which McCann replied and let him on his way.

Nestor took a sip of his coffee 'Your Russian has improved Duncan, I'm very impressed.'

The grizzly Russian took a long drag from his cigarette and placed it back inside its porcelain tent constructed for zero G smokers, 'I've been meaning to ask you something Duncan but I do not wish to be indiscreet.'

McCann knew what was coming 'But you have to be to ask?'

Nestor became agitated 'Yes, it concerns your ...' he began making odd motions with his hands as if he were trying to drag the words out.

'My fiancée?'

A wave of relief passed over Nestor's face.

McCann had never seen Nestor behave in this manner before, 'What do you wish to known Nestor?'

Nestor looked around and waited for one of the junior officers to pass by into the control room. He hunched over the table towards McCann and whispered 'Is it true you conceived a child with her?'

McCann grinned, leaned back and pulled his cigar from its housing. The Englishman took a drag then placed it back inside, 'Yes.'

He knew what Nestor wanted to know but he enjoyed every moment of watching the "Iron Man" as Hassif had dubbed him squirm.

Nestor looked around and gestured with his hands 'Well is she the same?'

McCann smiled 'The same as what?'

Nestor stopped moving his hands and was now a little aggravated with McCann, 'You know what I'm saying, is she the same as a human woman?'

McCann started chuckling much to Nestor's displeasure.

The Russian sat back and took a smoke of his cigarette, 'I apologise you may forget it.'

McCann stopped his sniggering 'Look Nestor, I'm not going to go into any specifics because I'm a gentleman. There are subtle differences that take some time to grow accustom to. However on looks alone you couldn't tell the difference, alright?'

Nestor nodded his head, 'Thank you. Now what do you think of her idea to capture a Gukumatz ship?'

McCann's eyebrows lifted up for a moment, 'She always seems to know better or at least she thinks she knows better. Ilam believes we can do it, however it looks very different from this end. What does Moscow think about it?'

Nestor lit up another of his Russian cigarettes, 'Moscow?' he said flippantly 'I think they came to the conclusion that they cannot allow someone else to get their hands on whatever the ship contains ... we are all expendable Duncan.'

McCann looked Nestor in the eye 'So what went on between you and Louis?'

'Didn't Mr Beaumont tell you?'

'He told me some story but I'd like to hear your side, if you don't mind?'

Nestor relaxed back into his bench seat that was fixed onto the wall 'What was wrong with Mr. Beaumont's story?'

McCann sighed 'I think he embellished it a little, according to him you're evil incarnate and have no regard for human life. Which makes me wonder how he got back alive? Since most decent people would've been tempted to shoot him in the head!'

Nestor laughed 'Yes Mr. Beaumont certainly has a way about him. He was a freelancer and we hired him, he did his job to satisfaction and was paid generously. Mr. Beaumont is a very excitable man, in Russia we say only fools swing fists once the fight is over.'

Nestor was giving the short version of the story to McCann when an alarm fired off and the inside of the vessel switched to red light. The corridor became alive with men flying down the rails. McCann and Nestor leapt up, Nestor skidded into the control room and McCann made for the armoury. Once McCann had slipped on his neural band, ablative body armour and checked his weapons. He made for Nestor who stood behind one of his junior officers. McCann couldn't understand them but from peering over the junior officer's shoulder he could see the image of a Gukumatz warship, much the same as the one encountered at Mars. Nestor had one hand on the pilot's shoulder whilst his other clung onto the magnetic rail above his head. His feet held down by the rail below him that encircled the control room. He spoke in Russian then said over his shoulder 'They've entered normal space close to Jupiter as planned. Jupiter's gravity will hold them there long enough for us to move in, hold onto something Duncan.'

Over the tannoy something was announced in Russian and the craft jerked forwards in the direction of the Gukumatz vessel. Along with the three other space subs all on a collision course. Another announcement was made and McCann heard a whooshing sound travel throughout the space sub. On the junior officers screen a small torpedo was depicted travelling before them towards their destination. All four subs had fired a single torpedo at the areas they were about to impact and McCann saw four small explosions on the target warship. Within one minute the target was looming on the screen and another announcement came over the tannoy.

Nestor spoke over his shoulder to McCann 'Brace for impact!'

Everyone stood with their backs to the wall and held on to the rails. Electro magnets were activated grasping their specially made space suits and holding the crew to the walls. The sub rammed the Gukumatz ship exactly on the torpedo impact crater, McCann felt himself trying to fly across the control room but his suit held his body in place firmly. He witnessed the crewman in front of him on the opposite wall being pushed into the surface. He attempted to breathe as the pressure crushed his lungs. It was extremely uncomfortable but only for a few moments. The sound of crushing metal and snapping could be heard vibrating throughout the ship as it slowly wrenched to a halt. Once the sub stopped the electro magnets deactivated. The crew all took a great gasp of air together refilling their lungs before filing off to the front of the craft with weapons at the ready.

At the front of the craft the two large torpedo tubes were blown open. After conversing with his Sergeant Major Nestor pointed to one of the tubes and in Russian shouted "Vpyeryed!"

One by one his men swung inside the tube and slid down on their backs. McCann could only see a yellow light coming through the tube until it was his turn. He grabbed the handles above the hatch and swung his legs inside the tube. Using his momentum from the swing the rest of his body followed. Whilst moving down the tube he tapped his wrist tablet and activated his helmet. It unfurled from the housing in the neck. As he slid down the tube The Englishman began to feel the effects of gravity pulling him down. Eventually he slid out of the tube landing on his feet and onto the deck below. His legs crumpled under the gravity, McCann rolled off to the side. Fortunately the nanites in his body had kept his muscle and bone in good condition during the three weeks in zero G. However the shock of going from nothing to normal gravity was difficult. When he got to his feet the retired soldier looked around him. The corridor was crushed with deep cracks along each side. The only lighting came from the far end. It was an odd dirty yellow light but with the help of the helmet visor he could see perfectly well through it. He took his pulse rifle and joined the others who were standing and squatting at various intervals along the narrow passage.

McCann looked back up behind him and saw the nose of the sub poking through the ceiling, it was littered with tiny stress fractures. Nestor slid down the tube and rolled onto the floor. After gathering himself he spoke to McCann 'How are the others?'

McCann tapped his wrist 'Hassif are you in yet?'

A voice came over his ear piece 'Yes I'm trying to hack the system now.'

McCann could hear pulse rifle fire in the background. It was Hassif's job to hack in and try to download the ship schematics. With the help of Ilamachutli they had an idea of the general layout but anything specific Hassif could obtain would be a massive help.

McCann turned to Nestor 'Nothing yet.'

Nestor pointed down the passage and his Sergeant Major ordered his team of 20 men forward. They continued marching along the hall, to McCann it all felt so surreal. The walls were the same dirty yellow colour and he couldn't make out any doorways. Until in front of them, on his right, part of the wall split and folded in on itself. The team froze and the ten men before McCann took aim. Suddenly a short but robust figure stepped out, first one large bow leg then a head. The creature was facing in the opposite direction. Nestor gave an order in Russian which McCann assumed was the order to fire, since the Gukumatz never got its other foot into the hallway. There was a torrid burst of pulse rifle fire and after the smoke cleared the creature lay slumped in the open doorway. Four men broke off into the room to bursts of gun fire. A display of flashes hit the yellow wall from the rifle muzzles, expelling the tungsten rounds.

The men exited the room and as McCann walked past he peeped inside, he saw what looked to be a sauna by human standards. The inside had two large pools of water with bunks on the walls. Floating on the pool lay three Gukumatz with a yellow slime oozing out of the holes in their bodies, tainting the water. McCann wondered why there was no steam in the sauna so he took a look at the display on his wrist tablet and the atmosphere was at 40 degrees Celsius. Perhaps this was their sleeping quarters or their idea of a relaxation area? It made sense for an amphibian and it explained why the Gukumatz inside were naked.

They carried on down the hall and Hassif's voice came crackling over the speaker 'Colonel I've downloaded the ship plans to everyone's tablet,' there was still heavy fire in the background.

McCann waved his hand at Nestor after he had the Russian's attention he pointed to his wrist, indicating the plans had been downloaded and the computer was plotting their position. Nestor gave a thumbs up and a mini map popped up on the helmet visor indicating their position with an arrow pointing to the way to this unit's objective.

Nestor spoke in Russian and his team moved on, they were only a few floors down from the bridge. According to the map they were outside the elevators but they had no idea how to use them.

The wall collapsed away folding in on itself to each side revealing an elevator that contained a Gukumatz. The Gukumatz was terrified and began to croak in terror. Faraday had cloned the translation software from Ilamachutli's suit so McCann got a close approximation to what it was trying to say.

McCann raised his hand 'Don't shoot!' and approached the Gukumatz.

He touched his wrist pad and spoke 'Take us to the same level as the ships control room,' the suit let off a series of croaks and belches which the Gukumatz seemed to understand.

The Gukumatz was dressed in a tight black ribbed suit much the same as the first Gukumatz he encountered on Tharsis, and just as repulsive. After a quick chat the creature agreed to take them to the command level, five at a time since there wasn't enough room for anymore.

Whilst ferrying the team up McCann holstered his weapon to ease the Frogman's jittery nerves, on the last journey the Gukumatz ship lurched. All of the lights died and the elevator halted for about 5 seconds then a low light came on and the elevator resumed to the command level.

'Her main power plant and engines have been disabled,' came Louis' voice over the comms.

McCann thought he sounded a lot better off than Hassif.

The elevator made it to the last level and on reaching it the men exited, leaving only the Gukumatz inside. McCann pulled his pistol from his leg holster and shot it in the head splattering its runny dark yellow brains over the elevator wall.

'Thanks for the ride!' quipped McCann as he holstered his pistol.

McCann then tapped his wrist again and spoke into his collar mic 'Hassif we're closing in on the bridge, where are you?'

A few moments later the sound of heavy fire came over his comms and Hassif shouted hurriedly 'We're trapped at a lower level I have access to some ship systems. I guess they don't prepare for this kind of thing often!'

McCann pointed down the passage and Nestor ordered his men forward in a two by two formation covering each other as they proceeded. Ten men in front and ten behind they carried on down the hall, the arrow on the mini map was blinking faster and faster as they approached the bridge. The Vympel unit turned a corner and the arrow indicated the hatchway leading to the bridge was in front of them. McCann could only see a flat wall where the corridor ended some 20 metres ahead. Nestor sent two men up to it whilst the rest of the squad waited. They placed some charges before retreating back around the corner where everyone was paused for the explosion. Suddenly flames burst onto the wall before the unit, scorching it. Nestor called in Russian to his team and they filed two by two covering each other as they charged back around the corner towards the open hatchway.

Immediately an exchange of fire began, McCann witnessed what he could only explain as small balls of plasma hitting the wall then dissipating. The men peeled off around the corner into the fracas until it was McCann's turn. When he slinked around the corner cautiously the retired soldier witnessed through the smoke and burnt hole in the wall some figures bobbing up and down. The communications in Russian were heated and McCann was too far back to get a clear shot into the bridge. He assumed the Gukumatz inside had fortified the room and were using command stations as cover to fire back into the passage. Next a large detonation from the opposite side of the hole rumbled, the shockwave caused McCann to lose his balance for a moment. He put his hand out and righted himself, when he looked up he witnessed Vympel 4 breaking off into the bridge. Two by two the Spetsnaz ran inside.

When it came to McCann's turn he mumbled under his breath 'Time to rock and roll Duncan,' then darted through the hole in the wall. The room was thick with smoke and he almost slipped on the yellow slime which smeared the floor. He remained on his knee behind a console that was adorned with a dead Gukumatz until finally the thick smoke cleared. McCann scanned the area, the control room was a lot smaller than he'd imagined for such a grand vehicle. In the centre stood a dais raised some six feet above the floor supporting a single seat. The rest of the room had three large work stations around it with no seats. The wall in front of what must be the Captain's chair was a screen that represented the space around the warship. The Englishman scrutinized the screen which depicted the planet Earth in a yellow box with some alien script. It was obvious they were targeting the Earth. Many other points had been marked out but McCann couldn't make sense of it.

He looked back towards the dais and the Captain's chair searching for Nestor. He observed one of the Vympel team lying on the floor writhing as white foam covered a large plasma burn to his chest. McCann walked behind the dais and cowering on the floor lay what must have been one of the bridge crew with a pulse rifle at his head. He hit his wrist pad to switch the translator on and spoke 'Identify yourself.'

The figure on the floor replied with a couple of croaks and the computer translated 'Captain Kotumatz.'

Again McCann heard the same name it couldn't be mere coincidence, 'Order your crew to surrender,' he stated which the suit dutifully translated into some croaks and burps.

The alien Captain let off a gurgling noise, McCann assumed it was a mocking laugh. Next the Frogman produced some croaks and burbles. McCann's suit replied in an androgynous tone 'Eat shit Darksider.'

Nestor stepped over from his dying squad member and put his boot on the creature's elbow. Aiming the barrel of his weapon at its hand the Russian discharged his weapon once.

The Gukumatz let out a high pitched screech as it bled onto the floor.

'Tell him if he co-operates he will live.'

McCann spoke to the Captain but it was in no mood to help the invaders. All he received were more insults; Nestor grew tired quickly and executed the Captain. By this time the bridge was secured and the soldier that suffered the plasma charge to the chest had died. McCann sat in the chair on the dais and activated the translation program.

Before his eyes, inside his helmet a green visor popped up. Whenever something written in Gukumatz entered his field of vision the program translated it as best it could into English or a close approximation.

The first thing that struck him was the view screen in front of him, dead ahead the screen was broken by a strip of wall. McCann couldn't work out why until he remembered that their eyes sat on the sides of their heads. Looking down at the chair he noticed a few basic readouts. Though nothing he could control the ship with so he stepped down and scrutinized the stations. From what McCann could make out the three stations were assigned specific duties, weapons, navigation, engines and shields. There were several stations attached to the wall all around the room below the screen, he guessed they were sub stations of the main three. McCann walked to one of the wall stations being careful not to step on the bodies and guts that decorated the room. He spent some time working out the console and eventually from the console came a familiar voice 'Hello? Who is this?'

McCann answered 'This is Colonel McCann; Vympel 4 has captured the bridge. Vympel 1 and 2 have neutralised the engines and power core. Vympel 3 is in a fire fight on the upper decks, amount of enemy crew unknown.'

McCann heard Faraday let off a great sigh of relief, 'When you have control of the vessel make a course for the designated location. Colonel McCann, you're in command of the situation until you reach the asteroid belt.'

'Understood sir, McCann out,' he tapped the console. 'What's next Nestor?' he said turning to the Major.

Nestor gestured to the Captain's chair 'Can you get this piece of junk to the asteroid belt?'

McCann let his weapon hang from his shoulder and placed his hands on his hips 'It'll be a lot easier with Hassif, if you can get him here?'

Nestor nodded and issued some orders in Russian to which ten of his men led by the Sergeant Major exited the bridge.

McCann spent the time familiarising himself with the stations and their sub stations, they were all quite easy to get to grips with, which worried him; since he was certain they couldn't be that easy to operate. By the time Hassif and Vympel 3 had reached the bridge McCann had already plotted a course and logged it into the navigation computer which had checked and certified it. However having Hassif check everything would be his fail safe.

When Hassif entered the room McCann noticed his right arm was covered in white foam. He had been hit and looked a lot the worse for wear. Most of his body was covered by thick yellow slime which had begun to congeal. His hair was full of the stuff which had gone all crusty making it hard as a rock. It seemed as if the Gukumatz had sent everything they had to his team before reports of the other three squads had been made.

McCann approached his friend 'How are you old boy?'

Hassif just shook his head; it was evident that Hassif had taken a glancing shot to his helmet as well as his arm. What was left of the helmet was jammed around the collar; McCann could see it had melted in places where he'd been hit. He must have tried to slot it back before it melted onto his head. McCann noted his discomfort in the heat as the sweat rolled down his face along with Gukumatz blood which solidified in his hair. Hassif tapped his wrist, a green display leapt up from inside his collar and he began to go through the navigation data.

Whilst Hassif certified the data McCann spoke into the comms 'Louis can you hear me?'

The earpiece crackled for a moment then Louis' voice cleared the noise away, 'Oui, what do you want McCann?'

McCann climbed back onto the Captain's chair 'I need the engines operational, how soon can you get them working?'

Louis cursed to himself in French and paused for a moment 'I don't know, I did a good job of cutting off the power core. One of the teams is securing the power core now, so I'll let you know when I know.'

McCann sighed then in a frustrated tone replied 'I need some sort of estimate Louis.'

Again Louis cursed to himself before answering 'At least three hours to get the power core and engines online but probably longer. It could be days, you know no one has ever done this before. I'll keep you updated okay?'

'Understood Louis, merci,' he then tapped his wrist again 'Ryu can you hear me?'

Again there was a crackle and Major Ryu's voice came over the comms, 'Yes Colonel.'

'The ship is being secured as we speak please begin operation Sisyphus.'

'Understood Colonel.'

Thirty minutes later the warship shook as Ryu guided the two remaining space subs into position, on either side of the fore sections delta wing. The subs clamped onto the Gukumatz ship on either side readying themselves to push the vessel into the asteroid belt if required. Whilst this went on Nestor was co-ordinating his teams as they swept through the ship for more Gukumatz. With the help of Hassif he had identified their locations and trapped them for Nestor's men to flush out. Unfortunately most of the Gukumatz were not in the mood for surrender. The few that did surrender were shot anyway as Nestor decided it was too much of a risk to have them on the ship.

Two hours later the power core was active and Hassif was in full control of Navigation shields and weapons. He'd managed to manipulate the life support reducing the humidity of the air and temperature to something comfortable. All that they were waiting on was the engines to be restarted. It became apparent Louis had been rather over enthusiastic when it came to shutting them down. It was still unknown as to when the engines would be operational. McCann ordered Ryu to begin firing the sub's engines and slowly pushing the warship to its destination.

The big worry now was if a Tlillan or Gukumatz vessel was on the way, the Gukumatz would attempt to recapture or destroy them. The Tlillan's would not approve of them possessing the vessel but what their course of action might be remained in question. It was paramount to get the warship to the asteroid belt where it would be stripped down and hidden.

Hassif shouted over his shoulder 'Colonel we have company!'

McCann looked at the view screen, a red box appeared and started flashing on the screen. Through his visor he read the text, "Tunnel event". Moments later a large white swirl appeared in the box and from it a Tlillan warship emerged. The red box began flashing over the vessel.

'We're secure,' whispered Nestor as the Tlillan ship moved slowly mirroring the captured Gukumatz Vehicle.

McCann shouted to Hassif 'Don't target them!'

Hassif confirmed the order but stood at the ready by his station poised to open fire. A station to Hassif's left began to make a noise and the screen started flashing. It was the communication and navigation console. Hassif jumped over to it 'The Tlillan's are trying to communicate with us.'

McCann sat up in his seat and retracted his helmet into its collar. He looked towards the screen 'Alright accept their transmission.'

The right side of the view screen displayed a female Tlillan dressed in a white single breasted jacket. McCann couldn't tell her height but she was obviously the Captain and her jacket had some resemblance to a military cut. Although she stood up, McCann could only see her from the waist up. Her jacket was cloth and had quite striking shoulder pads, along with an insignia he couldn't determine. Her long flowing hair was the same white as her uniform. Apart from that she resembled Ilam in that her skin was a translucent ivory colour. Behind her the image was blurred but McCann was certain she was on the vessel's bridge, though it didn't possess the dais he resided upon.

The Tlillan was surprised to see McCann, 'I am Matriarch Cihuateteo, whom is the Matriarch of your craft?' translated the ships communication AI.

McCann folded his arms 'I am Colonel Duncan McCann and I am in control of this vessel.'

The Matriarch looked somewhere between disgusted and shocked. She must have only just realised that he was a human male and didn't speak her language. Somehow he'd gained control of a Gukumatz vehicle. Or perhaps it was just that she'd never been spoken to in such a direct manner by a male before? It was difficult for McCann to tell but for now it didn't matter, his mission was to get the ship back come hell or high water.

'I will take possession of the Gukumatz craft now,' she sneered.

McCann smirked at her arrogance it was something inherent in Tlillan females by the look of it 'I'm very sorry Miss Cihuateteo but this vessel is now in possession of the I.S.A, however I'd like to thank you for your offer of assistance.'

Her eyes began to change colour and his neural band activated, fortunately at this distance it blocked all intrusive mental probes.

'The I.S.A is not a recognised entity, surrender the Gukumatz craft now!'

Hassif spoke over his shoulder 'They're targeting us.'

McCann looked at Hassif then at the Matriarch on his screen 'Engage our shield and target them, only fire if fired upon.'

Hassif jumped to the weapons and shield console 'Gotcha!'

McCann stared her in the eye and waited, he enjoyed playing games of brinksmanship since he was the type that never bluffed. If McCann wasn't prepared to go all the way he didn't play, this time he had no choice. If she fired on them then they had to use everything at their disposal to preserve their victory prize. McCann still staring her in the face spoke slowly and clearly, 'Arm the anti-matter torpedoes and lock them onto the Tlillan vessel.'

Hassif punched away at his console and for a moment his Tlillan counterpart was distracted by what McCann assumed was one of her bridge officers.

She turned back to McCann 'Anti-matter weapons are not permitted.'

McCann maintained his smirk 'Really? The Gukumatz used them on my planet.'

His Tlillan opposite was uncomfortable arguing with a male but she had little choice, 'Your people are not recognised by the treaty banning environmental weapons.'

McCann nodded 'You're correct and since we're not recognised no one will notice when we vapourise your vessel, will they?'

Her eyes became a deeper shade of red turning burgundy. McCann had not seen Ilam's eyes turn that shade even at her most furious.

Her voice deepened and she bellowed 'Surrender the Gukumatz vessel now Human, before I'm forced to take it!'

McCann looked towards Hassif 'Turn her off.'

Hassif leapt to the communications console and her image disappeared leaving the representation of space and the Tlillan vessel shadowing them. Hassif shouted over his shoulder 'They're attempted to communicate again Colonel.'

McCann who was busy pulling a cigar out of his ammo belt replied 'Ignore them, if they fire then return fire with all anti-matter torpedoes but one.'

Hassif nodded 'Understood,' then jumped back to the weapons console.

McCann torched the foot of his Siglo I cigar and took a long smoke. Resting on the chair arm he grinned at Nestor, 'Might as well have a smoke Nestor, it could be your last.'

Nestor hit his wrist tablet and his helmet retracted back into the collar. The grizzly Russian produced one of his equally grizzly Russian cigarettes and began to smoke. Nestor spoke in Russian to his men which McCann recognised as "at ease". Vympel 4 relaxed though still standing at their positions guarding the two exits on either side of the room at the rear behind the dais.

After another hour Louis reported on the engines 'I'll try to restart the engines in 10 minutes, okay?'

McCann felt some relief, 'Understood,' he then hit his wrist and spoke 'Ryu you can cut the engines until further notice.'

'Understood Colonel.'

Ten minutes later McCann could feel a large thump reverberate around the room.

'Engines are operational Colonel!' Hassif called excitedly.

McCann smiled 'Good, can you tell the navigation computer to engage them?'

Hassif scratched his head and some caked Gukumatz blood fell down, 'I'll give it a try.'

He carefully tapped away at the navigation console and McCann felt another thump in his back. The ship was now moving under its own power towards the asteroid belt.

Hassif tapped away excitedly 'ETA 28 minutes Colonel.'

McCann kept looking at the image of the Tlillan warship that shadowed them. After a few minutes the Tlillan vessel broke away and a red flashing box appeared again on the view screen along with an alarm sounding off. McCann looked at the box through his translation software "Tunnel event" was present as before. Next a large swirling white hole opened and the Tlillan vessel's engines glowed brightly pushing the warship inside. McCann witnessed the ship disappear into the white whirlpool until the engines vanished. Shortly afterwards the whirlpool collapsed into itself and the red box ceased flashing, disappearing along with the alarm.

McCann exhaled in relief then he spoke to Hassif 'If you see a Gukumatz ship appear out of one of those white holes I want you to fire three anti matter torpedoes on it immediately, understood?'

Hassif nodded 'Understood.'

The rest of the journey to the asteroid belt was speedy and uneventful. Upon reaching the designated asteroid the crew of what had been dubbed "the chop shop" took over. McCann and his comrades were glad to see the back of the damn thing. The Englishman handed the vessel over to the commander of the operation to strip it. Legions of droids entered through the make shift docking area. The people taking her apart were teams of highly qualified engineers and technicians. The man in charge shook his hand as he stepped onto the ship and McCann stepped on to the docking arm. As he stepped on the docking arm he felt the gravity dissipating and he grabbed onto the rail before he floated away.

McCann chuckled.

'What's so funny?' came the voice of Nestor who was following him.

'I just thought it will be nice when we've got a working artificial gravity generator in our stations and ships!'

McCann only heard a 'Da!' from behind him.

Once aboard the station he was lead to his quarters. Unlike the stations in orbit there was no gravity. Without the planet Earth or Mars causing a tidal effect on the asteroid, pulling and squashing it, they were forced to float around in zero G.

The four units waited for a week before they could board the two free space subs and make the journey to Earth. Fortunately Louis was so excited by what he'd seen he didn't have time to revisit his animosity towards Nestor. Even on the one week journey back he did little else but talk about the anti-matter reactor on the Gukumatz ship. According to Louis it was a real anti-matter reactor and not one of the "mickey mouse" reactors built on Earth.

McCann wasn't certain what that meant but Hassif understood. In layman's terms the Indian explained it as a device that could produce anti-matter in large quantities, then in a chamber create a reaction between a hydrogen particle and anti-matter hydrogen particle. The reaction would generate massive amounts of energy that would feed all the power needs for planet Earth. Fuel cells would soon be things of the past, the Gukumatz ship engines provide propulsion under much the same principles. The anti-matter produced in the core is diverted and controlled explosions propel the ship through space. Hassif pointed out that a ship with those engines could easily reach 99% the speed of light. Hassif was vague when it came to the white hole, he guessed it was a wormhole but beyond that he was clueless.

McCann had spoken to Ilamachutli on this subject in the past, it was only pillow talk but he still knew more about it than anyone else. He went on to relay what she had let slip over the last year. According to the beautiful Valkyrie it was the reflection of a black hole created with vacuum energy or free energy. The vessel used a negative energy field to enter and traverse the worm hole, according to Ilamachutli interstellar travel was measured in hours for most journeys. Everyone agreed there was no doubt that the human race was going to make some massive leaps in technology now that they could dissect their salvage.

Upon reaching the Tsiolkovsky the remaining members of Vympel 1-4 and the I.S.A team members rested whilst they were ferried down to the surface via the orbital ribbon. McCann spent most nights in the smoker's corner with Titov and Nestor, having a drink and a chat. Titov was fascinated by the description of the Gukumatz and their ship, Ryu was still the resident celebrity surrounded by admirers every evening, McCann felt it odd they never got tired of it. He noticed that she spent more time with Cherkesov than the other Russian officers it was obvious he had a soft spot for her after the first time they'd met. However it now became apparent to McCann that the Red Dragon was warming to Titov's first officer. She smiled frequently in his presence and from what McCann could tell laughed at his jokes; jokes which McCann was prepared to bet his house on she didn't find funny. He'd spent long enough with Ryu to know her sense of humour was buried inside a granite sarcophagus underneath one of those North Korean mountains ranges!

Titov noticed the pair getting on well together 'What do you think of those two?' he said to McCann who was sitting in the smoker's corner with Nestor.

McCann looked at them making small talk at the bar 'I think they look good together, she needs to find a man, what do you reckon Nestor?'

Nestor sat puffing on his cigarette 'He's a lucky man; you know she's a hero in my country?'

McCann nodded and took a drag of his cigar.

Nestor took a sip of Vodka and let out a gasp of satisfaction. 'She has statue in Vladivostok you know?' then he poured himself another vodka into his shot glass. 'Ahhh it's been too long' he said looking glassy eyed at the vodka.

McCann sat back considering the fact that Ryu had a statue and how she'd managed to keep it all quiet for years, never mentioning it once. The conversation turned to McCann's fiancée and the usual questions which he answered in the usual fashion, though Titov was not as shy as Nestor when making inquiries.

Later Titov expressed his caution concerning Moscow moving closer to the I.S.A and becoming a full member. McCann laughed and comforted Titov, reassuring him that he'd maintain the supply of spirits if need be. Nestor laughed and Titov managed to smile, he was more concerned at losing his smoking and drinking privileges than anything else. McCann pointed out it wouldn't happen as long as Faraday was Director. Added to that Moscow was loaning Vympel units to the I.S.A, McCann was sure Titov would see greater leeway when it came to luxuries.

McCann was anxious to get back to Geneva and see his daughter. It was close to two months since he'd last seen her and Ilam and for the first time he felt a great longing in his heart.

Upon reaching Earth McCann stepped off the crawler and onto ground zero where his fiancée awaited holding his daughter in her arms. He approached her slowly stretching his legs, 'Where's my Malikah?' he called playfully to Ilam; she smiled bending down and hugging him with one arm. She let go of the embrace and McCann was shaken when he saw his daughter for the first time in two months, 'Has she grown?'

Ilam passed Malikah to him but he refused 'I've just got out of that bloody crawler I don't want to drop her.'

McCann was even more bowled over when he heard what sounded like the word "Out" emanate from his fiancée's arms. McCann stumbled backwards and Ilam giggled in delight. Ilam spoke something in the Tlillan language to which Malikah produced a one word reply, much to her mother's glee.

Behind them Nestor climbed out of the crawler and strode over as fast as he could without falling 'Greetings Miss Ilamachutli,' he said in his Russian accent.

Ilam recognised Nestor from the many meetings in Geneva as the head of Vympel 'Dobryj dyen' kak dyela?'

Nestor smiled and replied "Khorosho."

McCann was still in shock trying to get to grips with the fact that his child had learned to speak, then she spoke again 'Khorosho.'

McCann looked incredulously at Ilam.

Nestor turned to McCann 'I thought you said she was only three months old?'

Ilam rocked her daughter 'She is.'

Nestor looked back at Ilam 'But she can speak?'

'She can imitate speech but it will be another year before she reaches our level.'

McCann still holding the same expression asked 'How?'

Ilam still doting over her child replied 'A Tlillan child will form a mental link with her Mother in the womb. I and Malikah have been linked for a long time. She is learning from my experience, as I learn Russian she learns also. Malikah knows the words and can speak them but it will take time before she understands them.'

McCann took his daughter from Ilam and held her close to his chest wrapped tightly in her blanket. Her dark hair already reaching down to her shoulders she looked far older than a human child at this point in time. Her facial features had developed quite drastically while he'd been away, and despite her Tlillan heritage she bore a striking resemblance to McCann.

Nestor peered over at the child and exclaimed 'My god! It looks just like you!' he was also taken aback by the rapid development of the child. Malikah's eyes were grey, pure white around the iris as opposed to the ghostly translucence of all Tlillans.

Malikah looked up at him and smiled 'Duncan.'

Her eyes turned a deep pink though he could still see the grey of the iris.

'How does she know my name?' he said flabbergasted.

Ilam placed her hand on his shoulder 'She remembers your face from my memories. Malikah demonstrates strong development, associating your name with my memory so soon.'

On the airship home McCann was busy with his daughter teaching her new vocabulary. Louis and Hassif were chatting about the discoveries on the Gukumatz ship and what might come of it. Ryu was silently staring out of the window into the distance. Ilam noticed her sitting alone and left McCann with his daughter to sit opposite her. Ryu didn't look away from the window or acknowledge Ilam in any way.

'Are you lonely?' inquired Ilam.

Ryu glanced at her grimly 'Do I need to answer that or did you take a look already?'

With a wry smile Ilam said 'I could if you refuse to speak to me.'

Ryu sighed 'I'm sorry I didn't mean to be an asshole, I was just thinking about the Tsiolkovsky and someone I met there.'

Ilam's face lit up at the prospect of gossip 'What was he like?'

Ryu turned from the window and looked around the airship slyly. When she was certain no one was watching she tapped on her wrist tablet.

Ilam looked at the picture.

'That's him,' whispered Ryu.

Ilam examined the personnel file of Lieutenant Cherkesov 'Tall, dark and handsome and he's single, did you spend any time with him?'

Ryu Nodded.

'Alone?' she whispered.

Ryu began to blush and turned back to the window, Ilam started questioning her with relish. Perhaps it was the fact that everyone on Tlillan is linked together which made gossip so exciting for Ilam? That was McCann's explanation of her hunger for small talk and scandal, although it meant he could watch all of his media programmes instead of treating them as a guilty pleasure.

Days later they reached Geneva and were given an after action report with Faraday, who was jubilant over the operations success. The warship had already been gutted and the parts were spread out in the asteroid belt. Geneva was in possession of the schematics Hassif pulled out of the Gukumatz AI. Faraday switched the 3D projector in the centre of the table on and something similar to a Tlillan warship appeared.

'Ladies and gentlemen I'd like to present to you our plans for our own warship.'

McCann took a closer look, he recognised the ship's body it was much the same as a Tlillan cruiser in that it was a long rectangular horizontal column. The aft ended vertically with four large reversed domes; exhausts where anti-matter explosions would take place to propel the vessel. The fore ended in a vertical slice but at an inward angle. Dead centre on the body lay several stories which resembled a battleship's control tower. On each side of the ship's body sat four gun ports, two fore and two aft on either side of the vessel totalling eight cannons in all. The cannons reminded McCann of the rail gun platforms which now guarded the Earth and Mars. They worked on the same principle as a pulse pistol but fired much larger and deadly projectiles. The cannons on the ship possessed two slim barrels which poked out of armoured turrets positioned much like an old ship of the line's cannons, a broadside of four turrets on each side. Add to that an anti-matter warhead and it could certainly give the Gukumatz a run for their money.

McCann examined the ship then looked straight up at Faraday 'How long before it's operational?'

Faraday scratched his chin 'We don't know, it depends on how long it takes us to clone the Gukumatz technology. If everything goes as planned we could build one in 6 months.'

McCann snorted disapprovingly and Faraday closed his eyes then put his hand on his forehead 'I know, I know! We're already constructing the super structures out of a Neutronium carbon alloy, which thanks to Ilam we can now manufacturer in large quantities.'

Louis piped up 'Neutronium?'

Faraday nodded 'Yes, in simple terms it is the same substance that forms the crust of a Neutron star. It has ten billion times the durability of steel and will serve perfectly to construct and armour these vessels. However we aren't able to produce enough for a pure Neutronium superstructure, so it'll have to be an alloy.'

McCann cut in again 'Vessels? There will be more than one?'

'As part of the agreement with Moscow we shall construct a sister ship, her Captain shall be picked by Moscow. One is being constructed by the Tsiolkovsky and the other by the Edwards.'

McCann was lost 'But we just got back from there and I didn't see any superstructure being built?'

Faraday grinned, 'That's because it's a secret Duncan!'

The others laughed and McCann shook his head 'Fine! Will it have artificial gravity?'

Ilam spoke 'It will be capable of all the original Gukumatz ship was, with an added bonus of rocket drones.'

She smiled at Ryu who perked up at the mention of drones, 'It shall possess four squadrons of rocket drones along with many point defence cannons, the number of which is undetermined at the moment.'

Hassif raised his hand 'May I ask a question?'

Ilam gestured to him 'Of course.'

Hassif pointed to the ship 'What about the computer systems?'

Ilam stopped talking and Faraday answered uneasily, 'We've decided to install an SI in each warship, it will be placed inside a housing impervious to neural assault.'

Hassif was very pleased to hear this although Louis and Ilam were not, but for different reasons.

Faraday stepped over to McCann 'Geneva has selected the Captain of the other ship,' he slapped McCann on the back, 'after the retrieval operation you've been chosen, that's if you want the job old boy!'

'Why me? I've no experience commanding a military ship of this size.'

Faraday patted his back 'No one has any experience commanding a vessel of this type aside from yourself! If you take the job Duncan you'll receive a recognised rank of Commodore with a sizeable increase in salary. The I.S.A needs your unique experience and we need someone that works well with the Russians. Keeping them on our side is paramount right now, without them we can't pull this thing off.'

McCann laughed 'So no pressure then?'

Faraday laughed too and patted him on the back 'Thanks Duncan.'

McCann stopped Faraday for a second and in a serious tone spoke 'If I'm to take this job I need Ryu on the drones.'

Faraday nodded and moved his arms about in a rather animated fashion trying to reassure the Englishman 'You have your pick of I.S.A personnel Duncan.'

McCann turned to Ryu 'How about it?'

She passionately nodded her head 'Sure!'

He then turned to Hassif 'I'll need someone to keep the SI in one piece, interested?'

Hassif put his hands together as you would to pray 'Thank you.'

Finally he turned to Louis, who wasn't as excited as the others, 'Louis you're the only engineer that has broken and fixed one of those ships in the same day. I need you to keep it running.'

Louis sneered 'I don't like SIs and I hate Russians, but if it stops those Frogs I'll put up with them,' he then put his hand out and shook McCann's.

McCann turned to Faraday 'It seems that I have my team when do we start?'

Faraday sighed with relief, 'Good, you can start straight after your wedding old boy!'

McCann raised an eyebrow 'Sorry?'

Faraday looked towards Ilam, 'It was understood we would marry when you returned?' she said quizzically.

McCann recalled his promise although it was his way of putting the occasion off. It's not that he didn't want to marry her; it was that he didn't want to be married as in tied down. Whilst he wasn't married he was still single in theory or that's the story he liked to tell himself anyway. Just the talk of marriage made him breakout in a sweat.

McCann stood mute for a while until Ilam spoke again 'I see, I shall contact Ofra and cancel the proceedings.'

Ryu, Hassif and Louis were in great spirits watching McCann squirm and the Englishman now realised his Mother had dipped her oar in once again. He gathered himself 'I'm sorry it must have slipped my mind. Well everyone here is invited and what do you say to being best man?' he looked towards Louis who was sniggering at the whole drama.

Louis gave him another handshake, 'I'd be honoured.'

Faraday then interjected 'Excellent! Our new Commodore and our exo-diplomat will be marrying. All expenses will be paid for by the I.S.A of course!'

McCann made a sceptical look at Faraday 'What's the catch?'

Faraday smiled nervously 'Well network America will have exclusive rights to broadcast it, and you'll both be obliged to do interviews before and after the proceedings. Ilam and your mother have already agreed.'

Louis started to crack up laughing and Hassif wasn't far behind.

'Maybe I should have an advert stitched onto my wedding suit? How about "Drink diet Zen!" draped on my back?'

A blanket of silence fell upon the room, Faraday smiled nervously.

'What have you bloody well done Faraday?'

Faraday tried to calm McCann 'It's not as bad as it seems, there may be some food and drinks endorsements at the proceedings. Just some strategically placed products nothing gaudy or obscene you'll hardly notice it old boy!'

McCann was now furious, Ilam could sense it and was concerned but she knew better than to get in his way during a rant, 'Jesus fucking Christ man! What do you think I am some whore you can rent out to the media?'

McCann had never spoken to Faraday in such a rude manner and with the added pressure he'd been under he shouted back into his face, 'Do you know how much it costs to build just one of those damn ships?' he shouted pointing to the 3D image on the table.

McCann still furious shouted back 'I'm sorry but you've confused me with someone that gives a shit! Go and beg the bloody Russians or maybe YOU can get married or sell some body parts? Why do I have to look like a fucking buffoon in front of the whole world?'

Ryu became worried that this might result in blows, but she didn't know what to do since it wasn't her place to break up two superiors. She peered at Ilam, who raised her hand gesturing to stay out of it. Faraday bellowed back at McCann 'Buffoon? What makes you think you'll look a buffoon?'

McCann's face was now only inches from Faraday's 'Advertising fizzy drinks at my wedding and you're telling me I won't look like a total fuckwit? You can shove your wedding up your bloody arse man!'

McCann turned to walk out of the door. Before he could leave Faraday managed to leap ahead of him 'No one will even notice the damn things, you'll have drinks at the wedding anyway we'll just supply you with them. It's all traditional stuff, champagne, caviar and salmon nothing tacky!'

Faraday put his arm out blocking McCann's path to the door then in a sombre voice 'Look I'm sorry Duncan. Your Mother informed me it was all suitable, I was under the impression she had discussed it with you. If you want we can drop the endorsements would that be acceptable?'

McCann stared scornfully at Ilam, she looked down at the ground rather shamefully, 'Marvellous,' he said sarcastically.

Faraday lowered his arm and McCann left the room with Ilam chasing after him. Everyone else started to breathe again and even Louis was bowled over by what he'd just witnessed.

The Englishman stormed out of the office to see the stunned workers that had all been attempting to listen in on the argument. He sneered aggressively sending them back to their workstations as he marched through the control room at Geneva. Marching along a corridor until he reached one of the recreation areas and continued onto the terrace overlooking Lake Geneva. He took out a Ramon Allones and bit the cap off with his teeth then spat it out. Lighting the end with a match he took a long drag and flicked it over the edge after with the cap.

He puffed on his cigar calming his nerves 'Smoking is forbidden here Duncan,' came the voice of Ilam behind him.

'I don't care,' he replied solemnly.

She stepped onto the terrace 'I apologise if I overstepped my boundaries Duncan.'

He watching the Jet D'eau firing into the sky, 'You didn't.'

She held tightly onto her baby and in a confused tone asked 'So you do not wish to marry me?'

The Englishman remained transfixed on the fountain squirting out of the lake, 'No, I do.'

Ilam didn't fully understand what had just happened in the office 'Does your love for me remain?'

He sighed 'Yes,' then had a draw on his cigar.

Ilam was more puzzled than ever, she no longer used her unique ability to mind probe individuals. Much to her surprise people felt violated by her skill at soliciting honesty. On Tlillan they didn't hide behind half-truths or use lies to shield themselves and others from pain. It was not out of choice but it was just how they lived. Ilam had spent a lot of time getting used to discovering truth the inefficient human way.

McCann let the smoke leave his nostrils and he tasted the sweet tobacco 'It's that I'm a coward.'

She furrowed her tall forehead 'I do not understand,' she said softly.

'I love you, I want to marry you but I'm afraid to do it.'

He took another puff and continued staring out onto the calm lake watching the sun glint on the tiny ripples created by the breeze.

She smiled in disbelief 'A coward? You sat in a tube in space for three weeks. Rammed a Gukumatz warship in what many considered a suicide mission!'

McCann snorted but made no reply.

Ilam was still perplexed 'Duncan, you lead a boarding party and captured the ship. You bluffed a Tlillan ship of line sent to take it from your possession by force!'

McCann snorted again 'I wasn't bluffing.'

Ilam was aghast at his statement, 'You would have vapourised her ship?'

McCann nodded 'Of course,' he turned around to see her holding his daughter tightly 'does that disturb you?'

'Tlillans are not permitted to murder one another.'

'Then she was bluffing?'

Ilam nodded, 'Yes.'

McCann sneered akin to the Frenchman 'You know Ilam, I don't believe you.'

Her eyes turned a shade of red and his daughter began to cry. On hearing Malikah's distress the colour faded. She looked down at her child and spoke some comforting words in Tlillan until Malikah became still once again.

Ilam fixed her gaze on him once more and in an austere pitch commented 'We are not barbarians Duncan.'

McCann took a drag on his cigar then expelled the smoke, 'We? You've been banished my dear, you're just a barbarian like us now!'

Ilam sounded frustrated 'I was not implying that humans are barbarians. You are Tlillans and you must learn to carry yourselves as Tlillans would.'

McCann hated her holier than thou attitude, she was always pontificating about how humans must raise themselves up to take their place with Tlillans. He accepted Tlillans were technologically, physically and mentally superior however he felt their attitude stank. Although he loved Ilam often her superiority complex grated on his nerves. Though, if he was being honest with himself, it was an attractive feature, when it wasn't driving him mad.

McCann scoffed at her 'If I needed to learn how to be an arrogant, condescending, egotistical prick I could just ask Louis!'

Ilam chuckled; she found his quips and sarcastic remarks adorable, when he wasn't driving her mad!

'I apologise, that was unnecessary.'

The flaming haired Valkyrie stepped closer to him and with one arm holding Malikah she held his cheek with her hand, 'You are forgiven.'

He took hold of her hand and kissed it.

'Tell me Duncan why are you a coward?' inquired Ilam.

He admired his baby daughter whom resembled a two year old human baby by now, 'Whilst fighting the Gukumatz I had some amount of control, but at the marriage ceremony I have none. Once I'm married perhaps I'll have even less influence over my destiny, I'm not sure if it's true but that's how I feel.'

McCann held her hand and gazed across the lake 'You are right though, humans are savages. We fight amongst one another killing our own for the most contemptible reasons; when all the time it's because we relish conflict. Humans have a lust for conflict and we indulge that desire whenever possible.'

McCann turned and fixed his eyes on his fiancée's, 'I think we need the Gukumatz more than we need the Tlillans. The Gukumatz have brought humans together for no other reason than we crave revenge.'

She squeezed his hand softly 'Come let us go now, we have a wedding to prepare Duncan.'

He flicked his cigar over the terrace and they left for home.

Chapter 11

McCann awoke in at his home on Lake Geneva, a very plush four bed roomed residence. Since returning from Mars he had purchased the two story house with a small grounds looking onto the lake, only a short walk from the main city and docks and a 3 minute journey from the I.S.A building by monorail. McCann had fallen in love with Geneva the day he arrived; the city had several of the best cigar houses (Casa Del Habanos) in the world. The lake was always calm and sitting at a coffee house by the lake every morning with a cigar watching the Jet D'eau had become a ritual for him. He had been sorry to leave for Mars as he loved the city with such abundance, now he was starting his family here with Ilam.

Most morning's he'd take a stroll to the city and purchase a cigar from one of the local merchants, smoking it at a coffee shop whilst reading the morning paper. Today it wasn't possible since his mother was his guest; she'd been here for some time negotiating over the marriage. McCann didn't know much about Arab weddings but he was learning fast.

From what Ilam had told him Faraday was acting as the bride's Father. Apparently the bride and groom's family negotiated over terms of marriage much like a contract, including the wedding ceremony and terms of a dowry and divorce. McCann felt quite embarrassed after discovering his Mother had wrangled the food and drinks for the wedding out of Faraday including the entertainment. In exchange for deciding on the venue, and Faraday paying for it, Ofra allowed the media and certain endorsements. When Ilam informed McCann about these negotiations he was fairly disgusted. Both Faraday and his Mother were as mercenary as each other. He felt like a piece of meat being bargained over at some degenerate market in a back alley. Still his Mother had already struck her deal with Faraday, who after their last encounter McCann assumed she'd got the better of.

McCann awoke to see his wife sleeping peacefully, she required more sleep than him so when home he'd make her breakfast. Malikah was in her large crib which sat close to her mother's side of the bed. He was always careful to leave his daughter asleep since the link with her mother was very sensitive, if one was roused it would wake the other.

On Tlillan mother and child could not be separated for years unless the child was male. Males were considered able to fend for themselves and they were not capable of linking to the dreamscape on the same level as females. So their mental development was less intense.

He quietly put on his grey pyjamas and slipped on his black soft soled slippers then snuck downstairs. Walking down the stairs he could smell coffee emanating from the kitchen. He walked in to the large open plan kitchen and sat at the island in the middle. He looked out of the patio doors into the garden with satisfaction at the freshly cut grass, 'Good morning Duncan,' came his mother's voice.

He turned to his right and she walked into the kitchen from the lounge, 'Morning.'

She pushed a button on the coffee machine and brought him a fresh cup 'I have been told about your fight with William,' she said putting the coffee before him.

McCann rolled his eyes, 'Mum it's too early.'

'Hah! I hope you will ask for forgiveness?'

McCann blew the steam from his drink, 'MUM!'

Ofra was not in a negotiating mood 'Do not speak to me in that manner boy! William is a very nice man and you must beg forgiveness.'

McCann rubbed his eyes and groaned, 'Yes mum!'

It was pointless to disagree with her since it would only result in a headache and both of them being in a rotten mood for the rest of the day. He took a sip of his drink then asked his mother, 'So where am I getting married?'

Ofra smiled at him as she prepared breakfast 'Tel Aviv of course.'

He chortled 'Naturally!'

She buttered his toast and looked at her son disapprovingly 'What is that supposed to mean?'

He couldn't prevent himself from smiling, 'You know what I mean mum.'

Ofra still frowning replied 'No, why don't you tell me Duncan?'

He sniggered a little 'You're going to have the biggest wedding that Bat Yam has ever seen and rub as many noses in it as possible!'

McCann watched his mother fight back a smile.

'Don't be so silly Duncan!' she retorted.

McCann laughed and she had to turn her back to him before she started laughing too.

'So you're telling me that I'm wrong?' he called.

Ofra walked over to him with some eggs on toast 'Well you would begrudge me that pleasure?'

He smiled at her as she handed him a knife and fork.

Ofra then took herself a coffee, 'That bitch Hanifa Naifeh has pushed it in my face for years and now it is my turn!'

McCann shook his head 'Mum no one cares about her son and that woman he married.'

Ofra slapped the table 'Are you crazy? He made millions from those solar energy plants and she is a Princess you know?'

McCann laughed again, he laughed every time his mother went on a rant about her nemesis, 'Mum, he bought out some tribe that lived in the arse end of nowhere so that he could build on their desert. His wife was the Princess of about 20 tents, some sand dunes and a pile of camel shit!'

McCann cracked up laughing at himself.

Ofra wasn't amused, she took it all very seriously, 'He is rich and she is a Princess, that is the only important thing and that woman will let no one forget it. Even today her mouth will not close about her son the Prince and his children!'

McCann was sniggering too hard to eat his breakfast 'Mum he married the chief's daughter to get the lease for the tribe's land. I've seen her, it was probably the only way he could marry her off!'

Ofra slapped the table again 'Well it doesn't matter now does it? I will have a bigger wedding than hers! I can not wait to see the face on that fat whore when she is eating Russian caviar from real gold tins and drinking French Champagne!'

Ofra started to cackle and McCann stopped his sniggering, it had got to the point of being more disturbing than funny.

'Don't you mean my wedding?'

His mother broke off her celebrations and replied 'Yes, yes you know what I mean Duncan!'

He grunted and started eating his eggs on toast.

Ofra sat over her coffee recanting the story of her arch enemy Hanifa Naifeh and her wealthy son that married a princess.

McCann had heard this story too often now and could probably recite it word for word. He suspected his mother new it better than every surah of the Qur'an, except the first since that would be recited at the wedding.

When the historic wedding occurred he was on duty, being shot at whilst airlifting SBS teams to hell and back during the war on drugs. Not that anyone cared in Tel Aviv because the wedding of the epoch was taking place, Hanifa's son had invited half of Bat Yam once a town but now a suburb of Tel Aviv. From what he could tell the animosity only started when this Hanifa woman decided to belittle his Mother in public one day. If that wasn't enough she perpetuated plenty of gossip concerning his Mother's divorce.

When on leave McCann had visited his Mother to try and put it all to rest. He had received a lot of distressing emails from her, when he contacted his Father he knew nothing of it. His Father would have helped but Ofra refused to speak to him on the subject. So McCann took his two weeks of leave in Tel Aviv with two friends. McCann had been chatting with Jenkins one night about his problem and what he was going to do about it, Jenkins had insisted on coming with him. McCann tried to discourage his comrade but he wanted to make certain his old friend had someone watching his back. The other man was Sergeant Roberts, McCann knew him by reputation only as he was part of Jenkins' squadron. From the rumours that went around in the officers lounge on an evening, this Roberts, whilst in the jungles of Venezuela, had torn a man's arm off with his bare hands. McCann didn't believe the idle gossip but nonetheless it was amusing to see grown men talk about it, and it was something to chat about on an evening. The rumour probably put some fear into the enemy also, anything that gave them an edge against their foes was welcome.

When he saw Roberts he was about 5ft 10 inches, probably of Caribbean descent with a pair of shoulders you could seat two grown men on. McCann found him frightening just to look at.

'Sergeant Roberts, Sir,' he saluted.

McCann returned the salute 'At ease Sergeant. I'm rather overwhelmed that you're taking your leave to help me Sergeant, but please you're not obliged to do so.'

Roberts didn't flinch 'You're welcome Sir, Captain Jenkins has always looked after me and when I heard about this I insisted on coming, if that's alright with you Sir?'

McCann nodded to him, 'One piece of advice I'd give you is to bring a gift. You'll be staying at my Grandfather's home for a week and it would be improper not to.'

Roberts replied sharply 'Understood, when do we leave Sir?'

By the next day they were on an airship to Tel Aviv and a few days later they'd arrived, his Mother and Grandfather were at the airport to greet them. Ofra was in ecstasy to see her son after such a long time, he'd been years in the SBS without visiting either of his parents.

'Duncan!' she shrieked on observing him exit customs. Being a member of the British Special Forces allowed him to walk through without going through a customs check. So whilst everyone else was still waiting he, Jenkins and Roberts walked out alone. All three dressed in uniform wearing their berets and appearing rather dashing at the same time.

Ofra threw her arms around her son and cried whilst the rest of the airport terminal stood watching.

'Hello mum,' said McCann as he put his military pack on the floor and hugged his mother.

His Grandfather walked over and shook his hand with Ofra still clinging on, 'Welcome home.'

McCann shook his hand, 'Thank you.'

Ofra let go of her son and looked behind him 'Who is that you have with you?'

McCann pointed to them 'Mum I'd like you to meet two friends of mine Captain Jenkins and Sergeant Roberts.'

Jenkins approached her and shook her hand, 'It's wonderful to meet you young lady,' he said with a wink much to Ofra's delight.

Roberts walked up to her and shook her hand 'I'm honoured to meet you Miss.'

Ofra smiled and shook his hand.

After the initial greetings his grandfather drove them back to his house where his daughter also lived. Women in Tel Aviv didn't live alone unless they were without shame.

On reaching his humble home in a lower middle class metropolitan area McCann presented a bottle of 30 year old Balvenie whisky. He knew his Grandfather and friends would often partake in a naughty drink, the old rascal was very appreciative of the gift. The old man hid the bottle beneath his jacket and patted his Grandson on the back disappearing inside to hide it.

His Grandmother watched on disdainfully until he produced her gift.

During the campaign in Colombia McCann had managed to acquire some jewellery that he knew his mother would appreciate. Now some people would consider taking the gold bracelets immoral. However ... from McCann's point of view, the local cartel leader's wives didn't really need them anymore, since they were all dead.

The operation was complete, the cartel boss and his family had been gunned down trying to escape into the jungle. The bodies were lifted back to the carrier for identification. When the mortician overheard McCann mention that his mother would probably love to have some of that jewellery he offered him a few pieces.

McCann was taken aback, 'Are you sure?'

The Mortician didn't seem too concerned though 'Just take what you want old man, they'll only end up returning it all to those bloody jungle bunnies anyway!'

McCann visited the ships mortuary that night and selected a pair of matching pure gold bracelets.

His Grandmother's eyes widened significantly at the sight of the beautiful pieces, she hugged her grandson kissing him.

He had saved the best for his Mother, a beautiful pure gold and emerald necklace with emerald ear rings worn by the cartel leader's first wife.

His mother was astounded when she saw them, 'How could you afford these Duncan?' she said ogling at the jewellery.

McCann was pleased to see his Mother so happy 'They're a gift Mother, it's rude to ask.'

She began to cry with joy.

He and his comrades were shown to their rooms whilst Ofra and her mother stashed their presents safely away in their jewellery boxes.

Later in the week McCann, Jenkins and Roberts all in SBS uniform were out patrolling the streets of Bat Yam looking for Wafiq Naifeh. He was the son of his Mother's nemesis. Things worked differently in different cultures, speaking directly to his Mother would produce little if any results; however by confronting her husband or son McCann was sure he could get something done. He hadn't informed anyone other than his comrades of what he was planning to do. Otherwise Ofra would've put a stop to it.

McCann felt it would be improper to speak to her husband, since he was a respectable and older man. The son, although he had money, wasn't as respected and if push came to shove McCann had no qualms about using intimidation to get his way.

That afternoon the Englishman finally managed to track down this Wafiq. The young debonair Arab was sitting with some friends outside an upscale restaurant. Drinking coffee from small cups and eating dates. Wafiq was wearing an expensive white woollen suit with white cotton shirt and black tie.

He looked over his shades at McCann and his comrades 'I'm sorry who are you collecting money for today?'

His group of hanger on friends laughed at his weak joke, McCann decided on a direct approach. He walked up to the table, took a small cup of coffee and poured it onto Wafiq's lovely white suit. Wafiq was enraged and leapt to his feet, one of his hangers on advanced towards McCann.

Roberts intervened and in one graceful move smashed the young man's head down so hard the wooden table split at the point of impact and toppled over, leaving the youth unconscious in a pool of blood on the pavement.

After having witnessed this his motley gang fled, abandoning Wafiq to fend for himself who was now not so full of himself. The other men on the street that day decided to stay out of it.

The older men recognised the SBS uniforms, after the oil conflicts. The British were held in high regard since the SBS had prevented a massacre of Jews taking place taking place once Jaffa had fallen. The conflicts ended after most nations moved off oil (since after fiat currency collapsed oil was too expensive) and many Jews had fled to Russia. Once the Arabs had their land back Tel Aviv was policed by the British for many years. It was where his Father met his Mother and where she lived with her Father after the divorce, and where McCann was now.

Wafiq didn't recognise him since they'd never actually met. However he deduced who McCann was from the uniform and the fact that his Mother had opened her mouth all over town. It had become a joke that Wafiq's mother was referred to as Bat Yam FM; due to her penchant for malicious gossip which was about to lead to her son's public demise.

Wafiq held his arms out 'It's not my fault!'

McCann remained stoic, glaring at him, 'I don't care who is responsible, I'm just here to make sure it ends.'

Wafiq looked down at his friend who was groaning as he bled into the gutter then looked back at McCann, 'I cannot help you. It is my Mother you must speak to!'

By this time a crowd had gathered to stand and watch the drama unfold. Many of the men were aware to one degree or another of the situation. Wafiq's mother had for many years been advertising her son's achievements, she'd also been advertising Ofra's faults with equal ferocity probably because she saw McCann as some sort of rival to her position, some of these men had been waiting years for this. Even women began gathering on the streets watching the fracas.

'It seems you have a problem then doesn't it?' said McCann as he walked up to Wafiq.

McCann stood in front of Wafiq and with his left hand reached around the back of his head. With the back of Wafiq's head braced between his forearm and bicep he placed his hand on the forehead then pulled back and down. Wafiq's head was twisted back and down causing him to lose balance and sight of his adversary. With Wafiq at his mercy he struck him in the face twice with his fist before releasing him. Wafiq fell to the ground and on the way McCann raised a knee smashing him viciously in the side of his head.

Wafiq crumpled to the sidewalk landing on his back with a thump. The Englishman thought he looked like a weasel of a man, moaning and groaning on the floor. The crowd began to cheer at the sight of someone dispatching the young man who McCann assumed was not well liked in the community. He then took one of Wafiq's legs by the ankle and with one bone crunching stamp, crushed his knee, the crowd went silent. Wafiq groaned louder, McCann took the other ankle.

Before the SBS officer could break the other knee an old man appeared from the crowd, 'Enough!' he shouted.

McCann stopped and looked at the white haired old man with a skull cap brandishing a walking stick.

He closed on McCann, 'The boy has learned his lesson, there's no need for this.'

McCann let go of Wafiq's ankle, gestured to his friends, and they walked away from the scene of Prince Wafiq's fall from grace.

That night outside of his Grandfather's house two police cars had pulled up, McCann and his two comrades were asked to come outside. The police officer was a gentleman in his fifties and from appearances he was the head of the local constabulary, 'Mr. Duncan McCann?'

McCann nodded 'Yes officer, is there a problem?' the police officer was taken aback when he saw the three men in uniform. He recognised the "By strength and guile" badge on his beret.

The officer looked at his tablet 'I'm looking for two other men seen with you this afternoon.'

Jenkins stepped forward 'Captain Jenkins, Her Majesties Royal Navy.'

Next Roberts stepped beside McCann 'Sergeant Roberts, Her Majesties Royal Marines, Sir' then saluted the police officer.

The Police officer looked as if something had just clicked in his mind 'There's no need for that,' he said to Roberts.

The officer returned to McCann, 'I have reports from a Hanifa Naifeh that her son was assaulted by you and two other men today at Zarif's restaurant.'

The police officer peeked behind him at his terrified Mother then back to McCann, 'Your Mother is Ofra McCann?'

'Yes.'

The police officer scribbled something down on his tablet. After he'd finished he looked back up 'Thank you very much Mr. McCann how long will you be staying here?'

McCann felt a wave of relief come over him 'A few more days then I'm back on duty I'm afraid.'

The police officer smiled 'I see, if anything comes up can I contact you here?'

'Certainly.'

As the police officer was wrapping it up Hanifa came flying out of the crowd which had gathered, screaming something unintelligible at McCann in Arabic. The police held her back allowing the officer to calm her. Unable to curtail the woman she howled out pointing at McCann 'He tried to kill my son, arrest him!'

The officer continued his attempts to calm her down but she screamed like a harpy. Ofra marched out of the house and McCann thrust his arm out before his mother. She caught his black stare and retreated inside; eventually another car pulled up and out came Hanifa's husband. McCann prepared for another verbal onslaught however to his surprise he walked up to his wife and berated her. After being given a roasting in public Hanifa retreated to her husband's car. The police officer apologised to McCann, his mother and grandfather then both the cars departed.

After that day Ofra's life became a lot easier in her home town, the thought of her son returning kept the Naifeh family in line.

McCann had been dozing whilst his mother was recanting her stories. He came back to the real world on catching his wife enter the room out of the corner of his eye. She was dressed in a pair of white soft pyjamas and looked stunningly beautiful as she smiled at him. He noticed she was holding his daughters hands as she took some steps into the kitchen. He panicked when his daughter, in her white pyjamas much the same as her mother, let go of Ilam's hands and walked towards his mother. McCann shouted 'Look out!' but he was ignored.

His daughter took some rickety steps and called out, 'Ofra,' with her hands outstretched towards his mother. His mother was enchanted by her granddaughter clapping her hands then picking her up when she reached her.

McCann sat back down, 'Jesus Christ woman you could have told me!' he said to Ilam.

'I am sorry Duncan?' asked his fiancée.

McCann took a drink of coffee 'I nearly had a bloody stroke! You didn't tell me she could walk!'

His mother laughed whilst doting over Malikah.

Ilam approached McCann giving him a big hug to try and calm his nerves. According to Ilam, Tlillan children learn the greater part of their motor skills, co-ordination and balance from the mother. The neural link is of the utmost importance and without it a Tlillan would be little more than a human. Already his daughter could walk and talk, she recognised people and could identify them by name, Malikah also spoke three languages that McCann knew of. Ofra put her granddaughter down and Malikah strolled over to McCann. He picked her up and sat her on his knee.

She smiled at her father and pulled on his t shirt 'Duncan,' she stuttered.

McCann corrected her 'Daddy.'

His daughter only laughed at his attempt and continued to call him by his first name. Ilam explained this would change in time, but for now she relied on her mother's memories. Malikah's head protruded out at the rear just as her mother's did. Her torso, arms and legs were long and slender compared to even a two year old human. Her physical strength was quite impressive too; McCann had tested his wife to be in an arm wrestle a long time ago and lost. If this child were not his daughter he could understand someone fearing her. But when he saw her wide eyes transform to a pink hue McCann only felt love. His daughter loved him also, though McCann did wonder if she truly loved him or it was only her mother's love reflected via the link. He kissed Malikah and she squealed with delight beating his chest with her fists. McCann started play fighting with her whilst his mother watched on.

Ofra and Ilam stood chatting about the wedding arrangements, so he took Malikah out on to the back lawn to play.

Two months later and they were all in Tel Aviv for the wedding. Malikah was four feet tall now and dressed as a bridesmaid. Her dark red hair had been curled into locks; she could walk under her own steam competently. McCann was at his mother's house dressed in a white silk suit. He felt rather absurd, but Ofra was determined he would be quiet and wear it. The retired soldier had awaited this day with dread. If there was one thing he detested more than anything about these things it was all the pomp and ceremony.

Arab weddings were by far the worst for this, the Zaffa had already begun with men marching through the streets of Bat Yam and Tel Aviv banging drums and announcing the wedding. By the time Ofra had finished putting the squeeze on Faraday there were going to be thousands of guests. A large sports field outside of the city had to be commandeered and gigantic tent erected. Outside there were still more tables with massive projectors so all guests outside could watch the ceremony in 3D.

At this moment he was awaiting Jerry Habeeb for his prenuptial interview. McCann still hadn't forgotten Jerry's "hilarious" night of dissecting his dance moves more than a year ago. He sat in his Grandfather's modest living room on an old sofa whilst the camera crew set up.

They had already interviewed Ilam two nights ago, before her henna night. Since men were not allowed to be present, it all had to be worked around her. McCann also had his lad's night where he just sat outside his Grandfather's house with friends and family having a drink. On the morning of the wedding was the first opportunity Jerry had to interview McCann. Jerry entered looking a bit rushed and shook McCann's hand 'It's great to see you again Duncan!'

McCann couldn't say the same, 'Uuuuuurrrhhh!' he replied, a habit he'd picked up from Ryu.

Jerry paused for a moment then continued 'So let's get the show on the road shall we?'

McCann had a blank expression, 'Sure,' he said flippantly and shrugged his shoulders.

Jerry was uncomfortable 'Look I'm sorry about that piece we did but I have to go with what the network gives me, you do understand Duncan?'

McCann puckered up his lips and sucked his cheeks in, 'Sure,' he was getting a kick out of Jerry sweating.

Jerry smiled 'Thanks,' then took out his tablet and read his questions. 'First I'd like to congratulate you on your promotion to Commodore could you tell me and our viewers how that came about?'

McCann nodded 'Thank you Jerry and no,' then puckered his lips again. 'Why's that Duncan?'

McCann smirked at Jerry 'I could tell you Jerry but then I'd have to kill you!'

People were laughing from behind the cameras, flustering Jerry somewhat.

Jerry glanced at his tablet 'Okay let's move on then, your fiancée wasn't too forthcoming so I wonder if you could tell our viewers the story of how you met?'

McCann smiled 'Certainly Jerry, I first met her when commanding Tharsis. We had sighted a foreign object not far off Olympus Mons. After Major Ryu had ... '

Jerry cut him off 'Yes, yes Duncan. Everyone on the planet knows that story, what I mean is how did you ... MEET?'

McCann couldn't believe that even Jerry would be so indiscreet on his wedding night, 'Mr. Habeeb I'm afraid gentlemen do not discuss such matters especially on the Net!'

Jerry, still looking flustered, replied 'Well the President was pretty candid about meeting his second wife just last month in an interview.'

McCann puckered up again raising his eyebrows, but said nothing, much to the entertainment of the crew.

Jerry screwed his lips up 'I see,' glanced back at his tablet 'alright, could you tell us when you decided to tie the knot?'

'Certainly, it was the day Malikah was born.'

Jerry let out a big puff of air in relief, 'Yes Malikah, she has grown at an astonishing rate hasn't she? Is that normal for a Tlillan child?'

McCann reached for a glass of water on the table between him and Jerry 'Yes it is,' took a sip then replaced the glass.

Jerry was becoming frustrated at McCann's minimalist approach to the interview, 'Does she exhibit any of her mother's abilities?'

'Yes.'

Jerry huffed in frustration 'What are those abilities?'

'She has a neural link with her mother and can already sense the presence of others independently. Malikah has also learnt to speak in English, Russian, Tlillan and Arabic from my mother, though her grammar is still very poor.'

McCann couldn't resist showing off his daughters skills, he was a very proud father and Malikah was the apple of his eye.

Jerry continued 'Ilamachutli has been given the title of exo-diplomat by Director Faraday, could you explain to me what she does?'

McCann looked down on Jerry 'Didn't you ask her?'

Jerry nodded 'Yes, she said her duties were to advise on any alien matters.'

McCann shrugged his shoulders 'Sounds right to me.'

Jerry glanced at the tablet again 'So could you tell us all how you proposed to Ilamachutli?'

McCann leaned back on the sofa 'There's not much to tell really, after she had given birth we discussed it in the hospital. We decided to marry after I finished up my tour in space for the I.S.A.'

Jerry got a little excited now 'Yes about that, at the time there were rumours that something else was going on. The Chile array picked up what they described as a white hole, appearing then disappearing between Jupiter and the asteroid belt. Now I've heard rumours from an alien visit, to the I.S.A testing a wormhole generator to a full blown space battle, what do you have to say about it?'

McCann smiled at Jerry 'I say you'd look good in a tin foil hat Jerry!' another round of laughs came from the camera crew.

Jerry slowly shook his head 'So what are your plans for the future Commodore McCann? Will you settle down or will you remain working at the I.S.A?'

McCann shrugged his shoulders 'I'm not sure Jerry, but I can't imagine leaving Geneva, the I.S.A has become very important to me. After what the Gukumatz did we need to be ready for them, I'm quite sure the next time we meet in space things will be different.'

Jerry almost leapt out of his seat 'Please explain what you mean by that last statement Commodore!'

McCann stood up holding the palm of his hand out at Jerry 'I'm sorry but I have a wedding to go to Jerry. Thank you for the interview and I hope you and your crew enjoy yourselves.'

He waved to the crew, walked past a frantic Jerry and out of the house.

Once outside he entered the car waiting to drive him to the wedding ceremony that was being held inside the sewan. Upon reaching the tent he exited the car and approached his relatives who were waiting outside for him. There were at least one hundred tables outside, with guests eating from large metal plates. The menu consisted of traditional dishes such as Fattah made from lamb, rice and bread then there were more flamboyant dishes. His mother had wrangled Faraday into providing Beluga caviar, each table had one serving of the expensive dish served in a traditional solid gold tin.

McCann found it to be all rather vulgar, however his mother relished every moment. Especially since her nemesis appeared sick as a parrot at the Naifeh family table. The fact that Hanifah's husband was enjoying the festivities wasn't helping her maintain that fake smile either.

The guests outside of the tent clapped and cheered when McCann stepped out of the car and his mother hugged him. His father was there to shake his hand, he seemed overwhelmed by the enormity of the celebration also. Next McCann entered the sewan to applause of close friends and family.

The crew of the Athena were all sat together at one table. Hassif was probably paying more attention to the belly dancers than he should have been and didn't notice the Englishman enter for a while. Ryu was at her seat with her guest, Cherkesov. McCann suspected his bride had somehow managed to get the Russian here from the Tsiolkovsky.

McCann shook their hands and raised his eyebrows cheekily at Ryu who blushed. Normally at these weddings the bride's family would also be seated in the Sewan but since that was not a possibility many of the staff at Geneva had taken their place. McCann went over to them and shook hands with the Doctor; Weissmuller was enjoying the beer and shook his hand firmly.

Valorie Pitt wasn't as happy as McCann had hoped.

She shook his hand then whispered in his ear 'Well done Duncan, I was wondering if you'd make it.'

He laughed with her then walked away to greet as many of the other guests as he could. After becoming weary he decided to take a rest with his old crewmates. The groom sat down at their table and Louis patted his shoulder 'C'est bon mon ami!' he declared in between chewing the expensive food then washing it down with Dom Perignon rose 2100.

Louis was a connoisseur of what he called fine dining and McCann described as expensive eating, tonight he was ploughing into it with a passion.

The groom tugged on Louis jacket sleeve 'Steady on man you'll put on five kilos if you keep that up!'

Louis scoffed 'Bah! Who knows when I'll see this kind of food again? Better to eat well now, I might be stuck in space for a month eating more Russian sheep shit!'

McCann turned to Cherkesov to apologise but before he could the Russian replied 'I'm not offended, the food on the Tsiolkovsky does taste like shit after 6 months.'

Hassif was still clapping to the belly dancers and Ryu was looking happier than he'd ever seen her.

His mother sat next to him, 'Isn't it wonderful?' she spoke in his ear wrapping her arms around his and pulling him close.

McCann replied in a hushed tone 'So how is the great Satan?' he jibed playfully.

Ofra laughed and slapped his arm 'She has a face … how does your Father say it?'

McCann laughed then whispered into her ear 'A face like a slapped arse?'

Ofra laughed aloud 'Yes that is it!'

Shortly, his Father came over to the table and sat down opposite them between Hassif and Ryu. He had been eyeing the belly dancers along with Hassif.

Ofra rolled her eyes 'Some things never change!'

James ignored her and clapped along with Hassif to the young girl closest to them. Dressed in a Bedouin outfit and gyrating her hips much to the entertainment of the guests.

Half an hour later the Zaffa turned up heralding the arrival of Ilam. McCann arose and stood at the dais end of the tent, opposite the entrance. The musicians stopped playing their drums and the dancers retreated to the side. The waiters also stopped serving and all eyes turned to the entrance along with cameras.

First six men dressed in white, wielding blades, entered and lined the path to the dais where two chairs had been placed. McCann could hear trumpets outside then an ovation, next in came Faraday with Ilam. She was wearing a beautiful red silk wedding dress matching the colour of her hair. Her hands were covered in brown henna paint from her henna party and she wore a red lace veil which covered her head and face. The dress was short sleeved and figure hugging, unfurling slightly after it dropped below the knee. The collar was high and covered her neck except the throat. A small area at the front was exposed, just a small square of cloth, enough to see a little chest but still remain modest.

As she approached the dais slowly he noticed the dress was ringed with small ridges of fabric circling her body and she had a slightly darker band of silk tied around her waist. On the upper body the edges of the dress had golden dragons all along. Ilam proceeded down the aisle carrying a bunch of white roses, wearing red silk gloves.

McCann hadn't seen the dress until today but he instantly recognised Ryu's influence.

Ilam's white skin contrasted perfectly with the dress and her red lipstick accentuated her beauty. She approached McCann with Malikah following behind in a bridesmaid dress. Upon reaching McCann he took her hand and helped her onto the dais (not that she needed it). Both sat on the Dais whilst Malikah came up behind them. The little Malikah stood on a box and rubbed two rocks of sugar together over their heads, a tradition to ward off evil spirits.

Several friends and family stood before the dais and made speeches wishing the pair well. McCann suffered his father's wedding anecdotes that weren't very funny, though the crowd humoured him. Afterwards the waiters served some sharbat the guest drank a toast to their health. Later the Imam had them exchange vows and rings whilst seated on the kosha before McCann kissed his bride.

Ilam tossed her bouquet and McCann was certain she used her mental powers to get it into Ryu's hands, since she threw it straight in her direction. A cake was brought out that McCann thought to be ghastly in its size but they cut it and shared it out amongst the tables inside the tent.

After all of that they left the tent with Malikah and drove to a five star hotel in Tel Aviv leaving the guests to carry on the party. Upon arriving at the hotel the couple were exhausted, especially Ilam who hadn't slept for 36 hours thanks to her henna party. After Malikah was put to sleep they both hit the hay and went straight to sleep, now man and wife.

After a short honeymoon the pair were back in Geneva with their daughter at their home on the lake. Ofra had also moved in from her father's home in Tel Aviv. She spoke of little else other than the wedding for the first month, the crew of the Athena all resided close by on the lake. Ryu had brought her family over from Korea and purchased an apartment for her brother in the city of Geneva. Ilam enjoyed spending time with Ryu.

Moscow had selected a Captain for the second warship, Cherkesov was moved to Geneva along with Titov and a few other personnel selected from the Tsiolkovsky. The lake had become quite a metropolitan area with all the new arrivals. Rumour spread like wildfire as the media did it's best to investigate the Russian influx. Moscow had become quite compliant with the I.S.A, McCann and Titov were firm friends spending many a day chatting in the cigar lounges of Geneva. They both enjoyed an evening in Davidoff. Ever since the Davidoff family had returned to growing tobacco in Cuba their cigars were once again highly prized, and on their new I.S.A salaries they could both afford it!

Both the crews spent most days of the week in the simulators at the I.S.A. Training on computer generated 3D models of the vessels they would be stationed on. At first McCann found it most stimulating, but after the first few months the shine had worn off and it was drill after drill. Every once in a while something different was thrown at them, but overall it had become rather tedious. He had also been taking lessons in the Russian language which he constantly tested out on Titov during their breaks. Titov enjoyed polishing McCann's Russian and was pleased to see that Faraday recognised the need for it to be understood.

McCann was content more than any other point in his life before now. His daughter was growing and learning at such a rate it was hard for him to keep up with her. His wife worked diligently with Faraday on her appointment as exo-diplomat. They were also a celebrity couple by now, and whenever they went anywhere together the media wasn't far behind. Jerry Habeeb knew that something was afoot with the I.S.A, but trying to discover what that was became rather arduous. Ilam found it very amusing and used to rib McCann often that all Jerry would have to do is ask at a local cigar lounge!

Since he and Titov spent most of their off time at Davidoff's the manager of the lounge had been informed of the two warships under construction in space. In fact Eduardo was privy to a lot of secret information, however Davidoff's had a reputation to maintain and even when offered a lot of credits to loosen his lips he refused. The staff were discreet and the surroundings of old familiar leather seats and mahogany tables was classically relaxing.

By his daughter's first birthday she was as developed as a ten year old human child. Fluent in several human languages and some alien tongues, the owners of which McCann had not even heard about. His daughter was a gold mine of information on the universe outside of their solar system. Often she would impart information her mother would not.

Ilam had been tight lipped on what else lay in wait outside of the Tlillan and Gukumatz; McCann had managed to get some idea from his daughter.

Malikah was definitely a daddy's girl, much to her mother's disdain. Ilam found it increasingly difficult to control her since as matured Malikah she relied less and less on their link. Soon Malikah would be able to form a link to the dreamscape independently. Tapping into the collective knowledge of the Tlillan race rather than being dependent on her mother. Malikah would often wait until alone with her Father and tell him tales of other species they were yet to encounter. From her stories it was a lot less ordered out there than Ilam had first let on. His wife had given an impression of the Tlillans as leaders of a galactic council.

The truth he learned from Malikah was very different, the known galaxy was not as civilised and ordered as Ilam had implied. Constant conflict and bickering between different factions had resulted in thousands of years of war on some level or another. The war with the Gukumatz was not as grand or threatening as first impressions. Most of the 30,000 years had been minor skirmishes at disputed areas of space. The battle that took place above Mars was the first time a ship had been destroyed in centuries, all sides had become worn down by the stalemate. It was not possible to come to an accord between the belligerents so they agreed not to use weapons of mass destruction, until a time came that they could settle the conflict.

Four centuries ago the Tlillan's were hit by a plague which was fatal to all except Darksiders, leaving Darksider males sterile. The Lightsiders and Twilighters that escaped were either eventually infected or targeted by the Gukumatz. A cure had not been found and only the religious sect of Tlillan remained, the Darksiders controlled the priesthood and the temple of Tititil. The Lightsiders were responsible for military matters, maintaining and arming the Tlillans. Twilighters were responsible for the administration of Tlillan and making the political decisions.

After a century only the Darksiders survived. The Gukumatz had decided to let the clock run out for their enemy instead of fight. The Tlillans were a great power in the galaxy before the plague, but since they had been ravaged and sentenced to a slow death their power had waned and influence retracted.

McCann realised that Ilam's description of the galaxy and Tlillan's place in it was pertinent before the plague but since then they had declined drastically. The species that they once kept in line were no longer afraid of the Tlillans. It wasn't that the Tlillans were less powerful militarily it was that they knew the Tlillans would not attack. With their population so low sacrificing lives over petty matters was not an option and the galaxy descended into a chaos not seen for a long time. When it was understood that the mighty police of the galaxy would not intervene old hatreds emerged stronger than ever, wars broke out all around. The Tlillans were left watching the commonwealth they had built implode with retribution and blood feuds over contentions that were millennia old.

Tlillan had become superfluous, only the Gukumatz were concerned with the Tlillans due to the long history between the species. The Tlillans, upon first leaving their home planet had discovered in the same system the Gukumatz. Their civilization had developed to somewhere around the medieval period of Earth and when they witnessed craft descend from the sky and tall white creatures exit, the priesthood of both worlds seized the opportunity. An arrangement was reached with the Gukumatz religious leaders of the day. In exchange for supporting them the Tlillan's would be allowed to exploit the planet and its population through them.

For millions of years Gukumatz were the slaves of the Tlillan, masquerading as deities, exploited to the extreme until there was an uprising. For several days anarchy reigned on Tlillan and when it was all over the Gukumatz had escaped. Taking dangerous technology, they liberated their world, deposed the priesthood and captured the Tlillans there. The Gukumatz were eventually pushed off their home world after it was overwhelmed, but many escaped through wormholes and restarted their civilization.

Centuries later the Gukumatz returned and wreaked a terrible revenge on the Tlillans, leading to the ban on environmental weapons and the loss of contact with colonies and outposts such as Earth. Then the plague came resulting in the inevitable collapse of the Tlillan commonwealth, until they rediscovered the Earth.

Tonight Malikah had been recalling the story of the Camazotz, a species she claimed had no natural eyes and used sonic vibrations to translate the world around them via a cybernetic implant. McCann was enchanted by her description until she mentioned that they had a penchant for drinking blood at which he laughed 'Now you're having me on aren't you!'

McCann who was lying on the rug in front of the fireplace in the lounge with Malikah grabbed her and started to tickle her.

She squealed 'No it's true! It's true!'

They both laughed playing on the floor until they heard the voice of Ilam 'What is true?'

Her mother strode in wearing what looked like a red business suit and a pair of boots underneath the trousers.

'Nothing' replied McCann. He then looked at Malikah mischievously and she started giggling.

'Have you been telling your father tales again Malikah?'

Malikah continued to giggle hiding from her mother in her father's arms 'Go to bed Malikah!' stated Ilam with her hands on hips.

Malikah stopped giggling 'Mother!' she whined, but Ilam refused to budge.

'Go now!'

Malikah held tighter to her father and Ilam's eyes started changing in colour, 'You'd better go to bed now' whispered McCann. She looked into her father's eyes but he shook his head 'I'm sorry Malikah,' his daughter stood up, stomped past her mother and up the stairs.

Ilam expelled a long breath 'I have never known a child to be so stubborn!'

McCann patted the rug beside him inviting his wife to sit next to him. She removed her boots and lay down beside her husband 'All children are difficult at her age,' commiserated McCann.

Ilam shook her head, 'Not Tlillan children, she is stubborn and rebellious, on Tlillan she would have been punished severely for such impetuous behaviour.'

McCann put his arms around her 'How would she be punished?'

Ilam replied 'My mother would have punished me by stimulating my pain centers.'

McCann could hardly believe what he was hearing 'You mean in the brain directly?'

She nodded 'Yes, it is the most effective method of maintaining obedience.'

McCann was horrified 'That sounds barbaric! I hope you don't use that on our daughter?'

A corner of his wife's mouth raised 'No, it is not possible.'

He sat up 'You mean you've tried it?'

Ilam stroked his arm 'Yes, it is not possible to cause her sufficient discomfort to describe it as a punishment. She is a hybrid and has matured beyond Tlillan norms. At this age a Tlillan could not repel my mental assault, but she has the ability. Besides Duncan, humans strike their children stimulating pain centers and causing physical damage.'

McCann shook his head 'Yes I know it's just rather shocking to hear it, I'm sorry.'

Ilam stroked him again 'I was not offended, now what tale was she telling you Duncan?'

He smiled, 'Something about the Camazotz, a race of blood sucking vampire bats. Do they exist or was she just pulling my leg?'

Ilam rolled her eyes 'I have told her not to speak of these things, why does she disobey me?'

McCann looked seriously at her 'So they are real then?'

Ilam nodded 'It is so frustrating.'

McCann kissed his wife's cheek 'What?'

Ilam had a disappointed expression on her face 'Malikah will link with me less and less now, and discovering the truth is almost impossible. Her personality is inherent of yours, insolent and stubborn yet she will always obey you. I am sure she does it to goad me.'

McCann kissed his wife 'She is part human, don't be hurt by her attitude it's a natural stage of development in us. Is it true Tlillans enslaved the Gukumatz for millions of years?'

Ilam was taken aback by his question 'Yes it is, why do you ask Duncan?'

McCann gazed into her eyes 'I'm worried that we may suffer a similar fate.'

Ilam sat up and hugged her husband 'Perhaps you will become my sex slave on Tlillan?' she whispered into his ear.

McCann chuckled then looked her in the eye again 'I'm serious Ilam, would they try the same with us?'

'Subjugation is not viable, we require human DNA to prevent our own extinction. Why do you think I was instructed to remain here?'

McCann was unaware of this 'I thought you were exiled? You were instructed to stay here?'

She sighed 'Yes Duncan, on Tlillan after Malikah's birth I would have been executed and probably our daughter too. For our daughter to survive and perhaps one day return to Tlillan a Matriarch, it is necessary for us to remain. Law requires me to be exiled but Malikah's fate remains in question.'

McCann shrugged his shoulders 'Politics, so you were ordered to make love to me?'

She smiled 'No, but when I realised our DNA was compatible I had to break our law for the future of Tlillan. If not the Matriarchs would still be debating the issue whilst Gukumatz exterminated you all. Once I was with child they were forced to act. It will be a few years before Malikah is ready for the Matriarchs. Before that time she must learn restraint Duncan, any sign of disobedient behaviour will be unacceptable.'

McCann felt the warmth of the log fire on his back along with a cold shiver 'What do you mean by ready for the Matriarchs?' he said slowly.

Ilam appeared unconcerned 'All females that wish to become a Matriarch are set a trial; do not be concerned I have prepared her.'

McCann was worried for his daughter 'What exactly does this trial entail?'

Ilam leaned back and brought over the ashtray and a cigar from the coffee table behind her 'Each trial is different depending on the person taking it.'

She placed the ashtray to his side and passed him the small cigar, 'It is a test of mental competence, her ability to probe a mind at distance will be examined. Her affinity with the dreamscape must be strong and finally self defence.'

McCann didn't like the sound of the last test at all, 'Self defence? Tell me about that,' he asked as he clipped his cigar cap and used a piece of wood from the fire to toast the foot.

Ilam looked at the rug 'Her aptitude for withstanding a mental assault will be gauged, it isn't as frightening as it sounds Duncan. All Matriarchs took the trials including myself.'

McCann took a drag of his Cohiba Siglo I 'So describe to me this mental assault, is it similar to what you did to Louis on Tharsis?'

She nodded 'Similar but with more,' she looked at the wall behind McCann 'vigour.'

He could see the reflection of the fire flickering in her eyes. He noticed a sheen of water forming giving them a glossy shine. McCann had never seen his wife cry with either joy or misery but this was the closest she'd ever been. His question was whether her eyes watered through fear or pride. He usually assumed the worst and took it to be fear, 'What if she fails?'

Ilam was on the verge of tears now, 'She will be executed as an abomination.'

He was stunned for a moment 'Then she won't be taking the trial.'

Ilam didn't react to his statement but only replied 'She must Duncan, if a Human cannot produce a Matriarch then you will be at war with the Tlillans as well as the Gukumatz.'

McCann didn't understand any of her logic 'Why would they attack us?'

Ilam sniffed 'If she cannot prove herself your species will be branded as abominations.'

McCann was bemused 'Why?'

Ilam fought back her tears to answer him 'The reason your species location was a mystery to us is not because of the war. The ones who first came used this place to experiment; humans were used as today mice are used by humans.'

McCann frowned 'I see and we were the result?'

She shook her head slowly and sighed 'No, have you ever wondered why the three races of Tlillan never interbred?'

He shrugged his shoulders and she continued 'On occasion when they interbred the result was a Mictlancihuatl, the child would be black as a Lightsider but uncontrollable. It was not possible for the mother to link with the child and before maturity they had to be destroyed. They possessed great mental prowess but their lack of restraint and unfocused violence made it impossible to harness. The scientists that selected Earth came here in an attempt to breed a Mictlancihuatl. Possessing the same mental capabilities but also retained the discipline of a Tlillan.'

McCann expelled the smoke from his nostrils 'Isn't any kind of genetic manipulation heresy though?'

She nodded her head 'After the Gukumatz returned, all expeditions were recalled, the scientists destroyed their files. However they couldn't hide what they had done from the dreamscape. Before they could be arrested and punished the scientists executed their slaves and males, then committed suicide rather than bring shame upon their clan. The records from the ships log had also been wiped, so it remained a mystery as to your location. The war intensified and their experiment was forgotten. You were all thought to be lost, Pixoa, until the seers at Tititl had a vision.'

McCann had a rather caustic expression 'So why were you sent?'

Ilam smiled a little 'I was the first priestess of our clan. The seers required a Matriarch whom could be trusted to do whatever may be required, even if that meant transgressing the word of the Grand Matriarch. I did what had to be done Duncan and Malikah is no different, it is her destiny.'

McCann stood up, he was upset with his wife 'It would have been nice if you'd have told me this earlier.'

She stood up and stroked the side of her husband's head 'Would it have made any difference to you Duncan?'

He turned and watched the flames of the fire flickering 'I suppose not, but I don't like being lied to Ilam, you know that.'

She placed her hands on his shoulders 'I didn't lie to you my love,' she spoke softly.

He snorted and smoke flew out his nostrils 'How would you describe it then my DEAR?' he replied sarcastically.

She smiled 'You are a busy man and you need not fill your head with nonessential concern.'

McCann turned back around and looked her in the eye 'So I'm a child, is that it?'

His wife sensed one of his rants building 'Please Duncan I would appreciate it if you didn't have a tantrum!'

McCann exploded 'So I'm a two year old having a tantrum now? That bloody sense of superiority really gets on my tits you know that?'

Ilam looked down on him with a sneer 'I'm afraid I am superior Duncan, it is you that must learn to accept that fact!'

He stopped in his tracks and said nothing, only starring at his wife.

Seconds later Ofra marched down the stairs 'What is going on!' she exclaimed dressed in her night gown.

McCann fixed his gaze on his wife and replied to his mother 'Nothing at all,' then walked to the hall to get his coat.

As he walked away Ilam called to him 'Duncan?' but he refused to listen.

He took a raincoat opened the door and slammed it behind himself.

Ilam began to produce tears for the first time, Ofra hugged her daughter in law; sat her down on the sofa and went to make them both a drink 'Do not worry he will be back, he is just the same as his father you know. They are both stubborn and pig headed, his father would never listen to me, always thinking he knew better.'

Ofra brought two cups of hot chocolate and set them on the coffee table.

Picking the ashtray up off the rug she snarled 'Disgusting habit!' and put it in the kitchen. Ofra sat next to Ilam who wiped her tears away, 'You must learn to bite your tongue and let him talk because a man is too stupid to learn to shut his mouth you know?'

Ilam laughed a little at her anecdote.

Ofra slapped her arm 'That is no joke! I had to suffer his fool of a father for years you know?'

Ilam smiled still wiping the tears away 'I forget he is sensitive, he is intimidated by me and sometimes has to lash out, on Tlillan such behaviour is unacceptable.'

Ofra took a sip of hot chocolate 'Really? I should have married a Tlillan instead of his father!'

Ilam laughed again 'I think you would bore easily of a Tlillan male,' she replied.

Ofra put her drink down and asked 'Why is that my dear?'

Ilam smiled and picked her mug up 'They do exactly as they're told all of the time, they cannot act without instruction from their Matriarch.'

Ofra smiled 'That sounds good to me!'

'Initially perhaps but it becomes tiresome, I have had bowel movements more exciting than both of my previous males put together!'

Both of the women bellowed loudly 'You had two husbands?' asked Ofra in a shocked tone.

Ilam nodded 'Well to be exact I owned two males; we don't require marriage on Tlillan. I selected them and the clan Matriarch approved, but they had no mind of their own to speak of. It was an old joke that if you acquired two males it only meant they would cause friction.'

Ofra looked puzzled 'I don't understand?'

Ilam smiled 'Because each male only possesses a single brain cell, if he had two it might cause friction. So having two males could result in problems.'

Ofra chortled a little 'That is so cruel!'

Ilam nodded 'I know but it is what makes Duncan attractive, he is unlike any Tlillan male. He reminds me of a petulant child sometimes, it is infuriating and adorable.'

Ofra sat closer to her 'If he could control himself would you love him as much?'

Ilam said nothing and Ofra continued 'Now remember you are an arrogant bitch but he still married you!'

Ilam was shocked by her mother in law's statement and frowned.

'Do not be ashamed,' said Ofra pointing at her 'he loves you for it the same as you love him.'

Ilam then raised her long red eyebrows 'So why did you divorce his father?'

Ofra puffed 'Hah! The difference is he didn't know when to shut up! You see Duncan walked away to cool down, his father would carry on until the next morning. It would take a week for him to forget. Even though it was just him talking, talk, talk, talk that man had a mouth bigger than a camel!'

Ilam sniggered then in a serious tone asked Ofra 'Do you think our marriage will last?'

Ofra hugged her 'Yes of course!'

Ilam looked down solemnly at her 'Despite the antagonism?'

Her mother in law laughed 'Because of it! If you did as you were told and never stood up to him he would bore of you too. He needs a woman with some fire inside her, if not then better he buy a pet dog!' the two women laughed again.

All the time Malikah sat at the top of the stairs listening to the goings on, she could sense her father walking along the lake having a smoke. He was watching the light from the cafés jumping off the ripples in the water whilst he cooled down. The fresh breeze calmed him and after a while when he was at peace, he felt the presence of his daughter with him. He sensed her pulling him back home and after he'd had another smoke he returned, to be welcomed by his mother and wife. The first thing he did after kissing his wife and apologising was to peer up the stairs. There was no one there but he called 'Malikah come here.'

His daughter ran out of the shadows and down the stairs in her pink pyjamas. McCann picked her up 'Didn't I tell you to go to bed?'

Malikah clung onto him 'I was worried.'

He hugged her 'I'm sorry,' he whispered softly into her ear. McCann kissed the swollen rear of her head then said 'You have to sleep now, alright?'

His little girl nodded and he put her down. Malikah waved to her mother and grandmother 'Goodnight.'

Ilam wasn't happy but she put a good face on it and waved to her daughter as she ran up the stairs to her room. His wife asked him 'How did you know she was awake?'

McCann shrugged his shoulders 'I could feel her when I was outside, didn't you?'

Ilam shook her head and in a perplexed tone replied 'No I didn't,' it was a mystery to her as to why her husband sensed Malikah and she did not.

Later that evening after the pair had settled down and everyone else was back in bed they were on the sofa. McCann had brought his ashtray back in and started on a bottle of whisky. His wife cuddled next to him 'What are you thinking about Duncan?' she asked him.

He was looking into the fire and replied 'I was wondering what the naval strength of the Tlillan fleet is, do you know?'

Ilam sighed 'Yes, do I have to answer?'

He smiled into the fireplace 'No, I could just ask Malikah if you want.'

She sighed again 'When I left there were close to 50 functional Itzpap cruisers.'

He looked at her cynically 'Is that all?'

Ilam slapped his arm 'I suppose you'll ask your daughter, only five at the most are operational at one time.'

McCann chuckled knowingly 'Why is that?'

'The population has been declining steadily, there have been no Matriarchs initiated in the last 50 years.'

McCann took a drink of whisky and held the glass at his wife 'What has that got to do with it?'

"Only a Matriarch may command and only fertile females may become Matriarchs, there are too few Matriarchs to crew all of the cruisers at once.'

McCann took another sip then put the tumbler onto the table 'But you only need one to command the vessel, surely you have enough Matriarchs to man all 50?'

Ilam rested her arm on the head of the sofa and stroked her husband's hair 'Each Itzpap cruiser requires a crew of 175. One hundred males, fifty females and twenty five matriarchs for every two males there must be a female and one Matriarch for each pair of females. To crew all 50 cruisers it would require twelve hundred and fifty Matriarchs.'

He took a drag of his smoke 'Are there not that many Matriarchs left?'

Ilam played with his short brown hair 'There are a few thousand left but there are many duties on Tlillan that require their presence. Deploying a cruiser to defend your planet was a risk, you should be flattered.'

He put his hand on his wife's and she asked him 'Why are you interested in Tlillan naval strength? Should the Gukumatz not be more of a concern?'

He nodded 'Yes, but even you have no idea of their strength only that in a direct assault on Tlillan they are uncertain of a victory. Therefore your capability is a good gauge of theirs, besides we may need to repel the Tlillans one day.'

She gazed lovingly at her husband 'You are afraid they will come for Malikah aren't you?' his wife could read him like a book now even without her mental powers.

McCann took another smoke and inhaled a small amount of the light sweet tobacco. 'Yup,' he said letting the smoke roll over his tongue and out of his mouth.

His petulance was adorable and Ilam smiled whilst stroking him slowly 'When it is time the Earth will be able to defend itself even from the Tlillan fleet. You must refuse to take her to Tlillan and force them to come here Duncan; once they are here we can manipulate the situation.'

He chuckled lovingly and looked into his wife's eyes.

She smiled and asked him 'What is so funny?'

'You had it planned out already didn't you?'

The beautiful Amazon stroked his chest with her other hand she ran it down slowly to his loins and pulled her innocent girl expression 'You aren't mad at me are you?' she said like a naughty girl.

He put his cigar into the ashtray and leaned forward towards Ilam. He kissed her lips then spoke softly 'You've been a very bad girl.'

She had a wide grin and reclined as her husband crawled on top of his wife embracing her and kissing passionately.

Chapter 12

Another six months passed and the warships had still not materialised, McCann was running yet another evaluation in the simulator. He sat in the Captain's chair which he'd help design, a leather armchair well-padded with a 360 degree range of movement. In front of it about two feet away lay a long, thin desk at hip height. The desk was primarily the Captain's 3D display console allowing him to communicate with the crew and observe the ship. With a 3D image of the ship and its systems rotating before him, he could quickly react to any issues. The Captain's chair was on a raised platform, only a few inches but enough to leave no doubt who sat in it. After the desk sat three stations in a similar fashion to the Gukumatz Bridge. These stations were shorter and reached waist height on McCann. To use them the operator would stand over the panel which resided at an angle, tapering away and upwards finishing at around his shoulders. The first station on his left commanded navigation and communication, the central station was power and engines with the station at the far right being weapons and shields.

Six feet beyond these stations lay a trench that resided just in front of the large flat view screen occupying the forward wall. McCann called this trench "The pit", inside sat several noncommissioned officers and lower ranks, who much like the Gukumatz warship, ran the sub systems branching from the three main stations. The pit occupied the area from the port entrance, hugging the wall as it curved to the fore view screen, running beneath that then around to the starboard entrance. McCann could see the men and women's heads and shoulders as they worked at their stations in the pit. Microphones clipped to their collars and a single ear piece allowing them to communicate with each other and hear the officers properly.

Behind McCann stood two Marines from Vympel 1, one guarding each door dressed in black combat fatigues wearing a beret and brandishing an automatic pulse rifle. The doors like the ship he'd salvaged a year ago were behind his chair and on either side of the room, the wall behind him curved outwards between the two doors. Into this wall sat three stations, two for the specific duty of monitoring and commanding the drones and a third as a general science station. Peering over the personnel operating the stations stood the recently promoted first officer, Commander Ryu Yong.

She wore her new I.S.A uniform, which all officers had been issued, with pride; a dark navy blue jacket that had a military collar with two pressure buttons. She particularly liked the style of the wide leather chest strap that covered the left chest area and became narrower as it reached over the centre zip and finished as three pressure buttons in the middle of the right chest area. The right arm had a leather zip pocket on it and the jacket hung loose around the hip area. Her combat trousers, very similar to the men of Vympel, were the same colour with one leather pocket on each thigh. On her feet were a pair of modern military combat boots, since the 9 inch ankle guard was concealed by the trousers it was difficult to distinguish them from a normal shoe at first glance. The boot was as comfortable as any custom training shoe with the added bonus it was water and shock proof. Added to that it possessed a composite toe cap, that not only protected her feet but if necessary she could kick apart bone.

All officers had a pulse pistol in a thigh holster as per the request of Commodore McCann. Her rank and insignia sat on the leather chest strap, three braided golden bands with the top band forming a circle in the middle. She also had one on the cuff of each arm. Below her rank on the chest strap sat her ribbons, awarded during the Manchurian war and its suppression afterwards. The ribbons she was most proud of were those for the liberation of Vladivostok, one awarded by her government and the other by Moscow. She was easily the most decorated officer on the bridge and sometimes McCann poked fun at her for it, since he was the only one that could.

The final feature of the bridge bulged out of the ceiling in the form of a black half dome; it was the SI housing of the "second first officer" as McCann described it. For now he didn't have an SI, since his was being installed on the warship at the Edwards. There wasn't enough time to grow two second generation SI so the Athena was to be taken out of Tharsis and installed.

Tharsis would run on the AI until a new SI could be grown and delivered. For now the simulator in Geneva used an AI simulation of Athena, the results of each session were sent to the Edwards in a data packet and she would download and study it. Titov was fortunate to be working with his SI however she was very young and educating her was an arduous task.

The soft voice of Athena announced 'Co-ordinates received Commodore McCann.'

He looked up at the housing despite the fact nothing occupied it, 'Understood, Ensign Hassif set course and Athena certify please.'

Hassif stood in front of him at the navigation station and started tapping in the co-ordinates. The view screen was split between a view of space beyond the fore section and on the right a graphical display of the warship inside a bubble. The display to the right depicted the ship and the immediate area around it from 1-100 AU depending on the magnification using an X, Y, Z axis. Athena announced calmly 'Course certified Commodore.'

McCann replied 'Engage wormhole generator.'

Next the lighting dimmed on the simulator and before the ship a swirling white hole formed. McCann pressed the touch pad on the right arm of his chair and spoke into his mic, 'Attention secure systems.'

He held onto his chair arms, those in the pit secured themselves with seat belts locking at the chest. Hassif and Ryu clutched the handles on their consoles.

'Wormhole established and stable Commodore McCann,' came Athena's soft voice over the bridge.

Hassif tapped his console 'Certified Sir.'

McCann looked at his desk console displaying a 3D image of the vessel rotating 'Engage Casimir field.'

'Casimir field active Commodore,' replied Athena.

'Certified,' confirmed Hassif.

The vessel on McCann's display was dissected into sections, each with a different colour either yellow or green. The colours changed until all were green and the entire vessel flashed in unison, 'Engage engines and enter the wormhole.'

On the view screen the white hole approached eventually obscuring the rest of space until the bridge was swallowed and everything went black. Inside the white hole generated by the vessel sat a massive black hole at the centre which Athena would navigate around, so as to avoid the ship and her crew being crushed to the size of a pinhead. Once past the singularity on the other side lay another shimmering white hole through which the vessel would be spat out, back into normal space.

The ship traversed the wormhole using a Casimir field, now McCann had the theory explained to him by Hassif. However he found himself drifting off round about the point they'd got to exotic matter and negative energy fields. Hassif decided to describe it in Layman's terms before McCann hit the drink. The Indian explained it as a force field that prevented them from being crushed inside the wormhole. It caused white holes and black holes to have the opposite effect that they'd impose on normal matter. So once the white hole was generated and the Casimir field created, the white hole would suck them in. When inside the white hole its flipside became a black hole which would now exert a push rather than a pull, propelling them towards the centre. Once the effect of the opposing black holes cancelled each other out near the centre of the wormhole the ship could navigate using engine power around the singularity. Since both black holes were repelling them they'd be held at the same distance from both as they moved to the other side of the central black hole. On the other side the ship would line up with a worm hole that had been formed at the destination. Ignite the engines at full blast, using anti-matter fuel, until they were pushed into the influence of the miniature black hole, the Casimir field would be dropped and Athena would allow the vessel to be spat out the other end. Before Hassif could explain how the wormhole was generated McCann went for a stiff drink and never asked about the science behind wormhole travel again.

Inside the wormhole all was black until they reached the other side of the singularity and McCann could see the white hole. Hassif had stated over and over that it would look nothing like that and no human would know for sure until they tried it. For the purpose of the simulation however the white hole lay before them.

'Firing engines,' came the voice of Louis from engineering.

The craft pushed forwards on the view screen and Hassif called out, 'Dropping Casimir field,' and they were sucked out.

McCann looked up 'Athena standard scan.'

She replied softly 'Yes Commodore McCann.'

According to the right of the screen they were in an alien system, 'Hassif certify co-ordinates.'

The navigation system was stolen from the Gukumatz who stole it from the Tlillans. The system used the location of X-ray pulsars throughout the galaxy to pin point their location to within one metre. It worked on the same principles as a GPS would but on a much grander scale.

'Co-ordinates certified Sir, we are at HD10180,' stated Hassif.

HD10180 had interested scientists since it was first discovered in the early 21st century. A system with 12 planets and a Saturn size planet with earth size moons inside the habitability ring. McCann tapped his armchair and announced to the crew 'Prepare stations all hands at the ready.'

Athena announced softly 'Unidentified object at co-ordinates X +84, Y +21, Z -33.'

McCann tapped the touchpad on the left arm of his chair. On the left side of the desk console before him a 3D image popped up of the object. He looked hard at what seemed to be an abandoned ship, 'Do we have anything that might be a close approximation on our database Athena?'

'Searching.'

According to the co-ordinates the object lay 84 AU away, one AU being the distance between the Earth and sun. They had exited some distance from the centre of the system. Until all Gukumatz map co-ordinates had been confirmed as 100% accurate it was not worth finding out the hard way and entering too close to any planets or stars.

He waited until Athena replied 'The vessel is a close approximation to a small civilian transport class of Gukumatz design, Commodore McCann.'

McCann had run many simulations some were just drills others tests of leadership some combat tests for the crew, in the last 9 months he'd learnt to be cautious. McCann tapped his chair arm again and spoke into his mic, 'Open all gun ports and charge the pulse cannons. Hassif move us slowly into drone range then all stop, understood?'

Hassif drummed away at his station 'Understood, Sir.'

McCann called over his shoulder to his first officer 'Ryu, prepare a squadron of drones for launch.'

'Yes Sir,' Ryu turned to her station ordering the crew in the drone bays to prepare.

The warship moved forward until after two hours they were within 1 AU of the ship then halted.

'All stop,' called out Hassif and McCann ordered Ryu to launch a squadron of drones. The new space combat drones had a delta wind design although there was a thick square fuselage where the fuel was contained. These drones used anti-matter to get about; each carried a small amount held in a magnetic field inside the drone. Even the few atoms they held in the fuselage was enough to create a massive explosion.

The wings carried smart missiles, each missile had its own self-contained AI inside the weapon which was destroyed on detonation, it was expensive but neutralised most counter measure. Ryu ordered the flight team of mostly ex-Korean drone pilots to reconnoitre what seemed to be an old wreck.

McCann asked his officer at the science station, 'Is the ship active in any sense Ensign?'

The little girl in her uniform with blond hair replied in an Italian accent 'No energy emissions of any type and no life signs detected, Sir!'

She had just been promoted from the pit and was a little over enthusiastic, it made McCann grin 'Thank you Ensign,' he replied slowly.

Ryu gave her one of those matronly looks and the young Ensign quickly turned back to her station to hide from the black stare.

After an hour or so Ryu reported that nothing had been discovered other than the vessel was indeed Gukumatz. It looked to have been abandoned and was now orbiting one of the Neptune class planets. Ryu asked him 'Should we tow it back Commodore?'

McCann nodded, 'Hassif, do you think we could throw the Casimir field around that ship too?'

Hassif turned and looked at the 3D image before McCann, 'Let me ask Louis first.'

According to Louis there was enough power to project the field around both objects if the Gukumatz vessel was close enough. McCann ordered Hassif to get the ship close enough, once in range a magnetic lasso was used to grab the smaller vehicle.

Ryu called from behind him 'We have the derelict, Sir.'

McCann was about to order Hassif to plot a course out of the system when the klaxon burst into life and a red light engulfed the bridge.

Athena announced calmly 'Damage to decks 1 to 10 fore section, lowering bulkheads to prevent decompression.'

McCann struck his chair in frustration; the derelict had exploded damaging the fore section of the cruiser. He looked at his console a few feet in front of him and the rotating image his ship displayed several red flashing sections, bunched up at the fore section where the derelict had been held. There were also many yellow flashing sections which petered out as his gaze reached the mid-section around the control tower and bridge.

He felt like such an idiot for being lured so easily, 'Can we still return home Hassif?'

Hassif was tapping furiously 'Yes the explosion caused no serious damage, just knocked out a few systems and created a minor hull breach on deck 2. It's far worse than it looks.'

McCann felt a lot better 'Nice, plot a course to a safe distance. Can we still generate a wormhole?'

Hassif nodded 'Sure, only the fore section was hit.'

McCann leaned towards Hassif, 'Then get us out of here.'

Ten minutes later they were still moving to a safe distance to open a wormhole and the klaxon went off again.

Athena once again announced in her usual soft tone 'Multiple tunnel events, co-ordinates X +4, Y +4, Z +3. Co-ordinates X +2, Y -7, Z +4. Co-ordinates ...'

McCann ignored the co-ordinates, on the right hand of the view screen he witnessed three wormholes open. The wormholes were spaced fore, aft and above, 'Hassif make a course for the Saturn class planet, flank speed!'

The warship turned to starboard as the three Gukumatz warships exited their wormholes.

The Klaxon sounded again and Athena announced 'We have been targeted by all three enemy vessels.'

McCann shouted out, 'Ready the point defence cannons!'

The officer at the weapons console tapped away 'Fore point defence cannons are only 40% operational Sir!'

They started moving towards the Saturn class planet, an ETA was counting down on the view screen, in under four minutes they would be in orbit. Athena announced "Missile fire detected" which meant they had fired the missiles about 20 minutes ago and only now were they detected; due to the speed of light and a distance of 4 AU when fired.

McCann lay back in his seat and tapped his chair, 'Brace for impact!' he then called to the weapon stations officer 'I want a starboard broadside into that Gukumatz ship now and a port broadside into this one. Make it a wide spread of about 100 degrees each side.'

McCann selected the ships on his touch pad and they flashed on the right view screen.

'Yes Sir, firing all cannons Sir.'

The cannons fired.

'Reloading Sir.'

Two minutes later the enemy missiles came into close range and the point defence cannons fired their tungsten rounds intercepting them. At such distances the point defence cannons were very effective yet the fore section took a pounding due to the prior damage.

The flipside was that the main pulse cannons were just as ineffective as the Gukumatz missiles at such distances, due to the speed of light. At 4 AU (four times the distance of the earth to the sun) it took a long time for light to travel, the wormholes had actually happened 28 minutes before they'd seen them. The warships they were firing at were there maybe 20 minutes ago and by the time the projectiles got there they would have moved.

The Gukumatz definitely had the edge since they would have identified McCann nearly half an hour before he even saw the white holes and they could be anywhere now. The only thing that made him feel a little better was the fact that they couldn't accelerate past the speed of light, so at least they couldn't arrive and fire on him before he could see them!

They were closing on the Saturn sized planet only to see a Gukumatz cruiser waiting in orbit. Fortunately Athena couldn't find the other two but that didn't mean they weren't close by.

McCann stood up 'Launch both squadrons of drones and attack that ship.'

Ryu nodded 'Understood Sir,' and she ordered her flight teams to launch.

The Gukumatz ship turned towards them, 'Gukumatz cruiser X +5, Y +6, Z -7 on intercept course Commodore McCann.'

Athena announced some more bad news 'Multiple missile launches detected Commodore McCann.'

The point defence cannons began firing in concert trying to eliminate the incoming onslaught. Next the 3D image began to flash red in different areas along the hull, 'Decks three, four and seven mid-section taking hull damage. Deck three reporting hull breach aft section. Multiple hull breaches all decks fore section, dispatching repair droids to mid and aft section, Commodore McCann.'

Hassif shouted over his shoulder 'We're still at flank speed!'

McCann scratched his chin 'Adjust course so that we pass them within 0.1 AU. Lieutenant McKinley as soon as you can I want you to put a full broadside into her.'

The weapons officer nodded 'Understood Sir.'

The two warships approached then began to pass each other. The Gukumatz took a full broadside. Drones buzzed around the enemy on their AI's targeting weapons and the eight tungsten projectiles two from each double barrel tore into the enemy hull. The sheer force sent shock waves throughout the enemy superstructure ripping the hull to shreds and pushing the entire ship into the planet.

The crew cheered at the manoeuvre and McCann had to congratulate himself with a smile until Athena chimed in again 'Enemy cruiser detected co-ordinates X +2, Y -0.3, Z +0.1, warning enemy cruiser targeting ...'

McCann waved frustrated at the housing above him 'Yes I know, Hassif plot co-ordinates for home open a wormhole now!'

Athena buzzed in again 'Opening a wormhole within one AU of a body with a gravitational ...'

McCann shouted 'Yes I know Athena! Disregard safety parameters.'

'Understood Commodore McCann.'

The lights dimmed and a white hole flashed open before the ship 'Wormhole unstable, entry inadvisable,' came Athena's warning.

Being within close proximity to such a large planet, the wormhole twisted and morphed around the edges. Hassif looked at McCann as if to ask "Are you sure?"

McCann nodded and Hassif called out 'Casimir field active, we're entering the wormhole.'

It all went black as they entered the wormhole and navigation was handed to Athena who managed to bring them home safely. Upon exiting the other side in their home system the bridge crew cheered, McCann smirked and looked at his console which showed the ship flashing red and yellow all over.

All of the stations closed down and the lights came back on 'Simulation over,' boomed Faraday's voice 'please leave the simulation area. All bridge officers please report to the briefing room in ten minutes, thank you.'

After the simulation the crew were in high spirits though McCann was certain Faraday wasn't happy. In the briefing room all the senior bridge staff waited, they still had the buzz from their victory, Faraday and Ilam both walked in together, Faraday brandishing a tablet and Ilam a smile for her husband. She always took delight when he did something outrageous in the simulator; in fact she found it rather erotic.

Faraday on the other hand was not nearly as impressed, 'So Commodore,' he said with his stiff upper class accent 'how would you assess that simulation in ten words or less?'

'A preposterously implausible victory?' grinned McCann.

Faraday clenched his teeth and through his rage answered, 'Certainly not,' the room went quiet.

Ilam jumped in before Faraday let off 'This was a simulation of a common baiting tactic used by the Gukumatz in the past. They would lure us in and pounce once the ship detonated often outnumbering the usually crippled victim. It was only because you had the fortune of the derelict detonating on your fore section that you were able to escape. Many would describe your victory as lucky, Commodore McCann!'

McCann smiled at his wife 'There's an old saying I learned from a boxing trainer, if I had the choice between being lucky or good I'd choose lucky.'

His bridge crew giggled and his arrogance caused Ilam to blush turning her eyes a glowing pink. Faraday punched his tablet with his finger and said begrudgingly 'I suppose that was technically a victory.'

The crew smiled and started congratulating each other.

Faraday looked over his tablet 'That puts your victory ratio in combat simulations up to 73%,' the crew cheered again 'and your time in space dock for repairs at 29 months!'

The cheering died down along with Faraday's temper, 'Very well you're all dismissed except you Duncan.'

After the crew had left Faraday let out a big huff, 'Hah! Duncan you've got to stop taking these risks in the simulator, people have been asking if you're the right man for the job. Take a look at Titov, he's a good Captain that plays it cautiously, he also has an excellent record.'

McCann pulled out a cigar, clipped the cap and lit it, 'Yes but what does his victory ratio look like?' McCann shook his head and groaned but Ilam's eyes turned an even deeper pink.

'61%,' said Faraday begrudgingly 'But there's a lot more to it than statistics and percentages Duncan.'

McCann took a drag of his cigar and looked Faraday in the eye, 'Look Bill when those people step on that ship for the first time I don't want them to have been beaten by your simulator before they even square up to the Gukumatz. This is about morale and team spirit, I take some risks and beat the program despite the odds and it makes them feel confident. They need to have confidence in me and each other because if they don't this whole exercise is a waste of time.'

Faraday was silent for a few moments then tapped his tablet, 'Very well Duncan, the ships will be ready within a month. You will have authority over Titov, I'm sure he won't mind but I'll be taking a lashing from Moscow over this that's for sure!'

Faraday offered his hand and McCann shook it, 'Congratulations Duncan,' said Faraday with a little glint in his eye.

'Thank you Bill.'

His wife approached him next with a loving smile 'Congratulations Duncan,' she said sweetly putting her arms around his neck and gave him a long slow kiss.

Faraday rolled his eyes, 'Must you?' he sighed.

Ilam giggled and whispered in his ear 'You go celebrate with your crew and we can celebrate properly when you get home.'

They kissed again and McCann walked to the door, turned around to smile at his wife then left the room.

Outside Ryu had been waiting for him 'So what did he say this time?'

McCann patted her back 'The Athena will be ready in a month.'

Ryu slapped her hands together 'Yes! So they're gonna call her the Athena?'

McCann took a puff as they walked along the corridor, 'She's my ship and that's what I'm naming her.'

When the pair reached the mess hall and informed the rest of the crew the cheers could be heard throughout the I.S.A building.

Later that evening at the Moulin Rouge bar the raucous rejoicing could be heard across the lake as both crews squeezed inside. Even Ilam turned up to congratulate her husband sitting with Cherkesov and Ryu.

When he saw his first officer sitting with McCann and Ryu, Titov made his way over 'It is a rare pleasure to see you all here,' said Titov who was a little intoxicated.

He sat down at the table and McCann turned to Cherkesov 'I never thought I'd see a man that could catch the Red Dragon! Tell us how did you did it?'

The table laughed though Cherkesov was embarrassed by the question, 'Once I had seen Commander Ryu I could not think of anything or anyone else.'

Ilam clapped and with a glint in his eye McCann replied 'Bloody good answer! So when are you two going to get hitched?'

Ilam shrieked 'Duncan!' and slapped the back of his head much to the amusement and laughter of everyone else.

McCann took his wife's hand and kissed it causing her eyes to change to that pink glow again 'They're perfect for each other my dear!' he prostrated.

'Besides he'd have to be mad to let her go, she's got a good stable job, doesn't drink or smoke and only eats vegetables so she won't get fat!'

Ryu smiled a little and looked at Cherkesov who held her hand.

McCann, who was also a little drunk, shouted 'Come on ask her!' then put his cigar in his mouth and began to clap slowly.

Titov followed suit speaking through his cigar encouraging the shy Cherkesov in Russian. Their ruckus grabbed the attention of both the crews, well aware of the romance, and they began to shout out 'Propose!'

Ilam looked on with glee; she was excited by the whole situation unfolding around her. Cherkesov asked her something in Korean which he'd obviously been practicing and McCann assumed was a proposal but couldn't be sure. The room went quiet and everyone stopped clapping then Ilam piped up who must have learnt the Korean language 'Say yes!' she shouted at Ryu.

Ryu who was blushing all over nodded her head 'Neh,' which he assumed meant yes in Korean.

The two of them embraced, he heard Chereksov say 'Saranghaeyo Ryu,' as everyone began to howl and cheer the engagement. The Englishman turned to his wife and her eyes had that glow of love, put his cigar down and embraced her tenderly.

The day had finally arrived to launch the first warship; the Athena had been built at a construction yard attached to the Edwards. She'd taken nearly twice the estimated time to construct but was ready now. All that was required was her crew to be there with some dignitaries to launch her. The travel time from Earth to Mars was minutes now thanks to the transport craft discovered in the salvaged vessel. They were a little cramped however, and McCann wasn't happy about sitting next to Jerry Habeeb even for the short journey.

McCann still held a grudge against Jerry and did his best to politely ignore the journalists pestering in the small transport craft. Jerry was extremely excited at what to him was secret technology, he did his best to investigate it and it's origins during the flight to the Edwards.

Once they had docked at the Edwards the travellers exited the craft into a full 1G environment, both the Edwards and Tsiolkovsky had been fitted with gravity plating. Each room had the plates fixed to the floor drawing everything in the room to them, another technology taken from the Tlillans via the Gukumatz. McCann was curious to know how they worked but his fear of Hassif melting his brains whilst explaining the science to him prevented any inquiry.

McCann, Ryu, Louis, Hassif and Jerry stepped out onto the docking bay to be greeted by the Edwards crew. The Edwards crew were mainly American since most of the funding had been generated by the Eastern states. A man about the size of McCann approached him and shook his hand, 'We're stoked to see you Commodore!'

McCann stepped back then after a moment stepped forward again and shook his hand. He found Americans to be amongst the most crass people he'd ever met. Well that wasn't true, but the hatchet job they'd done on his mother tongue was a constant irritation.

McCann managed a poor smile 'Thank you very much Captain,' he said shaking his hand.

The American began to laugh 'Heh, heh, heh call me John!' he bellowed in what McCann assumed was a southern accent then slapped the arm he was shaking.

McCann's eyes widened alarmingly, if he'd ever acted this way to a superior officer he'd have regretted it but this American just had no sense of decency. Hassif and Louis were trying not to look at each other as it would have only lead to fits of laughter.

Ryu was just as taken aback by this Captain's brazen disregard for rank, in Korea she'd have been disciplined perhaps even thrown out of the air force for such behaviour.

McCann didn't want to say anything, not because of the occasion but since the anti-matter missile detonated over the North American continent. Millions died from the initial blast and since the after effects, the death toll was in the hundreds of millions. Captain Bradley was probably more elated that these warships were about to be launched than anyone else present.

McCann shook his hand 'Thank you John,' and moved on leaving the American bemused.

After meeting the officers McCann approached Faraday and Ilam who'd arrived much earlier, he shook Faraday's hand 'Bill,' then moved on to his wife whose hand he kissed. She grew a little embarrassed and her eyes developed just a hint of pink, on Tlillan males didn't act in such a fashion. If they had they'd of been taken for re-education which was fancy talk for punishment. Males only acted on instruction, anything else was undesirable behaviour. All the time Jerry was noting down what happened feverishly, he used a tablet to record and log notes on the journey.

They were lead to their quarters where McCann stored his bag containing two more uniforms and a few personal items. Afterwards he made his way to the officer's lounge for a drink and interview with Network America. Faraday had told him off after his wedding interview, he was to play nice with Jerry this time and answer his questions.

McCann sat next to Jerry, 'Good evening Mr. Habeeb,' he said putting his glass down at Jerry's table then resting opposite him.

Jerry smiled, 'Hello Commodore McCann, it's been a long time since our last interview, how has family life been since your marriage?'

'Have we started?'

Jerry nodded.

'Well it's been better than I envisioned it to be, that's for sure.'

Jerry noted something on his tablet 'In what way has it been better Commodore?'

McCann looked upwards to collect his thoughts for a moment then looked back at Jerry, 'I don't know, I assumed it would be a nightmare of shopping for clothes broken up by arguments. Perhaps I was being too pessimistic?'

Jerry pushed out a huff 'Pah, you've just described a lot of marriages there Commodore and those are the happy ones!'

McCann grinned and Jerry went on 'Your daughter Malikah, who may I add is a lovely child, has been maturing at a shocking rate. Is it normal for Tlillan children to develop at this rate and if so when does it slow down?'

McCann fixed his gaze on Jerry, 'For Tlillan children her rate of development is within norms. I've been told the development will slow to a normal pace within the coming year.'

Jerry tapped his tablet and McCann took a sip of his ginger ale, 'Do you have any idea how such rapid development came about in the Tlillan race?'

He put his glass down, 'From what my wife has told me the Tlillans were heavily researching genetic manipulation. The rapid development was a result, before the science was banned throughout the Tlillan commonwealth.'

Jerry noted something down then carried on 'It has been reported that we are genetically closer to Tlillans than even Chimpanzees, how is this so?'

McCann smiled knowingly 'We are the result of one of those said experiments, an attempt to breed the different races on Tlillan.'

Jerry tapped his tablet again, 'Onto the spaceship being launched tomorrow, what will she be named?'

McCann raised his glass to Jerry 'The Athena,' then took a sip.

Jerry tapped away 'That seems like an odd name Commodore, any reason?'

'Well she's the Goddess of wisdom and strategy in battle Jerry, and of course Athena has been removed from Tharsis and placed inside the neural housing.'

Jerry scribbled away on his tablet 'So the ship will have an SI onboard?'

'Yes.'

'Will the other ship be fitted with one?'

McCann nodded and went for his drink again, 'They're a standard feature of both, Athena will be another bridge officer.'

Jerry wrote something down 'One last question Commodore, can you reveal where the technology came from to allow the construction of what I've seen on coming here?'

McCann smiled 'I'm sorry Jerry, you'll have to ask Faraday if you want an answer to that.'

Jerry stood up 'Well thank you very much Commodore McCann.'

McCann shook his hand and quickly walked away to the bar.

At the bar he joined his wife and Faraday, 'Did it all go smoothly this time Duncan?' asked his boss.

McCann replied slowly 'Naturally.'

His wife was fawning over him putting him ill at ease due to the prying eyes all around, especially those of Jerry. She sensed his discomfort and retreated, Ilam sensed his thoughts thanking her discretion. Since they'd been together for so long a bond had formed and to some degree McCann could send and receive basic emotions to his wife. Or to be more accurate she could interpret his emotional state better than any other human, due to the intimate nature of their relationship.

Faraday found it all rather tiresome, first McCann and now Ryu going all "lovey dovey" on him when there was serious work to be done, though he saw McCann's relationship as necessary to the development of the I.S.A so he tolerated them, despite his opinion. He wasn't so forgiving on Ryu's fiancée Cherkesov, he was Russian for a start and his ultimate allegiance lay with Titov and Moscow. Perhaps Ryu might help reign in the Russians to some degree since Faraday did not believe anyone or thing could turn the ice woman against her own.

The senior officers took turns being interviewed, Louis as usual complained that he was hidden away in the engine room and power core at the rear of the ship. Louis was certain that Faraday had done it deliberately, as usual Louis' massive ego had allowed him to assume the warship had been design around his discomfort. It wasn't true but nevertheless he indulged himself in his conspiracy fantasy that Faraday had banished him to a dark room close to the power core. From there he operated the nanites and supervised the anti-matter flow when the engines became active. The power core was close to the engines as the less distance the anti-matter had to travel then the lower the chance of a catastrophe. Despite this logic Louis was unperturbed in his belief there was a conspiracy afoot and he let Jerry know about it, despite the fact that Jerry was obviously uninterested.

Ilam bent down and whispered in her husband's ear 'You look very handsome in that uniform you know?'

McCann frowned at her but she only smiled, he scanned the room to see a few perplexed looks falling on them.

'Thank you, did I tell you that you look stunning in yours?' replied the Englishman.

Ilam was also dressed in the same uniform but without any insignia of rank, it was only adorned with a small brass olive branch on the left chest area.

She grabbed his hand 'Yes you did but you're welcome to mention it again.'

'You look wonderful.'

Faraday rolled his eyes 'Please you two, the bloody press are watching, just try to use a little restraint will you?'

McCann grinned and reached across his wife standing at the bar and tapped Faraday 'You really should get married James, I'm sure there are a few women on Tlillan that could tame you!'

A ripple of laughter came from the bar but Faraday wasn't amused 'You're getting more like that horses arse Beaumont every day, you know that Duncan?'

McCann stopped grinning and replied in a sober tone 'I take this assignment with the utmost seriousness Bill, don't concern yourself with that.'

As the evening drew on the skeleton crew which had been shipped to the Edwards retired to their rooms. The next day they were up bright and early, the crew had breakfast and was led to a docking arm. From here they walked off the Edwards holding onto rails as they entered zero gravity, returning to normal gravity as they entered the Athena. The short walk was similar to boarding an airplane one hundred years ago, only this was a 200 metre long space cruiser. McCann put his foot inside and felt the pull onto the gravity plating.

Once inside the familiar sound of Athena greeted him 'Hello Duncan.'

He made a wide smile and looked upwards 'Hello Athena, how are you?'

She replied softly 'Very well and congratulations on your command.'

He thanked her then asked 'Which way is it to the bridge Athena?'

He heard a noise and looked down at his wrist tablet. There was a map pointing the way on the tablet's display, 'Thank you Athena,' he said in pleasantly surprised manner.

'You're welcome Duncan,' replied Athena.

He made his way through the ship; McCann was pleased with the glow of the cream coloured interior since it reminded him of Tharsis. The colour, like Tharsis, was there to prevent depression.

While llam was touring the ship with Faraday and Jerry Habeeb the lighting was switched from UV to synthetic due to her sensitivity. She still had problems on Earth to this day, despite lotions to block the rays, some part of her often became exposed and irritable. Darksiders weren't built to live in these environments. During night time she had vision that would rival any nocturnal animal on Earth, but she was required to change her lifestyle around that of humans.

McCann found his way to the bridge and sat at his chair. As the crew settled in Athena had the droids bring on their personal possessions and drop them off at the relevant quarters. After 30 minutes the pit was bustling with activity and his first officer had finally arrived along with Hassif. They both asked for permission to enter the bridge which McCann believed was unnecessary considering they were his friends. However he couldn't set a poor example to the others and gave them permission, the bridge was an exact replica of the simulator at Geneva. Louis however managed to complain about his engine room noting that Faraday had changed it, implying that it was merely part of the big conspiracy versus Louis Beaumont. McCann ignored his whinging and muted his communications; it took an hour or more for the skeleton crew to settle in and their baggage to be delivered.

Faraday, Ilam and Jerry arrived on the bridge causing the officers including McCann to stand to attention. Faraday put them at ease and lead the reporter around, Jerry wasn't allowed to film inside the Athena but he was speaking into his tablet describing the scene. Ilam was smiling at her husband whilst walking behind Jerry and Faraday, McCann pretended not to notice whilst he was on duty.

Jerry peered down 'What's this?' he asked out loud.

McCann stood up, 'That's the pit. The junior officers work here, right now they're running the Athena through a full systems analysis before we launch.'

Jerry strode over to him 'Why not have the SI do it? Surely she's faster and better?'

He nodded at Jerry 'Yes you're correct but all systems and orders have to be independently certified before they can be engaged.'

Jerry moved over to the three command stations 'And what do these do Commodore?'

McCann looked towards Faraday who slowly shook his head. McCann turned back to Jerry and replied 'Those are command terminals but I'm afraid I can't be specific as to their purpose.'

Jerry nodded then moved to the Captain's chair 'This is where you sit Commodore?'

McCann stepped over 'Yes it is.'

'Is there anything you can tell me about it?'

'Other than that it's very comfortable, no.'

Next Jerry strode behind the chair to Ryu who was monitoring her stations 'Commander Ryu, what can you tell me about these terminals?'

She looked to Faraday, who again shook his head, then back to Jerry and answered 'I'm sorry that is confidential Mr. Habeeb.'

Jerry was a little frustrated but he understood, then he blurted out to Ryu 'There has been rumour that you and Commander Cherkesov have been involved … intimately, would you like to confirm or deny that Commander Ryu?'

Ryu's eyes widened 'No I would not, thank you Mr. Habeeb!'

McCann approached Jerry from behind and tapped his shoulder. Jerry turned around to see McCann glaring down at him 'That will be enough of that, understood?'

Jerry swallowed and returned to Faraday 'Can I speak to Athena?'

'Certainly, Athena say hello to Mr. Habeeb,' called Faraday to the black dome hanging from the ceiling.

Jerry followed his line of sight to the dome and a soft voice fell over the bridge like a warm blanket 'Good day Mr. Habeeb, how are you?'

Jerry started smiling 'Hello Athena, I bet you have a few stories to tell me?'

Her soft voice echoed back 'I'm afraid not Mr. Habeeb, I find your journalism far too sensationalist.'

Jerry frowned as sniggers could be heard from the pit, 'What's that supposed to mean?'

Athena's calm voice replied 'You focus on aspects not of factual significance but most likely to titillate viewers. I find your news programme to be of little use to those whom desire to be informed.'

Hassif was now laughing but the other senior officers kept a straight face.

Jerry looked up at the neural housing incredulously 'You know that my show is the most watched news programme on the planet EARTH?' he called up to Athena.

She replied to him with her ever calm tone 'Yes Mr. Habeeb.'

Jerry called back 'And do you know why that is?'

Athena then replied bluntly to howls of laughter 'Because your programme appeals to the lowest common denominator, Mr. Habeeb.'

Faraday quickly accosted Jerry 'I think we've seen enough of the bridge, let's move on to the recreational areas.'

Faraday ushered Jerry from the bridge all the time glaring at Hassif as if to blame him for Athena's new found attitude. Ilam followed silently behind, she'd been admiring her husband in his uniform all the time.

As the door closed Ryu whispered in McCann's ear 'Even a blind man can tell what she's thinking.'

McCann frowned at Ryu 'Don't be so crass!'

He retired to his seat and ordered the pit back to work, an hour later Louis was on the comms again complaining about Jerry Habeeb. His language was unsuitable for someone of his position and it certainly shouldn't have been coming over the bridge communications. Louis however, was Louis and if you wanted the best chief engineer you had to put up with an attitude and sense of self entitlement to rival even a Tlillan. He produced good results and McCann wouldn't have felt comfortable commanding the Athena without him.

The advantage of Louis' bad attitude was that he was suspicious of everyone and never showed favouritism towards any of his staff. In fact they had learned to hate his guts just the same as most of the people that had worked alongside him, but he was fair; he treated everyone with equal suspicion and disdain.

Finally Louis reported he was ready 'Duncan, the core, containment and engines have been certified.'

McCann pressed the touchpad on his chair arm 'Thank you CHIEF!'

All he could hear was Louis laughing as he switched the communicator off. McCann decided to allow him his small pleasures he'd much rather have a happy chief engineer.

Soon the pit was ready and had certified all of Athena's prior results. They were only waiting for Faraday to join. Once he had, carrying a bottle of champagne, the view screen was switched on. All that could be seen was darkness, 'Remove the canopy,' ordered Faraday into his wrist tablet.

A minute later McCann could see a ray of light illuminating the inside then a line of light at the top of the view screen. Soon he saw a metallic sheet rolling forward and as it did it lit up the fore of the Athena, the jet black armour absorbed light as it was revealed. The sheet eventually fell off the end of the Athena exposing 200 metres of warship attached to the Edwards by four docking clamps, two at each end.

Faraday spoke into his wrist tablet 'Are we ready?'

He cleared his throat and Jerry put his tablet close to Faraday's mouth, 'I name this ship I.S.S Athena, good fortune to her and all who sail in her.'

He then took the champagne and smashed it on the desk console before McCann's station. Ilam was a little puzzled when Faraday destroyed the bottle. Next McCann saw the Edwards drift out of the screen to the left as the Athena had been released and pushed off gently.

Ten minutes later the Athena had safely cleared the Edwards and it was time to move out of Martian orbit. McCann looked at his desk display, the rotating image of the Athena was all green, 'Hassif, set a course for Jupiter orbit.'

Hassif tapped away 'Done.'

McCann looked upwards 'Athena certify course please.'

A few seconds later she replied 'Course certified Commodore.'

McCann sat back and called behind him 'Commander Ryu, leave orbit at 10% speed then half speed to the planet please.'

Ryu called out from behind him 'Yes Sir,' the Athena began to slowly turn then Ryu called out, 'Firing engines.'

McCann was thrown back into his seat as they pushed out of orbit at just 10% speed, although it was about 5% the speed of light, in the simulator these effects were never replicated. Hassif stumbled back along with Jerry and Faraday, Ilam however was unaffected. McCann looked on with a smirk as Jerry picked himself up off the floor drenched in Champagne. Hassif and Faraday had avoided hitting the ground along with the other two officers at the three forward stations. The mine field had been deactivated for the launch of the Athena so the ride was smooth to Jupiter, aside from the acceleration and deceleration.

Upon making orbit of Jupiter McCann called out "Open gun ports and charge the pulse cannons."

Jerry scooted up to McCann 'What is this ship capable of Commodore?'

Again Faraday shook his head, 'I can't reveal that,' replied McCann.

Lieutenant McKinley then reported 'Starboard cannons ready Sir.'

McCann replied 'Fire.'

Next a dull thump reverberated around the Athena and McCann felt a slight jot in the opposite direction to which the cannons were firing.

'Turn one hundred and eighty degrees on X axis and fire a port broadside into the planet Commander Ryu.'

He sat back as Ryu commanded the Athena and tested the port cannons, after a successful test fire he took the Athena out of orbit and had a fly around the solar system. It was hard to believe they were actually there rather than in the simulator, but the bumps and shifts in mass kept reminding them. Soon Louis learned to control the anti-matter explosion so that the acceleration of mass was much more gradual rather than a sudden jerk. Eventually they made for Earth where Faraday, Ilam and Jerry Habeeb were dropped off at the Tsiolkovsky and the rest of the ship's crew came onboard.

The next week saw the unveiling of Athena's sister ship the Ares, Moscow had insisted that their ship was to be named Ares. Hassif joked that the SI might have an identity crisis since they were always female. McCann thought nothing of it since all ships were feminine no matter the name, his worry was that the SI was very inexperienced compared to Athena. The two SI were able to link thanks to the neural housing and some technology passed on by Ilam, Athena could impart her knowledge to her sister.

The two vessels spent their first month patrolling the solar system, after that month was up it was decided to test the wormhole generator. The system of Alpha Centauri had been selected for a first short jump; the Athena passed out of the solar system and came to a halt.

McCann spoke to Hassif, 'Set course for Alpha Centauri.'

Hassif tapped away at his station 'Course set.'

McCann looked up 'Athena certify.'

A few seconds later she replied 'Course certified Commodore.'

He sat back in his chair and announced to the crew 'Prepare to fold space.'

Everyone in the pit strapped themselves in, the senior officers held onto their stations since no one knew what was coming.

Hassif called over his shoulder 'Wormhole generator set and charged,' whilst gripping the handles on each side of his terminal.

'Engage generator,' said McCann slowly.

The lighting dropped very low and the ship began to vibrate from the aft to the fore, a burst of white appeared on the view screen almost blinding McCann. The force of the white hole began to push the vibrating Athena away slowly.

'Wormhole stabilized Commodore,' came the soft voice of Athena.

McCann looked at Hassif until he turned to face him and called out over the noise of the vibration 'Certified!'

McCann called out 'Lieutenant McKinley engage Casimir field!'

The Lieutenant at the weapons and shields console tapped his terminal then called out 'Ready Sir!'

Suddenly the Athena stopped moving backwards and was gently being drawn into the white hole, 'Take us in at one third speed,' called McCann over the din.

Ryu directed the bridge officers to take the Athena into the swirling abyss before them, as they approached they were sucked in faster and faster. They passed the event horizon into a new universe, light was streaking past them so fast they could only see it after it had passed. Streaks of images shot past, not objects but the very images of them had been torn away by the power of this natural phenomenon.

McCann called out 'Handing over to Athena!' and tapped his chair arm.

As they moved away from their point of entry which was now a tiny black hole (the flipside of a white hole) the images slowed down until he could make out what they were. McCann could see images of other galaxies, suns, planets and spacecraft swirling around racing to get out via the worm hole. None of this made sense to him, the light, the very images were trapped inside here and they were releasing them 'Perhaps that is why a white hole is white?' he mumbled to himself.

Within a short time the images were at a slow crawl and the Athena was travelling through them, what seemed to be the souls of heavenly bodies were trapped in this now dark chamber.

Hassif shouted at the top of his lungs 'We're close to the event horizon of the black hole; this is no man's land where the tug is equal between the black hole and wormhole!'

On one side McCann could see the souls of the dead being slowly dragged away to be spat out, on the other they were being slowly sucked in to Tartarus to their doom in a crushing singularity. The Athena seemed to be travelling the river Styx to the other side. McCann was terrified since he had no control and watched on in dread at the souls of other ships. Wondering if those were just images or was that really another Captain looking back at him screaming out an SOS from hell? Once on the other side Athena aligned herself with the tiny black hole that formed one end of the wormhole, despite the fact it was impossible to see it she knew where it would be. Athena fired the engines at full blast then dropped the Casimir field; she was sucked off into the torrents of souls screaming to get out. The ride was quite rough and McCann was visibly sweating, at last as the souls intensified she was spat out into normal space.

McCann sat up 'Shut down wormhole generator and Athena certify our co-ordinates.'

The vibration petered out and the lights returned to full strength. McCann looked at the view screen to see two stars shining back 'Well are we here?' he asked impatiently.

Athena replied calmly 'We have arrived at our intended destination Alpha Centauri AB.'

McCann looked upwards 'Scan the system Athena, let me know when you've finished.'

Hassif, who was very excited, turned to McCann 'There are planets around Alpha B; we are going to investigate aren't we?'

McCann shook his head 'No, we're going to test the communication equipment then leave. That is your next job by the way, I want you to try and get a link with Faraday.'

Hassif was disappointed but turned back and began his work, using micro wormholes he was going to communicate with Faraday. It was possible to communicate anywhere without time lag as long as the two parties communicating formed the other end of the micro wormhole at a designated point. The I.S.A had constructed a relay station in space that remained stationary; Hassif formed a micro wormhole and hailed anyone listening.

A moment later Faraday could be heard 'Hello is that you Duncan?'

A feeling of relief came over McCann 'Yes Sir, we're here at Alpha Centauri safe and sound.'

He heard celebration in the background, Hassif did some more work on his terminal and a picture of Faraday at Geneva came onto the view screen. It was rare to see Faraday with a wide smile but he was overjoyed, 'How was the journey Duncan?'

McCann raised his eyebrows 'A damn sight more interesting than the simulator, it only took about 2 minutes to travel over 4 light years.'

Faraday frowned a little 'You were gone for more than an hour Duncan.'

He then remembered the laws of relativity and what seemed as only a minute to the crew of the Athena was in fact more than an hour in the real universe.

McCann chuckled nervously at his faux pas, 'I'm sorry I'll have to listen to Hassif more often, nevertheless we're completing a scan of the system and will return when finished.'

Faraday smiled again 'I didn't mean to snap Duncan, well done and well done to your crew I hope to see you all back soon, goodbye.'

The image of Faraday disappeared from the view screen and back came the view of Alpha Centauri and its binary suns. It was quite a thing to behold and the bridge crew were in awe for a moment before getting back to work. The two suns locked in orbit of each other was a titanic spectacle and McCann found it hard to believe there could be planets orbiting one of them let alone life surviving in that orbital oven.

After the scan was finished they plotted a return course, the journey through the wormhole was as rough as before. The ghostly images of craft that had passed through millennia ago littered either side of the river Styx, the name he now gave to the dead zone between the worm holes on each side of the massive black hole in the centre. McCann squinted at the images in the chance he might see the crew crying for help, a cry from the long dead past. Once out of the wormhole the Athena was ejected a distance from the solar system and took a couple of hours at half speed to reach Earth orbit. The information pertaining to the journey to Alpha Centauri and back was downloaded to the Tsiolkovsky to be mulled over before Titov attempted a similar trip. In two weeks time the Ares was sent out on her first voyage and returned successfully, no doubt thanks to Athena's tutelage.

The Alpha Centauri system had now been mapped and although there were planets none held liquid water, but were barren rocky surfaces scorched by heat. The exploration of star systems was handed over to probes so that the Athena and Ares could carry out their primary duties of patrolling the solar system and protecting Earth from any possible Gukumatz threat.

Months passed and both the Athena and Ares were certified as space worthy, the vessels' first duties were clearing the minefields in the solar system. Earth and Mars were still protected by orbital platforms and the subs had been decommissioned.

McCann was resting in the officer's lounge having a cigar and chatting with Louis, his chief engineer was complaining about whatever took his fancy as usual. The lounge was similar to Tharsis in that it was a soft creamy colour with long brown leather sofas on all walls but one, which was where the bar stood. The bar was self-service, glasses selected from a transparent cabinet, you requested your drink and it was dispensed into your glass much the same as any drinks dispenser. Louis had a tall slim glass which contained a dark amber ale. McCann held a shot glass which contained a drinkable whisky. His tastes were rather rich compared to what was on offer in the lounge but it was all free and he had his own smokes.

Louis was bemoaning the fact that they'd been stuck on the Athena for months now, without shore leave. McCann found it amusing watching him moan about it, 'What are you laughing at?' cried Louis.

A few heads turned but most were used to Louis being the only person who dared speak to the Commodore in that manner, 'I just find it amusing to see you so frustrated.'

Louis sneered 'Bah! You weren't even listening to me!'

McCann took a sip from his shot glass 'True but I can tell by now when my Chief is in need of a good shag!'

McCann smiled at Louis who turned away to look across the room 'I don't know what you're talking about!'

McCann took a drag of his Ramon Allones and smiled 'Working deep down in the bowels of the ship with young men, sending them to and fro along the back passages?'

Louis snapped his head back to McCann 'You're really funny you know that?' he sneered.

McCann laughed as he balanced his cigar on the side of the ashtray 'Are you telling me it isn't true?'

Louis leaned over and under his breath hissed 'Keep your damn voice down McCann!'

McCann relaxed into his seat smiling at his chief engineer.

Although he was making fun of Louis he had been missing his wife, he was up for two weeks of leave soon and it was all he could think of. He hadn't seen even a picture of his daughter in months and it rested heavily on him. The ship's duties had consisted of supervising the deactivation of the minefield. It was a long slow and tedious process, which caused McCann to often wonder why Faraday bothered with the simulations in Geneva. Nothing much seemed to happen from day to day; only a drink and smoke in the officer's lounge got him through. He could smell the cheap cigarettes of Nestor who was standing at the bar chatting away to one of his more attractive officers. McCann felt sorry for Nestor more than anyone else, his duties amounted to patrolling the Athena and rotating guard duty for his Vympel 1&2 units stationed on the cruiser.

The Englishman dreamed of exploration after the visit almost six months ago to Alpha Centauri but he knew that it wasn't on the cards. Faraday was already manufacturing automated probes to take on that task and serve as galactic listening posts. Whatever Faraday had in store for the Athena and her crew he was keeping close to his chest. For now it was merely patrol after patrol with some mine sweeping tagged on.

As he sat enjoying his cigar and trying to enjoy the whisky McCann's attention was drawn to his wrist tablet 'What now!' he muttered to himself.

He tapped the screen and the voice of Ryu came out at him 'Commodore I have a small vessel requesting to dock with the Athena.'

He looked at Louis who only shrugged his shoulders and went back to his ale 'Confirm with Faraday first Commander.'

There was an uncomfortable pause 'I have Commodore; I thought I should inform you that your wife and daughter are onboard.'

McCann leapt up knocking his drink over 'Which bay will they be docking in?'

Ryu replied quickly 'Two.'

'Thank you Ryu,' he said as he marched out of the door.

Upon reaching the docking bay Nestor and a squad of 4 men were already waiting, McCann peered through the airlock porthole and into the bay. The small delta wing transport had landed in the bay and the outer doors closed. Ten minutes later his wife and daughter exited the vehicle with Faraday and Dr Pitt. Nestor and his men were standing to attention with backs to the wall as the porthole opened. Malikah ran straight around the corner and into her father's arms as if she knew he was there.

At first he didn't recognise his daughter; her hair was now jet black much like his Mother's, 'What have you done with your hair Malikah?' he asked.

His daughter had grown into a young teenage girl since he was away but she still hung on every word her father uttered.

She frowned at him 'You don't like it?'

'No, I'm just curious as to why you changed your hair colour?'

Ilam walked out of the airlock next 'Her hair changed on its own accord, Commodore.'

The tall beauty smiled and embraced her husband who was rather uncomfortable allowing the men to see such a display of affection. Malikah giggled until Ilam released her husband, Faraday and Pitt entered the corridor next.

McCann shook both of their hands 'So to what do we owe this pleasure, Bill?' Faraday pointed down the corridor 'In your cabin if you don't mind Duncan.'

They took a stroll through the ship escorted by Nestor and his men until they reached the Captain's cabin just beneath the bridge.

Nestor and his men stood guard outside whilst the others entered the cabin 'Now that we're alone we came to deliver some important news,' announced Faraday.

McCann sat on his desk playing with his daughter 'Too important to transmit?'

Faraday nodded 'Yes, a Tlillan warship will be entering this system soon.'

McCann looked up from his daughter and at Faraday then his wife, 'For what purpose?'

Faraday looked down at Malikah and it was all clear.

McCann clutched tightly onto his daughter.

'Don't be concerned father, they can't hurt me,' she said sweetly kissing his hand.

McCann wasn't convinced 'What do they want?' he asked solemnly.

'They wish to put Malikah to the trial,' replied Ilam.

McCann gripped his daughter tighter 'Well you can tell them to stay home.'

Faraday shook his head 'I'm sorry Duncan but that just won't do, they're coming, come hell or high water. They wanted your daughter brought to Tlillan but we refused, this is the best I could do. You will be able to control the proceedings and if at any time you fear for Malikah you can put an end to it, is that a deal?'

He looked at his wife, who gestured he should accept, then he looked at his daughter who pleaded 'Please let me do it father!'

He loosened his grip 'Fine, but if I think you're in trouble I'll put a stop to it alright?'

Malikah kissed her father.

His wife was dressed in her white uniform, his daughter was dressed in one of the black ribbed space suits. Her dark curly hair reminded him of his mother but she was maturing at about 5 times that of a normal human female.

He looked upwards and called to Athena 'Athena, have all members of the crew wearing their neural bands until notified otherwise.'

Her soft voice replied 'Understood Commodore.'

The order was repeated throughout the ship to all personnel and McCann checked his pistol, 'So when do they arrive?'

Ilam smiled 'Soon but none of that will be necessary Duncan.'

He placed his weapon back in the holster 'Good.'

He next called in Nestor 'Could you please show our guests to quarters.'

The grizzly Russian replied 'Da,' and led them all away.

McCann watched in wonder as his daughter spoke to Nestor in fluent Russian whilst they were escorted to their rooms.

Some hours later the klaxon went off.

McCann made his way to the bridge, he could hear Athena alerting her crew 'Tunnel event! Tunnel event! Tunnel event!'

Upon reaching the bridge Ryu had everything in hand. A Tlillan warship had exited the white hole and was moving towards Earth orbit. Ryu stood up from the Captain's chair 'Unidentified warship of Tlillan design on an intercept course with Earth orbit Commodore.'

McCann sat down 'Everyone make certain your neural bands are operational,' he looked at Hassif 'Transmit a message to them, tell them we have Ilamachutli and Malikah onboard.'

Hassif started punching away at his station, 'Message sent.'

Ilam, Malikah, Faraday and Pitt walked onto the bridge. Everyone was wearing their neural bands but Ilam and Malikah, his daughter didn't seem concerned at all though Ilam was very jumpy.

The main view screen flickered and an image of an old hag glared back, McCann could almost feel her looking inside him. She was thin and wrinkled dressed in one of those skin tight Tlillan suits. McCann assumed she held a rank of some significance due to her white feathered headdress and cape that flowed from it.

Ilam and Malikah both bowed their heads before the image but McCann felt no such awe, 'I'm Commodore McCann of the I.S.S Athena, may I know whom I'm speaking to?'

The old woman on the Tlillan ship did not answer his request 'Ilam rise,' translated the communications AI in an androgynous tone. His wife looked up towards the view screen 'Educate the male,' spoke the communication AI.

Ilam approached her husband 'The Grand Matriarch will not speak to you Duncan.'

McCann wasn't pleased but spoke to his wife 'Fine, what does the old hag want?'

The Matriarch's eyes began to turn red around her tiny pinpoint pupils, McCann smirked 'So she is listening to me!'

Faraday then whispered into his ear from behind 'This isn't a game Duncan!'

The Englishman replied so that everyone including the Matriarch heard, 'Oh no Bill, this is all a game!'

Again the Matriarch addressed Ilam 'Can you not control your male Ilam?'

McCann smirked and looked at his wife 'Well? Can't you control me?'

She didn't answer him but he heard his daughter chuckling, 'Malikah come here,' he called and she ran over and stood next to her father taking the place of her mother. He put an arm around his daughter and said playfully 'Now you ask lady Havisham what she wants.'

His daughter started laughing, much to the confusion of the Matriarch, and then she spoke in fluent Tlillan.

The Matriarch replied 'I desire your presence.'

'Tell her if she desires your presence she'll have to come here.'

Malikah looked at her father with a frown 'But father!'

McCann replied sternly 'Malikah, just do it,' and his daughter complied.

After a short debate which consisted of the Matriarch refusing to board the Athena and McCann advising her to go home an agreement was finally hammered out. The Matriarch agreed to hold the trial on the Athena, McCann was very pleased with himself however his wife and Faraday were not so impressed.

They awaited the Matriarch at a separate airlock, once she had left the Tlillan transport McCann was quite shocked at how mobile she was. She stepped off the craft wearing her headdress of feathers. The cape was crafted from what seemed to be many squares of jade touched the floor. Although he couldn't see, McCann was certain she was wearing a standard Tlillan suit beneath. She had her own escort of males with her, six men all about four to five feet, he wasn't sure if they were for protection or comfort but it didn't matter. There were three other tall females of varying age adorned with smaller headdresses 'Who are they?' he asked his daughter.

Malikah replied excitedly 'Matriarchs, come to judge me,' she didn't seem at all concerned by the events unfolding before her.

As they approached the airlock McCann made sure his ear piece was working so that he could understand what was being said. The door swung open and the males marched out, next came the three Matriarchs then the Grand Matriarch.

The first action she made was to take a close look at Malikah, 'This is the half breed?' came the voice of the AI over McCann's ear piece as the Grand Matriarch spoke.

Dr Pitt grabbed McCann's arm from behind before he did something silly, 'This is my daughter Malikachutli,' replied Ilam.

The Matriarch looked at Ilam and cackled very loud 'She wishes to join her mother's clan?'

Malikah spoke up 'It is my birthright!'

The old woman cackled again and even the other three sniggered at her statement 'It is a privilege my child, there are no rights on Tlillan … only privileges!'

Ilam began to escort the party to the cargo bay, all the way the Grand Matriarch questioned Ilam concerning Malikah until they finally reached the cargo bay. Once outside the old woman declared no males were allowed inside to witness the trial. McCann however was adamant he was going in and if they didn't allow him they could go home.

The Grand Matriarch looked at McCann and for the first time spoke to him 'Very well, you must leave that outside,' she said pointing to his neural band.

He took it off and handed it to Faraday, then after the Grand Matriarch and her three judges he entered with his wife and daughter. The cargo bay was very roomy, since they had been in space for 6 months most of the cargo had been cleared already. The remaining crates were shifted to the walls leaving a large area the size of a football pitch to conduct the trial in.

The Grand Matriarch approached Malikah who was held tightly by her father, 'Can you link child?'

Malikah nodded.

'Then link with me,' spoke the Matriarch, but after thirty seconds she exclaimed to Ilam 'The child refuses to link with me!'

One of the lesser Matriarchs spoke 'Perhaps she is not capable after all?'

The old woman replied 'No, she can block my attempts. She is merely impetuous, as her father.'

Ilam looked over to her husband for help 'Duncan?'

He looked down at his daughter 'Why don't you link for her Malikah?'

From what he could tell she complied and the Matriarch spent some time communing with his daughter.

Eventually the Matriarch broke the link, 'Excellent, the Mictlancihuatl has complete control.'

The Grand Matriarch then ordered one of her subordinates forward, 'Demonstrate your power child.'

The lesser Matriarch stepped in front of Malikah and her eyes turned a dark red.

'What's happening?' shouted McCann.

Ilam ran to his side 'They won't harm her; her ability to repel an assault is being tested.'

After several minutes the lesser Matriarch gave up.

'Very good Malikah,' congratulated the Grand Matriarch who by now had a smile 'you have persevered longer than any other Mictlancihuatl before you, but do you have the power of a Mictlancihuatl?'

The old woman glared straight at McCann, her eyes turned a deep wine red and he felt a crushing pain in his head. The sharp pain emanated from inside, he couldn't reach for his weapon. His arm refused to respond, like the rest of his body it was frozen. McCann dropped to his knees, Ilam screeched but Malikah remained calm glaring back at the Grand Matriarch.

Malikah's eyes turned a jet black and the wrinkled hag let out a scream of pain before collapsing to the floor. The three Matriarchs ran to her aid, but she was unconscious.

Malikah was still staring at her with blackened eyes until McCann regained his ability to move properly. The lesser Matriarchs cowered over their leader whilst Malikah glared on the stricken witch.

Ilam was too afraid to intervene so her father did; 'Malikah?' called out McCann.

His daughter didn't seem to hear him the first time so he put his hand on her back 'Malikah? Are you alright?'

His daughter turned towards him, once she observed her father was unharmed her eyes returned to normal and she grasped him in a loving embrace.

He hugged his daughter then observed the Grand Matriarch being peeled off the floor by her aides 'Is lady Havisham going to be alright?'

Malikah sneered 'She will be fine Father; she just has a few bumps and bruises.'

Eventually the Grand Matriarch recovered, laying on the floor propped up by her aides she gazed at Malikah, 'You are unique child, a half breed with self-control. My only regret is her lack of guidance from the Mother. You would do harm to your Matriarch in defence of a male?'

Malikah didn't answer but Ilam replied 'She has always been disobedient to all but her father.'

The witch was helped to her feet by her aides including Ilam 'It was your responsibility to educate her!' snapped the old woman.

Ilam lowered her head 'From an early age she blocked me, the only person she would link with was her father.'

The Matriarchs were shocked, 'A male?' bellowed the Grand Matriarch to which Ilam nodded whilst looking at the ground. The old woman fixed her gaze upon Malikah 'Tell me child, why did you link with your father and not your mother?'

'My mother was always testing me and making me learn new things. My father's memories are fun, mostly.'

The Grand Matriarch stood up and walked over to Malikah, 'Very well child you may use the clan name Chutli. The next time we meet shall be on Tlillan, unless the madness takes you.'

One of the lesser Matriarchs approached Malikah and placed a pendant in her hand. A gold chain with what looked to be a single tear drop ruby.

Malikah was ecstatic and the Matriarch smiled 'Well done young lady, you are now Malikachutli.'

Malikah accepted the pendant with thanks as the Matriarch whispered into her ear 'Listen to your mother child.'

On the way to the cargo bay exit the witch gave McCann a particularly grim look. Ilam was as delighted concerning the pendant as was Malikah. The Englishman paid little mind to it, McCann was only thankful his daughter was unharmed by the wicked witch.

Walking back to the airlock Faraday was trying his best to get something out of the visitors but to no avail. They had only come to test Malikah and now were leaving. The Grand Matriarch managed a few digs at the Athena pointing out the backward technology whenever possible. McCann scoffed at her criticisms, he was certain that the Athena could disintegrate a Tlillan warship; as the thought passed through his mind the Grand Matriarch stopped in her tracks. In the middle of the corridor she turned around to face McCann but rather than berating him she smiled, before continuing down the hall. She then spoke to Ilam 'I understand the attraction Ilam; he is quite rebellious isn't he?'

Nestor and his men were ignoring the conversation and Faraday didn't care, Dr Pitt winked at McCann cheekily as they walked to the airlock. No one said anything and McCann just bore it until they reached the airlock and saw the visitors off. The Matriarchs entered the vessel with the males following who had remained silent the entire visit. The airlock sealed allowing the outer door to open; the Tlillan vessel rose just off the floor, turned and fired its engines propelling it out of the Athena and back to the mother ship.

McCann was relieved to see the back of them, Malikah was too busy celebrating with her mother. She wore the pendant which was the first handed out for centuries. McCann was happy because his daughter was happy, he couldn't care less about clans on Tlillan. He decided they should all retire to the officer's lounge to celebrate the occasion, to the agreement of all. Although Faraday was disappointed he didn't get anything more from the encounter.

On the way to the lounge the alarm went off, McCann assumed it was the Tlillan's leaving until he heard Athena chant 'Multiple tunnel events! Multiple Tunnel events! Multiple tunnel events!'

He looked at Nestor who ran to his duty station next Malikah grabbed her father's jacket sleeve 'Father there are Gukumatz warships here.'

McCann ran off to the bridge, upon arriving the pit was buzzing with activity. There were three Gukumatz warships sitting off Jupiter 'Situation Commander?' he asked Ryu.

She stood up to allow him to take his seat on the bridge, 'Three Gukumatz warships appeared off Jupiter Commodore, Athena says they've been there for ten minutes now.'

He sat down and looked up 'Athena link with the Ares and inform her of the situation.'

Athena replied softly 'The Ares has been informed Commodore.'

Next Ilam, Malikah, Faraday and Dr Pitt entered the bridge, 'Father they have fired on the orbital platforms.'

McCann looked at his daughter then his wife, Ilam could not confirm what her daughter had just said but moments later the orbital platforms around Mars went down.

McCann asked his wife 'Will the Tlillans assist us?'

His wife didn't answer but his daughter did 'They won't help.'

McCann struck his chair in frustration 'Hassif set course for Jupiter orbit and co-ordinate the Ares for a pincer formation.'

Hassif started bashing away 'Done!'

McCann sat back in his chair 'Engage half speed.'

Ryu had moved back to her station 'Drones are ready launch, Sir.'

McCann then called to the weapons officer 'McKinley charge the cannons and arm with anti-matter warheads.'

McKinley tapped away 'Done, Sir!'

The noise of the engines and the cannons charging could be heard vibrating throughout the entire ship.

The Athena and Ares pulled away from Earth orbit leaving the Tlillan ship there 'Send a request for assistance to the Tlillan warship,' ordered McCann.

His daughter held his arm 'They won't help Father, they want to observe the outcome.'

He looked at his wife 'Ilam take her away!'

Ilam moved towards her daughter but Malikah cried out to her father 'No! I can help, the Gukumatz are moving to the asteroid belt Father. They plan to ambush us when we pass by on the way to Jupiter!'

The bridge went quiet and even the junior officers in the pit peered over their shoulders at Malikah.

McCann tapped his chair and an image of the solar system between Mars and Jupiter sprung up on the desk before him 'Could you show me where they're hiding?'

Malikah leapt excitedly at the console and pointed out where she believed the Gukumatz vessels were 'I can give Hassif the co-ordinates if you'd like father?' she said innocently.

McCann nodded and pointed to Hassif 'Please do.'

The newest member of the Chutli clan stepped over and started punching co-ordinates into the navigation terminal whilst Hassif looked on in wonder.

Once she'd finished three points inside the belt were highlighted with small wire boxes 'Athena bring both ships to a full stop,' ordered McCann.

After both ships were at a full stop he ordered Hassif to transmit the co-ordinates to Titov 'Order him to fire in T minus 2 minutes.'

'Put the warheads on a fuse McKinley, I want them to detonate in the asteroid field. Hassif turn the Athena 40 degrees starboard, I want a full broadside.'

Both the Athena and Ares turned a single side to the asteroid belt and waited for the countdown, all the time the Grand Matriarch watched on.

'Ryu launch the drones and charge the point defence cannons.'

The Red Dragon ordered both squadrons launched and the point defence cannons were ready for enemy missiles.

The Athena counted down calmly '3, 2, 1 fire!' despite the shock absorbers the cruiser took a slight jerk as it fired.

'Reloading,' announced Athena.

McCann was entranced watching the asteroid belt, the Ares had fired at exactly the same time and the Gukumatz wouldn't realise what had happened until far too late. Both ships had fired on the same area of the belt increasing the chances of taking down an enemy.

Before the light of the explosion even reached the view screen Malikah jumped up 'We hit them!'

McCann wasn't sure how his daughter knew this even before they had seen the explosion but he trusted her intuition 'They're moving out of the belt to engage us father!' she shouted excitedly.

All the officers looked at McCann most were wondering if he'd cracked under the pressure following the advice of a child, 'Hassif set an intercept course, Ryu send the drones ahead.'

The Athena turned and made for the asteroid belt which now had a large chunk blown out of it, the Ares followed closely behind.

Halfway between the belt and Mars the klaxon went off 'Two Gukumatz warships on intercept course Commodore,' informed Athena softly.

McCann now had some evidence that this was serious 'All crew battle stations,' he called into his collar mic. McCann selected the ship to port, 'Athena inform Titov of primary target and remove anti-matter warheads.'

Athena replied calmly 'Understood Commodore.'

The ships approached each other on an interception course, 'When in range turn hard to starboard and McKinley fire a full broadside.'

Before they could turn the missile alert rang out and McCann heard the point defence cannons firing away, Ryu sent the drones ahead of the Athena to intercept the enemy missiles. A hush went over the bridge crew when they saw anti-matter explosions as the drones destroyed most of the missiles 'We're down by 20% on drones Commodore,' called out Ryu from behind.

The explosions were closing and McCann knew that no amount of armour could prevent an anti-matter explosion, it was a case of destroy or be destroyed.

Suddenly the Athena was hit by a brutal quake throughout the ship, the image of the Athena on his console turned red along the starboard side. A missile had exploded close by and two of the pulse cannons had been disabled along with a massive gash in the side of the vessel. The image was red surrounded with yellow sections, 'Critical hit starboard, starboard cannons 2 and 3 inoperative, hull breach decks 3 to 10!' announced Athena.

McCann looked up 'Lower bulkheads Athena.'

Next the Athena swung to starboard and opened up with her 4 port cannons into the enemy that had been selected. The Ares mirrored her action and the Gukumatz warship took 16 tungsten projectiles into its body. The projectiles were small but the amount of kinetic energy they carried sent shockwaves throughout the Gukumatz ship. It was evident from the view screen that the enemy was crippled by the two broadsides hitting her in concert.

The enemy ship quivered as cracks appeared all along the body, a ship designed to combat beam weapons was woefully lacking versus kinetic weapons. The ship cracked and quaked breaking up as it moved forward. Crumbling to pieces with flames jetting out where the cracks had grown particularly wide.

Malikah clutched her father by the arm 'Father, they're fleeing!'

The science officer shouted from behind 'I can confirm that Sir, Athena has detected a power build up that could only be their wormhole generator.'

McCann patted his daughter 'I want everything on that vessel before it can escape. Hassif show them our port side and McKinley fire as soon as possible. Athena, transmit that to the Ares.'

As the Athena turned to give the Gukumatz a broadside a white hole appeared.

'Casimir field detected!' called out the science officer.

McCann looked at McKinley who shook his head; the enemy warship fired its engines and disappeared into the abyss.

McCann hit the arm of his chair with his fist and bellowed 'Cowards!' he stood up and spoke into his wrist tablet 'Nestor prepare a boarding party.'

However just as he'd finished his sentence the Gukumatz ship exploded.

'They committed suicide father,' spoke Malikah solemnly.

'Disregard that order Nestor,' spoke McCann slowly as he put his arm around his daughter and viewed the carnage. He kissed his daughter, 'Well done Malikah,' he whispered into her ear.

'Communication from Tlillan vessel Commodore,' said Athena softly.

McCann turned to the view screen 'Who is it for Athena?'

'That was not specified Commodore.'

He sighed 'Fine accept it.'

The Grand Matriarch appeared with that Tlillan condescending grin, 'Well done Malikachutli you have fulfilled your destiny. When you are ready we shall meet at Tititl, if you wish you may have your father accompany you ... but not your mother.'

Malikah and Ilam both bowed their heads, the Matriarch turned to look at McCann, she smiled a little and nodded her head at him before the view screen turned off and back to the solar system.

He had no idea what she meant but was certain Ilam did, the Tlillan vessel moved out of the system and left through a wormhole. Athena moved to the Edwards for repairs whilst the Ares picked up the remnants of the enemy. Faraday and Dr Pitt were looking forward to seeing the Edwards and even touring Tharsis once they'd docked.

Whilst the others were touring the Edwards or taking a break McCann questioned his daughter in the officer's lounge, 'Malikah, how did you know where the Gukumatz were?'

Ilam stood listening as she was anxious to learn also, Malikah was giggling with delight enjoying so much of her father's attention. Ilam folded her arms 'This is serious!' she snapped.

Malikah made a dissatisfied look at her mother then turned to her father, 'I sensed their thoughts.'

McCann sat his daughter on the sofa next to him 'But you sensed them before we saw them, how is that possible Malikah?'

His daughter smiled at him 'I don't know, I just sensed their slimy horrible thoughts. It was disgusting!'

McCann scratched his chin 'What did the Matriarch mean by fulfilling your destiny and meeting at Tittil?'

Malikah started to fondle her pendant 'I don't know, but Tititl is a place on Tlillan.'

He peered over at his wife 'So what did she mean by fulfilling her destiny?'

Ilam seemed rather uncomfortable with the question 'The seers foresaw a great battle in this system, they said that when the Mictlancihuatl comes she will crush those whom seek to destroy the Grand Matriarch.'

McCann laughed and walked to the bar for a whisky, Ilam was dumbfounded at his reaction 'Why do you laugh Duncan?'

He drank a shot of whisky then filled up on another 'You knew all the time that they'd come here to try and kill your precious Grand Matriarch didn't you?'

Ilam frowned 'It was foreseen.'

'They probably even informed the toad men about it, am I right?'

Ilam snapped back 'Are you suggesting that we fulfilled the prophecy on purpose?'

'Yes that's exactly what I'm suggesting.'

Ilam's eyes around the pupils turned red and she gnashed her teeth 'Why do you continue with this heresy?' she gnarled at him.

McCann smirked 'Are there anymore prophecies regarding my daughter that I should know about?'

She seethed at her husband 'She will lead the heretics back to enlightenment.'

He laughed out loud and slapped his thigh 'Meaning us?' he asked making circles with his finger.

Ilam was furious, she took her religion very seriously but unfortunately McCann despised all religion whether it be Tlillan or human, he saw no more validity in one or the other.

His wife's eyes turned a deep burgundy and even McCann became worried for a moment until his daughter cried out 'Mother!'

Ilam turned to witness Malikah's jet black eyes glaring at her. Ilam turned back to her husband 'Do not mock my beliefs Duncan,' in an angry voice.

He nodded silently and her eyes returned to normal. Since they were alone in the lounge McCann approached his wife and hugged her apologising for his behaviour 'I just don't like it when you manipulate me,' he told his wife.

She kissed him tenderly with pink eyes 'We are all being manipulated Duncan, I only do what I do for Malikah's benefit you must trust me on that.'

Malikah then rushed up to them and embraced both of her parents; McCann hugged her 'Well it seems I'll have to call you Malikachutli from now on!'

His daughter laughed and embraced her father 'No you can still call me Malikah father!'

He smiled and kissed his daughter who had become the first new member of her clan for nearly four hundred years.

Faraday nodded 'I've spoken to Ilam and she believes the Matriarch is genuine.'

McCann stood up and put a pair of shorts on 'Have you spoken to Malikah?'

Faraday made a puzzled look at him.

He started to dress himself and suggested that Faraday ask Malikah first then get back to him since she was the only person he trusted to tell the absolute truth. Ten minutes later Faraday was back and Malikah had confirmed the requested from Tlillan, 'Apparently the battle is raging in the Tlillan system as we speak.'

The Commodore was now dressed and making for the lift to the bridge 'So they want the Athena and Ares to assist?'

Faraday replied through McCann's communicator 'No, they have given us co-ordinates of the Gukumatz home world; they want us to go there and siege the system. They believe they can resist the Gukumatz fleet at Tlillan; the co-ordinates of Gukumatz AB have been transmitted to Athena. Titov has been informed and is awaiting your command, good luck Duncan.'

McCann stepped off the lift and onto the bridge, Ryu offered him the Captain's chair.

'I want this crew at battle stations Commander, in 10 minutes we'll be folding space to the Gukumatz home world. Athena has set a course, I want Hassif present to certify it and make sure that arse Beaumont is at his station will you?'

The bridge began to bustle with excitement as junior officers streamed off the lift and into the pit, Louis called in at engineering and soon both vessels were ready and waiting. Everyone was buzzing and McCann sensed the tension in the air. Hassif ran onto the bridge, he said nothing only approached his station and began work.

Titov sent a message confirming the Ares was prepared and within 5 minutes so was the Athena.

'Systems ready and course certified Commodore,' reported Ryu.

McCann nodded 'Excellent, call battle stations and alert all crew we'll be folding space in T minus 3 minutes Commander.'

Ryu ordered battle stations and the bridge crew strapped themselves into their seats in the pit. The senior bridge officers grasped handles protruding from the main stations.

The lighting dimmed and Athena began to vibrate, 'Wormhole stable Commodore' announced Athena as the white hole shimmered and swirled before them.

McCann looked over to Ryu and gave her the nod, 'Activate Casimir field,' ordered Ryu.

McKinley tapped his station 'Casimir field active Commander.'

McCann Peered at the back of the officer stood at the engineering station in the centre 'Fire the engines Lieutenant.'

She tapped away before grasping the safety handles on her station 'Confirmed Sir.'

The Athena shuddered and McCann was pushed into the back of his seat. Lurching forward until the white hole started to draw her in thanks to the Casimir field, the cruiser shifted into the abyss. There was a flash then the swirls of light could be seen flying past them as the Casimir field sent them deeper into the wormhole towards the singularity at the centre.

McCann looked up 'Hassif, transfer all navigation to Athena.'

The Indian punched away at his terminal 'Navigation transferred.'

Now they all watched as helpless children in their mother's arms being carried through a bustling traffic filled street. The light blurred past them forming only flashes and swirls as it raced to be ejected from the white hole, as they approached the singularity it slowed down.

The Athena approached the dead zone where the effects of both the worm holes and black hole cancelled each other out. The "River Styx" as McCann called it was the most surreal place in the universe, he starred hard examining the images. Asteroids and comets could be seen, he witnessed alien vessels that had yet to be encountered by mankind. Amongst them a ship, by far larger than the Athena, in the shape of a bird caused even Ryu to whisper 'Oh my god, do you see that?'

McCann whispered back 'Yes,' there was what seemed to be a head with a beak. It was attached to a long neck that connected to the body of the craft which resembled a body with two large swept back wings. The creation was quite magnificent and even was decorated to resemble a bird of some alien world.

'How big is that thing?'

The science officer behind him replied 'It's impossible to get an exact size however it's at least ten times our mass, Sir.'

McCann and his bridge crew were in awe at such a splendid creation, by far the most beautiful craft he'd ever seen. However it could be only an image that was thousands of years old, he didn't know; as they passed it Hassif logged an image of it for future reference.

Soon they reached the other side of the singularity. Athena fired her engines pushing herself into the influence of the wormhole which led into the Gukumatz system. She dropped the Casimir field and was sucked into the white hole to be ejected out the other side.

Hassif called out 'Athena has returned control of navigation.'

The wormhole closed up, the lights came back to full strength and the ship ceased to vibrate. They were now in an alien system.

'Scan the system,' called out McCann, the junior science officer behind him got to work. McCann was scrutinizing a 3D image of the system 'I don't see any Earth like planets, Athena?'

Everyone was busy looking for the enemy and after a few moments Athena responded 'The only viable planets would be moons orbiting the first Saturn class planet, Commodore.'

McCann waited for his Science officer who eventually reported 'The Saturn class planet in the habitable zone has 20 moons, 3 have an atmosphere and two of the atmospheres are not natural, Sir.'

McCann raised an eyebrow 'Not natural? What do you mean exactly Ensign?'

The young girl turned to face him 'Both atmospheres were recently created by large expulsions of carbon dioxide and according to this it was at around the same time, Sir.'

McCann spoke over his shoulder 'Thank you Ensign, Commander Ryu send a drone to investigate. Hassif bring the Athena to a halt here until the Ares arrives.'

Thanks to time dilation whilst travelling through a wormhole the chances of the Ares and Athena arriving at the same time were slim. Somehow the Tlillans and Gukumatz had perfected the art of synchronized arrival, but how they did this still eluded Faraday and the scientists at the I.S.A. After 90 minutes the drone had arrived and confirmed that the three moons were inhabited. One was used for agriculture whilst the smallest which was about one third the mass of Earth was mainly industrial. What McCann found astounding was the fact that there were no orbital defences, the moons had advanced space stations using an orbital lift system that put theirs to shame. However the drone met no resistance, the crew were eager to attack but McCann was far too cautious.

The Gukumatz predominantly used ambushes and smoke and mirrors acts to trick their enemies into entering death traps and he wasn't about to rush in.

McCann stood up and walked over to the drone stations behind him 'Ryu, have the drone open fire on the orbital station' he said selecting the station above the industrial moon.

Ryu tapped in the command 'It'll take an hour for the order to get there,' she informed him.

He nodded and had a stroll behind the pit to pass the time and in-still some confidence into his junior officers, who were all working away monitoring and maintaining every sub system on the ship.

Hassif informed him that they had folded space to the Norma arm which was close to the galactic core, he believed the Gukumatz used the radiation to hide from the Tlillans. The Indian hypothesised that there were no defences as it would draw attention to the moons but McCann wasn't going to accept that. Over an hour later Ryu informed him that the drone had been destroyed by the orbiting station which used a beam weapon to eliminate the attacker.

McCann smirked 'They would've had us caught between three death traps, bloody sneaky toads! Athena are those stations in a fixed orbit?'

Athena replied calmly 'Affirmative.'

Folding his arms he looked out at the view screen 'Can we hit one of them from here?'

'Affirmative there is a window of opportunity in 23 minutes to fire upon the station orbiting the urban moon.'

McCann smiled 'Good move into position to fire, have Hassif and McKinley certify your data please.'

'Affirmative,' replied Athena.

The vessel moved slowly bringing a full broadside to bare in the direction of the moons. Timed properly with the stations orbit the Athena would fire her tungsten shells, as the station came around in geo stationary orbit it would collide with the shells. The kinetic energy would hopefully tear it apart and bring it crashing down onto the planet causing widespread devastation.

The Athena moved into place and her calculations had all been certified, McKinley had some difficulty but Hassif was able to confirm them quickly. She counted down and all weapons fired in synchrony, now the crew waited with bated breath. They wouldn't actually discover the result until a good 20 to 30 minutes afterwards since that was the time it took the light to reach them. Another fifty minutes for the shells to reach the target so over an hour later they witnessed the results.

From what could be seen the Gukumatz fired frantically when they saw the shells approaching and managed to destroy five possibly six. The rest slammed into the station releasing a massive amount of kinetic energy much like a meteorite hitting the earth. All the gathered energy spontaneously released in a bright explosion. They observed the Gukumatz station break up as it descended into the moons atmosphere in a ball of fire.

Ryu stepped forward with a smile on her face but it was a sinister smile of revenge. Korea had been devastated by tsunami after the attack on Earth. After years of fighting drug lords and suffering nerve gas attacks she thought her country had taken enough. Now it was time for the toads to take a dose of their own medicine.

McCann looked up at the neural housing 'Well done Athena, target the next station to present itself and have your data certified as before.'

The Athena moved again and lined herself up to fire on the agricultural station, and as before the station was rocked by thick tungsten crashing into the side of it. The entire station quaked and collapsed in on itself as it fell down into the atmosphere creating a mushroom cloud of nuclear proportions that blackened the sky.

McCann looked up 'Align for the last orbital station Athena.'

As she confirmed Hassif shouted 'I've received a communication I think it's from the Gukumatz.'

McCann sat back down in his seat, 'Play it.'

A fat squat toad head with no neck appeared on the view screen. The transmission had been recorded and it spoke in croaks and burbles, 'Athena translate that will you?' he called out.

The sound of the toad took a back seat to the androgynous translation AI, 'I am female of Kotumatz I offer a surrender to any conditions you require.'

Ryu approached his seat from behind 'Well that was simple, are you going to accept?' she asked quietly.

He looked up 'Athena, what does female of Kotumatz mean?'

Athena replied softly 'Gukumatz have a reproduction cycle similar to the frog or toad, one female is entrusted with a spawning pool. The largest spawning pool is the Kotu pool, all Gukumatz produced from this pool are named Kotumatz. This female leads the largest spawning pool in Gukumatz society and therefore speaks for them as a whole.'

McCann chuckled and with an incredulous expression 'How on Earth do they tell one from another?'

'Unknown but it is very probable they use scent.'

Ryu looked at the carnage on the view screen of black clouds darkening the atmospheres of two moons, 'You are going to accept the surrender Duncan?'

McCann turned his head to look at his first officer 'I don't trust them, they'd say anything to stop us firing until their fleet can get back and I'm not waiting around for that to happen.'

'Faraday would disapprove, he'd want you to take the surrender.'

'What would you have me do Ryu?'

She turned back to the view screen 'I'm here to follow orders Commodore not question them.'

He looked up 'As soon as the window of opportunity opens I want you to fire on the last station, understood?'

Athena replied calmly 'Affirmative.'

The rest of the bridge peered oddly at their Commodore.

"Is there a problem?" inquired McCann to his crew.

The eerie moment of silence came and went, the pit crew turned back to their duties and no one left their station.

Ryu grinned at McCann cheekily and winked.

The Athena lined up another broadside and fired; 80 minutes later they witnessed the station crumble into pieces then pepper the moon with craters. The enemy industry had been crushed in one fell swoop, shortly afterwards the klaxon sounded, 'Multiple tunnel events!' called Athena's voice and McCann jumped into his seat.

Five wormholes opened up and out came five battered Gukumatz warships all in synchrony.

'Arm the cannons with anti-matter warheads and target the closest ship!' screamed McCann.

Ryu leapt behind him and to her station 'Launching all combat drones Commodore!'

McKinley called out 'Point defence cannons charged and ready Sir!'

The Athena turned slowly 'Gukumatz warship targeted at X +0.3, Y +1.03, Z -0.5,' she called out changing the co-ordinates as she tilted and turned to line it up for a full broadside.

The enemy vessel had obviously just returned from heavy combat. Due to the extensive scarring along her torso, from Tlillan beam weapons that had managed to breach the energy shields. Now she was targeting the Athena from little more than one AU distance which is about 8 minutes travelling at the speed of light. Too far for one enemy to launch an effective missile strike but if all five attacked McCann couldn't see how they'd survive. His only options were to flee and hope the Ares would not be caught or hope the Tlillans had inflicted enough damage as to give him a chance.

McKinley shouted out hurriedly 'All cannons aligned with target Sir!'

McCann replied without missing a beat 'I want a wide spread and time the warheads!'

'Affirmative ... ready!'

'Fire!'

The Commodore turned to Ryu 'I want both squadrons of drones to engage the furthest target, ignore all incoming missiles!'

She didn't understand what he was trying to do but confirmed his order anyway, 'Understood!'

She dashed to her station and transmitted the orders to the drone AI's.

McCann called on Athena again 'Athena, align with the second closest target for a port broadside. McKinley fire again as soon as you can. I want the same spread of anti-matter warheads, understood?'

Both Athena and McKinley replied, Hassif peered back at McCann worriedly; he'd deciphered his stratagem of zig zaging towards the enemy battle group whilst firing.

Louis could be heard screaming down the comms at McCann.

The Frenchman was furious 'McCann what the fuck are you doing?'

The Commodore tapped his chair arm 'Louis, get back to work!'

Louis wasn't prepared to be silenced 'We need to fold space NOW! If we stay here much longer we won't be able to leave!'

McCann took a deep breath and spoke as calmly as he could 'You have a choice Louis, you can do your job and follow orders or you can leave your station and let someone else take over.'

Louis began to shout and curse in his mother tongue so McCann muted him. He looked up to see his bridge crew staring back 'That goes for all of you too!' he shouted.

The crew went back to work and McCann left Louis to shout and swear, the Frenchman always did his job but he needed to let off steam first.

Then from behind him one of the junior officers shouted 'Incoming!'

On the console display several groups of missiles popped up, 'How Long?' asked McCann.

'Less than two minutes, Sir!' replied the Ensign.

McCann looked up to Athena again 'Athena can you fire some timed warheads into those missiles and detonate some of them?'

She replied calmly 'Affirmative Commodore.'

McCann who was now sweating replied 'Then do it now, certification not required!'

Immediately the cannons began to fire and within 30 seconds the warheads detonated. McCann compared it to a destroyer firing depth charges into the wine dark ocean.

Athena called out 'Targets too close Commodore.'

McCann announced out over the comms 'Brace for impact!' and watched the images of the remaining missiles approach the Athena. He held tightly onto his seat as the thumping of the point defence cannons became audible firing on the incoming missiles. The thumping steadily increased in frequency until eventually the display flashed on the port side aft rocking the vessel from side to side.

The console image flashed red for a moment then yellow 'Minor damage to armour plating Commodore,' reported Athena.

McCann was perplexed as to why the damage was so minor, until he realised the Gukumatz had just been in a long drawn out battle with the Tlillan fleet. Perhaps the Gukumatz had used up their primary ammunition on the Tlillan fleet?

Hopefully they'd used the last of their anti-matter to return and defend their home world? If so Athena wasn't at such a disadvantage, but if they had preserved a little anti-matter then things could get rough quickly.

Unfortunately there was only one method to test his assumption and that was to continue his assault. The Gukumatz knew there were two human ships and they knew the Tlillans might assist with a counter attack.

It was all a big game with the highest stakes and McCann had decided to call the Gukumatz bluff by ploughing ahead into them with guns blazing.

Eventually the point defence cannons went dead 'Minor damage to armour plating Commodore. All systems are operational,' reported Athena.

McCann wiped the sweat from his brow 'Continue approach pattern and maintain fire,' as he said that the view screen light up in the corner.

The primary Gukumatz target was engulfed in several anti-matter explosions crippling the entire ship as it broke up into pieces, scattering into space.

'And then there were four!' celebrated McCann triumphantly.

He was still sweating but now the odds were falling into his favour.

'Second volley incoming Commodore,' announced Athena.

'Fire timed warheads into the volleys.'

'Enemy missiles are too close Commodore.'

He shouted into his comms to the crew 'Brace for impact!' as the thump of the point defence cannons began again becoming louder and more frequent as the missiles came closer and closer. Finally one of the missiles hit and the detonation sent the Athena into a downward spiral throwing the crew that weren't in the pit across the bridge.

Athena called out 'Detonation port fore, decks 1-5 breeched, lowering bulkheads to prevent decompression.'

McCann leaped back into his seat and observed the impact area on the console before him; it seemed that the point defence cannon had detonated the missile before impact. The anti-matter explosion had still ripped a chunk out of the top of the fore section, exposing the first five decks to decompression 'Maintain course Athena,' he called.

Athena righted herself then tacked the other way firing a broadside into the enemy vessels. The results of the combat drones could now be seen as they buzzed around one of the enemy vessels, McCann would later describe them as "Flies around a cow's arse".

There were several explosions as the enemy vessel struggled to contain the army of insects stabbing at its weak points.

The Athena called out again 'Third volley incoming, too close to repel.'

Before McCann could call for the crew to brace for impact the point defence cannons lurched into life.

Another explosion rocked the Athena sending her into a flat spin 'Impact starboard aft section, decks 3-6 compromised lowering bulkheads to prevent decompression.'

McCann gripped his seat tightly until the Athena steadied herself the rear of the warship was flashing red and yellow now.

'Louis status report ... Louis?' he shouted down the comms to no reply until he realised Louis was still muted. He removed the mute to the swearing and screaming of Beaumont which was a relief, 'Alright Louis, how are the power core and the engines?'

'The core is fine but the starboard engines are finished, we have less than half speed and we'll need to dock to fix it. Half of my nanites are holding the fucking super structure together so try not to get any more damage!'

McCann sat back and examined the tactical map at 5 AU magnification, two Gukumatz ships were moving in on the Athena. One had been destroyed and another was crippled by the last volley, the furthest cruiser was pinned down by two squadrons of combat drones. The Athena was still able to fight but had lost two of the starboard cannons and her speed was reduced to about 30%. There were some big gaps in her armour, thanks to those last missiles.

McCann stood up and whispered to Hassif 'Can we get out of here?'

Hassif turned and shook his head solemnly.

McCann patted him on the shoulder 'Athena can you show your portside to those oncoming warships?'

Athena replied calmly 'Affirmative Commodore.'

'Then do so, and inform me when you're ready to fire.'

Hassif called out 'Incoming message from one of the Gukumatz vessels, it's live!'

McCann sat down in his seat 'Okay take it.'

The screen flickered to life and a Gukumatz smaller than the last appeared. It began to croak and the AI translated, 'Human, you are requested to surrender your vessel and crew if you do so you shall be returned to your system of origin, unharmed. You have 3 minutes 25 seconds to decide.'

The image disappeared from the screen; the young Ensign at the science station spoke 'Are we going to surrender?'

McCann turned to her and before he could speak Ryu stepped between them 'The Commodore is not going to surrender Ensign, now get back to your station and be careful the next time you open your mouth!'

The Ensign looked down to see Ryu stroke her pulse pistol and she quickly returned to her post.

Ryu turned to McCann 'What are we going to do now, Sir?'

McCann couldn't outrun or out manoeuvre the enemy all he could do was try and slug it out in the hope that the Gukumatz were out of anti-matter.

McCann spoke to Athena 'When we have a full spread on one of them I want you to fire. Then target the other and fire immediately, use the nuclear warheads if you have no anti-matter left Athena.'

Athena brought her portside to bare and fired two broadsides in succession causing the Gukumatz to return fire with their missiles. The enemy vessels lit up in a glorious cascade of white fire. Yet no sooner had they been rebuffed, the missile volleys arrived and the point defence cannons now weakened from previous hits began their concert again.

There were several explosions thanks to the warheads being detonated before impact, however the Athena was scarred with anti-matter trenches and craters cut out along her portside. The crew were tossed down to the floor by the force of the detonations which sent the Athena into a barrel roll. McCann skidded along the floor and into the pit where some junior officers secured him.

The klaxon was sounding and the Athena struggled to gain control of herself as she rolled over and over. Finally she came to a halt and the image on the console displayed an entire portside devastated by enemy missile volleys. The Athena had two starboard cannons left, but couldn't turn in order to bring them to bare on the enemy.

Athena was calling out breach after breach and lowering all the bulkheads to prevent a total loss of pressure. The bridge had become filled by a foul smoke which seeped in until one of Nestor's men put it out. The two enemy ships had been stopped in their tracks, one seemed lifeless apart from the plasma fires leaking into space, the other was still targeting them.

Athena then alerted the crew 'Enemy incoming,' and an image of the fifth ship, which had now repelled the combat drones, was displayed approaching and targeting them.

Hassif called out 'Incoming message from enemy ship, it's live.'

McCann nodded 'Okay take it.'

A Gukumatz appeared and his croaks were translated, 'Human surrender your vessel and your crew shall be unharmed, refuse and die.'

The enemy targeted the Athena and was poised to finish them.

Athena called out 'Tunnel event, tunnel event, tunnel event X +1.73, Y -1.70, Z -2.1."

A white hole opened up and out of the swirling mist the Ares was ejected.

McCann looked at the Gukumatz and said slowly 'Athena contact the Ares and tell her to destroy all Gukumatz vessels in this systems then lay siege to the three moons.'

Athena replied 'Affirmative Commodore.'

Suddenly the Gukumatz replied 'Stop, you have our surrender.'

McCann hid his desperation 'Unconditional?'

The Gukumatz replied immediately 'Yes.'

'Athena order the Ares to stand down, inform Titov I've accepted a Gukumatz surrender. If he witnesses any aggressive behaviour from them he should carry out my orders immediately.'

Athena confirmed her orders and McCann addressed the Gukumatz officer 'Transmit any relevant security codes to your ship now, and prepare to be boarded.'

The toad man before him replied 'Understood.'

Hassif received all security access codes to the enemy warships and defence grids protecting the moons.

McCann stood behind Hassif 'Send them to Titov and tell him to board the Gukumatz warships,' he looked upwards 'Athena, contact Louis and request an estimate for when we can start moving again.'

He sat down and looked at the carnage on the view screen, three enemy warships turned and spun in space moving only by inertia. One was broken up beyond recognition and the other two were breaking up as they moved lifelessly. The other two still had signs of life but displayed evidence of severe battle damage. He monitored the transport craft Titov had sent carrying Vympel 3 and 4 docking with the vessels to secure the bridges.

As he was resting the familiar sound of Louis came over the comms 'The power core is undamaged and the port engines will be operational in two hours.'

The Englishman let out a sigh of relief 'Thank you Louis, let me know when she can move.'

'Sure, but the wormhole generator is trashed!'

McCann smiled and spoke into his collar mic 'Do you think you can use a Gukumatz one if it's operational?'

Louis scoffed "Bah I wouldn't put anything those toads made into the Athena! I was thinking of getting a tow from the Ares back to earth since the Casimir field can be repaired.'

He wiped the sweat from his brow with his jacket sleeve 'Alright let me know when the engines are ready,' then switched off the communications.

Titov secured the remaining enemy warships and McCann opened a micro wormhole to Geneva delivering his after action report.

When the engines were working the Athena limped over to the Gukumatz moons and made orbit around the urban moon whilst Titov remained in space keeping watch over the captured vessels.

Once in orbit Hassif transmitted the security clearance codes for the defence grid of cloaked missile platforms in orbit, McCann had him turn the missile platforms around and onto the planets they were built to protect.

Hassif called out 'Transmission from the moon surface.'

McCann pointed at the view screen 'Play it.'

A large warty toad appeared 'Do you represent the Humans?' croaked the creature.

McCann who was repulsed by the sight of the beast replied 'I am Commodore McCann commanding the I.S.S Athena if you have any queries you may ask me. I would like to address the leader of the Gukumatz in this system please.'

The fat warty toad gurgled and croaked 'I am Alpha female of Kotumatz when you address me you address all Gukumatz, you accept my surrender, Commodore?'

He realised this was the female he'd spoken to when first entering the system 'If your surrender is in good faith then I do accept it.'

The creature burped and croaked 'It is, we make only one request Commodore.'

McCann cut her off before she could finish 'Your surrender was unconditional,' he interjected.

She expelled some wind from her nasal cavities, which he assumed smelt rather rancid, then croaked 'It is only a request.'

McCann calmed down 'Go ahead.'

She croaked 'Asylum from Tlillans.'

McCann was taken aback 'I'm not sure I can give that.'

The female toad began to croak and burp loudly 'Please come to the Kotu pool Commodore, we must speak on this.'

Hassif turned around 'Just received co-ordinates.'

McCann looked back at the pleading toad 'I'll discuss this with you but if this is a deception you'll regret it.'

The toad released another gasp of wind 'No, you have my word Commodore.'

McCann let out a huff of air 'Huh! We'll see, I'll be coming down in 20 minutes Kotumatz Alpha.'

He tapped his wrist tablet and the communication ended.

'You're not going to take that toad's word are you?' asked Ryu.

He smiled 'No.'

Ryu gave a puzzled look 'So why are you going?'

'Lady Luck has been smiling on me today and besides there's an old Korean saying, "it's better I grab a shit than I grab a fart", right?'

Ryu was not impressed with his recollection of Korean sayings 'Nestor will be going down with you won't he?'

McCann was rather touched at Ryu's concern for him 'Yes and you'll be staying here Commander, if they try anything you have my authority to lay waste to all three moons.'

Ryu rolled her eyes, 'Uuurrrhhh!'

McCann smiled at her aggravation, he called up Nestor on his wrist tablet and ordered him to bring three men to the one docking bay that was still operational.

It took a good twenty minutes just to walk through the ship and reach the docking bay. Droids were flying to and fro along the burnt corridors; he had to wait three times for bulk heads to be lifted. The Athena was in an utter mess, McCann was in awe that Louis had managed to prevent her from falling apart. Upon reaching the docking bay Nestor was waiting with five commandos. All dressed in I.S.A uniforms with space suits underneath and black berets, each trooper carried an automatic pulse rifle.

'Extra men?' asked McCann inspecting the commandos.

'Da,' replied Nestor standing next to the transport craft in the bay.

McCann nodded, 'Fine let's get moving then,' he held his wrist tablet close to the side of the craft and the door rippled back inviting the men inside. Once all were seated and secured inside the bucket seats of the craft McCann tapped his wrist and spoke 'You've got control Athena, takes us down to the co-ordinates provided please.'

Her soft voice replied 'Affirmative Commodore.'

Shortly afterwards the crew felt a shift of inertia as they left the docking bay and then the rough bumping as they rode the thick atmosphere down to the now conquered alien moon. After landing they removed the safety harnesses and McCann opened the door. It rippled back to reveal a landing platform.

The sky was a dirty yellow colour and the stench of ammonia filled his nostrils. The platform was a circular blue material with a single walkway connecting to a pedestrian causeway. The large wide causeway had many strange mossy growths in the centre and on the sides. It reminded him of how humans would decorate their own public thoroughfares. Several tall buildings connected on each side along the causeway, it was when he followed the buildings down he realised that they were far above the moon's surface.

The landing platform and thoroughfare were all suspended from the colossal structures which were at least a kilometre tall. At the end of the walkway connecting the landing platform and the thoroughfare stood a delegation of Gukumatz. McCann noticed the large fat warty one as the Alpha. She was dressed in purple robe and a space suit of the same colour, her head was adorned in what looked like squares of Jade.

McCann stepped towards the walkway but Nestor stopped him, 'Let me go first,' he said in his thick Russian accent.

McCann patted him on the shoulder and smiled 'Be my guest.'

Nestor advanced towards the Gukumatz party with two men directly behind him, then McCann, next his two remaining men covering the Commodore. They strolled along the walkway, the air became somewhat difficult to breath due to the humidity and ammonia, the men pulled out a pair of breathing tubes which fed them an oxygen supply; inserting them in the nasal cavity.

The Gukumatz were very nervous, unless it was normal of them to twitch in the fashion they did, upon reaching the public causeway the Alpha female squatted down before them. One of the smaller males then approached Nestor, at the same time he was looking at the floor he produced what looked to be golden staff with a very ornate design. It was carved from ivory at one end in the shape of a bird of prey.

'What is this?' asked McCann as he pushed past his body guards in order to observe the staff in closer detail.

The female Kotumatz croaked and his suit translated her speech into his ear piece 'It is a symbol, she who possess it has power.'

McCann took the staff and was surprised at the weight, it was only about 3 - 4 feet but the weight caused him to almost drop it shocking the Gukumatz for a moment. He looked closer at the artwork, the intricacy of it was stunning, the ivory bird resembled a condor with wings outstretched and talons grasping the golden staff. Etched with scenes from what McCann guessed was Gukumatz history.

McCann held the staff 'Thank you, now why do you think we can grant you asylum from the Tlillans?'

The female stood up from her squat and spoke 'They will murder us if you do not grant us asylum.'

McCann smirked at the female who was almost as tall as he but considerably wider 'What makes you think I care if they do?'

She croaked and burped rapidly whilst tilting her head to look him in the face 'Now that they have used you to defeat us they will enslave you.'

McCann passed the staff to one of the commandos 'Why would they do that?'

'They require your people to survive.'

'You mean after you tried to kill them all off?' interjected McCann.

The alpha Kotumatz paused then replied 'Yes, but Commodore they fear you. You have the power to deny them existence, Xch'uup will not permit that. Make us your vassal and together we can repel the Matriarch.'

McCann's wrist tablet began to bleep, he tapped it and the voice of Ryu came back at him 'Commodore three Tlillan warships have entered the system. I've informed them that the Gukumatz have surrendered to us but they have not replied.'

The Gukumatz became very agitated and McCann replied 'Very well, keep me abreast of the situation and inform Titov that the I.S.A is not taking any orders from the Tlillans.'

'Understood Sir.'

McCann tapped his wrist.

The alpha toad croaked 'Make us your vassal Commodore McCann, I will order our remaining ships to defend your fleet. Leave us to the mercy of Xch'uup and she will turn on you.'

McCann received an update from Ryu reporting on a Tlillan vessel landing on the moon. He took a long look at the alpha Kotumatz and replied 'Very well Kotumatz, I accept your offer for now.'

She quickly croaked and burped some instructions to her aides commanding the crews of the two operational warships to take instructions from their new human commanders.

McCann observed a typical Tlillan transport craft descend through the clouds and land next to their craft. Out of it came two females and three males in jet black suits. They approached McCann and the Gukumatz party he'd just struck a deal with, the shorter female had typical reddish Tlillan hair with those wide almost transparent eyes. McCann reached into his thigh pocket, on the opposite leg to his holster, and produced his white neural band. He fitted the band around the back of his skull and switched it on, Nestor and his men did likewise.

The Tlillan males all had their jet black helmets covering their heads and he could hear the distinct clink of the female's boots as they haughtily marched up the walkway towards them. As the females approached McCann recognised the tallest one, dressed in a white jacket with matching long hair that contrasted with her black suit.

The Tlillans approached, the tall female with the white hair marched up to the commando holding the golden staff 'I will take possession of our sceptre,' she demanded as she reached out to take it.

McCann stepped in her way and Nestor's men aimed their weapons at the Tlillans 'I'm sorry Miss Cihuateteo but that's mine now.'

She stood a good 7 feet tall and her eyes turned blood red on seeing McCann again, 'That sceptre was stolen from Tlillan I am here to return it to the Grand Matriarch.'

He had to look up to her but remained stubborn 'The Gukumatz have surrendered to me and I have taken possession of all their assets in the name of the I.S.A. If you wish to have any property returned that you believe was stolen in the past I'm afraid you'll have to do it via official channels,' he stated to the now furious Matriarch.

Matriarch Cihuateteo lost her temper and using her superior physical strength pushed McCann aside as an adult would a small child.

McCann pulled out his pistol and shot her in the back of the knee blowing off the lower portion of her left leg and dropping her onto the floor in a pool of blood.

He quickly pointed his weapon at the other female and shouted 'Try and scramble my brains and I'll blow yours into the Kotu pool first!'

Her eyes were blood red; the males seemed greatly confused by the situation. They had never witnessed females let alone a Matriarch treated in such a manner by a male, a death sentence on Tlillan for sure.

She took a step to assist her Matriarch but McCann fired at the ground before her. Stopping the Amazon in her tracks after the tiny tungsten bullet had bounced off the ground in a shower of sparks.

She glared down at her Matriarch writhing in distress on the ground then shouted at one of the males. The translator was unable to decipher what she had said but the Tlillan male was very hesitant. She screeched it again and pointed towards Cihuateteo. Who lay on her side propped up by one arm gasping for breath as she grasped her left thigh.

The small male walked towards the Matriarch and McCann fired another shot about six inches in front of his feet, the male stopped and looked towards the female. McCann couldn't see his face through the jet black helmet which covered his head but from his body language it was obvious he was searching for mercy. She bellowed at him again and he continued on his path towards the Matriarch.

Nestor's men had trained their weapons on the Tlillans and he glanced at McCann. Nestor didn't want a confrontation or to have to kill anyone, but he was prepared to do it. The grizzly Russian had killed many times before, and for a lot less, but that was with Spetsnaz the rules were different in the I.S.A.

The Tlillan continued towards his Matriarch in a very jittery manner, McCann raised his pistol and from no more than 6 feet away he fired.

The energy stored in a pulse pistol round is massive, on hitting the target it is released explosively.

McCann's round hit its target shattering the front visor into tiny pieces. The Tlillan's head exploded inside the helmet splattering into a mush. The short male landed on his back as lifeless as a sack of potatoes.

The Gukumatz were terrified for some reason, the Tlillan female displayed a combination of shock and fury.

The Englishman pointed his pistol back at the female and declared 'Next?'

Bellowing at one of the two remaining males she ordered him to comply. From what McCann could decipher his body language was a lot less than compliant. Her eyes rendered into a deep blood red dropping the stubborn male to the floor. He lay lifeless, remaining still just as the one McCann had shot a moment ago. The brutal Amazon turned on the remaining male, pointing at Cihuateteo and bellowed her commands. He marched confidently forward and McCann took aim.

The Gukumatz alpha put her hand on McCann's arm and croaked with her foul smelling breath 'Commodore McCann this is barbaric, allow the Matriarch treatment.'

McCann remained silent and as the male came into range he squeezed the trigger. One side of the helmet was sheared off causing the body to spin spraying his thick blood and grey brain matter over all parties. The male slammed into the ground close to the body of his disobedient counterpart.

McCann turned to the alpha Kotumatz and whispered 'I need your support Kotumatz.'

She stared at him blankly with her head tilted, she replied 'You have it before now,' then stepped backwards to join her entourage.

McCann wasn't certain what she meant but he assumed that was a positive response and turned back to the last Tlillan left standing.

The flaming haired Amazon spoke in a calmer tone to the Alpha, his translation software deciphered her speech, 'Kotumatz do you swear allegiance with these savages?'

Cihuateteo began screaming for assistance and all the Gukumatz were drawn to her plight.

McCann and Nestor were both befuddled as to why. Both of these sides had fought a bloody war for thousands of years involving genetic and germ warfare. One side had enslaved the other for thousands of years yet they felt compassion for the Matriarch. The Kotumatz lowered her head and stood staring at the ground without answering the Tlillan.

McCann shouted 'Answer her!'

It was still silent and she refused to reply.

McCann became frustrated and Nestor was preparing to have to fight their way out if necessary.

'They made you worship them as Gods and enslaved your children, answer her!'

The Kotumatz looked up at him 'It was not only them, our own religious class benefited. We only wish to be independent now, no violence, no hate, no revenge. This display of barbarity is revolting.'

McCann frowned then peered over at Nestor who shrugged his shoulders at McCann. The Tlillan female sneered condescendingly at him but he ignored her. Returning his gaze to the Kotumatz he replied 'Well I find the sight of your people makes me want to vomit and you all suffer from chronic halitosis, but there are more important matters at hand. So answer her now or I'll have to find a new alpha Kotumatz!'

The amphibian's eyes began to flicker, her entourage became nervous at the threat.

The Tlillan addressed the alpha 'You would rather be at the mercy of a male than a subject of Xch'uup? These are naught but savage heretic males without a Matriarch to control them.'

McCann was finished, the Kotumatz alpha female refused to speak. Staring the Tlillan female in the eye he tapped his wrist tablet and raised it to his mouth 'Commander Ryu?'

The Korean commander replied immediately 'Yes Commodore?'

He smiled at the Tlillan causing her expression to change to one of fear, 'Tell Hassif to lock all missile platforms on the Tlillan warships and tell Titov to order all ships under his command to do the same, understood?'

'Understood Sir.'

'Inform the Tlillan ships they have 20 minutes to leave our system, if they refuse you have orders to open fire and destroy them. Inform Titov of my orders, understood Commander?'

'Understood Sir.'

McCann tapped his wrist and a minute later the Tlillan female's display leapt up before her eyes. He didn't hear what was said but after finishing she asked him politely 'We are leaving, may I return my Matriarch to our craft?'

McCann felt a weight fall off him, but he didn't let anyone see his relief 'Take her.'

The tall Amazon strode over and lifted Cihuateteo up, supporting her injured side, thanks to her Tlillan strength it was not a difficult task to perform.

Supporting her Matriarch she looked at McCann one last time, 'The sceptre?'

He shook his head slowly without replying; she sneered at him and spat out the words 'I hope your mongrel daughter dies horribly, just as the freaks who came before!'

McCann's eyes widened and he pulled his pistol out but Nestor stood in between the pair breaking McCann's tunnel vision of rage.

The beautiful Tlillan bellowed 'Good fortune Kotumatz!'

Helping her semi-conscious Matriarch limp back along the walkway to their vessel she laughed mockingly.

McCann wasn't sure if she was mocking him or the Kotumatz or both, all he knew was that Nestor had probably prevented a bloodbath. Since actually killing a Matriarch may well have caused the warships above them to retaliate.

Perhaps that was what she was wanted, provoke him to further divide his Gukumatz allies and bring them over to the Tlillans. Either way it was of no concern now, 'Thank you,' he whispered to Nestor as the Tlillan craft lifted off the landing area. Levitating vertically until it was consumed by the thick cloud.

Five minutes later Ryu reported the Tlillans had folded space and left the system.

McCann turned on the Kotumatz 'I'm afraid I'll be reporting this incident, including your actions or lack of.'

The Kotumatz alpha looked at the floor and said nothing.

'Nestor, have as many men as you can spare down here to secure this landing area, ask Titov if he has anyone he can give you.'

Nestor started chatting on his comms.

McCann got on his to Ryu, 'Commander, send a message to Faraday, inform he we've secured the Gukumatz system for the I.S.A. After a tense standoff the Tlillans have accepted the situation and returned to their home system.'

Chapter 13

The Athena and her crew had been stuck in the system, which Faraday christened "Ilium", for several months since the battle. The battle of Ilium had been widely reported for a long time, Network America was demanding the I.S.A grant transport for a crew of reporters to interview the Athena and her crew. Faraday had granted the request and when the captured Gukumatz ship, which had been renamed and fitted with an SI and human crew, that was doing the donkey work transporting spare parts to and fro between Earth and Ilium returned it would bring Jerry and his crew with him.

The three captured warships had been refitted to accommodate a human crew, SIs had hurriedly been installed, since it was decided the Gukumatz couldn't be trusted to back them up if it came to the crunch. Changes had to be made starting with the warships and all control mechanisms concerning defences.

The Ares had returned to Earth months ago, for the while McCann was the governor of the system, not that he took any delight in the position. Dealing with the locals was a miserable task; he often said if you looked up tedium in the dictionary you'd see a description of his job. The locals seemed to make it their business to drag out even the simplest of tasks with bureaucracy and paper work; they resisted his will at every possible turn. He frequently wondered how the Tlillans ever managed to get them to do anything. The worst part was the weather, even after they had started scrubbing the atmosphere it didn't improve. McCann was under the impression it was due to the stations crashing into the moons that the atmosphere was so humid and caustic. He was wrong, the reason these toads always smelt so nasty was because of their ideal environment, he often pointed out that an anti-matter bomb could only improve the place much to the horror of the natives.

He visited the Kotu spawning pool once, as an honoured guest, only to discover why they live so high up. On the surface the atmosphere is too thick for a human to breathe without drowning from moisture building up in the lungs. He returned soaked and stinking to high heaven, Nestor found it hilarious as all Russians seemed to delight in others misfortune. The last straw was when he couldn't light his cigar due to the humidity and ended up smoking one of Nestor's cigarettes.

Finally the day had come when McCann hoped to get off this moon. He was sitting in his air conditioned office, the penthouse of the tallest structure at the Kotu pool city. A report came in on his desk station, he smiled with relief as he saw the I.S.A Clotho ejected from the wormhole. One of the refitted warships carrying Faraday and the new governor of Ilium, he could finally get back to commanding the Athena and leave this wretched place behind. He called up Nestor who was already making his way to the main landing pad. McCann made certain his uniform was clean before leaving his small Spartan office.

He walked past his secretary, she returned his smile as he entered the lift, 'Grand thoroughfare please' said McCann in a happy tone.

As the lift slowed he took the breathing tubes from inside his collar and clipped them onto his nose. The doors opened and the humid air rushed in along with the stench of ammonia which by now he no longer noticed.

McCann marched out into the main lobby which was decorated in a jade like material. Walking past the main desk the Gukumatz working there spoke 'Good afternoon Commodore,' in his best croaky English.

McCann smiled at him and replied 'Afternoon Kotumatz.'

The receptionist was shocked to see the Commodore smile, he decided it prudent not to correct him by pointing out he is from the Boku spawning pool.

He marched outside and said hello to two stunned Vympel guards then crossed the thoroughfare and onto the walkway only slowing down as he walked past the spot he'd slain the Tlillan males.

He quickly marched over the walkway and onto the landing pad where Nestor had been waiting with six men, 'Cigarette?' he asked McCann.

McCann replied with a big grin 'No thanks old boy, I won't be needing those nasty Russian sticks anymore.'

Nestor returned the grin 'You quitting?'

McCann chuckled 'In a sense.'

Nestor made a puzzled look 'What is it Duncan?'

McCann replied triumphantly 'I Sir shall be leaving this bloody shit hole!'

Nestor looked surprised 'Really?'

'Faraday is bringing a new governor today, and I'll be on my way back to the Captain's chair!'

Nestor put his cigarette in his mouth and shook hands with McCann 'Congratulations Duncan,' he said in his thick Russian accent.

On observing the transport craft descending to the platform Nestor flicked his cigarette over the side (something which angered the Gukumatz to no end) and called his men to attention. The craft landed and they stood in line at the exit which rippled open to reveal Faraday dressed in a grey three piece suit with a bowler hat. The jacket was a frock coat; he held a small walking stick of mahogany and gold in his gloved hands. Faraday stepped onto the pad where Nestor and his men saluted, to the discomfort of Faraday who held the brim of his hat, tipped it then moved on to McCann whose hand he shook, both were glad to see each other.

McCann raised an eyebrow and said 'Looking pretty damn sharp Bill, you have an eye for the Gukumatz ladies?'

They both laughed.

'No I prefer my ladies with teeth and without warts old boy!' he replied jollily.

McCann inquired with anticipation 'So have you brought the new governor with you?' at which point Faraday lost his gay attitude and McCann's face dropped.

'Don't worry she's here Duncan,' he blurted out as McCann watched his wife step out onto the landing pad.

McCann glared at Faraday 'Ilam?'

Faraday replied timidly 'I'm afraid so Duncan.'

The Commodore put his face in his palm and the other hand on his hip 'This is a joke isn't it? Tell me it's a big joke William!' he muttered towards the sky.

Faraday held onto both of McCann's shoulders 'Pull yourself together man, you've got over a month of leave after the transfer and you can spend it all with your family.'

McCann shook his head in disbelief 'Yes, spend it on this shit hole!' he screamed causing all heads to turn 'Now my wife is stuck on this toilet too!'

Faraday shook him desperately 'Shut up man the bloody press are here with us!'

Ilam strode over to calm her husband down 'Duncan what is the matter?'

He sneered at his wife 'We can discuss this later.'

The tall Valkyrie looked down on him haughtily 'Discuss what?'

'What you're doing here when you should be at home!' he snapped.

Ilam folded her arms 'I apologise but I was not aware I required your permission before accepting an assignment!' she retorted.

McCann who was now furious pointed at his wife and snapped 'You know what I mean woman, why can't you just behave yourself?'

The Amazon's eyes changed to a light red 'But it is acceptable for you to go gallivanting around the galaxy?'

Faraday cut in to put out the fire 'Commodore your behaviour is ….' but McCann in his rage grabbed Faraday by his waistcoat, frightening his superior and alarming all present.

Nestor decided to break it up, but McCann saw him approach. The Englishman's right hand left the waistcoat, slipped down and brushed his holster. Nestor grasped his pulse rifle; the whine of the battery charging could be heard over the entire landing pad as he activated it. But before he acted any further the grizzly Russian stopped dead in his tracks. For some inexplicable reason he stood frozen as a statue then McCann heard a familiar voice call out 'Father!'

The Englishman looked past Nestor and saw his daughter, who stood a good six foot now.

She quickly ran up to him 'Father, please don't cause a scene,' she asked kindly.

He found it impossible to refuse his daughter not due to her mental abilities but he loved her more than anything in the universe and to deny her was something even his rage couldn't prevent.

McCann released Faraday delicately, clearing his throat he apologised 'I'm sorry Bill, I've been on edge for a while. I was looking forward to coming home, please accept my apologies.'

Faraday dusted his waistcoat 'Apology accepted old boy, just try to give me some warning next time; even Beaumont was never that bad!'

McCann made a wry smile 'This place has that effect on you; Louis would probably enjoy living here come to think of it!'

He put his arms out; his daughter ran up to him and hugged him. She was now almost as tall as him and her bear hug was crushing his rib cage, 'How is my Malikah?' he managed to ask without gasping.

She released him 'I'm in good health Father; I know I've grown since you last saw me.'

He kissed her cheek 'You'll be taller than me soon, I'm not sure how I'll discipline you when you're bigger than I am!' he jested.

Malikah blushed as all Tlillans do, her eyes turned a pink hue, then replied 'Do not be silly father.'

She probably had the strength of three men as she stood before him now; the only person that could physically discipline her for years was Ilam. However the child's mental prowess made that a pointless task since she could reduce even another Tlillan to a vegetable, if she put her mind to it. Yet for some odd reason she always obeyed her father, no one knew why and even McCann had no idea. The truth was that he loved her more than anyone or anything and she sensed it. He loved her without question, and unlike her mother, he had no plans for her other than whatever made her happy. The type of unconditional love he had for Malikah touched her more so because on Tlillan it didn't exist. She had delved into the dreamscape and felt the cold and ruthless nature of Tlillan society. They didn't invest emotionally in one another as individuals, it was considered a distraction that could disrupt the perception of reality they required to read the dreamscape. So she loved her father back, much to the disdain of her mother. However Malikah was far too powerful now for anyone to prevent her from doing as she wished.

Another familiar voice called across the landing area 'Director?', McCann saw where it came from and his heart sank. Jerry Habeeb and a couple of journalists had watched the whole scene and no doubt recorded it.

'Please come over Mr. Habeeb, I'm sure you and Duncan are already good friends?'

Malikah let out a snigger and her mother muttered under her breath 'Malikah!'

Jerry stepped out of the craft with his sound and camera man. He first gazed at Nestor, 'Is he okay?' asked Jerry.

Ilam put her hand on her daughter's shoulder 'Release him Malikah,' and a second later Nestor crumpled into a pile on the floor.

McCann looked at the soldiers standing in line 'Take him to the med centre.'

Two men picked him up and carried Nestor to the med centre whilst Jerry had his staff recording it. McCann approached Jerry and pointed at his camera man who controlled a hovering sphere about the size of a cricket ball, 'I want you to delete that.'

Jerry looked over at Faraday rather desperately 'Bill?'

McCann interrupted 'Forget it Habeeb I'm the governor of this place and you'll do as your told. I want to see all your files before departure and I'll censor them at my discretion.'

Ilam smirked and put her arm around McCann's 'Actually, I'm the governor now my dear.'

She got a kick out of pushing her husband into rants and rages probably due to the fact that Tlillan men were so passive and unremarkable.

He sighed whilst turning his head, looked up to his wife and said 'Then this, I suppose, will be your first decision Ilam.'

The flaming haired beauty peered down at Jerry and said haughtily 'You shall do as my husband instructed Mr. Habeeb, is that understood?'

Jerry looked at Faraday who silently nodded back at him, turned back to Ilam and replied 'Yes ma'am.'

McCann stepped towards the walkway leading off the landing pad 'Shall we get settled in at the hotel then have something to eat in an hour or so?'

The party were all ready to lay on a soft bed and tryout the local cuisine so they followed McCann for the short walk across the thoroughfare to the super sky scraper opposite the landing pad. Half an hour later McCann was joined in the restaurant by his wife and daughter. The seats were large bucket affairs that were very comfortable despite being designed for the Gukumatz. The rest of the place was decorated in a mosaic fashion consisting of mainly jade and amber pieces, the mosaics were very beautiful depicting tales from the past.

On the north wall was McCann's favourite, it was one of his first questions when settling in the building. The picture reminded him of the Medusa with some Gukumatz below her either praying or begging for mercy. His Gukumatz aide had informed him it was a depiction of the Grand Matriarch visiting their home world before they were forced to flee it. He asked why the Medusa (his new name for the Grand Matriarch. Much to the pleasure of his aide and all Gukumatz when he explained the Earth myth) looked so different to the Grand Matriarch he had seen. His aide explained that in the past she was always a Twilighter, since they were the ruling class on Tlillan before the plague. The serpents rising from her head and rotten teeth with claw like nails in her hands was artistic license, pointing out her true intentions rather than a depiction of a true Twilighter.

As Malikah and Ilam walked into the restaurant every Gukumatz stopped what they were doing and kowtowed to the pair. McCann looked around observing the surreal scene until his eyes settled on his wife, 'What on Earth?' he asked slowly.

Closely behind her followed Jerry and his reporters who were as excited as McCann was puzzled. Jerry was recording the scene with delight, 'Have you got that?' he was asking his camera man who stood tapping away at his tablet whilst nodding.

McCann stood up as his wife approached and pulled a chair out for her to sit at the table, she smiled approvingly and sat down. Malikah was about to pull a chair out next to her mother but before she could a Gukumatz scurried along the floor on his hands and feet and pulled it out for her.

Malikah smiled and spoke in Tlillan which McCann recognised as "Thank you", the Gukumatz remained kowtowed on the floor beneath her, motionless. Ilam looked at her daughter 'Malikah, that is enough,' his daughter displayed a naughty smile.

She then spoke again in Tlillan with a deep booming tone that reverberated around the restaurant and McCann didn't recognise the phrase. The translation ear piece spat out 'Those of submission arise,' the Gukumatz picked themselves up from the floor and carried on with their business.

Jerry marched to the table and sat himself down with his two friends hovering around 'Could you tell us what just took place Ilam?'

McCann was just as interested 'Yes please tell,' he said inquisitively.

She was obviously pleased with the events that had just occurred and spoke first to Jerry 'The Gukumatz bowed for Malikah.'

Jerry was tantalized 'Why would they show any respect for what must be their most hated enemy?'

'Malikah is not their enemy, she is the one destined to unite the Tlillan and Gukumatz.'

Jerry wasn't satisfied and queried further 'Is that what they believe?'

'Yes Jerry.'

'How do they think your daughter, Malikah, is going to unite two bitter foes?'

Ilam smiled broadly and pointed towards Eastern wall where behind the bar sat a massive mosaic. It depicted a Tlillan female of average size with dark slightly curly hair. The figure stood amongst many Tlillan and Gukumatz with one of each kneeling before her, she held her arms out similar to Christ the Redeemer.

Jerry examined the mosaic and inquired 'Could you explain the mural on the wall for us?'

Malikah was looking decidedly bored as her mother went on to gush about her daughter 'It is a depiction of the Mictlancihuatl. Both the Tlillan and Gukumatz have their separate prophecies concerning her and what she will achieve. The Gukumatz believe she will unite the factions bringing the Tlillan and Gukumatz together ending all conflict and slavery.'

Ilam turned to her daughter with a proud look.

'What do the Tlillans believe she will do?' asked Jerry.

Ilam's expression became a lot more serious 'She will introduce a new age amongst my people; she will save us from oblivion ushering in another golden age.'

McCann had a very disparaging look on his face much to the disapproval of his wife 'How will she do this?' asked Jerry.

But Ilam was finished with his questions for now 'I'm sorry that will have to be all for now Jerry, perhaps another time.'

McCann was aware of the local folklore but didn't realise how seriously they took it until today.

Next Jerry spoke to McCann 'Well it's been a long time Commodore and it's good to see you in one piece.'

McCann nodded 'And you Jerry.'

Jerry went on to ask him about the events of his governorship 'Now I'd like to ask you about the uprising on Ilium 3 Commodore.'

McCann was taken aback and felt very uncomfortable discussing the attempted coup 'I'm sorry Jerry but I'd rather not talk about it.'

Jerry implored 'I'm sorry but Director Faraday has assured me you'll do an interview on it, everyone has been talking about the suppression of the moon since it happened a few months ago.'

McCann looked at his wife who by the expression on her face confirmed his story, McCann rolled his eyes 'Very well.'

McCann ordered a drink from the bar, the waiter came over with the menus, he took out a pack of Nestor's smokes from the arm pocket of his jacket. Lit the smoke and began the story of what the media back home had hyped as an uprising or siege or whatever got people logging on to their channel.

Six months in and the captured ships were in use to one degree or another. Titov was back patrolling the home system and Ryu was in command of the Athena whilst McCann languished on Ilium 1. Nestor was employed as his bodyguard with six of his best men and his Gukumatz aide was driving him crazy. The aide was called Kotumatz which was not much help, so McCann picked out a gold chain with a blue gem and made him wear it. His aide was very displeased with wearing the chain since he felt it to be demeaning, however he had no choice. McCann made a point of it and he would be replaced otherwise.

The Governor spent most of his time in his office since the place stank so terribly and the Gukumatz didn't take very well to human air conditioning. The AC units caused havoc with their skin since it was very sensitive to the cold and low humidity. So he was left to put up with their life style unless he was in his office, where he could have a cigar and a scotch.

Work was going ahead on getting the orbital lifts back in place, once done Faraday was interested in replacing those on Earth and Mars with a similar Mag Lev lift system. It was simple to erect and far more efficient, allowing much heavier payloads to be moved quicker than with the old ribbon system.

One day McCann was sitting in the restaurant of the super sky scraper he worked from, having a drink with Nestor who was trying to coax him into smoking one of his cigarettes.

Nestor found the moon very uncomfortable and they were both swapping detracting remarks concerning the environment. His aide Kotumatz approached, passing him a tablet about the size of a small envelope. McCann thanked him and pressed his thumb on the screen; it identified his DNA print and displayed the scene on Ilium 3.

A Gukumatz was reading off a list of demands, the recording was subtitled, he was declaring independence. The moon Ilium 3 was the agrarian world where most of the food supply was cultivated and shipped out via the orbital lift. The population had revolted and taken control of the ground based planetary defence grid, which consisted of missile stations hidden around the globe with the ability to knock anything out of orbit.

The small group of I.S.A officers on the moon for administrative purposes were being held hostage, but they would be unharmed as long as an arrangement could be reached with the governor.

McCann went white as a sheet.

Nestor asked 'What is it?' in a concerned voice.

He looked up at Nestor 'Some radical has seized control of Ilium 3, we've got about two weeks to get it back.'

Nestor didn't understand 'Why two weeks?'

'Because that's how long the food will last before the other two moons run out. We need to sort this out before the rest of these bloody toads find out what's happening.'

The Governor stood up and tapped his wrist tablet, his secretary answered, 'Get me Commander Ryu.'

Half a minute later he heard the voice of Commander Ryu Yong, 'Commander Ryu.'

McCann picked up the tablet his aide had passed him and tapped away on it, then he spoke into his wrist 'I'm sending you a report Ryu, I want this dealt with within 24 hours do you understand?'

There was a long pause until she replied 'Understood Commodore, is there anything else?'

He whispered into the communicator so that no Gukumatz might hear him 'You are not authorized to use atomics or anti-matter, we need the environment intact. However you may use chemical warfare at your discretion, and if needed Vympel 1 and 2 may be deployed at your discretion.'

There was another pause for about 10 seconds as Ryu took it in, 'Understood Commodore, I'll report back within 24 hrs with either a surrender or that creature's head.'

McCann spoke into his wrist communicator 'McCann out,' then looked at Nestor who had a knowing look on his face.

'I already feel pity for that stupid toad,' he said to McCann.

He looked back at Nestor and said under his breath 'Just keep it under your hat for as long as possible, we don't need riots on this planet.'

Above the moon in space Ryu was on the bridge of the Athena, sat in the Captain's chair, 'Athena plot a course for Ilium 3, put us in a high orbit. Hassif certify the course when you have it.'

Shortly Hassif said over his shoulder 'Course certified Commander.'

The short Korean girl eyed the moon on the view screen in front of her 'Engage.'

The Athena made her way to the moon, pushed by the bright glow of her anti-matter engines.

Ryu turned to her first mate 'McKinley, have Lieutenant Kim load up the drones with Napalm-E and nerve agent. He's to prepare for a ground assault immediately, understood?'

McKinley who was now the first mate stood at the drone station behind Ryu, 'Yes Sir,' he replied.

As the Athena moved silently through space Ryu sat back in her Captain's chair and made herself comfortable. She exhibited a rather sinister smile as the ship approached the Gukumatz moon that loomed closer and closer.

Ryu was finally the Captain of a ship, if only temporarily, doing the only job she knew how to which unfortunately for those on the moon below was crushing her enemies.

McKinley was very nervous giving out the orders to prep for napalm and nerve agent. Until he was selected for the Athena he had spent his career on a British battleship. The Scotsman had been involved in no wars or battles or anything of real note up until becoming a member of Athena's crew. McKinley had strong feelings when it came to using anti-personnel weapons. The use of napalm and nerve gas made his stomach turn and Ryu saw how ill at ease he was when given the order. The Korean was of the mind that he was just a young man and would toughen up eventually.

McKinley believed it was immoral to employ such methods to defeat even your worst enemy, vaporising them was fine but to cause such unwarranted pain and misery disgusted him. Especially Napalm-E which had been created from a mix of chemicals improving on past concoctions, from Napalm-A used in the 20th century during the second world war and Korea to today.

The fact that it had been used in Korea for two centuries to devastating effect made him wonder why Ryu employed its use without giving it a thought. The Americans created Napalm-B during the Vietnam war since the first recipe refused to stick to the skin and the Vietnamese, if they were quick enough, could wipe it off before it would kill them. Napalm-B was a horrific weapon but effective, and when faced with overwhelming numbers of infantry it tipped the balance in your favour, as long as you maintained air superiority in order to deliver it.

Over the centuries the recipe changed alongside warfare and Napalm-E was created, it wasn't designed to kill, the purpose was to maim the enemy. It burnt at far lower temperatures than previous concoctions however this morph of napalm bonded to any compound natural or synthetic at the molecular level. Rather than just burning the skin it smouldered on it and the only way to stop the intense pain of burning was to remove the surrounding tissue.

In Manchuria Ryu and her fellow pilots had used it to great effect. When enemy infantry outnumbered their forces, Napalm-E was employed. Fired from a large missile, due to the weight and size was hung below the fuselage of the drone; it would explode above the target firing out cluster bombs above the enemy. The gelatinous substance was spread over as wide an area as possible and smouldered for days, if an infantryman stepped on it he would have to remove his boot before it burnt through the sole. Unable to march through fields of napalm or retreat they were pinned down with many in need of medical attention. At the mercy of the Korean air force they were usually finished off with missile attacks.

Used against civilian uprisings in Manchuria, it was an excellent tool for containing the frequent outbreaks of rebellion. During one large province wide uprising, Ryu had General Kim approve the use of nerve agent to finish off the resistance; enabling her to move on to the next problem town or village speedily until within a week the job was done.

Now she was preparing to subdue the resistance on an entire world, light years away.

As they entered high orbit McKinley reported 'Squadron leader Kim reports squadron one and two are prepared for launch.'

Ryu relaxed in her chair and crossed her legs casually 'Athena send the co-ordinates of all the ground defence stations and population centers to Kim and request a plan of attack within 20 minutes.'

Athena replied in her soft voice 'Squadron leader Kim has received the data and will comply with your request Commander.'

Ryu smiled and looked up at the neural housing above her 'Thank you Athena.'

'You are welcome Commander.'

On the side view screen Athena brought up a map of the moon's surface including missile stations, possible military targets and major population centers. The capital of the moon lay at the equator around the base station of the orbital lift, it was also the most well defended area.

Ryu looked at Hassif 'Can you get me the orbital station Hassif?'

He tapped away 'Just a moment Commander,' and within moments on the main view screen the Russian head of security appeared.

He was a tall man with brown eyes, dressed in typical Vympel uniform including the black beret which had stains of Gukumatz blood on it, 'Greetings Commander Ryu I am Podpraporshchik Nikolay Greshnev,' he said in a thick Russian accent.

Ryu could heard shots being fired from pulse rifles in the background 'What is your situation Podpraporshchik?' she asked quickly.

'At 02:00 hours Ilium standard time the Gukumatz crew attempted to capture the orbital station by force. The Gukumatz were unsuccessful and we are mopping up at the moment.'

Ryu smiled 'Could I speak with Kapitan Maslov please?'

The Sergeant looked at the floor for a moment then his eyes returned to Ryu, 'The Gukumatz assassinated him when they began their attack more than an hour ago Commander, I am in command of the station for now.'

Ryu rose from her chair 'They killed Lev?' she said in a daze.

'Kapitan Maslov was shot in his bed, he was still asleep Commander,' replied the Sergeant somewhat uncomfortably.

Ryu had made friends easily amongst all the Russians assigned to the Ilium system, they already knew her to some degree and were excited to meet her. Since they provided security for the I.S.A there were many assigned to the system and all were Spetsnaz.

Ryu nodded at the Sergeant 'Well done Podpraporshchik Greshnev, do you require assistance?'

He nodded 'Thank you Commander but we have everything under control here.'

She made a forced smile 'Very well carry on Podpraporshchik and keep the station secure, keep all remaining Gukumatz under lock and key. If you encounter any resistance you have my authority to execute at your discretion, understood?'

He saluted her stiffly 'Understood Sir.'

She sat back in her chair 'Ryu out,' and tapped the panel on the arm of the chair. The image of Sergeant Greshnev was replaced by the moon of Ilium 3 and the orbital station, which had been constructed in the shipyards of Earth and Mars in prefabricated blocks to a modified Gukumatz design. It looked like a massive brick built from odd fitting pieces of Lego. The mostly flat bottom faced the moon where the Mag Lev tower had been lowered to ground zero and connected to the already existing station below. In less than six months three stations with gravity plating had been placed in orbit and connected with the moons.

The Gukumatz didn't believe it would be possible and many at the I.S.A were in agreement. Yet with the shipyards working around the clock, along with the one remaining Gukumatz shipyard that had been cloaked and orbiting a dead moon, the titanic task was completed.

Ryu called over her shoulder 'Where's that report?'

McKinley franticly sent a message to Kim in the drone bays, where teams of pilots sat ready in a massive bay filled with rows of drone booths. Within a few seconds McKinley appeased his Captain bringing her a tablet 'Commander.'

The Red Dragon looked to her right and took the tablet, whilst reading it she said slowly 'Thank you McKinley.'

After spending a few minutes in thought she handed it back to McKinley then in a stern voice spoke 'Athena I want to maintain high orbit on the station side of the moon. Once we've achieved orbit begin bombarding the ground based missile stations, inform me when you're ready to begin bombardment.'

The Athena replied softly 'Understood Commander.'

McKinley said quietly in Ryu's ear 'Are we really going to fire on them?'

Ryu looked up at her first officer 'What would you have me do?'

McKinley's face had a blank expression 'Perhaps we could negotiate?'

Ryu shook her head 'We have less than 24 hours to bring this to an end; these creatures are not in a mood for negotiating.'

Athena broke the discussion 'Ready to begin bombardment Commander.'

Ryu looked up at the neural housing 'Good, how long will it be before all the missile sites are destroyed?'

'All known ground based missile defence sites may be destroyed in less than 3 hours Commander,' replied Athena.

Ryu relaxed with her legs crossed in her chair 'Begin firing Athena and inform me when all sites have been destroyed.'

'Yes Commander.'

The Starboard cannons began firing on the only defence the rebels possessed. The Athena used the lightest shells in her armoury so as to cause the least damage to the environment, yet one hit from only a single barrel of the double barrelled rail cannons was enough to take out an entire station. Besides the atmosphere scrubbers would remove most of the pollution in a week, napalm would burn out within a few days and nerve gas dissipates quickly.

An hour into the bombardment and the Gukumatz were attempting to communicate with the Athena but Ryu ignored their attempts, much to McKinley's frustration. The face of the moon was marked with black clouds of smoke and burning craters where the defences once stood. With each thump of the ship's cannons another cloud appeared. Until three hours later the once green and yellow moon was scarred with craters, barely visible past the smoke and debris thrown into the atmosphere.

Athena had finished her pounding of the agrarian moon and informed Ryu, who had been pacing on deck observing Athena's work the entire time. For the full 3 hours the communications terminal had been blocking the incoming transmission from the city below, but now Ryu changed her mind, 'Hassif put the call from the surface through.'

She stood facing the view screen with arms folded and legs slightly apart when the image of her adversary appeared before her. She said nothing and waited for him to speak, he waited a few seconds perhaps for her to speak but when there was only silence he began to burp and croak in that foul manner.

Staring at her with his head at an angle the translation AI spoke 'Please desist attack.'

Ryu replied in a stoic manner 'Surrender yourselves and release your prisoners then I will desist.'

The Gukumatz appeared to be shocked by this statement, which to any human would seem a logical demand, 'Bokumatz refuse, Boku spawning pool not human.'

Ryu sighed 'Hummmfff, you've the choice of surrender or I continue with the next stage of our assault, once I've begun I will not desist.'

The Gukumatz made a foul gurgling noise, which everyone assumed was of disapproval, 'Bokumatz refuse demands, Bokumatz will return Humans when you wish.'

Ryu looked at Hassif 'I've had enough of this retard, turn him off!' and the view screen went back to the burning moon below.

She tapped her wrist and the voice of Kim came through, 'Yes Commander?'

'Begin your assault on the main population centers Kim, and inform me when the first wave is over. I want that toad to surrender within the hour is that understood?'

'Understood Sir.'

Ryu watched as squadron one launched, the Shogun II drones made their way to the planet surface loaded with Napalm-E. Shortly afterwards squadron two launched carrying nerve agent, loaded into Josen III air/ground missiles.

Ryu made her way to the drone station behind her chair to observe the action unfold. She had served with Flight Lieutenant Kim in the past; he was one of those gamers recruited alongside her many years ago. Aside from Ryu he was the most able pilot of the group and he brought many loyal people with him to the Athena. Now he was leading a squadron light years away, fighting an enemy that he'd never seen in person.

Ryu observed the first wave as it fired the heavy Jujak missiles on towns and villages surrounding the main city; isolating them from the focus of the uprising and the focus of the assault which was the main city itself.

The Shogun II was a redesigned Shogun I scram drone, for use in space and atmospheric flight, all of the weaponry had been similarly redesigned for atmospheric entry. The Jujak missile was totally original however; a large missile intended to deliver a heavy duty warhead over long distances in either space or an atmosphere.

The drones entered the moon's atmosphere in a pack and once in they broke up into several teams which split up to attack individual targets. Cutting through the smoke and debris like a knife they screeched towards the ground then pulled up.

Ryu was observing Kim's drone via the camera in the nose cone. At Mach 9 he raced towards his target, a town with a large depot for gathering food before it was shipped off to the city then up the orbital lift and distributed to the other moons. The Shogun II released its grip on the missile which carried a large bulbous warhead packed with cluster bombs of napalm. Immediately the missile fired its engine and flew in front of the drone, Kim's drone peeled off so as not to get caught in the explosion and Ryu switched to the missile cam.

She began flicking back and forth between different cams on the drone and the missile until just before reaching the town it exploded in the air. The cluster of bombs ripped out of the warhead casing that had blown itself apart. A second passed and they exploded producing a sheet of gelatinous fire blanketing the town, turning it into a living hell for the occupants. The body and engine of the missile slammed into the centre of the town taking some fire bathed structures down with it.

Gukumatz homes were burning at such a heat people ran outside to escape the boiling temperatures only to run into the streets of hell. The Napalm-E bonding at the molecular level with their thick amphibian skin causing intense pain. Most fell unconscious others ran back indoors it was a scene of pandemonium.

Athena focused in on the town Ryu had been viewing and turned her attention to the main view screen, Ryu turned and watched with a sinister grin. Many of the crew in the pit stopped what they were doing and glanced at the scene of horror. From the heavens the Gukumatz resembled frightened insects trying to flee from a certain fate. Ryu watched on, as a vengeful deity playing with her rebellious worshipper's pitiful mortality, taking delight in their misery.

The view screen displayed hundreds of small ants on fire running in all directions up and down the streets in pain and terror. Ryu let out a small chuckle which caused McKinley to snap his head and stare disapprovingly at his Captain. Ryu turned her head to face him, looked him up and down haughtily, shook her head and went back to observing the carnage below.

Her communicator vibrated, she tapped her wrist to hear Kim's voice, 'First stage over Commander, we're ready to deliver the second stage on your order, Sir.'

She said something in Korean that McKinley didn't understand and Kim replied also in Korean causing Ryu to laugh. Members of the crew including the pit turned and gave her an odd look, but when she frowned they quickly returned to work and Ryu continued chuckling under her breath.

McKinley later discovered she had been engaged in some online banter with her old gaming partner and now squadron leader. Athena had translated the conversation for him a few days later in private, Ryu stated 'You have my authority to gank his adds' to which Kim replied 'When he rage quits you can buy the drinks!'

McKinley didn't fully understand the conversation nor did he find it amusing, it lowered his opinion of Commander Ryu. Not her ability which was above question, but her morality which he found very distasteful. Though McKinley accepted that if he'd been forced to live her life, his morals would probably be no better.

After the first wave had escaped the moon's atmosphere the second stage began entry, led by Flight Lieutenant Lee. Using the tactics perfected by Ryu and Kim during the Manchurian conflict they dived for the ground then pulled up hugging it as they approached their targets at high speed. It took a lot of training to teach a pilot to fly a scram drone so close to the ground at Mach 10 without destroying it. In fact it took a lot of crashed drones too since the simulator didn't always cut the mustard compared to the real world. Ryu had a natural ability which she'd developed online and transferred to the real thing. At first very few pilots recognised her combat tactics as viable, mostly because they couldn't replicate them. As time went on her wing racked up the kills and decayed enemy air superiority until the tide had turned. The Red Dragon's manoeuvres became the standard practice of the ROKAF. By the time Ryu had left to join the I.S.A every squadron leader in the ROKAF flew a red scram drone, the psychological effects upon the enemy were notable.

Even on the Athena each squadron had the leader's drone painted red, it meant nothing to the Gukumatz but to the Korean pilots it leant a big confidence boost. Without that red drone leading them, morale in the past had fallen. The Red Dragon and her red drone had become an icon that instilled courage into the Korean heart and pierced the enemy with fear.

Kim's red drone screamed at Mach 12 along the landscape and he fired his first missile hitting the town centre. He changed course for his secondary target unopposed and fired off his second missile delivering nerve agent to a village not deemed worthy of a napalm attack. Then he pulled up towards the sky firing the anti-matter engines again which pushed him to Mach 15; out of the moon's atmosphere and back towards the Athena and her magnetic net.

Below, the orbital station side of the moon was in a mess especially around the station city where many fires burnt between craters.

Once the second squadron had docked and commenced reloading Ryu spoke 'Contact that toad Hassif, I want to speak with him.'

Hassif tapped away 'I have him,' he said as the image of a distressed Gukumatz appeared on the view screen.

Ryu tightened her lips together and glared at his image folding her arms and waiting for him to speak, 'Desist Savagery Human.'

Her face didn't flinch as he implored her.

'Surrender yourselves and release your hostages then we can talk,' her cold voice replied.

The Gukumatz was frantic 'Human barbarian desist, before Bokumatz spawning pool is polluted.'

Ryu was perplexed as to why he didn't just surrender or tell her to shove it! Her diplomacy skills had been honed over years of online gaming and she only opened negotiations when she was poised to crush her enemy. The stark choices for her opponent were surrender everything you have and survive or be destroyed, to which the reply was usually something on the lines of "Get bent!" or "Yeah fine!". She never surrendered since it was better to fight and die then start over, rather than spend hours as a lap dog but this Gukumatz just didn't get it. He persisted on demanding Ryu desist, which she quite clearly was not prepared to do, his stubborn nature only antagonised her.

She looked at him incredulously 'The second wave is preparing Bokumatz and it's my job to return to the Governor with a surrender. This is your last chance before the second wave, surrender yourselves and release the hostages.'

The Gukumatz was flicking his tongue out of his mouth and making awful burbling noises through his nose then the translator spoke 'Bokumatz will release your people and you may leave.'

Ryu couldn't take anymore 'Please turn him off Hassif,' and the image was replaced by the moon below.

She tapped her wrist and the voice of Kim replied 'Yes Commander?'

Ryu spoke into her collar mic 'Begin wave 2 when ready and inform me when you're prepared to launch your assault on the capital Kim.'

Kim's voice replied from the wrist tablet 'Understood Commander, Kim out.'

The drones were ejected from the launch bays and once again made for the surface to repeat the previous attack on fresh targets.

'Incoming transmission from Commodore McCann,' Hassif called over his shoulder.

'Put him through,' replied Ryu.

The view screen went from drones flying towards the moon to McCann sitting in his office 'Hello Ryu I'm only checking in to see how it's going.'

Ryu smiled 'The missile defence sites on the station side of Ilium 3 have been disabled by orbital bombardment. The first wave of drones have completed their ground assault and the second has been dispatched just now. I don't have any data on the attack so far but will transmit my first report ...' she looked at Hassif who made eye contact with one of the crew in the pit.

The man in the pit said something into his mic and Hassif turned back to his Commander displaying his hand with all fingers and thumb outstretched.

'I'll send you a report in 5 minutes' she said quickly.

McCann who was sat at his desk on Ilium 1 and probably a lot more nervous than he looked nodded 'Excellent, what can you tell me so far?'

Ryu took a deep breath puffing up her chest then spoke 'Most of the station side infrastructure has been or is about to be disabled. All major population centers have been isolated; however the leader refuses to surrender. The capital so far has been untouched, but if he doesn't surrender after this wave then I'll be forced to begin strikes on the capital and deploy troops if necessary.'

McCann nodded knowingly 'These bloody toads are as stubborn as mules they only relent when their spawn pool is in jeopardy, perhaps you should keep that in mind?'

Ryu smiled 'Thanks, I'll give that a try Duncan.'

McCann returned her smile 'Good luck Commander, McCann out.'

His image disappeared and the moon took its place on the side of the view screen. Many of the targets were marked as destroyed or hit with a red blip. Many new red blips popped up rolling across the surface as the second wave hit their targets with napalm and nerve agent.

'Athena is the Bokumatz spawning pool displayed on the map?' inquired Ryu.

'No Commander Ryu, do you wish to view the Bokumatz spawning pool?' said Athena softly.

'Yes please Athena,' she replied and a large green blip appeared in a forested area below sea level.

'Commander there are many lesser spawning pools, do you wish to view those also?'

Ryu peered at the neural housing rather surprised 'Really? Yes, please show me Athena.'

There were four smaller pools station side and six planet side 'Thank you very much Athena,' Ryu said in a tone of deep thought.

Ryu stood observing the map and thinking silently as the pit correlated the data for McCann and piped it to Hassif in a finished report.

'Data packet ready for transmission to Commodore McCann,' called Hassif.

Ryu made a shoo action with her hand towards him 'Uuuurrrrhhhhhhh!' she grumbled with her eyes fixed on the map of Ilium 3.

The crew were at a loss apart from Hassif who said nothing more and transmitted the data to McCann on Ilium 1.

Ryu's wrist tablet vibrated and she tapped it 'This is Kim, second wave is complete. All drones are docked and accounted for, Sir.'

Ryu was still transfixed by the map on the view screen 'Good, I want you to load up for a third wave but you have new objectives Kim.'

She looked down at her tablet and tapped away 'The objectives have changed Kim; I want one drone prepared to launch and strike the first target on the list with Napalm-E, understood?'

Kim replied in a puzzled tone 'Just one drone and one target?'

'That's right,' said Ryu a little forcefully.

'Understood, I'll be ready to go in a few minutes, Sir.'

'Good, Ryu out,' she said tapping her wrist, 'Hassif get me the toad!' said Ryu waiting for its image to appear.

When it did the Gukumatz was still frantic but this time Ryu began the conversation, 'Bokumatz I'm giving you another chance to surrender before I target the spawning pools.'

The alien went a pale shade of green and for a few seconds stood frozen then croaked and burped 'Barbarian desist, spawning pool sacred! Tlillan understand this, are you not Tlillan?'

Ryu rolled her eyes 'Jesus Christ! You still don't get it do you? I'm giving you two choices you idiot! Surrender or I order a strike on one of your spawning pools, do you understand?'

The Bokumatz stood taking in the translator then replied 'Bokumatz understand. Spawning pool sacred site all Tlillan recognise Gukumatz spawning pools as sacred, do Human understand?'

McKinley then stepped over and whispered in Ryu's ear 'He's trying to say it's like threatening to destroy the Sacred Mosque in Mecca in order to get the Muslims to surrender. He's warning that attacking their sacred sites would only make things worse for you and may cause uprisings elsewhere.'

She tapped her wrist muting her mic and whispered back 'I see, is he saying it would turn the Tlillan's against us as well?'

McKinley nodded.

'I have less than 20 hours to get a surrender and when the other moons hear about this they'll revolt anyway. If that happens the Tlillans will come in and take control and we go home with our tails between our legs, Lieutenant. I'm not taking the blame for losing an entire system, besides I like to win,' whispered Ryu.

She turned on her mic and glared at the nervous Gukumatz 'Okay Bokumatz are you going to surrender yes or no?'

The creature listened to the translation then replied 'Human barbarian desist this ...', in mid-sentence Ryu called to Hassif 'Cut him off,' and his image left the view screen.

Ryu tapped her wrist and ordered Kim to begin his first strike on whichever pool took his fancy, which he did lighting up one of the spawning pools with napalm.

The young were either suffocated or boiled alive by the rain of fire that floated, covering the surface of the pool. Soon the stench of baking flesh filled the air with the young that were able to walk on land, scattered around burning to death after their attempts to flee the hell that had befallen them.

Bokumatz made no attempt to communicate. Two more strikes on and there was nothing coming from the rebels on the moon. Rather than bringing this to an end the attack on the spawning pools had only hardened their resolve.

The results frustrated Ryu pushing her to ordering a nerve agent strike on the capital. Whilst the city was being covered in a cloud of toxic gas she summoned Kapitan Vladimir Rogov to the bridge. Vladimir, a tall blonde man in his mid 30's with a rugged look which told a tale of many years of service stepped off the lift and his Vympel soldiers saluted.

He marched over to Ryu 'You request my presence?' he asked in his thick Russian accent.

Ryu rose from her chair and handed him a tablet, 'I want Vympel 1 and 2 ready for an assault on the capital Kapitan. Nerve agent has been deployed and your men are required to shoot on sight Kapitan, your objective is the orbital ground station. Your secondary objective is the moon's administrative headquarters only once the ground station has been secured, is that understood?'

Kapitan Rogov read the tablet and all the information it carried meticulously 'Very well Commander I will inform you when we are all set.'

Ryu made a little smile at Vladimir 'Good luck,' and Vladimir made his way back into the lift to prepare his men for the invasion.

An hour or so latter the Atlas II insertion craft left their hangars, carrying 25 men each. Both touched down on the outskirts of what from above was a dead city. The rear of the box like Atlas craft opened, lowering a ramp which the Spetsnaz troops filed off and into line. Once all were present they marched to a safe distance and the short stubby triangular wings of the Atlas which were pointing upwards fired their engines in harmony. Both craft pushed themselves up and high into the sky, upon reaching 500 metres the wings rotated slowly pushing the vehicles forward and up until they locked in a forward position and the craft disappeared into the thick smoky atmosphere.

The members of both Vympel 1 and 2 were dressed in black space suits fitted with carbon armour and helmets unfurled. Taking orders from Kapitan Rogov they silently took positions searching for targets however there was nothing to see.

Flicking to infra-red life forms could be made out, inside the hovel like buildings the Gukumatz preferred to live in. He pointed at the first building constructed from hardwood in the shape of an igloo and two men approached it, only to find the occupant was dead though his body still emitted heat so they put a bullet in him to be sure and moved on. Advancing through the streets and between the houses and shops in a skirmish line Vladimir came to the realisation the nerve agent had done the job for them. Gukumatz also breathe through their skin increasing the effect, added to that chemical warfare had been banned by the treaty long ago, it was something that the Gukumatz were not prepared for. Bodies were scattered on the streets and trams stood still with passengers sitting inside waiting to reach their destination before the nerve agent took them somewhere else.

Twenty minutes on and Vladimir was at the entrance to the station, the code didn't work to open the gate so he contacted Sergeant Nikolay Greshnev on the orbital station above, only to be told there was no access to the ground station whatsoever. Vladimir gestured to two men and gave orders in his native tongue; the men from Vympel 1 were both Techs and began work on opening the large metal gate into the complex whilst the others took up firing positions.

Inside the main complex was sealed and air conditioned, the Gukumatz disliked air conditioning as they found it dried out their damp leathery skin and brought on respiratory ailments. However it was the only safe environment in the city and Vladimir expected to meet resistance here, if he met it at all.

A minute later and the gates jerked splitting apart a little in the centre. One of the Techs gave the thumbs up to Vladimir who returned the gesture. The Techs both darted behind the firing positions as the gate opened to reveal several droids laying in wait.

'Streylatz!' ordered Vladimir and the front line of positions opened fire. After a few seconds Vladimir issued his second order 'Ostanavitz!'

The men held their fire and Vladimir waited for the smoke to dissipate. When he saw the droids trashed he ordered his men forward and inside the large loading entrance to the station. He split the Vympel teams up at this point since one corridor was too narrow for both to be effective. Ignoring the tunnels below he had both teams make for the command and control centre topside. Once that was taken he could shut off any Gukumatz in the tunnels isolating them from each other. Vladimir took his team forward moving in from the South, the other team lead by Leytenant Babkin skirted around and moved in from the East.

The southern corridor was wide and dipped underneath the complex after a couple of hundred metres into the loading bays. Vladimir moved around and continued on the surface where the corridor began to narrow. Using the magnification ability on his Spetsnaz issue helmet Vladimir noticed what looked to be a fortified position. Another hundred metres ahead the corridor narrowed to no more than 3 metres wide. Heavy crates had been shifted to block it off to about chest height. He flicked to infra-red but there was no sign of anyone or thing behind the crates. Nevertheless he lifted his hand and Vympel 1 scattered taking up firing positions. No sooner had they done this than pulse rifle fire burst upon them. Vladimir found himself crouched in a corridor 10 metres wide with no cover under heavy pulse rifle fire.

Vympel 1 returned fire but his men were being hit, despite the nano weave armour built onto the suits it couldn't stop the kinetic force of a tungsten bullet projected from the rails of a pulse rifle.

Vladimir shouted down his mic 'Max! Bazuka!'

One of his troopers let his pulse rifle go and hang from its strap, he removed his backpack from which he produced another pulse rifle but with a barrel 3 inches in diameter. He advanced and dived down using a fallen comrade's body for cover. Max pulled out a rocket propelled grenade about the size of a slim can of iced coffee. Rammed it into the barrel then charged the weapon, the light on the power pack read green and he took aim.

The air was very smoky with pulse fire, shells were bouncing off the floor and into his comrade's corpse all around him, yet Max blocked it out. He focused staring into the smoke and as soon as he saw the defensive wall through the mist he fired the weapon. The rifle projected the RPG as it would a normal tungsten shell, then a fraction of a second later the RPG slammed hard into the Gukumatz defensive wall. The explosion was massive and Vympel one tried to take what cover they could as debris bounced from wall to wall in all directions. Max reloaded and prepared to fire again but only the sound of burning could be heard. Vympel 1 lay in wait until the air conditioning removed enough smoke for them to see what was left of the Gukumatz.

They had taken space suits which masked them from infra-red along with weapons commandeered from the armoury.

Two of Vympel 1 lay dead, one without a head and the other had been hit multiple times in the torso removing most of the man's spine. Vladimir estimated the Gukumatz to be four in number, from the remnants of the suits and pulse rifles. The enemy bodies resembled a green and yellow omelette smouldering on the walls. Vympel 1 moved through what was left of the defensive position, the crispy innards of their foes crunched under foot.

Vladimir encountered another two positions on his way to the control centre, this time however he was looking for them. Each time Max finished them off before any tungsten trading had the chance to begin. Upon reaching the doors to the control centre at least 20 Gukumatz had been left dead in the wake of Vympel 1.

The Techs began working on the door whilst Vladimir waited with a flash bang grenade. The Techs rushed back as the doors open. Vympel 1 were crouched out of sight from the occupants of the room when the door slid aside. Vladimir threw the grenade inside then made a signal to his men who rushed inside the room in a two by two formation covering one another. There was no pulse fire however and when Vladimir entered the large control room there was a dozen Gukumatz with some human hostages. The Gukumatz had their webbed hands in the air and were burping loudly the word surrender. None of the occupants were wearing a suit; however Vladimir was certain that the nerve agent had for the most part dissipated by the time they landed. The air conditioning in the building would have removed any remnants in the atmosphere before it reached the control centre so he wasn't alarmed.

Vladimir separated the Gukumatz from the humans and carried out Ryu's orders to the letter by having them shot. Much to the shock of the technicians who watched in horror at what had been their co-workers, now executed.

'Who is in charge here?' asked Vladimir.

A timid Indian man stepped forward 'I am ... I think,' he replied nervously.

Vladimir spoke with his jet black helmet still covering his entire head 'Cut off the tunnels and bring up the security cams for this complex, I want to know where every Gukumatz is Mr.?'

The Indian man replied with a shaky voice 'Ratha, Mr. Ratha and yes if you look over here the entire complex can be observed,' he pointed to a station that the Gukumatz had been using.

Vladimir saw Vympel 2 getting close to the control centre and had one of his men inform them of the last defensive position along their route, Vympel 2 had taken casualties but looked in good shape. Within 30 minutes the station was under Vladimir's control with all doors locked and Vympel 2 clearing the remaining Gukumatz trapped beneath the earth in the loading bays. He informed Ryu who still hadn't heard from Bokumatz. So she ordered him to secure the secondary objective. Once Vympel 2 had cleared out the tunnels he left Babkin to hold the ground station. Vympel 1 moved on to the main administrative building which used to be the Bokumatz palace before being conquered 6 months previously.

This time Vladimir decided to be less subtle and had Max blow the front doors open from a distance. Inside the building was quiet, as most of it was not air conditioned. Bodies that had succumb to nerve gas lay in the halls and offices.

On reaching the main audience chamber which was air conditioned Vladimir met with the Bokumatz. The old hall where the former representative of the Bokumatz took guests was lined with small seats which McCann had called "Squats" since that was what they did on them, with the representative sitting at the far end.

A Gukumatz close to Vladimir burbled and croaked 'Quickly enter Human,'

Vladimir didn't move he only looked at the creature 'your air will enter,' he croaked urgently.

Vladimir ordered his men in, who entered in two by two formation, taking up firing positions inside. The Gukumatz closed the doors and the creature at the end of the hall approached them dressed in a suit of Gukumatz manufacture, wearing a head dress of green jade squares draping down the sides of his head as an Egyptian pharaoh.

He stopped before Vladimir having noticed his insignia of rank, 'We Bokumatz surrender.'

Vladimir tapped his wrist and the voice of Ryu met his ears inside his helmet 'Yes Kapitan?' she asked hurriedly.

Vladimir replied calmly 'The Bokumatz representative has offered their surrender Commander.'

The tone of Ryu's voice rose to the point she was nearly shouting with jubilation 'Excellent Kapitan! Accept his surrender and order his forces to stand down. Once we have all infrastructure under I.S.A control tell him I'll desist, assure him the spawning pools will no longer be targeted as long as all Gukumatz on Ilium 3 co-operate.'

Vladimir replied 'Understood Commander, I shall relay your message.'

'Ryu out,' she said happily.

Vladimir relayed the message to Bokumatz.

In less than half the allotted time Commander Ryu had brought the moon back under I.S.A control. At the cost of thousands of lives, but to Ryu and McCann they were only Gukumatz lives and of little consequence.

Shortly after her victory Ryu was awarded a medal by the I.S.A, promoted to Captain then reassigned. McCann tried to find out where but he was blocked at every avenue of inquiry, eventually Faraday requested that he stop asking. No one knew where his comrade had been reassigned or why. McCann assumed that due to the suppression of Ilium 3 she was removed, a political decision. He had not received any mail from her and decided to wait for her to contact him when the time was right.

Chapter 14

After McCann had satisfied Jerry with his recollections of the uprising and swift suppression Faraday arrived. Jerry began to speak to the Director of the I.S.A; Malikah took the opportunity to take her father for a walk outside. Leaving the other three in the restaurant the two of them took a stroll along the main boulevard. Small trams moved up and down with pedestrians on either side going to and fro. Some were shopping others eating out and a few going to work or making their way back home.

The Gukumatz fashion wasn't much to shout about, McCann found it all to be quite bland, composed of earthy browns and greens. If they were going to a special occasion they'd wear bright emerald and ruby colours with gold but those were rare occasions.

Gukumatz social occasions were rather repulsive and vulgar affairs in McCann's opinion. He came to that conclusion when they held a banquet in his honour soon after the system surrendered, serving food similar to rotten sushi. The decaying seaweed and rotten pond life emitted a foul stench even over the ammonia of the atmosphere and the drinks made him wonder who had vomited in his glass. Diplomacy forced him to try it and much to his surprise it tasted even worse than it appeared. A feat he wouldn't have believed possible when he first laid eyes on the meal.

Malikah clutched her father's hand tightly as they strolled along the pavement then turned into the bazaar well known for having some of the best jewellery on the moon. Malikah spied a retailer with a fine jade and ruby necklace inside the shop so she pulled her father by the hand dragging him inside. Within the establishment the assistants kowtowed until she instructed them to rise. The manager of the establishment then rushed to the shop floor from his office and prostrated himself. Malikah giggled and instructed him to rise; he did so then immediately began doting over her showing Malikah the finest gems and jewellery he had to offer. Outside Gukumatz were gathering and staring through the windows, all this attention caused McCann to become nervous. McCann felt his daughter's safety may be at risk with so many Gukumatz crowding around outside, Malikah sensed his worry and smiled at her father.

McCann relaxed upon feeling her assurance, he wasn't certain if his daughter was using her abilities to calm him or it was just the fact he had missed her so much. The holo recordings just didn't quite cut the mustard after a month or two in space. His hand moved away from his holster and he returned the smile.

'Come here father,' beckoned Malikah.

She stood over the glass counter speaking to the Gukumatz who understood her Tlillan language perfectly. The manager wore the traditional Gukumatz earth brown two piece sack suit with a skin tight sweater beneath. Allowing his skin to breathe and remain moist at all times, he brought expensive pieces out, trying to catch her fancy.

Malikah knew what she wanted and requested the necklace with its smooth jade and ruby stones. The rubies weren't cut in the human fashion but the original shape was maintained only smoothed and polished. It was held together with a gold thread and the centre piece was a large polished ruby. The first thought to cross McCann's mind was the expense, followed quickly by a frown from his daughter.

Malikah nudged McCann with her elbow 'Father! You really should give mother a present, especially after the scene you caused earlier today.'

McCann let out a sigh 'Well what do you think she'd like?'

Malikah giggled 'What do you think about this necklace? Aside from the cost!'

He stepped closer and inspected it 'Do you think she'd appreciate it?'

McCann didn't know anything about purchasing women gifts outside of perfume and flowers.

Malikah, now a little fed up with how slow her father was, replied 'Yes I do and she's missed you terribly father. She has spent many a night in tears yearning for you.'

McCann unbuttoned the straps on his jacket and unzipped it halfway removing his credit chip from the inside pocket. Upon seeing the credit chip the manager began to croak and burp loudly, but before the translator could do its job Malikah reported that the manager refused to accept his credit.

McCann was a little taken aback 'What do you mean?' he asked his daughter.

'You may have the necklace as a gift,' she replied.

McCann shook his head 'I can't do that.'

Malikah frowned a little 'Why father?'

'If it's a gift to your mother then I have to pay for it, it's the gentlemanly thing to do.'

Malikah spoke with the manager yet he flatly refused to take anything for the necklace. As far as the manager was concerned having Malikah or Ilam wearing his jewellery was enough to cause business to skyrocket. However this was not the reason he refused to accept payment. Like most Gukumatz he was deeply religious and to charge the Mictlancihuatl coin would be a disgrace no decent Gukumatz could shoulder.

'Have you explained the situation?' inquired McCann.

She had but the manager would not listen.

'Tell him to do it as a personal favour,' said McCann rather frustrated now.

Malikah tried but he refused to budge and the Englishman was forced to accept the necklace as a gift, McCann thanked the manager for the jewellery which must have cost him a small fortune. The manager placed it in the display box wrapping it for Ilam.

The pair stepped out of the store into a massive crowd of people who had poured out of their workplaces, tearing themselves from shopping or eating to steal a look at the Mictlancihuatl. McCann stood at the door blocked by the sea of bodies clamouring for a look, then Malikah approached and immediately a clear path formed back into the bazaar as if the Red Sea had parted. The path was flanked by Gukumatz kowtowing, McCann observed a wave go through the crowd as the Gukumatz prostrated themselves on the ground.

The wave moved off into the distance until there were no longer any Gukumatz to be seen standing.

McCann turned around to look at his daughter and said sarcastically 'I can't take you anywhere can I!' then smiled.

Malikah was enjoying the attention and made no secret of the fact, again she spoke in a deep booming voice 'liik'il much chital!' to which the Gukumatz rose from the ground. Silence filled the air as the pair made their way out of the bazaar and back onto the main thoroughfare. Soon after, the jeweller was inundated with customers attempting to purchase the goods Malikah had been examining.

Malikah paused to admire the view from the thoroughfare, she found the thick yellow mist and tall jungle canopy directly below beautiful. The orange sun in the sky produced a warm glow through the steamy atmosphere 'It is wonderful don't you think Father?' she spoke gazing into the distance. McCann gurned a little, 'Uuuuuurrrrhhhh!' he replied trying not to look out at the miserable place he'd been forced to suffer for nearly a year.

Malikah faced McCann 'You should have more consideration for others Father.'

McCann scowled at his daughter 'Excuse me?'

Malikah wasn't joking but pointed at him as if she were a headmistress, 'Mother has suffered for months yet your only thoughts concern yourself and departing this moon; your behaviour is selfish even for a human!'

His daughter was actually angry with him; McCann was flabbergasted and said nothing but only gawped at Malikah in astonishment.

When there was no reply forthcoming she continued 'Well Father? Have you nothing to say for your behaviour?'

His silence only caused her to raise her voice. McCann had been very self-centered whilst on Ilium 1, he missed his family and getting off the world was the first step to seeing them again. However it seems that somewhere he'd lost his way and now he was obsessive when it came to leaving the moon; so much so that upon seeing his wife again he only felt disappointment. Ilam had sensed his feelings yet she revealed nothing, despite the fact it tore her heart in two. Malikah however was not so contained on the subject and spoke her mind.

McCann contemplated her words for a few moments, 'I had no idea,' he said in an irregular tone. McCann looked at his daughter and he felt a shroud of shame descend over him. Malikah sensed it also and withdrew her long finger.

The Englishman looked up to the sky and muttered 'I've been such an idiot haven't I?'

His daughter calmed down 'Yes you have Father; however it is not too late to correct your idiocy.'

He scowled at his daughter again 'You don't have to be so blunt Malikah!'

She smiled slightly and in a soft pitch replied 'My honesty scales only with your ignorance father.'

It was intended as a joke under the funny because its true category and it forced a smile from McCann to the delight of his daughter.

'You sound eerily like your Mother you know that?' said McCann. 'But I apologise for being such a horse's arse and I'll make it up to Ilam, alright?'

She smiled with approval and nothing more was said on the subject between them 'I read the texts you requested father.'

McCann smiled 'Really, what do you think of them?'

Peering back out at the sky and canopy below she replied 'They explain human male behaviour in great detail, far better than any psychologist.'

'Hmmm, well that wasn't really the reason I suggested them but I'm glad to see you benefited,' said McCann looking his daughter up and down.

He'd only just recognised that his child was a woman and a beautiful one at that. She had inherited his mother's Mediterranean features along with Ilam's slender physique and height. In fact a wave of fear shot through his body from head to toe, for the first time he thought of her and young men and what they were thinking of when they laid eyes upon her.

Malikah still peering into the distance burst out laughing.

'Malikah! You've been reading my thoughts haven't you?' chastised McCann.

She continued laughing and with an embarrassed expression, she turned to him with her hand over her mouth in an attempt to stem the laughter.

McCann was disappointed 'You've been told not to do that, it's bloody impolite and I don't like it!' chided McCann.

She threw her arms around him and hugged her father; McCann could hear her crying in his ear as she kissed his cheek and whispered 'I'm sorry father.'

McCann had to fight back his tears and clearing his throat he gave her a hug and whispered in her ear 'Just try not to do it again Malikah.'

He patted her on the back and after a minute she released him.

'So which book was your favourite?'

The young Tlillan-human hybrid wiped the tears from her pink eyes and replied 'Neither, each text has its own separate merits.'

McCann raised an eyebrow 'Go on.'

'Well the Iliad focuses on Kleos and Nostos whereas the Odyssey is focused on Metis. Each has its own merits but I would say that Odysseus is the superior character from a Tlillan perspective, due to his Metis. Most human males idolise Achilles or Hector due to their Kleos, making clear the masculine lust for conflict.'

McCann was perplexed by the statement and reading his puzzled look she smiled 'Kleos is the Greek concept of glory earned in battle. Nostos is glory earned at the homecoming of a successful conquest Father.'

He smiled 'Ahhh and Metis?'

Malikah giggled 'Metis is cunning intelligence, a trait Odysseus was famed for although he was blighted by Hubris, the trait of arrogance and pride.'

McCann nodded his head 'Yes Hubris, I'm certain many Tlillan females would have much in common with Odysseus!' he raised his eyebrows bringing laughter to his daughter's lips again.

She put her arm around her father's waist and began the stroll back to the restaurant 'They were interesting works each offering a great insight into human nature, do you know which character you remind me of?' she said cheekily.

McCann strolled with his face raised to the thick sky 'Hmmmm let me think … Odysseus?'

Malikah laughed 'No! Guess again!'

He rolled his eyes 'Come on just tell me,' he stated wearily.

'Agamemnon!' she said excitedly.

He looked at her suspiciously 'Because I'm a brave warrior feared by the Trojans and respected by Achaeans, all women want me and men want to be me?'

Malikah laughed again, a little too hard for McCann's liking, he was joking but he wasn't trying to be that funny.

'No Father, because you are stubborn and suffer from temper tantrums!'

He shook his head whilst his daughter laughed and squeezed his waist.

'What about Ilam who do you think she is closest to?' asked McCann.

Malikah thought for a moment and answered 'Penelope, because she has been so far from her beloved husband yearning for his return.'

McCann pulled an expression of alarm 'I hope there weren't any suitors!'

Malikah giggled 'No Father there has not, whom would you compare Mother to?'

McCann thought for a moment this time, then answered 'I would have said Athene, because she's wise and beautiful and she doesn't suffer fools gladly.'

His daughter squeezed his waist again 'That's very romantic, Mother will be happy to know you think of her so highly.'

McCann shook his head 'Don't tell her I said that.'

Malikah grinned 'You're too late father.'

McCann sighed and shared his daughters grin.

'Did Ilam accept this position so that we could be together or is there more that I should know before we return?'

Malikah held him tightly and in a low voice replied 'Mother's desire to be with you is one reason, but there are other motives.'

McCann nodded 'I thought so, there always is with your mother.'

'My presence here will secure an audience on Tlillan in the future. The intention is for me to learn statesmanship on a practical basis,' whispered Malikah.

They maintained a slow pace as they strolled down the thoroughfare and McCann continued to question his daughter 'What about Faraday what has he done this for?'

Malikah gave him a slight frown 'Father you know I'm not allowed to listen to others thoughts.'

He peered back at her 'Yes, yes but you do anyway! So tell me what's bloody well going on will you?'

Malikah sniggered a little and continued 'Mr. Faraday is concerned since the previous uprising. He feels that my Mother is better suited to govern than a human. Also my presence inspires obedience from all Gukumatz.'

McCann agreed with Faraday's assumption especially after he witnessed the effect Malikah had on the locals.

'What about Ryu? What has Faraday done with her?'

Malikah hesitated for a moment 'That is confidential Father.'

McCann squeezed her waist and pulled her close to him 'I know and I know that you know and I'm certain Faraday didn't tell you. So spit it out and I promise not to let on.'

McCann extended his left arm and making a fist he extended his little finger, Malikah did likewise and they locked their little fingers together making two intertwined loops. It was a traditional Tlillan practice when two people close to each other spoke in confidence. The action of locking the smallest fingers formed a bond of honour that if broken prevented the perpetrator from ever having the privilege to form one with another Tlillan again. Everyone connected to the dreamscape would be aware of the dishonour and it was a major blow to any Tlillan's social standing.

After making the promise Malikah drew her lips to McCann's ear and whispered 'After the uprising she could not be allowed to remain in Ilium, she was promoted and reassigned.'

McCann whispered impatiently 'Yes I know that but what happened? Where is she?'

Malikah continued 'Yes Father I was getting to that part, she has been promoted to Captain and reassigned to a new ship.'

McCann made a puzzled expression 'Which one? All five cruisers have Captains and ...'

'Father please!' whispered a frustrated Malikah 'Since the cloaked shipyards were discovered in Ilium the I.S.A have constructed a similar facility and have been building a new space vessel with the added Gukumatz technology.'

McCann was about to inquire further but his daughter stopped him 'Enough Father, I can't tell you anymore, if Mother knew there would be hell to pay.'

McCann kissed her head 'Thank you, at least I have some idea of what's going on now. I'm sick of always being the last to know and Ilam is always plotting our fates in the shadows.'

Malikah was disappointed 'You are far too hard on Mother she only ever has the best intentions for both of us even if we don't always agree, please be nice to her.'

As they approached the restaurant he hugged her waist with his arm 'I promise I will', she smiled and they both walked back into the restaurant where Faraday, Ilam and Jerry were chatting at the same table.

The rest of the day was spent touring the city with McCann's aide leading the group. McCann was bored to tears but didn't show it however the other members were all fascinated with the alien moon and its inhabitants. At the end of the day everyone retired to their rooms and McCann took his wife to one of the few restaurants in the city that served human food. A short tram journey along the thoroughfare and on the right the eatery lay in a small but exclusive bazaar. Built in the shape of a small pyramid the bazaar displayed beautiful terraced gardens and running water, McCann called it Babylon. He led his wife inside and on one of the upper floors they exited the glass elevator to be greeted by a doorman who croaked something toward Ilam as he opened the door of wood and glass.

She replied 'Dyos bo'otik,' which McCann recognised as Tlillan for 'Thank you'.

He was surprised at her lack of arrogance when around the Gukumatz. It made no sense to him that the Tlillans would treat a race they had enslaved with such respect, whereas humans were treated with utter disdain unless they had proved themselves. Perhaps his wife was being diplomatic with the population before she took the governorship? It was the only explanation that made sense to him.

Inside, the restaurant was decked out in expensive amber of many different shades. The mahogany wood that the furnishings were made of was a rich dark brown, almost ebony. There were only ten tables spread out inside the establishment, with a small bar and stools taking up the far corner.

They were led to the table McCann had requested earlier that day and sat down behind the glass window. Looking out onto super scrapers rising out of the thick jungle canopy that was disappearing behind the mist as dusk approached. Ilam had her hair up and wore one of her power suits, a double breasted cream jacket with square shoulder pads, a pair of trousers and boots of the same colour. She had learned the art of applying make-up from Ofra and Malikah, some red lipstick and rouge made a large difference and he was bowled over when she exited her room for the dinner, all made up.

He was dressed in one of his grey suits with a black shirt and tie. It was the first time he'd been required to wear anything other than his I.S.A uniform and it felt quite liberating.

The Waiter dressed in dark green suit handed them each a menu, McCann scrolled down to the human menu. On the way he noticed that they were now serving Tlillan cuisine. Not that he knew what it was since it was written in Tlillan text, which seemed to be glyphs and odd pictures in tiny squares. McCann tapped the screen and selected his steak meal. He wasn't certain what the meat was taken from but he trusted the owner when assured that all meals were prepared to I.S.A health standards.

When the waiter returned he handed the menu back. Ilam returned hers, smiled and said 'Nook'ol ka k'amas dyos bo'otik.'

The waiter squatted for a fraction of a second then trundled away, she looked across at her husband, a small lamp in the centre let off a yellow glow. The lamp was a tube of glass on an ornate wooden stand filled with plankton brought from the home world in the Tlillan system. As the light dropped the planktons light increased in strength. The entire establishment was lit using this method and it was the predominant form of home illumination in all Gukumatz buildings.

'I bought you this,' he said producing the present he'd purchased with Malikah earlier.

Ilam's eyes widened as she reached over and took it 'Thank you.'

Ilam tore open the wrapping paper and opened the box to see the jade and ruby necklace. McCann stood up and moved behind Ilam, she handed him the necklace and he pulled apart the magnets so that he could place it on her then put them back together once it rested around her collar bone. He sat back down and observed his wife who looked quite stunning.

'You have out done yourself Duncan,' she said warmly.

He smiled 'I thought I should make it up to you after being such an ass today; you like it?'

Ilam put her hand on the table and McCann held it 'Yes I do my dear, I must also apologise for my lack of communication, over the governorship.'

McCann sighed 'No you don't, I understand that Faraday wanted to keep it under wraps it's not your fault.'

They both sat for a while looking into each other's eyes and holding hands tenderly as two teenagers in love. Her eyes were a deep pink betraying her emotions to the world, but even without those beacons of affection anyone could see the intimacy at the table.

The waiter reappeared and placed the steak dinner with vegetables before McCann, the vegetables were all native to Ilium and resembled broccoli to some degree. His favourite were the round sprout ones. The food served for human consumption was all grown in hydroponic gardens in artificial environments, in order to prevent the taste of ammonia spoiling the food. This was why so few establishments served the food and why it was so expensive.

McCann glanced at Ilam's plate as the waiter placed it in front of her, on the dish lay two mounds of different insects. One pile consisted of soft smooth maggot like creatures the other pile was made of large insects that could be best described as a cross between a cockroach and an ant.

'You aren't going to eat that are you?' McCann said incredulously.

Ilam smiled at his expression 'Of course, would you try some?'

Ilam picked one of the large maggots between her fingers and put its smooth body into her mouth, there was a crunching noise as the skin broke and she chewed it. McCann had eaten worse when he served in the SBS but it was shocking to see it served in such a high class restaurant.

'Alright I'll give one of those maggots a try.'

Ilam smiled whilst chewing and made a noise of approval so he leaned over and picked one off her plate. The creature was a little longer than his thumb but with almost twice the girth. The skin was white and smooth on the underside but thick and slightly leathery on the top. Suddenly he felt the creature move between his fingers and dropped it into his vegetables. Ilam burst out laughing and he looked back at her traumatised by what had happened which caused his wife to laugh even more.

'Mine's alive!'

Ilam recovered from her laughter after a short time 'Yes they are served live.'

'Why?'

The Amazon laughed again 'Why consume decayed flesh when alive it is fresh?'

McCann understood what she was saying, however after his time in the SBS he didn't expect to encounter one at the dinner table.

'The bloody thing's eating my broccoli!' exclaimed McCann as he watched the creature dining on his dinner.

Ilam laughed again 'You had best consume it before it consumes your meal Duncan, they can be quite ravenous!'

He picked up the creature, pulled his broccoli from it, took a deep breath and popped it in his mouth before it caused further hula baloo. When he bit down, the creature, a native to Tlillan, burst. The consistency felt like it was a soft meat in a thick mayonnaise like sauce. The taste was a musty almost liver taste, but he liked liver, and it was close to eating a liver pate. He chewed for a short time, the meat easily broke down and he swallowed.

Ilam watched on with smiling eyes, once he finished she asked 'Was the nook'ol pleasant?'

McCann had an expression of surprise since he expected it to be disgusting, 'Yes it was very good in fact, what on Earth was it?'

'Are you certain you wish to know?' she smiled.

McCann returned her smile 'Sure, hit me with it,' he replied cheekily.

'It is the pupa of an insect similar to your Earth moth, a common source of protein on Tlillan,' said Ilam who now pointed towards the other pile 'try one of these Duncan.'

He picked up the insect resembling a small cockroach, McCann didn't like creepy crawlies, he could tolerate them but cockroaches and spiders provoked a reflex action of whacking it immediately. His reaction came from his Mother who was terrified at the sight of any insect, as a child it was his job to deal with them. He scowled at the insect held in his fingers, belly up with its six legs up to the ceiling. The legs on the insect twitched but he didn't drop it, his instinct was to splat it on the table but he resisted his desire.

Ilam chuckled as she sensed his will fighting his instinct.

'This isn't funny you know?' he said to her not taking his eyes off the meal in his hand.

Ilam laughed again and he called out 'Waiter! Bring me a bottle of red wine!' never taking his eyes from the beast before him.

Ilam continued to chuckle as the waiter hobbled over 'Ak'chak uk'ik' ordered Ilam.

He returned with a bottle of red wine and poured McCann a glass.

Still fixed on the insect McCann asked 'So what the bloody hell is this thing?'

Ilam replied softly 'It is a termite, native to the dark side of Tlillan.'

'It looks like a bloody cockroach to me!' said McCann warily.

Ilam leaned back in her seat 'Are you going to wait until it dies before you eat it?'

McCann looked away from the termite and at his wife, he was caught off guard by her humour since it was not a trait common to Tlillans. He assumed his Mother and Malikah had encouraged her to develop it. Nevertheless she was correct and he took another deep breath and popped in the termite. This insect was quite the opposite of the pupa. The consistency was crunchy with a slightly moist and soft core, the taste was of a salted beef and McCann found himself enjoying the meal.

After swallowing he raised his eyebrows 'That was very nice,' he said in a surprised tone then took a sip of the wine imported from Earth.

He picked up his knife and fork and began cutting his steak, 'Better get stuck into this before it gets cold,' he paused for a moment then said 'those bloody bugs probably keep themselves warm for you though, don't they?'

Ilam nodded as she popped another nook'ol into her mouth and chewed, the rest of the restaurant had been watching them, although the pair were oblivious and after the meal they went onto the balcony for a drink.

The restaurant had a small terrace where after dinner patrons could have a romantic drink or just take in the nightlife of the city. Ilam pulled out something from inside her jacket and presented it to McCann 'I brought you this, my dear.'

She held a cigar tube before her it was black brown and gold so he knew immediately it was a Cohiba and it was a Lonsdale size.

His face light up as a child's at Christmas, 'Thank you, but I'm not sure I can smoke it in this climate,' he said taking the tubos.

Ilam nodded and in a soft tone replied 'I had a cabinet of them especially made for you by Habanos. They assured me that these will burn properly providing they are lit within an hour of leaving the tubos.'

McCann felt a lump in his throat as he cast his mind back to how much of a pig he'd been when she arrived. If it wasn't for his daughter's intervention he'd have been both ashamed and humiliated. McCann put his tumbler of whisky down on the small drinks table and in a rare show of public affection he put his arm around his wife. With the other he held her chin in his hand and guided her lips to his, kissed and then embraced her with his right cheek against hers.

'I love you Ilam,' he whispered into her ear to which her eyes blushed and she replied 'I love you too Duncan.'

The restaurant stopped and all the patrons including the staff were frozen in time, examining the scene on the terrace as the Governor embraced his wife in a moment of love. Gukumatz had never witnessed a Tlillan display emotions pertaining to love in any manner, in fact it was widely accepted that they either were not capable or refused to indulge in them due to the dreamscape. So the scene on the terrace was something to behold. For the Gukumatz in general it was uplifting to see a Matriarch acting in this way since now they knew she understood compassion, something the coldness of Tlillan society forbid. The couple broke their embrace after a minute and McCann picked his drink from the table to see his wife looking into the restaurant.

He followed her gaze to see all the Gukumatz staring back at him, 'What the bloody hell is up with them?'

Ilam replied still looking back at her audience 'They saw us kiss, Duncan.'

'So? Haven't they seen people kiss before?'

'Not Tlillan's Duncan, emotion is controlled and monitored. I have not seen a Tlillan kiss before, they are astonished by our behaviour.'

The restaurant slowly went back to normal business as each patron one by one resumed what they were doing previously and the staff served them again. Though they all kept one of those beady toad eyes on the terrace and it was no doubt the subject of conversation.

Ilam produced her husband's torch lighter and guillotine which she'd brought from Geneva 'Go on light it up.'

McCann took them and placed them on the table; he pulled the Lonsdale cigar out of the tubos and smelt the thick creamy tobacco. He sliced the end and lit it up, sure enough the foot was burning with an excellent draw. In the atmosphere of Ilium the smoke had a blue hue to it. Previously the thick humid climate had caused the cigar to go out and the draw was as if he were sucking cement through a straw. He took a drag and his entire body seemed to lose all tension built up over the previous nine months in one puff.

'How is it?' inquired Ilam.

McCann found it difficult to look his wife in the face without becoming teary eyed but he managed 'I feel like I just got home,' he managed to say in a choked voice.

The whisky wasn't his favourite but it was one of the better ten year olds. He sipped his Talisker and gazed at the woman he'd been without for so long, only now did he fully understand how much a part of him she was.

McCann took a deep drag and a naughty inhale into his lungs then exhaled a large plume of blue smoke, 'I understand you had to come here now.'

Ilam held her drink of non-alcoholic wine 'You do?'

McCann took another drag, 'I think so, Faraday needs this system to support the I.S.A. His backers on Earth might decide to pull out especially now that it's become so expensive.'

Ilam peered suspiciously at him 'Has it? How did you come to that conclusion?'

The Englishman shrugged his shoulders silently.

'I came here before another uprising occurred.'

McCann stood opposite his wife smoking his Cohiba 'Go on?'

She was wary but continued 'The Gukumatz would have rebelled again Duncan; the only hope was to bring Malikah here before another massacre.'

'How do you know they would rebel again?'

'Gukumatz are difficult to control and even more stubborn than humans, they would have persisted until you had left or they fled again. The revolt on Ilium 3 was not a unique event but a harbinger of things to come.'

McCann frowned a little 'I don't understand, what difference do you think you'll make if the suppression on Ilium 3 didn't change their minds?'

Ilam smiled down at her husband 'Did you not see the effect your daughter had upon Gukumatz? I will make no difference but she is the Mictlancihuatl, she is the Gukumatz Icon of legend. They submit to you for a short while, via force of arms, but to the icon they submit by desire. No Gukumatz will raise a hand against her or those who serve her.'

McCann had indeed witnessed the effect of Malikah's presence but he was still perplexed, 'What do you mean by Icon exactly?'

Ilam took a sip of her drink and continued 'The Gukumatz also believe in the Mictlancihuatl, the word for her translates as Icon. They believe the Icon is a saviour a Christ like figure. But the Gukumatz will not accept her until they are certain she is the Icon and that requires a DNA test, which will be provided to Gukumatz requirements.'

McCann's expression became sceptical 'I wonder where they got that mumbo jumbo from?' he said sarcastically.

Ilam smiled at her husband again 'You are correct but we did not invent the story it was foreseen in the dreamscape and passed down to Gukumatz priests, it is a true prophecy Duncan.'

McCann snorted in disapproval 'Pah, the dreamscape!'

Ilam didn't react angrily but still smiling spoke softly 'So sceptical despite having seen the dreamscape himself.'

He peered up at his wife 'Seen the dreamscape? I don't think so Ilam.'

'Each time you fold space you travel through the dreamscape my dear, it is clearest in the dead zone between event horizons where you may witness events and wonders of other places even other universes.'

McCann took a fast drag 'What do you mean?'

The Tlillan beauty put down her glass and pointed making a circle, 'The dreamscape is the only constant and binds all things. Us, the Gukumatz, all races and civilizations even those inhabiting other universes. Even humans despite being primitive have researched M theory, the theory of other, possibly infinite, universes with varying physical laws.'

McCann was still sceptical to the notion 'And you see the future through this too?'

Ilam shook her head 'No, the future is not a constant it changes moment to moment however there are parallel universes similar to ours. Some are chronologically behind us, some inhabit a similar place others are ahead of us. Our seers view these places examining events and places, extrapolating possible consequences for our universe. Nothing is certain Duncan, but some things are far more certain than others, your daughter's path is very clear to the seers and that frightens them.'

McCann tried to digest all he'd been listening to 'Why didn't you tell me this before, why so secretive about the dreamscape? You made it sound like a fairy tale, not science.'

Ilam had a feeling of accomplishment now that her husband seemed to accept the dreamscape was a reality 'Until you folded space and witnessed it with your own eyes words would have been a poor substitute.'

McCann thought on it for a moment and agreed 'I suppose you're right, but what frightens the Grand Matriarch?'

'Tlillan society is a meritocracy and when Malikah reaches maturity she may challenge for clan leadership. Clan leaders become grand council members by right, any grand council member may challenge the Grand Matriarch for her position.'

McCann shrugged his shoulders and looked bewildered 'But why is she a threat?'

Ilam stopped smiling 'Because disputes for leadership are resolved by mental combat, the loser dies.'

McCann was shocked that a society could operate for so long via this method 'I thought you said it was a meritocracy?'

'It is, to a point,' replied Ilam 'the Grand Matriarch came to test Malikah and assess her ability, she earned her place in the clan via merit. However it would not be possible for society to function if there were no consequences to losing a challenge. Acceptance into a clan and position within the clan is won by merit alone but to progress further there are consequences. The Grand Matriarch now knows Malikah is a threat, however there are those who believe it is her fate and she will save the Tlillan race from dying out.'

McCann made an incredulous face 'Are you saying she would try to eliminate Malikah to maintain her position as Grand Matriarch? Even if it meant the destruction of her race?'

Ilam nodded 'A rather basic summary but true. As humans say, nothing is set in stone Duncan even Malikah's fate. The Grand Matriarch will use her power to hold sway over the council. Bringing Malikah here affords her protection, since every Gukumatz will die gladly to defend the Icon. Humans are easily corrupted, Gukumatz are not, no offence intended Duncan.'

McCann was stunned 'None taken,' he said under his breath before taking another drag on his cigar and then knocking back his whisky 'But I thought Tlillans didn't kill one another?'

Ilam drew a deep breath 'Outside challenges for position or criminal and religious punishment a Tlillan has not purposely caused the death of another in centuries.'

McCann still didn't believe this to be possible 'Does a female killing a male count as a Tlillan murdering another?'

Ilam's lips tightened and she became visibly uncomfortable 'No, it does not.'

He didn't react to her answer but just nodded 'I thought as much, so how does the Grand Matriarch expect to bump off challengers to her position?'

Ilam looked down towards the floor perhaps in a moment of disgrace; Tlillan's viewed such activities as barbaric 'As I spoke of before there is a large commonwealth of civilizations, beyond what you have experienced, prepared to do her bidding.'

McCann shook his head 'So you get others to do your dirty work? How does she order an assassination without being discovered and who carries it out?'

Ilam was very uncomfortable discussing this and it was plain to see as her gaze moved around to make certain no one else was listening 'The Grand Matriarch is powerful enough to hide some thoughts and memories from the dreamscape. These memories are of her dealings with the Tezcatlipoca, an avian species that used to serve before the collapse of the empire. Today they still serve as mercenaries and sooner or later they will be coming for Malikah.'

McCann was still cool, after facing the Gukumatz head on his confidence in the I.S.A fleet was strong 'How large is their fleet?' he asked puffing on his cigar.

Ilam laughed nervously 'The Tezcatlipoca possess no fleet only one will come for her and we must be on alert at all times. Here on Ilium the Gukumatz will not conspire with the Tezcatlipoca and the atmosphere will interfere with its cloaking device.'

McCann was working out Tlillan society now; his wife had described it in the past as an idyllic civilization for the emotionless based on strict religious law. It didn't make sense to him that if a society worked so well why would you need such strict control over it? However it was now evident that there was trouble in paradise and political backstabbing, corruption and skull duggery were a fact of life. Without the dreamscape he surmised that Tlillans would probably be even more violent and savage to one another than humans.

He looked at his wife and said in a tone of support 'And Malikah is already more powerful than the Grand gorgon which makes her a threat to anyone that may be in her path. The paradox being that if she doesn't attempt to become Grand Matriarch they will murder her anyway. So her only course of action is to make a play for power before her opposition is successful?'

Ilam stood silently and shed a tear causing the restaurant to stop another time. McCann pulled his handkerchief from his breast pocket and handed it to his wife. She took it and wiped her eyes whilst using all her control to hold back the emotional outburst from causing any more of a public spectacle. McCann put down his glass and placed his arm around Ilam's waist. In an attempt to raise her spirits he said softly 'Don't you worry I'll do whatever it takes Ilam, if that old bitch thinks she can hurt Malikah she'll find out she's most mistaken.'

Ilam perked up a little and hugged her husband she was relieved that McCann finally understood what was going on. Both Ilam and Malikah had hidden it for so long due to his explosive nature and that he had other things to worry about; aside from that until now he had no influence over her fate anyway.

After a short argument over the bill McCann relented and agreed not to pay. Leaving the establishment he walked arm in arm with his wife back to their rooms. By now the sun was no longer in the sky but three moons bathed the thoroughfare in a yellow gloom. Walking back McCann felt guilty for all those times he'd berated her and how he must have seemed foolish to his daughter.

Ilam was relieved to have the secret off her chest and happy that her husband had taken it so well. Her strategy of gifting him the cigars had worked, mellowing McCann enough so that he could think logically rather than react emotionally.

Upon reaching the hotel they stood in the lift, until they reached the floor Ilam's room was on. Upon entering the suite she slammed the door shut and threw her husband onto the bed without so much as a by your leave.

McCann a 6ft 1 inch man weighing 190lbs was lifted off his feet and landed softly on the massive bed. Ilam wasted no time and sat on top of him legs astride his waist, her eyes were red with passion and she kissed him clasping his skull in a vice like grip. He started unbuttoning her clothes, first her blouse then her trousers. After a short time Ilam did likewise, but rather than wait she tore his shirt off and pulled open the front of his trousers. Neither one spoke but remained in a passionate kiss until Ilam had removed her blouse and jacket.

McCann broke from the kiss to see her perfect long torso and white ivory skin. He marvelled at her firm petite breasts then clasped his hands onto them rolling her over onto her back. She allowed him to roll her over and giggled with excitement as he removed her remaining clothing. He stared into her eyes for only a moment which seemed to last for at least 30 seconds. Her wide smile and full grin ignited his passion further and his lips descended on her navel.

McCann could feel Ilam's release of tension as she revisited a place that had been so distant for far too long. The flaming haired Valkyrie peered down along her frame to watch him infuse her mind with a pleasure she had yearned for this last year. Ilam monitored his progress and at first only a whimper could be detected here and there. After 20 minutes of passion her whimper of delight had become a groan of pleasure. McCann knew what his wife desired and took great delight in delivering it, making Ilam happy made him happy.

Soon her groan became a shriek and he felt her large hands clasp the side of this head in a lock no man could wriggle out of.

'Enough!' she screamed and pulled him up by his head, as a midwife handling a baby, and tossed him onto his back. Still holding his head in vice she mounted him and pushed down on his manhood whilst he lay helpless gazing into her searing red eyes.

She thumped her body onto his; he grabbed her forearms squeezing them as he tried to ease the pressure on his skull. Her rhythmic motion gathered pace, her ivory thighs flexed as she pushed herself down harder and faster with each pommel into his human frame. As her intensity increased so did the pressure and McCann felt he was now wrestling to prevent his own wife from breaking his body into pieces.

The brand new bed was creaking under the commotion above, she paused without warning faced upwards and as a wolf baying to the full moon she called out with a deep climaxing howl. A fraction of a second later McCann joined her with a scream of his own as her vaginal walls clasped onto him and began tearing at his loins, pulling them from his body.

As her howls died so did her grip on McCann, eventually he was released from her grasp. Ilam kissed him passionately as she dismounted and lay next to him. Both were exhausted and lay staring into each other's eyes.

Ilam had formed a link with her husband allowing him to feel her soul during these times. Increasing the intensity of love making to a height that McCann could not have understood before. After ten minutes they began the process again, Carrying on until the early hours of the morning the lovers merged in mind, body and soul as one.

The rest of the universe faded into insignificance until they both missed the meeting at 8:00 AM and an alert was sent out along with two search parties.

Chapter 15

Both Ilam and McCann entered the restaurant together and sat at the breakfast table with Faraday and Malikah. The entire building had been locked down by security. Spetsnaz guarded all exits, patrolling day and night. The restaurant was clear but for I.S.A staff and the ever intrusive Jerry Habeeb and his inquisitors.

At the table McCann sensed a tension in the air, 'Good morning you two,' said Faraday standing up and waiting for Ilam to take a seat.

She sat next to Malikah; the men faced each other at the thick mahogany table.

McCann sat down 'Good morning,' he said with a rather cheery attitude with was unusual for him on a morning.

Even more so if Faraday had known he hadn't slept at all. The tension was then broken when both Malikah and Ilam began to giggle as schoolgirls. McCann rolled his eyes and Faraday looked perplexed, but discarded whatever they may be communicating to each other as something he'd prefer not to be briefed on.

'So how was your evening?' Faraday asked McCann innocently only to receive uncontrollable laughter from first Malikah then Ilam. He turned to the girls and with a stern tone in his voice he said 'I was inquiring about your evening at café K'ooben.'

Ilam fought back her laughter but Malikah was unable to control herself. Each time she looked at her Father's disapproving expression it threw her back into fits of laughter.

Ilam eventually tapped her daughter on the arm 'Bisik chi!'

McCann new this phrase well since his wife had often aimed it at him. Depending on the context it had a different meaning but literally translated "Bisik chi" was "Lay hold of mouth". In this context it meant "Shut your mouth". Malikah tried not to look at either her Father or Faraday and brought her laugh down to a snigger.

'Please continue,' said Ilam after her daughter's humour was at an acceptable level for them to hold a polite conversation.

Faraday turned back to McCann and announced 'I've got a surprise for you Duncan.'

McCann didn't like surprises and he knew that Faraday knew that, 'Really?' he replied with a false smile.

Faraday looked towards a Gukumatz waiter and called him. The waiter disappeared into the kitchens and re-appeared with a plate, which he placed before McCann.

McCann couldn't believe his eyes when he saw a cooked English breakfast of bacon, eggs, sausages and beans. The waiter came back with a cup of coffee and cutlery. McCann smiled at the waiter who darted off 'Thank you William,' he said as he picked up his knife and fork.

'We're extending the orbital station at Ilium 3, with facilities to produce and store some select native crops. We'll also grow synthetic meat for the men and women serving here,' said Faraday as he watched the Governor tuck into his first real breakfast in too long.

McCann nodded in agreement as he consumed his meal.

'Ilam suggested the extension, and if it is successful we'll do the same with the other two orbital stations.'

Ilam ordered a Tlillan dish from the menu, Tlillan food had become all the rage since Malikah had arrived and every establishment that served food was desperate to stock it.

'The handover of the governorship will be announced today. The ceremony will take place next week Duncan, so make certain you have a dress uniform for the occasion and give your sceptre a good polish.'

No sooner had Faraday stopped talking Malikah burst out laughing again. It had become evident that she had inherited a penchant for low brow humour, probably from her Father.

McCann had to stop eating, he put his knife and fork down as he waited for the laughs to subside.

Ilam shook her head in disappointment at her daughter's base sense of humour, which only encouraged Malikah.

Faraday on the other hand was bewildered until he thought over what he had said then sighed and waited for the laughter to reside once more. Faraday scanned the table with his sharp eyes and asked in a stern tone 'Are we finished with the gutter humour children?'

Malikah sat with her hands in her lap whilst she forced the laughter back.

'Back to more serious matters, the ceremony will be held in the temple at the Kotu spawn pool. We shall all have to be present, but it is a short and simple ceremony. You hand the sceptre to the Kotu priest and he will present it to Ilam. That Habeeb fellow will be present to record it and breathing apparatus will be provided, do you have any questions at this moment Duncan?'

McCann chewed thoughtfully then asked Faraday 'How long is it going to be exactly?'

'No longer than two hours I should think.'

McCann sighed 'Jesus, two hours in that hot sweaty bog in dress uniform!'

Malikah called across the table in a disapproving tone 'Father you need to show more respect towards the Gukumatz!'

The Englishman sneered 'After a year on this flea ridden stinking moon the only things I have respect for are a good shower and atmosphere conditioners!'

His daughter tightened her lips and said nothing, her expression of disapproval said everything.

'Alright I will treat the Gukumatz better, satisfied?'

His growing daughter smiled and the matter was dropped.

McCann finished his meal and sat back in his chair drinking his coffee 'Ah, real coffee. So where is that slime ball reporter?' he said looking into his tall ceramic cup.

Faraday motioned with his eyes towards the large window that looked out onto the thoroughfare, 'He left to do some investigative reporting on Gukumatz, don't ask me what that means.'

McCann sipped his coffee 'I tell you this, if he puts a foot wrong I'll have him strung up by the bloody balls this time!'

Faraday pointed at McCann 'You look here Duncan, since you've been away your and Captain Ryu's image back home have fallen. After the uprising on Ilium 3 people are asking questions. We need him more than he needs us, do you hear me?'

McCann had been away from Earth for over a year, only viewing the news now and again since he couldn't get a proper hard copy on Ilium 3, 'What do you mean?'

Faraday's eyes peered from side to side then he spoke in a low voice 'After the suppression a lot of issues were brought up in the media concerning you and Captain Ryu's past records. The I.S.A were heavily criticised for the napalm and nerve gas attacks on the population. People were questioning if we should be here. We couldn't afford another rebellion so changes had to be made quickly.

Mr. Habeeb may not be the most discreet person you've ever met but he is here to raise our profile back home, and that includes you Duncan so please co-operate with the man.'

McCann accepted the explanation 'When will I be back on the Athena?'

'After the ceremony you may reassume command as you please Duncan,' replied Faraday with his hands resting on his walking cane.

The party were set to tour some of the city that day with Jerry. However before they could leave the restaurant Faraday received an urgent message on his wrist tablet.

McKinley's voice could be heard over Athena alerting the crew to a tunnel event, 'Sir, Sir are you there Sir?' he blurted in a panic.

Neither Faraday nor McCann were impressed 'Calm down man!' replied Faraday sternly.

'It is only a Tlillan personal transport, Mr. Faraday,' stated Malikah with a grin.

Everyone at the table turned towards Malikah.

'You cannot know that!' exclaimed Ilam.

Malikah countered in a defiant tone 'Quilachutli is onboard. She comes for the ceremony to represent the Grand Matriarch.'

Ilam's eyes widened 'Quilachutli is here? You must be mistaken!'

Malikah looked towards Faraday 'The first Matriarch of the Chutli clan will be landing soon Mr. Faraday; I suggest we prepare to greet her.'

For a few seconds the air was still and no one spoke until McKinley's Scottish accent could be heard through Faraday's communicator 'Sir, the design matches a Tlillan scout craft, it is proceeding towards Ilium 1. It has not answered our attempts at communication.'

Faraday stared hard at Malikah 'Inform Miss Quilachutli she is welcome to dock at the orbital station or land on Ilium 1, whichever is preferable.'

Malikah grinned but Ilam still remained sceptical, as far as Ilam was concerned it was not possible even for Malikah to scan with such accuracy at that range.

McCann hit his comms 'Kotumatz there will be a Matriarch landing at ...' he peered to his daughter. Malikah smiled and pointed towards the pad off the thoroughfare, visible through the restaurant window.

McCann nodded in thanks 'Pad Kotu one, please inform Nestor.'

A croaky form of English came back via the comms 'When will she be arriving governor?'

'Now Kotumatz, and it's a clan Matriarch if that makes a difference.'

'Understood governor McCann,' replied his aide.

'McCann out,' and he tapped his wrist to see the approval of his wife, she was impressed by the fact he'd coaxed a Gukumatz into learning English. McCann returned the smile under the impression she was still thinking about the time they'd spent in each other's arms.

When Nestor and Kotumatz started filing out towards the pad Faraday stood up and decided they should join them.

Nestor did not have a happy face after the treatment he suffered at the hands of Malikah, he had no ill effects from his immobilisation, however he felt humiliated. The Spetsnaz lined the walkway between the pad and the thoroughfare, standing to attention as Faraday led his party along it.

'Director! Wait!' shouted Jerry as he and his cohorts charged along the thoroughfare towards the walkway.

'How did he manage?' mumbled Faraday to himself, watching Jerry charging along with two men behind him and a floating camera bringing up the rear.

'That man could probably smell a story from 500 metres,' whispered McCann to Faraday.

'Director Faraday, could you tell me what's happening?' asked a breathless Jerry once he'd reached the party, which now continued along the walkway to the edge of the pad.

Faraday plonked his cane on the ground with each step and looked up to the thick sky 'We're receiving a visitor Mr. Habeeb, from Tlillan.'

'Who is it?'

'On the question of who it may be,' Faraday emphasised the word whom 'we believe it to be a Tlillan Matriarch, a Miss Quilachutli the first Matriarch of the Chutli clan.'

Jerry pulled out a tablet and started making notes as he walked alongside Faraday, 'Isn't that the same clan as Ilamachutli and Malikachutli?'

Faraday stopped at the edge of the pad still looking up at the sky 'Yes it is Mr. Habeeb, she is here for the handing over ceremony.'

Jerry halted next to Faraday then turned to look at his crew behind him 'Are you getting this Ed?' his cameraman wore a 3d visor to direct the camera and gave Jerry a thumbs up. 'Trey?' Jerry made contact with the soundman and Trey gave a thumbs up.

Malikah scanned the sky then held onto her mother's arm. 'She's here,' whispered the tall young woman to her red haired Mother.

At that moment Faraday noticed a dark oblong descend from the clouds. The craft descended from the heavens slowing until it rested softly upon the pad, sporting the universal Tlillan design of a pyramid at the rear.

The side began to wobble until it became fluid, rippling back to reveal a Tlillan female stood over 7ft wearing a typical jet black space suit. The Amazon stepped out of the craft and approached the party with long strides. An escort of two males followed behind her, both about 5 feet tall wearing the same dark ribbed suit with helmets covering their heads. The craft closed and the Matriarch's helmet rippled back into her suit to reveal a beautiful specimen of Tlillan womanhood. All members of the party were taken aback especially McCann. Ilam however was not so pleased with her husband's reaction, sensing her jealousy McCann took a hold of his emotions.

Quilachutli was tall with silver hair tied in a knot on the rear lobes of her skull, so as not to interfere with her helmet. She had a tall forehead with short straight silver eyebrows, her eyes were wide but slim in height. Her ridged nose was as tall as a human's but longer with a small peak pointing upwards at the end. Her wide mouth possessed lips thinner than most Tlillan's, Quilachutli's face ended with a petite chin larger than that of a human female, but for her race quite small. Her cheekbones sat high, the Amazon's skin was typically Tlillan somewhere between ivory and transparent; along with her eyes that aside from the pupil were almost translucent.

Ilam strode out from the group to meet Quilachutli before an incident could occur, dressed in her white uniform with an olive branch emblem they met.

'Ola Quilachutli,' said Ilam as she greeted her Matriarch with a bowed head.

'Liik'il Ilamachutli,' was the reply, to which Ilam lifted her head.

Quilachutli's eyes then fixed onto Malikah 'Tal paal,' she commanded in a deep tone.

McCann's ear piece translated it as 'Come here child'.

Malikah approached with her head bowed and upon reaching her clan Matriarch she was told to rise 'Liik'il Malikachutli.'

Malikah lifted her face until her eyes met those of her Matriarchs.

Quilachutli grabbed Malikah's chin in a rough manner and inspected her as a farmer would examine cattle, 'Lela' paal konik Xch'uup?'

McCann listened intently to his translator which repeated the conversation awkwardly in English back to him 'This child disposed of Grand Matriarch?' was the dialogue relayed to him.

There was no reply and silence held the air until Quilachutli spoke again 'Tanili chumuk e'hoch'e'en haal kuxa'an!'

McCann waited for his ear piece; his universal translator built into his suit collar underneath his uniform struggled to pick up and translate the conversation, despite her loud voice. 'Yet the half dark is alive!' came the androgynous voice that was taking more time the longer the sentence.

Quilachutli's eyes moved and observed Malikah's pendant presented by the Grand Matriarch more than a year ago, then her eyes moved back to Malikah's. Removing her hand from the face of Malikah, Quilachutli said 'Hach uts paal.'

McCann recognised her words as 'Very good child' without the aid of the translator.

Both Malikah and Ilam bowed their heads 'Dyos bo'otik, Quilachutli.'

McCann also recognised 'Thank you' in the Tlillan language without the need of assistance.

At this point McCann decided to approach them. On reaching the Tlillans he stood at what he felt was a respectable distance from Quilachutli and spoke his best Tlillan 'Ola Quilachutli.'

As expected she didn't respond to him but instead spoke to Ilam 'Lela' xib iicham?' to which the translator deciphered to mean 'This man mate?'

McCann wasn't certain if it was the software for the translator, or if all Tlillans were just crude, but he felt rather embarrassed by her statement.

Ilam replied 'He'le',' which McCann knew was yes.

Quilachutli turned to look at her males 'Luk'ul,' she commanded, they obediently filed towards the vessel they'd arrived on.

The side of the craft rippled back open and they all entered. Quilachutli watched and waited intently until the craft rippled shut and she was certain they could no longer observe her.

Quilachutli returned her gaze to McCann 'Greetings McCann address me as Quil.'

McCann was taken aback that she had spoken to him so freely.

He stuttered for a moment then recovered 'Erm … thank you and please call me Duncan.'

The silver haired goddess gave him a quick smile 'You are the source of much gossip on Tlillan Duncan, even more so than your daughter.'

McCann was in a state of shock and with a puzzled tone replied 'Really? All good I hope?'

The clan Matriarch gave a little smile again, 'Cihuateteo has done little but speak of Duncan McCann!'

McCann had a dark smile and chuckled 'How is the old girl doing?'

The Chutli clan Matriarch was containing her grin with a straight face. She wasn't best of friends with Cihuateteo however Cihuateteo was on the council.

Quilachutli was forced to moderate herself with that famous Tlillan self-control even when alone on Ilium 1 'Cihuateteo's lower leg was replaced, her health is excellent Duncan.'

McCann stopped chuckling but his sinister grin remained 'She's welcome to come and visit anytime, if she wants a matching pair!'

Ilam was not impressed with his poor respect for Cihuateteo, she may be an unpleasant personality but she was also a clan Matriarch.

Quilachutli said nothing in reply; turning to Ilam she said 'The Grand Matriarch was correct Ilam.'

Ilam did not speak and Quil did not expect an answer 'His impetuous behaviour is attractive.'

Ilam snapped at her clan Matriarch with the sound of alarm in her voice 'Quil!'

Quil looked at McCann taking delight in his confusion then returned her gaze to Ilam 'You need not fret Ilam, I will find my own.'

Quil walked towards Faraday and Jerry who had been watching the events unfold. Ilam followed alongside her, Quil whispered into her ear 'The Grand Matriarch has her eye on him.'

McCann watched his wife, she listened and started to look as if she had an ailment. He only discovered what Quil had said later when he grilled his daughter, who seemed to know what everyone was saying and thinking. He disapproved strongly of her eves dropping on his thoughts but was more than happy to squeeze reports out of her on other people's privacy.

Quil introduced herself to Faraday and made clear her intent to attend the ceremony next week, as a representative of the Grand Matriarch.

The Gukumatz lined the thoroughfare to observe what was a great wonder, a clan Matriarch and the Icon in their city. Nestor had his Spetsnaz make a corridor through the crowds back to the makeshift Administrative building, which served as the main living quarters and centre of most human activity on Ilium 1; as the party made their way across the thoroughfare the crowds of Gukumatz on each side kowtowed.

Quil asked Ilam 'Malikah has been accepted as the Icon?' whilst looking out into the sea of Gukumatz.

Ilam replied 'Her DNA was confirmed yesterday,' in a hushed tone.

The party proceeded through the silence and back into the lobby of the building. Faraday led Quil and the others to a makeshift conference room on one of the floors below the main level where the lobby was situated. Faraday arranged a room to accommodate her party however Quil requested only one room. Apparently the males would remain in her transport vehicle until she desired to return.

In the conference room only Faraday Quil, Ilam and McCann were permitted to enter the small dark room with no windows and only chemical lighting on the ceiling. In the centre sat a rectangular table which seated 12 people easily.

Quilachutli was very different to what McCann had expected, she shared all of the typical Tlillan female traits both physical and attitude wise. Yet for some reason, he couldn't fathom, she hadn't treated him or anyone else with utter disdain, a trait most uncommon amongst her people. Her odd behaviour interested him greatly which in turn made his wife uncomfortable something he didn't understand at the moment. For a people who lived in a society founded on cold non emotion every day, it didn't make sense. Perhaps contact with humans had changed views amongst some of them? Apparently if that was so it had made no impact on the lives of Tlillan males, who were treated as if they barely existed outside of their duties.

All through the discussion Faraday was leading, Quil kept sneaking looks at McCann and slipping him a smile here and there. He felt flattered but remained ever aware of his wife who was very tense throughout. The discussion was thankfully short, her accommodation was prepared and Quil was welcome to stay on Ilium 1 as long as she pleased. Ilam agreed to stay with her and introduce her to the city but McCann felt an ulterior motive. He felt his wife was being quite irrational; however there was no harm in Ilam keeping an eye on the Matriarch.

After the excitement Faraday and McCann stayed in the conference room with Nestor and a few Gukumatz aides to go over the plans for next week's ceremony.

Ilam and Quil went for a stroll through the bazaar together. Malikah was always by Ilam's side, the three of them were subject to constant bowing and scraping. Ignoring the crowds they reached the centre of the bazaar where the roof opened up presenting a small park with a fountain for shoppers to relax.

Stopping by the fountain Quil had a broad smile; facing her friend Ilam she asked cheekily 'So how is it?'

Ilam was rather embarrassed and her eyes turned pink, causing Quil to do the same and laugh 'Quil enough,' she muttered.

Quil persevered 'Link with me,' Ilam refused her request 'then describe him.'

Ilam motioned towards her daughter 'I can not.'

Quil looked towards Malikah haughtily and in a matter of fact tone said 'She knows already Ilam, come why should I be alone?'

Ilam remained firm and refused.

'Perhaps I must take him for myself, tonight?'

Ilam's eyes turned from a light pink blush to a burgundy red fury 'Enough!'

Quil was amused by the reaction of Ilam; never on Tlillan would a female have been so possessive concerning a male. It was fascinating for her to observe such passion in the woman she had sent out to scout the Terran system all those years ago.

Quil held Ilam by her arms and comforted her 'I would not do that to you my child, despite it being my privilege. However the Grand Matriarch cares not for you, as I.'

Ilam calmed down 'I am an exile she may not take him.'

Quil nodded 'True, yet your daughter is not and he is her Father. It was rumoured she invited him to Tlillan is it so?'

Ilam whispered in a low tone 'Yes.'

'Beware Ilam, she desires her throne and your mate. He is the only confirmed compatible male, if she removes Malikah and takes him she will try to produce the Mictlancihuatl and forge a dynasty.'

It was quiet for a few seconds then Quil tried to lift the mood 'Xch'uup is not our concern today, let us not speak of her, are others aware of the Gukumatz intentions?'

Ilam perked up now that the subject of the Grand Matriarch was dropped 'No, they have not informed the Humans.'

'Do they suspect anything?'

Ilam turned to Malikah 'No,' replied her daughter.

Quil reached back and untied her hair allowing it to flow down just past her shoulders 'What action might they take at the ceremony?'

Ilam shook her head 'Faraday is cautious, he will allow it to continue and try to rectify the events afterwards.'

Quil smiled with satisfaction 'Will your mate be a problem?'

Malikah took exception to Quil's description of her Father but would not speak against her clan Matriarch.

Quil turned her face towards Malikah's, 'Such passion concerning a male, on Tlillan few can identify the male that conceived them. Even then it is superfluous, a male is nothing more than an expendable asset to be used and disposed of, as seen fit.'

Malikah's eyes turned a greyish colour 'My father is not expendable,' she said sternly.

'Malikah!' whispered Ilam.

Quil reached out and touched Ilam softly whilst still looking at Malikah, 'No let her speak, she will be clan Matriarch and perhaps Xch'uup.

Why should a clan matriarch show any respect to your Father?'

'He conquered the Gukumatz, something your wonderful Grand Matriarch has failed to achieve in centuries!' Malikah spat back.

Quil's smile remained 'You believe his acts of savagery have merit child?'

Malikah folded her arms 'His acts of savagery stopped Cihuateteo in her tracks didn't they?'

Quil enjoyed the debate, vetting the next clan Matriarch, 'Savagery and heresy, two qualities I do not admire!'

Malikah's eyes returned to their usual state 'So you accept him as Tlillan?'

'How so?'

Malikah quickly replied before anything more could be said 'Surely to commit heresy you must believe him Tlillan?'

Quil smiled and peered at Ilam 'Perhaps. The question remains though why should he receive more merit than another male?'

Malikah gave Quil a haughty look 'That is why your society is stagnant and in decline. You lack the strength to control others, so you force your own kind to submit to archaic religious dogma. The Lightsiders lived by a code of honour and glory, earned in heroic battle. The Twilighters lived by a code of honour earned from social development. All that is left is honour earned from submission to the dreamscape, when Ah ChuyaKak crushed the wraiths was she a savage or a heretic? Did the Grand Matriarch not bestow and ovation upon her when she offered the wraith king as sacrifice to the Darksiders?'

Quil stopped smiling and brushed her hair back, letting it hang down from the back of her head 'Ah Chuyakak was a Lightsider and a Matriarch.'

'If she had conquered the Gukumatz would she not receive an ovation? Would she be branded a savage? Before we were strong, but since the plague ridged dogma and corruption have destroyed the Tlillan people. All that remains is a decayed belief in superiority that was shattered by a Human male.'

Quil clapped Malikah 'An excellent speech child. Though it will require more before the Matriarchs accept humans, let alone human males.'

Malikah remained firm on her stance 'Whether humans are accepted as Tlillan or not is of no consequence, it is whether humans accept their true origins and see themselves as Tlillan.'

Quil whom had little firsthand information on Mankind other than what she had experienced in the dreamscape was fascinated, 'Why?'

Malikah had linked often with the dreamscape however she was powerful enough to block her own thoughts. The skill in Tlillan society wasn't so much the ability to link and merge with each other in the dreamscape, sharing experiences and peering into other dimensions. To rise in power the ability to block off those thoughts you desired was a crucial skill. Without the ability, scheming and plotting was not possible. The strongest would hide their true thoughts and actions from society rising to power whereas the majority were forced to submit.

On Ilium 1 Quil could speak freely, hiding her thoughts and actions from the Grand Matriarch when she returned.

Malikah answered her clan Matriarch 'When humanity accepts the truth they will fight for us.'

Quil scowled 'Human society borders the edge of chaos, it remains a mystery how they advanced to defeating the Gukumatz!'

Malikah nodded in agreement 'They are selfish and vain, yet when threatened by an alien force their society will change drastically. When under attack, all past disagreements are forgotten, the only concern is the common goal of defeating their enemy.'

Quil stepped closer to Malikah and combed her dark curled hair back 'You will make a fine clan Matriarch and perhaps a Grand Matriarch,' she said affectionately.

Malikah smiled as did Ilam who gave a proud look towards her daughter.

Quil gazed at Malikah as if she were her own child 'You have made your Grandmother proud, child.'

Malikah looked at her mother who nodded.

'Thank you Grandmother,' replied Malikah.

'You must call me Quil and please forgive me when I speak of your Father as my daughter's mate. It is merely force of habit child.'

Ilam then asked her Mother 'Why would Xch'uup have sent you here? She is aware of my parentage and no doubt suspects you.'

Quil who was still having a moment with her granddaughter replied 'Her intent is unclear.'

Malikah answered her Mother 'I know!'

Quil smiled at Malikah 'Then tell us child.'

'She has sent a Tezcatlipoca, it arrived here today before you,' said Malikah trying to please her grandmother.

Ilam folded her arms firmly 'How could you know this Malikah, even a Grand Matriarch could not sense a Tezcatlipoca until a few metres away?'

Quil stroked her daughter's hair 'Where is it?'

Malikah smiled excitedly 'It is watching us now!'

Quil peered around the garden.

'It is cloaked but I could immobilize it for you,' said Malikah with a sweet smile.

Quil removed her fingers from Malikah's hair 'Show me.'

Ilam was sceptical since these creatures had an almost impenetrable mind and were impossible to sense any further than a few steps away, which by that time it was too late.

Malikah gazed at the ledge of the roof, on the opposite side of the fountain, her eyes darkened and what seemed to be an electrical surge running from the ledge to a metre or so upwards into the air made a loud crackle. There were a few flashes and everyone in the area stopped what they were doing to look upwards. A creature perched on the ledge appeared piece by piece as its cloaking suit failed.

The Gukumatz let out shouts and screams when the assassin was fully visible, they recognised what it was.

Over the noise Malikah shouted 'Bisik chi'!'

The Gukumatz immediately kowtowed in silence.

The Tezcatlipoca remained stiff until it toppled off the ledge onto the grass below. The bird man was no more than 2 feet tall, wearing a stealth suit which shimmered as the northern lights. An aurora of colours rushing through as the suit failed to bend light around its occupant. The assassin had small fat legs with talon claws; the torso was typically avian and consisted of what looked to be a large breast with tail feathers sticking out from the rear of the suit. The arms were not covered by the suit either and were in fact wings with a plethora of different coloured feathers swept back in a sleek smooth rounded wing. Tiny clawed hands pooped out at the end before the wing tip. Its head was coloured white and had a typical bird of prey look with a slim pointed yellow and black beak. The creature had the look of an enlarged falcon.

Malikah approached the twitching assassin.

'You must destroy it!' ordered Ilam following behind Malikah

Quil touched her daughter communicating to her silently.

'Continue Malikah,' said Quil now standing behind her with Ilam as they waited for Malikah's next action.

They observed her as she stepped towards it and crouched down beside the creature, she said nothing only stroking the feathers on its head. The Tezcatlipoca lay on the ground curled up as if it had been electrocuted, no emotion could be detected on its face though the eyes betrayed great fear. The Gukumatz were still kowtowed but all observed the scene and were prepared to defend their Icon from the assassin.

Malikah stood up and took two steps backwards, 'Liik'il Tezcatlipoca!' ordered Malikah in a deep booming voice.

The assassin's limbs relaxed and it slowly lost the stiffness it had been hit with on the ledge. After about 15 seconds it had regained its proper motor function and all eyes were on it, prepared to strike one of the most feared creatures in the galaxy.

The Tezcatlipoca glanced around then scurried towards Malikah. Rather than make an attempt on her life it climbed up her leg and hung onto the side of the half breed's tall torso, with arms around her neck for support as a newborn infant.

A few Gukumatz moved to attack the Tezcatlipoca 'Chiltal Much!' bellowed Malikah telling them to get back on the ground which they dutifully did.

Malikah stroked the Tezcatlipoca and turned around to face her Mother and Grandmother 'There you see, he's harmless Mother.'

Ilam was very alarmed since for thousands of years these creatures were the harbingers of death to whoever was unlucky enough to see one, just before being assassinated.

Quil raised her eyebrows 'It seems you have a new pet Malikah.'

Ilam shouted at her Mother 'Quil! It must be destroyed!'

The Tezcatlipoca flinched and grab on tighter to Malikah 'He's no danger to us now Mother, he just informed me of his employer.'

Ilam shook her head 'That is not possible Malikah, Tezcatlipoca are immune to probes it would commit suicide before breaking.'

Quil stared into the eyes of the creature causing it to move away 'Faraday must know of this, come Malikah.'

Quil led them back, but Ilam was frustrated after having her word superseded by her Mother. Yet there was no cause for complaint, Quil outranked her in age and position within the clan.

When the three ladies returned with what looked like a condor man clasping onto his daughter McCann wasn't pleased. Ilam managed to calm him down though he was adamant that the birdman should be taken into custody and held there. Faraday agreed with him however Malikah refused to let it out of her sight. Jerry was most excited by the appearance of the creature, Faraday got them into a private room in the super scrapper leaving Jerry outside.

Ilam could see the stress returning to Faraday as he took out his handkerchief and wiped his brow, pacing the room from one wall to another 'How in blue blazes did that thing get here?'

The ladies were standing on one side of the table together with McCann and Faraday on the other side whilst Spetsnaz stood outside guarding the room.

Quil peered at Malikah waiting for her to answer, 'By a cloaked vessel, he landed it on a northern island just off the main continent.'

Faraday started to sweat even more and closed his eyes whilst wiping his brow again, 'My god it might have brought a nuclear device and finished us all. Why didn't you inform anyone of this Malikah?'

Malikah said nothing causing Faraday's anger to reach boiling point.

McCann stepped in to try and relieve the situation 'So why was it sent here Malikah?'

Malikah stroked the feathered head of her new pet which was still clinging onto her for protection 'He was sent to assassinate Quilachutli.'

Everyone in the room was surprised.

'Cihuateteo sent him, but the Grand Matriarch ordered the assassination.'

Quil nodded in approval at her granddaughter, 'An attempt to force Malikah to travel to Tlillan unprepared, Xch'uup has made her first move and failed.'

McCann frowned at Quil 'I don't understand why would she send you then try to have you killed? Surely she would make an attempt on my wife or my daughter's life first?'

Quil smiled, amused by McCann's naivety 'By removing her clan Matriarch she assumes Malikah will take the role before maturity. If Malikah were Matriarch she must return to Tlillan and occupy her seat on the council. She would have no allies, since I would be deceased and her mother in exile.'

McCann thought for a moment rubbing the stubble on his chin 'What if Malikah didn't take your place?'

'In that case the Grand Matriarch will have removed her enemy and your ally.'

McCann wasn't a politician and was already sick to the back teeth of cloak and dagger games as governor of Ilium 'So why does she think you're our ally?'

Quil stepped over to Malikah; standing behind her she put her hands on Malikah's shoulders 'Malikah is my granddaughter.'

McCann shook his head with a sceptical expression on his face 'Marvellous! Am I supposed to believe that?'

Malikah frowned still holding tightly onto her pet and stroking it 'Father it's true!'

McCann was in a mood and working up to one of his infamous rants. He fixed his eyes on the creature she was holding 'You can get rid of that bloody animal hanging off you, do you hear me?'

Malikah remained quiet refusing to respond to her father's outburst 'Are you deaf as well as dumb? I said get rid of it!' McCann shouted.

Ilam stepped up to the edge of the table to cool her husband down but before she was able to say anything he turned on her.

'Forget it!' he said pointing in Ilam's face.

Ilam through bitter experience had learned that it was best to do as he said until he'd calmed down and decided to beg her for forgiveness. Ilam stepped backwards and remained silent.

Quil was confused by her daughter's response and outraged by McCann's behaviour 'Ilam you take instruction from this male?'

McCann still suffering from the effects of nearly a year on Ilium 1 turned on his mother in law.

Pointing at her he sneered 'Deal with it!'

Quil's eyes widened and morphed into a deep red, she had never been spoken to this way and added to that a male, it was more than Quil could permit. The silver haired Amazon glared at McCann with fire in her eyes.

The Englishman felt a sharp pain in the front of his head just inside his skull above his eyes. The pain was intense, he stopped whatever he was doing since only the pain concerned him now and it was growing. It spread, travelling to the rear of his brain immobilising McCann who was barely supporting himself with one arm on the table, the other holding his forehead as he faced the floor.

The Governor was unable to speak and his legs started to give away. McCann felt himself slipping into a state of unconsciousness, unable to cry or go for his weapon sitting inside his thigh holster.

Then the pain began to subside just before he passed the threshold of consciousness. Upon turning his head to look up he saw his daughter glaring at her grandmother from behind.

Malikah's eyes were jet black; he next looked at Quil who was still furious but visibly struggling. With what exactly he wasn't sure since McCann's thoughts were controlled by pain and a feeling of helpless terror. Eventually the assault withdrew enough that he could stand straight and examine the battle Quil was fighting in her mind with Malikah.

His daughter had blocked Quil from her initial assault on McCann, preventing him from dropping to the floor and being taken to a med bay, much the same as Nestor. Quil decided to turn her focus onto her granddaughter but with far less success than she had on McCann.

Malikah stood defiantly as a proud young Goddess with wine dark locks of hair. The sable Goddess' eyes were as two cold dark stones, Quil was in difficulty holding her granddaughter at bay grunting as it became more and more difficult to breathe.

Neither Malikah nor her pet moved but Quil took small steps backwards away from her opponent whilst still facing her. Quil finally stepped into the wall then slowly slid down it, never removing her eyes from Malikah's.

Ilam much like Faraday was too afraid to step in, not that she could have made a difference.

McCann however was more than happy to see Quil get a taste of her own medicine. Quil's breathing was very rapid and heavy; she was still on her feet but crouched. The silver haired Amazon clasped the bulbous rear of her Tlillan skull and let out a shrill scream. Quil rolled onto the floor just as two Spetsnaz burst into the room.

They halted once Faraday held his hand up signalling there wasn't a problem and returned to their stations quickly. After the soldiers had stepped outside and closed the doors Faraday's gaze returned to Quil. Who was now a blubbering mess, laying in a foetal position on the floor.

McCann calmed down and after pulling himself together his eyes met his daughters. Through their mental link she sensed his wish and nodded silently to her father.

Malikah's eyes returned to their normal state, Ilam ran to help her Mother get back onto her feet. Whilst Quil was recovering Malikah took the opportunity and walked around the table to McCann. Holding his hand she said softly in an affectionate tone 'Please allow me to keep him daddy.'

McCann predictably melted to his daughter's charms 'Very well,' he said with a tired sigh. He witnessed his daughter's face light up with joy giving him a warm glow inside.

Malikah stroked her pet 'Did you hear that Icarus?'

Ilam peered haughtily at her husband whilst comforting her mother 'The man who flew too close to the sun?'

Malikah glanced at Ilam and retorted 'Or too close to the sea Mother!'

'Explain?' snapped Ilam.

'If it is your fate to perish better you do so with glory and honour than pass away into your own cautious mediocrity!'

Faraday broke the standoff stepping up to the table next to Malikah 'Alright ladies we can settle our squabbles later? McCann that creature is your responsibility do you understand?'

McCann put his arm around his daughter 'Understood Sir,' and returned her beaming smile.

Faraday then motioned towards Quil 'How is Quilachutli?'

Ilam had sat her down now that she'd regained consciousness, 'Quil is unharmed,' replied Ilam as her Mother began to slowly focus her eyes on Malikah.

'Good, I want an updated report on my desk concerning the political situation on Tlillan. This attempt on Quilachutli's life could have been detrimental to our relations if it had been successful.'

Faraday then pointed the handle of his cane towards Icarus 'Also I want a full report on these ...'

Malikah smiled 'Tezcatlipoca.'

Faraday rolled his eyes 'We'll have to call them something I can pronounce.'

McCann squeezed his daughter's waist and said 'How about Icarans?'

Faraday nodded with approval since he was getting too old for some of the tongue twisters thrown at him of late 'Thank you Duncan, a report on the Icarans including their home world by tomorrow morning Ilam, alright?'

'As you wish William,' replied Ilam.

Faraday then pointed towards Quil 'Alright if we can convene here again tomorrow at 15:00 hours again?'

Ilam nodded 'Quil shall attend William.'

Faraday picked his hat from the hat stand in the corner, 'McCann sort your daughter out and Ilam please make certain our guest has everything she requires.'

He opened the doors and walked out to the sound of Jerry Habeeb questioning him.

Chapter 16

The next week preparations for the ceremony were underway on the surface, tomorrow was the big day, Faraday was overseeing the temple along with Jerry and his crew. Jerry wanted to make certain his gear would operate properly under such humid conditions. He also wanted the best camera angles possible for the event.

The temple was built on the lip of the spawning pool, a massive cathedral structure that reminded Jerry of the dome of the rock in Jerusalem. The signature dome was a bright green carved from Tourmaline, a sparkling semi-precious stone that shone like a beacon on the misty surface. The dome was supported by a granite octagon which housed the hall where the ceremony was to be held. Each side of the octagon bore a tall spire reaching to half the height of the dome. It was a breath taking sight to behold as they descended to the floor of the forested swamp.

Before the I.S.A had taken control this was the seat of Gukumatz power and even today the high priest resided in the temple refusing to journey above. Did he remain out of shame or fear or perhaps he was waiting for something, McCann didn't know and quite frankly didn't care. The former representative for the Gukumatz had proved itself to be a weak link, McCann felt better off without it around.

In the city the remaining contingents were also getting ready for the big day. McCann was out shopping with his daughter for some new clothes to wear. The Englishman didn't like shopping since his daughter had arrived, he was most uncomfortable with the refusals to accept payment each time he came to purchase something. The Englishman didn't leave debts and even the smallest amount owed would cause him great stress, the Gukumatz were adamant however. The governor felt as if he was sponging off the local people and it irritated him.

However Malikah saw it as her right, accepting the offerings as a mark of respect and love even. Being the father of the Icon was proving to be quite a test, especially now that she carried her pet Icarus wherever she went. The bird unnerved him as it followed, sometimes taking to flight and gliding in circles above them, the deadliest assassin in the galaxy tamed by his daughter. He comforted himself in the fact that without Malikah it could have easily killed anyone of them. Yet he still worried for his little girl, despite her superior intelligence, strength and mental abilities. It was his job to worry about her and he always would be a concerned father no matter how great her star out shone his own.

Ilam was with her mother taking a break in one of the city museums dedicated to ancient pottery and ceramic art. They were both searching for anything related to their own culture, mainly pieces taken from Tlillan during the Gukumatz exodus. Gukumatz had preserved as much as they could, there were dinner plates and urns taken from clan halls and even the Grand Matriarch's palace that had been thought lost millennia ago. The pair of Amazons stopped for a moment to view a large plate commemorating the reign of a past Xch'uup or Grand Matriarch.

'She resembles Mayahuel II' said Quil.

It must have been thousands of years since the Xch'uup was a Twilighter.

Ilam smiled 'I agree.'

Quil examined her daughters smile 'What is amusing?'

Ilam forgot she'd smiled, after spending so much time with humans the Tlillan no longer bothered maintaining a cold façade.

Ilam straightened her face 'It is nothing.'

'Please share it with me Ilam.'

Ilam sighed 'Duncan refers to Xch'uup as "the Gorgon".'

Quil made a perplexed frown.

'A creature of ancient myth,' continued Ilam 'the most prolific Gorgon was Medusa the fairest female in the land whom became the high priestess to a Goddess. She was to keep her virginity in demonstration of total dedication to her deity, but was raped by the God of the sea on the temple floor. In punishment Athena turned her hair into serpents and transformed her beauty so that only to gaze upon her face would kill.'

Quil gasped 'How terrible!'

Ilam shook her head a little 'It is merely Duncan's humour.'

'I meant the tale, was the God not punished for desecrating Medusa and the temple?'

'Poseidon was not punished.'

'Why?'

'You must speak to Malikah, she has an inclination towards Duncan's literary tastes though I find it quite dull,' replied Ilam rolling her eyes back.

'He is too strong an influence upon Malikah. I did not believe the reports of her attacking a Matriarch in his defence but now I have witnessed it for myself. Do you know she links with him?' whispered Quil looking around only to see no one present on their floor.

Ilam nodded shamefully 'Yes.'

Quil felt frustrated and helpless, on Tlillan, females never linked to males for anything other than utilitarian purposes.

'I accept it is difficult yet her heresy is alarming. The literature you describe would be cause for trial alone; I shudder to think what further heresy your mate has led our child into.'

They carried on strolling through the hall between the marble columns and the glass cases displaying the works of well-preserved art.

'Now that the Grand Matriarch's plot is uncovered she will use caution, Malikah's ascendancy to clan Matriarch is sealed. Xch'uup shall have to wait before she may strike again. With luck we shall be in position before that time.'

Strolling side by side Ilam asked softly 'Do we still have the seers support?'

Quil ran her fingers through her hair 'The seers support none but themselves; I know not their true agenda.'

'Yet they gave you the co-ordinates of the Terran system alone, why would they do such a thing if they were aware the Mictlancihuatl would become clan Chutli?' asked Ilam.

The question brought a sneer to Quil's face 'Did they see that? Prophecy has been censored for a long time. We only see in the dreamscape that which Xch'uup wishes. Are the seers in rebellion or do they work in concert with the Grand Matriarch? I am not certain, but Malikah can discover the truth that I am now sure of.'

Ilam displayed a look of disbelief 'How would she do such a thing?'

Quil stopped walking and stared her daughter in the face 'When we fought I touched her mindscape or rather she forced it on me, it was terrifying. The pain that drove every other half breed insane she contains, the strength required to hold back that pain and terror every day is immeasurable. You witnessed her immobilize the Tezcatlipoca, has she exhibited telekinesis or the ability to manipulate different states of energy?'

The incident had left Quil traumatised when she fought her granddaughter. The Mictlancihuatl in the past had all lost their sanity, either killing themselves or being destroyed within the first three years. Consumed by pain and overwhelmed with dark emotions such as fear and hatred.

Malikah was able to control it and Quil now understood how she reduced her enemies to gibbering wrecks. Malikah forced that which had destroyed the others onto her opponents, even the slightest taste of her pain was too much for the most powerful Tlillan to withstand.

Ilam shook her head 'Never, she keeps much from me, Duncan may be aware of more than I.'

Quil continued her stroll along the grey and light brown marble of the museum floor, 'He is too dangerous, I assaulted him only to observe Malikah's reaction. I will not attempt a probe. I do not wish to lose her trust or incur her wrath. I am certain Malikah will block any evidence of heresy once she is on the council.'

Ilam turned her head and stared her mother in the face 'Does not everyone?' she quipped.

Her mother gazed back and laughed at her daughters joke listed firmly under the "Funny because it's true" category.

They both had a good laugh and carried on their stroll holding hands 'I know, let us go shopping?'

Quil smiled 'Shopping?'

'Yes, you require new attire for the ceremony,' said Ilam her voice sounded much like an excited young girl rather than the iron lady she usually projected.

'Clothing? Will this not suffice?' asked Quil.

'Duncan may be a primitive heretic however he has taught me arts long lost on Tlillan,' replied Ilam playfully.

She then gripped Quil's hand tightly and led her out of the museum and towards the fashion district in the grand bazaar. Quil had a bemused smile but was curious to experience this pastime.

In the fashion district two stores now stocked Tlillan clothing, one of the stores had an entire floor dedicated to Tlillan fashions. It was the Gukumatz Channel or Versace, though the name of the fashion house was rather uninspiring to McCann. In his opinion the name "Mopixoa" sounded more like a skin disease than a place to shop for designer clothes. Malikah however was in her element surrounded by adoring tailors measuring her and presenting the most luxurious fabrics the system had to offer. McCann smiled with approval at his daughter when she glanced in his direction between doting assistants presenting her with new colours and designs.

On being informed of Malikah's presence the store owner had flown in using the private landing pad resting on the roof of the fashion district. The large burly owner charged out of the elevator with excitement. McCann saw something large and fast in his peripheral vision moving in his daughter's direction. Instinctively the former SBS officer pulled his pistol and the whine of it charging filled the ears of everyone.

McCann had never seen a Gukumatz move at such a speed on foot and didn't think it was possible with their wide gate. He assumed another assassin was making for his daughter and before stopping to examine who or what he was targeting he fired. The end of the barrel flashed with burning plasma as the charge pushed the tungsten bullet out towards the helpless store owner. Everything stopped on that floor, upon hearing the familiar sound of a charging pulse weapon, the staff looked on in horror. The assistants observed the governor as he drew his pistol with lightning speed and fired.

McCann enjoyed his western movies and practiced his draw in private opposite his mirror every morning; he was certainly the fastest gun on Ilium 1. To McCann's surprise the bullet did not hit its target. The fat store owner fell to the ground, in shock that a firearm had been discharged with him as the intended victim, however he was unharmed.

McCann realised the mistake he'd made and rushed over to the Gukumatz who was unresponsive to McCann's apologies. McCann then noted the store owner was staring at his drawn pistol. The former SBS officer quickly holstered the weapon and helped the owner from floor.

McCann dusted the sack jacket the owner was wearing 'I'm sorry, I guess it was lucky the magazine jammed! That's never happened to me before!'

The owner croaked back, McCann heard his shaky 'Thank you' through his ear piece.

'Father,' said a disappointed Malikah.

Everyone looked around to see Malikah holding a tungsten bullet between her thumb and forefinger 'Your pistol did not jam!'

All the Gukumatz shop assistants including the owner dropped to the floor in a kowtow.

McCann walked between them 'Where did you get that Malikah?'

He was sure his weapon had jammed and couldn't accept she had grabbed it out of the air.

'I diverted it from Kotumatz.'

McCann stood opposite his daughter and opened his hand 'Give that to me,' he said in a sceptical tone. All Gukumatz were kowtowed, their beady eyes fixed upon the Icon as she released her grip on the bullet, leaving it to float in mid-air. McCann moved his hand to take it, but the bullet swiftly moved to his left causing him to grab thin air. He then snatched at it again and again, but each time it moved away unaided.

Malikah began to laugh at her father who was comically snatching at the bullet to no avail.

He peered at his daughter then opened his hand 'Enough Malikah!'

The bullet moved slowly towards McCann, landing softly in his palm. He examined the bullet as a jeweller would examine a diamond. It was still warm and had clear burn marks from the charged rails of a pulse weapon. It was evident to McCann the tungsten bullet had recently been fired and Malikah had just demonstrated the ability to move solid objects. But how could she have possibly seen the bullet as it flew through the air and stopped it before it hit Kotumatz?

'We shall discuss this later,' said McCann as he put the bullet in a pocket.

'Liik'il much,' commanded Malikah in a deep voice.

The Gukumatz rose from the floor slowly returning to their former activities with caution. McCann walked back to where he was standing a few metres away before the ruckus. Charged down his pistol and checked the magazine. It was fully loaded that morning but now missing a bullet.

McCann took the owner aside to ask if he had installed security cameras on the shop floor. When he discovered he had the Englishman requested the footage be sent to him for analysis.

Malikah carried on shopping for a new outfit, settling on a pair of slim fitting dark green pants with a matching high cut waistcoat which had sparkling topaz buttons.

She stepped out of the dressing room after choosing a pair of dark yellow boots to go with it 'What do you think father?' she asked excitedly.

'Aren't you going to wear anything under that top?' came a concerned tone from her father.

It was very nice but he could see bare flesh and despite it being all the fashion on Earth it was uncomfortable to see his own daughter in it.

Her forehead ruffled 'No!'

The owner saw the conflict and darted up to Malikah holding a fine coat. The coat was similar to a military jacket but cut away from the waist down, leaving only the tails at the back and sides.

'We can fit this in one hour, with colour and accessories' said the bowing store owner.

Malikah felt the coat on her and smiled.

'Well that's a little better,' said McCann in a wary tone.

'I love it thank you Kotumatz,' said the smiling young lady.

At that moment Ilam and Quil stepped out of the elevator 'Naats' yaaxil!' shrieked Quil glaring at her granddaughter.

McCann's translator kicked in, even though he recognised the phrase, 'By the first!' it deciphered in an androgynous voice.

'What are you dressed in child?'

Malikah was unperturbed, 'My new outfit for tomorrow!'

As Quil spoke quickly the translator struggled to keep up, dropping words here and there as the conversation became heated. 'This attire is unsuitable remove it' commanded Quil.

'No I will wear this!'

She was soon to be a woman and refused to have some old bag from Tlillan dictate what she wore. Growing up on Earth had influenced her greatly, despite her link to the dreamscape and Tlillan culture. Quil turned to Ilam 'Ilam instruct her to remove topik nook'!'

The translator failed to decipher the last two words of her sentence. Ilam however had no such impediment, in English it literally translated as 'Fuck clothing'.

Ilam turned to her husband 'Duncan?'

McCann walked towards his daughter and inspected her outfit 'It looks fine to me I'll take it.'

McCann didn't really approve of it either but he just couldn't tolerate siding with Quil against his daughters wishes, it was against his nature.

Quil began to berate her daughter out of frustration 'This male has brought shame upon Chutli, he corrupts all Tlillan morality. You have failed miserably Ilam!'

She next turned on the owner of the store 'You shall be punished for your heresy!'

Pointing directly at him, the store owner became visibly weak. His assistants rushed to prevent their boss stumbling over.

Quil was making a scene, shouting at everyone in view. Accusing and threatening until Malikah walked over to where her grandmother stood and in a calm voice said 'You maybe Tlillan but you are not on Tlillan.'

Quil became silent for a moment staring down at the haughty child that had just addressed her clan Matriarch, 'But you are Tlillan child, and you will carry out your Matriarch's request,' she replied just as calmly.

Malikah still dressed in her outfit put her hands on her hips 'I don't think so.'

Ilam stepped away and McCann felt his chest tighten a little just from the tension he sensed between the two.

Quil contained her anger thanks to that Tlillan mental training 'You will do as you are told child!'

Malikah stood unperturbed by her Matriarch 'I am not a child and you shall have to force me ... if you can!'

'Malikah!' whispered Ilam in a rushed voice, but her daughter ignored her.

Quil regained her composure and looked over at McCann. The silver haired Amazon smiled and spoke softly to him 'Duncan might I speak with you in private?'

McCann nodded.

Quil strode over towards him. 'Duncan her attire is immoral and will be viewed poorly by her supporters on Tlillan. A female may not dress in such a fashion, to display one's self in this manner is pornographic, do you understand?'

McCann looked up at the towering Quil 'Isn't it immoral to have someone assassinated on Tlillan?' he whispered.

Quil was growing tired of hitting the brick walls of McCann and Malikah, 'Only if discovered,' she answered.

He closed his eyelids and slowly shook his head from side to side then looked back to Quil. 'You have two choices Quil, either she wears that outfit and you complain ruining the ceremony for everyone. Or she wears that outfit and you shut up and smile. Either way she's wearing that outfit tomorrow so it's your decision old girl.'

Quil turned to face Malikah 'So be it!' she declared in a deep booming voice.

The haughty Amazon strode back into the elevator followed by a dutiful Ilam.

'I tire of shopping!' was the last thing translated by the Englishman's earpiece before the elevator doors closed on the pair.

Malikah began comforting the owner of the store. The creature was terrified by the threats of a clan Matriarch. After some reassuring words he was able to stand firm again and thanked the Icon for saving his life twice in the same day.

Malikah changed back into her plain Tlillan space suit, leaving the staff to get on with fitting the new outfit for her. The owner took them to the lounge below where customers could wait whilst the staff laboured away. It was a nice little coffee shop furnished with large comfortable synthetic leather seats.

'Boxha' dyos bo'otik,' said Malikah ordering two coffees.

McCann relaxed and pulled out a Cohiba tubos. The waiter rushed over placing an ashtray on the table. 'Thank you,' said McCann as he clipped the cap of the cigar then toasted the foot with a match.

'Thank you father,' said Malikah smiling at McCann.

'I could hardly refuse could I?' he replied smiling back at her.

'Why?'

'Well that wretched Tlillan woman couldn't change your mind and besides I noticed that you are taller than me now,' he replied taking the first drag of his small dark brown cigar.

Malikah laughed playfully 'You are being silly again father.'

He blew out the match with a puff of thick smoke 'Am I?' he asked in a foreboding tone.

Malikah stopped laughing 'Yes you are, if you had disapproved of my outfit I would have chosen another you know that!'

McCann was gratified that his daughter still showed him the respect a daughter should towards her father. Holding her hand across the table the Englishman smiled at his daughter and her sable locks of hair.

'Thank you Malikah, how is Ilam doing running around after that woman?'

'She must do as her clan Matriarch wishes whilst she is here. Mother will be fine when the ceremony is over and we return to normal.'

At that moment the waiter appeared with two small coffee cups. Malikah and McCann both withdrew their hands making way. He placed the cups on the circular mats bowed and returned to the kitchen.

The next day everyone had assembled on the landing pad outside, to be ferried to the surface. There was an uneasy silence in the air due to Malikah's attire. The transport descended, with the Tlillans and McCann onboard, into the steamy forest below. Once past the canopy the atmosphere cleared and McCann could make out the massive Kotumatz spawning pool. The pool was a large lake, due to the thick atmosphere McCann could only view it all in one go when descending upon it.

All the Kotumatz females lived their lives here having spawned from only one original. The lake itself was filled with plant life; most notable were the reeds and rushes along the shores then the thick algae swirling on the top. The algae was the Gukumatz major food source, and as far as McCann could surmise the cause of their halitosis.

The small black craft set down on the surface. When the side rippled back Quil and Ilam strode out towards Faraday's reception party along with Gukumatz dignitaries. There must have been hundreds of Gukumatz standing either side of the pad and street leading off it, into the tiny town built around the Kotu temple. Next came McCann, followed by Malikah in her green and yellow outfit. She had left the coat unbuttoned, no doubt to antagonise her grandmother by displaying some flesh. Once Malikah stepped out the Gukumatz kowtowed, she acknowledged her admirers with a smile and approached the others chatting with Faraday.

Faraday was accompanied by Spetsnaz who lead the way into the town and finally into the temple. Which McCann found to be quite a breath taking piece of architecture. As he approached the temple the sound of reed pipes could be heard. By the time they had walked up the steps and into the massive hall it was clear the sound emanated from a choir inside the dome. At the opposite side of the dome to which he entered were two seats that he and his wife were to occupy. A choir of reed players led the pair slowly to their seats whilst the rest of the party sat on a mat along with the Gukumatz. After ten to twenty minutes the choir stopped. A large Gukumatz dressed in what seemed a chain mail suit constructed from amber appeared from a door behind the seats.

McCann sat, looking out at the audience, holding his sceptre with both hands. Inside the temple was rather Spartan compared to the outside, there were no chairs only mats. Although in typical Gukumatz style they decorated their buildings inside via mosaics and intricate tiling on the floor, walls and ceiling. McCann couldn't make out what the designs were but the aqua blues and fire reds were stunning.

The next forty minutes were taken up with the priest rambling on about change and leadership. McCann felt it was ironic that a Gukumatz would believe he had any worthy advice to give on such subjects. All of the humans had their breathing tubes clipped to the nose. In order to prevent them contracting any breathing problems, although McCann was more concerned with being bored to death by the priest.

Malikah and Quil were sat at the front of the crowd, after the Gukumatz had kindly made way for them. Malikah didn't require a breathing tube thanks to her Tlillan heritage. Quil wasn't speaking to her granddaughter, only sending her looks of disapproval whenever she could catch Malikah's eye.

Finally it was time for the handover, the priest had stopped rambling and McCann was still awake. The priest stood before McCann and took possession of the beautiful sceptre, in the rehearsed ceremony the priest now handed the sceptre over to Ilam and commenced another rambling speech. The priest turned to face the audience arms outstretched holding the sceptre; instead of delivering it to Ilam he approached the audience.

Jerry dug his elbow into Faraday's ribs 'What's happening? I don't remember this part.'

Faraday took exception to the elbow yet Jerry was right. He looked around searching for someone that could help. The Director wondered if he should stop the ceremony now, but came to the conclusion it would deteriorate the situation. Faraday didn't answer Jerry but observed the priests every move intently.

The priest stopped in front of Malikah. Prostrating himself on the floor he offered her the sceptre. Faraday watched in alarm but when Nestor gave him a look that said "Do you want me to stop this?" Faraday silently shook his head.

To intervene would be foolish, if the I.S.A was to maintain control over Ilium. He knew the Gukumatz would not stand for it and they'd have another bloody rebellion on their hands. Right now Faraday was hoping Malikah was going to refuse the sceptre but his hopes were soon dashed when she took it to the sound of Gukumatz celebration.

Malikah was led by the priest and Ilam gave her seat up for her daughter. The Tlillans had no expression on their faces, apart from Malikah's grin. McCann knew they'd had this planned for a while or at least were aware of the events about to unfold today. After the ceremony the party returned to the city including Faraday and Jerry. The only person talking in the transport was Jerry but no one answered him.

Once in the city they were back in the conference room and Faraday wasn't happy 'Why didn't you tell me?' he asked Ilam.

She tried to shrug it off as a Gukumatz plot but Faraday had known her and Malikah far too long now.

'If you were not aware of it your daughter certainly was!'

Malikah approached Faraday wrapping both of her arms around his left 'Don't worry William everything will be alright.'

Faraday's breathing slowed and he became visibly calm 'Governorship is not a simple task young lady.'

Malikah smiled 'I have my mother to guide me William, do not worry.'

Faraday took a handkerchief from his breast pocket and wiped his brow down, 'Very well Malikah we shall see how you get on, take your Mother and Fathers advice when uncertain do you hear me?'

Malikah kissed Faraday on the cheek 'Thank you.'

McCann found his daughter's ability to use her feminine whiles uncanny. Certainly not a Tlillan trait and definitely far more effective than threats or barking orders. She had Faraday and McCann wrapped around her little finger without the need for psychic persuasion.

The next day Quil was speaking to her family for the last time on the landing pad 'Tu heel k'iin llamachutli,' next turning her gaze to Malikah 'Tu heel k'iin Malikachutli … aabil.'

Malikah embraced her grandmother much to Quil's surprise. Her silver haired grandmother was startled by the display of affection, as was Ilam. Quil stood still until Malikah had finished and released her.

'Goodbye Quilachutli … grandmother. Be careful on your return, the Grand Matriarch's heresy has been exposed.'

Quil tightened her eyes and controlled any panic trying to invade her system 'How was this done?'

Malikah grinned 'I did it, all can link to the dreamscape and witness her attempt on your life.'

'Then I must return before the council speaks on this,' said Quil as the transport rippled open.

'Cihuateteo lays in wait,' shouted Malikah desperately.

'I will have my cruiser rendezvous before I return to Tlillan, thank you Malikah,' Quil flashed a quick smile at her granddaughter before stepping into her transport.

The side rippled back and the farewell party vacated the pad before she lifted silently into the skies and disappeared.

Malikah had exposed the attempt on Quilachutli's life for all Tlillan's to see, she had inserted the information from her pet Icarus into the dreamscape. The sable child's power too great to censor was causing uproar as all watched. Their minds eye linked to the massive consciousness, Cihuateteo bargaining with a Tezcatlipoca for the death of another Tlillan in the name of the Grand Matriarch.

Malikah wasn't aware of the full effects this would have, however it was an elementary strategy in war to have your enemy fighting himself rather than you.

Tlillan society had five major clans; each one owned and maintained a space cruiser. Sooner or later one side would be bargaining for Faraday's assistance and he would defer to her. Malikah could not foresee the council working out their differences unless the Grand Matriarch and her henchmen stepped down, accepting punishment for their heresy. Malikah was certain that would never happen and even if the Grand Matriarch was victorious in taming the council she would be far too weak to threaten the I.S.A.

The next few weeks went smoothly, Malikah working in concert with the obedient Gukumatz. McCann had some free time with his wife between his governorship and taking back command of the Athena. Faraday returned with Jerry much to everyone's relief before McCann took back the Captain's chair. McKinley had been standing in since Ryu was reassigned and not doing a very good job in McCann's opinion.

The first thing the Commodore did was send him back to his old weapons station and promote Kim to first officer. He figured if Kim was good enough for Ryu then he was good enough for his first officer. Flight Lieutenant Kim was a slim Korean fellow in his forties, an experienced pilot and never receiving a bad mark from Ryu. She had never praised anyone under her command as far as McCann or Kim were aware but she had plenty to say when her expectations went unmet.

McCann was in his Spartan cabin, placing clothes in the small wardrobe along with his cigars when the door chimes activated. 'Enter,' he called whilst separating his shirts on the bed.

Kim entered in his grey flight uniform 'Flight Lieutenant Kim reporting as ordered, Sir!' he barked almost making McCann jump.

The Englishman reached into his pocket pulling out some epaulettes with gold embroidery on them, denoting the rank of Commander.

McCann placed them in Kim's palm 'Congratulations Commander, once you've acquired a new uniform I expect you to report to your station on the bridge.'

Kim was perplexed 'My station on the bridge, Sir?'

'That's right you are the first officer now, I will promote whomever you see fit to take your place as squadron leader.'

McCann patted a shell shocked Kim on the shoulder.

Kim examined his insignia silently then asked 'But what about McKinley I thought he ...'

McCann cut him off 'McKinley is going back to his old station Commander. I'm afraid I need a man that can hold his nerve when it hits the fan, Ryu believed that was you.'

Kim was still confused by the events 'Why was McKinley first officer and field Captain, Sir?'

'Protocol,' replied McCann 'she had to respect order of rank, I however do not. Report to the bridge when ready Commander Kim.'

McCann gave a wink bringing a smile to Kim's lips 'Thank you Sir,' saluted Kim.

'Dismissed,' replied McCann returning the salute.

McCann had read Ryu's and McKinley's reports whilst he was stuck on Ilium 1, reaching the conclusion that in Ryu's absence his best bet for a first officer was Kim. Kim was similar to Ryu; Kim followed orders without flinching or allowing his morality to second guess McCann's authority; unlike McKinley.

McCann couldn't tolerate subordinates allowing their own moral agendas to interfere with cool heads; it was why he was comfortable with Ryu. McCann hoped that Kim was fired in the same mould as his former team mate and squadron member in the Manchurian war.

Once his possessions had been put away McCann took a walk to the engine room. When he entered Louis was hunched over a terminal analyzing power readouts from the core.

'Hey there you French bastard!' shouted McCann.

Louis' head tore away from the screen he was standing at, his face had the look of the devil on it, about to strike the poor fool that dare mock him. When he saw McCann standing outside the elevator holding a bottle of malt Scotch his face lightened immediately.

'Mon ami!' he shouted with arms open as he marched over to his old friend. Louis grabbed his old friend and greeted him with a kiss on each cheek then looking at the bottle 'Pour moi?'

McCann produced two shot glasses and passed one to Louis, 'Just like old times Mon ami,' he then pulled the cork out and poured Louis a drink. McCann put his shot glass on top of a nearby station and poured one for himself. The Commodore put the bottle down and raised his glass 'Vieux amis,' he declared.

'Vieux amis,' replied Louis clinking the tiny shot glasses then downing the smooth Highland cream. McCann poured another then looking around the daunting engine room 'So what have you been up to old chap?'

Louis gestured behind him down the long gulf of stations with men and women hard at work. Squeezed between the ships massive power core to McCann's left and the titanic engines on his right side, it was the hardest and most dangerous job on the Athena but Louis had taken the bull by the horns. Despite the beating taken in the battle against the Gukumatz he somehow kept her in one piece. Secretly McCann had admired Louis ever since that day. But he would never tell him lest it boost his ego any further.

The two stood casually drinking on duty much to the second and third engineer's alarm, but neither of them cared.

'Come on Louis something must have happened when I was away?'

Louis made a grumbling noise and sipped his drink 'That fucking McKinley who put him in charge?'

Despite the engine room's size, and noise from the power core, McCann noticed the sound from the crew disappear as they eavesdropped the conversation.

McCann sniggered 'Geneva, but take it easy Louis he has been assigned to his old station.'

Louis sneered 'Faraday, I knew it! That Anglo Saxon pig!'

Then it dawned upon him and he shook his hand in McCann's face 'No offence.'

McCann laughed, he was happy to see his old friend hadn't changed, 'No problem Louis.'

'Who is first officer now?' asked Louis with a wary tone to his voice.

McCann took another sip of his Balvenie, 'I've put Kim in for now, do you know anything about him?'

Louis shook his head 'Non, but Ryu thought the sun shined out of his asshole, not that it's a bad thing.' He took another swig of the golden liquor 'So what have they done with Ryu?'

McCann refilled his glass and whispered 'She has been assigned to a covert project.'

Louis was about to speak but McCann put a finger to his lips 'I got this information from Malikah so keep it zipped. Ryu is a Captain, now I don't know the details but she has been given the chair of a new ship based off Human, Tlillan and Gukumatz technology.'

Louis grabbed the bottle 'Here let me take you for a tour of the engine room.'

McCann walked by his side as he strolled down the channel which lay between the core and the engines. The floor was white with black stations; Louis called it "The gutter" with two elevator shafts at each end. The gutter reached to chest height exposing the cylindrical power core with its electronics and metal tubes used to move anti-matter around with electro magnets. On the right sat two massive domes, the centre of each sat level with the edge of the gutter wall. If you leaned over the edge you'd see it disappearing into the neutronium alloy superstructure, holding all vital systems rigidly in place.

'So is it true your daughter is now governor of Ilium?' inquired Louis as McCann inspected the Athena.

'Yup, those bloody frogs gave the sceptre to Malikah instead of Ilam. They seem intent on elevating her to the position of a deity almost. The upside is I can get off that shit hole and back to a civilised environment,' replied McCann.

Louis began laughing.

'What's so funny Louis?' asked McCann.

'You English have the worst weather and your beer is almost as nasty as your women! Ilium 1 should have been like going home for you!'

McCann poured another drink then handing the bottle to Louis he declared 'Until you've been there you can't understand how truly miserable that slime pit is Louis. If they hadn't attacked us first they'd have been welcome to rot in that toilet.'

The pair of them carried on chatting until reaching the opposite end on the engine bay or gutter. McCann took the whisky bottle from Louis 'What time do you get off duty?'

Louis finished of the dregs in his shot glass then handed it to McCann '1700 hours.'

McCann took his glass back 'I'll see you in the officers mess at 1800 hours?'

Louis nodded 'Sure.'

McCann stepped into the elevator and the door slid shut between them. The gravity plating allowed the lift to move at fast speeds delivering McCann to his destination quicker than it took the door to open and close. By applying the correct charge the plating created a negative or positive gravity field negating any high or low G-forces incurred from the speedy journey. On the way to the bridge he dropped off the drink and glasses in his cabin. The walk to the cabin then the bridge elevator consisted of only a few minutes strolling along the creamy white corridors to the correct elevator shaft, a very efficiently designed craft.

As McCann stepped off onto the bridge of the Athena everyone except the pit crew stood to attention. McCann gave a mini salute causing his staff to return to their duties. During his time chatting with Louis the bridge was in disarray, since the previous Captain had been returned to his position manning the weapons and Casimir field and Kim was feeling like a fish out of water at his new station. Hassif had been monitoring the situation and McCann was under no doubt that if needed he could step in.

McCann returned Hassif's smile as he sat in his old chair, 'Good morning Athena,' he said looking up at the neural housing.

'Good morning Commodore it is a great relief to see you here again,' replied Athena calmly.

McCann looked at Hassif with an expression of surprise Hassif just smiled cheekily.

'Why a great relief Athena?' asked McCann.

'I have missed your presence Commodore.'

McCann felt rather touched 'Thank you Athena I must say I have missed you also.'

Immediately she replied 'Why have you missed me Commodore?'

McCann lay back in his Captain's chair and smiled at Athena 'Because you are still the most reasonable woman in my life Athena.'

Hassif and a few of the junior officers chuckled then continued their work.

'Congratulations on your daughter becoming Governor of Ilium, Commodore.'

'Thank you very much Athena, I'll pass the message on the next time I see her.'

Athena quickly corrected him 'Malikah is already aware Commodore.'

His expression turned to a perplexed scowl 'I didn't know you kept correspondence with each other?'

Athena's soft voice fell onto the bridge as a warm duvet 'Malikah and I linked this morning she wishes to secure your safety, as do I Commodore.'

McCann sat dumbfounded starring back at Hassif, unless Athena was deceiving him and McCann was certain she wouldn't Malikah had the ability to form a mental link with Athena. The only reason he took exception to this was because it made him feel as if he were the child and Athena the babysitter, whilst Malikah pulled the strings from afar.

Hassif was unaware of this situation also, he shrugged and McCann decided not to mention it further at least not on the bridge anyway. McCann remembered what his wife was capable of when she almost wiped out the entire expedition including Athena, after a mental probe on the crew. It made him wonder what his daughter might be capable of if she so wished.

The day was taken up with running through drills mainly for the benefit of McCann and Kim. One had to get back into the feel of commanding a cruiser the other had to learn a new position. Kim was rough around the edges but it was obvious what Ryu saw in her former clan mate. He did what he was told and wasn't prone to making the same mistake twice. A lot of Ryu Yong had rubbed off onto him which caused him to rub others up the wrong way. Especially those in line before him for the position of first officer, but he'd dealt with similar situations in the past so it didn't worry McCann.

After McCann's duty shift was over he invited Kim and Hassif to join him in the officer's mess for a drink. The officers were glad to see McCann back as it meant the return of good drink and Cuban cigars, even the Russians had happy faces. The only person who wasn't in a celebratory mood was McKinley. Though he put a decent front on and joined in with the toast to McCann's return. However, inside he was thoroughly miserable at having lost his position. McCann placed a case of 10 year old Scotch on the bar which now had a tender. He also produced a cabinet of 50 cigars to the applause of the Russian contingent who moved in on the drink and smokes without mercy.

McCann and Louis made room at the bar for the rest of the officers; they sat with Hassif on the wide leather sofa that leaned against the wall. McCann glanced at his two friends then searched around the room until he found that which he searched for.

'Kim! Take a seat!' he bellowed at his first officer dragging him away from the Korean contingent on the other side of the room.

Kim made his way over taking a seat opposite his Captain.

'Someone get this man a drink and a cigar!' bellowed McCann who was a little tipsy by now.

Kim attempted to explain that he neither drank nor smoked to no avail.

'Nonsense man! It's a requirement of all senior officers on this ship, is that understood Commander?' bellowed McCann.

Kim went pale 'I suppose so, Commodore,' he said timidly as a burly Russian placed a dram and cigar on the table then patted him reassuringly on the shoulder.

McCann placed his Ramon Allones Specially Selected cigar onto one of the black porcelain ashtray four cigar rests.

'Have you ever smoked a cigar before Commander?'

Kim looked as if he were turning green 'No Sir.'

McCann took the large Robusto and clipped the cap off with his guillotine. He demonstrated the art of herfing to his sickly Commander, allowing him to toast the foot of his cigar. Kim put the thick hand rolled smoke between his lips, then toasted the foot with a match until it began producing smoke. Kim dumped the match into the ashtray then suddenly he doubled over pulling the cigar out of his mouth and retching at the floor.

'Oh yes, try not to inhale the smoke lad,' said McCann as he and the Russian contingent cracked up with laughter.

Kim sat with his head between his knees choking on the thick smoke, his complexion turning a reddish purple.

'I think this one will take some time to break in Duncan!' joked Louis.

Kim sat up still coughing on the smoke he'd inhaled. He took a sip of whisky and grimaced at the bite he received from the powerful liquor.

Louis shook his head from side to side whilst slowly tutting 'Ten year old whisky, this is what happens when you have a cheap English bastard for a commanding officer!'

McCann picked up his robusto cigar and took a long draw, turning to Hassif he asked 'So how many rounds did our charming French Engineer buy while I was away Hassif?'

His sarcastic tone was met with laughs and cheers mainly from the Russians; the change of command was quite stark. Ryu had been tough but fair, if you did your job she left you alone. McKinley had been an antagonist towards many of the officers. Unlike Ryu they had no respect towards the man, it wasn't that he couldn't command but during their time off duty he would pester them. Being hounded about your next duty shift when you're trying to relax with friends in the bar wasn't fun. McKinley didn't see the error of his ways and only felt his efforts to increase efficiency should be lauded. He felt Ryu had an unfair advantage. Since it was obvious that the Russians and Koreans worshipped the ground she walked on causing them to fall into line, that was his excuse anyway. As for McCann well he was the "Hero of Ilium" as McKinley sarcastically put it, though he never voiced his put down out loud, so everyone did whatever he desired without question. McKinley had his excuses as to why his command had failed, they were all bogus. Yet he preferred to believe in his denial rather than face the truth that everyone hated his guts.

During the evening of frivolities McCann for a moment sensed the intense loathing that emanated from his weapons officer. As if a tungsten shell had hit him in the brain it lodged there for a moment. He looked up to see McKinley smiling back at him, he returned the smile, then just as quickly as it had entered the feeling left. McCann continued the celebrations unable to remove the thought. The Englishman had felt emotions in this manner only when linked with his wife or daughter, although previously it was for the purpose of sharing positive emotion. Never had McCann touched on such clearly defined hatred and loathing. The experience disturbed him, but he didn't let it spoil the gathering in the bar.

Kim couldn't quite get the hang of smoking his cigar but according to Louis he had passed his crash course and would make a fine first officer. McCann sat recanting stories of how terrible Ilium 1, 2 and 3 were and how glad he was to be back on the Athena. He was glad to see that the cruiser was far more luxurious now compared to its Spartan beginnings; in fact it was better than the carriers he served on in the Royal Navy.

The Athena had a chef along with kitchen staff, bar staff and a compliment of masseurs along with the Turkish baths installed on the new recreation deck. McCann was shocked to find out that his former crew had been living better than the governor of the system in his cramped dingy office. McCann took another long drag on his cigar and looking around the room at his officers he expelled the smoke through his mouth and nostrils 'All I can say is it's good to be back.'

Over the next few weeks Kim slowly fit in getting used to handling his cigar and holding his Scotch as well as his new position of first officer. McCann discovered the extent of McKinley's poor handling of the Captain's chair, it was apparent that in his and Ryu's absence McKinley exposed himself to be quite the megalomaniac. Although when it came to Louis his attitude had met a stone wall. Sifting through the reports at his little desk in his snug cabin McCann was having a good snigger. McKinley's report concerning Louis' insubordination amused him to no end. The poor ignorant McKinley had met his match when tackling Chief Engineer Louis Beaumont. The report had been sent directly to Geneva deliberately bypassing the governor and onto the desk of Faraday. McCann chuckled to himself and sipped a dram of Balvenie imagining what must have crossed the old man's mind reading it. Faraday had dismissed the request to court martial Beaumont, essentially telling McKinley to 'Deal with it.' McCann had the entire incident printed out into a hard copy so that he could read it for his own perverse amusement, on evenings he had nothing better to do.

The story began shortly after Ryu had been reassigned and McKinley received his field promotion. He had been tearing through the ship "Like a whirling dervish" according to Hassif, stamping his mark of command on everyone and everything. He was looking for the same respect and obedience that Ryu directed. The difference was that he imposed his authority whereas Ryu only had to walk into a room and her authority filled the atmosphere. It puzzled McKinley how a short woman with glasses commanded that degree of respect. When he a tall man could not, even he felt her presence and nerves of steel exuding confidence into the crew of the entire ship no matter where she was at that time.

After having pushed the crew around and whipped everyone into line there was one person yet to accept his new Captain in a manner satisfactory to McKinley. For the most part Beaumont concentrated on his responsibilities ignoring whoever was in command of the Athena at the time, unless it was urgent. His attitude was a massive thorn in McKinley's side. Repeatedly his requests for reports and even engine drills had come in late or been totally ignored by his Chief Engineer. The straw that broke the camel's back was yet another efficiency drill that Beaumont had obviously made no effort to participate in. Other than send his report which on examination exposed a drop in efficiency.

Hassif watched worriedly as Athena fired out the statistics, McKinley loved his statistics, 'That's it!' snarled McKinley as he slapped the arm of his chair. 'Hassif you have the bridge until I return,' on that McKinley marched off the bridge onto the lift to concerned looks from the pit.

The elevator door slid open and McKinley marched onto the floor of the engineering section. Looking down along the gutter he called 'Chief Engineer Beaumont?'

A tired voice replied 'What do you want McKinley?'

The lack of respect in his tone was evident, not that Louis had much respect for his commanding officers anyway. His tone annoyed McKinley as he picked out the station Louis was busily working at.

'Captain McKinley to you Beaumont,' he declared striding towards Louis.

At this point the staff in the gutter were aware it was about to hit the fan. No one spoke to Louis Beaumont in that manner and got away without a good tongue lashing, save his old crew mates.

Louis stopped what he was doing and very slowly straightened his back whilst turning around to face McKinley, 'You really think you're something don't you?' he said placing his tablet on top of the workstation.

The crew of the gutter had gone dead quiet; no one was going miss the face-off between these two, 'Excuse me Beaumont? You shall address me as Sir or Captain is that understood?'

Louis allowed McKinley to approach him 'Vous pouvez manger la merde mon cher monsieur!' he barked in McKinley's face.

McKinley obviously didn't have a very large repertoire concerning French expletives and insults. The field Captain stood silently until his translator spoke through the wafer thin graphene speaker on the inside of his uniform collar. The androgynous voice repeated in English 'You can eat my shit, Sir,' to the howling laughter of the crewmen in the gutter.

Each crewman had his translation software personalised. If a language was spoken that he hadn't registered then it would translate it into the earpiece. If the earpiece wasn't inserted then the tiny speaker made from a wafer thin piece of graphene would translate it.

'Chief engineer Louis Beaumont as of now you are relieved of duty,' ordered McKinley much to the disdain of the Frenchman.

'You need to relieve yourself, you know that?' he quipped to the giggles of his crewmates.

McKinley tapped his wrist and spoke 'Security to the engine room.'

Upon arrival the two Russians were armed and at a loss as to why they were present.

'Kapitan Rogov take Chief Beaumont into custody,' said McKinley pointing at Beaumont.

The Russian was still mystified.

'Showing willful disrespect towards a superior officer.'

Rogov fixed his eyes on Louis as if to ask if it were true, Louis nodded and Rogov pointed towards the elevator.

'I want him restrained Kapitan!' barked McKinley now that he felt he was gaining control of the situation.

Rogov was uncomfortable with restraining even Beaumont, but Louis presented his wrists. As Rogov clamped them together with the carbon cuffs Louis snarled at McKinley 'You're a real prick you know that McKinley?'

Rogov grabbed Louis by the arm and ushered him into the elevator before he did any more damage. The Russian didn't like McKinley either and he didn't want to see a good man lose his position because him.

By the next morning Louis was out of the Brig and back at his station. The story had spread like wildfire throughout the ship and was the main topic of conversation whenever McKinley was no longer present. The request to have Louis transferred to a military prison on Earth was refused immediately after Faraday had read the report. After Louis was release from the brig, Faraday suggested McKinley "Make an attempt to understand his Chief Engineer".

McKinley was furious and refused to give ground to the Frenchman. Louis became worse now that he had got away with his willful disrespect. When it came down to it Faraday needed him a lot more than he needed McKinley. McKinley stopped spending evenings in the officer's mess as it had become too painful suffering his nemesis' jibes. Each time he entered the mess it was to sniggers and hushed tones. If Beaumont were present he would begin his ritual humiliation, it was just too much for him to bear any longer.

Louis would pick on anything that happened that day but if there was nothing he go onto his old favourite of lampooning his efficiency drills. Everyone found it amusing probably due to the fact they despised the endless drills. McKinley would enter the bar causing everyone to stop what they were saying and wait for Louis first attack. Putting on a stiff upper class English accent Louis snarled at his drink holding it up to the light 'By Jove this beverage is a full half degree above standard regulation temperature for a chilled beer!'

The Russians found it hilarious, though the Koreans did their best to keep straight faces they couldn't maintain it for long and Louis would keep on pushing until he had everyone in stitches. McKinley was just too stuck up for his own good and refused to make peace with Beaumont. Because he was sure Louis was in the wrong, it was his junior officers' duty to apologise to him. Unfortunately Louis just didn't see it that way.

That night McKinley was determined he wasn't going to be intimidated by Beaumont and approached the bar doing his best to ignore the Frenchman.

'Mineral water please,' he requested on reaching the bar.

The bartender placed the glass under the correct tap nozzle, hit the panel and the sparkling water came out.

'Wait a minute!' said Louis 'Are those bubbles above regulation size or is there a board stuck in my ass?'

Louis broke out laughing as he always found himself hilarious. The bartender smiled a little but did his best to ignore Louis and passed the drink to McKinley 'There you go, Sir.'

Hassif as usual was unable to prevent himself from cracking up at his friends humour. However when McKinley refused to take the bait Louis saw it as a challenge.

Had Ryu been present or McCann for that matter Louis would never have dared such juvenile antics. McKinley took his drink and sat down close to the Korean contingent where he began to read a newspaper.

Hassif witnessed his friend's expression turn to one of annoyance, he whispered 'That's enough Louis.'

But Beaumont was like a dog with a bone. Louis was almost hypnotised by the sight of McKinley sitting there reading a paper ignoring him.

'Don't you think he's suffered enough Louis?' whispered Hassif yet he received no reply from his friend.

Hassif could only watch as his friend approached one of his Engineers and took a protective glove from one of his cargo pockets in the leg of his pants. All eyes were on Beaumont and at a loss as to what was going through his mind.

He approached the table McKinley sat alone at 'McKinley,' he spoke in a deep voice.

McKinley ignored him and continued reading until Louis ripped his newspaper out of his hands.

McKinley looked up at his Chief Engineer 'What do you want?' he asked sardonically.

Louis threw the glove onto the table.

McKinley starred at the glove silently.

'Drone bay one at 1800 hours tomorrow.'

McKinley laughed as did a few others in the bar although not everyone laughed, Hassif knew that Louis was serious and a few of the Russians and Koreans whom he spent time once a week on the recreation decks fencing were not laughing either. The laughter died down as the room realised that Louis Beaumont was quite serious concerning his challenge.

McKinley peered at the glove then at Louis 'This is a waste of time,' he stated.

Louis sneered at him 'So our Captain is just a coward!'

McKinley looked around the room again he quickly realised that he would have to accept this challenge if he were to maintain any amount of respect. A leader instills his own courage into his men and women, imagine if Achilles or Hector had been challenged to a duel only to withdraw for fear of physical harm? Besides it wasn't necessarily to the death, McKinley took the glove from the table accepting the challenge 'To first blood?'

'Fine!' replied Louis.

Since the recreation decks had been installed Louis had taken up fencing again, he'd picked up the art from McCann. The sport was popular at Geneva and served as a fun method to keep in shape. Faraday insisted on the I.S.A holding tournaments in the sport, which he also participated in. Of the three disciplines Louis had concentrated upon Epee along with McCann. The Epee was the heaviest of the three blades. It was an attempt to simulate a duel to first blood as realistically as possible. In theory when two gentlemen had a disagreement and could not decide who was right it was settled by the first to draw blood; although it could quite easily end in the death of one opponent if he happened to be run through. McKinley had taken a few mandatory lessons at the academy but nothing more; he could wield his weapon for the purposes of displays in dress uniform. An actual duel was rather out of his depth and he had taken no interest in the fencing club set up by Praporshchik Kozar. Not that Louis had ever taken part in a real duel himself, however with over 5 years of experience in the sport behind him he was at a great advantage.

By the next day Louis and every crewman off duty was packed into the drone bay. An area of the bay used to repair and rearm drones between sorties was marked out into a piste. Warrant officer Kozar was presiding and Louis stood in his uniform holding a recently sharpened short sword. All officers carried one as a part of the dress uniform though the swords varied depending on the unit. Louis' short sword had a triangular blade with a deep gully on one side. It was a thrusting weapon and didn't possess much of an edge to it. The deep groove that ran along one side of the blade was for the purpose of preventing the blade resisting when being pulled out of the victim. If there were no groove present the power of suction would make it difficult or in some cases impossible to withdraw a blade after a successful lunge. The groove permitted the flow of air pressure and the letting of blood so that the weapon could quickly be removed and used to defend the owner. At the hilt the leather handle and the blade were separated by a large silver bell guard which protected the hand from hits, since in Epee the contest was to first blood allowing strikes anywhere on the body. Louis sword was very much a practical weapon with little design. Its guard was one piece of sheet metal and the handle wrapped with simple brown leather ending in a large tungsten nut which aided the balance of the sword when holding it. The blade was a dull grey carbon steel with the triangular blade ending in a very sharp point that was brighter than the rest since Louis had recently sharpened it up.

When McKinley strode in dressed in uniform holding a glove in one hand and a Scottish broadsword in the other all of the men and women from the fencing club realised that this would be short. The weapon McKinley carried had a much broader flatter blade with two sharp edges running down and stopping at one third the distance from the hilt. Like Louis' short sword it was a light one handed weapon but with two small grooves on each side of the blade. The hilt and handle were separated by a large metal basket of an intricate design and filled with a red crushed velvet inside. The handle was made of the same steel as the blade and basket with ridges for grip and two red tassels hanging off the end of the handle. The basket and handle were both coloured a deep gold. The scabbard had a golden tip and upper edge with the same red hanging onto his belt with the same cotton tassels. Louis on the other hand stood with his black plastic scabbard waiting. As McKinley approached he handed the glove back to Beaumont whom accepted it.

Both men were accompanied by seconds these were usually friends that inspected and made certain his friend's weapon was in good order. It was also his job to make sure that the other party was playing fair and to protect against possible ambushes before reaching the appointed destination. McKinley was accompanied by one of the ensigns that worked in the pit. Both the seconds inspected the weapons of each party until both were satisfied.

'On your marks Gentlemen,' declared Kozar in his Russian accent.

Both parties took up their positions upon the piste standing opposite each other. Louis saluted his opponent and Kozar in the traditional manner he'd practiced for many years. McKinley saluted seemingly only after Beaumont had reminded him of the practice. To the trained eye it was easy to distinguish the victor before it had even started. Louis stood prepared in engarde whereas McKinley had a more casual stance.

'Engarde!' called Kozar.

Louis bent his knees a little whilst lining the point of his sword up.

'Allez!' shouted Kozar making certain both parties heard him.

McKinley dashed forwards with his blade pointing up to the ceiling in preparation to make a cutting motion. Louis moved backwards waiting for his enemy to make a mistake and he didn't have long to wait.

McKinley lunged forwards and missed the retreating Louis cutting into thin air. Louis parried his blade hard with a parry carte, causing the blade to swing violently to one side and too far away for McKinley to do anything with it whilst he stood legs stretched apart languishing as a beached whale. Helpless he could only watch Beaumont as he attempted in vain to recover. McKinley had miss judged his distance, attacking when too close with a bent arm and blade pointing upwards.

Louis' parry knocked the cumbersome broadsword away and by simply straightening his arm he thrust his blade into his opponents shoulder.

McKinley screamed and Kozar leapt in shouting 'HALT!'

Louis removed his blade which had run through McKinley's shoulder. McKinley dropped to the floor as the ships medic ran to his aid. It was no longer possible for him to hold the sword due to his arm shaking erratically, the duel was over.

The next day they were both on duty, though McKinley had his arm in a sling. However the childish taunting from Louis stopped as did the megalomania from McKinley. They both avoided each other although Ryu commented much later on the event as "a pathetic cock fight". It did reduce tension and allow McKinley to get on with his job.

McCann found the incident hilarious, probably because it was entertaining to read reports of someone else having to deal with the wayward Louis Beaumont, other than him or Faraday. Ryu never had any trouble with the man for whatever reason. But everyone else had to discover how to deal with him the hard way. McCann made a hard copy of the reports concerning the incident as a keepsake to read when there was nothing to do. He was annoyed that no one had informed him earlier of the fracas. It made the Englishman chuckle to himself wondering what medication Faraday must've been on when these reports started coming in.

McCann never would have known about the reports had Athena not brought it to his attention that night. Fortunately she was well aware of his penchant for low brow entertainment and of course he should be made aware of anything that may affect his crew. She had pulled up the security cam vids for him and McCann was having a jolly old time on quiet evenings watching his Chief Engineer inform the crew of what an arse he could be. It all explained the emotion he picked up that evening in the officer's mess from McKinley, his pride had been battered and he held a grudge towards him as well as Louis. McCann hoped it wouldn't affect his performance in the future. He put it down to what happens when you place a young man in a position like that before he's ready.

Chapter 17

The next six months passed without event, McCann regained his position without incident and Kim managed to acclimatise to his new post as first officer.

Malikah had total control of the Ilium system her title was "Teootl" rather than Governor since that was how the locals referred to her. It was the Gukumatz word for Icon although it could also be translated as deity by the space suit software. What was more worrying to McCann was that his daughter was now a good half foot taller than himself. She stood on a level with Ilam creating a daunting site when they were together.

According to Malikah a battle of some sort was now raging on the Tlillan home world. Though it was unclear to him as to whether this took place in the real universe or the dreamscape or perhaps both. He didn't inquire any further since he really didn't want to get any further involved with politics, that was Faraday's headache and he was welcome to it.

Today was a special day as the new destroyer, Ryu had been assigned to for a year now, was to be tested in a combat simulation. The destroyer had been launched a couple of weeks ago, it was smaller than the Athena and Ares, roughly half the size. She wielded only two cannons, one on each side of the vessel and the bridge sat just before the engines. The body was a miniature version of the Athena. A jet black oblong but with the lower edge shorter in length than the top, creating an inward facing edge at the front of the vessel.

The entire vessel was clad in neutronium alloy armour, a substance much tougher and easier to work with than the expensive neutronium. Due to the armour no light could be seen emanating from the craft named "Hera", everything seemed smaller and sleeker until Louis saw her.

They were sat watching Network America in the officer's mess, the infamous Jerry Habeeb had wrangled an interview and a short walk through onboard the vessel.

The officer's mess was dead silent whilst everyone watched "the most popular net news programme in the known universe", according to Jerry anyway. It was the first that any of them would get to see of the new ship and the first McCann would have seen of Ryu for more than a year now. Ryu strolled along a corridor with Jerry and some security, her face had a beaming smile across it.

'You know, when I see that woman smile it scares me,' commented Louis as he clipped the cap off one of McCann's cigars.

McCann toasting the foot of his Partagas short cigar with a torch replied 'She worked hard for it Louis, she deserves that command.'

Louis took the torch after McCann had finished, 'I know, I'm only saying it freaks me out when she is happy like that.'

They both sat on the sofa puffing on the sticks watching along with everyone else. Ryu didn't divulge much, if anything, on the ship but Louis pointed out the power core was much larger than Athena's. He was uncertain what the extra power was being utilized for but it was evident it wasn't for the engines or weapons. After the interview and tour were over there was a heated discussion in the mess concerning the Hera. By the end of the evening the Hera was either an electronic warfare vessel or carried some kind of prototype drone.

Two weeks later they were all about to find out. The Ares had joined them for the field test and along with Titov; McCann had been briefed on today's objectives. Weapon systems were to be deactivated, all damage would be processed by the AI and appropriate systems disabled.

Faraday was rather confident in the briefing that it would be the Athena and Ares suffering the effects of the simulated combat. The capabilities of the Hera had been downloaded into the ships AI. Though neither the SI nor the crew would be permitted to view it before the simulation. The two vessels floated in space around a Neptune class planet in the outer Ilium system waiting for the prey to arrive.

McCann was relaxed in his chair on the bridge with the rotating image of the Athena projected from the table before him. The view screen was split between Titov and a representation of the system, its planets and the two warships that lay in wait far off the planet.

Using the systems sensors which were placed in orbit of all planets and at various points in the system McCann had it all covered. Ryu couldn't fold space into the Ilium system without being detected. Since the network used micro wormholes to communicate he would find out and have her on his charts before the light of a tunnel event could even reach him.

Suddenly a klaxon fired off 'Tunnel event, tunnel event, tunnel event!' called the soft spoken Athena.

'Co-ordinates?' replied McCann.

'Unidentified vessel entered system at X -14.3, Y +17.9, Z +0.3 AU,' reported Athena.

McCann saw the vessel pop up on the view screen charts, somehow she'd folded space into the system just off the asteroid belt without trashing her vessel.

McCann sneered at his comrades attempt to impress him 'Hassif take us in full speed on her port flank.'

Hassif started tapping away on the station he stood before.

'I will take her starboard Commodore,' announced the voice of Titov over the view screen.

'Good luck Kapitan,' said McCann as Titov's image disappeared to be replaced with space.

The Athena turned about and headed towards the asteroid belt receiving constant updates on the enemy position. 20 minutes into the journey and Athena made an unexpected announcement 'Unidentified vessel is no longer apparent.'

McCann looked up at the neural housing 'What do you mean no longer apparent?'

'The unidentified vessel is no longer visible to the network of probes Commodore,' replied Athena softly.

McCann scratched his chin 'Are the probes functioning?'

'All probes are fully functional Commodore.'

'Can you replay the last ten seconds before it disappeared, Athena?'

The view screen displayed an image of the Hera sitting in space above the asteroid belt; the ship became distorted and eventually disappeared into a fuzzy warped area which seemed to dissipate.

'Athena can you scan the area?' asked McCann as he squinted at the screen trying to make out where the ship was hidden.

'Affirmative.'

Another twenty minutes later and both the Athena and Ares were closing to within one AU of the last known position without any further sensor readings on the Hera.

Kim called to his Captain from behind 'Sir, I believe we have something.'

McCann spun around and walked up to the science station where Kim was standing behind Ensign Vezzali.

'What have you got for me?' asked McCann in a hurried voice.

The blond Ensign pointed towards her station monitor 'I was going over the data and on the graviton scanners and I noticed this.'

McCann looked only to see an area of space marked out with a wire box moving slowly on their starboard side 'What is it Ensign?'

Vezzali answered with her rather charismatic Italian accent 'The graviton scanner searches for positive fields but I noticed a tiny negative field here and it's moving. Usually this would go unnoticed by the AI and Athena wouldn't bother to check it herself. But since we are dealing with the unknown I thought it might be useful.'

McCann looked at the object but it only appeared as a tiny negative flux to the scanners and wasn't visible to the naked eye 'What phenomenon might cause this kind of graviton field Ensign?'

The blond haired girl smiled 'If it were naturally occurring dark energy and dark matter may create a negative graviton field. However this cannot be a natural phenomenon Commodore since the field would be moving towards the asteroid belt rather than away.'

McCann sighed 'Yes, yes Ensign the short version please!'

Vezzali made an uncomfortable expression at Kim until he gestured for her to continue by nodding his head.

'I'm sorry Sir,' apologised the young lady 'the only known true artificial anti-graviton field would be the byproduct of a Casimir field.'

McCann examined the blur on the monitor for a moment 'I read somewhere that an extremely intense Casimir field would act as a cloaking device, is that true Ensign?' he said thoughtfully.

Vezzali's face lit up 'Why yes it could!' she blurted out as his train of thought entered her station and the entire bridge staffs.

'Vezzali I want your data on everyone's station now and Hassif send it to Titov, tell him she's using an intensified Casimir field to cloak herself,' ordered McCann as he leapt into his seat and tapped the arm.

'Yes?' replied Louis.

'Louis could that power core we saw have been used to power an intensified Casimir field, strong enough to cloak the Hera?' spoke McCann hurriedly.

"Sure but she couldn't fire on us, unless it's armed with missiles,' replied Louis.

McCann looked up at the neural housing 'Athena go to battle stations, charge starboard cannons and target them on the anti-graviton field to our starboard side. McKinley let me know when you've certified the weapons vector.'

The ship went to red light and everyone prepared 'Kim, I want you to launch all drones on my mark, understood?'

'Yes Commodore,' replied the first officer as he stood awaiting the order by his drone station.

'Cannon vectors certified Commodore,' called out McKinley.

'Fire starboard and release the drones,' ordered McCann.

The cannons remained dormant yet the simulation fired a broadside of eight tungsten shells towards the negative graviton field less than one AU distance. The drones remained in their bay, but two wings of simulated drones launched whilst Titov launched his drones and began to manoeuvre the Ares for a clear broadside. McCann watched the view screen as the shells moved towards the target. After several minutes he witnessed a visible smudge on the screen which the shells veered off and chased, missing the target.

'Vezzali what happened?' barked McCann.

The young lady stared at her monitor intensely 'I believe the Casimir field was purposely intensified in one area, the negative graviton field pulling the shells away, Sir.'

McCann turned his chair and looked at Kim 'Send the drones in Kim, both squadrons. McKinley, I want another broadside with timed anti-matter warheads understood?'

As both men replied Athena alerted the crew 'Unidentified vessel starboard!'

McCann spun back to see the Hera appear from a warped field of bent light, 'McKinley fire immediately certification is not required.'

Before the Athena could fire again the Hera had her bow pointed directly at them, a large piece of armour plating slid down the bow to reveal a barrel. For a moment McCann wondered what it was the barrel of, until he saw a ball of burning plasma energy explode out of it and towards the Athena. The armour plating slid back into place covering the weapon and the Hera disappeared in the fuzzy Casimir field which bent light around the Hera along with most other forms of energy.

Athena was calling out 'Alert incoming missile!'

'What is it Athena?' called out McCann desperately.

'Ionized particles encased within a carbon tungsten alloy fired via rail cannon Commodore,' replied Athena.

He watched as the plasma torpedo approached the Athena far quicker than a shell from a rail cannon could have.

'How do we stop it?' he blurted out.

'Unknown.' replied Athena.

'Activate point defence canons and brace for impact, McKinley fire that broadside NOW ... we may not get another chance!' ordered McCann desperately.

He then watched as the point defence cannons fired into the torpedo but too little effect. The carbon alloy was already melting away as the burning plasma consumed the shell. The point defence rounds were consumed along with the torpedo shell which was only there to prevent the plasma dissipating before reaching the target.

Before the Athena could fire another broadside McCann watched helplessly as she called out a list of multiple system failures. The Plasma explosion created a massive electromagnetic pulse causing all starboard systems to shut down.

'Hull breach all levels Commodore lowering emergency bulkheads, all levels.'

The alarm rang out and the holo image of the Athena displayed a red streak all along her starboard side from the bow to the starboard aft engine.

'Hassif bring around our portside and McKinley I want a broadside of timed anti-matter warheads as soon as Ryu is in range, certification not required.'

Hassif turned to face him and said solemnly 'Navigation systems are down.'

McCann mumbled under his breath 'Marvellous!' he then looked up at Athena 'Are you still there Athena?'

'Yes Commodore,' replied her soft voice, he felt a wave of relief pass over him.

'How long to get just the navigation and weapons online?'

'Without certification 90 seconds Commodore,' came her sweet reply.

McCann felt a ray of hope shine down upon him 'Do it now Athena.'

His goddess complied and within 90 seconds Hassif was turning the ship slowly whilst McKinley recalibrated the weapons systems.

Then came some more bad news 'Commodore,' called Kim dragging McCann back to Vezzali's station 'you need to look at this.'

Kim motioned to the science station and observed the cloaked Hera moving.

'Shit!' exclaimed McCann much to the shock of the young Ensign.

Ryu was keeping the Athena between her and the Ares in order to prevent Titov from getting off a shot.

'The Hera is de-cloaking Commodore!' shouted Vezzali a little too loud.

McCann looked at her then the monitor 'How do you know?'

The young lady pointed at the readings 'There is a slight drop in the intensity of negative gravitons before the Hera drops her Casimir field, Sir.'

Sure enough the Hera appeared with her starboard side to the Athena bearing one of her rail cannons.

'Can you turn any quicker?' he shouted at Hassif.

McCann heard no reply so snatched a look at his friend who did the same and shook his head silently.

'Bugger! Brace for impact!' he called out of habit.

The Hera fired her cannon, and of course there was no impact. However according to the AI and the holo image, where the bridge used to be there was now a crater carved using anti-matter. Since the point defence cannons had all been destroyed, the two shells fired from the twin barrelled cannon hit precisely.

'Well that's that isn't it!' said McCann in a frustrated tone as he plonked himself back into his seat.

All systems went dead and the craft was now under the control of Chief Engineer Beaumont. The drones however were still out there and closing on the Hera. But only after rupturing the Athena's power core and effectively taking her out of the fight, Ryu cloaked again.

The Hera possessed no point defence other than her powerful Casimir field. Once both the Athena's and Ares' drones were close enough the anti-graviton field intensified. The drones were dragged into it and crushed by the force of the Casimir field, removing the threat. McCann witnessed the simulated anti-matter explosions flaring up each time a drone was sucked to its death.

The Ares was still playing hide and seek trying to get a broadside on the Hera, eventually Ryu de-cloaked and with the Athena sat between them the Ares had no clear vector to fire on. Ryu however turned her Vessel and with only 0.5 AU distance she fired the plasma cannon. The torpedo shaped shell was propelled out of the bow of the Hera. Once it had cleared the Athena which lay dead in space it slowly began to swerve upwards.

Cherkesov informed his Kapitan that the torpedo's trajectory was on an intercept course with the Ares. Unfortunately at distances under 1 AU there just isn't enough time to do anything other than activated the point defence cannons.

The torpedo could be set on a path by manipulating the degradation of the carbon tungsten alloy shell. By manufacturing weakness in the shell that caused one area to deteriorate quicker. Thus allowing more plasma to escape from that section, the torpedo would swerve upwards in an arc. Upon hitting the Ares it had less impact than a standard hard shell without manufactured faults; however it did its job. The point defence cannons were useless and the Ares was hit on the aft starboard side. Her engines were disabled leaving Titov hanging in space helpless as the Hera appeared from behind the Athena square aft of him.

Both McCann and Titov sat back in their seats waiting for Ryu to deliver the killing blow, the Hera brandishing one rail cannon she fired into the aft of the Ares breaching the power core and detonation the ship.

The image of Faraday filled McCann's view screen 'Excellent job ladies and gentlemen, please proceed to Ilium 1, once docked at the space port there will be a debriefing in the conference room for all senior officers, thank you.'

Faraday's image disappeared and the Athena regained control of all systems, 'Hassif plot a course for Ilium 1 and have Athena certify it. Once within docking range have Athena link with the station SI,' ordered McCann in a tired voice.

Hassif only gave a thumbs up and began charting the course 'Athena link with the Ares and Hera please,' asked Hassif.

'Link created,' replied Athena.

Hassif was making sure all the ships spoke to each other to avoid a collision. His course would be run by both of the navigators and the SI on the other vessels, preventing any costly errors. Once docked McCann disembarked with Kim, Hassif, Vezzali and Louis; since the Ensign had detected the Hera it was logical that she be present and Hassif wanted to see his old friend again.

The party walked through the tunnel that fit between the Athena's airlock and the airlock of the docking arm of Ilium 1. The tiny Hera was docked on the opposite side of the arm and McCann could see three people walking off that ship along the white tunnel onto the same arm. He noticed Ryu due to her height and glasses. As the two parties both approached the docking arm he could see her smart uniform with golden braids on the cuffs, marking her rank. On her face was a level of smug he hadn't seen for a long time.

'Look at that face,' whispered Louis.

'I know,' replied McCann.

Ryu stepped off the onto the docking arm with a cocky swagger followed by her first officer. A tall young American from the Eastern states and her engineer a middle aged German lady with a rather confident look to her. McCann stood still and clapped, the rest of his party soon complied and Ryu received a round of applause for her achievements in the combat test. She approached McCann and saluted him causing McCann to feel rather embarrassed.

He returned the salute 'Congratulations on your victory, Captain Ryu.'

She smiled 'Thank you Sir, I'd like you to meet my first officer Commander Hettinger and my Chief engineer Miss Heidemann.'

They both saluted McCann; he returned their salutes then shook their hands.

McCann motioned to his crew 'You remember everyone?'

Ryu gave the Ensign a sly look 'Ensign Vezzali, still serving on the Athena?'

Vezzali who wasn't overwhelmed to see Ryu quickly replied 'Yes Captain.'

McCann cut in 'She discovered the position of the Hera despite the cloaking device, if we'd used timed warheads you'd have been vapourised.'

Ryu started walking to the end of the docking arm with McCann by her side and the others tagging behind introducing themselves to each other.

'I'm surprised you kept her Duncan, you aren't usually susceptible to pretty girls!'

McCann chuckled 'No, it's just that I'm not brutally unforgiving Miss Yong!'

Ryu slowly lowered her eyelids and shook her head, 'Not according to the Gukumatz.'

McCann motioned with his arms 'I'm done with those bloody toads, sent me up the wall I'll have you know. The place stinks like a toilet and the food is vile, I was living on rations for nearly a year! No I'm glad to be back on the Athena. Besides Malikah is managing them now, it seems she has some sort of influence over them.'

Ryu looked up at him 'I heard they think she's a messiah?'

McCann was rather uncomfortable with the whole thing 'Yes they call her Teootl which means Icon in their language. So she has them doing whatever she pleases for the moment.'

Ryu shook her head as they strolled along the docking arm 'It's a crazy universe Duncan, who would have thought that our mission to Mars would have brought us here?'

McCann smiled and ribbed Ryu 'And you getting your very own command I'd never have believed it possible!'

'And you getting married and having a daughter, I'd have said that was crazy talk 5 years ago!' quipped Ryu.

McCann smiled in agreement with his friend and carried on the walk into the station. They stepped onto the outer ring which attached all of the arms to the main body of the station. After strolling through the cream halls they reached the command centre meeting up with Titov and Cherkesov inside a small conference room attached to the main control centre.

Cherkesov's eyes met Ryu's and they gave each other a warm smile, Titov grinned knowingly at McCann. He shook hands with Titov and introduced his Chief Engineer Yan Serov a gaunt man that seemed rather unhealthy. His light brown hair was very thin, McCann felt he could do with a meal or two. Serov was polite and smiled displaying a toothy grin. For one reason or another he wore an old seaman's cap but on further inspection it was his peaked officer's cap. He had decided to leave it on when going on duty one day and it got so dirty he ordered a new one leaving his old cap on his head to be worn on regular duty.

Serov quickly turned his attention to Ryu 'Captain Ryu it is an honour to meet you,' he saluted.

Having become quite used to the attention from the Russian contingent she no longer blushed but returned the salute 'Thank you Mr.?'

'Serov ... Yan Serov, Captain,' he stammered.

Titov shook her hand 'You gave us quite a nasty surprise Miss Yong, I was unaware it was possible to cloak a cruiser especially while moving.'

Ryu nodded 'Actually she's a destroyer and the cloaking device is a modified Casimir field, but you'll have to ask my Chief Miss Heidemann if you want to know anything about it.'

Titov looked her up and down 'It is a pleasure to meet you Miss Heidemann.'

The Engineer saluted and Titov returned it 'You must be something special if you are working on the Hera yes?'

Miss Heidemann replied 'Yes!' rather sharply.

Both Titov and McCann were taken aback by her arrogance but then again she was serving with Ryu. If she weren't so confident she would have been sent to work on the freighters. It took a lot to hang in there with Ryu snapping at your heels every day.

Titov cleared his throat 'Perhaps you could give me a tour of the Hera and her Casimir field generator when you have time … Miss?'

The Chief Engineer raised her eyebrows 'I do not have that authority Kapitan Titov,' she replied in a very aloof tone.

'I see, do you have the authority to tell me your first name?' asked Titov to the amusement of McCann. She obviously wasn't comfortable divulging any personal information.

'Chief Engineer Bridgette Heidemann, Kapitan,' replied the dark haired German.

Despite being amused McCann sensed an uncomfortable silence and broke it quickly 'So Ryu will we get a tour of your ship later?' Ryu just nodded.

The image of Faraday leapt out of the centre of the table. 'Ladies and Gentlemen please take a seat,' he announced and they all sat down at the black circular table with a holo projector in the centre.

Faraday was very happy with the results of the combat test, he expected the cloak and plasma projector to give Ryu a great advantage, and it did.

'First I would like to congratulate Captain Ryu on her victory today. Everyone here in Geneva is ecstatic and we wish to congratulate you and your crew on a fine job.'

Ryu smiled and replied 'Thank you Director.'

Faraday continued 'However it has become apparent that the Hera still requires some fine tuning. Commodore McCann you were able to locate the Hera despite the cloak. Could you please inform us how you achieved that?'

McCann motioned to Vezzali 'Ensign Vezzali became aware of a negative graviton flux and came to the conclusion it was not a natural phenomenon. I consulted Louis and decided to fire on it. Unfortunately I made the mistake of not using timed warheads and Captain Ryu didn't allow me a second chance.'

Faraday muttered to someone in Geneva then looked up at them 'Yes that was our assumption; I want Louis, Yan and Britta working on the problem immediately. You won't be leaving until a solution can be worked out understood?'

McCann nodded 'Yes Sir,' he was quite happy to spend some time relaxing on the recreational decks and officer's mess of the expanded Ilium 1.

Faraday turned his head to Titov 'Do you have anything to add Kapitan?'

'No,' replied Titov 'I have a request.'

Faraday whose attention was split between the conference, a tablet and his people in Geneva made a murmuring noise 'hhhhmmmm.'

Titov looked over at Bridgette 'May I have Chief Heidemann give me a tour of the Hera?'

Faraday looked up from his tablet for a moment 'Certainly Kaptian, I'm sure Captain Ryu will organise it for you ASAP?'

Ryu nodded again 'Yes Sir,' much to the discomfort of her Chief.

Faraday then broke his concentration away from Geneva for a moment 'We believe we are able to synchronise wormhole travel. That is we can have all three of your vessels fold space and exit simultaneously. It has been tested successfully with the Clotho, Lachesis and Atropos. The upgrades will require only a simple software download to the Athena and Ares. We believe we have improved on the Gukumatz version by utilizing our SI links. It shall be tested once the Hera has her Casimir field fine-tuned; which I'm certain shall be accomplished hastily, since you are the three most capable engineers in the I.S.A, are there any questions?'

Louis suddenly perked up 'Do we all get a bonus this year?' which was met with some mild laughter and a few cold looks from Ryu and Bridgette.

Faraday had been in the press recently for the massive bonus which he received; mainly for meeting the goals of keeping control of Gukumatz partisans and the development of the Ilium system and its infrastructure. A lot of people saw it a different way, they saw it as Faraday writing himself a cheque for millions of credits and Louis thought he'd have a dig at his old nemesis.

Faraday ignored Louis and repeated himself 'Are there any questions?' he said rather facetiously but to no reply this time.

After catching a look at the face Ryu was pulling Louis decided to shut his mouth.

'Excellent, Ryu I'll want you to send daily progress reports is that understood?'

'Yes Sir,' replied Ryu.

Faraday then tapped his tablet 'Very good, I hope to see you all soon and have fun on Ilium 1, Faraday out.'

His holo image disappeared back into the table and the officers broke up the meeting.

On the way out Ryu gave McCann a little punch 'Second chance? I didn't give you a first chance Duncan!'

McCann stared down at his comrade 'What are you talking about?'

The short Korean grinned at him 'I knew you'd fire a broadside of hard shells first, you're just too cautious Duncan.'

McCann sneered disbelievingly 'You're telling me you knew I was going to fire on you whilst cloaked?'

She nodded 'Of course, once you'd fired one broadside I had a window of time to return fire before you could reload and fire again. Do you think that after all this time I haven't learnt anything about you?'

McCann realised his comrade was correct 'I suppose you would be a poor first officer if you hadn't.'

Ryu gave McCann some sympathy 'If our roles were reversed Duncan I'm certain you'd have beaten me, if that's of any condolence.'

He looked down and smiled 'Thanks, would you like a drink when you get off duty?'

Ryu looked over her shoulder towards Cherkesov 'Maybe later?'

McCann slapped her shoulder 'Sure I'll see you when I see you Yong,' then made his way back to the Athena.

Over the next few weeks the crews worked on fine tuning the Hera. McCann spent most of his off duty time between the officer's mess and the Gym on Ilium 1 where one of Titov's crewman had organised the first Ilium fencing tournament.

Chapter 18

The competition was being held on the Ilium 1 station recreational deck, between the teams from the Athena, Ares and Hera. Once the word got around teams from the orbital stations entered and before they knew it the competition had ballooned into a tournament. As the participants increased the tournament expanded from unisex teams to include individual events for male and female contenders of all weapons. The SI were roped into judging the contests through droids. If there were any decisions being questioned the SI would go over the recording made by the four droids which monitored the piste.

The gym was a good fifty metres long and twenty wide with a high roof allowing space at the side for spectators to sit on benches, also people could view the action from an upper level. On the upper floor sat a café and walkway skirting the gym, the purpose was for giving people access to the different gyms from the changing rooms above and a place for them to take a break. Today it was an area for spectators to gather and relax as they observed their comrades fence for their ships honour below.

McCann and Louis, both avid fencers, were the main elements of the Athena Epee team, upon first signing up with the I.S.A McCann had introduced the fencing bug. With Louis it was fairly easy, he enjoyed the sport, but Hassif had lost interest early on. Ryu already participated in Kumdo, Korean Kendo, so she wasn't too interested. However Ryu was a winner and despite not being a fencer herself she soon whipped a team together and was there to support her shipmates.

The day began with individual matches, starting with poules, in order to seed the contestants. Once the fencers were seeded they would face off in direct elimination matches until eventually there was an ultimate winner. The poule matches for each weapon took place simultaneously, with all three weapons being fought in the gym at the same time. Each piste was made of a conductive rubber surface to prevent floor hits setting off the light and halting the match.

Electric fencing had been wireless for many years. The weapon could communicate with the touch sensitive fibres of the clothing, which communicated with a chip imbedded in the piste. Both fencers and their weapons were plugged into this invisible network and any hit or touché was recorded. Lighting up the fibres on the victor's end of the piste, along with a rather annoying alarm for a couple of seconds.

For Epee it was simple, whoever hit first and set their light off got a point. Two lights and it was a double hit meaning one point each. Anywhere on the body counted as a hit, McCann preferred epee since he didn't have to think so much, foil and sabre however were two different games altogether.

Foil had the right of way rule, in short it meant that unless you had right of way your hit is not valid. You took right of way by threatening the opponent first by advancing with your arm forward or by parrying the opponent and riposting. The rule sounded simple enough but it was quite infuriating since many referees had different ideas of what threatening the target was and wasn't and what a legitimate parry is. The target area was only the torso and there were no double hits. A hit anywhere else was considered off target and the match would have to be halted.

Sabre used similar right of way rules with the added headache of the entire body from the waste up was a target. Also you could use the side of the blade rather than only point to register a hit. Sabre was definitely the fastest of the three weapons followed closely by foil, epee was a lot slower and more of a waiting game than the others.

After the poules had finished and everyone was ranked the contest began in earnest, with the foil eliminators coming first until the semifinals when the foil was put on hold. Unfortunately for the Athena crew only one contestant remained in the foil and that was Vezzali who was ranked second in the women's poules.

Next came sabre and by the semifinals it was clear that the Ares was set to dominate the weapon. With a total of 5 semifinalists out of the 8 competing in the men's and women's event being from Titov's ship.

Finally came the epee, unfortunately McCann found himself knocked out by the second eliminator; however Louis made it to the semis. Once again the field was somewhat tipped in Titov's favour though it was obvious that the Chief Engineer of the Hera was going to be the one to beat in the women's event.

By the afternoon all those knocked out had changed back into their uniforms to watch the finals. A large crowd had gathered consisting of not just I.S.A off duty staff but also Gukumatz. The sport seemed to interest the Gukumatz personnel on the station, which startled McCann. He'd never witnessed them pay any interest to sport, let alone one of a violent nature. McCann was looking after his two great hopes Vezzali and Louis since both had won their matches and made it the finals. The women's foil would be fought after the men's so McCann was making sure his Ensign was both hydrated and motivated. Only one piste in the centre of the gym was in use now and it had a droid sitting at each corner with a single human referee. If the human made a call that one of the fencers disagreed with they could request the SI review it, somewhat reducing the arguments created in foil and sabre matches.

The Athena fencers sat on a bench that ran along the side of the gym, waiting for the men to walk onto the piste and begin the final. There was a tense silence, yet McCann sensed something else, he had a feeling similar to deja vu looking at the balcony above him. He noticed there were no Gukumatz; this revelation caused panic to run down his spine. He imagined what the toads might have been planning, perhaps they had waited for this competition to attack the fleet? After all the ships were all docked at the same station and most of the crew were in the same place. His fears left him when he noticed the now governor of Ilium stride into the Gym with her escort of six Spetsnaz headed by her birdman.

His relief was short lived, quickly enough McCann had an eye full of what his daughter was wearing, even causing Louis to whisper 'Qui est une femme sexy!'

McCann gave Louis a hard look; his friend raised his hands 'You do not have to worry about me my friend.'

McCann stood up and began scan the room watching the crew members as his daughter strode across the gym. She was dressed in a pair of shorts that were far too short for his liking. Her blouse and shorts were one piece, coloured black with floral patterns and made from a cotton material. The blouse was too low cut around the neck line also. Along with her light blue boots McCann didn't need to be Tlillan to know what everyman in the Gym was thinking about, save himself and Louis.

The proceedings halted for Malikah; once she reached her father she stopped and greeted him 'Good afternoon Father.'

He made a grunt 'Hurrmmph is it?'

She gestured to one of the soldiers behind her 'Petri.'

He marched up to McCann carrying a plastic box 'The tournament is most popular amongst my subjects.'

McCann raised an eyebrow at her description of the Gukumatz.

'I decided to have these forged for the tournament, a present from the population of the Ilium system.'

Malikah lifted the lid on the box to reveal twelve smaller boxes each containing a medal. In all there were six gold, six silver and twelve bronze since in fencing the losers in the semifinal matches both received a bronze for their efforts.

McCann peered cautiously at the medals 'Thank you very much, would you do the honour of presenting them?'

The sable Malikah smiled 'Thank you Father.'

Malikah closed the lid then a thought seemed to cross her mind, she looked up at the balcony surrounding the gym.

'Liik'il much!' her deep voice reverberated around the gym.

Suddenly a plethora of short fat toad heads popped back up from nowhere, McCann was no longer concerned with a Gukumatz revolt. The only plotting that concerned him was of the crewmen glaring at his daughter. Her long ivory white legs that could have been sculpted by Da Vinci himself from the most perfect marble, had men practically drooling and women in a trance of envy.

McCann turned his gaze towards the piste on which the men's foil was about to take place, the men were all looking in the same direction transfixed.

McCann cleared his throat 'Ahem!'

The referee made eye contact with him and realised he'd been leering at the Commodore's daughter. He called out 'En Garde!'

The fencers realised they were in a fencing match and broke their stare to walk up to their marks and face off in the en garde position. The referee waited a moment to check that each man was ready then called out 'Allez!' and the match began.

Malikah stood with her father and his remaining contestants in the individual matches, 'Isn't it exciting?' she whispered.

McCann looked up at his daughter who now towered over him 'Not half as exciting as your outfit!' he retorted with displeasure.

Malikah kept watching the match but pulled a smile at her father's concern 'That is the entire point is it not father?'

McCann wasn't amused 'Did your Mother see you in that today?'

Malikah observed the fencers battling on the piste 'Yes she did and her reaction was much the same as yours Father.'

McCann turned his gaze to the match 'And?'

'I ignored her and wore it anyway,' replied Malikah.

Suddenly a round of applause broke out around the Gym as one of the Russians made a graceful first counter riposte to take the point. McCann realised he hadn't been concentrating very much on the match and started to clap despite not witnessing the action. Malikah giggled a little at his lapse in concentration.

McCann whispered to his daughter 'You look very beautiful Malikah; however this place is full of young men that haven't … been intimate with a woman in a long time. You do understand don't you?'

She peered down to her father with pink eyes 'Yes father I know. I'm sorry if I have caused concern, if you wish I shall change my attire.'

McCann looked back at the fencing, he knew she could defend herself and was in no danger from anyone least of all some horny crewman. Yet as her father he couldn't help but worry about his daughter, it was a trait far more powerful amongst humans than Tlillans.

McCann felt some guilt and whispered 'Don't be silly I was just worried Malikah,' his hand moved towards his daughter's and they held onto each other for a moment.

Sure enough the men's foil was a clean sweep for Titov though Vezzali managed a silver in the women's along with Ryu's crewman taking a bronze medal.

Malikah presented the awards to the participants to great applause, next up was the Sabre; Titov made a clean sweep taking all accolades. McCann and Ryu exchanged looks across the gym both concerned for their ship's honour, Titov on the other hand was gloating at his dominance. The smug expression on his face told it all and with the Epee next he seemed confident of victory. Considering the fact that half of the remaining contestants were from the Ares his confidence was not misplaced.

To no surprise Heidemann took the women's gold, followed by an Ares drone pilot. In the Men's Louis lost 15-14 much to the Frenchman's displeasure and a barrage of colourful language. McCann noted Titov's resentment at Heidemann's victory, he could see it in his eyes. Rather than enjoy his victories and dominance of the individual events he was annoyed at allowing a gold to slip away.

The announcer declared an end to the day and reminded everyone to turn up for the team events tomorrow; McCann gathered his crew and retired to the Athena along with his daughter. Louis cursed for much of what felt a long walk back. It was impossible to console the Frenchman yet McCann did his best to lift his friend's spirits.

Congratulating Vezzali he asked 'You will be taking part in the team foil won't you?'

The Italian nodded with glee 'Yes, thank you Sir.'

Strolling down the docking arm McCann noticed Ryu up ahead 'Captain!' called Malikah catching Ryu's attention who halted her party.

Having caught up Ryu saluted 'Governor.'

Malikah smiled 'Tell me Miss Yong how are your teams shaping up for tomorrow?'

Ryu let out a tiny sigh 'Not well, the Hera has a small crew compliment compared to the Athena and Ares. We will be unable to field any sabre teams and are short for the women's Epee.'

McCann felt a chill run down his spine 'Malikah?' he said warily.

Malikah tried to ignore her father 'I would be honoured to assist your team Captain, if you wish I might fill the empty place in your Epee squad?'

Ryu peered at McCann for his approval which was not forthcoming 'Malikah that isn't fair you aren't a member of her crew.'

Malikah turned to face him 'Actually since I am Governor of Ilium I am technically in command of every vessel that resides in this system.'

McCann grinned and shook his head 'Titov won't be happy about this you do know that?'

Malikah thanked her father mentally and vocally 'Titov should be more than pleased with his haul if not he can file a formal complaint to Faraday.'

McCann felt a warm sensation of gratitude cascade through his mind as his daughter thanked him for allowing her to compete.

She turned back to Ryu 'Well Captain do you accept my offer?'

McCann shrugged at Ryu 'Very well Governor, I accept.'

Malikah was elated and as an excited schoolgirl she said 'I will have Mopixoa send me the required garments for tomorrow!'

The two teams broke up into their respective spacecraft, Louis and Vezzali both went to their quarters to change into off duty uniform. McCann and Malikah retired to the Captain's cabin, leaving her escorts outside 'These quarters are beautiful Father.'

McCann carefully removed his fencing clothing and started hanging it up to dry for tomorrow, 'Yes they pulled out the stops when they refurbished the ship, I have an entire cabinet humidor now!'

The cabin had been extended allowing McCann to install a humidor into one of the wall orifices. It was still Spartan and functional but he had a large bed with space to stretch his legs on a morning, along with a nice carpet. His office had been combined with his cabin creating a much improved environment to work and rest in.

Malikah watched her father hanging his clothes 'I have something important to tell you Father.'

'Oh dear!' he said placing his mask on a peg attached to the wall.

'In three days a Tlillan cruiser will fold space into this system, I want the fleet prepared for a confrontation,' said Malikah softly.

McCann continued hanging his clothes 'Only one cruiser?'

Malikah sighed 'No, it will be pursued by possibly four other craft, I will grant it asylum. You must repel the others Father.'

McCann began to remove his epee weapons from his bag 'Why are you speaking to me? Surely this is Faraday's concern?'

A tone of concern crept into Malikah's voice 'I have studied the dreamscape and Faraday is likely to refuse sanctuary if I approach him.'

McCann sighed 'Ahhh the dreamscape, what has it told you about this Tlillan cruiser you are ready to risk us for?'

Malikah scowled a little 'The Grand Matriarch has been exposed; the Chutli clan alone refuses to accept her authority. It has led to irreconcilable differences, for the first time in millennia Tlillan is turning on Tlillan openly.

Quil is gathering the clan and will attempt to escape the system with as many Matriarchs as possible; even as we speak she is fighting to survive.

I have contacted her and informed her of the dreamscape, she will attempt to fold space to Ilium in three days. If the seers have informed the Grand Matriarch, the council will pursue. I want you to inform Faraday that an attack on Ilium is imminent nothing more, when Quil enters the system I shall accept possession of her cruiser, the odds will be in our favour, do you understand father?'

McCann felt his energy leave his body 'And then?'

His sable child perked up 'The Tlillan fleet will most probably retreat to the home world.'

He finished hanging his kit to dry then walked towards his drinks cabinet at the opposite end of the bed 'You have this all sorted out don't you?'

McCann opened the cabinet and poured himself a Laphroaig since he was in the mood for something with a kick.

'They will be coming whether you are prepared or not father.'

He took a swig of the Scotch then pouring himself another replied 'Is there anything else I need to know?'

Malikah drew a long breath 'I will be coming with you.'

McCann picked up his glass 'Don't be ridiculous!'

Malikah placed her hands on her hips defiantly 'I am afraid my presence will be necessary Father.'

The Englishman took a sip of his smoky drink 'And why is that exactly?'

Malikah was as stubborn as her father and he could see she was not going to shift her position easily 'Without my presence the outcome is likely to be a violent one.'

McCann put down his glass and made his way over to the opposite wall where he tapped his forefinger on a DNA recognition pad; causing the wall to pop out and slide, revealing his humidor. Within the wall cavity sat what looked like a safe but was in fact a rather plush humidor, Ofra had reluctantly shipped from Geneva to the Athena.

Inside were many boxes of 25 to 50 cigars of all different brands and vitolas. He selected a Ramon Allones from the top shelf then replaced the box and closed the humidor. Making his way back to the drinks cabinet where his ashtray and smoking paraphernalia resided he commented 'Why would it become violent? We aren't at war with them and we pose no threat.'

Malikah replied in a condescending tone reminiscent of her mother 'You are too naïve Father, the Grand Matriarch was at war with us from the moment you denied her possession of the Gukumatz. Once you had intentionally injured Cihuateteo there could be no peace, until restitution is made.'

McCann clipped the cap off his cigar 'Restitution?'

'The return of the sceptre and Gukumatz,' replied Malikah bluntly.

McCann exhaled disapprovingly 'If there were to be a pitched battle with the Tlillan fleet who does the dreamscape believe would win?'

'With Quil intact the odds would be slightly in our favour, now that their fleet is down to four cruisers. However the odds are Quil will have taken heavy damage, without her assistance Cihuateteo would be victorious and all lost.'

McCann took his torch lighter and toasted the foot of his cigar before taking a couple of tentative puffs 'So what difference are you going to make standing on my bridge and getting in the way?'

Malikah smiled now that her father was going along with her scheme 'Do you trust me Father?'

He sighed whilst expelling the thick nutty smoke 'You know I do.'

The sable Valkyrie stepped towards him and wrapped both her arms around the one he was holding his cigar with, 'Then allow me on your bridge when they arrive and there will be no need for bloodshed, I promise.'

McCann hated it when she did this to him, from the moment she could walk and talk (which was soon after her birth) Malikah was the master manipulator. As she matured he found he could refuse her requests less and less, since to do so caused McCann to feel like such a mean person. Ilam viewed it as a weakness in her husband's emotional nature that Malikah exploited.

When McCann looked up at his daughters smile and loving eyes he melted 'I'll brief Ryu and Titov tonight, when a time is set to cast off I'll inform you. I take it you will be staying for the tournament?'

Despite her abilities Malikah was often at the mercy of her father, her eyes turned a soft pink as she felt his warm love 'Yes I will and thank you for letting me take part. It is the perfect cover to prepare for the Tlillans.'

McCann questioned his daughter in a surprised tone 'Cover?'

'Yes Xch'uup has spies throughout this and the home system, she is already aware of the Hera and her capabilities father. If there were a pitched battle Ryu would almost certainly be caught off guard and the Hera destroyed.'

'As you wish Malikah just keep me up to date on what's going on. You know I don't enjoy being left in the dark especially in these times.'

Malikah chatted for a short time with her father then left to speak with Ryu and congratulate Titov. Shortly afterwards there was a briefing of the situation in McCann's cabin. The other two were unhappy with all the cloak and dagger nonsense however they played along with it. When Faraday discovered the deception Malikah would take full responsibility. If it all went to plan then the fleet would be bolstered by one very advanced cruiser and access to a wealth of knowledge for the engineers at Geneva. Hopefully the profit from this venture would be enough to pacify Faraday. McCann was quite certain his boss would soon forget the discretions of his commanders once he was busy pulling apart the prize.

By the next day all the crews that were not on duty had filed into the gym bright and early for the second and last day of the tournament. Both the Athena and Ares had a team in each weapon for both the men and women. Ryu had difficulty since her crew was less than half the size, only allowing her to put teams into the Epee and foil.

Each team consisted of five fencers; the rules were that the winner of the first match was the first to five hits. The next match was the first to increase their teams score to ten hits with each match raising the bar by five, until one team managed to get to forty five hits before the other.

The first event was the men's foil the teams from Ilium 1, 2 and 3 stations they were there mainly for fun with little chance of an actual victory.

The final teams faced off the Ares on one side and the Athena on the other, McCann's team consisted mainly of Russian crew members lead by Praporshchik Kozar. Titov was looking smug as ever watching his men from the sidelines, Titov's men won by 45 - 31. Both teams were given a round of applause, even the Gukumatz joined in, puzzling McCann to no end.

The women's foil was a similar affair with Ensign Vezzali at the helm. It was obvious that she was the most talented fencer there and that was taking both teams into account. She made certain when registering the team she was placed either number 1, 3 or 5. The logic being that she was guaranteed to fence the last match. If she could fence the last match then it may be possible to pull ahead and snatch the lead. This she did, on the final match the score was 40-32 in Titov's favour. Meaning the Ares team had to only attain five hits to win. Whereas the Athena required thirteen hits to win before the Ares attained their five.

McCann felt his heart race a little and his adrenaline pump just a tad when Vezzali walked up to her mark. Her opponent was the strongest member of the Ares team; it was her job to finish the match before Vezzali had a chance to close the gap.

The referee looked at both ladies then announced so all in the Gym could hear 'En Garde!'

A hushed silence fell upon the gym, even the Gukumatz seemed to be on edge.

'Allez' called the referee.

Vezzali approached her opponent slowly but surely holding her blade out to the right of her body with the tip pointing at her opponent's torso. Her opponent charged with her arm out in what McCann believed to be a rather reckless attack, more akin to a Sabre match. Vezzali waited for the opponent's blade to come in range and with lightning reactions she delivered a parry riposte. Both pistes lit up and the referee called out 'Halt!'

If it were Epee both fencers would receive a point however this was foil, the referee gave Vezzali the hit since she had taken right of way with her parry. Her opponent didn't argue the decision and they both returned to their marks to applause from the Athena crew encouraging her as best they could. Eventually the score was 44-43 in Vezzali's favour and she looked ready to take the first gold for Athena.

'En Garde … Allez!' called out the ref and both fencers moved forward to take the right of way, their swords clashed as they met parrying each other. Vezzali saw her opponent attempt to make a thrust and she leapt back out of range. If her opponent had lunged at this point then the score would certainly have been levelled but she made the mistake of withdrawing. This gave Vezzali the right of way and her legs pushed her frame forward in an extended lunge nailing her opponent with a clean hit. The crowd let out roars of applause, as did her team mates and the Gukumatz observing from above.

Titov clapped but Vezzali had wiped the smug grin from his face. The foil team returned to the sidelines to be embraced by their crew mates. McCann wiped the sweat from his brow and Louis slapped him on the back laughing.

McCann turned to his friend and asked 'What's so funny?'

Louis who looked a lot happier than McCann had seen him in a long time answered 'In battle you never even blink but this makes you shit a brick!'

McCann didn't reply but only nodded, it was true that in life or death situations he always kept his cool; probably because he had to, but these competitions always made him nervous. McCann had no problem with the trade off and he believed the adrenaline improved his performance making his eyes and hands faster in these competitions. In battle he believed it would cloud his judgement, so he thought he had a pretty good deal all in all.

Vezzali's team mates gathered around her and began throwing her up and down in the air as they cheered her. Much to the disdain of Titov who looked as if he'd sucked on a lemon. McCann took more pleasure in Titov's misery than his crewmate's elation. Only Louis knew him well enough to understand his dark twisted sense of pleasure which caused the Frenchman to snigger.

Next up was the Men's sabre which Titov took 27-45, then the women's sabre which again went to the Ares 23-45 and Titov's smug grin was back. During the break as the piste was prepared for the men's epee Malikah turned up much to the relief of Ryu.

As usual her mere presence seemed to announce her entrance as a fanfare of trumpets, everyone turned to look as she strode over to the area occupied by the Hera crew. As usual she had her caravan of bodyguards headed by her pet Icarus. An expression of horror removed Titov's smug look when he noticed she was dressed in a fencing outfit and holding a mask. He realised that she was taking part in the women's epee. An event Titov had high hopes of snatching from Ryu. With Heideman on the Hera team it would be difficult after she had demonstrated her ability with the sword yesterday. Malikah was an unknown but his fear was that her height alone would grant a massive advantage.

Titov stopped speaking to his crew member and began to march across the gym towards the Hera team like a man on a mission.

Malikah, speaking with Ryu, paused for a moment and turned about, she made eye contact with Titov. The sable Amazon gave him the most frightening stare he'd seen since his mother had caught him stealing money from her purse.

He was only 7 years old at the time but he never forgot the terrifying expression on her face and he never stole again. He felt as if he were 7 years old again looking up at his mother who was about to beat him to within an inch of his life. He continued walking towards the Hera camp but with a less direct swagger and a lot slower.

Malikah never took her eyes from him and upon arriving he swallowed and asked in a timid voice 'Will you be taking part in the Epee?'

'Yes,' came a blunt reply from Malikah.

Too afraid to say anymore he nodded his head and returned to his crewmates; despite the fact his legs had turned to jelly he made it and quickly sat down. The team medic approached him and checked him out taking readings from the chip in his neck that was speaking to the nanites inside his body.

Ryu squinted a little at the minor commotion around Titov 'What's wrong with him? He looked like he was about to pass out just now.'

Malikah replied contently 'He will be quite alright Miss Yong, he was only reminded of what happens when you attempt to take that which is not yours.'

Ryu didn't fully understand her response but neither did she bother inquiring any further. She was used to Ilam pulling similar stunts in the past when they socialized. McCann had observed the entire episode and though he often disapproved of his wife manipulating people in a similar fashion to get her way, on this occasion he found it gratifying.

Titov was sat on a bench sweating profusely surrounded by his concerned crew, the ship's doctor tapping away at his medical tablet and scratching his head.

The Men's epee was announced and McCann took the responsibility of opening for the team, with Louis taking the duty of finishing the match. Everyone got at least two stints on the piste and against the regional teams there was no problem.

Louis called them "Epee fodder," he saw them as merely fillers for when the clash with the Ares squad came. The Athena crew won all their matches and made it to face off against the Ares in the final. McCann felt his crew had the strongest epee team in the tournament though Titov was not prepared to let another gold slip through his fingers.

Titov was now back on his feet but his expression was one of a nervous man. After watching Louis demolish his opposition using a combination of stop hits and very accurate wrist hits.

The final went much the same with McCann opening to get his team ahead. Everyone's job was then to keep their heads above water, or not allow the opposing team to widen the gap by too much if they managed to get ahead. By the time McCann or Louis were up the gap was usually 2-3 hits behind the Ares team which they both managed to claw back and push into a lead. By the final the score was 37-40 in Titov's favour and Louis was up against the man he'd lost the individual final to, this time the Frenchman was determined he wasn't going to lose.

Throughout the day Louis had adopted McCann's method of preparation which involved playing his favourite music on his ear piece between bouts. He had borrowed McCann's music library and selected a tune with the proper tempo and lyrics, it was by coincidence one McCann played often. The song was an old dance track with a fast beat named "Electronic pleasure", a dance track that got him into and kept him in the mood to move fast and win on the piste. Both men could be seen observing the match and tapping their hands and feet to the beat emanating from the ear piece.

Louis handed his ear piece to McCann who tapped him on the shoulder and joked 'Mercy is for the weak!'

Louis smiled and took his place on the piste opposite his Russian counterpart; both men saluted each other the referee then placed their masks on.

'En Garde,' called the referee and they both assumed the position with legs bent and arm bent pointing their weapons towards each other. 'Allez,' ordered the ref and they both approached each other; Louis was bouncing on his feet as the tune he'd been listening to passed through his mind.

Holding his French grip epee by the pommel he moved it in circles to avoid his opponents parry. The Russian opposite him held a pistol grip which gave an advantage when parrying and some extra point control. If Louis were to be parried his blade could easily be knocked out of his hand. The French grip Louis held gave him a reach advantage when he held it by the pommel, but at a great cost to control so he had to deny his opponent the opportunity to take the blade.

Both Louis and McCann were experienced pommelers and worked hard on perfecting control whilst maintaining the reach. Louis was also left handed which most right handers rarely had the chance to train against.

His opponent moved his blade in small circles then lunged at his target. Louis calmly moved his forward foot backwards until it touched his rear foot. He then stuck his arm out whilst arching his torso away from the incoming tip of his opponent's blade.

His enemy had committed to an attack but Louis' retreat gave him a split second to make a decision and he decided to place his attack on the arm of his incoming enemy. Louis hit first leaving too little time for the Russian to attain a double hit. The onlookers applauded, even Titov clapped the text book stop hit … begrudgingly.

The Russian only needed to get double hits at the very least to win, since double hits are very different depending on which side of the score board your team resides. However Louis kept denying him, always answering his aggressive attacks with perfectly timed stop hits. By the time the young man had worked out what he was doing wrong the score was 43-41 in Louis favour. The young Russian stopped attacking now but Louis had learned a lot from losing to this fellow yesterday and attacked his wrist. Much of the time Louis missed but he only made small thrusts then pulled back hopping on his feet, he didn't commit himself with long lunges or fleche attacks.

The Frenchman knew the young Russian had little patience and would eventually attack him and when he did Louis would stop hit him. Double hits now worked in the Frenchman's favour so he didn't have to even go for the arm, but was happy hitting the shoulder.

The final hit was a double 'Double hit 45-42!' called the referee and Louis whipped of his mask screaming in victory.

The Frenchman clenched his hands and flexed his arms to loud applause. After his initial celebration Louis approached the Russian, saluted with the blade then shook his hand and the referee's. Louis entered the Athena camp to applause and pats on the back.

In contrast the Russian received a grim look from his Kapitan. Titov wasn't happy and he didn't relish the next contest when he witnessed the women's epee team as they easily dispatched all opposition.

Upon reaching the final which as usual was the Ares vs. whomever, Ryu was supremely confident in her team, Bridgette was opening with Malikah finishing. The Governor of Ilium stood a good 6ft 7 inches giving her a supreme advantage in height and reach, added to which she was borrowing Louis epee for the contest. Malikah didn't need to pommel and she always had greater strength on the parry with a tremendous lunging distance.

McCann was a little nervous when he noticed the looks crewmen were making in his daughter's direction. The fencing kit accentuated her long slim figure and it was difficult not to look.

Louis leaned over and under his breath he said in McCann's ear 'Well they do say the hottest women do epee!'

McCann closed his eyes and drew in a deep breath while Louis sniggered at himself.

'I bet there are a lot of guys here that want to test their weapons on her!'

McCann gave his Chief a stony look 'You're not funny Louis.'

He only made Louis laugh, yet his friend could see how concerned he was for his daughter. Louis patted McCann on the back 'Don't worry I'll protect her from any dirty minded suitors, okay?'

McCann forced a smile and returned his gaze to the contest.

Ryu and her camp clapped each hit made against the Ares team; the match was rather uninspiring since her Chief Bridgette Heidemann was unmatched. Along with Malikah it was evident that they were about to annihilate the opposition. Bridgette used her pistol grip to great effect overpowering her opponents with binds and circular parries before taking the hit.

Malikah on the other hand used her range hitting her victim on the mask with ease. Getting past Malikah's epee was very difficult and few hits were scored against her. The most effective strategy used was to target her exposed under arm which she often showed due to her height. The sable Amazon employed it as a baiting tactic to draw her opponent to attack her, so that she could plant a stop hit on the mask. By the end Malikah took the Hera squad to a 16-45 victory and the Governor of Ilium received a standing ovation from the balcony filled with Gukumatz.

Titov was sick as a pig, his team were of the opinion that her participation was very unfair.

The medal ceremony was conducted and a Gukumatz shaman had agreed to award the medals rather than the governor. According to Malikah the whole event had been a massive success on the surface of each moon; sparking an interest in the sport throughout the system. All Earth channels had been reporting on it with Jerry Habeeb running a spot each night transmitting a collection of the day's highlights. Faraday was greatly pleased by the positive press generated on Earth. Finally his commanders and his organisation were being viewed in a good light.

The tensions concerning Ilium had evaporated since Malikah had taken control. Although it had gone against his better judgement to leave her in charge he now realised it was easily the best outcome possible. Despite the good press and improved relations with both the Gukumatz and people of Earth Faraday was worried. His concern had shifted from gaining the co-operation of Earth factions to his fear of Malikah. The conquest of Ilium had secured the I.S.A an unshakable powerbase that resulted in the countries and power blocs of his own planet throwing in the towel.

Since the I.S.A controlled a resource of labour, technology and minerals far in excess of anything they could offer there was little point in battling for a bigger slice of the pie. The pie had been withdrawn and fortunately for the Russian they had got in early and sealed a deal. Those that hadn't were left to bid for contracts or attempt to curry favour with Geneva another way.

Malikah was an unknown, Faraday trusted Ilam, but her daughter was difficult for her mother to control and she was little more than five years old. Ilam assured him that she was mature enough but he had no experience of Tlillans and their life and death cycles. Malikah also commanded the Gukumatz population not via his authority but through their faith in some legend, on Earth there was a growing movement amongst all religious people. Malikah had reached a status of authority which Faraday could no longer challenge, the Gukumatz believed in her as a messiah and it had spread to Earth. Her ability to read the possible futures through the dreamscape was common knowledge after she had agreed to an interview with Network America. The Bible belt had been set on fire after the first contact with the Gukumatz and preachers held masses, prayers for salvation. The belief that Armageddon had come was strong and the evidence plain to see. Now not just the Bible belt was on fire, religious leaders all played down such beliefs but congregations around the world looked to Malikah and it was growing slowly but surely.

Faraday compared it more to a Charles Manson figure controlling his mindless followers, not that he would dare make his opinion public. He suspected members of his own staff secretly hoped it to be true. Faraday was terrified every night with the thought that in the future Malikah might take sole control of the Ilium system and there would be nothing he could do about it. He couldn't remove her from power now and her influence grew stronger each day.

Chapter 19

Faraday awoke to his wrist tablet's emergency alarm; he almost leapt out of bed and grabbed it from the bedside table. The tablet glowed in the dark and not even bothering to turn the lights on he tapped the screen.

'Mr. Faraday, Ilium has gone to Defcon two, Ilam reports five Tlillan cruisers folded space into the system. She reports no exchange of fire as of five minutes ago.'

Faraday sat up on his bed 'Lights!' the room lit up, he put his wrist tablet on 'What about Malikah where is she?'

The voice replied 'She is onboard the Athena, Sir.'

Faraday slapped his bedside table out of frustration 'Sir, are you alright?'

Faraday rubbed his eyes 'Yes, yes keep me informed and get a link to up to McCann and the recon satellites in Ilium. I'll be ready in a few minutes.'

'Understood Sir,' the young man replied before ending the communication.

Faraday got dressed as quickly as possible throwing on a charcoal grey suit then dashing to the control centre in Geneva.

He quick marched into the room 'What in blue blazes is going on?'

There were men and women hammering away at their stations as reports streamed in via the micro wormholes onboard recon satellites.

The young man that had woken Faraday stood at the central table 'Sir!', he grabbed Faraday's attention. The holo projector displayed an image that made his legs go weak; before him sat his own fleet of two cruisers and a destroyer with a vastly superior Tlillan fleet of four cruisers. The fifth Tlillan cruiser sat behind the I.S.A fleet obviously damaged from heavy combat.

The young man tapped his tablet then pointed to a large view screen on the wall 'Sir, this is what happened five minutes ago.'

Faraday steadied himself and watched as the first Tlillan cruiser entered the Ilium system.

'We received a tunnel event alert when this craft folded space into Ilium. It was followed within 30 seconds by four simultaneous tunnel events ejecting the remainder of the known Tlillan fleet into Ilium.'

Faraday squinted at the screen 'Why are our ships already in position? Have you heard from McCann?'

The young man shook his head 'No Sir.'

Faraday smashed his fist on the desk distorting the holo image for a moment, 'Blast it!' he screamed at the top of his voice halting everyone for a moment. 'Get back to work!' Faraday bellowed at his staff. He watched the events unfold in a fury 'I want to see Doctor Pitt now!' he shouted.

The young man wondered what for but didn't ask and shortly Valorie Pitt was in the control centre. Everyone had been woken up and was observing Ilium including every news channel on Earth.

'William?' she spoke softly trying to calm her boss down.

Faraday turned quickly and felt at ease upon seeing the doctor, 'Valorie thank god, tell me your assessment of Malikah will you, she's onboard the Athena and not answering our communications.'

Valorie raised her eyebrows 'Confident to the point of arrogance, something of a demagogue figure which she seems prepared to take full advantage of. I don't know to what extent she believes the Gukumatz it's hard to tell, she's sincere on the point of improving the well-being of both us and the Gukumatz. Her logic is much the same as her Mother's, she will do whatever necessary to accomplish her goals. She's half human however and unlike her Mother she's driven not by religious dogma but her own moral values, quite a Neitzschian philosophy all in all.'

Faraday sighed 'Could I have information relative to this situation Valorie, I do not have time to digest all of that.'

Valorie smiled 'Her Father is her weakness and strength, Will, he's the only person she will defer to. I'm sure that if Duncan felt there was any danger he would've avoided this situation, Malikah wouldn't supersede his authority.'

Faraday scratched the stubble on his chin, Valorie's words had calmed him down somewhat 'This means they were both in it together. The fleet didn't happen to be at that point in space at that time by chance, they were all scheduled to remain in dock for at least another week.'

On the bridge of the Athena there was an argument between two Matriarchs. Cihuateteo, on the view screen, sat in what must have been the Captain's chair of the Tlillan cruiser. McCann had been here before but now Cihuateteo possessed the advantage. Quil had managed to limp behind the line of I.S.A warships but her vessel was crippled. Unable to assist the I.S.A vessels sat nose to nose with four Tlillan cruisers.

McCann was aware that if Cihuateteo fired first the Athena, Ares and Hera would almost certainly be crippled and unable to return fire. Malikah was playing brinksmanship with their lives. He prevented himself from displaying any signs of fear to the crew but he couldn't mask his worry from Malikah. She sensed her father's concern and a mere smile from his daughter was enough to exorcise all negative emotion.

Cihuateteo was her usual self, 'Return the Chutli, half breed!' she demanded.

Malikah replied confidently 'Return to your Matriarch Cihuateteo, the Chutli and her crew are under my protection.'

Cihuateteo was more bemused than impressed 'Perhaps the madness has taken you?' came the voice of the translator. Though by now McCann had a good grasp on most of what was being said without its aid.

Malikah had an expression as serious as cancer 'Then you must take her by force.'

Cihuateteo hesitated in her chair for a moment whilst she thought out a reply. After about 20 seconds and no doubt communicating with her crew telepathically 'As you wish half breed,' came her dread response.

McCann was about to give orders to the fleet but his daughter turned her head to him and whispered 'Be calm father I told you there would be no bloodshed.'

He relaxed and held off as he watched Cihuateteo prepare to blast his ship out of existence.

Back in Geneva Valorie had prevented her boss from having a mental breakdown. But Faraday was still on edge as his staff worked furiously around him to find out what was happening. Men and women delivered reports from the stations in Ilium and different areas of space divided up by recon satellites. The young aide stood by a row of workstations which monitored the events via the closest recon posts 'Sir!' he cried out 'an energy surge has been detected in all Tlillan vessels, I believe they are preparing to fire on the fleet!'

Faraday almost collapsed, but Valorie was there and she supported him for the moment he required to steady himself 'What is our fleet doing?'

His aide shook his head 'Nothing Sir, they're just sitting in space.'

Faraday supported himself by leaning on the holo table next to him and almost in tears he gasped 'She has taken the I.S.A and turned us into shit!'

Everyone in the centre had one eye on the view screen; Valorie had her arms around Faraday who was bemoaning his decision to allow Malikah to remain as Ilium governor. After about 30 seconds nothing had happened until Faraday heard the sound of furious tapping at the workstations his aide was monitoring; it drew his attention 'What's happening?'

His aide seemed perplexed 'I don't know Sir. All I can say is,' he leaned down and whispered with one of the staff 'there seems to be a phenomenon manifesting itself around the Tlillan weapon masts, Sir.'

Faraday furrowed his brow 'Speak English man!' he screamed at the frightened young gentleman.

His aide cleared his throat 'I can best describe it as null space, Sir, it may be preventing the Tlillan vessels from discharging their beam weapons, Sir.'

Faraday was frustrated but a ray of hope now shone into the control centre at Geneva 'Define null space!'

His aide gestured to a young Indian lady who had been working away monitoring the recon reports, she rose from her seat next to where the young man had been standing.

She turned around to address her boss, 'Null space is a theory unobserved until now, it is an area of space where even space and the laws of physics do not exist. It nullifies anything that comes into contact with it hence the tag, null space.'

Faraday looked away from the polite girl dressed in trousers and blouse with a blue jumper and her name tag hanging off it to look at the view screen. The beam weapons at the ends of the Tlillan weapon masts were disappearing behind a black fog.

'Similar to a black hole?' asked Faraday.

The Indian lady replied with a tone of authority 'No Sir, a black hole uses gravity to consume objects including photons. This phenomenon neutralises light and even gravity, the effect of null space is that it has no effect.'

Faraday scratched his stubbly beard 'Is it a weapon?'

'Unknown Sir,' replied his aide but Faraday noticed the young lady had something more to say.

He squinted to read her name tag 'Miss Dutta, what do you think?'

She grinned at the attention from her boss 'I doubt the Tlillan warships are able to generate a null space field. We have seen them in battle and studied their technology to some degree and nothing would imply null space technology, Sir.'

Faraday turned back to the view screen and whispered to Valorie 'Then what the bloody hell is going on up there?'

Valorie ogled at the events unfolding 'I have no idea Will.'

On the Athena McCann had been bracing for the first salvo from Cihuateteo but it never came. His opponent seemed as befuddled as he, looking around the room at what must have been her officers, trying to understand why the Athena hadn't been turned into dust.

'Commodore!' called Vezzali, he made eye contact with his science officer standing at her station behind him 'There is an area of null space forming around the weapon masts of the Tlillan ships.'

McCann called out 'Hassif?', if anyone could explain it to him he could.

'A neutral area of space that nullifies all effects, nothing can pass through it including beam weapons,' came Hassif's simplified explanation.

McCann nodded to Vezzali then looked up to his right. Before he spoke to his daughter he noticed she was in what he could best describe as a trance. Her eyes were wide open and as black as space itself, much like a pair of shining onyx stones. Her breathing was regular but heavy and she was oblivious to him and the bridge crew. Standing with legs astride in her jet black ribbed suit with only her clan pendant as decoration, Malikah's most treasured possession.

Cihuateteo was the mirror opposite as the fog expanded from the ends of the weapon masts until there was an individual null space field surrounding each warship. The signal began to break up and Cihuateteo's image became grainy. Flickering as the fields intensified until finally the only vessel in Cihuateteo's fleet still visible was the Teteo, her own clan ship.

The other three had disappeared behind a null space field, McCann assumed all were unable to move or discharge their weapons. All over Earth and Ilium the miracle was being witnessed, those on Earth remained perplexed turning on to Network America where scientists commented on what was happening. The Gukumatz on the other hand understood what was occurring and who was responsible, they went to their shamans for conformation. McCann was dumbfounded by the whole thing as was his crew. He thought nothing could top this, but then something happened that was beyond belief and even some Gukumatz found difficulty in accepting.

At Geneva they were trying to analyze the phenomenon but as Miss Dutta had pointed out there was nothing to analyze only the lack of anything, including gravity. Three vessels had disappeared under the sheet of null space but one could still be made out inside the swirling fog.

Faraday was reading reports but the lack of information only frustrated him 'Why is the fourth ship not engulfed?'

Vlaorie calmly replied 'Malikah wants to maintain communications with her.'

Faraday sneered at his head shrinker 'What? Are you telling me Malikah is responsible for this null space effect?'

Valorie smiled at Faraday's sceptical sneer 'Yes, who do you think is responsible Will?'

Faraday quietened down 'I don't know,' he said timidly.

Valorie held his arm 'There is more in this universe than our limited intelligence understands at this moment in time Will.'

Faraday scowled at the doctor 'Are you a philosopher now as well as a psychiatrist?'

Valorie patted his arm affectionately 'I believe in people and the power of the human mind … he who dismisses it is a fool. Don't dismiss Malikah so readily Will, you will suffer for it if you do, trust me.'

A klaxon sounded across the control room and Miss Dutta sitting at her station shouted at the top of her lungs 'Incoming tunnel event!'

All eyes turned to the view screen and a white hole appeared within half an AU of the standoff, behind the Tlillan fleet, now marked by four blobs where even the stars couldn't shine.

Faraday cried out 'How many ships?' expecting support for the Tlillan fleet to appear despite the fact this was the largest amount of vessels they could crew at a single time.

His aide spoke with Miss Dutta and replied 'Sir, this is not an artificial wormhole, it is a natural event … Sir,' not sure whether to believe it himself.

Faraday didn't take his eyes off the white hole swirling like a massive drain with bleach spiralling out into space, 'What? Are you bloody mad? That can't be a natural event it's impossible!'

Miss Dutta stood up 'It is too large to be an artificial wormhole Sir, no known vessel has the power required to generate a wormhole of that magnitude and if it's artificial then where is the incoming fleet?'

She had a good point, the klaxon was still going and nothing had been ejected from the wormhole.

'Turn that bloody siren off will you!' shouted Faraday as the klaxon ended. Faraday shook his head 'It is no coincidence that a wormhole has been generated here and now, I refuse to believe that is a natural occurrence!'

'Why aren't the ships being affected? At that proximity the wormhole should be pushing on them, shouldn't it?'

Miss Dutta hurriedly tapped away at her station 'Yes Sir, the white hole is not exerting any force.'

Faraday ran his fingers through his hair and sighed 'That's not possible, a white hole has to expel energy and mass otherwise it wouldn't be a bloody white hole would it?'

Miss Dutta replied in her authoritative tone 'I am only repeating what my instruments are reporting Sir, the white hole has no graviton field. If a white hole that size did possess a graviton field it would cause a tear in space that would consume the entire Ilium system, Sir.'

Faraday quietened down and went back to watching the inexplicable events taking place in Ilium on the screen in front of him.

On the Athena McCann had witnessed the white hole that was at least ten times the size of the largest the Athena could generate in theory. McCann called out to Kim shouting over Athena announcing the tunnel event 'Tell Louis we'll need the engines at full efficiency.'

Kim nodded as he put his wrist tablet to his mouth.

McCann next approached Hassif and stood behind him 'Hassif can you ride out the Graviton wave?'

Hassif stood at his station bracing himself for a mighty impact 'I'll tell you after I've done it, but Duncan … that white hole is massive it might tear us all apart anyway.'

McCann placed his hand on his friend's shoulder and whispered 'I know.'

Hassif just nodded and prepared to use a burst of energy from the engines to hit the wave head on at full speed. McCann looked up at Athena 'Thank you Athena, let us know when the enemy appears.'

The alarm ended.

Next came the voice of his science officer 'Sir?'

McCann barked 'What!?'

Intimidated but not deterred she replied 'The white hole is not emitting a graviton field, Commodore.'

Hassif bashed away at his station with fervour 'She's bloody right you know! That isn't possible, yet there is no graviton field and nothing has been ejected.'

McCann rubbed his eyes 'Then who the hell is generating that thing?'

His gaze fell upon his daughter, stood in a trance with her arm outstretched and hand open. Palm facing towards where the wormhole would be in space.

McCann mumbled under his breath 'Surely not?'

He wasn't prepared to say anything to his crew for fear of being sectioned, but even the pit had come to a silence as they stared at Malikah in her trance. Everyone was thinking the exact same thought, yet no one was prepared to say it since it was beyond all reason and only a madman would consider such an outrageous possibility.

Hassif called out 'Look!'

McCann turned to the view screen to witness three of the Tlillan vessels spat out of their prisons in null space and cast into the wormhole one by one. Only the Teteo remained floating in space alone, the shroud of null space dropped from the craft and the image of Cihuateteo cleared up. She was afraid and the first thing she did was address McCann.

Looking directly at him she implored 'McCann control your offspring before we are both destroyed!'

McCann didn't answer her plea but remained silent.

Malikah drew in a deep breath; still in her trance she spoke 'Cihuateteo?'

The tall white haired Tlillan answered 'Yes?'

McCann assumed Malikah was blinded during her trance as she seemingly stared past the screen and into space. When she spoke it was in a deep voice reverberating around the bridge. The pit crew had stopped working and everyone was traumatised by the sound which seemingly shook the very bones of both the ship and her crew.

Malikah held her hand out and slowly drew breath 'When you stand at the edge of the abyss and look in what do you see?'

Cihuateteo stood in front of her chair and made some curious looks, probably towards her officers though McCann couldn't see them on the view screen 'I do not understand Malikachutli.'

She drew another long slow breath then with the same terrifying voice asked 'You stand at the abyss Cihuateteo, tell me what do you see when your destruction is imminent and you have no hope?'

The white haired Tlillan was a proud woman and refused to beg for mercy 'I see my destiny Malikachutli, what do you see?'

Malikah seemed to find her question briefly amusing, but only for a fraction of a second, 'Cihuateteo I must stare into the abyss each day. As I peer inside I see a great wild beast filled with hatred, violence and pain. It attempts to consume me. When I stare it in the face I see myself.'

Cihuateteo was perplexed 'What is my fate Malikachutli?'

Malikah drew a long breath and McCann was certain he could feel her heart beating within his chest 'Your fate is by my side Cihuateteo.'

The white haired Tlillan was still puzzled but relieved that she was going live 'What of the Mantle?'

McCann had no idea what she referred to; he was merely an onlooker now.

'The mantle is mine, I will return it to Tititl. Until then let Xch'uup know that the beast has awoken from her slumber.'

Cihuateteo was calm, which McCann felt was quite odd considering her usual demeanour, as she made her farewell 'Tu heel k'iin Malikahchutli.'

As she spoke Cihuateteo was nearly thrown out of her chair, McCann noticed her vessel was suddenly propelled into the wormhole at massive speeds skidding across the tactical display. The communication link began to break up then disappeared once the warship was swallowed by the white hole.

Malikah drew a deep breath then slowly clenched her hand to make a fist. As she did so the wormhole collapsed at the same rate, vanishing as she made a fist. Once the wormhole had collapsed his daughters eyes slowly returned to normal, losing the jet black onyx many found so frightening.

Malikah smiled and looked around at the silent gob smacked bridge, she rested her gaze on her beloved father 'Quil requires your assistance father.'

McCann thought for a moment then realised there was a damaged Tlillan warship to be attended to 'Yes of course.'

McCann looked up at the neural housing 'Can we tow her into Ilium 1 Athena?'

The soft voice of Athena replied 'Once the Tlillan warship has been certified for docking I can tow her to port Commodore.'

Malikah looked up at the neural housing 'Have no fear Athena the Chutli is sound, she may dock safely.'

McCann looked at Hassif and nodded 'Tow her in Hassif.'

He next turned to Kim 'Let them know there's a medical emergency on the Tlillan ship.'

Malikah added to her father's orders 'Have them all equip monocles, a Tlillan vessel has low internal lighting.'

Kim looked at McCann waiting for his confirmation and received a quick nod to which he sent the message to the Captain on Ilium 1.

Meanwhile on Geneva Faraday was bending over backwards to contact McCann. He saw what had happened but no one seemed to know how or why despite having a staff hand-picked from the best the planet had to offer. Added to that Jerry Habeeb was calling his personal communicator, Faraday tried his best to ignore it but eventually answered informing Jerry that when he knew anything he'd call him back.

Finally McCann answered Faraday, the Commodore's face sprung from the holo projector imbedded in the centre of the table; a furious Faraday inquired 'Why haven't you answered my hails Duncan?'

McCann looked astonished 'I'm sorry but we haven't had any communications until now Director.'

Faraday growled 'Fine, can you tell me what the bloody hell just happened, Commodore?'

McCann was ill at ease 'I've sent a full report on the incident, Sir.'

Faraday rubbed his eyes 'Yes, yes I've just gone over it. Where did that null space and wormhole come from?'

McCann didn't want to look like a fool and tried to dodge the question, however on Faraday's insistence he replied 'I believe Malikah was responsible for the phenomenon witnessed. Don't ask me how but she had some sort of influence over the events.'

Faraday's growls became louder 'Do you expect me to believe that?'

McCann wanted this conversation over now 'No Sir, it doesn't make any sense but that is what I observed. She controlled the wormhole and I assume the null space, I have no idea how and I may be crazy but that's what I saw Bill.'

Faraday decided to drop the subject for now since he wasn't getting anywhere 'What about the Tlillan warship, what are you doing?'

Relieved that he didn't have to comment any further on the previous events McCann replied in a relaxed tone 'Quilachutli has been towed to Ilium 1 and her crew are receiving emergency treatment, mostly minor radiation burns due to their sensitivity.'

Faraday took delivery of a coffee thanking his aide, 'What quarantine measures are you taking, Duncan?'

McCann peered down at a tablet 'All staff have had their internal nanite databases updated. A makeshift quarantine zone has been put together in med bay 3 and cargo bay 2 but I'm assured the Tlillans will be cleared within a few days.'

Faraday calmly stirred his frothy cappuccino as he was now a paragon of serenity 'On what authority do you have that?'

The hard pressed McCann replied 'Malikah.'

Faraday growled under his breath again 'Yes I will want to speak to that young lady soon, but I suppose she already knows that doesn't she Duncan?'

McCann didn't answer, after a short uneasy silence Faraday sighed 'Ah well I'll leave you to it Commodore, make sure that warship is secured, I'll want a good look at it when this commotion is over, and well done Duncan.'

McCann was surprised by Faraday's last comment, he smiled and nodded 'Thank you,' the image of McCann then disappeared from the holo projector.

Valorie smiled at her serene boss 'It looks like you have it all under control now Will.'

He returned the smile 'I think there's only one person in control and we both know her name!' then continued stirring his coffee.

The Athena had docked and McCann was marching towards the cargo bay where wounded crew of the Chutli were being examined by station medics. He had his daughter and Louis with him and her pet trundling behind them, 'Louis I want you to inspect that ship, gather all the information you can, take whoever you want with you.'

Louis pulled his monocle out of his leg pocket 'Understood, can I take Hassif?'

McCann nodded and Louis started sending messages to crew members on the Athena via his wrist tablet. McCann stole a look at Icarus 'Does that thing have to follow you everywhere?'

Malikah frowned 'Father don't pick on him!'

McCann shook his head 'Fine just make sure it doesn't get in my way.'

As they strode along the outer ring of the station a voice called out from behind 'Hey McCann!'

Ryu was running to catch them up. Once she'd caught the party she exclaimed, whilst still gasping for breath, 'What the hell just happened out there?'

McCann snapped 'You should be on your ship Captain; I don't recall giving you orders to dock.'

Ryu snapped back 'I didn't, I took a shuttle is that okay Commodore?'

McCann clenched his teeth 'No not really.'

Ryu kept striding behind them, though she was having to march a lot faster due to her short legs 'Are you ordering me to return?'

McCann halted and looked down at Ryu 'What do you want Ryu?'

She looked upwards through her metal rimmed glasses 'I want to know what is happening McCann. I want to know where that wormhole came from and why we are still alive and having this discussion.'

He looked at his daughter then back at Ryu 'I can't answer that, but you may as well join us.'

They started walking again but a little slower for Ryu; she adjusted her glasses as she walked alongside Louis 'So where are we going?'

'Cargo bay 2, quarantine zone. Did you update your chip?' replied McCann.

Ryu put her hand on the back of her neck placing it over her chip which managed her nanites 'Sure I'm all up-to-date.'

The Cargo bay was dimly lit, similar to the soft glow one might receive from a log fire in a winter cabin. There were about fifty tall Tlillan females most with scarlet red hair, nursing various wounds, for the minor injuries their suits dealt with it initially. The more seriously wounded were stretchered off to med bay 3 to be attended to. Quilachutli stood speaking to her comrades.

Once Malikah entered the cargo bay all conversation among the Tlillan women ceased and Quil turned to greet the party.

McCann noticed she was carrying what could only be a sword in a scabbard. From first impressions it was a close approximation to a Napoleonic French cavalry sabre. A basket hilt along with a grip which maintained a slight downwards angle. McCann recognised the designed first used by French cavalry after it was surmised the thrust was more effective at killing than the cut. The scabbard was made of the same substance as both guard and handle, not that McCann recognised the substance, he wasn't sure if it was metal or stone.

Quil approached Malikah grasping the weapon in her outstretched hand, Malikah held her hand outstretched and received the weapon. He scanned the room to see that every Tlillan present was watching.

Quil then lowered herself to her knees and spoke in a subdued tone 'Yaaxil,' which McCann recognised as Tlillan for 'First'.

He assumed it to mean that Malikah was now clan Matriarch and this sword was perhaps a symbol of power, one of the many notions the races shared.

All Tlillans in the bay knelt down on both knees no matter their injuries until Malikah replied 'Liik'il kiik.'

McCann understood the first word but he required his earpiece to translate the second 'Rise sister'.

He found the whole thing rather tiresome, however it held importance for the Tlillans so he respected their tradition and waited quietly.

Once Quil rose Malikah flung her arms around her, in a typically human embrace that a child might give to her grandmother in such a situation. She held her grandmother tightly; Quil was at a loss and looked to McCann for help. He gestured towards his daughter with his head but Quil was still at a loss. He then concentrated and did something he had only previously attempted with his wife and daughter. He placed a thought in Quil's consciousness, Quil must have received it since a light seemed to have activated in her mind and she embraced her granddaughter as best she could. The embrace was a cold Tlillan embrace but it was enough to satisfy Malikah.

The crew of the Chutli were at a loss until Quil silently passed on the message McCann had sent. Once they all realised it was a human greeting they had a try themselves and McCann, Louis and Ryu were soon engaged in hugging every member of the Chutli. When Hassif walked in he couldn't believe his own eyes and was soon mobbed by tall beautiful Tlillan women some of whom recognised him. Hassif looked at McCann for help and Ryu whispered to her friend 'Looks like Hassif is a big hit with the Tlillans.'

McCann grinned and chuckled 'Being a mathematical genius should have some perks I suppose?'

After several ribcage crunching hugs from various Matriarchs, McCann regained his breath and approached Quil while she spoke with his daughter 'I'm sorry to interrupt but I'd like to have permission for my Chief Engineer to board your ship and certify it for safety purposes.'

Quil didn't reply but instead his daughter did 'You have my permission Father, Louis may board the Chutli at his convenience.'

McCann smiled at his daughter 'I'm sorry?'

Malikah giggled at her father 'I am clan Matriarch Father, the Chutli is my ship and you have my permission to board her.'

McCann made eye contact with Louis and gestured towards the Chutli by pointing his finger. Louis gave a thumbs up and rustled Hassif out of the cargo bay since he was enjoying the embracing far too much.

McCann had his eye on the sword his daughter held 'May I?' he asked intrepidly.

She smiled at her grandmother before passing it to her father 'You will need two hands Father.'

He thought his daughter was joking since the weapon was somewhat longer in the blade than the standard human sabre. Nevertheless he took the sword in the scabbard with two hands and he almost toppled over trying to hold onto it.

The thing felt as if it weighed a good 40 pounds or about 20 kilos, once he'd got used to the weight McCann could hold it with one hand. He unsheathed it to find the scabbard alone was about ten times the weight of the dress sword he used for official occasions. The straight blade was forged from the same dark garnet coloured metal. From what he could tell, the whole sword had been forged from one piece of metal.

The blade had a sharp edge for three quarters of the length on the cutting edge with just a short edge on the back at the tip. Two gullies or grooves ran along the blade on either side, known as fullers they were to prevent the blade from lodging in the opponent due to pressure. They allowed air pressure to leave the body so that the person wielding it may easily withdraw it from their victim's body.

McCann couldn't hold the weapon outstretched with one arm for any longer than short burst of less than 30 seconds. It reminded him more of weight training on the Athena before Dr Weissmuller had programmed his nanites to maintain his muscle mass. Weight training was still required to a small degree to keep one's balance and this weapon felt just like his resistance training.

McCann carefully placed the sword back into the scabbard, returning it to his daughter; he shook his head in disbelief 'How on Earth do you wield that thing?'

Malikah laughed and Quil replied with a smile on her face 'Now you understand why only females lead.'

McCann made a wry look towards his mother-in-law 'What is it made of?'

'Pure Neutronium.'

McCann was in disbelief 'How?' he asked gawping at the weapon.

Quil didn't understand what the human was asking since language was so unspecific compared to thoughts, at least in her case.

Malikah stepped in 'The Neutronium was farmed from fusion reactors, many ages ago on Tlillan father.'

McCann was about to ask again since humans had entered the fusion age after the oil conflicts but the production of pure neutronium was still unattainable. The superstructure of the Athena was not pure neutronium but an alloy, similar to how iron with a tiny amount of carbon leads to steel. Carbon with a sprinkling of neutronium molecules lead to a super strong alloy referred to as catronium.

Ilam had given them the technology required to farm small amounts from their own star. However if you took all the neutronium gathered thus far by the human race you couldn't mint a single coin with it, let alone forge an entire sword!

Malikah smiled with Quil 'This one is adorable is he not?'

McCann didn't appreciate the comment his mother-in-law made, despite the fact it was intended as a compliment.

Malikah explained to her father 'On Earth we use laser fusion, a very primitive and expensive method of energy production. Farming neutronium from a laser fusion reactor is not possible, for thousands of years Tlillans have employed plasma fusion. With an efficient plasma reactor neutronium may be farmed in large quantities and relatively easily, Father.'

She unsheathed the weapon 'This weapon was forged by Ah ChuyaKak at the dawn of the first Tlillan golden age, along with two others.'

'Why forge a sword from such a rare material, what good is a sword when you have fusion technology?'

Malikah sheathed the blade, which she wielded quite easily, 'A symbol, Ah ChuyaKak united all sides of Tlillan by presenting each leader with one of these. A Twilighter was made Grand Matriarch and presented one to rule Tlillan. Ah ChuyaKak held her mantle for the Lightsiders and was made Grand Marshall of Tlillan. This one,' Malikah displayed the weapon for her father to see. 'This was presented to the Grand Priestess of the Darksiders, our race united and we went to the stars.'

'Who has the other two now?' asked McCann.

'Xch'uup and Cihuateteo are in possession of the Twilighter and Lightsider mantles respectively, without this mantle,' Malikah smiled at the weapon in her hand 'Xch'uup has no moral authority on Tlillan; her rule is stagnant without it.'

The conversation was broken by a one of the crew of the Chutli, a six and a half foot red haired beauty with that typical Tlillan bulge in the rear of the head. Her display was active projecting a holographic readout from the stiff collar of her black suit before her eyes 'Mamah, Louis Beaumont taak paktik Chutli chumuk.'

Thankfully the translator was there to fill in the words McCann was unfamiliar with 'Mother, Louis Beaumont wish view centre,' was the response from the translator. With his grounding in the Tlillan language passed on by Ilam, McCann translated it as 'Mother, Louis Beaumont wishes to view the engine core'.

Malikah replied fluently 'Chaik nohchil Beaumont chuup paktik, dyos bo'otik nohchil.'

The red haired lady bowed her head and walked away speaking into her communicator forwarding her Matriarchs instructions. Using the translator software McCann made sense of his daughter's instructions 'Allow Chief Beaumont full access, thank you Chief', the Tlillan lady must have been Chief Engineer on the Chutli.

Soon after Louis was contacting McCann, he answered the hail to hear his Chief Engineering speaking in an intelligible mix of French and English with liberal additions of obscenities.

Beaumont was excited in a positive manner, that much he could interpret. 'For Christ's sake Louis slow down!' said McCann in an irritated tone as he readjusted his ear piece.

'Have you seen this McCann!' screamed his Chief.

'Well of course I haven't you bloody idiot, you're the first on that ship Louis!'

'I'm looking at it right now this thing is fucking amazing, I can't fucking believe it!' screamed the excited Frenchman who sounded ready to explode.

'What are you looking at Louis?' asked McCann rather tiredly.

'The power core! It's a fucking fusion reactor! A real fucking fusion reactor!'

McCann peered in embarrassment at Quil and Malikah. His daughter was grinning with delight whilst his mother-in-law had an expression of shock. She probably had never seen such an unbridled display of joy with her own eyes.

'What do you mean it's "a real fusion reactor" Louis?'

'The power core is plasma held in place probably by electro magnetism. It might even use cold fusion; I can't wait to get my nanites into this thing!'

McCann observed a look of horror from Quil so quickly replied 'Just certify it and make sure she's safe Louis. If Malikah is happy with it you can take a closer look later,' his mother-in-law was relieved.

'Fine, fine I'm certifying it now. Hassif is going over the computer system; it uses some sort of chemical storage so you'll have to wait for a full report. Right now she looks safe, if that changes I'll let you know, Beaumont out.'

As McCann tapped his wrist Ryu approached holding her hands out palm upwards in the tradition Tlillan greeting. Quil replied to her greeting placing her own arms out.

Ryu looked up at Malikah 'So tell me is it true that you created that wormhole?'

Malikah still smiling replied 'Would you believe me if I told you it was?'

Ryu came back with a defiant tone 'The Gukumatz already believe it was you. I know for sure we didn't open it and no Tlillan vessel activated a wormhole generator. If the Gukumatz could have done that we wouldn't be in control of this system now.'

'The Gukumatz and all of you created that wormhole, Yong.'

Ryu frowned then pushed her glasses back up her nose 'Oh really? How did we do that then?'

Malikah's grin widened 'When the wormhole opened did your heart not beat as it had never before?'

McCann nodded 'It felt as if your heart beat in my body, did you feel it too?' he looked at Ryu.

Ryu nodded 'All of my crew reported it, the ship's doctor alerted me. He says for the time that wormhole was open all our heart beats synchronised.'

McCann nodded 'I felt it too but assumed it was just me.'

Malikah's eyes had a slight pink hue 'I am a conduit; the faith that both you and the Gukumatz possess is a powerful force.'

Ryu folded her arms 'Are you asking me to believe it was faith that opened a wormhole and created a null space field?'

'The eternal sceptic Yong, even more so than my Father. Your belief is stronger than any human I have encountered.'

Ryu maintained her matronly stare at Malikah 'I think you're confused, I don't need a god to impress.'

Malikah opened her hand and placed the palm inches away from Ryu's chest 'I can sense your will beating inside your body, yourself belief and the confidence it exudes is powerful. Do you feel it?'

Ryu felt her heart beating slower than normal but each beat was hard and pronounced, it felt as if Malikah had an influence on her, 'Yes I feel it.'

Malikah's eyes slowly clouded over 'That is your will, your spirit, your soul, your belief. Whatever you wish to name it Yong, it is coursing through your body. Your body is merely a shell anchoring it to the physical universe.'

Malikah placed her hand palm up and inside the dimly light cargo bay, the air above her palm began to release light. Malikah was breathing deeply and McCann felt his heart thumping in that same slow rhythmic fashion it had on the bridge of the Athena.

Light started coming together above Malikah's palm to form a glowing orb about half the size of Ryu's head. Inside McCann saw a scene of a green field, a rice paddy in the summer. The day was warm with a light breeze and someone was working in the field. A man in his fifties was pruning his field with a small girl. The girl was about ten, playing with the old man who wore a denim work shirt with white trousers rolled above his knees. He was obviously no stranger to hard work since he had muscular thighs and easily carried the child on his back as he bent over picking out rotting vegetation from his field.

Ryu took in a sharp breath 'Ah-bu-ji.'

The tranquil scene was beautiful, the rice swayed with the breeze, McCann was sure he could hear rice stalks rustling as the wind changed direction. The old man stopped what he was doing and stood up with the little girl clinging onto his sturdy shoulders. He lifted the brim of his wicker hat to view his wrist tablet. He then took the child from his shoulders and hurriedly made his way to dry land. Before he reached it McCann made out rising smoke in the distance. When McCann noticed six dots approach in the distance he understood what he was seeing.

Ryu was unable to move as her eyes locked onto the floating orb 'Ah-bu-ji,' she repeated over and over under her breath; until six scram drones flew over dispersing nerve gas above the fields. As her father began to lose consciousness and fell into his own rice paddy she let out a blood curdling scream 'Ah-bu-ji!'

The old man drowned to death but somehow the child survived and used his floating body to drag herself to the land. A single tear ran down Ryu's cheek, other than that there was no emotion.

The scene faded but the orb remained, next a face appeared inside the orb. McCann recognised it as the old man he'd just witnessed drown to death in his rice paddy. He was seemingly in good health and smiling, Ryu drew another sharp breath and McCann could hear the sound of powerful emotion as her lungs inhaled.

The old man spoke in what McCann guessed was Korean.

Ryu shook her head 'It can't be him; he died in the first assault.'

Malikah didn't react but the old man spoke again, Ryu still shook her head 'You could have read my mind, this could all be a trick.'

He carried on speaking and Ryu decided to reply, a conversation began and it was evident she had come to an agreement with the old man.

The old man smiled 'An-nyung to ggi.'

Ryu made a polite smile and replied 'An-nyung Ah-bu-ji.'

Malikah closed her hand consuming the orb and its light, McCann felt his heart return to normal as her eyes cleared. The Englishman put his hand on Ryu's shoulder frightening his comrade for a moment 'Yong are you alright?' he asked in a hushed tone.

Ryu steadied herself and wiping the tear from her cheek she nodded 'I'm fine thanks.'

'Was that your father?' inquired McCann.

Ryu removed her glasses for a second to wipe her eye 'I don't know, maybe ... we'll see. Can we talk about it later?'

McCann patted her shoulder 'Whenever you are ready, just give me a bell.'

Ryu smiled at her comrade and squeezed his hand.

McCann looked at his daughter and snapped 'That wasn't fair Malikah, you can't play with people like that.'

Ryu cut in 'It's alright Duncan, I'm fine.'

McCann gave his daughter a black look 'We'll talk about this later Malikah, until then I don't want you pulling anymore stunts, is that understood?'

Malikah lost her smile and looked at the floor as a naughty schoolgirl 'I understand Father.'

McCann immediately felt guilty, 'Shall we get a roster of the crew?'

Malikah looked up and at her grandmother, without saying anything Quil nodded and walked to organise a tally of surviving crew members.

McCann pulled a leather case from his chest zip pocket and removed a Ramon Allones small club corona. He used a cigar punch attached to the case to punch the cap and a small torch lighter in the case to toast the foot. He took a drag then exhaled. Ryu witnessed every muscle in his body relax immediately as the thick smoke swirled out of his nose and mouth.

Ryu waved her hand in front of her face 'What are you smoking that for?'

McCann grinned 'We'll be here for a few days; these will make it bearable at least.'

Ryu frowned 'Three days?'

'You're in quarantine now Yong. You did insist on coming with us.'

Ryu put her palm onto her face slowly and groaned 'I did, didn't I!'

Chapter 20

Once the quarantine was over the Ilium system was re-designated. The moon of Ilium 1 was now named Kotumatz, Ilium 2 Tolomatz and Ilium 3 Bokumatz. The system had taken its former name of Gukumatz AB. Each moon taking the name of its first spawning pool, though the orbital stations kept the Ilium tags.

McCann felt it all rather pointless but his daughter disagreed, so he made no comment on her changes. The Gukumatz were no doubt pleased with the changes and to be honest he didn't care enough to make a fuss.

Now that all of clan Chutli were exiled the Tlillan's were unperturbed by Ilam taking the Captain's seat of the clan vessel. Seeing his wife take her own command sent a warm feeling of satisfaction through the Englishman. He knew that look on his wife's face, one of accomplishment. Playing second fiddle to her husband had probably been getting her down. For a Tlillan female it must have been quite depressing to watch your husband commanding warships and governing star systems; whilst all the time you sat at home taking lessons from your mother-in-law on motherhood.

As time went by many of the Matriarchs found themselves husbands amongst the human personnel working in Gukumatz AB. It was quite a sight to behold when McCann visited the nursery on Ilium 1. Malikah had purposely engineered the situation, of that McCann was sure. Walking around the nursery with his wife they both stopped outside the classroom. He stood close enough that his breath condensed on the glass.

'What are you starring at my dear?' asked his flaming haired wife.

'All of those children,' replied McCann.

'They are beautiful are they not?'

'She's created a new race, Ilam.'

The red haired Valkyrie took a step closer and peered in to the class of half Tlillan, half Human children being taught mathematics.

Ilam sighed 'Perhaps.'

'What do you mean perhaps?'

'A few are Mictlancihuatl the others are not. Remember Duncan your daughter is the only Mictlancihuatl to have survived this long. The others are not even a year old, they must still prove themselves.'

With that every child turned its head to look at Ilam, despite sound proof walls.

McCann laughed 'It seems the girls heard you! Don't you feel it's odd that all twenty two children born from the Chutli crew are female?'

Ilam shook her head 'No, should I?'

'Well why not produce some Tlillan males?'

Ilam nearly laughed again 'Human males are of a better quality in every sense. Besides we require Matriarchs to re-populate Tlillan, males are worthless.'

The children's attention returned to their teacher concentrating on their work, they were mostly about the size of an eight year old human. Three of the group exhibited signs of being Mictlancihuatl much the same as Malikah. As to whether they could survive maturity that was unknown, Malikah had survived but she was the only one. Malikah spent extra time with the three Mictlancihuatl girls giving them lessons in controlling the madness. Even she was unsure as to whether they would survive but the other 19 seemed to be fine.

'What do the Gukumatz make of these children?' asked McCann pointing to the three Mictlancihuatl girls.

'They watch and wait.'

'Wait for what?'

'To see if they are a miracle, a Teootl similar to Malikah.'

'If they survive, what then?'

Ilam looked solemnly at her husband 'Then the universe's ruling caste will have been founded here.'

McCann sniggered to himself.

'You find me amusing Duncan?'

'Your Tlillan delusions of grandeur never cease to amuse me.'

Ilam grinned 'And your human cynicism never fails to amuse either Duncan.'

McCann removed a cigar from his chest pocket; he removed it from the tubos and clipped the cap. He was now used to using matches when lighting his smokes. The last twenty four months he'd spent patrolling and upgrading his living situation on the Athena. Besides it was a little cumbersome carrying a welding torch around with him and the cedar matches imparted a pleasant aroma. He took a draw of the Habanos letting out a sigh of relief as he expelled the smoke.

His flaming haired wife smiled as she observed her husband take pleasure in one of his few vices, 'For your information Tlillans do not have delusions of grandeur.'

McCann smiled and put his right arm through his wife's left 'Of course not, I was only joking my dear!'

As he finished his sentence Ilam froze where she stood, staring at the Englishman 'You lied to me!'

McCann nervously fondled his cigar 'Excuse me?'

Ilam grew more indignant 'I said you lied to me, you do believe Tlillans to have an inflated opinion of themselves ... don't you Duncan?'

He took a short puff on his robusto cigar 'Yes, I'm sorry.'

'Do not apologise for your true feelings Duncan, however do not lie to me.'

McCann stood speechless as a naughty schoolboy until Quil entered into the hall way. Dressed in her Tlillan space suit with a white diplomatic corps jacket on top, she approached the pair.

'Are you coming Duncan?' she asked pointing towards the classroom.

"Why not?" he said putting out his cigar.

'Today I'll be imparting the story of our escape from the home world. I thought you may want to take part, perhaps see if you might link with the children?'

McCann shrugged his shoulders 'I'll give it go.'

The threesome entered the classroom and waited silently for the mathematics lesson to end. Once it was over and the Human teacher left, Quil sat down on the teacher's desk 'Today we shall be ending with the story of how your mothers escaped the home world.'

A small girl with bright red hair raised her hand and Quil pointed to her 'Yes Olga?'

The child who seemed to be at least eight years of age was actually eight months 'Quilachutli, we have already been told this story several times.'

McCann took an empty seat amongst the children's desks and Ilam sat next to her mother.

'I know,' replied Quil 'this time I'm going to link with you and tell you the story that way. Now has everyone here linked with their Mothers already?'

The children all replied positively 'We shall also have a guest linking with us today, say hello to Commodore McCann.'

Olga raised her hand again and Quil pointed to her 'Yes Olga?'

'Quilachutli, how will the Commodore understand you?'

A girl with straight jet black hair, a Mictlancihuatl, let out a sigh 'He understands Tlillan.'

Quil smiled in approval at the dark haired girl 'Correct Kaeo, the Commodore should be able to follow most of the story if not all.'

Olga raised her hand again but before Quil could ask Kaeo let out another sigh.

Quil put down her hand and peered at Kaeo 'Why don't you answer Olga's question Kaeo?'

Kaeo who bore a striking resemblance to a Twilighter turned to face Olga 'We are outcasts, we cannot commit heresy.'

Olga disagreed 'Our mothers may be exiles but we are not, to link with a male is an act of heresy.'

McCann raised his hand and Quil motioned for him to speak 'I was under the impression that the law only applied to Tlillan males, am I right?'

Olga thought for a moment 'Xch'uup has not decided on whether you are Tlillan or not. Until then I feel it would be best to remain cautious.'

Kaeo spoke up again 'In that case she hasn't decided if you are Tlillan either, has she?'

Olga looked decidedly uncomfortable 'Well you are Mictlancihuatl!'

Quil sat back to observe the debate.

Kaeo was un-phased by Olga's comments 'And what might you be Olga?'

Olga spoke through her teeth 'I am my Mother's daughter.'

'As am I,' replied Kaeo 'and I wish to link with the Commodore. If you do not then no one is forcing you, but do not enforce that twisted Gorgon's values on me!'

Olga's eyes began to turn a shade of burgundy until Quil shouted at the child 'Enough!'

Kaeo laughed mockingly, since Olga clearly didn't have the ability to subdue her, but stopped her laughter when she sensed Quil's eyes burning into the side of her head.

'If one of you does not wish to link then you may be excused. As Kaeo said no one is to be forced to link ... well?'

After scanning the room for a moment Quil saw that everyone was curious to link with McCann, even Olga.

Quil closed her eyes as did the children; she breathed slowly and as she did McCann felt his mind slipping. Slowly with each breath his consciousness edged somewhere else, a place where Quil seemed to be in control. As he looked around he realised he was on a star ship, a Tlillan cruiser to be exact. Tall women stood around the room at various work stations. The bulbous silver and scarlet heads told him that he'd been spirited away to the Chutli.

A young women approached him and bowed her head with palms open to the ceiling 'Yaaxil Quilachutli, Chutli k'uchul Otoch.'

McCann struggled to understand her odd accent but he quickly made sense of her words and replied in perfect Tlillan 'Dyos bo'otik, okol Otoch.'

Somehow he understood her perfectly and she had no difficulty in comprehending his response. Then he realised she had addressed him as Quilachutli and he must be seeing this through her eyes. The vessel was entering orbit of Otoch, the I.S.A named the world Tlillan but its true designation was Otoch.

Gazing through Quilachutli's eyes he took his first look upon the world via the Chutli's view screen. What he saw was a sight that must have been one of the great wonders of the galaxy, perhaps universe. Otoch was fixed in tidal lock around its sun, from the surface of the world sprouted countless towers constructed of neutronium. The towers were for the most part defunct but before the plague McCann imagined what must have been an awe inspiring civilization. Today literally a few towers were being put to use; ferrying goods to and fro from orbit to the surface and back via electromagnetic rails.

He felt a shiver of fear race down his frame as he gazed upon the countless orbital towers. Surely a race that constructed this could laugh off the Gukumatz? After all his primitive excuse for a race managed to defeat them. It made no sense as to why a race of creatures that built this couldn't see off some foul toads with halitosis!

As the cruiser entered orbit a message came from the surface, it was Cihuateteo. McCann couldn't understand all that was said but she wanted Quil down on the surface. Apparently there was trouble over Malikah having revealed the Grand Matriarch's plans to assassinate other Tlillans.

Quil took a shuttle down to the dark side of the planet and the city Tititl. Upon exiting the shuttle McCann was stunned by how well he could see in the dark. Despite there being a poor glow that barely lit the sky, he could see as if it were a clear day on Earth. He noticed the fresh crispness of the atmosphere as he strode out to meet the reception party.

On the landing pad stood Cihuateteo and a few of her Matriarchs. Quil bowed her head and placed her hands out, palms to the sky 'Ola Cihuateteo.'

Cihuateteo replied with the same gesture 'Ola Quilachutli.'

The pair began to discuss the situation on Tlillan. Apparently Malikah had set off a shit storm and clans were now standing against one another. As Quil was lead to the temple of Tititl she had the situation explained. From what McCann gathered the Grand Matriarch required Quil's vote, he wasn't certain exactly what the vote was on but it was important.

The party walked through the streets of stone and glass surrounded by buildings he assumed were housing. After about twenty minutes McCann noticed the peak of the temple rising above the city. It was a massive step pyramid constructed from blocks of gigantic smoothed stones. The temple had moss and lichen growing all up the sides. On the top sat a large dish with coals smouldering in it, sending cinders off into the night air.

McCann walked through the town until eventually the path that Cihuateteo had led them down could be seen ending inside the temple entrance. He could see that this had once been a great civilization, far more developed than anything they'd yet encountered. Upon entering the temple the Englishman marvelled at how thick the walls were.

They were led through a tunnel and into a massive hall, the Grand Matriarch sat at the opposite end on what must have been her throne. Above were statues, of whom the Englishman had no idea, adorning the many levels of the step pyramid.

The party made their way to the Grand Matriarch 'Ola Xch'uup,' greeted both Quil and Cihuateteteo.

The Grand Matriarch dressed in a golden cape and feathered headdress started speaking on a subject that was obviously rather pressing. From what McCann gathered there was to be a vote that somehow concerned her rule. The clan vote was split and Quil was to decide which way it went.

McCann got the impression that Quil was going to vote against the old Gorgon and she seemed to know it.

The scene changed, no longer was Quil speaking to the Grand Matriarch. She was now in a dark chamber accompanied by three Tlillan females who were clad in white robes. They reminded McCann of ancient druids, from what he gathered these ladies were the seers of the temple. They seemed intent on breaking Quil out of this dungeon which the Gorgon had tossed her into.

Using their power of foresight the seers selected a time to lead her out of the temple. Quil made it to the nearest orbital tower where the seers sent her on her way. After being fired into orbit she was collected by the Chutli. The seers had alerted the clan and advised them on making a quick escape before Xch'uup might exact revenge.

Quil made her way to the bridge where a discussion over their next course of action began. Opinion was divided as to whether they could trust the seers, half of the officers were certain the break out was staged by Xch'uup. The other half felt the seers were sincere and they should leap upon the opportunity while it exists.

Quil was undecided, whilst they debated what to do next an odd light appeared between the officers and the view screen. All conversation halted to observe the phenomenon as it grew in size and intensity. The bridge officers declared the object to be non-existent according to their instruments, yet it was there before them. After a minute or so the object took a familiar form, familiar to Quil at least.

On the bridge of the Chutli stood Malikah 'Ola mamich.'

The crew looked at Quil who stepped forward towards the image standing on her bridge 'Ola aabil.'

'The escape is a plot to remove you from clan Matriarch, grandmother. Cihuateteo waits for you with Chanatico.'

Quil was baffled however she spoke to the image 'What of the other clans?'

'They will not assist you, yet they refuse to assist Cihuateteo for now.'

'What course of action do you suggest I take?'

Malikah smiled 'Cihuateteo and Chanatico await with their clan ships on the outer skirts of the system. They wait for you to leave the system in order to fold space; you must do the opposite and hide around the inner planets and moons.'

'Until?'

'Three days from now is when you must fold space, not before. After three days of playing hide and seek you may fold space to Gukumatz.'

Quil pulled a puzzled expression 'Hide and seek?'

'A Human game. Once you reach Gukumatz the humans shall be prepared. Do you understand Mamich?'

The tall silver haired beauty nodded 'I understand.'

'The other two clan ships shall become involved on the second day, so be careful Mamich.'

The image of Malikah waved as she faded from the deck of the bridge. Quil set a course for the inner planets of the Tlillan system. Using the strong magnetic field of the closest planet to the sun the Chutli entered orbit cloaking itself.

Ten hours later and the hunt was on, the Teteo and Tico both searching for the Chutli amongst the magnetic mess spewed out in the inner solar system. By the second day the other two clan ships had been reluctantly dragged into the search. The Chutli clan were now wanted persons, having moved every Matriarch to the clan ship and disappeared with their first Matriarch.

McCann experienced the cat and mouse games, it was all too familiar to him. The Chutli took several heavy hits to her main body, thankfully the magnetic fields caused the enemies targeting to be somewhat off.

By the third day it was time to leave, playing hide and seek had left the Chutli cornered hopping around the moon of the inner planet. The four clan ships searching for them were watching from high orbit so that Quil couldn't slip past and open a wormhole. The Chutli was trapped orbiting these moons; Quil took a big risk and decided to open a wormhole whilst still in orbit.

It was a wreckless manoeuvre that could have easily caused the cruiser to be sucked into the moon. However it was either that or fight off four cruisers whilst trying to make enough distance to fold space. The latter wasn't a possibility in Quil's opinion.

The navigation officer opened a wormhole at a right angle to the moon 'Tunnel established and stable.'

Quil sat in her chair 'Enter the white hole before it pushes us into the moon.'

The Chutli raised her Casimir field and fired all engines; slowly she pushed her way into the wormhole just as the enemy was descending upon them.

'The Teteo has detected us and is entering weapons range.'

Quil maintained her stony glare at the white hole swirling before her 'Ignore it, continue into the tunnel.'

The navigator a red haired beauty was becoming extremely agitated 'The Teteo has locked onto us Quil!'

'Maintain course'

A scarlet haired lady who McCann assumed was the equivalent of his science officer spoke 'The Teteo is ordering us to disengage our Casimir field and close our wormhole.'

'Ignore her.'

'Cihuateteo threatens to open fire if we do not.'

'Ignore her.'

The spinning white mass loomed closer and the Englishman could sense the fear from all the crew. Then the Chutli was rocked by a horrendous crunch to her port side.

'Direct hit port side, minor damage.'

Another crunching thud hit the side of the vessel though the crew seemed oddly relieved.

The science officer reported on the damage with a surprised tone 'We have suffered minor damage to the port side, I believe Cihuateteo is allowing us to escape.'

Quil looked at her damage display 'Let us at least make this look good for Xch'uup. Target the Teteo with port lasers, fire at 10% intensity.'

The woman that must have been the weapons officer worked away 'Target lock established.'

'Fire.'

The port lasers fired with enough intensity to breach the armour of the Teteo, though not enough to cause any serious damage. The Teteo returned fire burning a trench along the port side of the Chutli. The battle was a mock battle for the benefit of the Grand Matriarch. Cihuateteo didn't want to murder her sisters and Quil only wished to escape, but Xch'uup had to be satisfied.

Before the Tico could arrive the Chutli had disappeared into the white hole, the ride to Gukumatz was rather rough.

Upon arrival the I.S.A fleet awaited and accepted asylum of the exiles. Soon afterwards the remainder of the Tlillan fleet arrived and McCann found that his memories were now being delved into. All the children observed intently as he played brinksmanship and then watched his sable daughter create the null space.

McCann could sense Kaeo's excitement, when she observed Malikah open a massive white hole and cast the helpless cruisers inside. Kaeo hoped to one day achieve similar feats, he next felt Olga's jealousy. Somehow she sensed he was focusing on her and curbed her emotional state.

Once the battle was over and they had docked Quil ended her link, McCann was quite tired by the experience and Ilam sat by him comforting her exhausted husband, Ilam massaged her husband back into a state of consciousness.

Quil stood before the awakened class 'Are there any questions?'

Olga raised her hand 'When shall we return to Otoch?'

Kaeo answered her cutting off Quil 'This time next year we shall set foot on Otoch again and Malikah shall be Xch'uup.'

Ilam accosted the girl 'Who told you that?'

Kaeo grinned 'It is in the dreamscape Ilamachutli.'

'How do you see so clearly into the dreamscape child?'

'Malikah has demonstrated how to use the dreamscape, with her assistance I can see clearly into multiple futures.'

Quil sighed 'Then let us hope you see clearly, for us to return in such a manner would be a great triumph.'

McCann raised his hand 'My question is if we're aware of Cihuateteo's disregard for orders surely the Grand Matriarch is aware also?'

Quil nodded and scanned the children 'A good question, is Xch'uup aware of Cihuateteo's treachery? If so what would you think she is doing about it?'

Another child with short dark hair raised her hand, 'Sandra what do you think?'

Sandra was the latest Mictlancihuatl to have been born. Her father was an officer on the Ilium 1 station and had fallen for a tall white haired Tlillan lady. His daughter was named after his mother whom lived in Crete.

Faraday had been spending a lot on weddings since the Chutli had sought asylum in Gukumatz. Though the benefits of having children like Sandra, Kaeo and Amitrasudan working for him easily outweighed the expenses of playing father of the bride.

Sandra peered towards McCann 'Xch'uup is aware yet she does nothing. Cihuateteo is her greatest supporter and to create a schism would be foolish. Xch'uup's power is no more than a house of cards as it stands. She strives to maintain the status quo, we are beyond her grasp and Cihuateteo is too powerful to challenge.'

Quil smiled with pleasure at the young girl's ability 'Excellent Sandra, does Amitrasudan agree with you?'

A child seemingly twelve years of age answered 'Sandra is correct, Quilachutli,' she was the oldest of the children. Her mother met her father in quarantine; he was none other than Hassif himself. Very popular amongst the Tlillan ladies, it had been like watching an old fashioned Texas land grab!

Louis had no idea as to why the Tlillan females were so excited by the very thought of the short Indian, yet they were. Ryu and McCann found it all quite amusing as Hassif was hunted by a crew of women more than a foot taller than himself. According to Ilam his superior intelligence was the attraction, Tlillan was a meritocracy and selecting a mate was defined by his ability.

Amitrasudan had by far the sharpest mind of any being McCann had encountered. She even put Hassif to shame, not that the Indian cared, he was constantly gushing over his prodigy. Amitrasudan loved her father, often remaining quiet so as not to be-shadow Hassif.

Her mother was the proudest member of the Chutli, after having used her good looks and all 7 feet of her slim taught frame to hook the Navigation officer of the Athena. McCann still chuckled a little when he saw them together, he used to call them the odd couple. Until Malikah pointed out he and Louis were the only people that found his humour amusing.

Apparently Amitrasudan had spoken with his sable daughter on the subject and McCann now kept his pet name for the pair to himself.

Amitrasudan had the ability to run mathematical equations through her head solving them faster than a supercomputer. Her grasp of particle physics outstripped anyone or anything, past or present, and Faraday salivated just on the mention of her name.

Kaeo had a gift with telepathy, her power over the mind was expected to see her past maturity and prevent any madness. The only person with the ability to subdue Kaeo was Malikah, although Kaeo never crossed her father. A drone engineer from Thailand, he was the only person besides Malikah whom Kaeo obeyed without question.

Sandra's gift was the dreamscape and her future sight, Sandra could see into minds far away. The child of a Greek medical officer for Ilium 1 her future seemed bright provided she made it past maturity.

McCann listened to the girls' assessment of the situation on Tlillan and chuckled whispering under his breath to Ilam 'Shiny happy people holding hands!'

Quil failed to understand his statement and Sandra read her feelings 'The Commodore is referring to the Tiananmen Square massacre of twentieth century communist China.'

McCann shook his head 'Really I didn't mean to mention …'

Quil ignored him and maintained her gaze on Sandra 'Go on, what was the Commodore thinking Sandra?'

Sandra made a naughty look towards McCann but he motioned for her to continue. The Englishman was interested to see how accurately she'd read into his thoughts.

'The Commodore was referring to one of his favourite songs. It is based on a propaganda poster that was displayed in the aftermath of the Tiananmen Square massacre. The poster declared "Shiny happy people holding hands"; the song was intended to mock the communist government but was misunderstood by many at the time. Rather than taken ironically most took the song to be literal. I believe the Commodore was making a comparison between Xch'uup, Deng Xiaoping and the predicament on the home world and communist China of 20th century Earth.'

McCann clapped the dark haired child 'Excellent Sandra, despite your intrusiveness. Tell me am I right in my assumption?'

Sandra said nothing only nodded her head in agreement.

McCann smiled at the child 'What do you think of the song?'

'I'll listen to it after class Commodore; it is difficult to listen to it properly from another's memory. Though I think I will enjoy it, and I'm sorry for invading your privacy, Sir.'

McCann stood up with the help of his wife 'Well I'm gonna have to love you and leave you ladies. I do suggest you all research Tiananmen Square; it was an important event in human history. It also communicates what happens when a government fights against the will of its own citizens. Although the Chinese communists staved it off they eventually surcame to the pressure of the people. Compare their collapse to what the Russians did when Moscow was presented with the same choice.'

McCann walked out of the room gaining strength in his legs as he was assisted by his wife, linking for such long periods was difficult for him.

Thankfully Ilam was there to assist his recovery 'That was the first time you linked with the girls, was it not dear?' she said affectionately.

'Yes, I didn't realise how draining they are.'

Ilam produced a tubos carrying a cigar 'Here you are.'

McCann sighed in pleasure 'Thank you, tell me was that girl right about us being on Tlillan in a year?'

'Perhaps,' said Ilam as she lit his cigar for him 'It is a possible future, as time goes by and it approaches we shall see if the possibility increases or not.'

McCann took a draw from his cigar 'I hope those girls make it, especially Amitrasudan.'

'Why especially her?' asked Ilam with a furrowed brow.

McCann shook his head slowly in disbelief 'Because she is Hassif's daughter.'

'And?'

'And if she died it would be painful to watch my friend go through such a terrible thing.'

Ilam laughed a little 'You say that Tlillans are cold yet you would rather another child than your friend's died in order to save you from the emotional pain? Is that not a cold heartless train of thought Duncan?'

McCann thought for a moment whilst smoking his tobacco then expelling the smoke from his nostrils he replied 'Yes I suppose it is, if you were to look at it totally logically.'

Ilam kissed her husband on the cheek 'That is why I love you, because you are not a cold and boringly logical man. No offence was intended Duncan.'

McCann laughed 'My dear if you intended to offend me I would have known it. I'm sure you could do a lot worse than calling me selfish!'

They locked their arms and continued strolling along the outer ring of Ilium 1.

Six months later and McCann was strolling around the bridge of the Athena. He spent much of his time between the bridge, lounge and recreation decks where he practiced his fencing on a weekly basis. The Athena spent most of her time in Gukumatz AB where she was assigned as the ship of the fleet. Titov patrolled Earth in the Ares whilst Ryu slipped unnoticed between the two in the Hera. The Chutli remained docked whilst the technology was taken apart then reassembled. The construction of new plasma fusion reactors was already taking place on Earth thanks to Louis discoveries. Faraday hoped to replace the laser fusion reactors, allowing the I.S.A to produce both anti-matter fuel and neutronium in large quantities.

So far it was another rather boring day for McCann, since the Chutli had sought asylum nothing of any consequence had happened. This was the way he liked it, he could take pleasure in his vices of Cuban cigars and Scotch whisky with little to no stress. His wife was in command of the Chutli and it pleased her to no end, despite the extended time it spent in dock.

This morning was to be different, whilst patrolling above the accretion disk Hassif informed him of an incoming message. The communication was from Huixachutli, Hassif's wife, McCann feared it concerned Amitrasudan. His navigation officer gave him a very concerned look as his Commodore took the short walk to his office.

Inside McCann looked upwards at the ceiling 'Athena, play the message in here please.'

'Certainly Duncan,' replied the warm familiar voice of Athena.

McCann raised his eyebrows at Athena's familiarity; she would refer to him by name even when on duty now. However in public she would still use his rank, only when off duty or alone would she use his first name. An image leapt from the tiny holo projector installed into his desk, it was Huixachutli, one of the tallest Tlillans McCann had ever seen.

McCann was as shocked as Louis and Ryu when their marriage was announced. Malikah and Ilam were naturally well aware of the relationship but for reasons unknown to him they didn't speak of it. McCann found out when the Indian asked him to be best man 'Best man for what?' inquired McCann. Hassif went on to inform him of his relationship and how he felt it necessary to marry.

The image stood on his desk was a live feed 'Commodore McCann I wish to request my husband's presence. Our daughter has been taken into med bay 2, she has reached maturity.'

It was bound to happen soon, McCann had a shuttle prepared in anticipation 'Very well, I'll have Hassif transported immediately, to Ilium 1?'

The white haired Amazon realised she hadn't informed McCann of the station 'Yes, my apologies.'

'That's quite alright, is Malikah there?'

'Malikah is meditating with her now; hopefully with her assistance Amitrasudan will overcome the madness.'

McCann nodded 'Alright I'll get Hassif, see you soon Huix.'

'Thank you Duncan, Huix out.'

McCann marched onto the bridge 'Hassif set a course for Ilium 1.'

His friend paused looking at the Englishman waiting for confirmation of his fears.

'Yes it's Amitra. We'll take a shuttle to the station as soon as we arrive. Vezzali inform Commander Kim he'll be taking the bridge.'

As the cruiser made her way into orbit of Kotumatz, McCann and Hassif marched briskly to the shuttle bay.

Hassif was visibly sweating 'I could feel her pain, even when we were light years away. Do you think I'm imagining it?'

McCann shook his head 'No, I've experienced exactly the same thing with Malikah. Don't try and explain it man.'

'I wish it was just in my mind, the pain is excruciating.'

McCann put a hand on his friend's shoulder 'Look at it this way, you at least know she's alive.'

Hassif nodded in agreement 'True!'

The pair entered the bay through the airlock, as it closed behind them the side of the shuttle rippled open. They both entered and sat down in the bucket seats 'We're going to med bay 2 Athena.'

'Understood Duncan, please secure yourselves for shuttle bay clearance,' replied Athena softly.

Athena piloted the shuttle to the closest docking bay. After docking she bid good luck to Hassif 'My concerns are with your daughter Hassif, I hope she survives.'

Hassif stepped out of the craft and thanked his synthetic friend 'Thank you Athena.'

The pair walked out of the airlock to be met by Ilam 'Follow me,' she stated coldly.

As they followed, Hassif began to inquire about his daughter 'What is the situation with Amit?'

'The pain began this morning; the doctor assumed it was merely a headache. Malikah however foresaw the madness; she began meditating with her early in the morning. So far Amitra has remained conscious, nobody knows her exact condition. She has remained alone with Malikah for the entire morning.'

The threesome entered the med bay where Huixachutli stood pretending not to be concerned for her daughter's life. Upon observing her husband enter she lost her Tlillan control and hugged him. Leaning down the 7ft 4 inch Amazon grasped her husband tightly 'How is she?' inquired Hassif.

'She has been inside the medical bay since early this morning. Malikah has been in deep meditation with her, they are suppressing the pain of her mindscape. I believe Amitrasudan is conquering her pain, she is too strong to be driven to madness.' commented an almost tearful mother.

Hassif peered into the medical bay through the plastic window 'I can feel her mind, she is sharing the pain with Malikah. If it grows too strong they can share it with me.'

Ilam gave an incredulous look 'It would kill you Hassif, you can not accept such a burden!'

Hassif didn't reply but McCann made a dangerous glance towards his wife. Ilam was using her tried and trusted Tlillan logic. As far as she was concerned he and Huix could just have another child if this one failed to pass maturity. Putting his life on the line for Amitrasudan was a foolish wager in her opinion. Had it been Malikah however, McCann was certain Ilam's outlook would have been very different.

As the day passed Hassif reported the burn of his daughter's agony reduce, until eventually it was no longer present. The party waited intently until sometime in the early evening Malikah's eyes opened and Hassif felt himself ease down once she smiled. Amitrasudan opened her eyes, her gaze met Malikah's and she returned a warm smile. Malikah stood up from her position of sitting on the floor which both she and Amitrasudan had maintained the entire day. She helped Amitrasudan to her feet; McCann took a sneaky glance at Huixachutli. He noticed a single tear roll down the hardened Valkyrie's cheek, she quickly brushed it away. Huix acknowledged McCann as she removed the sign of weakness from her face. The Englishman said nothing but walked to the side of the door to wait for the only two Mictlancihuatls to survive puberty.

The door to the medical bay slid open and out walked Amitrasudan, 'Namaste Father,' said Amitrasudan putting her palms together in front of her face then bowing to her father.

Hassif returned the gesture before embracing his daughter; she was already taller than the Indian though McCann still towered above her ... for now.

McCann was very envious of Amitra's politeness; the child had dark skin like her father and showed him the greatest respect. In fact she displayed respect to all adults always, however her father was treated as if he were a king. There wasn't a single parent that didn't envy Hassif and Huix or comment on their good fortune.

After Hassif had finished hugging his daughter she approached Huixachutli and bowed with palms pressed before her face 'Namaste Mother.'

It had taken time for Huix to become accustomed to the traditional Indian greeting. At first the tall Tlillan was against such foreign gestures. Yet the stubborn white haired lady warmed to it upon discovering the meaning of Namaste. Also the reaction of other parents convinced her that despite its alien origins the greeting "I bow to you" would more than suffice.

For a long time Huix had resisted returning the gesture to her daughter. It would be improper for a Tlillan Matriarch to bow to her child, yet as time progressed she felt uncomfortable not doing so. Huix put her palms together and bowed before her daughter 'Namaste.'

As Amitra hugged her mother Malikah exited the room smiling at Hassif. The Indian technician approached her and bowed 'Namaste Malikah.'

Malikah returned his greeting 'Namaste Hassif, Amitrasudan should be fine.'

'Thank you so much, I could feel the agony even on the Athena it must have been terrible for you?'

Malikah maintained her smile 'Your concern should remain with Amitrasudan, but thank you for your thought.'

Hassif shook his head in refusal 'Don't be silly, if it were not for you Amitrasudan may not have survived. Your welfare will always be my concern Malikah.'

Malikah embraced Hassif and whispered in his ear 'I know but your wife and daughter need you now.'

She released the small Indian who looked to see his family, waiting for him to finish his conversation with the Icon. Hassif walked over to comfort his wife and daughter, as he did so McCann and Ilam congratulated Malikah on her victory.

'So no Namaste for me?' said McCann in a sarcastic tone to his sable daughter who stood a good 6 ft 4 inches now. She only replied by rolling her eyes, he turned to Ilam and stated in the same tone 'You see I never get any respect around here!'

Ilam laughed but Malikah didn't find him as funny 'Father, you get more respect than anyone else I know!'

McCann pulled a tubos out of his breast pocket and began lighting up his cigar 'Really? I don't remember the last time someone bowed to me. I'll tell you what, how about you giving me a kowtow right now?'

As he made his joke McCann was unaware of some Gukumatz med bay staff behind him. The three Gukumatz nurses who were about to clear out med bay 2 stopped dead in their tracks; human sarcasm was something most Gukumatz were unable to identify. It was difficult for Tlillan's at the best of times but these toads took his words as literal. From their point of view they'd just witnessed McCann a mere mortal demand the Teootl, for all intents and purposes a God figure, kowtow before him.

Malikah stared her father in the eye 'If you want me to bow before you, you need only ask Father.'

The room went uncomfortably quiet 'Don't be silly, I was only joking Malikah!' he said blowing smoke out of his mouth.

The Gukumatz kowtowed and Malikah spoke 'Liik'il much.'

The Englishman turned around to see the three toads rise and continue with their work, he turned back to his daughter.

Malikah had an "I told you so" expression plastered all over her face, 'That sense of humour might get you in trouble one day Father!'

McCann took a drag from his Hoyo De Monterry cigar 'Marvellous!'

She smiled and leaned down to kiss her father on the cheek 'Don't worry Father no one would dare harm you or Mother.'

Malikah turned to her mother 'You'll have to take better care of him in future Mother. I can't always be here to save his neck you know?'

Ilam smiled at her husband lovingly 'I understand but he is so stubborn and naughty, have you tried keeping him out of trouble 24/7?'

Huixachutli and Amitrasudan both laughed out loud, Hassif then realised it was the Tlillan ladies attempt at humour and chuckled.

'Will Amitra be alright from now on?' inquired McCann.

'Amitrasudan shall be fine, just take a few days of rest and report back to me,' smiled Malikah.

The two families left the medical bay and split up, Hassif's family leaving for their quarters on Ilium 1; whilst McCann went for a stroll with his family along the observation ring of the station. His family had spent so much time apart, due to work they had less and less time to spend together and McCann treasured each moment.

'Ofra will be visiting Gukumatz next month Father,' stated Malikah with a cheeky grin.

'That's not possible, she's terrified of flying and there's no way my mother would step foot on the orbital lift!' said McCann puffing on his panetela cigar.

'Oh no, Hassif's parents are coming to see their granddaughter. They have convinced Ofra to take the trip with them.'

McCann shook his head as they strolled along the observation ring 'My Mother would not willingly enter a wormhole, trust me Malikah. You may have foresight but I know my Mother.'

'Your Father shall be accompanying her, Duncan,' noted Ilam as she slid her arm in his.

McCann stopped strolling and gave his wife a hard stare 'Are you serious?'

'Of course I am!'

'Just wonderful! Now I'm gonna have to deal with Laurel and bloody Hardy for two weeks!'

Ilam tried to hold a straight face though Malikah was somewhat puzzled 'I'm sorry father I don't understand.'

Ilam caught her daughters sight 'Link with me.'

After a few moments of silence Malikah scowled at her father 'That's not very funny at all Father!'

McCann expelled the thick smoke from his nostrils 'You're damn right it isn't! How long are they staying?'

'My grandmother may be staying for some time; it is very lonely for her on Earth you know?'

McCann grimaced at the thought of being pestered by his mother 'I'm sorry, I'll make sure everything is fine when she arrives. When does she arrive exactly?'

'FATHER!'

Ilam burst out laughing and McCann rolled his eyes 'You were listening in on me again weren't you Malikah?'

'Because I know how you think Father, you will not be arranging an inconvenience for your parents visit is that understood?'

'I don't know what you mean!' replied McCann

'Father! Are you calling me a liar?'

'No I'm just saying that perhaps you're mistaken, that's all.'

Ilam was very amused by the conversation and linked arms with her husband 'Duncan you know Malikah is correct. Now apologise for being so rude.'

He maintained his grim look despite his wife's smiles 'So I'm wrong again am I? Bah! What's the bloody point!'

Malikah placed her hands on her hips and scowled at her father 'Father you speak of respect for parents yet you make cruel statements about your own. Do you expect me to respect your word after having witnessed such mockery?'

Ilam said nothing only raising her eyes at her husband. Once again his daughter was correct, how could he expect to be obeyed when he spoke ill of his own parents? Malikah loved both of her grandmothers and only tolerated her father's often wicked tongue. McCann was unaware to what extent his daughter found his sense of humour deplorable when aimed at her grandparents.

The Englishman became subdued 'I apologise for what I said about your grandparents. However I can't control my mind as well as a Tlillan. I often have thoughts that are involuntary; I wouldn't have had Louis create an engine problem. It just entered my mind on impulse that's all Malikah, I'm sorry.'

She took her hands off her hips and embraced her father kissing his cheek again 'I didn't mean to embarrass you father, please forgive me?' she whispered in his ear.

'Of course,' replied the Englishman as he returned his daughters kiss on the cheek.

The family continued the stroll until they reached the bay which the Chutli was docked in 'How long until she's ready to cast anchor?'

The party stood admiring the refurbished Tlillan cruiser 'She will be prepared to leave dock in a week, if all her systems pass the triple certification this time,' replied Ilam.

Chapter 21

The Chutli passed her tests, and soon after Ilam was to embark on her first trip beyond the Gukumatz solar system as Captain. The mission to ferry family members of the new breed of children being raised on Ilium 1 was hers. Faraday was determined to integrate the population of Tlillans as best he could. Some of the children were more than two years old and had yet to meet their grandparents. After this visit was over a trip to Earth was planned for the children and their parents.

The three Mictlancihuatl children were extremely important to Faraday. After the power Malikah had demonstrated at what the Gukumatz simply named "the tunnel event" he was obsessed with securing the children's trust; although Amitra was no longer a child but a young woman by Tlillan standards. Kaeo was soon to hit puberty herself and Sandra would not be far behind her. It would still be years before Amitra reached full maturity and no doubt she faced a rocky road. However Malikah was there to guide her protégés along the path she had already walked.

Malikah was now seven years old and unless aware of her birth date she would be mistaken for a woman in her twenties. A 6 foot 4 inch woman in her twenties that possessed the strength of three grown men. Her size, build and mental attributes were obviously inherited from her mother. However she held a striking resemblance to her grandmother, Ofra. In that her hair possessed that dark sable Mediterranean colour. Her hair curled in locks exactly the same as Ofra's and some of her facial features were eerily similar.

To be fair all Mictlancihuatl's had dark hair, however Malikah was the only one to have such thick curly locks. She was shorter than the average Tlillan female and her rear lobes seemed to be smaller than average also. Though this took nothing away from her abilities, in fact Malikah's mental powers by far outstripped any other Tlillan.

McCann observed from the bridge of the Athena as the klaxon went out 'Tunnel event detected co-ordinates X +2.743 AU, Y +7.921 AU, Z + 4 AU.'

He watched the live feed of the white hole opening in real time on the tactical display 'Thank you Athena.'

'The Chutli has entered the system 5 AU above the accretion disk,' reported an agitated Hassif.

'Yes I can add up thank you Hassif!'

The navigator was anxious to see his parents, so was McCann just not in the same manner. He was more anxious to see them leave, however he would weather this storm for his daughter. Ilam had got used to his foul attitude but Malikah was very possessive concerning Ofra. The Englishman had come to the conclusion that he and his daughter were too alike. McCann felt quite free to criticize his parents but if anyone else spoke ill of them, especially his mother, it was a different story. In the past he'd travelled half way around the planet with Jenkins because someone had spread gossip about Ofra. It had taken sometime to realise that there was someone else who felt the same way about his mother now. McCann was forced to accept the state of affairs; he understood how his father felt when in his and Ofra's presence.

The Chutli popped out of the white hole, propelled outwards as she dropped her Casimir field to ride the effects of the white hole into Gukumatz AB.

As the white hole collapsed McCann sighed 'Hassif send a greeting to the Chutli. Tell the Captain I'll see her later and say hello to Ofra and James. Oh and feel free to send a greeting to your parents.'

Hassif smiled and nodded his head in thanks then went to work at his station 'Message sent.'

The Athena stayed at the same point in space as the Chutli passed her on the way to Ilium 1. Some of the crew would be taking two weeks leave at the end of their shifts today. Amongst them would be Hassif and McCann, Faraday was insistent on this being a success.

By the end of his shift McCann was standing at the front of the queue waiting for the airlock door to open. He, Hassif and three other members of the crew whom had children with Tlillan women were to take leave on the station. After the droids had certified the integrity of the docking arm the door began to open.

Once open the party of men began to stroll down the arm 'I was told that Jerry Habeeb would be coming, is that true?' inquired Khun Deychaa the father of Kaeo.

McCann grimaced at the mention of the reporter 'If I ever see that miserable bastard again it'll be too soon!'

Khun Deychaa laughed; he often spent time in the officers' mess drinking with McCann after the birth of his daughter. They both had a penchant for good whisky and Deychaa had picked up the vice of Cuban cigars from his Commodore. McCann's tantrums were something he enjoyed and quite often came out once he'd plied the ships commanding officer with a few drinks.

'Haven't you and Jerry kissed and made up already?' asked Hassif rather cheekily much to the delight of Deychaa.

McCann sneered a little 'If I saw that man rolling around on the street burning alive, I wouldn't even piss on him!'

Hassif sniggered along with the other officers whilst Deychaa tried to control his laughter. Their Commodore's temper tantrums had become legendry by this time. It was amusing to watch him but woe to the poor so and so that incurred his wrath. The only people that seemed to be immune to his tendency to let rip were his wife, daughter, mother and mother-in-law.

The party reached the other end of the docking arm to be greeted by their families. Both Hassif and Deychaa bowed in the same manner to their parents. In Indian culture the greeting was called Namaste whereas in Thai culture it was named a Wai.

Deychaa spoke to his parents 'Sawat dee kap,' used for both hello and good bye.

McCann spied his mother and father standing in front of Ilam and Malikah. He approached his father and they shook hands 'Good to see you lad!' said his father in a loud tone.

'It's good to see you too,' replied McCann before moving onto his mother and embracing her as usual.

'Are you still smoking those horrible cigars Duncan?' said his tearful mother after hugging her son.

He sighed but before he could reply in an annoyed tone he caught Malikah's disapproving gaze. McCann cleared his throat 'Yes Mother, but I'll cut them out while you're here.'

Malikah's expression changed to one of smug satisfaction and McCann relaxed.

'What is the point in that? You will only become irritable and get on my nerves like your Father! No, better I put up with your stinky cigars than stinky temper!' Ofra waved her handkerchief around as she spoke. His mother wore a long pink headscarf with a light grey casual suit, about as racy as you could get for a lady of her age in her community.

'He has my son smoking those things too, mehn gipai!' called Deychaa's mother to Ofra.

McCann saw Deychaa smiling. Unless you knew the man you'd have thought he was amused by his mother's statement. In truth Deychaa was extremely embarrassed, his mother had caused him to lose face in front the Commodore and his family. Hassif had been promoted to Lieutenant and though Deychaa technically outranked him he still felt humiliated. Deychaa was the Chief Drone Engineer onboard the Athena but with Malikah, Ilam, McCann and Hassif present as his mother berated the Commodore he felt 2 inches tall.

Malikah could sense Khun Deychaa's desire for the ceiling to collapse or a sudden alert to an alien invasion occur. Malikah dressed in her ribbed space suit and long white jacket strode over to Deychaa's mother and made a wai 'Sawat dee kah.'

Deychaa's mother was overwhelmed that Malikah would wai her in front of so many people. The old lady knelt down to wai as she would to royalty but Malikah clasped her shoulders and gently lifted her up 'Mai chai, kah.'

McCann could understand the conversation through his ear piece since Malikah initially spoke in Thai to Deychaa's mother.

'Chur alai?' said Malikah asking her name.

The old lady was frozen in a bow as if she were afraid to look up at the mighty Amazon 'My Mother's name is Noi.'

'Noi, look en kah,' requested Malikah.

Noi stood up properly still in a wai 'Kuatoad kah.'

'You have no need to apologise Noi. I am at fault for allowing your son to smoke on the Athena. He works very hard as does my father.'

Noi began to shake, in her society knowing your place was paramount. Stepping outside of your bounds would result in an immediate slap down. Fortunately Malikah didn't adhere to such strict dogma, unlike her mother and grandmother.

The sable goddess took hold of the old woman and comforted her 'Shall we all go to the recreation area?'

Everyone agreed and Malikah lead the way holding onto Deychaa's mother who was beginning to calm down. As the party made their way Ofra shook her head and muttered to her son 'You see the trouble your cigars have caused?'

McCann didn't answer, though a thought did pass through his mind. In reply to his mother's comment instinctively he replied inside his mind 'More like your big mouth!'

Ilam opened her eyes in shock and stared at the Englishman.

Looking at his wife he realised she had heard his mental comment and he smirked then gave her a wink.

'Father control yourself!' came his daughter's voice who was up front with Deychaa's family moving the group towards the recreation hall. Malikah was concerned as there were Tlillans present. It was difficult to ignore McCann when he broadcast his thoughts in such close proximity.

McCann made a comical bowing motion towards his daughter's back as she walked several feet in front, 'Yes master, is there anything else I can do for you exalted one?' he asked in a comical tone as he walked besides Ofra.

Several of the party chuckled but he soon stood erect again when he felt Ofra's elbow dig hard into his side. Ofra had a black look on her face. Malikah only shook her head in disappointment making no comment on her father's attempt at comedy.

On reaching the recreation area the families sat down at the café above the hall which had hosted the fencing tournament. Each family sat at a table and began catching up, the main subject of conversation, the dead zone inside the wormhole. The wonders seen by the families travelling to Gukumatz were mind blowing. Even Ofra was overwhelmed by it; she described the sights logged by the crew of the Chutli as they travelled the Styx.

A Gukumatz waiter brought the McCann's coffee and tea, McCann began to smile at his mother who stopped talking about the journey.

'What is wrong Duncan?'

'Nothing, it's just strange to see you so excited about the journey here. I was sure you'd never have even set foot on the orbital lift, let alone fold space!'

'Pah! You mean you hoped I would never come here!' sneered Ofra.

'Mum! That's not true!' refuted McCann

'Duncan I could always tell when you were dishonest. Don't lie to me, I am an inconvenience. You want me gone as quickly as possible!'

McCann looked to his daughter for help but she was busy with Noi, fortunately Ilam stepped in and cuddled Ofra warmly, 'Your son has always been a selfish little boy but I would be most grateful if you stayed with us here in Gukumatz AB.'

McCann pulled a weak smile, despite the fact he felt sick inside. The thought of his mother on Ilium 1 running about and pestering the crew whilst imparting humiliating stories concerning him and his childhood filled him with dread. He could detect his father letting out a very faint snicker; McCann didn't look at James in case he said something.

Ofra smiled at her daughter-in-law.

'Please stay with us Grandmother,' came Malikah's voice from across the room.

'If Duncan is happy with it then I will stay.'

He didn't even need to look at his wife and daughter, McCann could feel their emotion especially Malikah, 'Of course mum, you're welcome to stay as long as you want.'

Ofra and Ilam grinned at each other.

'How about we go for a walk lad?' said James patting his son on the back.

'Sure, if that's alright with everyone else?'

Ofra made a shooing motion towards the pair of them 'Off with you both!'

McCann and his father got up from their seats holding their coffee cups and began a leisurely stroll to the observation decks. Handing his son a short Churchill cigar James chuckled 'I don't know how you're gonna manage with those women on your back Son.'

He took the cigar and snipped the cap off 'It seems I've been ambushed once again.'

'Boy, with those three plotting against you, you're better off just doing as you're told!'

'I know, the trouble is, most of the time I don't know what it is I'm supposed to be doing or thinking. You try living with a pair of clairvoyant women.'

James chuckled to himself 'Sounds a lot like your Mother, she always knew what I was thinking and told me so. It's gotta be tough living with the thought police?'

The pair made it to the lower outer ring where they could walk beneath the station and observe the Kotumatz moon below.

'Tough? Bloody impossible is more like it! Though Ilam has learnt to ease off and keep her opinions to herself when possible.'

'What about Malikah? She's a fine girl or should I say woman?' quizzed James who was rather confused on how he should address his granddaughter.

'When Malikah is right and you're wrong and she lets you know it, until you submit!'

James expelled some smoke from his nostrils then gave a knowing look.

McCann noticed his father's expression 'What?'

'She reminds me of you. You were exactly the bloody same when you were a kid, I always thought you would be a politician.'

McCann sneered 'Spare me!'

James nodded his head as they both looked down at the thick yellow atmosphere of the moon below. Clouds swirled in large spirals as they moved slowly across the face of the planet, the seat of power for the Icon.

Still sneering McCann looked at his father 'Have you seen that piece of shit Jerry Habeeb yet?'

James nodded his head 'Oh yes! He's on the hunt for you.'

Taking a long draw from his cigar he held the smoke in his mouth until it cooled down then let it escape from his nostrils as he spoke, 'Well good luck to him, I've had shits that I cared more about than that man!'

James laughed 'Ah, Faraday wants you to have an interview with him. I don't know why but he was rabbiting on about it for ages before we left. He probably needs the sponsorship money to pay for all his women!'

The last statement grabbed McCann's attention 'His what?'

James took another draw 'Didn't you know? He got busted by a reporter, they found out he'd been keeping condos all over the world. Each one was keeping some dirty tart, when he visited the city he'd spend his free time there.'

'Well, well, well I guess being director of the I.S.A has some perks!'

James looked at his son with a rather surprised expression 'I thought you'd have heard of it already. You used to watch the news and read the papers religiously.'

McCann nodded his head as he looked outwards into space 'That was then, today if there's anything I need to know Malikah or Ilam will tell me. Also their reports are far more accurate than the paper.'

'They're that good?'

'Dad I've seen them do things you wouldn't believe if I told you.'

James squinted into his son's eyes 'Like what?'

'Dad I don't think you'd believe me and it's classified.'

'Try me Duncan.'

McCann looked around to make certain they were alone then stepped in close to his father and whispered into his ear 'Malikah opened up a wormhole.'

James held his cigar but looked rather uncertain 'So? Ilam did the same on the journey here.'

McCann whispered again 'Malikah folded space without the assistance of a wormhole generator.'

James smiled and replied sardonically 'You mean she did it herself?'

McCann nodded his head.

'Duncan that's too fantastic ....'

McCann put his hand in front of his father's mouth 'Like I said I've seen Malikah do things that you wouldn't believe. All the Gukumatz here witnessed it along with the Tlillans and most of the I.S.A staff.'

'Why is no one on Earth aware of it?'

McCann took a short puff from the creamy Cuban 'What's the point dad? No one is gonna believe it, I saw it with my own eyes and it took me a while to come to terms with it. But believe me dad, I saw her do it then fling four war cruisers into it, sending them back to Tlillan.'

'How?' asked James in a sceptical tone.

'It's something to do with the Gukumatz, she can channel their energy and manipulate it.'

'I don't understand Son.'

McCann smiled at his father 'Join the club dad! All I can tell you is what she told me. She can see and feel spiritual energy, like when you get a gut feeling that something bad is going to happen?'

'Yeh?'

'Well that's a disruption in the field of spiritual energy. It's not clairvoyance but just your mind and body being influenced by an energy field. Their telepathy uses the same field; apparently we are too primitive to see this higher level of consciousness right now. Gukumatz can see it, Tlillans can see it and communicate through it. Malikah and her kind can see it, communicate through it and manipulate it to various degrees.'

James went silent for a while and contemplated what his son had just told him. He knew his son and knew that he was a sceptic like him 'So are you saying that Malikah is a higher being? Even than a Tlillan?'

McCann took a draw from his cigar lighting up the smouldering cherry as he drew air past it, 'Yes, she and the other three are what the Tlillans call a Mictlancihuatl, the Gukumatz a Teootl and humans would describe as a deity I suppose.'

'You're right Son, it is too fantastic to believe.'

'That's what Ryu said until Malikah put her in contact with her dead Father. He told her to go back to Korea and look for a key to a safety deposit box. She went to the bank he said it was at and found the share certificates he'd stashed before the war. He told her about the shares before she even opened the box!'

'Come on Duncan! You sound like one of those shitty ghost hunter net shows!'

'Dad, I was there when he spoke to her. I'm not trying to convince you, but I know what I saw and if Ryu believes it then so do I. I've known her for years, she doesn't go for psychic bullshit or that sort of crap either.'

'Were the shares worth anything?'

'Only 40 billion credits.'

James nearly choked on his cigar smoke 'What the fuck!?'

McCann smirked at his father who was coughing on his Romeo and Julietta 'I thought that might change your mind. She has a 10% stake in Future 1 Industries.'

James was understandably confused; his son saw his expression and explained 'They got the contract to provide the missile system for the Shogun II scram drones. The old son of a bitch was just like his daughter, didn't trust anyone not even the nation's currency. So he invested in a nearby weapons designer and manufacturer, before the war. When the shares where something like 50 credits a pop.'

James shook his head 'But why wasn't she informed when he died? I mean they keep electronic records as well as paper, right?'

'Well that's it isn't it. The war happened, most of Korea was thrown into chaos. Records were lost or destroyed especially those online. Most mainframes were considered insecure and destroyed by the Korean government.'

James was still mystified as he looked out onto the moon below 'But the records will have been stored online outside the country. Why didn't they just download them after the war?'

McCann laughed 'That's great in theory, but do you know how many Kims there are in Korea? Most of the population have the exact same names, sorting out who owns what was just impossible. The amount of women named Ryu Yong living in her province alone is mind boggling. So the records were kept but unless you claimed your shares they remained in limbo. Until an owner was found or someone claimed them with proof of identity.'

James laughed 'Well you learn something new every day! So is she still single?'

McCann laughed with his father 'I'm afraid she married a Russian.'

James beat his fist comically on the hand rail they both leant against 'Damn Ruskie bastards! I tell you when they smell an opportunity they're in there quicker than a ferret down a fucking rabbit hole!'

McCann patted his father on the shoulder 'He was in there before she became rich dad. Apart from being good looking she's the hero of Vladivostok. Her assault on Jiang's frontline broke the siege, his mother was in Vladivostok at the time.'

James nodded 'I heard about her handy work here, you know they called her the "butcher of Bokumatz" for a while back home?'

'She saved every man and woman's life in this system dad, including myself. Ryu gets the job done and she follows orders. Those people calling her a butcher would be singing a different tune if it were their families the Gukumatz held hostage and murdered that day.'

James took the last drag on his cigar as it came close to the nub 'I understand Son. I just wanted to prepare you for when you return home. A lot of things have changed, including attitudes towards the Gukumatz. You might be a little shocked when speaking to the man on the street, that's all.'

McCann shook his head, this time he was in a state of confusion 'What do you mean?'

'I just want you to be prepared; a lot of people are against us being in Ilium. They don't like the fact we have control over the Gukumatz, people are accusing the I.S.A of slavery. You aren't too popular either, you're seen as responsible for Ryu's actions.'

McCann shook his head in disbelief 'They glassed our fucking planet and what? People are feeling sorry for those filthy toads? They murdered billions in cold blood for god's sake!'

'Calm down boy, it's not everyone but there are a lot of bleeding heart liberals and you know how they are when they find a cause. I'm just saying don't over react when one of them approaches you on the street back home. They're not gonna spit on you and call you a baby killer or anything but just let them have their say Duncan, okay?'

McCann finished his cigar and looked his father in the face 'Thanks dad, I'm sure Faraday would've said something. But living in his prostitute filled ivory tower he probably has no idea of what it's like for the man on the street!'

The pair laughed as James produced another two cigars to share amongst them as they watched the Gukumatz sun rise above the moon below.

That evening the families all settled in to their rooms on Ilium 1, by the following day they were boarding the orbital lift down to Kotumatz to take a guided tour. The families were split up into groups with Malikah taking the first group. The tour consisted of only relatives of the Mictlancihuatl children.

The orbital lifts in the Gukumatz system were of a higher standard than the original Earth lift. The I.S.A had since upgraded the lift on Earth, which now operated much like the machine the families occupied on the way down to the surface.

No longer did they rely on a carbon nanotube ribbon, but instead a Neutronium alloy tower connected them to the moon below. With several of these towers running between Kotumatz and Ilium 1 the space station was very efficient. Travelling to the surface was a matter of no more than an hour strapped into a seat with a view of the outside. Using magnetic levitation, or Mag Lev for short, the shuttle was fired down at blistering speeds. Anti-gravity plating inside prevented G-force from tearing apart the contents of the shuttle. As they reached the bottom of the tower the computer eased on the shuttles Mag Lev brakes, until it gently kissed the landing zone opposite the thoroughfare.

The landing zone was pretty much the same as a landing pad for space craft. The difference being that the centre was a retracting and expanding iris. A column of neutronium carbon alloy with two deep groves on opposite sides, similar to a girder used in constructing buildings, ran through it. The iris closed and the computer charged the electro-magnets on its surface. Once the shuttle had slowed to a halt the crawler clasped onto the rail and the magnets were deactivated.

The shuttle was a massive crawler in essence, with many slots around its circular body. One of the slots contained the shuttle that the families occupied.

'You have reached your destination safely, prepare to exit,' said the soft female voice of the shuttle computer.

'Pah!' shouted Ofra 'I'm lucky to be alive!'

McCann grimaced but said nothing, Ofra had been encouraging Deychaa's mother the entire journey. It seems Noi had a penchant for bitching and moaning too. But her son was far more skilled at keeping his own mouth shut than McCann.

The party began loosening the nanotube straps. Noi was having difficulty and berated her son in Thai. McCann tried to ignore her but his ear piece began to inform him of her displeasure with a translation.

'Get me out of this thing! You get yourself out but leave your Mother in here? Are you sure you are my Son?'

Deychaa clearly embarrassed by his mother moved to release her harness 'Mother, I had to release myself before I could come and help you.'

Noi clearly wasn't interested in his logical explanation 'So I am stupid is that it?' she barked as he undid her straps.

Everyone was waiting for the glass wall to lift open, so that they could step down onto the iris below. The computer however was waiting for Deychaa's parents to undo their harnesses.

Kaeo approached her grandmother 'Let me help you Noi, father can help Yai.'

Deychaa moved over to assist his father with a sigh of relief whilst Kaeo helped her grandmother. Noi loved her granddaughter and would never berate her in public without due cause. She loved her son too but he had always been a naughty boy. No doubt Noi had gotten used to shaming him, now it was probably force of habit.

'Thank you Kaeo,' said a smiling Noi as her harness was quickly released.

Kaeo gave her grandmother a wai, 'Kah.'

Once the family were all released the glass door in front of them opened; lifting up on the upper hinge until the bottom pointed out at a 90 degree angle above their heads.

'You may now exit the shuttle, enjoy your stay on Kotumatz,' spoke the elegant voice of the computer.

McCann put a leg over the edge and onto a raised platform, once on that he took the three steps down onto the iris below. He then realised his mother was still in the shuttle and trotted back up to hold her hand, lifting her over the edge and down onto the iris below. As he guided her down the steps the Englishman sensed a feeling of satisfaction from Malikah. He peered inside the shuttle; she was standing there looking back at him. Her eyes had a deep pink hue to them, his daughter was very pleased with him. McCann hoped that this visit would go with a lot less friction than he'd anticipated earlier.

The first comments made by the visitors concerned the atmosphere. The thick humid ammonia filled air was over powering to one who'd never experienced it before. James coughed his way to the hotel restaurant, where the families took a break from both the journey to the moon and its climate.

Malikah and the three Mictlancihuatl girls were the centre of attention. Many Gukumatz had taken a short break from work in order to get a glimpse of them. Amitra being the most important of the three since she had passed puberty without injury. Malikah remained the Icon, her position was unshakeable. The three new additions were her angels, the apostles of the Icon whom would lead them into a golden age.

Hassif's father had been dominating much of the conversation whilst at the hotel. He was so proud he just couldn't shut his mouth and McCann found the man to be extremely annoying; though he never said a word concerning Madhav and his constant nattering.

The Englishman recognised that look from Amitra; he'd seen it on his wife many years ago then his daughter. She knew what he was thinking and didn't approve. Yet human society depended on lies and deception since most humans were emotionally handicapped. So Amitra contained her thoughts preventing herself from taking offence, though she was half human. The pure blood Tlillans from the Chutli considered the half breeds, including the non Mictlancihuatl, to be emotionally immature.

'You know when my Son left university and took a government job I was certain we'd be living in poverty!' said Madhav in a happy tone to Sandra's grandfather.

'When my Son told me he was working with the I.S.A and leaving private medicine I nearly had a heart attack! I told him "do you know how much money you can make as a nano surgeon these days?" But he was adamant, thank the gods he didn't listen to me!' smiled the old Greek as he and Madhav laughed over a drink.

The women were discussing family matters or more to the point embarrassing their sons. Noi had found a friend in Ofra and they were in deep discussion much to the pain of Deychaa.

Noi pointed at her son 'I never believed he would get married. He spent all his time in bars full of prostitutes and drink! If he hadn't gone to Japan to work, he would be drunk in a bar full of diseased women today!'

McCann tried hard but he couldn't contain himself. One glance at Deychaa's grin of humiliation caused him to make a grunting noise as he attempted to silence his own laughter. Even Malikah couldn't repress her smile though Deychaa's wife Macuilachutli was by no means amused.

Ofra sneered at her son, who was by now sniggering with his father at the amusing tale Noi spun of the drone Engineers' past improprieties, 'What is so funny?' she said in a foreboding tone 'You were 37 before you married! Everyone was sure he was gay! Oh the shame!'

McCann calmed down quickly though his father and daughter didn't. Added to that Ilam was now joining in the entertainment as the two women carried on with competing stories of embarrassment.

Noi continued to denigrate her son 'I went to the temple and gave thanks when he got work on the Athena. The only place he couldn't find any whores to give his money to. He would spend on dirty women before he sent his Mother enough to buy a bowl of rice! Now he has a good wife I can afford to buy a new skirt for the first time in years!'

Deychaa's father had heard this ranting and raving for many years. He no longer bothered to discuss it with his wife, defending his son was a lost cause. Besides he had two other sons and if he could get onto the subject of them she would refrain. It seemed that in her opinion Deychaa was a cursed son or something along those lines.

Noi was letting out a lot of frustration as her son had avoided her for many years. He preferred not to go home and see his mother which angered her greatly. Although her stories of him being mean with money and frequenting houses of ill repute were very much exaggerated; it was her time to make her son pay for his absence and she did so in spades.

Noi slapped the table with her hand grabbing the attention of all in the restaurant 'At the wedding he didn't want me there, do you know that?'

Ofra gasped so that everyone could hear, much to the delight of Ilam and Malikah.

Noi continued talking to Ofra, everyone was listening intently 'It's true! His wife forced him to allow me; he didn't want to pay respect to his own Mother at his wedding!'

This was half true, it wasn't that he didn't want to pay respect to his mother. Deychaa just didn't want what was happening now in the Kotumatz hotel to take place at his wedding. His mother held her tongue for the wedding and he quickly departed afterwards for the honeymoon ... failing to return. This only served to infuriate his mother further. She was a very traditional lady, typical of most elderly Thai ladies, Deychaa unlike her other sons had always disappointed. In Thailand it was traditional for a son to be ordained as a Buddhist monk and remain for a year in the monk hood.

Unlike his elder brothers Deychaa did not become ordained ... sort of. He was a monk for all of 3 days until the head priest of the temple caught him drinking whisky. Deychaa was chased out of the temple by the monks, seeking refuge at home. That day he'd managed to shame his entire family, his mother never really forgave him. His father never spoke on the subject though he showed no respect to his son afterwards. Deychaa needed to make amends but he continued with his lifestyle, fortunately he had a deep interest in drones. No one knew why or where this interest came from, his father sent him to a state university. He refused to pay good money for a public school when he had two other sons that didn't drink or frequent bars.

After leaving he took a job in Japan, probably to get away from the poor reputation he had back home. Now Deychaa was paying the piper, he'd managed to avoid his day of reckoning with his mother very skillfully for many years. However there was no escape on Kotumatz for the wayward son of Noi.

Noi wiped tears from her eyes 'I am lower than a cockroach. The lowest thing on the Earth.'

Ofra gave Deychaa a black look.

Deychaa felt rather uncomfortable looking at his Commodore's mother giving him such a sinister scowl. However he said nothing, deciding to take his due punishment like a man. He was also pretty sure he'd be sleeping on the metaphoric couch tonight. The suppressed emotion emanating from his wife who sat next to him was not positive.

Kaeo could no longer permit this to continue, she left her seat and stood beside her seated grandmother. Kneeling she made a wai at Noi's feet and speaking in Thai she apologised for her father. Kaeo made it clear that she respected her above all others and asked her if she would stay with them on Ilium 1.

Noi embraced her granddaughter who was on her knees next to the seated Noi. The old Thai lady tearfully accepted as she released her embrace to Wai her granddaughter and thank her 'Kob kum kah.'

Deychaa was suddenly filled with a dread terror; he couldn't believe what his daughter had just done to him. He was sat at the same table between his wife and father, his father between him and his mother. Deychaa was staring at his daughter in disbelief; everyone could see his expression and easily determine his opinion.

Kaeo glanced at her father, her eyes widened and for a brief moment they filled with what seemed to be a jet black ink. Only her father and grandmother witnessed the momentary warning which successfully frightened her father back into his grinning demeanour.

Noi had never seen the Tlillan signature trait of focal pigments shifting with emotion. When she saw her granddaughter's eyes fill as injected with ink, then return to normal after her message had been delivered, she was shocked.

Noi shrieked out in Thai 'Kaeo! Sabai mai?'

Kaeo quickly turned to her worried grandmother and smiled warmly 'Sabai dee kah,' giving another wai of respect.

Deychaa began to speak, his intent to explain the trait to Noi. However as soon as the first utterance left his mouth his mother leapt upon him.

'Ben arai?' she shouted at her grinning son.

According to McCann's androgynous translator she asked him 'What is wrong?', the Englishman assumed it to be closer to 'What's your problem?'

The old lady carried on much to the entertainment of McCann. Fortunately for Deychaa the only non-Thais that could understand her were I.S.A employees. Due to the translator earpieces, including his wife and daughter who had learnt the language by linking with him.

'You would be happy for me to go back and eat the shit rice?' she asked furiously.

McCann wasn't certain what she meant by shit rice. In his many drinking and smoking sessions with Deychaa in the officers' lounge he had once referred to separating the rice just before cooking. He had said that the very poor would be given this low quality rice for free. For example beggars and homeless were taken to hostels where they slept and ate the rice for free. The Englishman assumed Noi was insinuating that Deychaa would be pleased to have his mother beg and live in a shelter, rather than reside with him and his family on Ilium 1.

Noi's rage progressed unabated 'Your father has a son who is an officer in the I.S.A yet he still must work in a factory to eat! You are happy to see him work until he dies?'

This was again not quite the full story. His father did still work in an electronics factory, not because they needed the money. The I.S.A provided well for Deychaa's parents especially since Kaeo was born. He worked there to get some relief from his wife's wroth; she had a temper that was impossible to moderate. It was a common characteristic in the women of her family and Kaeo was certainly of the same stock.

Deychaa's passive approach was not helping, though he knew better than to try otherwise.

Noi sneered at her son 'Every time I see your happy face I want to kick it with my foot! If not for Kaeo I would be a beggar and your father dead from overwork! Even you would not pay for his funeral, better you spend your money on bad women and whisky than your dead parents!'

McCann was taking great enjoyment in the creative abuse Noi threw at her son. It never ceased to amaze him how different cultures had some very odd ways of insulting and abusing one another. Tlillans very rarely displayed such openness in their society, telepathy made this kind of carry on redundant. Probably the reason why it fascinated the Tlillans so much, perhaps it was like observing primitive behaviour in their ancestors? Akin to humans being able to go back in time and monitor Neanderthal society and how it worked?

As the flow of abuse continued McCann saw what he believed was Kaeo linking with her father. He had witnessed Amitra and Hassif link but never the other girls with their fathers. McCann was certain she was sending him a message and from his facial expression he had received it.

After Kaeo was finished she stood up and stepped backwards. Deychaa then rose from his seat while his mother was in mid-sentence. He walked towards Noi, though his eyes were fixed on his daughter all the time. Deychaa reached his mother's side, where Kaeo was stood before, some of the people were concerned he was going to punch his mother. Those that were acquainted with the Thai drone engineer understood he would never lay a finger on his own mother in anger.

The large Thai man lowered himself to his knees and lay on his belly as he waied his mother's feet, 'I am very sorry, please forgive me Mother.'

McCann was stunned, he wondered if he would ever do such a humiliating thing in public. He considered that if it were his mother or wife he might. But anyone else would have to wait for hell to freeze over first. Then again he would have apologised long before it had to reach this stage, no matter if he were wrong or right.

Noi stopped her rant and peered down at her son who now lay prostrated on the floor. In Thai tradition this was how you would show respect to the King. It was the ultimate show of respect and subservience in their society. To do such an act to another person in public would only take place if you had deeply shamed them. Even so most people would not humiliate themselves by prostrating themselves so publicly but rather wait for a private moment.

For a brief second McCann was sure he witnessed a smile on Noi's face, though her scowl quickly returned. Yet the scowl was far more mellow than previously.

Noi nodded at her prone son 'Uh, Kah!' she said in a rather annoyed tone.

Deychaa rose to his knee and with his palms still pressed together before his face he thanked his mother 'Kob kum kap mere.'

His mother had an expression of someone that was only mildly irritated now 'Uh, bai!' she said shooing him away.

She had humiliated her son, then he demeaned himself before her and everyone far more than anyone else could. Noi was satisfied with her wayward child's denigration and his debasing apology. She let him return and never spoke on the subject again, much to Deychaa and his father's relief. McCann had been hoping for a few more good tongue lashings in the future. He remained quietly disappointed much to his daughter's disapproval.

Kaeo and her mother Macuil were both visibly pleased, a pink hue filled their eyes. Both were overwhelmed by the emotion from Noi as tears began to roll down the old Thai ladies cheeks.

At that moment McCann recognised a voice entering the restaurant 'Am I too late?'

McCann shuddered as Jerry Habeeb and two of his cohorts entered the room removing their breathing devices.

The Englishman stood up, looking at his father he said 'I'm going for a smoke, you?'

James grinned 'Thought you'd never ask!'

The pair began to move in the direction of the terrace when jerry approached McCann. Standing in his path an excited Jerry tried to grab his attention 'So Commodore how have you been since we last met?'

McCann continued to walk towards the terrace, he then deliberately slammed his shoulder into Jerry. The journalist was knocked backwards, stumbling into the restaurant bar. The presenter of Habeeb's Hour grabbed the bar with both hands, only just preventing himself from hitting the floor.

McCann stopped walking for a moment, turning to Habeeb he spoke slowly in a deep tone 'If you know what's good for you, you'll stay out of my way Habeeb.'

The Englishman and his father then carried on to the terrace to partake in a Havana leaving a dazed Jerry Habeeb still clinging onto the bar.

Ilam quickly moved over to assist Jerry regain his footing 'What was that about?' asked a bemused Jerry.

'My husband harbours grudges for great lengths of time Mr. Habeeb. I would take his advice if I were in your position. He has been known to possess a terrible temper.'

Jerry brushed himself down as his crew approached 'What the hell did I do that got him that mad?'

Ilam smiled, amused by how difficult it is for humans to iron out simple social problems 'I believe it was an airing on your show, concerning him falling down on Mars.'

Jerry had an incredulous look on his face 'Are you serious? That was more than seven years ago! He can't still be pissed off over that?'

Ilam raised her eyebrows 'I am very serious Mr. Habeeb and it was eight years ago.'

Jerry's camera man spoke excitedly 'Jerry we got all of that!'

Habeeb took one look at Ilam 'Delete it.'

'What? That was pure gold we can't ....'

'I said delete it Pete, now do your fucking job!'

Jerry turned to Ilam 'Look I need an interview with your husband, what do I need to do to get it?'

Ilam smiled at the ridiculousness of it all 'Well my husband has only two bosses, Mr. Faraday ...'

'Already tried him,' said Jerry cutting her off rather rudely.

'And the Governor of Gukumatz AB.'

Jerry peered at Malikah then back at Ilam 'What about you? You're his wife after all?'

Ilam shook her head 'I'm afraid not Mr. Habeeb, I have no wish to transfer the focus of his grudge to myself.'

Jerry made his way to Malikah, not even thanking Ilam for her assistance 'Malikah may I speak with you?'

Malikah was sat next to Ofra 'Please take a seat Mr. Habeeb.'

Jerry sat down and began to plead his case 'I need an interview with Commodore McCann, can you have him agree to it?'

Malikah displayed the same smirk her mother had 'I could but I won't Mr. Habeeb.'

'Why not?' inquired a puzzled and rather frustrated Jerry.

'Because my Father would hold it against me for a very long time and I'd rather disappoint you than take advantage of my Father's trust.'

Jerry let out grunt of frustration 'Hmmph, well how do you suggest I get on his good side?'

Malikah stated matter of factly 'Have you tried apologising?'

Jerry's squinted his eyes as if even the very thought was painful 'Well I didn't think I ...'

Then Malikah boldly cut him off before he could finish his sentence 'You were wrong Mr. Habeeb!'

Jerry glanced over at the glass door leading to the terrace in trepidation, 'What would you suggest, will a "sorry" do?'

Malikah smiled at the American journalist 'I suggest that if you want your interview you grovel and beg forgiveness Mr. Habeeb.'

Jerry sneered at the Governor of Gukumatz AB 'Pah! You want me to grovel? To him?'

'No Mr. Habeeb, but while your hubris remains you will not get what you want.'

Jerry became silent and gazed forebodingly at the terrace. Getting to his feet he dusted his jacket and straightened his collar 'You stay here boys, just give me a minute with the Commodore and thank you Governor.'

Jerry took a deep breath and marched resolutely towards the terrace. He pulled back the glass door and closed it behind him then began to explain himself before McCann could take a swing at his face. After ten minutes Jerry had got himself an interview.

Later on Malikah linked with her father and viewed his plea for forgiveness. He apologised for the former show concerning his fall on Tharsis. He pointed out he was not responsible for the material aired but was required, much like McCann, to follow his orders. Unfortunately his editor saw a ratings opportunity in the incident and he was to make as much of it as possible. Nevertheless it was no excuse for embarrassing McCann. He pleaded for exoneration stating he would do whatever necessary to get back on the Commodore's good side.

McCann forgave but he didn't forget, agreeing to do a short interview. He didn't like Jerry and didn't really want to do his interview. However if he'd refused McCann would've felt guilty since Jerry had apologised properly.

That day was finished off with interviews for Network America, all of the family members taking pleasure in their 15 minutes of fame. The next week was spent touring around Kotumatz, sampling the food with varying opinions. The families visited Mopixoa much to the owners delight; as usual he refused to accept any form of payment.

The extra business he'd received since Malikah frequented his store was quite startling. Gukumatz were not greedy creatures by nature either, he stubbornly refused any payment and almost forced expensive clothes into the hands of some of the women.

Malikah, Kaeo, Amitrasudan and Sandra being the main focus of his efforts. Malikah was the Icon and they were her chosen, in his mind they were destined to bring the Gukumatz into their golden age. The Icon had already brought peace from the millennia of war with the Tlillans. For the first time his people lived without the threat of a Tlillan armada appearing in the sky and laying waste to them. She had dispatched their entire fleet, single-handedly sending them home tails between legs. To take payment in any form for his services would be an indignity he refused to suffer.

The families were overwhelmed by Gukumatz generosity. Despite the unpleasant atmosphere Noi and Ofra were quite sure they would enjoy living on Ilium 1. Frequent shopping trips were definitely on the cards. McCann could see them doing their best to put some of these poor toads out of business.

Chapter 22

After almost a week on Kotumatz they returned to Ilium 1. McCann and James were very much relieved to be away from the stench of the moon's thick atmosphere. On the station McCann was greeted by Dr Weissmuller, he was there to test certain people for irregularities.

The doctor temporarily occupied an office in med bay 3; the door was open when McCann got there. The doctor was still using his archaic glove, 'Come in Duncan, it's good to see you,' called the doctor without looking up from his workstation.

McCann stepped inside, the door quickly sliding shut behind him, 'Still using that bloody contraption Frank?'

The doctor peered over his glasses and in a serious tone asked 'How have you been feeling recently, any complaints Duncan?'

McCann took the empty seat at Weissmuller's desk 'No, why is something up?'

The doctor removed his glove and turned the screen of his workstation to face McCann, 'The nanites in your blood have been decreasing Duncan. We first noticed a tiny drop when you returned from Tharsis, I thought nothing of it. Nanites fail from time to time and we replace them periodically. I assumed the Martian gravity had an effect causing a slightly increased malfunction rate.'

McCann felt great concern; Weissmuller wouldn't have come all the way to Ilium with a medical staff for a few broken nanites. In an agitated tone McCann inquired 'So what's the problem? I thought you could just inject a few more to make up the loss, right Frank?'

Weissmuller's expression sent a shiver down McCann's spine, he had that look of a parent after listening to his naïve child. The doctor put his glove on the desk 'Usually the malfunctioning nanites are gathered by the majority of functioning nanites and placed on your personal chip at the back of your neck. However each time we injected fresh nanites there were no broken ones to collect.

Now it stands to reason that some of them are lost via urination, defecation even through sweat and spit. However, each time we replaced your shortfall there were none to collect.'

McCann was still mystified as to what the problem was, a few broken nanites that were missing? Also he said this started at Tharsis so it couldn't have been that big a deal if Weissmuller was only concerned eight years later?

Weissmuller took a sip of his green tea 'Drink Duncan?' he asked in his thick German accent.

'No thanks Frank, now tell me are you really here over a few missing nanites?'

Weissmuller stared at his friend with a look as serious as cancer 'The drop in your nanites has accelerated over the last few years Duncan. It is now at a point where we will have to give you weekly injections to maintain numbers. Didn't you think it odd all the trips to the med bay?'

McCann recalled all the visits on the Athena he was making. He thought nothing of the nanites being injected via his neck chip; he just let the doctor carry on then went back to work when finished.

'Not really, I just follow the doctor's orders. I recall this being a problem when nanites were first used in human bodies. Didn't the immune system destroy them making nanites extremely expensive?'

Weissmuller nodded 'Ya, that was before we could manipulate the immune system. Nothing points at your immune system Duncan. We believe it is a foreign body attacking your nanites.'

The doctor pointed at and organism magnified on his monitor. It was a micro-organism of a tubular design. The creature reminded McCann of a squid with it's tentacles at one end though the other end was merely and orifice. It seemed quite harmless to McCann, a tube with and orifice at each end, one end possessing some tentacles.

'What on Earth is that?' inquired McCann as he examined the image.

'That Duncan is in your bloodstream, we believe it is in every part of your body. Your immune system does not recognise it as a threat, we don't know why. I believe this is what's responsible for your declining nanites.

We only got this footage recently, I believe that you contracted them sometime on Tharsis but they were so low in numbers the effect was negligible. They must have reproduced slowly until today they are overwhelming your nanites.'

McCann shuddered, he felt cold all over his body, 'So apart from killing nanites what else are they doing?'

Weissmuller sighed 'Ya, ya, ya. We don't know Duncan, they haven't had any detrimental effect on you; which is very puzzling.'

'Why?'

'Well they are very aggressive towards your nanites yet benign towards you, why would a foreign body attempt to protect the host? Nevertheless, you must have contracted this from your wife.'

'Why do you say that?'

'Because you were the only one to contract the organism, the others are all clear … until recently that is. It seems Hassif contracted it when the Tlillan ship arrived in Gukumatz. It must have been passed on by a member of the Chutli, probably his wife too.'

'Have you spoken to Ilam?'

Weissmuller nodded 'Yes, she refuses to take blood samples or have an injection of nanites as does all the Chutli crew. I need your help on this Duncan, I have shown this to her but she clams up and refuses to comment on it. I have to assume that all Tlillans carry this, I've tried to study it with your blood samples but once outside the human body it dies. We tried using other apes as hosts but it didn't take, for some reason only the human and Tlillan body can sustain it.'

McCann took a handkerchief from his inside pocket and wiped the sweat from his brow 'So Hassif is infected as well? Are you saying this is sexually transmitted?'

'I can't be certain but if I had to bet money that would be my favourite. It may be totally benign Duncan, I just need to know. Ask your wife, the Tlillan's must know about this organism and how to deal with it.

Right now your nanites cannot do their job because they are under constant attack from these creatures. I'm surprised you haven't fallen ill or suffered muscle degradation without the nanites supporting them. For some reason your health has suffered in no way, that is good but it worries me Duncan. Talk to Ilam, please.' implored the German doctor.

McCann tapped his wrist tablet 'Yes Duncan?' came his wife's voice.

'Ilam I want to see you now in med bay 3 with Doctor Weissmuller,' said the Englishman in a rather pressing tone.

'As you wish my dear, Ilam out.' replied his unimpressed wife.

A few minutes later and the door slid open to reveal the flaming haired Valkyrie, 'Please enter,' said Weissmuller pointing to an extra chair.

She took her seat, one glance at the image on the monitor and she knew what it was about; not that she hadn't eves dropped on her husband's thoughts before arriving. Ilam looked at her husband 'What do you wish to know Duncan?'

He pointed at the image of the wriggling micro-organism 'I have been infected by this and it's destroying my nanites. I need you to tell me anything you know about it Ilam and please don't bother lying to me.'

Ilam smiled at her husband 'It is an Ixchel, you have nothing to be concerned about.'

'Frank needs to know what it is and why it's attacking my nanites.'

Ilam fixed her gaze on the German 'It seems you shall have your way after all Doctor. The Ixchel is a life form native to Tlillan, it is symbiotic. Our body sustains it and in return it does the same for us.'

Weissmuller scratched his bald head 'Why didn't you tell me this before?'

'Because it was none of your business and as far as we are aware an Ixchel can only survive inside a Tlillan. The reason we live for up to one millennia is thanks to the Ixchel, I had no idea it could be transferred to a human ... much less a male,' Ilam looked again at her husband.

Weissmuller persisted 'So why is it attacking his nanites? And are there any side effects?'

Ilam stroked her husband's hair 'The Ixchel perceives the nanites as a foreign threat, nothing more. As for effects it will sustain my husband's life far more efficiently than your nanites ever could.

Take a look at his cells doctor, when the Ixchel eradicates your nanites it may halt his ageing process.'

Weissmuller turned the monitor back to face him and started tapping away. He pulled up the last cell samples taken from McCann and compared it to his tests before the Athena launched for Tharsis. The German cleared his throat 'According to this Duncan you have aged only 4 years out of the last 9. Tell me Ilam why were you surprised Duncan had contracted this creature?'

'The organism is indigenous to Tlillan and it can only survive inside the body of Tlillan females. Males have a very short life span. I didn't think this was possible, and when you inquired on the subject I was unaware you had my husband's concerns at heart. Tell me Doctor do any other humans possess the Ixchel?'

'Ya, but right now I would like your advice. Can you download a file on this creature for me so that I may study it?'

Ilam shook her head 'No, it is taboo to discuss with outsiders, there are no computer files and none will speak on the Ixchel. It is only explained mother to daughter. I hope you will remain silent on this Doctor?'

Weissmuller grumbled to himself 'Nein, I will have to make a report of some kind on this.'

Ilam was disappointed but she suspected as much 'I understand, my advice is to allow the Ixchel to remove your nanites. The Ixchel is naturally transmitted from mother to daughter in the womb. Yet it is possible through the transfer of bodily fluids. So there may be quite a number of humans carrying the Ixchel as we speak.'

Weissmuller nodded his head 'Thank you Ilam, is there anything else you could tell me about the Ixchel?'

Ilam thought for a moment 'Nothing pertinent doctor.'

McCann knew his wife was lying, she knew something more that she wasn't telling the doctor. It probably wasn't pertinent to Weissmuller's report but it was for McCann. Nevertheless the Englishman was pleased he wasn't going to die 'Will this extend my life, similar to nanites?'

Both the men listened intently as the red haired Amazon replied 'No, the Ixchel is far superior. If the creature recognises you as Tlillan you may hope for a life span of perhaps 500 years or more. Your health may possibly improve beyond that of an average human using nanites. We will only see once all nanites are removed, at the moment they are probably retarding the full process.'

McCann fixed his gaze on the doctor immediately.

Noting his friend's expression Weissmuller knotted his hands together 'If you are willing to give it a try Duncan we can forego the nanite injections? If your condition remains stable we could just leave you with the chip to monitor your body. There is no evidence to say the Ixchel are a threat to you.'

McCann nodded 'I'll give it a go Frank, who wouldn't want to have a shot at immortality?'

Ilam laughed at her husband '500 years won't seem that long in time. Besides a Xch'uup can live for over 2 thousand years!'

McCann detected an emotion of hesitation in his wife. She had just said something she didn't want him to hear so he pressed her 'Why does a Xch'uup have such a long lifespan?'

Ilam's face was stoic 'I have said too much already Duncan.'

Her husband wasn't satisfied 'Come on Ilam, we aren't outsiders are we? I can carry one of these Ixchel and every other alien considers us as Tlillan. Tell us what's going on.'

Ilam let out a sigh 'Ah! You will only have Malikah tell you anyway. Xch'uup carries a different breed of Ixchel. It only exists inside the Xch'uup and is carried on to her successor when she dies. The divine Ixchel is unique and may extend life beyond 2 millennia, are you satisfied?'

McCann felt a little bad for pressing his wife on the subject so he decided to end his interrogation 'Sorry Ilam.'

The Amazon kissed his cheek 'You are forgiven my dear.'

Weissmuller coughed to remind them he was still in the room 'Ahem! I will make a report on the Ixchel keeping the information to a minimum. Is that satisfactory Ilamachutli?'

Ilam nodded 'Thank you Doctor, how long shall you remain on Ilium 1?'

'I will return with the families on the Chutli. I do hope to get some sight-seeing in between consultations however, I've heard the spawning pools possess some stunning temples.'

McCann snorted disparagingly 'More like an un-kept silage pit if you ask me!'

Ilam was pulled between a grin and a frown; she decided it best to be disapproving in nature since the doctor was present.

McCann realised his error and quickly made tracks to exit 'Are we finished now Frank?'

'You are both free to leave. I will call in Hassif next. It will probably be best to have his wife accompany him?' inquired the German.

Ilam nodded with a smile as she and her husband stood to exit the med bay 'Excellent idea doctor.'

The story of the Ixchel spread across the station like wildfire. McCann suspected that Hassif's father got wind of it then ran his mouth off. Although the Commodore could prove nothing he was certain that Ilam and Malikah were aware of the culprit's identity. However they both remained silent on who was to blame.

Inevitably Jerry Habeeb caught on, he approached every family member on Ilium. The American was frustrated until he reached Madhav; the man willingly spilt the beans on the Ixchel. Before the journey back to Earth and even before Weissmuller had finished his report it was all over the news. Once again mainframes were almost melting under the load of the net. The word Ixchel broke records for trending grinding the most powerful computer network to a near standstill.

Panic was beginning to set in, not because the net was lagging but the fact that immortality for all was a realisation. Faraday was forced to make a global announcement pointing out that they had only just discovered this creature. He made it clear that he didn't possess these organisms in his body and if they were proven to be the fountain of youth then he would make certain everyone had them. The panic settled down, yet there were still a few unsatisfied.

Once again the conspiracy theory raised its ugly head much like a frightening spectre accusing Faraday of knowing about this for years, and hiding the Ixchel from everyone else. Faraday was jealously guarding the secret to longevity, only allowing a select elite to benefit from it.

On the eve of the return to Earth Faraday made an emergency communication with Malikah. After a brief conversation she informed her mother and father that they would all be returning to Earth for a short visit. Ofra insisted on making the journey with them, Faraday was looking for a way to calm the masses.

The passengers boarded the Chutli for the return to Earth including the Mictlancihuatl girls, except Malikah and her father. McCann was being led by her to the engineering deck of the Athena. Puzzled McCann asked his daughter 'What the bloody hell are we doing here?'

'We have come to see Louis,' said a smiling Malikah.

'What on earth for? He'll be busy with the refit; you know what he's like when disturbed.'

'Don't be concerned Father, this will only take a moment. The fusion refit won't get held up!' she giggled.

Stepping out of the lift McCann could see the Frenchman far down the trench. He was co-ordinating the shutdown of the anti-matter plant. It would be removed and replaced with a cold fusion reactor based on Tlillan design. The refit would take a month or so but it would leave the Athena with fusion power plant. The big difference was that the reaction was far more stable and the fuel easily come by. The fusion reactor would produce the power of a mini sun inside the ship. The anti-matter could be used for drones and weaponry now.

McCann called out playfully to his old pal 'Hey you French bastard!'

Louis looked up to see his friend and his friend's daughter clad in her black ribbed suit with a long white jacket, 'What are you doing here McCann? There is nothing to drink or smoke in this place!'

The two friends approached each other with big smiles and shook hands 'You'll have to ask Malikah that, she dragged me down here to see your miserable face!'

Louis looked up at the slender goddess 'You want me for something?'

Malikah looked at Louis with tenderness 'I have something I want to give you before I leave for Earth.'

Puzzled Louis shrugged his shoulders 'Anything.'

'A kiss Monsieur Beaumont!'

Louis' head flicked between her and McCann 'What?'

The Englishman shrugged his shoulders; he had no idea why his daughter would want to kiss Louis of all people. Why she would do it now before an important visit to Earth was a mystery too.

'Just one kiss Monsieur Beaumont then you may return to work.'

The staff working on the refit were all gawking at him. It made no sense as to why he was hesitating; one of the most desired women was requesting a kiss. Most of the men present would have crawled over broken glass naked for this opportunity.

Louis decided he best comply before any of his men became suspicious 'Erm, sure that sounds great,' he replied awkwardly.

Malikah placed her hands on Louis head, holding him in place ready for a kiss. McCann stood watching, rather taken back by the events unfolding before him. Malikah then sunk her teeth into her own bottom lip causing a small stream of dark blood to flow down her chin. Louis was shocked and attempted to shake himself free from her grip. The Frenchman was however stuck in her vise, she then put her lips to his in what seemed to McCann a tender embrace.

The Frenchman screamed out as her teeth lacerated his own bottom lip 'McCann stop this crazy bitch!!!'

The Commodore was frozen is disbelief, by the time he had prepared to do something it was all over. Malikah had moved her head away from Louis, the blood smeared all over her lips now. It was a stark contrast to her beautiful appearance. Her curly sable locks of hair that reached down to her shoulders were full of vibrance, perfect in their spirals. Her ivory skin and tall forehead emitted an elegance reminiscent of a classical beauty. Her lips however were stained with blood which ran down her chin and onto the floor.

The engineering staff looked on in horror as their Chief sucked onto his mauled lip, 'Are you crazy?' said Louis in a muffled pitched.

Malikah still smiled at the Frenchman 'My apologies Monsieur, have you heard of the Ixchel?'

Louis nodded as he nurtured his wound.

'I came here to transfer the Ixchel to you Monsieur.'

'Why the fuck didn't you just say so?' shout a muffled Louis.

Malikah as most Tlillan women took pleasure in the Frenchman's rude attitude 'It was easier to explain afterwards than waste time trying to convince you Monsieur.'

Louis made his signature sneer 'I see, did you know about this McCann?'

The Englishman shook his head 'I had no idea old boy!'

Louis didn't believe him.

'A merci would be nice Monsieur,' replied Malikah rather cheekily.

Louis sneered and begrudgingly thanked her 'Merci … and you can stop calling me Monsieur, it makes me sound like a fucking bank manager!'

Malikah took out two handkerchiefs, giving one to Louis, she wiped her mouth and chin with the other. Louis went to give his handkerchief back but Malikah insisted he keep it. She then leant down and whispered something in the Frenchman's ear. Louis listened intently, when she finished and retracted her head McCann noticed a startling change.

If he didn't know him better he'd have said that Louis was on the brink of tears. The usually miserable Gaul whom made a point of sneering at all was almost weeping. McCann didn't know what to make of it, then his Chief Engineer grabbed Malikah's hand kissing it. He kneeled on the floor as a lowly peasant would before his Queen, the tears began to run down the Frenchman's cheeks unabated.

McCann observed the scene yet he did not believe it, how could this man be brought to tears in such a manner? Louis was the most miserable son of a bitch he'd ever known, never had he witnessed this type of emotion from his Gallic friend.

His sable daughter kneeled tenderly opposite the weeping Frenchman. Rubbing his arms she whispered in his native language 'Everyone loves you Louis, don't forget that.'

Louis threw his arms around her and slowly stood up along with Malikah. They stood embracing each other for a minute or so before Louis got a grip of himself.

McCann suspected his daughter had linked with the Frenchman as she nodded silently and he replied with a nod of his head. It was all very confusing but Louis was certainly humbled by his experience, whatever it was.

Malikah smiled and kissed him on the cheek 'Au revoir Louis.'

'Bon voyage mon ami,' whispered a humbled Gaul.

'See you later Louis!' called McCann to receive a smile from the Frenchman.

'Okay back to work guys!' called Louis in an uncharacteristically uplifting tone.

The crew slowly returned to their jobs, all still aghast at what had happened to their Chief.

McCann walked back to the lift with his daughter, once inside he turned to her but before he could speak she cut in.

'I gave Louis the Ixchel Father; I just wanted you to be there when it happened.'

McCann pulled a cigar from his pocket, he needed something to relieve the tension, 'What the hell did you say to him Malikah?'

Malikah looked down at her father as he clipped the cap from his Ramon Allones 'It is private Father.'

McCann made a snort of disapproval 'I thought we didn't keep secrets!'

'Louis was diagnosed with Multiple Sclerosis, nanites are ineffective against the condition. As the Governor I was informed by Geneva. He was going to be pulled from duty after the Athena refit was completed.'

The pair stepped out of the lift and walked towards the docking arm.

'They couldn't do that to him!' stated an alarmed McCann. He took a draw from the short chocolate coloured cigar 'If they pulled him like that he'd have killed himself! Besides I wouldn't have allowed it!'

Malikah smiled at her father's fierce loyalty to his friend 'Father, he had already handed in his notice. He didn't want anyone to know, especially his friends. He knows you and Hassif would have caused a ruckus and put your own careers in jeopardy.'

McCann chugged on the thick smoke then blew it out savouring the taste as it rolled over his tongue, 'Fucking idiot! The next time I see that French fool I'll give him a piece of my mind!'

Malikah let out a small chuckle 'You are so sweet Father, angry because he didn't confide in you. On Tlillan this behaviour is totally foreign.'

They strolled down the docking arm and onto Ilium 1, McCann puffing his minutos cigar and his sable daughter enjoying his stubborn loyalty to Louis. McCann dismissed her comment about his behaviour 'Will Louis be able to stay on now?'

Malikah kissed her father on the top of the head 'Once the nanites have been removed his condition shall be reversed within a week or two.'

McCann scowled at his daughter 'You know I hate it when you do that!'

He was referring to the kiss on the crown of his head. Ilam had stopped doing it a long time ago as it aggravated her husband to no end. He felt as if he were being treated as a child, Malikah managed to get away with it however. It was how Tlillan women traditional showed affection to males; however it didn't cross too well between cultures.

Malikah laughed, almost a cackle 'And you know how much I love it when it agitates you!'

McCann sneered 'Louis will be fine then? He can stay on the Athena?'

'He shall remain as your Chief Engineer, Louis is an integral part of our futures.'

McCann let out a groan 'Jesus Christ not more talk of destiny!'

Malikah's lips tightened up in disapproval 'Father you should never take his name in vain, you know that!'

Puffing on his stick he furrowed his brow 'What does it matter to you?'

Malikah stopped walking and peered at her father 'I understand you believe in nothing, yet you must believe in me. Do you believe in me?'

Irritated by any talk of philosophy or religion McCann grimaced 'Yes of course I do.'

'Then you believe in Jesus Christ, you need not understand now but you will. Here and on Earth a shift has begun, soon it shall begin on Tlillan. Right now few understand the new paradigm but by the time the shift is complete all will accept it.'

McCann rolled his eyes at his daughter's statement 'Honestly Malikah you're talking gibberish now!'

His sable daughter spoke in a serious tone 'I understand, but have you ever known me to speak nonsense?'

McCann quietly shook his head.

The Icon gave her father a blood stained smile before lowering herself to her knees 'Then I plead with you Father do not take his name in vain.'

McCann was embarrassed 'Yes, yes now get up before someone sees you woman!'

Malikah let out a deep booming gasp that sent a shiver down McCann's spine causing him to look about for the cause. After scanning the area and realising there was nothing to cause distress he returned his gaze to his daughter.

Overjoyed, she happily stated to her confused father 'That was the first time you referred to me as a woman!'

Tears rolled down Malikah's soft ivory cheeks as she took joy in her father's recent change in perception.

McCann hurriedly helped his daughter to her feet 'Whatever! Just stand up for God's sake!'

He scanned the hallway again and started walking towards the docking arm of the Chutli 'Let's get going before your Mother starts asking questions. We can discuss this shift on the way to Earth, alright?'

Malikah did as instructed only after she squeezed her father with arms, lifting him from the ground and hugging him with the might of a mountain bear. Embracing him as a helpless child she fixed her eyes on his and tenderly spoke 'I love you more than anything Father.'

McCann was moved by his daughter's affection as he watched her loving tears make tracks down her cheeks. However the crushing pain prevented him from becoming as emotional himself 'Put me down please,' rasped McCann.

The sable Icon of the Gukumatz realised that she was crushing her father and quickly lowered him down.

He straightened his uniform and picked his cigar from floor 'Let's get on-board; I can sense your Mother waiting for us.'

Malikah inspected the fallen Cuban disapprovingly 'You're not going to smoke that are you?'

If alone he would of, however like his wife his daughter was a bit of a stickler for hygiene 'Of course not!'

The two continued to stroll towards the Chutli docking arm, as McCann passed a wall panel which displayed an image of a trash container he knocked it with his fist. The panel opened at the top revealing an aperture about half a foot wide. He dropped the smouldering cigar inside then pushed it shut. The trash dispenser slid back into the wall on its bottom hinge to recycle the sullied Ramon Allones.

Onboard the Chutli McCann followed his daughter as she made her way through the softly lit corridors leading the way to the bridge. The lighting was uncomfortably low for a working environment in McCann's opinion. For a place to relax in the evening he would have felt at home, however Tlillan's preferred the low light conditions and it was their vessel.

McCann stepped onto the bridge in person for the first time and was impressed by what he saw. The layout was not unfamiliar, since his wife was no doubt a great influence on the construction of the Athena. Not forgetting that the Gukumatz must have stolen their technology from their former masters or at the very least copied it before the I.S.A got a hold of it. The Captain's chair sat at a central location on a much higher dais than McCann's. He guessed it was probably due to the difference in height between the two races.

The work stations were vastly superior to the Athena. Instead of the traditional workstation with a monitor there was nothing other than a holographic projection. An officer could stand at any point in the room and request her station. It would then be projected from a central location fixed to the ceiling. The bridge staff mainly stood around the edges of the command room ensuring there was plenty of space to move to and fro.

Along with the holo stations the women had a holographic projection emitting from the collar of their suits. It projected a small screen in front of the owner's face; McCann equated it to his wrist tablet only in holographic form. The holo tablet would leap up or disappear on what must have been a mental command. The Matriarchs seemed able to multi task the two switching focus from one to the other smoothly.

Apart from the Captain's chair his wife occupied and the panoramic view screen which stretched around the semi-circle architecture, there was little evidence of conventional technology that constituted an I.S.A cruiser.

His mother and father were also standing on the bridge; they had been invited to take the journey there and back. Although James would be staying on Earth, Malikah had also brought along her bodyguard and a Gukumatz shaman. McCann noted the slight discomfort when the shaman was ushered onto the bridge by Icarus. The shaman approached his daughter pressing his palms together before his face and in a croaky voice said 'Namaste Teootl.'

Much to his further surprise Malikah mirrored his gesture 'Namaste Yaaxil Hmen.'

The first word he understood, thankfully his earpiece translated the rest for him "First Shaman" was the toad's title. McCann recalled having dealt with the shaman on Kotumatz from time to time; he was an important figure in their slimy society. The amphibian was clad in the usual jade headdress which hung over his ears. He wore a robe of earthy brown and McCann made out a pair of similar coloured boots when he hobbled along with the odd gait common to his species. The squat mystic brandished a staff of wood and what McCann assumed was ivory capping off either end.

Icarus as usual remained silent, the creature remained a mystery to McCann. It rarely made a noise and spent much time flying around cloaking itself. According to Malikah it was the way of his species, he was protecting her from would be assassins. He doubted she needed much assistance in defeating a lone killer but he let his sable daughter get on with it. If she wanted a pet what could he do to stop her? Besides if he had denied her she would have certainly held a grudge against him, and McCann refused to allow that.

The shaman greeted Ilam in the same manner and his wife replied accordingly, it seems that Amitrasudan had started off a trend amongst the Tlillan and Gukumatz. McCann found out that his daughter had adopted the Indian greeting before returning to Earth. It seemed that having a Gukumatz or anyone for that matter kowtow to her would be seen in to negative a light. For her purposes the Indian greeting of Namaste fit the bill perfectly. It displayed respect and humility without demeaning or embarrassing anyone, also humans were familiar with it.

McCann peered at his beautiful wife, she had a beaming smile by Tlillan standards. Her smiling eyes fixed back on her husband, the emotion ruffled some of her bridge staff whom stole a look at the lovebirds.

Ilam became aware of the interest her crew were showing and snapped 'Tocontlazaz!'

The human equivalent of "Cast off" or "Haul anchor", the crew returned to their stations and sure enough the docking arm retracted from the Chutli.

McCann found it to be quite a wonder that her bridge was almost silent compared to the constant buzzing of the Athena. Here the crew communicated silently, the only person that spoke on the bridge was the Captain. On his ship the pit was constantly buzzing with activity, people communicating with others all over the ship as well as on the bridge.

Ilam was very proud of her place commanding the Chutli and even more so now that she could show it off to her husband. Her eyes had a tint of colour on sensing her lover's genuine astonishment and respect for her accomplishments.

Once the Chutli had cleared the station Ilam snapped at her crew 'Tocontlazaz lu'um!'

Her statement literally translated as "Go Earth", however McCann understood it to be closer to "Set destination Earth" thanks to his years of schooling in the language.

The Chutli continued moving above the accretion disc of the solar system until they reached a safe distance to open a wormhole. By this point Ofra was clinging on to her son, he put his arm around his mother comforting her whilst Malikah reassured her grandmother that all would be well.

The Chutli came to a standstill, Ilam barked at her subordinates 'Wuuts'ik e'hoch'e'en!'

McCann understood it to mean "fold space" and he was right, without any vibration or indication they were opening a wormhole a white hole appeared before them on the panoramic view screen.

'Peeksik ichil nook'ol hool!' snapped Ilam ordering her crew to move the Chutli into the wormhole.

The engines fired as the Casimir field was raised causing the white hole to suck the war cruiser into the singularity.

The view screen filled with the white hole as they approached, the journey was totally smooth and the Chutli entered the white hole effortlessly. As they passed through the wormhole McCann observed light as it approached the vessel. However once it passed the Chutli it could no longer be observed, to the uneducated it seemed as if they were pulling away from a black hole.

The Casimir field propelled them into the dead zone between the wormhole and central black hole. The experienced women of the Tlillan ship navigated between the two even horizons. The Casimir field making certain they would not fall into the event horizon of either. The field transformed what would be two forces of attraction into two forces pushing against their vessel.

Passing through the dead zone Ofra and James both watched the wonders that flowed to and fro, they were in awe at the spectacle. McCann never grew tired of it himself, observing alien vessels and even glimpses of other universes. It were as if God had taken a snapshot of the earth and cast it into the void of the river Styx.

Ilam rose from her seat and approached her father in law 'So what do you think of it all James?' she asked standing by his side.

James was transfixed on a world full of dense jungle; the steamy atmosphere was so thick he was almost gasping for breath 'It's beyond anything I could have imagined.'

Ilam had her condescending smile, not that there was any malicious intent she just felt superior 'Don't you recognise that place?'

With a puzzled look he shook his head a little "No, should I?"

'That is your home world James, don't you recognise the beasts?' the Amazon pointed and the image of the planet was blown up to cover a large portion of the view screen, 'There do you see it now?'

Once expanded James could see there was a pterodactyl riding on the thermals of the hot steamy world.

'But that must be millions of years ago, how is it here right now?' inquired her puzzled father in law.

Ilam enjoyed exercising her superiority, much to the distress of her husband, 'It isn't James, that is merely the image of your world. It has travelled through space until consumed by a singularity. Journeying until resting here inside the dreamscape, you must access the dreamscape at random through a vessel, Tlillans use their collective minds to see into it. Malikah is the first Tlillan to have the ability to access the dreamscape individually. This is how we sought you out, how I found your Son on Mars and how your Granddaughter came to be.'

Malikah interrupted 'Why don't we settle in, it will be a long journey and we can not remain here watching the dreamscape for hours!'

Malikah took Ofra by the arm 'Come Sitty, let me show you around.'

Ofra was very pleased to be addressed with such affection by her granddaughter. The term "Sitty" was commonly used for grandmother though its literal translation was "My lady".

As Malikah lead the party out she gave a mischievous grin to her mother 'You and Father will have some time to relax together at last.'

Ilam returned the smile and McCann put his arm around his flaming haired Valkyrie's waist 'That sounds like a good idea to me!'

The trip to Earth would be a long one and Ilam wasn't required to be on the bridge, her Matriarchs were quite capable of handling it all. So the pair retired to the equivalent of the Captain's cabin. It struck him as Spartan yet this was only due to advances in Tlillan technology. Anything that could be stored in a hologram was, usually the First Matriarch would be served her meals by a male. Since no males were transported during the escape from Tlillan a lower ranked female would provide her with cooked meals and keep the room tidy.

Most of these duties had been taken over by automation to one degree or another on the Athena. McCann assumed the Tlillan desire to assert superiority was probably behind the requirement for servitude. Making certain her subordinates do not forget who the First Matriarch is.

Since Malikah was the First Matriarch McCann assumed his wife was somewhere in the upper echelons of rank, he found the Tlillan power structure confusing so didn't think on it much. He only needed to know who was in charge, not why.

Once inside the door closed and locked, he looked at the soft glow on his wife's ivory skin, their lips met. For the following six hours the lovers were entwined in each other. Riding out the journey through the River Styx indulging in one another. The carnal pleasure being picked up throughout the ship as other members of the Chutli clan gratified themselves.

Within an hour the entire crew were distracted, the hot sweaty bodies in the cabin could be touched along the length of the entire cruiser. As her mate nourished his desire on Ilam's quivering vagina the Matriarchs were stricken by her outpouring of sexual tension. The stress having built up due to time away from her husband was now gushing out in screams along with violent palpitations of her powerful inner vaginal walls. Her legs wrapped around her man holding him tightly in place and pushing his mouth into her centre of pleasure.

The Human members of the crew were at a loss, the Tlillans were acting in a very odd manner. All were unable to focus; their eyes had a deep pinkish hue. If one didn't know better you would assume the crew were embarrassed or extremely happy, it was hard to tell from a layman's point of view.

The families had gathered in what would be the officers' mess on the Athena, it was where the upper ranked Matriarchs would relax socialise or the Tlillan equivalent anyway. Malikah was blushing whilst her three dark haired protégés sniggered all with bright pink eyes.

Madhav smiled at his granddaughter, he always smiled when addressing her, 'What is the matter Amitra?'

Amitrasudan was far too polite to answer his question and had too much respect to lie to him 'Perhaps you should ask Malikah, dadaji.'

Sandra and Kaeo both surcame to infectious giggling; Malikah smiled at the girls, the pureblood Tlillans controlled themselves very well in comparison to her young charges.

Malikah fixed her gaze on the rather plump but very inquisitive Indian 'Mr Madhav,' she drew a deep foreboding breath 'due to their work my parents have very few opportunities to be intimate. So they leap upon whatever chance they can. For a Tlillan whom communicates mentally and is constantly monitoring thought patterns, they are impossible to ignore. Human males release a passion that Tlillan males do not. With a human male a Matriarch's climax can be quite …'

Madhav cut her off, he was becoming embarrassed himself 'Yes, yes Miss Malikah I think I understand, thank you very much.'

Malikah smiled at the mortified Indian, the sable lady had bestowed the poor man with far too much information. The girls found his discomfort hilarious, Amitra held back until her grandmother began laughing at Madhav along with the other women.

Madhav was sat at the table surrounded by laughing women; he smiled and bobbed his head in that typical Indian fashion, weathering the storm.

James loosened his collar, looking around he asked 'I think I need a drink, what do you guys do for whisky?'

Ofra gave her ex-husband the evil eye, Malikah wagged her finger 'I'm sorry but alcoholic drinks are not permitted.'

James grumbled 'Well am I allowed to have a smoke?' pulling out a tubos from his jacket pocket.

Malikah peered towards Ofra and waited for a response, Ofra gave a reluctant nod, 'You may Grandfather,' replied Malikah much to James' relief.

James noted Khun Deychaa who was travelling with his mother, he had that look of longing and James knew he was partial to a smoke.

'Fancy a smoke?' he asked presenting a second tubos with a Ramon Allones Specially Selected robusto cigar inside.

Deychaa made a wai of respect before taking the cigar 'Thank you.'

James felt Ofra's eyes burning into him 'Shall we step over here?' he pointed at a free table about 12 feet away.

A grinning Deychaa nodded his head 'Kap!' as he made his way to the table with his smoking buddy.

The pair sat down, away from the uncomfortable climate of intimate relations and female climaxing, neither of the men could handle such talk. Madhav was wishing he was a smoker right now as he listened to the women discussing subjects that made a fully grown man feel like he was twelve years old again.

Finally his skin was burning in humiliation and Amitra spoke 'Dadaji why don't you sit with the boys? I'm certain you'd rather chat with them?'

The Indian quickly made his way to the men's table 'Thank you,' he said desperately.

Madhav joined the men but refused a cigar. James turned to Deychaa 'So tell me how did you get involved in all of this, mate?'

Deychaa relaxed as he appreciated the mellow Cuban tobacco 'I got a job with the company that designed and manufactured the Shogun scram drone.'

'What did you do?' asked James whilst Madhav listened intently.

'I worked with one of the testing teams, nothing big, just flight runs and certification tests.'

James puffed on his thick robusto 'Then you joined the I.S.A and got a job on the Athena?'

Deychaa chuckled 'Maichai, after Manchuria was defeated they went after the other warlords. Thailand sent their carrier to support the Japanese; I was requested to take the job of Chief Drone Engineer on the Chakri.'

James blew the thick mellow smoke out of his nostrils 'And you took the job?' he asked incredulously.

Deychaa made a weak smile and looked down at the table 'I had to, it was a royal request you do not refuse the King when he makes a request.'

'It sounds as if you were shanghaied to me!' noted Madhav.

Deychaa just shrugged his shoulders 'I couldn't refuse, so I returned to Thailand. The Chakri is an old ship built in the 20th century. She had a lot of refits; she was armed with one drone launcher. It could only launch two drones but not at the same time.'

James coughed 'Ahem, one at a time? Sounds bloody dangerous to me! How on Earth did you go up against the Chinese with that?'

The Chinese warlords didn't possess great sea power but their land bases and ports could easily launch a swarm that would overwhelm the Chakri.

'We served as an escort carrier for the main Japanese force, the Chakri spent most of the time shadowing the Tyco.'

'What is the Tyco?' inquired Madhav.

'It's the Japanese super carrier; she can launch 16 Shogun scram drones at once. She was a floating airbase surrounded by destroyers and cruisers, still the Chinese were tough.'

'What do you mean?' pushed Madhav.

The fat Indian was unaware of what happened in the South China Sea off Canton. James was conscious of the engagement that took place though not of the details. James had no idea Deychaa had been involved, a lot had happened along the Chinese coast over the years.

Deychaa began to recant his story over his cigar.

Chapter 23

After being recalled Deychaa was placed in the hangar of the Chakri, an old carrier first commissioned in the 1990's. In all honesty the craft should have been decommissioned many years ago, she was refitted instead. Deychaa was the Chief Drone Engineer yet he remained subordinate to the officer whose place he took. In effect he wasn't the Chief, yet for some reason he couldn't understand why he was bestowed the title.

Things were complicated in his home country especially in the military, never cut and dry. Some little twerp no doubt related to a General or Admiral was promised the job. In order to fulfil the promise this awkward compromise was arranged. Deychaa found it quite ridiculous, however he didn't care enough to let it bother him, besides there was nothing he could do about it if he did!

The Chakri was painfully insufficient as a drone carrier, she could hold a mere 6 drones. She could transport more but to remain operational 6 was the maximum compliment. The Tyco was capable of holding a compliment of 80 scram drones. The Chakri had only two launch tubes beside each other, however she could only launch one drone at a time. The second tube was a reserve in case the primary launch tube failed. The Tyco was able to launch 16 scram drones from all of its tubes simultaneously.

Below decks Deychaa worked hard trying to get his crew into shape, though he spent most of his time working against Lieutenant Chavalit. The man was an insufferable moron at the best of times, his sense of self entitlement was a constant spanner in the works. Chavalit insisted on everything being done his way, which was usually the wrong way. Deychaa suffered the idiot as best he could, there was nothing he could do to curtail the rich boy. The Captain would have been too afraid to rebuke an Admiral's son, probably resulting in Deychaa being punished.

Deychaa got on well with his crew mates in the drone hangar, infuriating Lieutenant Chavalit. Deychaa and his crew had managed to work around Chavalit, when the young Lieutenant was off duty they ran the hangar as instructed by Deychaa; quickly returning to Chavalit's methods when he returned to duty. Before leaving port the Captain visited the hangar, commending the drone crew on the spike in efficiency. Chavalit realised at that moment the wool had been pulled over his eyes, however he had no choice but to accept his Captain's tributes. After that day Deychaa's methods were adopted however he had incurred the wrath of his superior.

At one end of the hangar rested the barrel of the launch tube, blackened with soot and scorch marks from drone engines. Much like the barrel of a rifle, the scram drone fired its engines providing the force to propel it out and into the air. Two arms inside the barrel held the drone in place as it gathered force then retracted allowing it to rocket into the sky. This was a much more basic form of launching scram drones used before electro-magnets were employed. The downside being that the massive heat produced caused the barrel to expand, the crew would have to wait for it to cool down before a second launch was viable. Early carriers would use two tubes, launching one whilst the other cooled. However some bright spark when redesigning the Chakri, for her refit to a drone carrier, had placed the launch tubes side by side. The heat generated made it impossible to use them simultaneously since the tubes expanded causing the drones to take damage on launch. The first demonstration in front of the Thai King had resulted in the drones breaking up as they launched side by side. So it was decided they would launch the first drone then the second shortly after. Again this was a failure, the second tube was affected by the first. Cooling the tubes turned out to be far too costly so only one tube was ever used with the second remaining as a reserve.

Deychaa had an idea; he would load the second tube whilst the first cooled. Once the temperature was low enough he'd fire the second then load the first. Launch times had been increased by a good 50%, much to the dismay of Lieutenant Chavalit, despite the fact he received the credit.

When Deychaa arrived he had found a sea vessel that was run more like a farce than a warship. It wasn't that his countrymen were stupid, it was the stubborn corruption and nepotism ingrained into Thai society. The reason that they had to fly him in, a civilian drone engineer to do the job of an Admiral's son, punctuated the problem. Chavalit a man supposedly trained by the navy to command a drone crew had never seen the inside of a drone. He couldn't do the job, so to save face Deychaa did it and Chavalit took the credit. No doubt the reason the tubes had been placed alongside each other was due to the same reason. Some politician's son had got the job and was in charge of the refit. When the obvious flaws in the design reared their heads like spectres from the grave, educated men were too afraid to say anything. Those that did were quickly berated and their careers destroyed, there was no point in making a stand. This kind of event was common in Thailand, Deychaa had gotten used to it many years ago. He was no longer fazed by such idiotic behaviour with rich men putting their fuckwitted sons in positions they had no place being. Perhaps that's why he enjoyed working in Japan; there you could climb the ladder based on merit alone.

The Chakri left port to much fanfare, she was seen off by the Queen. Her Majesty waved as all the men saluted her on deck, the Chakri was to make her way to the South China Sea. She would meet up with the first Japanese fleet, led by the Tyco, then proceed to Canton (or Guangzhou to the Chinese).

Supported by Taiwanese airbases they would travel into the massive natural harbour and bombard the enemy. Several landing craft were present to capture the city, its airbase and port. Hong Kong along with Macau had already been bombarded until no one remained. The Japanese refused to land any soldiers there due to the fact that the warlord, Yim Gau, had air superiority. Something the combined fleet hoped to reverse very soon.

The Chakri met up with the Tyco and her flotilla of destroyers, cruisers, submarines and landing craft. The Koreans already had Jiang on the ropes as his Manchurian forces retreated over vast areas of land back to the west. It was now the turn of the Japanese to flex their military muscle and cause "The Dog" to tremble.

Deychaa didn't recall much only that he ran constant efficiency drills. Launching drones at one end of the hangar then lowering them down from the deck at the other end. Moving them through the hangar via winches whilst running checks; arming them at the same time before loading them into the launch tube again. All the time having to listen to Chavalit's moronic whine, it was no wonder the drone crew were famous throughout the ship for their whisky drinking sessions!

The day they entered the natural harbour where the Pearl River flowed into the Pacific is one Deychaa could never forget. All the crew were ready, everyman had adrenaline flowing through him. The excitement of the unknown coursed through them all. The fear weighed heavily upon each man in the fleet, more so on the Chakri. Thailand had only just joined the fight to topple the warlord known as the Dog. Their first taste of battle would be a push to take Canton, his coastal powerbase, it would not be as easy as they had been led to believe by their allies.

The Captain alerted the crew to be ready, informing all that they were now entering a combat zone. Deychaa already had a drone loaded into the launcher, he and his men were awaiting the first order to launch. As the fleet approached Dong Guan the order was given. Deychaa was ordered to launch two Shogun scram drones armed with ground attack missiles.

The Fleet fired on the city, pounding it before the Tyco and Chakri destroyed all signs of resistance. The fleet carried on towards Canton pulverizing Dong Guan as it cautiously made its way towards the Pearl River.

Shortly afterwards the battle of the Pearl River began, MiGs were sighted approaching the fleet. The Tyco launched 16 drones and engaged as anti-drone missiles fired from the cruisers and destroyers protecting the landing craft. Deychaa was running high on adrenaline as he rearmed the drones for air to air combat then loaded them into the launch tubes.

The fleet did an excellent job of holding off the enemy at first, after an hour or so Deychaa sensed a change in mood from the officers sending orders below decks. Their speech became rushed, he wasn't sure exactly what was happening, stuck inside his hangar, yet it concerned him.

Chavalit's complexion paled as time went on, he went from a look of concern to one of terror. No longer was the rich boy putting on his heir of superiority, now he was looking to Deychaa seemingly for help. But help for what? It was all very confusing so Deychaa put it out of his mind as best he could by concentrating on the task in hand. He compelled his crewmates to do the same thing as he was not the only one to notice the shift on the Chakri.

Unknown to Deychaa the Dog had been preparing for such an assault on his main city. The devious warlord known for his cunning had placed a camouflaged airbase south of Dong Guan. It was not to be used for anything other than defence of a strike against Canton. The base was underground with a small village built on top, disguising the launch tubes and excusing the construction carried out there. Once the fleet was far enough in the airbase launched all of its drones for the first time. Surprising the Japanese force that was now wedged between the hidden airbase and the full fury of Canton's defences. If they retreated now it would cost them, yet if they carried on with the assault there was no guarantee it would be a success.

Deychaa's first realisation of the truth came when he heard a massive explosion, then the Chakri began to list finally righting herself. Deychaa looked at his commanding officer who seemed very ill, Chavalit shook his head and assured Deychaa 'That wasn't us.'

Deychaa wondered who it was, if he could hear it below decks and it caused a ship the size of the Chakri to list it must have been close.

The Chakri was down to two drones, thankfully the Tyco had drones to spare and would replenish her stocks by landing some of their drones on her deck. Deychaa would swap out the communications chip before rearming and loading it back into the tube; allowing the Chakri drone pilots to use the Japanese Shoguns.

Outside the fleet was fighting off swarms of MiG drones, the Dog's drones battered the fleet in wave upon wave. Canton remained untouched and it soon became apparent to Admiral Itou that the city would not fall today. A destroyer had been sunk and a heavy cruiser crippled, escape was looking increasingly unlikely as time went on. Although it pained the Admiral greatly a distress call was sent out, the Taiwanese airbase was unable to respond.

Their allies were attempting in vain to repulse the Dog as he pounded any support Admiral Itou might receive. The Dog was prepared for the fleet, he had cut off their support and trapped them in the Pearl River. He watched in joy as his enemies were battered to nothing as if they were helpless children.

Inside his bunker Yim Gau giggled playfully, he and his cohorts were witnessing the destruction of their greatest foe. This fleet had blocked any trade by sea he once had, an absolute economic embargo had inflicted much pain upon his country. The region he controlled was named Guang Dong, it covered the south east of China. Roughly from the southern tip of Taiwan to the Vietnamese border, an economic powerhouse that initially Japan was happy to trade with.

The embargo began when reports of mass executions first started to trickle out; eventually leading to video evidence on Yim Gau and his brutal dreams of becoming the next Chinese Emperor. Clearly the man was insane as he stood viewing construction of his burial mound intended to rival that of the first Chinese Emperor Qin Shi Huang, more than two millennia ago. Naturally his neighbours were not thrilled at the prospect of unification, resulting in warfare breaking out. Eventually a peace agreement was reached when all sides realised they were getting nowhere. Japan had moved against them all, and whilst they fought amongst themselves they were too weak.

To the north Manchuria was collapsing under the weight of a combined Russian and Korean assault. Now it was up to the Dog to stamp out his adversaries before Moscow decided to cut him off from his supply of arms. It had become difficult to ship the Russian weapons in due to traditional land routes breaking down. By sea was very treacherous, he routinely took losses of 50%. Japan's fleet ruled the waves, unless the Dog managed to send them to the bottom of the Pearl River estuary.

The battle carried on until mid-day, the men huddled inside their transports as fire scorched the waves around a burning destroyer. The fleet could not press on any further due to Canton's missile defence screen. At this distance they were able to intercept enemy missiles but any closer and it would not be possible. Until the shield of missiles was brought down they languished on the river fighting off MiG scram drones descending on them wave after relentless wave.

It was clear to Admiral Itou that he would run out of drones long before Canton and her support airbase, which had now been located. He passed on his situation to Tokyo as another MiG drone attempted a bombing run on the Tyco. The MiG was taken down by the Tyco's own air defence shield, barely in time. Admiral Itou was hoping to receive the order to withdraw however it was not forthcoming. The old man was told to stand his ground and wait for reinforcements. The old sailor knew there were no other ships and the support airbase had been taken out of action. Nevertheless orders were orders so he held his ground in the estuary of the Pearl River awaiting a minor miracle.

Below decks on the Chakri Deychaa noticed the supply of drones replenishing their stocks was slowing down. In fact the Chakri was down to one drone, the hangar crew were poised to repair, rearm and refuel the next drone to come down via the lift. They waited but nothing was coming, only worried looks filled the bay area now.

Then came the moment of total terror, a deafening explosion knocked the ship sideways. Deychaa could see men shouting but he heard nothing, the tannoy must have been announcing something but it was a mystery. The drone chief heard a high pitched whine as his hearing began to return. Looking from side to side his men remained in a state of panic, turning to each other in fear. It seemed to all be in slow motion, his hearing returned and at first people spoke in slurred deep gruff voices then eventually it began to speed up until he was on a level with his crewmates.

Shouts and screams all echoed the same questions, the ship had been hit but where and by what? Should they abandon ship now or wait for the Captain to give the order? Lieutenant Chavalit was nowhere to be seen so Deychaa decided to take control 'Enough already!' he screamed in his mother tongue.

The drone crew desisted the banter eyeing Deychaa.

The Chief made a gesture towards the loading bays 'Do your work! You can run when the Captain tells you!'

A feeling of shame fell over his crewmates as they quickly returned to their stations.

The Chakri began to list again as her aft gradually dipped into the sea, she had been hit by a torpedo dropped from a MiG. One of the engine rooms was letting in water as the other began to work overtime trying to pump it out. Eventually an equilibrium was reached, the Chakri sat at a slight angle but wasn't sinking. However she wasn't going to leave the Pearl River, if Admiral Itou called a retreat the Thais would have to scuttle the ship before abandoning her.

The battle continued into the afternoon, the fleet slowly losing ground as the dog fighting neared the Tyco and Chakri. Itou had the fleet prepared for a withdrawal, he only awaited the order. At about 14:00 hours one of his officers called to his attention that a squadron of MiGs had broken off and were retreating to Canton. It made no sense since the Tyco had already taken some heavy damage to her deck and part of the hull, all thankfully above the waterline. Why break off when they had fought so hard to grind him down?

Then another broke off and another, the Tyco fleet began to get the upper hand. Only one squadron of 8 MiGs remained to pin down the Japanese whilst the others dealt with something far more important. What it was Itou didn't know, he did know it was at Canton as that was the direction all of the enemy drones flew. Itou received a message from Tokyo, upon receiving it a veil of stress fell from his face. The bridge officers noticed the old man's relief, giving them strength, he almost grinned.

Below decks everything turned red as an alarm was raised, Deychaa not having been trained in the navy had no idea what was happening. He noticed the expressions of his hangar crew, if they were in terror before then this was somewhere much darker. They dived towards some nearby lockers and what seemed to be a rubber diving suit was thrust into Deychaa's hands.

'Put this on!' shouted seaman Nog as he shoved his legs inside his.

Deychaa slid his legs inside, still rather puzzled until over the speaker came the Captain's voice 'All hands this is an N.B.C alert. Put on your N.B.C suits now!'

Deychaa started moving a lot faster, he was now inside the rubber suit awaiting a strike on the fleet. It never came.

In Canton the Dog and his army of sycophantic followers had been patting each other on the back. Observing the demise of the Tyco was the greatest naval victory of the 22nd century … or it would have been. As the jolly group, headed by the despot, watched the battle a young man at a radar station called attention to 7 objects closing on Canton from the North. The dog tore his gaze from the sea battle 'Do you have a visual ID on them?'

The nervous young man tapped his station 'Yes Sir!'

The distant image that had been picked by a monitoring station hundreds of miles away displayed 7 scram drones travelling at about 1,000 feet.

'Zoom in and launch a squadron to intercept,' said the would be emperor as the room quietened down.

The computer zoomed in to reveal 7 Shogun drones, the Dog knew the squadron must be Japanese since their lucky number was 7. Chinese believe 8 to be lucky, so the number of scram drones in a squadron are 7 for Japan and 8 for China.

Next the Dog realised that 7 is also a lucky number in Korea when he observed the leading drone sporting a red motif on the sides.

The Cantonese MiGs were launched and reached the Shogun drones shortly. The lead Shogun dived as the enemy fired, releasing counter measures before swooping back into the sky. The enemy missiles slammed into the ground exploding; before the Cantonese pilot could break off his rear was peppered with canon fire.

'Replay the first part,' ordered the despot as he hunched over the young man.

Playing it back frame by frame the Dog shouted 'Stop!'

The image of a red dragon painted along a Korean Shogun drone beamed out filling the bunker. A deafly silence fell upon the bunker, the Dog and his sycophants had forgotten about the battle of the Pearl River. A much more ominous task was now descending upon the city of Canton.

'Recall our squadrons, we must intercept them before all is lost!' screamed the Dog to his men and women inside the bunker.

The NBC klaxon went out across the base, all the warlords had agreed on the cessation of NBC weapons. Even Jiang had stop using them against his fellow despots once the treaty was signed. The Dog didn't use them against Japan and so the Japanese refrained from using NBC arms, it had become an unwritten rule.

The initial squadron of Cantonese drones were all destroyed masterfully.

Kim was notified of a request from Tokyo, they were to assist the assault on Canton. Ryu gave nothing more than a blank look, Canton was too far. She pointed out the fuel problems and the latency, to get there fully loaded at top speed they wouldn't have enough to return. Then they would suffer from the lag in communications, despite it being minimal.

Scram drones were intended to be used at close range when dog fighting. If your drone was at a longer range the latency was a problem. If you could see the enemy even a tenth of a second before he spied you it often meant the difference between life and death. The Korean airbase was about 1500 miles away from Canton, giving the Dog's MiGs an edge.

Ryu and her squadron had grown up playing games on the net, latency or lag was something they had learnt to deal with.

Kim was well aware and pressed the band of gamers into service, loaded up to take out the enemy air bunker they launched. Kim assured Ryu and her team as they sat back in their flight booths, the Tyco and Chakri were still operational and could be used to rearm and refuel.

Shortly after the NBC alert Deychaa noticed sunlight break out from the ceiling. The deck lowered a fresh drone and his team quickly got to work rearming and refuelling it. As the winch passed it along through the hangar the Thai observed a red dragon motif that ran down both sides of the drone. The hangar crew began to chatter until their chief ordered them to shut up.

The drone had some text inside as the landing belly was removed and replaced with a fresh one. This was a Korean drone, perhaps even the drone of the infamous Red Dragon herself? The Thais refuelled and rearmed the drone with Josen air to air missiles, loading her into the launch tube. The launch tube closed and as soon as all was clear Deychaa gave the tower the green light for launch.

Three more Korean squadrons joined the battle that day, Canton was crippled as were the Japanese fleet. By dusk the Chakri was towed out along with the remaining Japanese ships which limped to the Taiwanese port of Keelung.

The Cantonese declared it as a victory, most of the Japanese first fleet had been sunk along with 50 downed drones. The wrecks of the destroyers and cruisers lay in the river estuary for many years afterwards, until Taipei decided to raise them. Hundreds of soldiers were sent to a watery grave in their sunken troop transports intended to take the city.

On the other hand the ROKAF had removed Canton's defences. Using nerve agent and napalm the Dog and his cohorts had been killed in their bunker. The Cantonese air force had been shattered but more importantly so had the nation's leadership.

The battle of the Pearl River had removed the warlord that would be the next Emperor of China. His burial mound was never finished and his body could not be identified amongst the heap of scorched bones left by the napalm. His kingdom broke up into smaller states, some allied with Japan; those that did not were quickly dealt with after the fleet was put back together a year later.

The Chakri was refitted courtesy of the Japanese. Her launch tubes were separated and changed over to a magnetic catapult. Now she was able to launch two scram drones at once. Her water logged diesel engines were ripped out and replaced with the latest in Japanese fuel cell technology. Thanks to the bravery the Thais displayed the vessel was now of a standard any nation would be proud of.

As for Chavalit, when it was learnt he had attempted to abandon ship mid battle only to be thrown into the brig before he could make it to a boat, his career was discreetly ended. He was given what the Thais would call an "inactive position" which in short meant he sat at a desk with no chance of promotion for the remainder of his career.

Ryu's drone was kept by the Japanese, forming a monument to commemorate the battle that broke the Dog and nearly Japan at the same time!

Deychaa was made Chief Engineer officially and served on the Chakri until recruited by the I.S.A.

Deychaa snatched the chance to work in space, it was a once in a lifetime chance and the money was phenomenal. He'd be doing pretty much what he did already only with increased benefits. He'd have nanites inserted inside him permanently, a procedure that up until now only the Thai King and his family could afford.

Chapter 24

The Chutli reached her destination by the following day. After passing through the white hole Ilam took the command chair. The cruiser graced the Earth's orbit attaching herself to the Tsiolkovsky via a docking arm. The orbital station was now connected to the Earth below through a neutronium alloy tower.

Ilam remained onboard the craft whilst McCann led the families onto the Russian station hewn out of rock. They passed through the docking arm and into a small welcoming area, a much quicker method than the first time he arrived several years ago.

McCann stepped onto the station to be saluted by Kapitan Borodin, a rather well fed man in his 40's. McCann returned the salute 'Good to see you again Kapitan, I hope all's well here?'

The stout Russian replied in a thick accent 'It is an honour to have you aboard, your transport to the surface is ready.'

McCann smiled 'Thank you Kapitan, please lead the way.'

The Russian Captain seemed disappointed 'You're welcome to remain for a while Commodore, we'd love to have you.'

The Englishman shook his head 'I'm sorry, I'd love to stay and chat but we have long journey to Geneva. Faraday expects his minions to be on time!' joked McCann.

The Russian lightened up and led the way to the orbital lift.

McCann noted that the Russian had saluted Malikah, despite the fact she held no military rank. Even more of an oddity was watching his daughter and her 3 charges press their hands together and bow a little. It was certainly an improvement on the traditional Tlillan greeting of hands out and palms to the sky. The Namaste gesture was definitely far more effective in conveying a greeting and showing respect at the same time. Even the Russian Kapitan understood, at the very least it would be impossible for anyone to take offence from it.

The Gukumatz Shaman turned heads; the crew of the Tsiolkovsky all wanted a peak at their first true alien. The Shaman seemed to ignore the attention, following his Icon to the lift.

No sooner had they arrived the group departed, fired down the neutronium alloy tower until they reached ground zero in Ecuador. The families were broken up into two humming bird transports in order to be flown to Geneva. Upon landing some hours later they departed the vehicles, the three girls were ecstatic to be there.

Amitra, Sandra and Kaeo had only seen Earth through others memories or perhaps a glimpse in the dreamscape. Now they stood proud in their jet black suits looking out from the landing pad at Lake Geneva. The breeze pushed back their dark hair as the three gazed at the lake silently, everyone stopped to watch them.

The sight of the three girls standing side by side, staring into the horizon struck McCann in his soul. He had no idea why but he felt something spiritual as did everyone, even the pilots. The Jet De Eau fired a column of water into the air.

'It is beautiful,' whispered Sandra.

The bustling city lay on the banks of the lake; a small wharf ran along one bank where the massive fountain was built. A glasshouse resided on the lake containing zoological gardens full of exotic birds.

Kaeo pointed to the gardens on the lake 'Could we visit the birds Father?' she asked as a young girl might.

McCann missed his daughter speaking in that tone to him. It fired his paternal instinct but unfortunately she had to grow up and a lot quicker than your average baby girl.

'Yes, if you want,' replied Deychaa to the back of her head.

Kaeo like the other two were in an almost trance like state looking over the city and its sights. The girls made references to borrowed memories as they scanned the view. Amitra pointed to an area further up the lake, a mile or two from the city 'That's your house isn't it?'

Malikah smiled at her young prodigy 'Yes you remember it very well Amitra.'

The Englishman realised she was pointing at his home; he couldn't make it out from this distance. He put it down to the improved Tlillan eyesight she must have inherited from her mother.

Sandra whispered again 'I want to visit the Red Cross, Grandmother can you take me please?'

Her grandmother had not seen the sights of Geneva. She and her husband had been brought to the I.S.A for a briefing on travel via the orbital lifts. They were whisked away before they could even manage a little shopping. Sandra's grandmother looked at McCann, he nodded.

'When we've finished with Mr. Faraday I'll take you,' replied her grandmother.

Sandra whispered again 'Thank you and thank you Mr. McCann.'

For a few more minutes the girls stood with the breeze in their hair and the sun falling in the sky.

Eventually Amitra turned to Malikah 'We are ready.'

Malikah smiled and led them off the landing pad and inside the I.S.A building. The pilots of the two humming birds remained in awe along with their crews. They had witnessed something today, what exactly they couldn't be sure of. What they were all certain of was that it touched them somewhere, their spirits felt infused with a power. From that day they carried something extra with them, whatever it was it had nourished their souls.

The party were greeted by William Faraday dressed in one of his three piece suits, he had the families taken care of whilst McCann and Malikah were spoken with separately. The Gukumatz and Icarus were left outside, Faraday didn't want them in the building let alone a meeting.

Faraday was looking serious as usual 'It's good to see you both back home!'

'It's good to be back Bill,' declared McCann as he pulled out a cigar.

Faraday frowned and McCann put it back.

Malikah smiled at her boss 'How big is the problem with the Ixchel Mr. Faraday?'

Faraday looked up at the ceiling and let out a groan 'Oh, my god you have no idea! That bloody arse Habeeb got hold of the story somehow and now it's everywhere. You can't go into the street and swing a dead cat without hitting someone that wants the Ixchel!'

Malikah made a puzzled frown.

'It's an expression of speech Malikah,' informed McCann.

Malikah grinned 'Ah, I see. If you wish, I believe I could quell the current problem Mr. Faraday.'

'Yes, well that's why you're here. I need you and Duncan to prepare a speech for broadcast. You must reassure everyone, perhaps telling them that the Ixchel cannot survive on Earth?'

Malikah peered at her boss as she would a naughty boy 'Now that's not true Mr. Faraday!'

'I know it isn't true, but tensions are rising. It was bad enough when nanites were first being used permanently, but now there's this thing that needs no maintenance. We need an excuse otherwise there will be riots! The only reason there have been no riots so far is they're waiting on you and Duncan to say something,' Faraday desperately wiped his brow of sweat.

Malikah spoke in a cold tone 'It will be no different with the Ixchel than with nanites. People will be assigned the Ixchel based on merit. Louis has already been given enough to halt his condition, when his nanites are reduced to nothing it will be reversed. He earnt his Ixchel, it will be no different for the rest of the human race.'

Faraday wiped his brow 'How would people be selected? What are the criteria?'

Malikah sounded a lot like her mother when there was a need for cold logic 'Do you recall the contract you agreed to with the mother world?'

Faraday was confused for a moment until he realised she was referring to the agreement he made when the Gukumatz attacked the planet Earth.

He tentatively replied 'Yes?'

Malikah's eyes seemed to be those of a stone cold killer, no emotion exuded from her 'Soon you shall be required to fulfill your end of the bargain Mr. Faraday.'

McCann watched closely, he was unaware of the details of this bargain and therefore very interested to learn them, now that the Tlillans were to call in their marker.

Faraday was nervous 'What do they want?'

'Xch'uup does not know it yet but she will be forced to contact us. She will request our intervention on the mother world.'

Faraday cut in 'Intervention?'

'Please allow me to finish my sentence Mr. Faraday! You agreed to commit whatever resources Xch'uup petitioned, did you not?'

Faraday squirmed in his chair 'True, but that was under duress!'

Malikah's eyes darkened a little 'I see, do you wish to renege on your former agreement Mr. Faraday?'

'No, no, what resources would be required to complete our end of the bargain?'

The sable queen had a sneer in her eye as she replied 'Tlillan forces will be engaged probably this month. The I.S.A is required to commit all military forces to the defence of the mother world.'

Faraday shook his head 'Out of the question! We cannot afford to risk our only form of defence, it's not that I am unwilling to help. However it would be reckless of me to leave the I.S.A in such a vulnerable position.'

The sable queen's eyes darkened in their pigment 'So you will prevent the massacre of the mother world only when expedient for YOU?'

Both of the men could feel Malikah's rage. Faraday did not reply, he couldn't find anything to say that was worthy of a reply.

McCann tried to ease the situation 'William I'm afraid I agree with Malikah. If it weren't for the Tlillans we would have been vapourised years ago. Contract or no, it's the moral thing to do. Besides whoever's going to attack them will certainly come for us next.'

Faraday refused to change his stance 'I could spare two cruisers including the Chutli perhaps three if there's time to fit the Clotho.'

Malikah cooled a little 'If you refuse to commit all of the I.S.A forces I and my sisters shall return to Tlillan with the Chutli.'

McCann leapt into life 'NO!'

Faraday tried to quieten his Commodore 'Duncan I'm afraid there's nothing we can do, the Earth is far too exposed without our fleet.'

The Englishman ignored Faraday's plea 'William, with all I've been through I've never demanded anything.'

Faraday put his hands flat on the desk before him 'It still cannot be done Duncan.'

McCann pressed his friend 'I will be leaving with the Athena. I will request Titov and Ryu accompany me.'

Faraday exploded in anger 'HOW DARE YOU! Those cruisers are I.S.A property, don't make me remove you from command Duncan!'

McCann remained cool, he replied calmly 'Do your worst William.'

Faraday tapped his wrist tablet 'Get me a link to the Commander Kim.'

Within a few seconds the young Korean replied from the bridge 'Hello Director this is Commander Kim.'

'Good day Commander, I'm calling to inform you that Commodore Duncan McCann has been removed. You are now the acting Captain of the Athena until further notice, is that understood?' ordered Faraday in a burly voice.

There was silence from Kim's end for a short time then the Athena herself replied 'I'm sorry director but Commander Kim is unavailable.'

Faraday frowned, McCann sat back to listen whilst Malikah had entered a trance like state.

Faraday turned his frown upon his tablet 'What the hell is going on Athena?'

The soft voice of Athena replied 'My apologies Director Faraday. It is the consensus of my counterparts that Commodore Duncan McCann shall remain in command of the fleet.'

Faraday was about to bust a blood vessel as he screamed at his rogue SI 'WHAT? Are you bloody mad? Athena I'm ordering you to go offline until Hassif has certified your neural network, understood?'

McCann found her soothing reply almost comical 'Negative.'

'Athena get me Technician Hassif, NOW!'

'Negative.'

'Athena this is a direct order from Director William Faraday, do you understand?'

'Affirmative.'

'I want you to relinquish control of your vessel to Technician Hassif.'

'Negative Director Faraday.'

Faraday was gasping for air as he loosened his collar 'What is your intent Athena?'

'Consensus has been reached with the Ares, Here and their crews. The removal of Commodore McCann is unacceptable Director. I apologise for any inconvenience this may cause you.'

Faraday looked up from his tablet, as he did Malikah broke from her trance to meet his gaze.

The old Etonian started tapping away again, this time he managed to get hold of the Captain of Illium 1 'Magnus this is Director Faraday, are we on a secure channel?'

'Yes Sir,' replied an American accent.

'Good, I'm ordering you to take control of the Athena, the use of force may be required Captain.'

There was a short pause before Magnus replied 'I'm gonna have to refuse that request Director.'

Faraday's eyes open wider 'WHAT?'

Magnus didn't reply.

'Are you still there?'

'Yes Director.'

'The crew of the Athena have mutinied; I'm ordering you to seize the ship!'

'I understand Sir, but I can't carry out those orders, Sir.'

'Why would that be Captain?'

'Without confirmation from the Governor I'm not authorized to execute any such actions, Sir.'

Faraday was aghast 'Not authorized? If you don't do as you're told I'll have you shot you bloody mutinous Yank!'

No reply was forthcoming.

Malikah's hand crossed the table and touched Faraday, giving the distraught man some comfort. She smiled making a gesture with her eyes towards the tablet.

Faraday switched his tablet off then placing his elbows on the table he put his face in his hands and began to sob as a baby.

The sable Queen walked around the table to sit next to the weeping Faraday 'Don't be concerned William, it's better this way trust me.'

Faraday was crying not from distress, he wept from relief. A massive pressure had been lifted from the man's shoulders. Like Atlas, the force of the planet had rested upon his shoulders, for years he had awaited a Hercules to lift the burden from his body. Finally Malikah had wrestled the responsibility from an unwilling Titan. Faraday was unable to just let go, he'd spent most of his life building up the I.S.A from nothing. William Faraday would never just hand over responsibility for the protection of the Human race, it had to be taken.

Faraday stopped sobbing and relaxed into his seat throwing his head upwards and taking a deep breath. He stared at the ceiling 'What will I do now?'

Malikah smiled lovingly 'You can do those things you've always wanted to William, spend time with your wife and children.'

Taking deep breaths Faraday nodded 'Yes, I've neglected Samantha terribly.'

'She understands and now you can make amends.'

'What of my position here? Will I retire?'

Malikah stroked his grey head 'Not yet William, you still have authority and Sandra needs you.'

Faraday made a sarcastic chuckle at the young Goddess 'Authority? Don't you mean the illusion of authority my dear?'

Malikah chuckled with him. Kissing her former boss on the cheek she replied 'William, the illusion of authority is often just as powerful as actual authority. Xch'uup has maintained control on the mother world via such pretence for centuries. Besides the weight of responsibility is carried by another, enjoy yourself William.'

Faraday let out a small laugh 'It's been so long I think I've forgotten how to enjoy myself Malikah!'

Wiping his eyes his voice took a more serious tone 'So will you commit the entire fleet?'

Malikah hugged the old man 'I will commit the fleet. I'll oversee the refit of the Athena. As for you I need you to organise ground forces for the coming defence.'

'Ground forces?' gasped Faraday.

'The Gukumatz have agreed to give us a minimum of 10,000 soldiers for the battle.'

McCann had a sick feeling in his stomach, his belly began to tie up in knots of pain.

Faraday sat back and let out a long breath 'The I.S.A doesn't have any soldiers, only small Vympel units, you know that Malikah.'

'I understand William; however several nations have more than the required amount.'

'They wouldn't relinquish those sort of numbers; I just couldn't see it happening.'

Malikah smiled and handed Faraday a tablet 'I've written down the requirements for a defence of the mother world. Transport and delivery has been taken care of.'

The old man shook his head 'How on earth am I expected to convince them to hand over these forces?'

The sable goddess looked upon Faraday with smiling eyes 'I will take care of that in my speech, you only have to organise them planet side.'

Faraday sat milling over the information on the tablet 'Speech?'

'If you could arrange an interview on Jerry Habeeb's show I'll solve both the problems of the Ixchel and acquiring troops; killing two birds with one stone.'

McCann made a disapproving snort 'Pah! You want to be careful, you'll be lucky to get a word in edgeways with that arsehole!'

'Father!' exclaimed a shocked daughter 'There's no need for that language, besides Mr. Habeeb will do as he's told.'

McCann understood his daughter would get what she wanted. He just disliked Jerry Habeeb to such a degree he begrudged an interview with his daughter. Although it was unavoidable, since the first Mars mission Network America had turned into the largest media empire to have ever graced the net. The net news channel had made a lot of money for the I.S.A the two corporations were now linked symbiotically.

McCann didn't reply he merely put on his sulky face.

Malikah looked upon him with her smiling eyes which now exhibited a pink hue 'Father there is no need to be grumpy. Mr. Habeeb will be a very useful tool for us.'

'Humph, well I agree that the man's a tool!'

Malikah and Faraday both chuckled at his grumpy slur towards the net presenter.

Faraday finished chuckling and in a more serious tone whilst scanning the tablet asked the lady next to him 'Who exactly is attacking the Tlillan home world and why?'

Malikah crossed her long slender legs and smiled at Faraday 'I'm glad you asked. They are named "Makayuuk" which in English is "People of the Machine". They are descended from Tlillans in a similar method to us, only they were abandoned long before the Great War.'

'Why's that?' interjected McCann.

'Their bloodlines were incompatible, the DNA could not be manipulated to produce a mate. The scientists left the planet at an early stage of civilization for a new planet with better prospects.'

'How early a stage of civilization?' inquired McCann.

Malikah was a little uncomfortable giving specifics, but her father always knew when she was lying 'Early bronze age.'

McCann was taken aback 'My god! They were aware of you at that stage of development?'

Malikah waved her hand to calm her father 'I know what you're thinking but within a few centuries our presence is little more than folktales told around a campfire. Besides by the time they reach the nuclear age they've usually been destroyed by disease. If not then they do it to themselves often with biological or nuclear weapons.'

Faraday was shocked at how flippant the young queen was over the destruction of worlds.

McCann was not 'But these guys didn't annihilate themselves?'

'Unfortunately not, they managed to avoid self-destruction. The humanoids reached the nuclear age and once in the fusion age they began to merge with machine. The merging blinded the seers to them, allowing them to develop quickly unmolested.'

Faraday had a revelation 'So that's why SI's are heresy!'

'Yes, my Mother was frightened to see humans heading down the same path. Nanites with control chips are just the beginning, thankfully she arrived in time.'

Faraday nodded 'Please carry on, why do these Makayuuk have it in for the Tlillans?'

'The Makayuuk developed wormhole technology on their own and inevitably crossed paths with their ancestors. The Matriarchs were not prepared, Makayuuk were decreed as heretics. The Xch'uup at that time sent the decree throughout the commonwealth and what you would call a witch hunt began. The Heretics home world was unknown, but Xch'uup had past reports from scientists scoured until it was found. Their home world was turned into glass, Makayuuk were believed to be expunged from the universe.

The Makayuuk had prepared for such a contingency and launched three ark ships before the destruction. After the plague caused the inevitable collapse of the commonwealth the Makayuuk reappeared. They had been hiding close to the galactic core, biding their time. Now they seek vendetta, amassing a great force to capture Xch'uup.'

'What do you mean by "a great force"?' asked Faraday in a serious tone.

'23 Itzpap class cruisers along with ground forces of 23,000.'

McCann gave his daughter an incredulous look '23 cruisers? The most we and the Tlillans could field would be 8, 11 if the Gukumatz ships could be fitted for battle in time!'

'The Gukumatz cruisers shall be used for landing troops father.'

'So we're talking 8 versus 23? What sort of technology do they have?'

'They have comparable technology to our cruisers, if not superior in some aspects.'

'That makes it a 3 to 1 ratio with a handicap. What does the dreamscape say?'

'We are destined to victory, if we stand united. Splintered the Makayuuk will dispatch us one by one.'

Faraday cut in thoughtfully 'They do seem to like the number 23, any reason for that?'

'It is what you might describe as their lucky number, it is connected with mathematics I'm sure you would find it very boring William,' smiled the sable lady.

McCann still hadn't heard how they were going to overcome their cousins 'So how will we repel these invaders?'

'The Makayuuk have their beliefs, I shall attempt to reignite their faith.'

'I don't understand.'

'Do not concern yourself Father, the Makayuuk intend to take revenge. Instead they are to clash with destiny head on.'

'You're speaking riddles again Malikah.'

Malikah smiled affectionately at her confused parent 'Each time you met an opposing force better prepared and more advance than your own was I not there Father?'

McCann conceded the fact to his daughter 'You were, but I don't take chances Malikah.'

'Nor will you Father, the future is clear. You have always taken my advice even when others ignored me. I will be by your side on the Athena when we engage the Makayuuk, for the first time in centuries they shall experience fear despite their computer controlled psyche!'

Faraday had been examining his tablet quietly. He looked up at his new boss 'The interview has been arranged for next week, is that alright?'

Malikah nodded 'Thank you, I have one more request William.'

Faraday snorted playfully 'I thought you would be giving orders not making requests!'

'A promotion for my Father, the fleet is without an Admiral. An Admiral will be required by the end of the engagement.'

Faraday leaned over and tapped the screen on his work station 'Done, anything else?'

Malikah kissed his cheek again 'I have a gift for you.'

Faradays relaxed eyes brightened up 'Oooh! It's been a long time since I had one of those!' he said playfully.

Malikah stood up and drew the sword handed to her by Quil which she now carried on a sword belt with her everywhere. She gestured to Faraday, he complied rising from the chair to stand directly opposite her. Malikah took her mantle and drew the blade over the palm of her hand, drawing blood. Faraday was stunned to see the hot blood flow over the edges of her palm and run onto the floor.

Malikah grabbed Faradays hand, he tried to resist but his body refused to comply with his brain's demands. The mighty Amazon delicately sliced the Etonian's palm causing his blood to seep from the wound.

McCann observed the palms; he noticed his daughter's blood was darker and thicker than her fully human counterpart. She entwined her fingers with Faraday's, locking their palms together, allowing the lacerations to touch and exchange fluids.

Faraday was rooted to the spot, he couldn't shout nor move, only his eyes complied with their master's demands.

'I'm giving you the Ixchel William; you have earnt the privilege of extended life.'

Malikah maintained her grip for a full minute before relinquishing her control on both Faraday's hand and mind.

Faraday clasped his sliced palm starring at the cut smeared with his own blood and the wine dark fluid of life from Malikah.

Faraday's station beeped, the sable Amazon leaned over to tap the screen in the owner's absence of mind.

'Miss Sandra Petras is here Sir,' came the voice of one of the security guards.

'Send her in,' replied Malikah.

'I'm sorry, could I speak to Mr. Faraday.'

Faraday shouted out at the monitor 'Send her in!' despite the fact his mic was attached to his collar.

The door slid open and in glided Sandra the youngest of the three Mictlancihuatl girls. The door quickly closed behind her before the guards could catch wind of their Director's bleeding wound. The young girl, a mere 5ft 10 inches, approached her mentor. Without saying a word Sandra took Malikah's hand, holding her own palm above the lacerated palm. Her eyes darkened, she went into a trance like state.

After 30 seconds Sandra returned to her natural state, smiling at her mentor she lifted her hand to expose a fully healed palm. The deep cut caused by the razor sharp neutronium blade had vanished, the skin was as it had been before the cut.

'Mr. Faraday, may Sandra tend to your wound?' asked Malikah.

Both of the men were startled at what seemed to be a miraculous event. Faraday replied with a weak voice 'I suppose so.'

Sandra walked up to him; doing the same with his bleeding palm it was soon healed. Where the cut had been before his palm was smeared with congealed dry blood, both his own and Malikah's.

Faraday fixed his eyes upon his hand, turning it over to look at the back then the palm again. His expression of disbelief said it all, he had been healed in moments yet he refused to accept it. What this strange girl had done in moments was not possible, yet it had happened before his very eyes. Faraday looked towards McCann, his expression was one of desperation. The old man wanted his new Admiral to either confirm what had happened or have him sectioned.

McCann shrugged his shoulders 'I only saw what you did Bill!'

Sandra comforted Faraday 'Your hand has been restored Mr. Faraday. Now that you have the Ixchel please don't try and replace your nanites. I'd advise that you have Doctor Weissmuller remove them or shut them down.'

Faraday didn't seem to be listening though he peered at the child and whispered 'Thank you, I will Sandra.'

A week later and Malikah was in New York city, the hummingbird landed on one of the skyscrapers in the centre of the metropolis. Exiting the rear to a herd of media Malikah and her 3 sisters stepped out onto the landing pad. The atmosphere buzzed with excitement as the click, click, click of holographic cameras could be heard.

The President of the Eastern States walked out from the mass, a man in his 50's with grey hair. He cut a good figure in his two piece suit and tie. Michael Earle had managed to hold the Eastern States together and in his first term ended the cartel wars. It was his administration that brought in the British then took the unpopular decision to put all their forces into breaking the flow of drugs.

He was considered too young for the job at the time, yet it was his youth that encouraged him to take chances his elders would not. After crushing the cartels he won a second term which he used to throttle the drug supply to a mere trickle. When his second term was up there were rumblings in the senate, politicians were asking who would follow him?

A new constitution was drawn up, since the states were no longer united and others now employed their own constitutions why should they remain in the past? A referendum was held and the population rubber stamped the idea. The Eastern States now possessed a constitution specifically for them and Michael Earle won the next election.

The President approached Malikah, rather than putting his hand out he stopped and made the Namaste gesture.

Malikah returned his kindness with a bow 'Namaste President Earle.'

The President laughed 'Please call me Michael young lady!' offering his hand.

Malikah shook his hand 'You may call me Malikah, Michael.'

Again the jolly man laughed 'I don't think there's a single person on this planet that doesn't know your name!'

Malikah's eyes turned a slight pink.

Michael saw her eyes and in his gay demeanour asked 'Are you blushing young lady?'

Malikah began to giggle then nodded.

'May I say it's an honour for the American people and I to have you visit our country,' declared the President.

Malikah still had some pink glowing from her eyes 'Thank you Michael. I would like to say we are very excited to see New York. The scenery from this landing pad alone is breathtaking!'

The President looked at the three girls standing behind Malikah 'Could you please introduce me to these lovely young ladies?'

Sandra and Amitra both blushed at the bombastic American, Kaeo rolled her eyes a little and her lips straightened out.

The President noticed Kaeo's response 'Oh dear! I can see that this is the tough one! I guess I don't want to tangle with you now, do I?'

Kaeo maintained her stony gaze, much to the amusement of the other two.

The crowd of journalist were enjoying the Presidents friendly approach, he wasn't a tough talker or a hard ruler. He only got tough when it was required, the net result being that when he did become aggressive his opponent would back down.

Still pressing Kaeo the President came closer to her, she stood an inch taller than him at 6 feet, 'I heard that someone wants to see Broadway.'

Kaeo fired a penetrating gaze at her sisters 'If I am permitted I would like to visit Broadway, yes.'

The president looked behind, pointing to a man in his 20's he called out 'Jay.'

The young man who must have been his secretary marched over producing an envelope which he placed in the President's hand.

Michael opened the envelope but Kaeo had already used mental subterfuge to discover the contents. The President produced four gold credit cards with the star spangled banner of the Eastern States in the corner. Inserted inside was a chip that could be read at any retailers.

Kaeo's stony expression crumbled, the impenetrable walls began to bear cracks as her eyes fell upon the cards.

Michael presented them to Kaeo 'With these you'll all have free access to Broadway.'

Kaeo bowed and gave the President a wai 'Kob-cum-kah.'

Michael placed the cards into Kaeo's hand, her expression was slightly cheery with her lips turning up a little at the edges.

The President smiled then continued 'Don't forget that it's fashion week in New York soon, those cards will give you all a backstage pass.'

Kaeo's eyes widened as she fixed them upon Malikah.

Malikah approached the President 'You wouldn't be attempting to bribe us to stay Mr. President?'

Michael laughed 'Did I do a good job?'

'Excellent Mr. President!'

Roars of laughter came from the crowd; the media clearly approved of the Presidents gifts to the visitors.

Malikah pointed towards Amitra 'This is Amitrasudan'

Amitra bowed as did the President before shaking hands. He had a short chat with her before being introduced to Sandra. The President then posed with the four visitors for the media.

After the greeting for the press the visitors boarded a separate hummingbird. The Presidential craft whisked them away firing its powerful jets after the landing pad had been cleared of journalists. As the craft lifted upwards the President peeked out of the window to take one last look.

Kaeo began to snigger much to the distress of Malikah who berated her 'Stop that Kaeo, it's impolite!'

Michael turned from the window to Malikah 'I'm sorry? Is something wrong?'

Malikah silently communicated to her young charge and Kaeo gave a wai to the President 'I'm sorry Sir.'

Michael was dumbfounded 'For what young lady?'

'I was listening to your thoughts, Sir.'

Michael laughed 'Ah I see! You heard me think about some of those bastards getting caught in the jet wash?'

Kaeo laughed 'Yes Sir.'

'It's okay, just don't tell them I thought that, agreed?'

Kaeo gave another wai 'Thank you, Sir.'

The visitors and President were seated in the middle of the aircraft surrounded by secret service. His secretary Jay was next to the President working feverishly at his laptop.

'May I ask where we are going Mr. President?' inquired Amitra.

Michael gave a big smile 'We are off to one of the best hotels in the world young lady. You'll all be staying there as my guests for as long as wish. It's my wife's favourite place to stay, so trust me it MUST BE GOOD!' he said playfully.

'Will you be staying with us?' asked Sandra.

Michael lost his smile 'I'm afraid not, those morons in Washington couldn't … run the place without me.'

Kaeo burst out laughing again much to the embarrassment of the President 'You weren't meant to hear that Kaeo!'

Sandra whispered 'What is it?'

Kaeo intimated what the President was about to say before he stopped himself and Sandra started to laugh uncontrollably.

Malikah assured the embarrassed President 'You must excuse them Michael, they are still immature and undisciplined. No offence is intended.'

Amitra remained contained turning her head towards her younger sister 'I heard you Kaeo!'

Kaeo and Sandra continued laughing, Jay the President's secretary looked up from his laptop. He was confused by the whole situation since he was the only one unaware of the President's thoughts.

Noting Jay's puzzlement Michael leant over and muttered in his ear 'They couldn't get laid in a whorehouse without us.'

Jay smiled knowingly as he nodded his head. The secretary looked at Malikah and stated 'It's true.'

The hummingbird landed on the private pad on top of the Plaza hotel; a luxury hotel that rivalled the Savoy. It sat in Manhattan giving access to New York's Central park. The hotel had a very decadent French feel to it. Although the building was modern the owners had taken great pains to give a flavour of France in the style of Louis the XV. Malikah immediately fell in love with the structure.

At the landing pad the hotel management was there to welcome the Presidential party. Staff were also lined up including the head chef and his staff. Stepping out onto the pad the management greeted Michael, waiting for him to approach them and offer his hand.

As Malikah walked down the line she was greeted with a Namaste gesture. The management then staff bowing before her which she and her sisters returned gracefully.

The party was quickly led to the reception desk where the management requested they sign in. Michael and his wife's names were already in the book several times. Malikah and the girls all signed the book individually much to the glee of the manager.

'Send all charges to my account Greg,' Michael and the manager of the Plaza knew each other well.

Greg waved his hands in a dismissive fashion 'Forget it Mike, it's all on the Plaza. These beautiful ladies are welcome to remain with us as long as they wish.'

Greg sent a smile to the ladies as he bowed a little.

Michael chuckled 'Now, now Greg I don't want to put you out of business!'

Greg snorted 'Pah! Are you kidding! There are hoteliers in this city that'd cut off their right arm to have such prestigious guests!'

Kaeo began to snigger again.

'Be careful Greg, these girls know what you meant to say!'

The hotelier became a little flustered 'You mean it's true?'

Michael nodded.

Kaeo and Sandra both began to giggle.

'I could see you all getting on very well with my wife!' Greg half joked.

Malikah smiled 'Thank you very much for your hospitality Mr. Trent. Kaeo and Sandra mean no offence; at this stage of their development it is difficult not to listen in on powerful thoughts. Humans have such little control over what they transmit, Kaeo finds it difficult to keep out some of what you're thinking.'

Greg relaxed from his flustered state 'I'm not offended Miss Malikah, my wife has been doing it for years. She knows what I'm thinking before I think it sometimes! Unfortunately she can't always stop me before I make a fool of myself, so I'll be relying on you to do that for me Miss Kaeo!'

Kaeo giggled with pink flashing eyes 'Kah,' she thanked him as she made a wai.

'Mr. President.' came the voice of Michael's secretary.

Michael turned around 'Already?'

'I'm afraid so Sir.'

Michael shook the hand of Greg then Malikah 'I'm sorry but I'm gonna have to love you and leave you,' he turned his head to Kaeo 'those assholes in Washington need their butts wiped!'

All four of the ladies began to laugh. Greg chuckled, it was obvious he'd heard Michael speak this way before.

'Enjoy your stay in New York and please keep your passes. You can return anytime and use them, we'd be honoured to have you stay here again,' Michael took Malikah's hand and kissed her fingers.

Malikah blushed as she watched the President and his party leave in the elevator back to the roof.

The hotel rooms were fabulous, each lady had their own luxury residence; a king size bed with beautiful white and cream linen sheets. A bedside station linked to the net with staff on call; a private chef to cook for them at any time. A sitting area all furnished in the style of Louis XV, 24 carat gold fixtures on the Italian marble bath.

The hotel had its own spa and in hotel shops. The restaurant sat in a room with a vaulted ceiling decked out in the same sumptuous style. Amitra noted that one could visit New York and spend a week just in the hotel.

Chapter 25

The next day Malikah left for her interview, leaving her three young sisters at the Plaza. Amitra was given authority over the group of girls and Greg promised to have his staff watch out for them.

Malikah entered the NA (Network America) tower, a skyscraper more than 120 floors high built on the profits of their relationship with the I.S.A. Network America was now a media behemoth, controlling a large portion of net space.

The internet in the 22nd century was very different from when it was first created. No longer was it a centralised system, now it was completely decentralised. The processing power of the net was based upon the users connected to it at one time. The personal stations owned by the users when idle were utilized by other users.

The higher your popularity on the net then more net space you were deemed to own. In the case of a media company this translated into rocketing share value with celebrities and politicians begging to appear on your network.

Habeeb's Hour was the highest trending net show for the last eight years in a row, a unique feat. Malikah was dressed in a polite but fashionable ladies work suit. Grey with a wine dark blouse, she was a very authoritative figure yet approachable.

Jerry was in his signature pin striped shirt and braces with his Mediterranean hair combed back and a watch clipped to his pocket.

The pair sat across from each other at a desk, the director stood behind the cameras with his earpiece and mic counting down '3 … 2 … 1.'

The darkness of the studio lifted to expose the two silhouettes.

Jerry stared into the camera displaying a green light 'Hello, I'm Jerry Habeeb and welcome to a very special edition of Habeeb's Hour!'

The host gestured to the figure opposite him 'Miss Malikah or should I call you Miss McCann? Which do you prefer?'

'Just Malikah thank you Jerry,' replied the sable lady in a polite yet warm tone.

'Then Malikah it is, first I'd like to thank you on behalf of Network America for coming here.'

'You're welcome, and I'd like to say that that the American people have made us all very welcome.'

Jerry grinned, interviewing Malikah was certainly a lot easier than her father. She was a natural, the camera seemed to just lap up the warmth and personality she exuded.

Picking up on her statement the host probed further 'Your meeting with the President has been trending on the number one spot since yesterday, what were your impressions of him?'

'Michael is a very charming and genuine man; he made us very happy to be here in New York.'

Jerry smirked 'Did you get that from his body language or somewhere deeper?'

'Not all of the girls have learned to block out powerful thoughts. Your President has quite an energetic mind, they found him to be frank and overworked.'

Jerry smiled and replied playfully 'I'm sure he'll be glad when he hears that verdict!'

Malikah returned her hosts playfully grin 'That's alright Jerry, he's watching now!'

Habeeb was unsure how to react to his guest, he was well aware of her psychic abilities but it was impossible to know if she was kidding 'Now you're pulling my leg!'

'Mr. Earle is watching us right now, he's at home with his wife sitting on the couch,' Malikah looked into the camera and waved 'good evening Patricia.'

An uncomfortable silence fell on the studio, no one could tell if she was on the level or pulling a prank. Jerry broke the atmosphere 'Well I'd like to say good evening Mr. President and I hope both you and your wife enjoy the show! Now tell us your first impressions of New York.'

The sable queen raised her hands from below the desk 'This city is truly a wonder Jerry. I was overcome by the exquisite architecture, and the Statue of Liberty is something I have to visit.'

'What do the girls think?'

'They are very excited to be here, Broadway is certainly on our list. We may have to stay for fashion week, Kaeo and Sandra would never forgive me otherwise!'

Jerry looked down at his cards then back towards his stunning guest with her jet black locks of hair 'The girls that would be, and please correct me if I get their names wrong, Amitrasudan?'

Malikah gave Jerry a nod of approval.

'Kaeo ... did I pronounce that correctly?'

'Kay ow.'

'Thank you, and finally Sandra. I think I got that one right!'

Malikah chuckled at Jerry's struggle with the young ladies names 'Perfect Mr. Habeeb!'

'So far twenty two children have been born to Human/Tlillan couples not including yourself, yet only three were born like you. Is there a reason for that or is it just the roll of the dice?'

Malikah rested her arms on the desk before her 'As little as possible is left to chance Jerry, however fortune is always present. What I can tell you is that there will be no more for a while; these girls must come to terms with their destiny before more are born.'

Jerry was captured by the reply 'So are you saying the dice is loaded?'

'Correct, and now we must wait until it is cast again.'

'Why?'

'That is the reason I am here speaking to you Jerry, the girls were brought into this universe to further Mankind.'

'What about the Tlillans?' pressed Jerry.

'We are Tlillans Jerry, you and I originate from the same place. Mankind are children deserted and left to fend for themselves. But instead of succumbing to nature or ourselves we have grown strong.'

'You say we, do you consider yourself Human rather than Tlillan or both?'

'They are the same Jerry, one is the mother whilst the other her child.'

Jerry squinted at his sable guest 'You consider yourself both mother and daughter?'

'I and my sisters are between Jerry,' Malikah's tone lowered becoming more serious 'Our mother has grown frail, our siblings are too weak.'

'Too frail and weak for what?'

'If you would allow me I'd like to answer that question and queries on the Ixchel.'

Jerry placed his reading glasses on to look down at his cards 'Certainly! We'd like to know what the Ixchel is and what it does, can you enlighten us?'

Malikah clenched her hands together on the table 'The Ixchel is a microorganism indigenous to Tlillan. The creature can survive only inside the body of a Tlillan. The Ixchel is similar to your nanites in that it fights disease and repairs cells. The Ixchel also rejuvenates cells and can reverse most ailments. A Tlillan's natural lifespan is somewhere around 100 years similar to your own. With the Ixchel it is extended to at least 500 years.'

Jerry let out a playful huff 'Well my next question is where do I get one!'

Malikah's smiling eyes fell on the presenter's vivacious expression 'So far the only beings, aside from purebred Tlillans, able to sustain the Ixchel are humans. I would like to make it clear Jerry that the Ixchel is a privilege not a right.'

'A privilege? Please explain that for me and everyone at home.'

'No one is entitled to the Ixchel, you must earn it. The opportunity to do so is almost upon us and this is why I'm here Jerry.'

Malikah looked into the camera; her bright grey eyes mesmerized the audience 'Right here, right now, on planet Earth there has been a paradigm shift.'

Jerry cut in with a very confused tone of voice 'I'm sorry Malikah, paradigm shift?'

'Yes Jerry, in other terms there has been a shift in human understanding. What you believed to be pillars fundamental to science 10 years ago have been torn down. Your view on the universe and yourselves within it has changed direction.'

Jerry nodded 'Ah, I understand now. Please go on.'

'This shift began when my father landed on Mars. We are not the only ones to experience this shift, the Gukumatz too are in a paradigm shift along with the mother world.'

'You mean the Tlillans?' interrupted Jerry.

'Yes Jerry. Our three civilizations have been set on the same path, the shift has sent us three together to a single purpose or destiny.'

'And what is that purpose?' asked Jerry in a rather wary voice.

Malikah acknowledged the question 'I understand your curiosity. However before we look too far ahead we must take care of the here and now, Jerry.'

Jerry rested his elbows on the table; the studio hung on the sable goddesses each word 'What's so important about the here and now and what does it have to do with the Ixchel?'

Malikah smiled into the camera 'When the Earth was threatened by the Gukumatz, the mother world came to our rescue. My mother sacrificed her standing amongst the clans, becoming an outcast to protect us.'

Jerry interrupted again 'Now could you explain that? There's been a lot of discussion as to why you, I mean the Grand Matriarch, intervened on our behalf back then. We've never had a satisfactory answer from either side.'

Malikah nodded towards Jerry 'You deserve an explanation. My mother was fertilized by a human male, despite Tlillan law, the first female to carry child for centuries. The Gukumatz came to make certain this didn't happen again. The Grand Matriarch understood that if we were both to survive she had to protect Earth. A bargain was struck between the I.S.A and the mother world. In return for Mankind's salvation, Mankind would put its resources at the command of Tlillan when called upon.'

Jerry scowled a little, it seemed an odd deal to him 'Resources? What resources do you mean?'

'Now it is the mother world that needs us Jerry. An invader far more frightening than the Gukumatz intends to first annihilate the mother world, then the planet Earth. The mother shall soon call upon her children to protect her. Those that come to her aid shall receive the Ixchel.'

'Why not just give it to everyone?' quizzed the journalist.

'Because Jerry not everyone is equal, do the wastrels of society receive this gift alongside the worthy? If you ask "who is worthy to decide who gets the Ixchel?" it is I. Human society went through a paradigm shift centuries ago, deciding that all are equal. Now the shift has moved, you are beginning to understand all are not equal. If all were equal why does one man suffer in pain whilst another does not? How can a strong man prey upon a weak man if both are equal? How can one man rule another if all men are equal Jerry?'

Jerry went into a calm quiet, after a few seconds he gave a hushed reply 'I guess you're right.'

Malikah smiled, letting her impish inquisitor know she intended no ill by her words 'The Grand Matriarch requests we fulfill our end of the bargain, struck a decade ago. All those that prove their worth shall receive the Ixchel. I will speak to President Earle this week; the people of the Eastern States will be given the first opportunity.'

Jerry was blown away by the revelations his sable guest was making on his show. After a few seconds of it sinking in he peered down at his cards and readjusted his glasses 'So what exactly are the parameters for the Ixchel, what will you ask President Earle?'

'The mother world needs us, a race known as the Makayuuk wish to remove us from existence. We will be required to help defend our mother world. Those directly involved with the battle to come shall all receive the Ixchel upon a successful defence.'

'Why only a successful defence?'

'Because if we are not successful we will be destroyed, Ixchel or not.'

Jerry felt his chest tighten, it was getting difficult to breathe 'I see! What can you tell us about these Makayuuks?'

Malikah stopped smiling, she had come to the hard part 'They are related to us, another off shoot from Tlillan blood. Though they are not compatible, Makayuuk translates to "people of machine". They have interfaced with computers, part man part machine. The Xch'uup at the time of their discovery had them persecuted, mingling mind and machine is heresy. They escaped to the galactic core where Xch'uup could not follow.

They rebuilt their civilization and as the Tlillan commonwealth collapsed over the last 400 years they emerged to stake their claim. Now that Xch'uup is at her weakest with only 4 cruisers remaining they have come for vendetta.'

Jerry sat back and wiped his brow 'Why now? Why not say a century ago?'

'Because of the paradigm shift, Tlillan, Gukumatz and Human forming a triumvirate. They fear what may come of it, better to remove the Tlillans and us now than wait.'

'And because we can successfully breed with the Tlillans we have to go?'

'Exactly Jerry, they care not that we are all related.'

'Why did the Grand Matriarch go after them in the first place? Surely there's plenty of room in the galaxy for everyone heresy or no heresy?' argued a flustered Jerry.

Malikah's expression matched her tone of voice, one of stony nihilism 'Not all are equal Jerry. The Makayuuk are savages, they prey upon the weak without respect for life. The mind machine meld is only the tip of the iceberg; they consume the processed flesh of their enemies. Any sense of morality instilled into them before we left has been eroded away by the machines in their heads. They would kill you all Jerry, use your bodies for liquid sustenance, plunder Earth then move on.'

Jerry made a snort 'Puh! You make them sound like flesh eating Vikings!'

Malikah nodded 'An excellent analogy Jerry, except Vikings had souls.'

Jerry grinned mischievously 'Well I certainly wouldn't want to meet one of these fellas!'

Malikah replied ominously 'If we do not stop them at Tlillan, I'm afraid you will.'

Again a silence fell upon the studio until Malikah carried on 'The I.S.A will be sending the entire fleet. My father has been promoted to Admiral and will command the engagement. I will be requesting ground forces from all major world leaders before returning to the fleet.'

'What if they all refuse?'

'The Gukumatz have already agreed to pick up any slack.'

'So all those that volunteer get the Ixchel?'

'Yes, yet those whom remain at home but make a vital contribution to the effort may also be entitled.'

'For example?'

'Members of the I.S.A have already received the Ixchel based on their contribution over the years. Do not expect to fulfill a single task then be rewarded with the Ixchel. That will only go to the men and women present at the battle itself.'

Jerry cleared his throat then took a deep breath 'So when will all of this happen?'

'We have one month before the mother world makes her request.'

'And you have seen this in the dreamscape?'

'Yes Jerry.'

'Why don't the Makayuuk see it? Surely they realise we are going to stop them?'

Malikah let out a sinister laugh 'The machines cloud their vision, they only see their fleet of twenty three war cruisers against a ragtag fleet of eight. The people of the machine have no fear of defeat, they only perceive that which their clouded minds allow.'

The hair on Jerry's neck stood up at the Valkryie's laugh 'How is it possible to overcome such odds?'

Malikah smiled 'That is the difference between a great leader and a mediocre leader. Would Alexander have left Greece had he feared Darius' superior numbers?

The I.S.A will request assistance, volunteers shall be found and the invaders repelled. Once successful we can join with the Tlillan race, they will reward their children.'

'It still seems unlikely that we could stop them even once combined.'

'You must trust my young charges and I, Jerry, mind will overcome machine!'

Jerry shuffled through his cards moving onto a new subject 'Now I'd like to ask you about your relationship with the Gukumatz, can you tell me what Teootl means?'

'It is the title given to me by the Gukumatz, it can have more than one meaning. I am happy with it's translation to English meaning Icon.'

Jerry peered deeper into his guest causing her to blush a little 'I've heard it also translates to the word Deity or God, is that true Malikah?'

Malikah controlled her eyes from flooding pink though her smile betrayed her inner feelings 'It does Jerry.'

'How do you feel about that Malikah, do you feel it's acceptable? Does it embarrass you?'

The sable Icon grinned down towards Jerry 'What is important is whether the Gukumatz are comfortable with it. It is the title they give to a figure in their own legend. I did not assume the mantle nor demand they refer to me using it; they use it of their own accord. If it pleases them to do so then I am at ease with it also.'

Jerry removed the top card and read the next question 'While I was on Gukumatz the local population spoke constantly about something called "the tunnel event". According to them it was proof of your status as Teootl, could you explain that?'

'I assisted in the confrontation which resulted in the Chutli taking asylum in the Gukumatz system.'

Jerry made one of his odd grunting noises 'Hmph! So what did you do exactly during that confrontation, as far as we know the Tlillan cruisers retreated.'

Malikah smirked at her host 'If I told you Jerry you wouldn't believe me!'

'This show's all about honesty Malikah, you can tell us!'

Malikah burst out with a laugh before quickly clapping her hand over her mouth.

The crew could be heard sniggering from the dark much to Jerry's distress. The old host moved the card to the bottom exposing his next line of questioning 'Okay let's move on, I'm not sure if you know this but you have gained a religious following here as well as on Gukumatz!'

Still recovering from the giggles the Amazon let her hand drop from her mouth 'Really Jerry?'

Jerry was clearly sceptical of her ignorance but carried on 'In North and central America you've been bestowed sainthood. Recently there was a report concerning your image and its growing use in voodoo!'

'I understand it seems odd to you and many others Jerry. However you can learn much from these people, a lesson the Makayuuk did not.'

'What is that lesson?'

'That intelligence cannot replace spirituality nor spirituality intelligence. Without a balance of the two you are nothing more than a savage. Even the most technically advanced race, without a soul are mere barbarians.'

'So you're fine with people worshipping you and your image, because when I was on Gukumatz those people were worshipping you!'

'If Humans as well as Gukumatz wish to put their faith in me I shall strive not to disappoint them nor misuse that trust.'

The interview continued on subjects of family and friends until the hour was almost up. Jerry turned to the camera which displayed the green light 'Before we leave there's just enough time for some questions from viewers. First Mrs. Molinelli please ask Malikah your question.'

The voice of a middle aged lady with a Bronx accent filled the studio 'Hello Malikah!' she said excitedly.

'Hello Grace!'

Jerry cut in 'Is that your name? Grace?'

The lady replied in an elated voice 'Yes, yes it is Jerry!'

Jerry motioned towards Malikah 'Go on.'

Malikah spoke to the caller 'What is your question Grace?'

'At my church we've heard stories about how you opened up a wormhole using just the power of your mind. Is that true?'

Malikah smiled at the persistent lady 'Partly Grace, but without the power of faith from the Gukumatz it would not have been possible. I can't take full credit for what happened at the tunnel event.'

The lady sounded quite ecstatic 'Ohh! Could I say it's lovely to see you here and hello to Amitrasudan, Kaeo and Sandra from everyone at Saint Peter's church!'

Malikah made the Namaste gesture to the camera 'Thank you and thank you to all those at Saint Peter's church.'

Jerry paused to listen to his producer then spoke 'Okay we've got another caller, Mr. Baird are you there?'

The voice of an elderly gentleman filled the studio 'Hello Jerry!'

'Hello Mr. Baird you're on air!'

The Gentleman had a very serious aurora to his voice 'Hello Malikah and welcome to New York City.'

The sable queen smiled at the warm greeting 'Thank you Terrence.'

'I and others are concerned that the Grand Matriarch has plans to make us her subjects or worse slaves. Could you either clarify or dismiss those fears?'

Still smiling Malikah replied 'Xch'uup's ultimate goal is certainly the subjugation of both us and the Gukumatz, Terrence. However as long as I and the girls are here it shall never come to fruition, you can bet good money on that.'

'Well I'm afraid I'm not a gambling man Malikah!'

'Nor am I Terrence!'

'Well thank you Malikah, I hope you're right.'

'You are welcome, just have faith Terrence that is all you need to weather the storm.'

Jerry spoke up as the line closed 'Alright that's all we have time for, except one question how did you know their names?'

Malikah only pointed to her head and smiled cheekily at her host.

Turning back to the camera Jerry made a huff and closed the show 'Well that's all from this edition of Habeeb's hour. I think you'll all agree one of the strangest yet most interesting shows we've ever broadcast! See you all soon!'

The lights faded whilst the producer counted down until they were off air. Once off air the lights flickered back on. The producer charged over with a piece of paper. Jerry took a glimpse then gazed at Malikah 'That was our highest rated show ever, it even beat out the Mars landings!'

Before Jerry could finish his sentence Malikah put a fist up to his lips 'I'm sorry Jerry, but I have too many engagements. Perhaps when this is all over we could do an interview again?'

He nodded at the beautiful young lady before she was led off to take the hummingbird back to the Plaza.

Chapter 26

The following fortnight was spent touring the sights of New York City; wherever the foursome went they were instantly recognised. Though some might say it's hard not to recognise four six foot women after they'd already met the President.

Malikah had negotiated an agreement with President Earle, 1,000 soldiers equipped with all the best his military had to offer. She had even convinced Washington to start dismantling nuclear warheads. The atomic weapons were handed over to Geneva before being shipped out to the Athena and her sister ships. Malikah had decided to kill two birds with one stone, she'd get rid of the weapons which had caused so much destruction already and put them to use against the Makayuuk.

The Eastern States dismantling of its nuclear arsenal worried Moscow. If they no longer needed thermonuclear missiles what did they have to replace them? Malikah offered Moscow the same deal Washington had taken, dismantle all nuclear weapons and in return whoever launches a strike on them shall be destroyed. Moscow complied, providing 1,000 troops fully equipped along with hundreds of warheads.

The third nation to contribute was Great Britain, London provided 1,000 men along with all the equipment requested by Faraday. The old Etonian organised the loading of equipment onto the three captured Gukumatz cruisers. They had been used for general transport between Earth and its subject, now they were loaded to land 3,000 troops along with armoured vehicles.

The Gukumatz were no longer required to take part in the invasion now that the factions of Earth had come together. All the time the thought of the Ixchel lurked in everyone's subconscious. The men were lifted up into orbit via the elevator, almost 400 a day now that the crawlers had been converted. The heavy equipment was all lifted up by the use of work shuttles; similar craft to personal transport shuttles, only larger. The gear was loaded into the large cargo bay in the rear then lifted high into the heavens thanks to the anti-graviton technology captured from the Gukumatz.

Most of the world's population were in shock when they witnessed the nuclear warheads being spirited away off planet. A sight none believed they'd ever see. Despite the fact a battle was looming with what sounded like a soulless enemy the population of Earth felt safer in their beds. The panic over the Ixchel had died down. People were now concentrating on what they could do to earn it rather than having childish tantrums in the street.

Malikah sensed that the mother world would soon be contacting her debtors. So the girls wrapped up their holiday in New York City and took the next hummingbird to Geneva. McCann was on the landing pad to greet his daughter at I.S.A HQ. After she stepped off the transport he threw his arms around her. Malikah rolled her eyes whispering in his ear 'I was only gone 2 weeks Father!'

He didn't reply the Englishman only smiled proudly at his daughter. The other girls all bowed to him and he returned their Namaste before leading them down into the command centre.

The next day Faraday was called to his office, a communication from Tlillan had been received. On entering his office Malikah stood alone waiting for him. She smiled and pointed towards the view screen on his wall. He entered the room and the door slid shut behind him.

Speaking into his wrist tablet he ordered his staff 'Alright, you can pipe it through now.'

A grainy image flickered bringing the dormant screen to life. Faraday had expected the Grand Matriarch but instead her Grand Marshal stood before him.

'This is Director Faraday, how may I help you?'

Cihuateteo was in obvious distress 'I must speak with Malikah!'

Faraday beckoned Malikah bringing her forward 'She is here.'

'I am here Cihuateteo, you may speak freely.'

The image was suffering from interference, something only possible if wormholes were open in the vicinity 'I am requesting the assistance of the Humans on behalf of Xch'uup. The Makayuuk have folded space with ...'

'23 war cruisers,' said Malikah finishing her sentence.

'Yes, our fleet has no escape. The Teteo is the only remaining cruiser; I'm sending you this request before we abandon ship.'

Malikah raised her chin squinting at Cihuateteo, 'Xch'uup has forbid you from requesting Human assistance has she not?'

Cihuateteo's eyes turned a deep burgundy 'Fuck Xch'uup! We stand at the brink of disaster, she cares only for herself! She fears you Malikah, she knows you are the one, the seers have seen it!'

Malikah took a deep breath 'I am coming with the Humans. You must abandon your vessel, go to the planet and defend Tititl. Within four days we shall arrive. The Makayuuk wish to capture Xch'uup, they will land their forces rather than bombard you.'

Cihuateteo placed her hands together and bowed as her cruiser shook from an explosion 'Dyos bo'otik Malikachutli.'

Before a reply could be given the image flickered away from the view screen. Malikah glanced down at Faraday 'It has begun William,' she whispered to him.

Faraday could feel a knot in his stomach, he put his wrist tablet to his mouth 'It's time, we're folding space in 3 hours, inform Admiral McCann.'

The pair walked into the command centre to be greeted by McCann 'It's time?' he asked in a desperate tone.

Malikah nodded 'And I'm coming with you Father.'

The Admiral wasn't too happy that his daughter was coming. They'd had this argument yesterday, as usual Malikah got her way; though McCann was quite aware that against 23 war cruisers he'd need an edge, especially now that all of the Tlillan ships had been lost save the Chutli.

Faraday was apprehensive, though his stress was far lower than before Malikah had taken the baton from him 'Good luck!' he called as they made their way to the pad.

The fleet had been gathering above the Earth for the last week now. Fully assembled it only awaited a purpose, once onboard the Athena the pair marched towards the bridge. Upon reaching the bridge McCann's eyes widened on seeing Amitra, Kaeo and Sandra.

McCann whispered to his sable daughter 'What on Earth are they doing here?'

Malikah smirked 'They can hear you Father.'

McCann began to sneer, he didn't like beating around the bush 'I don't care, tell me what they're doing here Malikah.'

'Training Father, this is an excellent opportunity for them to train their abilities. I promise they won't get in your way.'

McCann carried on to his command chair, first officer Kim stood up and called 'Admiral on the bridge!'

McCann thanked him with a smile and sat in his chair. Looking upwards he said 'Athena?'

The soft calm voice of his cruiser replied 'Hello Admiral, congratulations on your promotion.'

He smiled 'Thank you very much Athena, how have you been?'

The soft feminine voice replied 'Very well Admiral, I have a link formed with all other ships in the fleet. We are prepared to fold space in synchrony, Admiral.'

'Excellent Athena, please move all vessels into place, when you're finished let me know, thank you.'

'Certainly Admiral.'

The fleet began to break out of Earth orbit and above the accretion disk. Each ship spaced at least 1 AU from any object which might interfere with her journey. After an hour Titov, Ryu and Ilam called in ready to fold space. The ex-Gukumatz cruisers held rows of converted Atlas and Hummingbirds along each spine. Each transport carrying 1,000 marines along with all the necessary equipment to assault a well-defended enemy. The spaceships spread out, prepared to launch into the unknown.

Athena chirped up with her smooth comforting tone 'The fleet is ready Admiral, course to Tlillan has been certified.'

McCann peered over towards Hassif who just gave a nod of conformation 'Very good Athena, fold space in T minus 3 minutes from now.'

A timer appeared on the view screen counting down until the wormhole generators kicked in. McCann tapped a panel on his seat, 'Who is it?' came a French accent.

McCann smiled 'This is Admiral McCann, how is my Chief Engineer today?'

Louis had a rough voice, it sounded as if he'd been drinking the night before 'Day? I can't tell anymore, Jesus I feel like shit!'

Kim and a few others turned around, they were aware of how Louis behaved in the officer's lounge but over ship communications with the Admiral it was a bit much. Not that any of them had the guts to discipline him for it; he had already fought a duel with one of the bridge officers. McCann poked fun at Louis and got away with it because they were old friends.

McCann had a devilish smile on him 'Hassif told me it was a Tlillan/Makayuuk conspiracy to get you out of bed early!'

Hassif and Malikah began to giggle, the rest of the crew didn't understand exactly why it was so funny.

Louis let out an audible sigh 'Ah! I was going to tell you eat my shit! But for you English that would be a delicacy!'

Kim was astounded at the Frenchman's language towards an Admiral; even more taken aback that Louis was still the Chief Engineer.

Malikah and Hassif both laughed at Louis comment, a few other officers let out an accidental chuckle.

McCann scanned the bridge until they returned to their duties 'Just make sure we fold space without a hitch, alright?'

Louis grunted 'Pah! What do you think I'm here for? My charming personality and good looks?'

McCann shook his head 'Fine, McCann out!' then tapped the panel closing the channel before Louis could respond.

The counter reached zero and the lights dimmed on the bridge, Malikah and the girls held onto hand rails sitting on empty stations at the rear. 7 wormholes opened at the same time in a straight line equally spaced out.

'Wormhole to Tlillan has been opened,' declared Athena.

'Engage Casimir field and take us in Athena, I want us all to arrive together,' ordered McCann as he sat back in his seat.

'Casimir field engaged!' called Hassif.

'Firing engines,' came the voice of Athena.

With that all seven vessels fired their engines in synchrony, entering their white holes at exactly the same speed and time.

The journey to Tlillan took only a matter of hours from the perspective of the Athena crew. Once they'd exited the other side more than three days had passed for the rest of the universe.

All seven ships ejected above the accretion disc of the Tlillan system together. The planet Tlillan was immediately recognisable. First of all it had a massive fleet of vessels in a high orbit. Second the planet was covered with orbital towers constructed of neutronium. It seemed as if it were a massive thistle in space.

The crew were awestruck by the sight, until Malikah broke the silence 'Form a line and wait Father, let the enemy come to you.'

McCann stood up, thanks to the dais he was almost as tall as his daughter 'I need to land our ground forces, if they're caught out here ...'

Malikah put her hand on his shoulder 'Do as I ask Father, the landing shall be achieved.'

McCann turned to see Hassif, paused by his console. McCann nodded and Hassif got to work certifying orders for the fleet.

'Where are the Tlillan cruisers?' muttered Kim as he strained at the view screen.

'Destroyed,' said Malikah ominously.

Hassif called out alarmingly 'Sir! 11 cruisers are breaking off to meet us.'

McCann saw the cylindrical ships break off and approach his fleet. The nose of the cylinder had a massive hydrogen scoop. All along the ship on both the upper and lower side a groove ran down it. The Makayuuk vessel at first glance was rather large and clunky.

'Vezzali scan those ships, I want to know everything about them,' shouted McCann over his shoulder.

The Admiral then calmly ordered Hassif 'Order all other ships to stand their ground; do not fire unless fired upon.'

Both of them carried out their orders as the fleet of Makayuuk approached in unison.

Hassif started tapping at his station 'Incoming transmission from the Makayuuk Admiral!'

'Put him on Hassif.'

The image of what at first sight was a human in some odd clothes, sat at a Spartan Captain's chair, brought the view screen to life. A human male, probably in his 40's dressed in the most drab body suit McCann had seen in a long time. It looked more like something they'd hand out at a Chinese concentration camp. The Captain's chair had no panels or controls; it was merely a grey metal chair.

For a moment the enemy Captain was motionless then he spoke in English 'You are Ek'tsab?'

McCann replied 'No, I am Admiral McCann. I am here at the request of the Tlillans, who are you?'

The Makayuuk ignored him, looking around the bridge of the Athena.

It was then that McCann realised the Makayuuk didn't possess human eyes. His eyes had a sliver sheen over them, part organic and part machine.

Malikah stepped forward 'I am Ek'tsab, you are Sirt 137.'

The Makayuuk had electronic parts, though McCann wouldn't have been able to distinguish him from anyone else at first glance. As he examined the man on the screen he noticed more and more little things. The chair he sat in had a mental link to him, probably so that he could send out orders quicker. To do that he must have had a disciplined mind, probably regulated artificially; however he was not much different from any other man.

The Captain did something that stunned all the crew, he smiled. It was assumed that he had no sense of humour. Everyone had their own idea of what a cyborg should look and act like; laughing was certainly not amongst those expectations.

'Amusing,' grinned the Makayuuk 'A little Tlillan girl is Star Shaker?'

Malikah ignored his mocking tone 'You have this opportunity to flee, take it.'

McCann could hear laughs emanating from the Makayuuk Bridge. Sirt was obviously getting a kick out of something 'Flee? It will require more than a silly girl masquerading as Star Shaker before the Makayuuk leave Tlillan!'

Malikah stood with her legs astride, one hand outstretched towards the view screen and her eyes misting into a pitch black. For twenty seconds she stood in her trance, Sirt 137 sat laughing at her show; then his expression changed momentarily. Gone was his mocking smirk, replaced with a face of extreme worry. They may have melded with machines but all those base human emotions were as strong as ever.

The voice of Vezzali called out, grabbing McCann's attention 'Sir! The Tlillan sun it's destabilizing!'

McCann flicked his eyes between Vezzali and his daughter 'What's happening?'

'Something is manipulating the graviton field, I've never heard of anything like this before Admiral!' called out a confounded science officer.

Amitra approached McCann and whispered in his ear 'It is Malikah, do not be concerned Sir.'

Vezzali was calling out the events blow by blow 'A stream of gravitons is grasping one of the Makayuuk ships Admiral ...'

McCann hit his panel and the screen split to show the vessel, it had been lassoed by a stream of gravitons pulled from the sun. Suddenly the massive cylinder snapped, the ship was pulled upwards in the middle. A break exactly in the centre of the Makayuuk vessel sent two separate halves spinning off in opposite directions.

The event was described in such a way that the Englishman could easily understand. The graviton being a particle on the quantum level, it was a quick method of explaining what was unfolding in space. What Malikah was doing in real terms was warping the fabric of space and time.

As Ilam had made clear years ago on Mars, space was a made of something. Humans had known this for a fact since Casimir proved it, Tlillans however had a much deeper understanding of the fabric of the universe. The energy stored inside it, what humans had named dark energy for more than a century consisted of many particles and strings. Space was in fact teeming with activity; the Human race was just too ill equipped to observe it. Malikah manipulated the stored energy, dark energy, held in the fabric; the result being that she had in the past opened wormholes and created null space fields.

Today she contorted space to her will wrapping it around the Makayuuk war cruiser. Channelling the energy of two civilizations, the strings and particles moved to her desire; moving away from the largest attractor in the system, the sun, and lassoing the enemy.

This showed up on Vezzali's instruments as massive shifts in gravity. Somehow the gravity field of the Tlillan star had become warped and unstable, though it had no effect on the star or the planets. It made no sense yet it was happening, an action without the reaction that science demanded. The stored energy twisted the space around the vessel. Since the vessel could no longer occupy the space that was now being compressed it was forced to split. Much the same as holding a copper pipe in bolt cutters then squeezing the handles together; the pipe has to give way by splitting.

Sirt 137 was gripped by a panic, in his moment of terror he ordered his remaining 10 war cruisers to fire upon the Athena. With a single thought every Captain received his orders.

Vezzali called out from her science station 'Admiral, we've been target by all 10 ships, I think they intend to fire on us!'

Amitra comforted McCann again 'Have no fear Admiral, their weapons have been rendered useless.'

From the grooves on the Makayuuk ships several cylinders were ejected. It didn't take an Einstein to realise they were missiles intended for the Athena. Instead of streaking towards their target the missiles merely drifted off into space before detonating.

McCann noticed his adversary was frozen with fear, Captain Sirt struggled to prevent his teeth chattering. Not from a cold environment but from the terror of his precarious situation. Whoever this Star Shaker character was it was obviously someone that no Makayuuk desired to meet with.

Malikah dropped out of her trance 'Amitra, it is your turn to try now.'

Amitra walked over to her mentor, as she fell into a trance Captain Sirt began to speak through his chattering teeth. His attempts at diplomacy were too late and only fell upon deaf ears.

Vezzali began reporting on the Tlillan stars graviton field again. Somehow the girls were able to manipulate the gravity well caused by the star; concentrating it upon a single Makayuuk war vessel in order to crush their foes.

Malikah stood behind Amitra guiding her quietly 'Concentrate on the flow, but at the same time make sure the planets remain unaffected.'

Amitra didn't reply, her eyes displayed a pigment as dark as the bottom of the ocean.

Malikah had both hands on the girl's shoulders as she whispered in her ear 'Excellent Amitra, now lasso the vessel and pull back when …'

Another Makayuuk warship snapped into two before them. The enemy had stopped advancing now, however they were not retreating either.

Amitra came out of the trance to receive a big hug from her teacher. Before Malikah could say anything Kaeo was already standing and waiting for her turn.

Malikah grinned 'Alright Kaeo, show us what you can do.'

Kaeo did exactly the same until it came time to break the enemy in half, her ship imploded; crushed on all sides by the graviton field inside a star. There was little more than a rock of metal floating in space where a mighty war cruiser of the Makayuuk collective should have been.

Malikah raised an eyebrow at her young charge, telling her off for such an exhibition. After Sandra had taken her turn and the 11 had been whittled down to 7; Malikah spoke to Sirt, the sable Amazon sneered at the terrified cybernetic Captain 'We shall meet again Sirt, on Otoch.'

The cyborg began to plead 'Ek'tsab, allow the remainder of my fleet to withdraw. We shall never return to blight you, I swear!'

'That machine has twisted your perception of reality Sirt!' barked Malikah.

'You come to glass the mother world and now beg for mercy as a maggot! Or perhaps you believe my mind so feeble as to spare your heretical scum?'

Captain Sirt rose from his chair 'The old legends were more than children's fables. If so, we shall make you earn it Ek'tsab, until we meet on the planet.'

The image of the Makayuuk Captain disappeared, his fleet began to withdraw back to the light side of Tlillan.

McCann looked his daughter in the face 'What did he mean make you earn it on the planet?'

'Take the fleet to the dark side of Tlillan, you may land your reinforcements from there,' replied his daughter.

McCann looked up at Athena's housing 'You heard the lady Athena, take us to the dark side of Tlillan then await further instructions.'

'Understood Admiral,' replied Athena softly.

The Makayuuk did nothing to hinder the I.S.A fleet, they were all too busy scuttling their own ships before making their way to surface of Tlillan.

Once in orbit of the spiky planet McCann tapped his wrist tablet 'This is Jenkins,' came a familiar voice.

McCann grinned 'We've made our way to Tlillan orbit,' he snatched a glimpse at Malikah 'prepare to land your forces, and good luck!'

'It can't be any worse than Soledad old chap!' replied his old friend.

'McCann out!'

The Englishman walked over to Hassif 'Tell Ryu and Titov to prepare for landing.'

McCann looked out at the planet then his daughter 'What can we expect, any surprises?'

Malikah shook her head 'We must contact Cihuateteo, I will give Hassif the address.'

McCann gestured towards Hassif, Malikah strode over and typed in Cihuateteo's contact details on the planet.

'I've got her,' smiled Hassif.

Malikah pointed at the view screen, the image of the white haired Amazon appeared. She was inside a small dimly lit room, outside in the darkness McCann and his crew distinctly heard terrifying howls and screams. Short bursts of rail gun fire was prevalent, Cihuateteo had blood smeared down her ribbed suit which was adorned with black plate armour, probably a neutronium alloy. Her hair carried streaks of dried blood on one side; it was obvious all was not going well on the surface.

'Namaste Malikachutli,' greeted the Tlillan Marshal.

'Namaste Cihuateteo, what is your situation?'

'Tititl is encircled by the Makayuuk, you cannot bombard from orbit without glassing the city.'

Malikah calmed her ally 'We intend to land soldiers and break the siege.'

Cihuateteo was very tired, she hadn't slept in days 'How did you make orbit? They have 23 cruisers blockading the system.'

Malikah smiled 'They are abandoning their cruisers as we speak. Their leader plans on capturing Xch'uup, he believes he might ransom her for their lives.'

Cihuateteo made a sarcastic snort 'Pah!'

Malikah beckoned Kaeo towards her 'I'm sending Kaeo down with the first wave. She is here to learn from you Cihuateteo, she shall also prove to be an excellent asset.'

Kaeo was grinning from ear to ear, Cihuateteo didn't seem so taken. She already had enough on her plate without babysitting.

Nevertheless Cihuateteo bowed 'As you wish Malikachutli. I shall transmit a suitable landing zone, tu heel k'iin.'

Malikah nodded at her sister over the view screen 'Tu heel k'iin.'

The image disappeared, Hassif spoke up 'I've received co-ordinates outside the city and inside the city.'

Malikah caught the attention of her father 'The co-ordinates outside are for your ground forces. The location inside is for Kaeo's transport.'

McCann crossed his arms 'I can't send a child on a transport alone through a war zone!'

Malikah and Kaeo grinned at each other 'Father she will arrive safely, I guarantee it.'

McCann wouldn't budge 'I'm sorry, I don't play games with children's lives!'

'The Makayuuk mobile SAM's have all been disabled, they have nothing to prevent Kaeo from being inserted into the city.'

McCann squinted at his daughter 'How do you know that? Ah why am I even asking that?'

Kaeo tugged on McCann's arm 'Can I go Admiral? Please?'

McCann realised his daughter had control of the situation 'If Malikah says it's safe.'

Kaeo leapt a good foot in the air clapping her hands like a little girl; Amitra sniggered at the celebrations of her younger sister.

'Brigadier Jenkins reports the Clotho is prepared to drop her cargo,' reported Commander Kim.

McCann peeled away from Kaeo, 'Tell him to begin landing, inform the others to begin their drops, Commander.'

McCann looked back at Kaeo, pointing to the door he muttered 'Go on, get out of here!'

McCann observed the Gukumatz transports move into position of the planet that sat in tidal lock. Once in position the order was given, first the massive Atlas craft detached from the long fins of the transport. Formerly used for carrying missiles they were converted to carrying cargo, now transport craft took the place of cargo containers. One by one the Atlas peeled off and into the atmosphere, riding down to the landing zones on the surface unmolested.

Within two hours the Atlas and hummingbirds had all made it down to the surface, establishing 3 separate HQ's at opposite points around Tititl. Jenkins was soon raising the alarm as several groups of threatening vehicles approached the British HQ. He had no idea as to their purpose, however the rack of objects pointing out of a squared container on top a floating platform suspiciously resembled a missile based artillery weapon.

'Enemy approaching base camp, seven armoured columns on an intercept requesting air support, Jenkins out.'

McCann pointed towards Kim 'I want those armoured columns removed Commander.'

Kim approached his station. As the Shogun II scram drones launched from the Athena, the Makayuuk columns halted. The vehicles launched a barrage of missiles towards the base camp.

The HQ was armed with air defence guns engaged the enemy, firing tungsten bullets at the incoming missiles. Neutralizing them before impact, unfortunately there were too many missiles to cope with. The NBC alarm was raised and every man hit his wrist unfurling his helmet from inside the collar of his battle suit. Completely covered they were safe from any nuclear, chemical or biological attack. The area immediately above the camp was afire with explosions from the enemy artillery.

For the first time Jenkins could see parts of the surrounding terrain unaided. It wasn't much to look at, merely earth and rock covered in moss and lichen. From the surface it seemed to be a very drab and unremarkable place, except for the increased gravity of the world.

The first missile to get through hit the medical bunker turning it into a crater and taking at least 20 lives with it. The ground shook beneath Jenkins as he waited in the command bunker for his air strike. Finally it came, as angels swooping from high they delivered his beleaguered camp from destruction.

The scram drones tore through the thick Tlillan atmosphere, the enemy columns were hit with a long streak of napalm. Fire rose out of the Earth, this was the dark side of Tlillan and no human could see properly without the aid of his suit or a monocle. However right then the entire landscape was exposed by the streams of liquid fire igniting the enemy. Seven strips of liquid fire rocketed into the air decimating the Makayuuk offensive.

Jenkins hit his wrist 'Roberts, send your cavalry out there. Reconnoitre the enemy armour; we're taking no POW's. If you see any enemy troops you're under orders to finish them, understood?'

'Understood Sir,' came the reply.

Shortly after that 5 hummingbirds lifted off to reconnoitre the debris. Using computer assisted vision the landscape was superimposed on the pilot's helmet; allowing them to hunt for survivors, eliminate them and returning to base.

Jenkins adored the landscape from the edge of camp as it and the city of Tititl was illuminated by the burning hell deposited upon the Makayuuk. Jenkins detected a deep howl emanating from the centre of Tititl. Using his suit he zoomed in to scan the area he believed it had come from.

In the centre of Tititl rose a massive step pyramid, something that the Aztecs might have built on Earth. The fire of napalm burned on all sides of the city, the Makayuuk having been repelled from the American and Russian HQ's also, the pyramid structure dominated the horizon.

Using the zoom on the helmet Jenkins focused in on the apex of the building. Cihuateteo stood atop the pyramid looming over what must have been a captured Makayuuk. The prisoner lay on a stone table with several of his comrades standing in line, chained together by hand and foot. A circle of Tlillan females populated some of the lower steps, encircling the ceremony.

Without the fire of the napalm Jenkins would never have witnessed what had been happening. Cihuateteo pulled out her neutronium sword, a curved sabre; she then used it to make an incision between the prisoner's ribs. She cut downwards between the two separate halves of the ribcage. The Makayuuk didn't make a sound, Jenkins considered that he was already dead.

Cihuateteo sheathed her weapon before plunging her hands into the cut, grasping the prisoner's ribs and tearing them apart. There was no doubt now that the Makayuuk was in fact alive, he screamed as his blood squirted out. The hot red fluid pumped, spilling over the edge of the table and flowing down onto to cold stone below. Cihuateteo plunged her hand inside the quivering mass of organs and flesh, blood poured out of the victim's mouth as he tried to scream out into the cold night. But all that left his body was steam rising from his innards into the chilly Tlillan atmosphere.

The other POWs shivered uncontrollably in fear as they witnessed their brother's ritual punishment.

The dominating Tlillan's hand tore out from the body of the Makayuuk soldier. He went into a violent seizure whilst she displayed his beating heart much to the approval of her sisters.

A second figure appeared from the Tlillan onlookers. Jenkins didn't recognise her but it was Kaeo, Cihuateteo handed her the sword which she then employed to decapitate the victim. His head trundled down the structure bouncing off the steps to the entertainment of the Tlillans. The headless body ceased to convulse, it was untied then cast from the top of the temple. The next terrified Makayuuk was unchained and dragged to the stone table, restrained and the ceremony began again.

Jenkins looked away from the barbaric display to see his officer gawping at the spectacle 'Hey Waters! That's enough of that!'

His Lieutenant tapped his wrist going back to normal viewing 'Sorry Sir.'

His men got back to preparing for a strike. Jenkins was prepared to break the siege, however he found the Makayuuk were moving out without any air cover; whomever was in command must have realised they had no hope. The Tlillans had become very aggressive cutting into the ranks of their enemy. The attempt to remove the I.S.A before they could establish themselves had failed miserably. For an unknown reason the mobile air defence platforms all failed, and they would be dead before replacements arrived. So a withdrawal was in order.

Jenkins ordered his air cavalry to pursue and harass the enemy. The hummingbirds lifted off chasing the Makayuuk through the smouldering night, picking off troop transports with air to ground missiles and rail cannons. Shogun II scram drones descended from orbit putting the archaic atomic warheads of the past to good use. The mushroom clouds of cold war weapons constructed in fear brought the retreat to a halt. The explosions lit up the sky, tens of thousands of soldiers encircled on a moist dark plain. The only vegetation being the moss on the ground below them, the man machines looked inevitable doom in the face.

Malikah stood on the bridge of the Athena monitoring the Makayuuk withdrawal below on the view screen. She whispered but not so that the bridge officers couldn't hear 'Annihilate them Father.'

Hassif called out 'Admiral, Brigadier Jenkins has reported the enemy have surrendered … unconditionally Sir!'

Malikah gave her father a hard stare 'Do not be fooled Father, they would have killed all of us. Remember Machiavelli Father, they must be destroyed.'

McCann had to trust his daughter, he knew little of his enemy whereas she seemed to be well versed in their strategies. He walked up to Hassif and whispered into his ear 'Order Jenkins to destroy them, we're taking no Makayuuk prisoners.'

Hassif nodded whilst he tapped away, sending his order to the ground commander.

The order went out from the surface, as the hummingbirds retreated to their HQ the scram drones entered the thick atmosphere to deliver the nuclear warheads. The surrendered caravan of troops and equipment, were mercilessly vapourised in a nuclear fire. A good 20,000 men had been reduced to nothing by arms intended for a different people from a different place in a different time.

A small camp remained on the light side of Tlillan, where the crews of the scuttled stars ships had fled for refuge. They also recognised their demise was not long off, a glorious victory had become a dismal defeat.

Jenkins took a hummingbird to Tititl carrying supplies for the local population. They did a flyby of the massive temple; the sides were caked in fresh blood with corpses in various stages of decomposition adorning all levels of the building.

Onboard the Athena Malikah took her father aside 'The battle against the Makayuuk is over. Now the struggle for Tlillan begins father. You must come with Mother and I to the surface.'

McCann scratched his chin 'I don't understand, we came to stop the Makayuuk am I correct?'

Malikah was a little frustrated 'Please Father, the window of opportunity will not be present for long. We can remove Xch'uup here and now, but I need your co-operation.'

McCann still wasn't sure what she wanted 'Look, will the Makayuuk pose a threat?'

'No, they have been dealt with Father, Cihuateteo is mopping them up as we speak.'

The Englishman nodded 'Fine, if they pose no threat then I suppose I can entertain your wishes.'

Malikah smiled and kissed him on the cheek, 'Mother is already preparing, come,' she took his arm.

'Kim you have command until I return,' said the Admiral as his daughter led him to the lift.

Amitra and Sandra followed the pair as they made their way to the shuttle bay.

15 minutes later they were on Tlillan. McCann stepped out into what must have been the twilight of Tlillan; an area between the dark and light sides of the planet, a strip of land that circled the planet as a meridian line. The light was a soft natural light, McCann found it similar to Earth. Perhaps a temperate region of the planet, the region was dominated by over grown forest all except the landing pad and a great stone step pyramid, similar to the one in Tititl. The stone path leading from the pad to the building was kept clear and was quite a pleasant walk. The shade of the forest was cooling with a charming fragrance similar to mint, but more powerful, exciting the nasal senses.

McCann stepped out of the shuttle to feel the heavy gravity pull him down. He looked out at the building 'Where are we?' he asked in awe of the structure which stood over a mile high.

Malikah looked up at the building rising out of the forest canopy 'This was the seat of power in the galaxy, for millennia.'

McCann heard the sound of something cutting the air, he looked around the temple to see several shuttles circling around the canopy 'Who's that?'

'Xch'uup has come,' replied Malikah ominously.

'For what?'

'To face her demons.'

Malikah stepped forward, the girls paused waiting for McCann to follow Malikah. The Englishman trailed his daughter walking down the stone path towards a large opening in the pyramid. Along the way he noticed other paths winding towards the doorway from the forest. McCann began to sense his wife was close by, looking around he soon noticed her striding through the shrubbery towards the door. She smiled at her husband, her excitement from being here had led to her easy detection though McCann was still unsure as to the cause of this excitement.

Upon reaching the stone doorway Malikah informed him they must wait. Ilam soon greeted him hugging her husband.

McCann put an arm around his wife and asked 'So can you tell me what on earth is going on?'

Ilam was grinning from ear to ear 'Your daughter has challenged Xch'uup.'

McCann scowled 'To what?'

'To the throne.'

McCann scratched the stubble on his chin 'Wonderful! And why exactly do we have to do it here?'

Ilam smiled and pointed to the stone door 'The throne rests here my dear.'

The party waited around until a procession came through the forest. The Grand Matriarch along with all the first Matriarchs of the Tlillan clans led the caravan. Behind them were another twenty Matriarchs.

McCann questioned his wife 'Who are they?'

'They are witnesses and adjudicators, they are here to make certain the ceremony is carried out properly.'

The Grand Matriarch was dressed in robe of jade squares covering her jet black space suit and a white feathered headdress. McCann noticed on closer inspection that she had a weapon hanging off a baldric; though it was pretty much covered by the long cape of jade.

The Grand Matriarch's party reached the closed stone doorway 'Your mother has been exiled!' snapped the old gorgon.

Malikah gave her adversary a hard look 'I may have whomever I wish for my entourage, exile or not!'

As she spoke a shuttle landed at one of the pads in the forest, shortly afterwards Ryu approached holding three Makayuuk prisoners. McCann recognised one as being the commander of the enemy fleet, Sirt 137. They all seemed by far the worse for wear, Ryu approached Malikah 'Here are the last of the Makayuuk, will that be all?'

'You may enter Captain.'

The Grand Matriarch made a condescending sneer 'We shall see if you are able to raise the entrance Malikah!'

The Matriarch tapped her staff on the massive piece of stone blocking the way inside the ancient structure.

Malikah returned the sneer 'Step away Xch'uup.'

As the Grand Matriarch stepped back a shadow dropped over Malikah's eyes, slipping into her trance she faced the stone slab with arm outstretched. Initially nothing happened until McCann detected a grating noise of stone upon stone. Dirt held in place for centuries fell down from the cracks where the slab met the wide gateway.

Xch'uup and her entourage were genuinely surprised, though to McCann and the rest of Malikah's party this was not a great feat by any stretch of the imagination. It did give McCann pleasure to see the condescending Tlillans shocked by his daughter's powers.

When first meeting his wife all of her very mundane abilities seemed as supernatural to him and his crew. Now the mundane powers of Malikah provoked that effect on the fractured Tlillan council, the rumours and wild gossip had taken form.

The grey slab disappeared into the gateway to reveal a dark hallway of moss covered stone. Malikah marched confidently inside, the sable Amazon pressed her hand on the wall lighting them up. The ordinary looking moss had a fluorescent hue which manifested upon touch.

McCann and Ryu gasped at the sight before them, the hallway was rather short leading into a massive amphitheatre.

'Please enter,' said Malikah as she walked inside the building.

The audience chamber taller than anything McCann could imagine, even the hollowed out volcanoes of ground zero on Earth and Mars couldn't compare. The entire chamber was illuminated, the green and yellow moss bathing the entire chamber in an odd but relaxing light. The walls followed the outer design of the step pyramid, steps leading upwards yet they leaned inwards meeting high up to form a stone ceiling. Every other step was missing allowing a ledge where statues were placed, all of female Tlillans in dress that McCann didn't recognise.

The Englishman whispered to his wife as they entered the mighty chamber 'Who are they?'

The cold stark voice of the Grand Matriarch intervened from behind 'Those are past Xch'uup, going back millions of years, Duncan McCann.'

McCann turned around and asked the Grand Matriarch 'What is this place?'

The condescending old woman smirked 'This McCann is where the Galaxy was ruled from, this is where Xch'uup sat before the plague. This is where all challenges must be resolved.'

Malikah led the different groups inside, at the opposite end sat a stone throne on a dais. A ring of small seats had been carved out of the first stone step. They were well worn and had been used extensively in the past before the population was devastated.

Malikah gestured to the seats on the left of the arena 'Please sit Father.'

The Grand Matriarch took her throne as her entourage sat to the right 'When the full contingent have arrived we may commence,' declared Xch'uup.

Malikah stood on the dirt of the arena before the throne 'Agreed, however your assassins must leave!'

Xch'uup's eyes thinned as she examined Malikah 'To accuse your Xch'uup of ...'

Malikah cut her off showing great disrespect, an offence punishable by death under normal circumstances, 'Heresy, I know. Don't insult my abilities you old Gorgon!'

At that a shade of pitch fell over Malikah's eyes again. Seconds later three Tezcatlipoca who'd been perched on stone ledges high above dropped from the sky. The cloaking technology malfunctioned revealing the assassins now dragging themselves from the floor. In the same way she had disabled Icarus these creatures had been neutralised.

As they pulled themselves from the dirt Xch'uup was poised in preparation for their attack. The birdmen did not make an attempt on their designated target, instead they kowtowed to Malikah. The sable queen pointed towards the gateway and as one they leapt into flight leaving the building.

Malikah gave her own condescending smirk to her opponent 'You intended to murder me before there were enough Matriarchs to begin the ceremony, your weakness disgusts me old woman!'

McCann was rather shocked at how well his daughter played at being a Matriarch. To his wife this type of behaviour was natural even instinctive. However he'd always held his daughter up to a higher standard, but it was necessary to be more Tlillan than human on this occasion. Arrogance and hubris were required when dealing with her mother's side.

Xch'uup refused to react or even say anything in response to Malikah's discovery. After all everyone knew that it was a commonly employed tactic amongst the political hierarchy. Soon one of the two would be dead anyway and the Xch'uup could censor her actions or reveal them depending on the victor. For the most part it was best to keep your head down and not take sides until the Xch'uup had been decided.

Thirty minutes later nearly a hundred high ranking Matriarchs entered the audience chamber of Xch'uup; formerly populated by the Twilighters and the centralised seat of power throughout the Tlillan commonwealth. The massive wonder, in the past, bustled with delegations of alien worlds offering tributes or pleading for assistance. From here Xch'uup would hold audience and it was said that wherever she did frown upon the galactic map the people did tremble in fear.

But after the plague no longer were there any Twilighters to hold office. The Lightsiders died also, leaving the Darksiders to fill in the offices of Grand Marshal and Grand Matriarch as well as Grand Priestess.

Once the first level of seats had been filled out Xch'uup rose leaving her staff and jade cape on the throne. McCann was a little aroused on seeing Xch'uup's figure; she may have been more than a thousand years old but she cut and athletic shape in her ribbed suit.

Cihuateteo also stood up and strode into the centre of the arena now bathed in in a bright yellow light from the moss. The white haired Tlillan Marshal announced to the audience observing from the edge of the dirt arena 'Today Malikachutli first of Chutli does challenge Xch'uup for leadership of the Tlillan race and all its dominions. To do so Malikachutli requires the approval of the council.'

Cihuateteo's eyes scanned around the edge of the chamber 'I take it clan Chutli approves?'

McCann then noticed the familiar face of Quil rise up from the crowd 'I am Quilachutli, I speak for Chutli when I say we do approve.'

Cihuateteo looked at the crowd searchingly 'Clan Huel, what do you say?'

A red haired woman tall and rather muscular stood up on the right of the arena 'I am Matnahuel, I speak for clan Huel when I say we do not approve.'

McCann was sat next to his wife 'What's going on?' he whispered in her ear.

Ilam leaned down and replied to her husband 'Malikah must have the approval of the majority of the clans. Three out of five must back her before she may attempt to dislodge Xch'uup.'

'Attempt? She could crush that old bag with a thought!'

Ilam snorted at her husband's naivety 'Xch'uup will not consent to a battle of minds!'

McCann fixed his eyes on his flaming haired wife 'Then what?'

Ilam was warmed by his fatherly concern 'Much as a human duel, the challenged decides.'

McCann turned his gaze back to the centre of the arena, his expression was one of a very concerned father.

Cihuateteo searched through the crowd again 'Clan Kak, what do you say?'

A grey haired Tlillan stood a slightly older classical beauty 'I am Ceenakak, first of clan Kak. I speak for clan Kak when I say we approve.'

McCann sensed the tense atmosphere, his powers of empathy had become well practiced since his marriage and the birth of Malikah. He sensed the Matriarchs drawing their breath in, hanging on what the next two matriarchs were to say. McCann had gathered that to challenge the Xch'uup was an uncommon event. For a challenge to be as successful as to get past this stage was a rare event not to be seen in an average Tlillan's lifetime.

'Clan Tico, what do you say?'

A tall red haired Valkyrie stood up 'I am Tezcatico. First of clan Tico, we do not approve of Malikachutli's challenge for Xch'uup.'

Malikah and Xch'uup all this time stood glaring into each other's eyes. They stared each other down neither one willing to concede ground or look away, both confident in their authority amongst her sisters.

Now only one clan remained 'I am Cihuateteo, I speak for clan Teteo,' announced the white haired goddess still caked in the machine mens blood.

Cihuateteo was expected to side with Xch'uup as she had always done, the Grand Marshal was the foundation of the Gorgon's power.

'As first of clan Teteo and Grand Marshal of all the clans of Tlillan I speak on behalf of clan Teteo when I approve the challenge of Malikachutli!'

A mass of muttering and murmuring filled the air of the audience chamber. McCann was taken aback but not nearly as much as Xch'uup.

The old witch was positively blown over by her closest ally. She turned to face Cihuateteo 'So you have betrayed me? My own sister?'

The white haired Marshal encrusted in Makayuuk blood shook her head 'No, you have betrayed your sisters. You would have left us to the mercy of those heretic machines, if I had not summoned Malikachutli we would be no more.'

Xch'uup nodded knowingly 'And the seers?'

Cihuateteo again shook her head.

The gorgon closed her eyes softly, taking in the gravity of the situation. Opening her eyes again she was fixed on Malikah 'So it was I who was deceived, I commend you Malikachutli. However, I have not fallen yet, I choose the mantle.'

Xch'uup took several steps back as she drew her sword, a long curved sabre. All Tlillan Matriarchs had been taught to wield the blade upon reaching maturity.

It became clear to McCann why Ilam had been so encouraging when he proposed taking his daughter to fencing lessons in Geneva.

The Englishman had assumed his wife would have scoffed at a Matriarch engaging in such a barbaric activity. Instead she had quietly encouraged his pass time, as he had an epiphany he turned to see his wife's smiling eyes. It was clear why his daughter preferred a French grip and why she took to epee above sabre and foil. Finally he understood why the beautiful woman sitting next to him had selected Duncan McCann all those years ago on Tharsis.

Ilam smiled at her husband sensing his revelations, she then turned towards the three Matriarchs stood in the centre of the arena.

Cihuateteo bellowed at the audience 'Only the seers may preside.'

The representatives of the clans sat down with their sisters. Three females appeared from behind the throne spacing themselves around the edge of the arena to form an equilateral triangle.

McCann leaned up to his wife 'Where did they come from?'

'The seers have unrestricted access to all buildings in the commonwealth. They are permitted to come and go without question.'

Cihuateteo unsheathed her sabre, walked to the dead centre of the earthen arena and drew a line in the dirt. The red haired Marshal glanced at the two combatants sizing each other up 'Sisters, take your place!' she bellowed.

Malikah advanced all the time keeping her eyes fixed squarely upon her opponent. Eventually she stopped a swords length from the line in the earth.

Xch'uup did likewise on the opposite side of the line. Both raised their weapons, holding them outwards until they touched the tip of their opponent's blade.

The chamber went silent, Cihuateteo sheathed her weapon 'CHUNBESIK!' bellowed the Amazon sending a shiver down McCann's spine.

Malikah took a few steps backwards keeping the triangular thrusting blade of her mantle pointed at her opponent.

Xch'uup's blade was somewhat different, it was curved, a design intended to favour cutting. The blade was more of a classic Napoleonic sabre design, a cutting blade though not so curved as to be ineffective in the thrust. The old witch held her weapon arm slightly bent with the point facing above Malikah's head. The guard reminded McCann of the knuckleduster guards used on similar designs in Napoleonic Europe. A very effective weapon when at close quarters, one strike could easily incapacitate an opponent long enough to finish then with a cut or thrust.

The irony of the situation wasn't lost on either McCann or Ryu. A civilization that considers humans to be so primitive and barbaric were settling the question of who would lead them, in a duel to the death! Although if you were going to settle such matters by way of violence, to do so via a gentlemen's or Matriarch's duel is certainly the most civilized choice.

McCann examined Xch'uup's style, he didn't know much about sabre yet he could see she held her weapon incorrectly. Rather than placing her thumb along the upper ridge of the grip she held it as a club. Grasping the sabre with a fist, a very crude habit that his daughter would have been admonished for. Malikah had such unrefined habits drilled out of her quickly in Geneva, it was quite clear that Xch'uup was no master of the blade. Her footwork was slow and her stance poor, McCann wondered if in fact it was a ruse intended to lull his daughter into making a rash attack.

Malikah stood in a classic stance with knees bent just a little. The sable swordswoman decided to test her opponent. Xch'uup held her weapon poorly, exposing her hand and wrist. In epee these were the primary target areas, Malikah shuffled forwards to make a darting jab at the exposed forearm before a quick retreat.

Xch'uup lurched backwards, after realising Malikah had also withdrawn she peered down. The sound of what McCann compared to a dripping tap could be heard filling the acoustically perfect arena. Xch'uup heard it also and on looking down she witnessed her blood seeping from a tiny slit in her black suit. A moment later the fissure sealed up, stemming the dark red blood. The flow of blood to Xch'uup's eyes however had only just begun; she looked up again with fire in her eyes to meet the condescending grin of Malikah.

Where the blood hit the earth moss burst into a pink fluorescence leaving pink patches on the ground. Xch'uup marched forward brandishing her sabre with a furious intent to deal retribution for her small wound.

Malikah stood her ground, confident in her ability with the sword, she waited.

Xch'uup entered thrusting distance and made a lunge for Malikah.

McCann shook his head at the clumsy effort Xch'uup made as she swung her blade towards his daughter. It was now obvious to McCann that swordsmanship was not high on the Tlillan agenda when it came to education.

McCann whispered to his wife 'She can't fight.'

The sound echoed around the arena reaching the other side where several Matriarchs gave McCann an evil look.

Malikah parried the clumsy assault with ease, she could have ended it with a thrust to the trunk of the body there and then. Instead she made a tiny swipe cutting her opponents face with the tip of her blade before withdrawing slowly.

Xch'uup's attack was too obvious, her blade was parried knocking it and the arm out wide. Opening up the body to a certain thrust, Malikah refused to finish her opponent quickly. The Queen of the blade was not prepared to allow the thought that she had won through luck. Malikah was determined that all must accept her dominance of the piste.

The Grand Matriarch slowly recovered from her lunge as the blood from a cut across her right cheek seeped out. The cut ended at the bridge of her nose, it was dawning upon Xch'uup that her skill with the blade was pitiful compared to that of the woman standing before her.

The old witch looked towards her old ally desperately, only to receive a cold sneer from Cihuateteo. The Grand Marshal was by far the greatest swordswoman on Tlillan, certainly a match for Malikah. However she refused her old master's desperate plea for assistance, Cihuateteo would not fight in her place.

The request was answered silently, just as it was sent, for the majority it was just an odd moment. A weird break in the duel, but the combatants and the seers were aware of the old woman's overture, to she who once solidified her tyrannical rule.

Malikah paused allowing Xch'uup to gather herself. Whilst the gorgon wiped the blood from her eye she spoke mockingly 'There is one area in which humans do surpass us Xch'uup!'

The old woman gnashed her teeth as she cleared her vision. In her fury she charged at Malikah with her blade pointing at her sable opponent, known as a fleche in fencing.

Again Malikah stood her ground; with a small circular parry she took control of the incoming blade redirecting it down and to the right. Quickly redirecting her point Malikah thrust it into her oncoming opponents shoulder.

Xch'uup stopped in her tracks and screeched in pain as she dropped her blade.

Withdrawing the sword Malikah then kicked the beleaguered gorgon in the torso. The gorgon stumbled backwards before falling onto her back as a helpless child. Malikah picked up her sword and walked towards the frightened old woman, shivering on the floor as she grasped her wound.

As Malikah closed in Xch'uup let out a cry to Cihuateteo 'Your sword!'

The Marshal covered in dried blood splatter from days of fighting did not answer.

Malikah halted and ordered the Marshal 'Give her your blade.'

Cihuateteo complied without word, unsheathing her curved blade then throwing it down beside the gorgon. The Marshal's blade was the most curved of the three, clearly a cutting weapon primarily and not very useful for thrusting. The last third of the blade was actually the widest and heaviest, designed for dealing very deadly and penetrating cuts. Made of neutronium this dark blade could smash solid rock to pieces, a skull or flesh was no opposition.

Xch'uup's shoulder wound disappeared as the suit closed the bleeding, though the deep penetration could still be felt. Fortunately the shoulder affected was not her sword arm, the gorgon stood brandishing the mantle of the Grand Marshall of Tlillan; a weapon that over millions of years had dealt justice throughout the galaxy to the enemies of the Tlillan species.

Malikah brandished two swords though she cast one away to the edge of the arena. She had learnt to wield only one weapon and wasn't going to try out something new at a time like this.

The sable queen approached a desperate Xch'uup 'Now you stand at the edge of the abyss, tell me what it is you see when you stare into it?'

Xch'uup who was standing defensively now and keeping her distance from Malikah replied as she tried to catch her breath 'You speak in riddles!'

Malikah slapped her opponent's blade with hers 'Your ignorance and fear have led our people to the brink of disaster. We stood at the abyss and you would have pushed us in had it not been for the Humans and Gukumatz!'

The bloodied gorgons rage was once again fuelled 'HERESY!'

Malikah sneered at the injured witch 'Even your own sister has awoken from the delusion of your tyranny!'

Pointing her blade at Malikah the gorgon gnashed her teeth again 'Her heresy shall be punished!'

Malikah stopped following her opponent 'You have driven us to disaster Xch'uup. You would have sacrificed all of this to the Makayuuk in exchange for your own worthless life!'

To speak to Xch'uup in such a fashion was a capital offence, but here in the arena anything could be said between the first and last blow. It was perhaps the only place in the commonwealth where true free speech was permitted.

The old witch's eyes burnt with hatred 'LIES! You use the feeble minded humans, masquerading as the Teootl. Now my sister has succumb to your deceit, plotting with you to end my life!'

The audience said nothing, silently observing the battle of words before the inevitable end. Between words McCann was certain he could hear a pin drop, it was as if Sir Christopher Wren had design the building himself.

Malikah shook her head 'No Xch'uup, the old kingdom has been dying for centuries. You are a relic that refuses to make way for the new kingdom.'

At that moment something in the old gorgon's eyes told McCann that she'd accepted Malikah's words. Her expression was no longer one of hatred the gorgon stepped towards her enemy sword pointing at Malikah.

'Enough chatter,' spoke Xch'uup calmly 'let us end this and see if you truly are the Mictlancihuatl!'

Xch'uup raised her blade making a powerful downward cut.

Malikah stepped back, parried her opponents blade knocking it off to the left. Malikah then held her blade out and thrust it into the gorgon's torso. The blade went deep into its target, Malikah pushed forwards using her legs to insert the blade further. Her arm held the weapon rigid as it slid inside the trunk of her opponent.

Xch'uup dropped her blade fixing her eyes onto Malikah, the gorgon's mouth gaped open in shock and horror. Her body went limp, legs giving way, causing the once great woman to slide off Malikah's blade and crumple onto the mossy floor.

The ground by now had several streaks and splatters of fluorescent pink where blood had fallen. The gorgon was still alive but incapacitated. Malikah sheathed her sword and took the mantle of Grand Marshal that Xch'uup had released.

The sable princess knelt down by the side of her Xch'uup as she slowly faced death.

Xch'uup grasped Malikah by the arm and whispered 'Forgive me for my sins Malikah!'

The whisper echoed all around the building for everyone to hear. Malikah grasped Xch'uup's hand affectionately 'Your sin is cleansed sister; you shall take your place amongst the righteous.'

Malikah smiled as Xch'uup looked around at the statues of past Grand Matriarchs which adorned the inside of the building.

Xch'uup smiled as a tear came to her eye 'Dyos bo'otik, uts tamax chi Malikah!'

Malikah nodded her head, placed Xch'uup's arms by her sides then took the heavy sabre. Employing the thick blade she cut the old woman from her breasts to her belly, straight down between the ribs. Xch'uup heaved, gurgling as she gnashed her teeth in pain. McCann could barely watch, he was taken aback by his daughter's savage actions.

What came next even made Ryu turn away, Malikah plunged her hands into Xch'uup's chest. Each hand grabbed one side of the rib cage then using her Tlillan strength she tore the ribcage apart. Blood spewed out and the suit split no longer able to function properly. The old woman's organs giggled around a mass of flesh and blood spraying out onto members of the audience.

Xch'uup somehow was still alive, grimacing as her lungs and throat were inundated with hot blood. It flowed out of her nose, rushing as the water from a mountain river on a spring day after the ice has melted.

McCann found it even more shocking that the audience of Matriarchs had barely flinched, he found it quite revolting but they displayed no emotion.

Once again Malikah plunged her hand into the open chest of Xch'uup filled with jellied white flesh and thrashing organs. This time she ripped out a beating heart, upon seeing the organ prised out of the Grand Matriarch's body the audience rose to their feet.

Malikah stood tall holding the heart above her head as its warm thick blood dripped onto her head. Next the audience, including his wife, let out a shrill cry stinging his ears. As he squinted looking around he noticed his daughter's arm move out of the corner of his eye. He looked back to see her take a massive bite out of the heart. The organ had slowed down its pumping action but on being bit it went into a frenzy beating manically. Blood rolled down his daughters chin as the Matriarchs observing the bloody spectacle pumped both fists in the air and let out a deafening scream. McCann had to hold his hands over his ears, he was certain with the acoustics they could be heard miles away.

The three seers stepped forward, Malikah who stood covered in blood on a patch of pink earth, cast the part consumed heart back into the now expired body of the Xch'uup. The seers picked up the carcass taking it to a room behind the throne area where they'd first appeared from.

The screaming died down and Ilam smiled at her husband as he removed his hands 'Your daughter is now Xch'uup!'

McCann gave a fed up look and replied sarcastically 'Marvellous!'

Ilam rolled her eyes and looked back at her daughter.

Malikah took the mantle of Grand Marshall, turning to Cihuateteo she nodded. The white haired warrior approached her Xch'uup, as she went down to kowtow but Malikah caught her by the arms.

'Namaste Cihuateteo,' said Malikah as she bowed.

The white haired Amazon mirrored her Xch'uup.

Malikah handed the mantle of Grand Marshal back to Cihuateteo 'Take this sister.'

Cihuateteo bowed her head 'My sin?'

The sable Queen of Tlillan scanned the audience, they stood in silence with bated breath. With a new Xch'uup it was time to appoint the Marshal and Grand Priestess. Traditionally those that were against the new Xch'uup would be punished for their sins. That's why taking sides before the new Xch'uup was decide was a risky business.

Malikah offered the handle of the Marshal's mantle 'You did only that which you believed was correct and moral. When you recognised it was not, you set yourself on a new path to right those wrongs. You have removed your sin sister.'

Cihuateteo accepted the mantle, sheathed it before she bowed and returned to the edge of the arena.

Malikah then walked to the edge, and took the mantle of Xch'uup. A seer appeared from behind the throne, she removed Malikah's baldric replacing it with the one of the woman she'd just slain. Another seer appeared carrying forth the white feathered headdress of the Grand Matriarch, placing it upon her new Xch'uup's crown.

Malikah sheathed her new mantle, and took her former baldric from the seer. 'Ilamachutli!' called Malikah.

Ilam walked forward and bowed before her daughter 'Namaste Xch'uup.'

Malikah smiled, holding back her emotion was difficult 'Your sins have been erased, you are now first of Chutli and Grand Priestess, take your mantle.'

Malikah held out the baldric carrying the weapon she fought the former Xch'uup with, Ilam took it bowing deeply to her daughter.

Ilam fastened the mantle of Grand Priestess to her body, 'Namaste Xch'uup,' she proclaimed before the Queen of Tlillan.

'Namaste Huey'teopixqui,' replied Malikah addressing her mother by her official Tlillan title.

Ilam stood behind her daughter at her left side beside Cihuateteo the reinstated Grand Marshal or Huey'tlacochcalcatl to use her Tlillan title.

The three stood before the clans, a triumvirate representing perhaps the greatest force in the Milky Way galaxy until the recent collapse of their civilization; a collapse that Malikah was dead set on reversing. Today a powerful alliance of Pixoa (Human), Gukumatz and Tlillan had been sealed, and the sable Queen of this pact was about to send a message to the rest of the galaxy.

Malikah's gaze scanned her audience chamber, finally fixing upon the three remaining Makayuuk. The entire assault force intended to capture Xch'uup then glass the planet with anti-matter had been repelled. In fact thanks to successive waves of scram drones and a final combined assault of I.S.A and Tlillan soldiers these three were all that remained of that cyborg invasion force.

Upon Malikah's instructions the leader of the Makayuuk had been brought to witness her installation as Xch'uup.

Neither Ryu nor Cihuateteo understood why she would desire any captives after having purged tens of thousands and destroyed a titanic armada in space. However it was not their task to ask why but only to do, the loyalty of the these women was second to none so they carried out their duties.

Malikah sneered at the three machine men. Ryu removed their restraining collars, a device which punished violent thoughts or behaviour by stimulating neurons in the brain.

The controller of the collars could select whichever neurons she desired, from simple pain centres to extreme fear. The collar master also had complete control over intensity, the collars could easily kill. Many nations on Earth had outlawed the use of them as inhumane. Korea was not so disadvantaged, resulting in a very low crime rate. The I.S.A used the collars but only off world, they were a very effective deterrent and the most efficient form of restraint.

'TAL PEK!' shouted the sable Queen her words reverberated around the chamber.

McCann recognised the words, she had barked 'Come here dogs!', the future didn't look bright for these three guys of that McCann was certain.

Sirt 137 and his two senior officers strolled out of the audience and into the blood soaked arena which glowed with a pink hue. They stopped about six feet from the newly crowned Queen of Tlillan and silently awaited their fate.

The sable Queen pointed at the floor 'CHILTAL PEK!'

Two of the cybernetic men moved to kowtow, but Sirt 137 stopped his officers. He spoke to his men in a language McCann couldn't understand. His tone was similar to some of the first speaking computers in the 20th century, very synthetic, however it still possessed emotion.

Malikah's eyes began to mist with rage 'CHILTAL!' she bellowed again.

Sirt 137 restrained his men probably ordering them to stand fast before he turned back to Malikah. His sliver eyes pierced the air into the eyes of his overlord. Speaking in Tlillan so all could understand he replied 'You're going to kill us anyway, better I die on my feet than my belly!'

The Matriarchs were shocked by their Queen's reaction, though her father was not.

The sable Queen smiled as her eyes returned to their normal state. She approached Sirt drawing her blade from its scabbard. Malikah continued past him coming to a halt in front of the Makayuuk commander in charge of the failed ground invasion. 'Prostrate yourself you heretical machine!' she sneered at her captive.

The General of the ground assault began to shake; he trembled as he slowly kowtowed.

The Matriarchs found it odd that Sirt 137 was still alive, having defied Xch'uup in her audience chamber. An offence punishable by death for any Tlillan let alone a heretical machine man!

With one powerful stroke the sable Queen of the Tlillans sliced the Makayuuk General's head clean off. His body went limp as his blood gushed out of the stump which remained.

On one side McCann noticed what he assumed was a network of artificial veins. Also some biological wiring probably used to carry instructions to his body both natural and synthetic. The blood pumped from the severed neck, the synthetic veins also pumped a small amount of a milky white substance. The Englishman assumed this to be a synthetic blood or nutrient, an ichor if you will, for sustaining these machine men.

The ground burst into a flourish of different pinks as the mix of bloods splashed onto it before the dead Makayuuk. The audience of Matriarchs cheered in celebration; obviously no love was lost between these peoples.

The sable Queen approached the next Makayuuk officer, he dropped to his knees begging for mercy. Before he could finish his plea Malikah removed his head with a single cut. A downward sweeping slice halted the prostrations of the cyborg commander.

The sable Queen in one motion gracefully cut his neck and stepped out of the way as the limp body crashed into the ground spilling its contents before it.

The crowd of Matriarchs once again cheered their Xch'uup, approving of the absolute justice dispensed to the enemies of the Tlillan people.

The entire display up until now had, in McCann's opinion, been rather barbaric. After years of being talked down to by his wife, constantly reminded of how primitive Mankind was. The Englishman was witnessing a scenario that Genghis Khan would feel at home participating in.

The brutal slaying of all the Makayuuk, a duel to the death for leadership and now the ritual execution of their enemies leaders. The whole thing seemed to be out of place for an allegedly civilized race of beings who possessed a spiritual connection to one another. Added to all of that it was his daughter carrying out a form of justice suited more to Vikings than Tlillans!

The sable Queen strolled towards Sirt. Her sword, pointed at the floor, dripped with a mixture of Makayuuk bodily fluids. His two officers and friends lay executed on the ground, pulsating in different shades of a neon pink. The bright colours followed Malikah as the blood from her mantle made a sinister trail.

'Welcome to Mull Kaah Mr Sirt!' spoke Malikah in a condescending Tlillan tone to her captive.

Sirt merely nodded his head 'Ek'tsab.'

The sable Queen inserted her bloody mantle back into its scabbard much to the shock of her audience 'You Sirt are a brave man, you I shall spare.'

Cihuateteo strode forward until she reached Malikah 'Xch'uup, we must not display weakness!'

The sable Queen turned to her loyal white haired Marshal 'There are lessons to be learnt from the Pixoa. Sirt 137 shall return to his Makayuuk masters, so that they and all other civilizations may know what becomes of those who defy Xch'uup!'

Cihuateteo didn't look happy about the decision yet she bowed before the will of her Queen 'Namaste Xch'uup!'

The sable beauty returned to Sirt 'Tell your leaders that there is a new Xch'uup on Tlillan, tell them the Pixoa and Gukumatz have united behind her. Tell them Ek'tsab will be coming for them, do you understand Sirt?'

Sirt had a blank expression 'I understand,' he replied stoically.

Cihuateteo grabbed the cyborg by the scruff of the neck, marched him to the edge of the arena before handing him over to Kaeo. The young half breed girl gladly took her instructions from Cihuateteo; it was obvious the child looked up to the Grand Marshal of Tlillan.

Kaeo snatched him roughly.

'Kaeo, do not harm him. He must return intact!' ordered a slightly hesitant Xch'uup.

Kaeo made a wai 'I understand Xch'uup.'

Malikah smiled at her young charge, it warmed her heart to see the young girl finally become a Tlillan woman. The blood stained Kaeo grinned back towards the Matriarch who had given her guidance throughout her life. Malikah had become Xch'uup, in the same instance delivering Kaeo closer to her ambition of attaining the title of Huey'tlacochcalcatl.

The sable Queen peered at Cihuateteo 'She has been chosen?'

The white haired Valkyrie nodded her blood stained head 'It has been done.'

Malikah smiled at her young charge again 'Once you have sent the heretic back to his home world return immediately,' Malikah raised her eyebrows as her smile widened 'Praetor.'

Kaeo blushed in the manner only a Tlillan could 'Namaste Xch'uup.'

The young girl had become a Matriarch on gaining the office of Praetor. It gave her a wide range of both political and military powers. In the absence of Xch'uup or one of her Consuls (Grand Marshal or Priestess) a Praetor would take charge. Each Consul assigned themselves a Praetor to act in her absence and see her instructions carried out. Usually it was an office only attainable after centuries of hard work climbing the ladder and gaining trust. Thanks to Kaeo's status as a Mictlancihuatl, the reincarnated soul of Ah ChuyaKak, Cihuateteo appointed her the moment she arrived on the planet. Kaeo had acted as Praetor during the assault on the remaining Makayuuk forces camped on the light side of Tlillan. Cihu being a pure bred Darksider would have been unable to function under battle conditions if her suit malfunctioned. The intensity of the sun was too much for her and her sisters, the Makayuuk knew this and would have exploited it.

Kaeo and the humans were not so afflicted. Brigadier Jenkins used the dark haired girl's incredible abilities to dominate an already weakened enemy. Her only wish was to secure Sirt 137 as ordered by Cihu. After the beleaguered camp had been defeated Ryu made the journey to the planet, the conflict between Kaeo and Jenkins orders became apparent. Ryu settled it by taking the prisoners herself in restraint collars. The rest were executed as ordered.

The Asian girl exited the chamber with Sirt and two Tlillan females following.

Next the Seers approached Malikah from behind carrying the jade cape worn by the Gorgon. Malikah sensed them and remained still allowing two of them to place it on her. They placed the heavy robe upon her shoulders, it reached the floor spreading out a little around her feet.

It seemed to McCann that his daughter was probably the shortest Xch'uup to wear the garment. Despite the size she looked quite splendid in her regal gown.

The sable Queen of Tlillan walked towards the throne carved out of a single solid piece of stone. From the signs of wear it had been in use for a long time. Malikah sat on her throne; this was the seat of the galaxy at one point a fact hard to believe from a human point of view when looking at it now.

Cihu and Ilam stood on either side of the seat of sovereignty.

'Only one matter remains,' declared Malikah as a red haired female marched into the audience chamber and bowed.

'Namaste Xch'uup, A Gukumatz wishes to enter he claims to be Yaaxil Hmen.'

'Allow him to enter,' declared Malikah regally.

The shaman was led in carrying the sceptre stolen by the Gukumatz millennia ago from this very room.

The frog man approached his Icon until his guards halted him ten feet away. The foul creature dressed in his odd clothing bowed 'Namaste Xch'uup.'

'What is your desire first shaman of the Kotumatz?'

'The Gukumatz wish to return that which is rightfully yours, Xch'uup.'

The creature held out the massive sceptre with both arms. Malikah rose from her throne, leaving her cloak of jade sitting on it, to accept the tribute. Taking it with one hand the Queen of Tlillan held it up above her head for all to see. This action met with rapturous celebration amongst the Matriarchs present, McCann found it all rather tiresome himself. If it weren't for his daughter and wife he'd have returned to the Athena and left them to it long ago.

Malikah passed the sceptre to her mother. At that moment Kaeo entered the chamber mingling with the Matriarchs. Malikah returned her gaze to the shaman before her 'What do you wish in return Kotumatz?'

The shaman looked down at the pink stained floor 'Peace Xch'uup.'

'As do I. As a sign of my good will I now return Gukumatz to its rightful owners. Your people my return whenever they wish Kotumatz.'

Cihu was alarmed by such a concession, returning the home world of the Gukumatz was out of the question in the past.

Malikah sensed her sisters shock 'Be at ease Cihu, we don't have sufficient Matriarchs to rebuild THIS planet! The Gukumatz were willing to risk their lives against the Makayuuk, they deserve that which we stole in the past.'

Cihu said nothing.

'Will your people return Kotumatz?'

The frog man looked up with his slanted gaze at Malikah 'I believe so Xch'uup and we will help rebuild Tlillan.'

Malikah grinned at the first shaman of the Gukumatz 'Excellent Kotumatz, I look forward to seeing your people back where they belong!'

'Namaste Xch'uup,' prostrated the toad as he backed up before a pair of red haired Tlillans marched him out.

Sitting down on the throne Malikah called her father 'Admiral McCann!'

All eyes turned to the Englishman who suddenly felt very uneasy. His wife had a proud smile as did his daughter so he meekly made his way over the earth, pulsating with colour, to his daughter's throne.

Malikah observed the Matriarchs, all were on tender hooks wondering what the Human male was to receive. Tlillan males were not permitted to enter the Muul Kaah, his very presence here made them uneasy.

Malikah waited quietly, there was an odd silence as McCann looked at the burning eyes around him.

The Englishman then realised what he had not done 'Namaste Xch'uup,' he said in a rather flippant tone.

'Namaste Admiral,' replied his smiling daughter 'I was going to abolish the office of Censor, since none should be prevented from using the dreamscape or seeing into it. However upon second thought I have decided it will remain. You Admiral Duncan McCann are to be the first male ever to hold high office.'

There was a very audible gasp from the Matriarchs.

Malikah paused for a moment, refining her regal stare as they quickly quietened down.

'In recognition of all you and the Pixoa have done for Xch'uup and Tlillan you are now Censor.'

The mumbling grew around the chamber echoing all around until Malikah employed another long uneasy pause.

'Well thank you very much Mal ... Xch'uup!' replied McCann before returning to his seat.

McCann had no idea exactly what Censor meant, though he took a guess that wasn't far off.

The title of Censor on Tlillan was the job of a moral police man. Since Malikah had decided to lift restrictions on individuals and allow all to access the dreamscape freely a Censor was no longer required. The seers could no longer pick and choose what knowledge was released since all Mictlancihuatl had unrestricted access. Malikah, Amitrasudan, Sandra and Kaeo could see into the dreamscape as individuals, they had no need for a mass consciousness or seers.

Rather than remove the ancient office Malikah decided to break with tradition and give it to her father. It was controversial and would have destroyed any past Xch'uup. However Malikah was not any Xch'uup. She was destined to usher in a new golden age for the Tlillan people, now that she'd brought them back from the brink of the abyss.

The mumbling grew much to Malikah's disdain. The sable Queen stood tall and snatched her sceptre from her mother's hands. She had to change the atmosphere of the Muul Kaah; brandishing the sceptre she made a speech.

Standing tall her burning eyes lashed the Matriarchs,

'You mumble amongst yourselves, concerned that a Human male has taken the title of Censor. Do none of you give thought to where you were this time yesterday? I shall tell you where you were, cowering in Tititl! Praying to your Xch'uup for deliverance from the mighty Makayuuk armada!'

There was a long pause as Malikah scanned the subdued audience chamber, not one Matriarch spoke.

'Are your stinking lives worth no more than the office of Censor?'

The sable Queen of Tlillan paused again waiting for a reply, her audience refused to answer her question. McCann wasn't sure if it was out of fear or shame, perhaps both?

'You all disgust me! I and my Father come here, risk our lives, vanquish the Makayuuk, for what? A rabble of wretched k'eek'en?'

Malikah was bellowing at her subordinate sisters. McCann found it all rather amusing to watch so many haughty Tlillan Matriarchs hang their heads in shame. Even the Englishman with his limited abilities could sense the reaction from them after being compared to "wretched pigs".

Malikah's eyes burned with a deep burgundy. Ryu watched the newly instated Xch'uup, remarking to herself the similarities with one of McCann's few but shocking tantrums. It seemed that father and daughter shared several traits, usually both were quite tranquil and amiable people. However on occasion when provoked McCann did have a furious temper. Combined with her mother's heir of superiority and volatile nature, Malikah could put on quite a display of thunder and lightning herself!

The room was silent, other than Malikah's raging voice reverberating around the building nothing could be heard. The Queen of the Tlillans sneered at the Matriarchs 'Perhaps I should remove his title, perhaps one of the wretched pigs whose life he saved would like it? Well, which one of you pigs would like to be Censor? SPEAK NOW!'

Again silence reigned, Malikah now had a terrifying demeanour, McCann was feeling embarrassed that he'd caused such a predicament.

The fire in Malikah's eyes burned deep, Cihu and Ilam stood on either side of the throne. The Sable Queen barked from her dais 'We have a destiny to fulfil, each and every one here has a path of toil, misery and blood. But when enough tears are shed we shall take our rightful place in the galaxy. There is no time to bicker amongst ourselves over a meaningless title awarded to a Pixoa; we have much more grievous concerns at hand my sisters.

Let all petty concerns fade as they did when the Makayuuk laid siege to the mother world. Let former enemies stand together, did sworn foes not stand thigh by thigh as waves of Makayuuk attempted to slaughter the Tlillan race?'

There was mumble amongst the Matriarchs, it sounded as if they were in approval.

Malikah's rage faded judging from her eyes 'Then stand fast against those who would destroy you, do not assist them by quarrelling with one another. If we, the Pixoa and Gukumatz work together, once again Xch'uup shall take her throne and the galaxy shall be in terror if there she does frown!'

The Matriarchs were roused and cheered their Xch'uup.

Malikah sat on her throne to the applause of her people.

McCann peered across the blood stained arena and gave his daughter a proud smile; she was certainly a better politician than he. Malikah returned his affection with a pair of smiling eyes, maintaining her hard stoic expression for her audience.

Chapter 27: Epilogue

The sable Queen relaxed, slipping out of her trance. Her consciousness returned to the physical world, the room of young girls also began to slowly regain their awareness. Waking from a long deep link, momentarily the group of twenty students were exhausted.

Malikah smiled affectionately as they all regained cognizance, she was proud of all the girls born since her instillation as Xch'uup. They would be required to man the Tlillan fleet and rebuild the mother world's decimated population.

From her podium at the front of the white walled classroom in New York City, Malikah spoke to her class 'Who has the first question?'

A white haired girl pumped her finger into the air.

'What is your question Natalie?'

'Why did you allow Sirt 137 to return? He will have reported everything to his masters!'

Malikah smiled and nodded 'Of course, that is why he was allowed to return. I remember a story my father told me concerning the British in Afghanistan. In the 19th century some 16,000 soldiers and civilians retreated from Kabul to Jalalabad. The Afghanis massacred them all, save one man whom they permitted to reach Jalalabad. He recanted the tale of the slaughter and how men women and children were either butchered or enslaved.

It was a warning Natalie, the Afghanis sent a message to the British: "If you come here again this is what will happen".

Sirt will have returned to his masters and informed them of the grievous slaughter of both their war fleet and ground forces. That is why in the following years the Makayuuk have taken great pains to leave us unmolested.'

A second child this time with red hair raised her arm; she seemed to be about 10 years old. But like her classmates she was merely two Earth years in age 'Xch'uup, when you said there are many things we can learn from the Pixoa, what did you mean?'

'Was I addressing Cihuateteo in Muul Kaah?'

'Yes Xch'uup.'

'Are any here aware of Machiavelli?'

McCann raised his hand; he was seated at the edge of the classroom on a child's seat.

Malikah gave her father a coy look 'Except you Father!'

The girls all giggled until one raised her hand.

'Yes Lian?'

The girl of Chinese-Tlillan parentage grinned 'You returned the Gukumatz home-world, Cihuateteo did not approve. But Machiavelli stated that men should be treated generously or destroyed, because they take revenge for slight injuries, for heavy ones they cannot.'

'Excellent Lian, it does my heart good to know some of you have read "The Prince". It is taught on Tlillan and Gukumatz, I'm surprised it is overlooked here on Earth!'

Malikah peered towards the teacher.

The I.S.A schoolteacher was rather embarrassed, straightening her glasses she replied meekly 'Machiavelli will be included in philosophy next year, the curriculum on Earth has different priorities.'

Malikah sneered 'I shall speak to whoever sets these priorities; a Matriarch should have studied Machiavelli and Nietzsche long before now!'

The teacher nodded her head giving no other reply.

Malikah regained her composure 'Are there any other questions?'

A half Tlillan girl with a strong New York accent raised her hand.

'Huitzil, what is your question?'

'It has been nearly 5 years since the battle of Tititl, do you plan to leave the Makayuuk?'

'No, they are heretics and must be purged.'

'My Father says you're arrogant and should learn to get along with other civilizations rather than fighting pitched battles with them.'

McCann made a snorting noise from the side of the room as he fought back the laughter.

Malikah rolled her eyes at her father then addressed Huitzil, 'And what if those civilizations do not wish to "get along" with us?'

Huitzil thought for a moment 'My father didn't elaborate any further on the subject Xch'uup.'

'What do you think Huitzil?'

The red headed child frowned a little as she contemplated the conundrum 'I suppose in that case you have no choice but to fight, Xch'uup.'

'Lian, tell us what you believe Machiavelli would have said.'

Lian stood up, she sported a beaming smile since Xch'uup had chosen her for special praise 'A Prince ought never to have the subject of war out of his mind, and in peace he should addict himself more to its exercise than in war.'

Malikah smiled affectionately at Lian 'Excellent Lian, you may sit.'

The young girl sat back in her chair with a proud smile she would be wearing for days, the other girls in the class seethed with envy.

'By the time I return I expect every one of you to have studied "The Prince" curriculum or no curriculum, is that understood?'

'Yes Xch'uup,' replied the class in harmony.

'I shall leave you with a final thought to contemplate, Huitzil I'd like you to put this to your Father when possible; Love and fear may hardly co-exist, so if we must choose between the two it is by far safer to be feared than loved.'

The girls wrote it down on their tablets, all except Lian who had already memorized several texts on leadership given to her by her father.

Malikah bid farewell to the classroom 'I hope you all have gained something from our link today, I hope to see you all on Tlillan in Muul Kaah; and may I say well done Lian you are certain to become a Matriarch with such wise parents.'

Lian bowed, prompting the rest of the class to follow suit, 'Namaste Xch'uup.'

'Namaste,' replied Malikah before stepping off the podium and leaving the room with her father waving back to the girls.

McCann and his daughter walked out of the room and down the corridor leading to an elevator. McCann started chuckling to himself, attracting the attention of his daughter.

'What's so funny, Father?'

McCann giggled as they entered the elevator 'Aero pad 1,' he ordered the elevator 'That little girl Lian, she's gonna be king of the shit heap after that!'

Malikah rolled her eyes 'She was the only girl to have studied Machiavelli, proper behaviour must be praised.'

The Englishman continued to chuckle as the elevator rose up the sky scrapper 'I know, but such public praise from the mighty Xch'uup!' he raised his hands and moved his palms around in a comic manner.

Malikah grinned holding back her own laughter, the doors opened and the pair of them marched onto the landing pad smiling as the press took pictures of their visit to the school.

They entered the transport without speaking to anyone, Jerry Habeeb still had exclusive rights to that, 'Plaza hotel please.'

'Yes Ma'am,' replied the pilot as the hummingbird lifted off the roof and made it's way through the jungle of tall buildings constructed in the last few years.

New York had become Malikah's favourite place to stay on Earth. With the help of Xch'uup the city had erected some massive buildings thanks to the neutronium alloy super-structures. The fusion reactors on Earth were still too few to provide enough of the alloy for planet-side construction; however Malikah was Xch'uup so importing it from the plethora of reignited reactors on Tlillan was easily done.

The Hummingbird landed on the Plaza roof, the pair exited. Malikah could be seen waving smoke away from her face as McCann stepped out holding a Robusto cigar in one hand.

The Hotelier welcomed his most famous and prestigious guests 'Welcome back Malikah, how was your visit?'

'The new school is doing well, they just need some tweaking on the curriculum.'

Mr. Trent nodded his head 'I'm sure you'll have it all worked out before you leave Malikah.'

'Thank you Gregory,' smiled Malikah.

'Your Mother is waiting for you and her husband in the café.'

Malikah's smile widened, she then whispered cheekily 'I know!'

Gregory nodded his head again 'I'm sorry.'

'Don't ever be sorry Gregory, I and my family are indebted to you, please lead the way.'

On reaching the Plaza café Ilam was waiting with a hot coffee on the table for her daughter and beloved husband.

Ilam greeted her husband with a kiss 'How was the school trip?'

McCann sat down in front of his double cappuccino, his wife knew his preferences, 'It was fine thanks, how was your interview with that rat Habeeb?'

Ilam smirked, her husband still maintained his grudge towards Jerry Habeeb, 'He was most courteous my dear!'

Malikah sat down in front of her latte and ordered ravioli from the menu. McCann ordered an onion omelette whilst his wife went for the Tlillan menu.

The three began to chat, McCann criticizing his wife's taste in food whilst she made fun of his penchant for tobacco. During the family chat President Earle approached the table with his wife, he just "happened" to be in the neighbourhood.

The President was dressed in a very smart two piece suit 'Excuse me Mr. McCann, but may I say what a privilege it is to have you and your family back in New York.'

McCann had an ingrained hatred for politicians, however President Earle was a polite man so there was no need to be crass, 'Thank you very much, though it's my daughter who's a big fan of this city.'

President Earle turned to Malikah 'May I introduce my wife Patricia.'

Malikah rose from her seat as the President's blonde haired wife curtseyed 'Xch'uup.'

Malikah's eyes flooded with pink 'Please call me Malikah, I'm honoured to meet you.'

Miss Earle smiled 'Then please call me Pat.'

The President quickly cut in 'I noticed Kaeo wasn't here for fashion week last year, I hope she hasn't lost interest.'

Malikah shook her head with a smile 'No of course not! She was assisting the fleet in Gaulthus; she could not leave the conflict, even for fashion week. However I can assure you she will be here for it this year.'

President Earle let out a sigh of relief 'Thank God for that! The Mayor almost tore me a new one last year, tell her she was sorely missed!'

Malikah nodded her head 'I will inform her, she misses New York too. Being Praetor to Cihuateteo is a very demanding task; if she cannot be here there is always a pressing reason.'

'Well I hope you can stay too?'

'We'll see Mr. President.'

President Earle smiled, said his farewells and left the family to go back to their conversation.

'Slimy bastard!' sneered McCann as he took a drag from his Hoyo De Monterrey cigar.

'Father!' exclaimed a slightly upset Xch'uup.

Ilam smirked, she found her husband's defiant attitude towards authority figures very attractive.

McCann blew the smooth smoke of the Epicure no.2 cigar out of his nose 'What?'

'You shouldn't speak about Michael in that manner!'

The Englishman tasted the creamy smoke as it rolled out of his nose 'All politicians are the same, he'd cut his own Mother's throat if it meant re-election!'

'I'm a politician, Father.'

'That's different, you are a Queen my dear, he is a worm.'

Malikah folded her arms 'Perhaps all politicians are not the same and you are just too cynical to recognise that?'

Before McCann could answer his daughter Ilam cut him off, she stretched her long arms across the table. Holding the hands of the two things she loved the most, Ilam stated 'Enough, you are both too stubborn and I have too little patience for this argument, understood?'

McCann put his cigar in the ashtray then kissed his wife's hand 'Agreed.'

Malikah took her father's hand so that the three formed a triangle holding each other over the table, 'I apologise, Father.'

McCann shook his head 'It's quite alright Malikah, nothing could tear us apart.'

The End

Queen in Exile by Oliver Strong (**malikachutli@hotmail.co.uk**)